Here the water is fresh

RIVER

Nothing but Rocks

HAWKESBURY

Broken Bay

April 13, '91
Tench's Prospect Mount

...untry
...Aug.t '90

...etched
...ushy

A Lake of muddy Water
about 50 feet wide.

...and still worse, almost
...ntirely overflow'd with floods.

...brushy

Land worse

...equent marks of the Natives

Very dreadful Country, the whole
that we saw on this Creek, the
ground cover'd with large
stones as if paved.
April 12, '91

This Country as far
as can be seen from the downs
on the Coast appears to be very Rocky.

Bad Country
April 11, 1791

Tolerably good land in
many places hereabout

A Patch of
good land.

...Prospect Hill
...ry bad Country

Redoubt
Rose Hill

North Head

Country worse

Bad full of brush

PORT
JACKSON
Sidney [ov...]

South Head

...f Coppices

Kangaroo Ground
good land

exceedingly
rocky, sandy
& barren.

Country Tolerable, frequent Ponds
of bad stagnant water.

Sandy, barren,
swampy Country

Tolerably good Country

Botany
Bay

Pt. de la Peyrouse
C. Banks

Pt. Solander

...ove of 10 or 12
Cassowarys

Swampy & barren

...ourse
...ver

THE TIMELESS LAND

THE MACMILLAN COMPANY
NEW YORK · BOSTON · CHICAGO · DALLAS
ATLANTA · SAN FRANCISCO

MACMILLAN AND CO., Limited
LONDON · BOMBAY · CALCUTTA · MADRAS
MELBOURNE

THE MACMILLAN COMPANY
OF CANADA, Limited
TORONTO

THE
TIMELESS LAND

BY ELEANOR DARK

THE MACMILLAN COMPANY

NEW YORK · 1941

PRINTED IN THE UNITED STATES OF AMERICA.

For my son

Michael Dark

PREFACE

*T*HIS book has borrowed so much from history that it seems advisable to remind readers that it is fiction. My aim has been to give a picture of the first settlement of Sydney which is always true in broad outline, and often in detail, but I make no claim to strict historical accuracy either in my dealings with the white men or with the black. With regard to the latter, strict accuracy would be hardly possible. There are many accounts of these people in the journals of those who came to Australia with the First Fleet; but as was inevitable between races unacquainted with each other's languages, and unfitted to appreciate the significance of each other's customs, there were constant misunderstandings, and, in the light of research which has been made in more recent years, one is bound to regard some of their statements with suspicion. That they recorded faithfully what they saw cannot be questioned; that they placed the correct interpretation upon it is not so certain. The aborigines, too, have a strongly developed sense of humour, and one cannot help suspecting that the early colonists had their legs frequently and diligently pulled.

Of the tribes which lived on the shores of Port Jackson at the time of the white men's arrival, less is known than of almost any other tribes, for the obvious reason that, being the first to mingle with the invaders, they were the first to disintegrate, and die out. Therefore, where I have wanted to introduce songs, words, legends, customs, for which I have been able to find no record for these particular groups, I have borrowed shamelessly from other tribes, often far distant. The result, from an ethnologist's point of view, must be quite horrible; but I am not really very repentant. These people were all of one race, and it is the quality of the race which I have tried to suggest, without regard to minor tribal differences. The important thing has seemed to me to be that these were the *kind* of songs they sang, the *kind* of legends they loved, the *kind* of customs and beliefs by which they ordered their lives.

A great deal of research has been done among them, and many books have been written to describe their way of life. What I have read has only served to make me increasingly conscious of my abysmal ignorance, and I must emphatically insist that my portrayal is not intended to be taken

vii

too literally. Many intensely important aspects of tribal life have been touched upon lightly, or left out altogether. The question of native "religion," in particular, has been here enormously oversimplified; to treat it fully (even if I felt myself qualified to do so) would have left no room in the book for anything else. The belief in the existence of a Supreme Being is vouched for by many authorities, as is also the belief that after death the spirit passes to the sky—but these are mere fragments of a huge and complicated structure of spiritual belief embracing the mythology which is, in a sense, the history-book of the aborigine, keeping him in touch with the "eternal dream-time," the unseen world from which he came, and to which he hopes to return.

Certain mistakes made by the colonists when they were first learning the meanings of aboriginal words have been ignored, as they would only be confusing here. In some cases I have deliberately used an incorrect word simply because it has become the familiar one—as, for instance, birrahlee and kangaroo. Kangaroo was a word quite unknown to the Port Jackson natives, being one which Captain Cook had learned from the Queensland tribes, and they naturally assumed that it was a white man's word. Indeed, Tench records that one of them, upon first seeing cattle, enquired whether these were kangaroos.

The beautiful lament which I have borrowed for the occasion of Barangaroo's death belongs by right, I believe, to a Western Australian tribe.

Among the native characters many are historical, Bennilong being, of course, the best known of them; the eastern point of Sydney Cove, upon which Governor Phillip built him his hut in 1790, is still called Bennilong Point. It will be obvious that my account of his life before the arrival of the First Fleet must be purely imaginary; after its arrival I have stuck to facts, but interpreted them freely. Booron, Nanbarree, Colbee, Caruey, Arabanoo, Barangaroo, Ballederry, Gooroobarooboolo, and several others are historical figures. Tirrawuul, Wunbula, and Cunnembeillee are imaginary.

The Australian aborigines had great virtues; in a fairly extensive reading I have been able to discover no vices save those which they learned from the white invaders of their land. Some of their customs seem cruel to us. Some of ours, such as flogging, horrified them. The race is nearly gone, and with it will go something which the "civilised" world has scorned too easily. I do not want to be taken for a "back-to-nature" advocate, nor for one who, in these disillusioned times, regards our own civilisation as inevitably doomed; but I do believe that we, nine-tenths of whose "progress" has been a mere elaboration and improvement of the technique, as opposed to the art, of living, might have learned much from a people who, whatever they may have lacked in technique, had developed that art to a very high degree. "Life, liberty, and the pursuit of happiness" —to us a wistful phrase, describing a far-away goal—sums up what was, to them, a taken-for-granted condition of their existence.

With regard to the white men and their doings there has been little need to embroider. The difficulty has been, rather, to choose and eliminate from the *embarrass de richesse* which is available in the early records of the colony. The characters of many of the officers are to be discovered between the lines of their journals and letters; I have tried to portray them as I found them there, realising that another student of those same documents might find quite different men. It is not easy to catch more than a glimpse here and there of Arthur Phillip the man, in the voluminous despatches and correspondence of Arthur Phillip the Governor. The comments of his contemporaries shed a little light—his actions and the results of his actions more still. Certain qualities appear too obviously to be questioned—physical courage and endurance, moral fortitude, a struggling humanitarianism, and a streak of illogical faith. Upon these qualities I have built what must be regarded merely as my own conception of the founder of Australia.

Where letters have been used they are quotations from genuine documents. The Prentice family and the Mannion family are entirely imaginary.

ELEANOR DARK

Katoomba,
July 29, 1940.

ACKNOWLEDGMENT

MY MAIN sources of information have been the published journals of members of the First Fleet, and the Historical Records of New South Wales. For my descriptions of aboriginal life and customs I have found material in the works of Professor A. P. Elkin, Dr. Phyllis Kaberry, Dame Mary Gilmore, Dr. Herbert Basedow, Mrs. Daisy Bates, C.B.E., and others. My grateful acknowledgments are also due to the Trustees of the Mitchell Library, Sydney, for permission to quote from the journal of Lieutenant Ralph Clark.

E. D.

1770-1788

BENNILONG and his father had come down to the cliffs again, alone. It was quite a long way from the place where the tribe was camped, and they had set out early in the morning when the heat of the midsummer day was only a threat, and the spider webs across their path were still glimmering with dew. Now it was after noon, and though Bennilong was six and expected to bear himself like a man, he was tired and sleepy and a little cross, and he sat in the shade of a rock with his copper-coloured legs thrust out in front of him, and his fingers idly making curly marks in the thin, hot sand. His head was bent, his lower lip protruded, his dark, liquid eyes were sulky. And yet, although this sleepiness, this crossness, lay upon his spirit like a weight, he had a sense, too, of a larger contentment which included it and made it trivial. He was conscious of the world, and conscious of himself as a part of it, fitting into it, belonging to it, drawing strength and joy and existence from it, like a bee in the frothing yellow opulence of the wattle. He was conscious of an order which had never failed him, of an environment which had never startled or betrayed him, of noises, such as the chorus of the cicadas, less a sound than a vibration on his eardrums, of scents which he had drawn into his nostrils with his first breath, and of the familiar, scratchy touch against his bare skin of sand and twig, pebble and armoured leaf. So that his sulkiness remained isolated in a mind abandoned to sensation—something which, for the present, would go no farther than the outthrust lip and the liquid darkness of the eye, while he absorbed, in absent-minded voluptuousness, his secure and all-sufficient world.

The sky was very blue; there was not a cloud in it. The sea joined it in a silver line, incredibly far away, and there was the noise of surf breaking on the rocks at the foot of the cliff. But these were not things to be thought about, or even to be noticed very much. They were so, they were eternal, unquestionable, like the tribe, like the moon, like Gnambucootchaly, the evil spirit. An ant dragging a dead fly laboured tremendously, backward, up the smooth, overhanging curve of Bennilong's leg. He watched it solemnly, finding that by contracting his muscles he could impede its progress; and then suddenly he became aware that it tickled him, and

3

killed it fiercely with a blow of his palm. The smell of it, hot and pungent, reached his nostrils, and he held his hand before his nose, sniffing, until he decided that he did not like it, and the small flicker of sensuous revulsion released his mood, and filled him with the formless resentment of overwearied childhood. A tear overflowed and slid down his cheek. He knew that if his mother had been there she would have understood that he was tired. She would have gathered him against her breast, scolding and soothing him with familiar words. "Woram-woram buna," she would have said, "worambil moium." But his father did not notice. Bennilong, from beneath his lashes, stole an upward glance at the motionless figure standing upon the rock in whose shade he rested, looked at the long, tireless legs, the broad chest, the upflung head with its matted hair and beard, the muscles standing out along the arm which held the shield and spear; and for a moment his gaze was held and his eyes dried, as he studied the grace and the strength and the pride of a man who had never known physical or spiritual humiliation.

Wunbula stood quite still. A darkly shining silhouette against the blue sky, nothing moved but his hair and his beard blowing in the sharp sea wind. The light struck downward on to his forehead and his cheek bones, making them gleam softly like unpolished bronze, and his eyes, narrowed to slits in the dark caverns beneath his brows, gazed out over the ocean, searching the horizon.

Thus reminded of the object of their journey, Bennilong's gusty sense of grievance faded once again before more absorbing thoughts. His father had not noticed that he was tired. His father had forgotten him. His father was watching for the boat with wings.

* * *

For long ago—a whole season ago, when the days were growing shorter, and one crept close to the fire at night, and left the 'possum rugs reluctantly in the morning—a strange thing had happened. Wunbula had gone with other warriors of the tribe to attend a ceremony in the towri of the Gweagal, who dwelt on the southern shore of another great harbour a little farther down the coast. It was an important ceremony whose attendant celebrations would last for several days, and at all important ceremonies the presence of Wunbula was held to be indispensable. For he was not only justly famed as a warrior and a hunter, but he was also acknowledged to be the greatest youara-gurrugin of his own or any other neighbouring tribe. Not even the Cammeraygal, proud and haughty and numerous as they were, could boast a maker of corroborees to vie with Wunbula.

Sometimes when the mood for making a song came upon him he would go away by himself, or sit apart, silent and brooding, and Bennilong knew better than to tease him at such times for stories or to be tossed in the air by his strong arms. And then suddenly words would come from his lips—wonderful words of celebration, battle, or death; words filled with the gaiety of feasts, or the wild triumph of victory, or the long wailing for the dead. Or with another element, dimly sad and yet compelling, stirring the heart—but whether with pride or sorrow his hearers hardly knew.

So Wunbula had gone to the towri of the Gweagal, and joined in their dances and songs, and made an entirely new and very magnificent corroboree for the occasion. But one morning when he had set out with his hosts upon a kangaroo hunt, he had realized that the mood for hunting was not upon him, and he had left the others and gone alone to the sea cliffs. His companions had watched him go, nodding their approval, for they understood that the words of a great youara-gurrugin come to him most easily in solitude.

But after all no words had come to Wunbula that day. For he had been only a few moments on the cliffs when he had seen something which made his heart leap in his chest and his pulse hammer with excitement. It was a magic boat. At first only a drift of white to his far-sighted eyes, he saw it come out of the south, and he was afraid, believing it to be a spirit sent by Turong, who rules the water; and he had crouched behind a rock watching it come nearer and nearer until he saw that it was in the likeness of a boat, but that it had great white wings which bore it along over the ocean like a bird. Fear was still strong in him, but stronger still was that quality which had made him a maker of songs, and he had felt himself shaken and enraptured by the beauty of this marvel, by the grace of its movement, and the billowy curves of its wings. He had stared and stared hungrily while it passed, and then, fearful of losing sight of it for ever, he had leapt to his feet and hurried along the cliffs. But gullies and indentations had so delayed him that it was soon out of sight, vanished around a headland. Presently he had fallen in with the hunting party and had told them, wild-eyed, what he had seen. At first they had stared—then laughed—then stared again, but finally they followed him; and when they reached the camp they had found it seething with excitement. For the magic boat had flown into their harbour, and, folding its wings like a seagull, had come to rest.

There it was. There for many days it had remained, and from it had come, in a smaller boat, mysterious beings with faces pale as bones, who spoke an incomprehensible language, and wore coverings not only all over their bodies, but even upon their heads and feet.

All this Bennilong knew because it was all in the corroboree which his father had made to tell of it—the famous corroboree of the Bereewolgal—which had been several times performed since by his own and other tribes.

And then, as suddenly as they had come, the strangers had departed. One morning quite early, when the creamy film of fog was just lifting from the bay, their boat had spread its wings again and made for the open sea. Wunbula was home in his own towri by that time, but it had so happened that about midday, standing upon these same rocks where he stood now, he had seen it pass, making northward up the coast, and he had stood straining his eyes after it until it vanished.

That same afternoon, Bennilong remembered, when his father had left the camp, he had followed at a respectful distance, for he had guessed that Wunbula was going to the flat rock to make images, and he dearly loved to watch this work, though he knew that he was not welcome at such times unless he sat very still and asked but few questions. So he had crept up to find his father already arrived at the great stretch of smooth, flat sandstone, which was half covered with the things he had made—a huge fish, an emu, very fine and tall, many shields and boomerangs—but, best of all, the whole story of a hunt, showing the two kangaroos with the spears of the hunters in their sides, and the hunters themselves with their arms upflung in triumph.

Wunbula, squatting on his haunches with his bit of sharp flint in his hand, was so still that if Bennilong had not been able to see the bright eyes, fixed and intent beneath their frowning brows, he might have thought him dozing. After a time he began to work, and the sound of the flint, *chip, chip, chip,* on the rock was so monotonous that Bennilong had fallen asleep and had not awakened until the shadows were long and he was beginning to feel cold. Wunbula was still there. Now his head was bent and his hands hung idly, and he looked so full of sorrow that Bennilong sidled up to him curiously and looked over his shoulder. There was the winged boat. Wunbula had made it quite large—larger than anything he had ever made before, except the whale-feast which had covered the whole of a big rock. It was indeed a very strange looking boat, Bennilong thought, for it had no paddles, and no men were to be seen in it. He breathed admiringly: "How fine it is!" But Wunbula only shook his head.

* * *

That was long ago. The tribe did not bother about the magic boat now. Except when the corroboree of the Bereewolgal was performed they never thought about it. It was gone. It had never been important to them in any case; it had not touched their lives for more than a few days, nor disturbed the centuries-old rhythm of their existence. Only Wunbula remembered it, and so often now that he had lost count, Bennilong had come with him to the high cliffs of Burrawarra to watch for it. Between them there was a faith unspoken: the winged boat would return.

Yet Bennilong's thoughts of it were different from his father's thoughts. He had not seen it as Wunbula had, swinging and lifting gallantly over the long swell of the sea, with its wings painted golden by the sunlight and the little plume of spray at its bows. His thought was that if these beings, these Bereewolgal, could make such a boat, could not he, Bennilong, when he was older, do the same, and so journey across the water out of sight of his own land, as (until this thing had happened) he had believed that no man could go, and live.

For, of course, every child in the tribe knew the tale of how, long, long ago in Wunbula's father's boyhood, three men had built a very large, strong bark canoe, and they had put out in it between Burrawarra and Boree, the gateways, leaving the sheltered water, and all the tribe had watched from these very cliffs, the women wailing with fear because now the canoe looked so small, and seemed to be from time to time engulfed, disappearing from their sight behind the wall of a great, lifting swell. But the men had paddled on and on until their canoe was only a speck, and then not even a speck, but lost, vanished in the great waste of shining water. And when several nights had come and gone, one of the women, walking on the cliffs farther south, saw the tiny boat almost below her, tossed in the surf, and in it the prone bodies of two men, not three. So she had summoned the tribe, and the men had climbed down to the rocks; and some, by feats of strength and courage still celebrated in corroboree, had dragged one of the men from the pounding surf when the canoe at last smashed to pieces on the rocks. He was very nearly dead; his bones almost pierced his skin, his blackened tongue was pushed between his lips, and only the whites of his eyes showed. But he had recovered at last, and all had waited about him to learn what lay beyond the horizon, for here was a man—the only man—who had crossed the water out of sight to the place where the sun dwelt. But when he was strong enough to speak he had declared that there was nothing beyond, only the endless water, so that when their eyes had lost the comfort of their own land there was no other, and they had grown afraid, knowing that now indeed they had delivered themselves into the hands of Turong. And Turong had been angered, and had sent sharks to pursue them, and had cast a spell upon one of them so that he stretched himself in the bottom of the canoe and died, and his companions had thrown his body to the sharks to appease them and their master, Turong. Then they had taken their paddles and paddled desperately towards the declining sun, where their home lay; and in the dawn of the next day they had seen it like a shadow on the horizon, but they were too weak to paddle longer. And the one man who remained had known no more until Turong had cast him into the arms of his comrades, that he might warn them of the unending water. . . .

Bennilong stared at it. The unending water. He looked up at his father's lean figure, still motionless, still watching for the boat with wings, and there was born in him a conviction which all through his boyhood was to tease him now and then—that the water was not really unending after all; that somewhere, far, far away, there lay another land; that someday he, Bennilong, not in a bark canoe, but in a boat with wings, would go in search of it.

* * *

In Wunbula's mind now, as he stood staring out to sea, there was a strange conflict of thoughts, a quickening of memories, a difficult striving with unfamiliar ideas, a faint premonition of peril and of change. Yet there could be no peril in this land which had not been clearly understood by his forefathers; and against all such assaults of evil, whether upon the body or the spirit, they had evolved and passed down through the centuries a thousand well-tried safeguards. Nor was the thought of change one which dwelt easily in the mind of a man who had never known it. This thought had come to him with the coming of the magic boat, with whose memory it was now painfully and inextricably entangled, and his brows knitted over his eyes with the effort of his concentration. Was there some hidden meaning in this persistent uneasiness which lay like a weight upon his heart? Some miraculous significance for his people and their land?

For them, knowing wealth as contentment, as freedom from hunger, as well-being in the tribe, it was a rich land. It was theirs, and they knew of no other save only, dimly, as a part of their ancestral legends, that their forefathers had come in some remote past age from over the sea. The planets which shone in the midnight sky were not farther from them than the rest of the Earth planet to which their land belonged; the stars, indeed, were neighbourly to them, but the other lands of their own world, unknown and unsuspected. The friendly and familiar heavens were an always open book in which they could read inexhaustible and imperishable legends, but the Earth was their land, and only their land, and they, borne upon the rhythm of succeeding generations, were its breath, part of it, so closely knit with it that they changed only as it changed, laying the quiet centuries behind them as the outer world laid its feverish years.

Here it was as if the pulse of life in plant and beast and man had slowed almost to immobility, taking its beat from the land itself, which had all eternity in which to change. Here life was marooned, and Time, like a slowly turning wheel, was only night and day, night and day, summer and winter, birth and death, the ebb and swell of tides. Nothing showed for the passing of the ages but a minutely changing coastline, an infinitesimal wearing away of mountains, a barely discernible lifting of coral reefs. Still the ancient grass tree thrust its tall spear towards the sky; still the platypus laid its eggs and suckled its young as it had done in primeval times; and still through the high tops of the gum trees the blue thread of smoke from the black man's fire wavered into the uncorrupted air.

Silence ruled this land. Out of silence mystery comes, and magic, and the delicate awareness of unreasoning things. The black men learned from it, having no other teacher, neither hunger nor danger, and what they learned was different from the learning of mankind in other lands where famine threatened, and wild animals, fierce and powerful, thrust upon it a feverish development of its only weapon—thought. Here thought was less a weapon than another self. A freer self—a communer with mystery. Thought made man one with his environment, knowing a tree as if it were a brother, hearing not only with his ears, weaving so finely from imagination that his creations stood before him, clothed in reality, like his fellow men.

There was nothing in his life which spurred him on to change. Eternity was ever-present to him, past and future interwoven with his own life by legend and unvarying tradition, so that all time was the frame for his mortality, and contentment his heritage. His thought-power, not teased by restlessness, looking inward rather than outward, turned to life as it was, not conceiving a different life, nor wanting it, but loving it as he came to it and as it received him, turning to it as instinctively as an infant to its mother's breast.

Here was unfailing nourishment. The quiet land was illimitable, unknown, mystery beyond the tribal borders. The black men's awareness of it was like the awareness of a seed for the changing season, of a cicada for the breaking heat of day, of a shellfish, sensitive to the wash of sea water over its rock pool. Magic was all about them, entering their lives, their bodies, bringing birth or death. There were many things for laughter —comical things, sounds, postures to be mimicked, children to play with. There were spiritual possessions, vast stores of legend bequeathed to them from a past too remote for their conception; laws, ceremonies, things not to be lightly spoken of, things to be guarded jealously, and passed on to future generations, still sacred and revered. There were songs and tales for firelight, hunting and foraging for noonday, the sharp ecstasies of mating in the dark. Battle was brief, sporadic, ceremonial, a fierce and simple thing of courage, hostility and skill. Death came hard and swift, like a flung spear. Food was for the seeking, and seeking it they wandered, needing under the mild sky no roof but a fragile one of bark and boughs, and leaving it lightly, as a bird leaves a twig where it has rested.

* * *

How, thought Wunbula, staring at the sea, could life change? Was it not eternal, unhalting, everlastingly renewed and yet everlastingly the same? When a leaf fell, brown and withered, to the ground, did not another, small, moist, and red as blood, appear to take its place? When the breath failed on the lips of a man, and his body was buried, carefully shrouded in boughs and leaves that it might not touch the earth, was not the strength and permanence of the tribe assured by a new life? Were not the days and nights already as full as they could be, rich in all things a man needs—hunting, mating, ceremony, sleep, fierce tests of courage and endurance, tenderness towards the young, reverence for age, compassion for infirmity? How else, cried Wunbula in his heart, could a day pass but as it passed for him, beginning at daybreak, when, from a 'possum rug in his mia-mia he could see the night fading between the tree-tops, and smell the wakening earth? Ending with darkness and the glow of dying firelight, with a silence hardly touched by the mournful note of night birds, with the familiar stars blurring as eyelids fell in sleep?

No, no, the way of life was fixed; what, then, could change? The Earth? But had it not from time immemorial nurtured their forefathers as now it nurtured them? Had not the grass tree yielded spear-shafts for the warriors of uncountable generations? Was there not always bark for a man to fashion his mia-mia, his canoe? Could the trees fail to produce his shields and wommerahs? Was it conceivable that there should be no more clay to adorn him for corroboree, no more stones to be sharpened into knives? How could the land change? Wunbula's wisdom was deep enough, primitive enough, to know that it could not. He knew that a camp deserted became no longer a camp; the bush took it back, dropping twigs and bark over the earth where it had been blackened by fires, trodden by the feet of men, sending new growth where the old had been torn or trampled. Nothing could change the land, the eternal land, to which each generation of men was but one breath of its endless survival.

Not they themselves could change, and not the earth. What, then? The Heavens? But had not man from the dawn of his existence watched the same stars move in their unaltering procession across the sky? Should Baiame, Maker-of-all, the Builder, no longer have his pleasant grove and stream where the broad, luminous band lay like a pathway athwart the midnight heavens? Where should the spirits of the dead go but there, to Baiame, to walk with him in happiness and plenty beside his creek whose waters never failed? Was it to be believed that Ngindigindoer, the laughing star, should vanish, and that the four warriors of Mirrabooka should be seen no more?

There was no sense in such thoughts. Man and beast, plant and bird, earth and sky were unalterable. Yet, because he was a youara-gurrugin, not only a maker of new tales but a lover of old tales made long since by other men, Wunbula was still unsatisfied. For he remembered now, and had continually remembered with vague uneasiness ever since the coming of the winged boat, that legends of such things already existed among his people. It was true that he had always felt them to be inferior legends, having no substance, no roots in the established verities of material or spiritual life. They were mere fragments of tales which had travelled, taking generations for the journey, from tribes far, far away. Tales told by a visitor from some more northern towri, learned by him from his father who had them in childhood from one who came from farther north again; forgotten for years; delivered once more from obscurity by some writing on a message-stick; living precariously but persistently, as legends will while men have tongues to speak and ears to listen. Always tales of strange boats which brought strange people with bone-white faces from the north—whence their own forefathers had come. What were they? Men? Returning spirits of black men long since dead, and now seeking their home again? And when had they come? A lifetime ago, a century ago, ten centuries ago—all were past, and a thousand years hardly more remote than one. For this, Wunbula mused, was the purpose of legends— to bind the past securely to the present; for this new tales were made—to project the present forward into the future, so that man's environment might be made stable, enduring, all-embracing, and the majestic continuity of human life be assured. Thus the story of their own ancestors, Mommon and Yaburog, remained always fresh and real. Thus every child became aware of his origin, and knew how his first forefathers had come to the land in a great canoe from across the sea, and how a woman on the shore made a song which wakened a storm, so that the canoe was dashed to pieces, and the men marooned. "Berrugen korillabo," began the tale, familiar as the sound of wind among the trees, "gerrig Mommon, Yaburog." Long, long ago they came, murri, "the men," the forefathers of their race, to go their separate ways, and found their separate tribes, and to make each his own corroboree to pass the story down the generations. . . .

Indeed, thought Wunbula, it was abundantly clear that no tribe could survive without its legends and its songs. How should a man live fully who had no song to sing with his fellows, stamping, grunting, acting the tale which it told? How should the hunt keep the full flavour of its virtue if there were no song afterwards in which to relive its great moments? In the corroboree a man felt himself exalted and renewed; celebrating his valour, he became more valorous, chanting his manhood, virility welled up anew in him; and in remembering a tale and telling it to his children he touched the fringe of immortality. . . .

Therefore he had been wrong to think lightly of those old, unreal tales, told idly sometimes by a dying fire, and soon forgotten. He had preferred robuster tales—of hunts and tribal battles, of storms and floods and great fires, of the machinations of spirits and the movements of stars, of how Piggiebillah, the prickly one, acquired his spikes, and why Dinewan, the emu, flies no more. Such things, he had held, were of the very stuff of life, and fit material for tales. But now, since he had seen the winged boat himself, those ghosts of legends had come suddenly and disturbingly to life. Yet one part of him remembered it ardently. How beautiful it was! In his memory it was a thing so lovely and so strange that its strangeness dimmed the outlines of its beauty, and its beauty shone through its strangeness like a star breaking through mist. He told himself that he had done his part. The boat had come and gone, but he had made a corroboree to tell of it, so that the knowledge of it would live in his tribe long after he was dead. And still he was uneasy.

His eyes left the ocean for a moment to stare down at Bennilong. Looking at his son, pondering, he was aware of many things in life never to be explained, and therefore magical—changing of seasons, ebbing and swelling of tides, wind waking out of silence, children coming to birth. Magic was always very near. The land was full of it, gaunt with it, burdened with the secrets of its incredible antiquity. With that inspired awareness which is the heritage of creatures who live and move to the rhythms of nature, Wunbula began to perceive that between Bennilong and the boat with wings there stretched a thread of contact—frail, invisible, intangible

—not to be too inquisitively considered. He knew that some power beyond his comprehension was at work—that in some destiny whose pattern and purpose were not for his understanding, Bennilong and the boat with wings would come together.

* * *

Bennilong did not really expect the boat to come today—he had been too often disappointed. But he liked these expeditions, for they made him feel important, and there were moments when his father's persistent expectancy reawakened wonder in him and set him scanning the empty ocean with an attention which the first dipping seagull easily deflected. But though he never upon any one occasion expected that the boat would come that day, he did not doubt that it would come someday—in a future too far away to be real or important to him now. Did not his father say so? And was there another in the tribe whose word was more regarded?

He sighed heavily, his finger still tracing curly marks upon the sand. And then suddenly he stopped, astonished, excited, for had he not himself made an image of life in the sand? Was not that coiling line Kuurang, over whose sinister trail his mother had lifted him when he was little, that its evil might not cause sores upon his feet? He began to be afraid. He looked up at his father again, and now tears welled in earnest and had to be hurriedly smeared away with the back of his hand, for he was not sure whether the thing which he had made had power to harm him or not, and he muttered: "Wi! Wi!" edging away from it. Then for one moment the blackness of a paralysing fear swept upon him, and he stared, his eyes round, his mouth round; for Wunbula had turned to him, and planted his great bare foot firmly upon the image of Kuurang, Kuurang himself, the trail of Kuurang—What was it? What would happen?

He stood close against his father's side, with held breath, and Wunbula's hand came down and lay comfortingly upon his head. Nothing happened but reassurance, the fading of that monstrous suspicion that perhaps even a little boy like himself might work an evil magic without knowing it. His breath went out in a sigh of relief, and he leaned contentedly against his father's side, his eyes heavy with sleepiness. Blurred, lazily unfocussed, they saw only colour—white, blue, white. The far-away white was the line of surf against the cliffs of Boree, the blue was the stretch of water, the nearer white was beneath his nose, and his nose as well as his eyes approved it. Where the water frothed it was white, and here was another kind of froth, smothering the shrubs, drenching the hot air with its honey-sweet scent. Looking more intently he could see the small brown body of Kuji, the bee, burrowing into one of the wide-open flowers.

Wunbula said:

"We will return to the camp. The winged boat will not come today." He looked down at Bennilong and gave his shoulder a little shake. "Would you be lazy and bring shame upon your father and your tribe? Come, walk swiftly, like a man!"

He strode off across the hot sand between the prickly shrubs, and Bennilong, squaring his shoulders, ran zealously to catch him up.

* * *

When they were nearly home they came upon Kuurang himself coiled upon a warm rock in the sun. As Wunbula leapt forward the long, brown shape ringed with darkish bands writhed into movement with astonishing swiftness, and Bennilong, dancing with excitement, yelled to his father to hasten. Just as the blow was about to fall Kuurang turned upon his attacker, and Bennilong saw the pale gleam of his underside as he lifted his malevolent head to strike. But Wunbula was too quick; there was a crack, and then Kuurang was dead, though he moved convulsively, lying there on the rock with his back broken, and would continue to move thus for a long time. Wunbula grunted with satisfaction, and Bennilong, jubilant, stood over the slain enemy with his hands on his knees, gloating.

There was a creek at the bottom of the gully along whose northern ridge they were travelling, so they left Kuurang lying there, and scrambled down the hillside for a drink. Here, in the shade, it was cool and secret-smelling; the rocks in the creek bed were thickly cushioned with green moss, and the water trickled round and between them with a pleasant sound. On the branch of a tall tree Gourgourgahgah was sitting, fat and fluffy with contentment, puffing his feathers out, his head, with its powerful beak and its wise, bright eyes, held a little to one side while he regarded them. Bennilong thought of the snake which they had killed, and which Gourgourgahgah would have dearly loved for his supper, and he cried gleefully to Wunbula: "He does not know, the foolish one, what we have just done!" And while they chuckled over this, suddenly Gourgourgahgah burst out, too, into his wild, harsh laughter, and it seemed to them so comical that he should thus join in their mirth against himself, that they laughed harder than ever, holding their sides.

When they had finished their drink and Bennilong had jumped into a pool and splashed himself all over with cold water, they climbed up the other side of the gully and set off for home again. It was almost sundown when they came to the camp, and they could hear the noise of the dogs and the shouting of the children, and see through the lengthening shadows the glimmer of the fires. The children were playing the game of thirrin-gnunna, and Bennilong could see his elder sister, Carangarang, standing in a clearing facing the last glare of the declining sun, while the others scattered through the shadowed bush to their hiding places. Presently their shrill calls came from a dozen different places, each like the echo of another, and a real echo, far away, bore the sound of their challenge down into silence as lightly as a leaf falling. But Wunbula's long stride did not falter, and they passed the children and came into the camp.

There were no men about—they were not yet back from hunting—and Bennilong, leaving his father's side, ran to the mia-mia before which his mother, squatting on the ground, was suckling his baby sister, Warreweer. It was fine and it was adventurous, he thought, to have spent the whole long day far from camp with his father, and because of it he felt a little contemptuous of Warreweer, who did not know how to walk yet, and even of Carangarang whom he loved, and who tended him only less devotedly than his mother. But now that night was coming, and there was to be felt in the stomach that empty clamouring which always came with dusk, it was good to be home again with the tribe. It was good to sit close to his mother's warm bare side at the doorway of his home, and to know that inside it soft 'possum rugs awaited him when, replete with the scraps from his parents' meal, he should feel moved to curl himself upon them.

Warreweer had ceased to suck, and was holding out her arms and making gurgling noises to Bennilong. Looking up at her, where she lay across her mother's shoulder, he could see the gleam of four tiny teeth in her gums, and he took her fat wrist, to which a kangaroo's tooth was tied, and guided it to her mouth as he had seen his mother do. She gnawed at the tooth placidly, and, suddenly, out of the midst of his contentment, Bennilong realised that there was a core of grief to this perfect day. For was it not to see the winged boat that they had gone to the cliffs of Burra-warra, and had not the winged boat failed to come? For the first time he was conscious of this failure as a disappointment to himself. Always before it had been his father's disappointment, and the emotions of grown people were strange and remote from him. But today, it suddenly seemed to him, he had wanted to see the boat himself. The desire to see it swelled in him like his rages did sometimes, till it felt as if his body could not hold a longing so fierce and violent, and suddenly he pinched Warreweer's foot viciously, so that she squealed, and his mother gave him a cuff which sent him sprawling and provided him with an excuse for the yells which were, in reality, only an outlet for the misery of his frustrated desire.

*   *   *

The camp was quieter than usual. The night was gathering around it, and each of the score or so of mia-mias was flickeringly lit by a small fire burning before it. The women were cooking such articles of food as their day's foraging had afforded, and Bennilong, feeling better once his tantrum had subsided, edged nearer to his mother again to watch her take the spoil of her day's fishing and foraging from the woven grass basket at her side. There were four big fish and a lizard and some oysters, and a handful of fat witchetty grubs—yes, it would be a good supper tonight—there should be plenty left for himself and Carangarang, even after their parents had eaten. From a coolamon filled with water came a honey scent which made his mouth water for the sweet drink which he would be allowed to sip when the time came. He knew better than to be importunate. Already he had been one, the youngest, of a party of children taken on a two-day foodless march, and he remembered with pride that when the women met them with a meal at the end of the second day he had quelled the clamourings of his ravenous stomach, and taken only what would have been his portion for one small meal. His reward was the commendation of the elders of the tribe, and Wunbula's laughing, prideful cry: "Here is the making of a fine man!" Carangarang, too, had come through the ordeal well. But Yambeetch, the oldest of the party except Carangarang, and she, after all, was only a girl, had failed, and had brought shame and disgrace upon himself and upon his father. For he had been caught trying to take more when no one was looking, and his father had beaten and scolded him, saying what would become of a tribe whose members could not learn to control their hunger, who could not practice endurance and self-denial?

But then Yambeetch was not much good anyhow. He was a great shame to his father and his mother and his brothers. For when the time had come, a little while ago, for the tribal marking of the older children, and they had been gathered round the medicine man to receive and endure their cuts, he had been afraid even at the sight of the shell knife, and when his time came he had struggled and cried out, so that now he was known as Yambeetch, "the unworthy." But Carangarang had stood straight and still while the three long, red cuts sprang out across her body, following the point of the knife, and afterwards, too, when the bleeding was stopped with charcoal and the wounds packed with white clay to make the scars stand out fine and beautiful. He, too, Bennilong resolved, would not move or cry out when his time came; and he sighed impatiently, feeling that life was endless, and that he could not be patient for his longing to be grown up like his father, Wunbula, strong like him, brave like him, a leader in the tribe.

For the truth was that Bennilong liked to show off a little. When he played with the other boys he always laughed louder and talked more than anybody else, and though the children were treated with great indulgence, his volatility had often brought him reproof or a blow. And he thought, upon these occasions, that there could be nothing finer than to be a man, free to come and go at will, free to eat largely of the best part of the food, free to lift his voice when he would, and to be heard with respect. Nor were these all the prizes of manhood. Of the others he thought not at all in the bright daylight, but only at night, when thoughts became merged with dreams, and between waking and sleeping he knew that great matters were afoot, a stirring and whispering among the women, a purposeful activity among the men, an awed anticipation, half-fearful and half-exalted, among the youths. Where did they go? Through a sleep as light as a dingo's, all his body, delicately alert, twitched a response to the high waves of nervous tension which enmeshed the camp. Coming up out of this haunted half-consciousness, opening his eyes fearfully upon a place deserted by all but its womenfolk and young children, he had heard from far away the wild roaring of the great spirit who made youths into men, and he had shut his eyes tightly, burying his face in the 'possum rugs, plunging back into sleep where these awesome and beckoning things would merge again into the half-reality of dreams. No child spoke of these sacred matters; no woman witnessed them. But at the back of Bennilong's mind the knowledge of them lay mistily, a promise, a threat, a dedication.

*   *   *

When Bennilong thought of manhood he thought of his father, Wunbula; but when he thought of his own manhood he thought of Colbee, a short and sturdily built youth, very strong, and with a decision of character which already marked him as a potential leader. Bennilong often watched him, and he noticed that though Colbee made no effort to claim attention he was given, as if by right, a leading part in the activities of the young men. Somehow, although he did not wish it to be so, Bennilong always felt his own noisiness clamouring for outlet more urgently when Colbee was near. He desired very ardently that Colbee should notice him (though he knew it to be ridiculous to imagine that so magnificent a person should ever notice an unimportant little boy), and he pushed the other children about, and boasted loudly to them, and capered and sang, all the time uneasy and unhappy, because he knew that not thus would Colbee himself behave.

* * *

Years, in that land, were marked only by the growing of children into manhood and womanhood, and the fading of men and women into age and death. Sometimes a season might be made memorable by floods of rain, or by long drought which dried the creeks to mere trickles, and set fires raging through the bush until the beasts fled, and lean times came upon the tribe.

Sometimes there were battles. When Bennilong was in the first stage of his initiation, certain warriors from a hostile tribe invaded their territory and stole two young women who were returning from fishing with their catch. One was Carangarang, who resisted with such spirit that she had to be clubbed into insensibility. Her avengers followed the trail all day; Bennilong and his friends, By-gone, Kuurin and Ballederry, sick with envy and excitement, watched them go. Towards evening the tribes met. Halted in a clearing under the slanting sunlight, they defied each other fiercely with songs and terrible grimaces. Stamping and grunting, brandishing their spears, they sang:

"Burran, burin, bilar bundi
Murala bera karni!"

Their voices rose in a frenzy of martial enthusiasm, their faces were contorted with rage, their spirits rushed to meet this moment which demanded a demonstration of their courage and their virility. Spears began to fly. Straight and hard and true, their shafts making a golden streak through the evening light, they glanced from skilfully turned shields, buried their points in the ground and stood swaying softly, or found their way into the naked bodies for which they were aimed. Every time this happened there was a crescendo in the shouting, and when Wunbula staggered and fell with a nine-foot shaft quivering in his side, his companions lifted their voices in a wild yell of fury.

For who was left to them now to make such songs as Wunbula had made? Who, for the glory of the tribe, was to record upon the rocks the story of their hunting and their tribal life? When the battle was over and the enemy had retreated, they hardly noticed the two causes of it who, bloodstained and limping, crept out from the undergrowth to join them. Carangarang crouched over Wunbula's body and wailed while the warriors rested and made preparations for their return. And suddenly out of her wailings words came, praise for Wunbula, maker-of-songs, maker-of-images, bold warrior, great hunter, tender father. Praise to Wunbula who in his life had brought much honour to his tribe, and who in his death had avenged its insult.

But the words faded as swiftly as they had been born. Smitten with fear of her own temerity, she glanced around apprehensively upon a ring of startled, hostile faces. They stared back at her suspiciously; were not these such words as Wunbula himself might have sung, and was it fitting that they should be heard from the lips of a woman? They said nothing, but she understood their condemnation and abased herself before its justice. For her and for her mother and for her little sister, Warreweer, there must be only the wordless wailing at sunset, the women's ritual of mourning. Humbly she followed them home.

*   *   *

It seemed to Bennilong that his father's death in battle accelerated his own progress to manhood. He grew stronger and taller than most of his fellows, and the tribal scars stood out proudly on his body. He became a fine hunter, and though he never learned to make images upon the rocks as his father had done, he did occasionally make songs. He almost forgot the magic boat now that Wunbula was no longer at hand to remind him of it; but sometimes, skirting the high sea cliffs, he would pause for a moment, remembering, and stare out at the horizon with a faint stir of expectation. In the tribe he was warily handled because of his sudden rages, and of his vanity which was easily affronted; but he was popular, too, for his light-hearted antics, his endearing self-importance, and his gift of buffoonery.

In his early manhood his tribe prepared for a great ceremony to celebrate the last stage of the initiation of a number of its young men. A messenger was sent to summon the neighbouring tribes. Elaborately decorated, and carrying a torch at night to frighten the evil spirits of the darkness, he passed through the land bearing his invitation, and in many camps a stir of preparation began. From farther down the coast came the Gweagal. From across the harbour, warriors of the Cammeraygal arrived, proud and a little aloof; from the north, travelling several days and nights, came the Awabakal from the shores of the great lake which gave them their name. Each party as it approached sent an emissary in advance, as courtesy demanded, bearing a message-stick to announce its arrival into the territory of its hosts, and upon reaching the camp was warmly welcomed and hospitably entertained.

While they waited for some of the more distant tribes they passed the days in hunting and the nights in corroborees in which both hosts and guests joined. Bennilong was proud to find that many of his father's most famous corroborees were well known to the visitors, and was wild with delight, when, as Wunbula's son, he was pressed to perform the main part in one of them. This he did with great spirit, enjoying himself hugely, and later he sang one of his own songs so that all his audience cried out in approval and congratulation. He thought, stamping and singing in the cleared circle, crouching, hitting his knees, leaping in the air, that life was indeed good, and could hold no greater joy than that of being a man. It was a warm, still night, and the sweat ran down his body as he danced. Behind the dim circle of onlookers the tree trunks rose straight and silver, and when he flung his head back he could see only a small patch of sky above him, with the white, misty line of Baiame's pleasant stream winding across it. Together, in a group, the women sat watching, their bodies touched warmly by the firelight, swaying and bending in time to the rhythm of his song, and Bennilong felt his eyes drawn to them, held for the moment by the lustrous brightness of a pair of eyes, or the play of shadow and firelight on a smooth shoulder or the alluring curve of a breast.

These things made him think of the child bride betrothed to him in infancy, and not yet marriageable, and there came to him, with an urgency which he had not felt before, the conviction that he must set about procuring a wife to cook his food and bear his children in the meantime. There were many good things in the life of a man, and now they were all his save this; and in this, as in hunting and fighting and corroboree, a man must prove himself. His thoughts, as he sang and stamped in the firelight, flickered about the women of his own tribe who were available to him. There were not many, for the rules which governed marriage were strict, and the penalties for infringement were severe. Most of the young women were already betrothed or married, and of those who were not, many belonged to his own kobong and were, therefore, forbidden to him. There was Peeka, the widow of one of the old men who had died, and there was Peecharn, but she was notoriously idle, and her catch after a day's fishing was always small. Then there was Kuumarneen, but although she had had two husbands she had borne no children, and it was evident

that the birth-spirit was not kindly disposed towards her. There was Ma-
neela, but she was ill-favoured, and there was Goonoolameear, quite im-
possibly talkative, and there was Barangaroo, also a widow, but her fiery
temper had already brought strife and trouble to one husband, and, besides, she was older than himself which vaguely offended his dignity, so
she was out of the question, too. . . .

Suddenly there she was, looking straight at him. Intruding so sharply
into his only half-formed thoughts of her, he felt his exuberance checked
and damped, and looked away, resenting this encroachment upon his
mood. He danced more and more wildly, leaping higher and higher into
the air; brave words poured resonantly from between his lips. His eyes
slid round again to seek her, and darkened with anger to find that she
was not looking at him now but past him into the night.

When his song was ended he flung himself down among the others,
exhausted, but happy in the acclaim which greeted him. Indeed, he
thought with joyful complacency, he was in a fair way to become, like his
father, Wunbula, a great youara-gurrugin, and his fame would pass over
the land to all the tribes. He lay flat on his back, staring up at the tree-
tops, his breath still coming quickly. He could see the four bright stars
which were the departed spirits of two chiefs and their brothers, and
smaller, paler, the fifth star which was the woman, Namirra, who had
brought them all to death.

* * *

Barangaroo wakened in the pale dawn. The night had been warm so
she had pushed aside her 'possum skins, and lay now on her back, blinking
and yawning, and thinking, almost at once, of Bennilong. Indeed, she
could hardly have done otherwise, for she had wakened not refreshed but
weary and ill at ease, because, while she slept, her Doowee, her other self,
had been abroad in that confused chaotic world which only the Doowees
could visit. And there it had encountered the Doowee of Bennilong, and
together they had made a stupendous journey whose details Barangaroo
could only dimly recall, and together they had faced appalling perils, and
the Doowee of Bennilong had performed prodigious feats of valour whose
nature she could not now remember at all, and no less prodigious feats of
love which made her feel weak with pride and ecstasy.

She sat up, pushing her tangle of dark hair away from her brows, and
glanced with distaste at the other occupants of the mia-mia. They were
both old women, widows like herself, but much too old and too ugly ever
to find husbands again. She looked down with a rather mournful pleasure

at her own coppery body, lifting her arms and watching the way the movement drew her breasts upwards, turning her head sideways to admire the smooth roundness of her shoulder, frowning at the spear wounds in her thigh, bending forward to approve the symmetry of the tribal scars across her middle.

Her hair fell into her eyes, and she tossed it back, drawing her knees up and clasping her arms round them, staring at the first pale glimmer of sunlight on the tree trunks, but not seeing it for the clamour and urgency of her thoughts.

She had been betrothed at birth to Koo-wee, a great man, and a leader, but by the time she was ready to marry him he had another wife who had scolded and beaten her a good deal. After a time she had borne two children, but both had died, and the older wife had persuaded her husband that Barangaroo had offended Wadahgudjaelwon, the birth-spirit, and that he should seek another young wife. So he had taken a girl called Tuupuun, and Barangaroo had been wild with jealousy, for Koo-wee was still a great man, strong and comely in spite of his grey hairs, and she had quarrelled bitterly and incessantly with her rival. She would show her husband, she thought fiercely, that she had not offended the birth-spirit; and aching with resentment, hungry for her two dead children, she had gone seeking others in the places where their spirits dwelt until suitable mothers could be found for them. There was no tree, no cave, no rock where they were known to wait that she had not visited, but Wadahgudjaelwon had not relented. Instead, he had placed a baby spirit in the body of Tuupuun, and when Barangaroo knew of this she became mad with grief and fury and rushed at Tuupuun and they fought like wildcats, tearing each other's hair and faces until the blood ran over their bodies. But Barangaroo was the stronger, and she had borne Tuupuun to the ground and beaten her with a yam-stick until she was senseless, and because of this the baby of Tuupuun had been born before its time, and born dead.

Then it was Tuupuun's turn to hate, and one night she had stolen one of her husband's spears, and had tried to kill Barangaroo while she lay asleep, but it was dark and she was still weak, so her aim was faulty, and the spear had passed through Barangaroo's thigh, pinning her to the ground, where she was left till morning, for everyone thought that it served her right.

And a week or two later Koo-wee had been killed, and they were both widows. When the time of mourning had expired Tuupuun had found another husband readily enough, but no man had wanted the fierce and sullen Barangaroo. By now she was used to being ignored by the young men of her tribe, but the coming of so many others to the camp had wakened an old unrest in her again, and she had gone to the corroboree last night full of sadness for the good things which had been taken from her—for her lost status as a married woman, for the two babies who had died, for the esteem of her tribe which was hers no longer.

For a long time now she had watched Bennilong. He was cheerful and noisy and full of an abounding vigour which called to her own rebelliously smothered vitality. Last night his singing had stirred her; she had hardly heard his words, but his voice and his leaping figure and the infectious excitement which he generated had made a warmth in her blood, an unevenness in her breathing, a brightness in her eyes.

Her brows drew together in a frown which her tribe knew, and into her heart came an enormous resolve. There was beauty and ripeness in her still; she was not old and withered like the two who snored beside her, but fit for any man. As if to confirm her decision with instant physical activity, she slid through the opening of the mia-mia and stood erect outside it, stretching luxuriously.

Through the trees the water was just visible, cool and grey in the morning light, and she left the camp and wandered down the hillside, stopping now and then on some rocky outcrop to look about her. She was hardly conscious of what she saw, for it was all too familiar; she looked at it, not to see it but to feel the stability which flowed from it to her. When she pushed through a grove of honey-scented wattle, or trod knee-deep among the pink boronia, she did not notice their fragrance—but its absence would have touched her nerves with warning. Her reaction to her environment was that of all her people, to whom the earth was simply cradle, hunting-ground, and bier. Because it had never occurred to them to coerce the soil, they lived in utter harmony with it. They did not demand that it produce and produce, exhausting its fertility, but were content with what it gave them, leaving undisturbed its serene cycle of disintegration and renewal. The trees which she passed clambering down to the water's edge she recognised as she would have recognised a man or woman of her tribe, and although their fallen branches would feed her fire and their bark fashion her canoes, they maintained, not in her thoughts, but more deeply, their place as fellow inhabitants of a land in whose earth both their lives and her own were rooted.

Coming out from the shadows of the bush, she stood on a rock overhanging the water; feeling the first faint warmth of the early sunlight touch her body like a caress, she thought again of Bennilong.

About noon that day Bennilong and his friends, By-gone and Balle-derry, took a party of their visitors across in their canoes to an island in the harbour called Mem-el, which belonged to Bennilong, and from its rocks they sported and amused themselves, diving and swimming and spearing fish. When they were weary of this they sat in the shade, and the visitors told tales of their own tribal territory. Some came from a place two days' journey to the westward, where a great river flowed; here there were many ducks which the warriors caught by binding leaves and rushes about their heads; then, swimming softly, they came upon their unsuspecting prey and dragged them beneath the water and broke their necks with a swift turn of the wrist. One of the young men sang a song which he had made about it:

> "Here a great water runs
> Pleasant as the stream in Baiame's grove;
> Behind it the hills go up into the sky,
> Far away they go. What land lies there?
> Is it the land of Tippakal
> He who comes in darkness
> And bears sleeping men from the mia-mia and the fire?
> Here is a better land where many ducks are;
> Many ducks sit upon the water,
> And the hunters catch them."

Bennilong applauded politely, but privately he thought that it was not a very good song.

When the afternoon was fading they took to their canoes and began to paddle back to the mainland. As they came round the point of the island they met the canoes of a party of women who had been fishing. Barangaroo, when she saw Bennilong, wound in her line swiftly; after a little while he noticed with annoyance that her canoe was keeping pace with his, though at a respectful distance. She did not look at him, but paddled steadily, her arms and her wet paddle flashing rhythmically in the sun.

Bennilong's arms moved faster, the great muscles of his shoulders strained. One of his guests was with him in his canoe, and soon they shot ahead of the others, but still Barangaroo kept pace, and behind them Bennilong heard a little screech of laughter and mockery go up from the other women, now left far behind. He stared thunderously across the intervening water, but Barangaroo did not even glance his way. He began to exert all his strength and skill. His canoe was large and heavy, and he had a passenger; Barangaroo's was smaller, and she was alone.

Nevertheless, it enraged him that he could not outdistance her, particularly as everyone had now accepted it as a race, and not only from the women but from the men behind them came shouts of mocking encouragement.

They beached almost simultaneously. Bennilong jumped out on the sand, his vanity smarting, his rage choking in his throat, and at this moment Barangaroo chose to look at him. She ran half-way up the beach, turned to laugh, pointing a derisive finger, and then ran for the shelter of the bush.

Bennilong, always the slave of his tempestuous emotions, lost his head entirely. Furious, he started in pursuit, leaving his guest, splitting his sides with laughter, on the beach. Barangaroo was fleet enough, but she was tired, nor did she greatly want to escape, though her heart was thumping with fear. He caught her just as she reached the rocky slope of the hill, and she turned on him like a fury, biting, scratching, kicking.

This was all in order, and easily dealt with. Already Bennilong's resentment was being transmuted into desire, his wounded male pride assuaged by the consciousness of his strength and dominance. He gave her a blow on the side of the head which reduced her to half-swooning acquiescence, and then, grabbing her by the wrist, he made off into the kindly shelter of the bush. She was too giddy to run behind him for more than a few paces. Then she stumbled and fell and was dragged along the ground. The stones bruised her body and the prickly shrubs tore her skin, but it is the fate of woman to be captured, and pain is her lot, so neither she nor Bennilong accounted her suffering as anything but the normal preliminary to his rough wooing.

* * *

When the dusk came quietly between the trees, he stood up and began to think of the fish he had speared and loaded into his canoe. He was very, very hungry. By now they would be prepared; they would be taken from the hot stones of the ovens and carefully released from their wrappings of wet grass and leaves, and the smell of them would be good in the nostrils of hungry men. Life was perfect and complete. He lifted his arms above his head and stretched his body taut in enjoyment of so excellent a world, in which a man had only to eat and sleep to renew the strength which he had expended on hunting and on love.

He looked down at the crouching figure at his feet and said with authority: "Come." But she did not move, and for the first time he began to realise that this was Barangaroo, the fiery-tempered; Barangaroo, unfavoured by the birth-spirit, a shrewish, violent, troublesome and rebellious woman whom no sensible man would have for his wife. If there was trouble to be made, he felt, without exactly thinking it, he was very capable of making it himself, and something warned him that here was a woman in whom his own choleric and impulsive nature might find its match.

She looked quiet enough now, humble enough, sitting with her hands clasped round her knees and her head bent. And Bennilong, hesitating, scowling, found himself shaken by an ecstasy whose echoes still flickered through his nerves, for she was straight and comely and ardent, her arms warm and welcoming. His brows cleared. His vanity, his love of creating a sensation, was suddenly intrigued by the thought of the stir which this marriage would cause. Indeed, he thought, no man fears to handle a 'possum, but there is courage needed in one who would take a wildcat to his bosom! He remembered how abruptly her kicking and struggling had ceased with his blow, how limply she had fallen where he had flung her on the green bracken, and he puffed his chest out and squared his shoulders, thinking that no woman lived whom he, Bennilong, could not master if he would. Soon she would be meek enough.

So he said again: "Come!" And added angrily: "It is time to eat."

This time she rose and followed him, but she kept her head down so that he should not see her small, victorious smile, and a gleam in her eyes which was anything but meek.

* * *

Bennilong's younger sister, Warreweer, was now come to womanhood. Carangarang, long since married, and the mother of two boys and a girl, viewed her with a good deal of disapproval, and so indeed did Bennilong, objecting austerely to those traits in her which were most conspicuous in his own explosive temperament. There was, perhaps, a touch of jealousy in Carangarang's disapproval. Ever since that strange moment, years ago, when she had felt wild words of grief and mourning rise like a flood in her, and pour from her lips in a lament for her father such as he himself might have made, she had been nervous and ashamed. Seeking to forget her own lapse into conduct so unseemly, she had become a pattern of docile wifehood, but Warreweer, though well past the age when most women found husbands and produced children, not only remained virgin, but shamelessly and persistently produced songs and tales instead. It was true that her fault was not so glaring as Carangarang's had been, for her songs were not such as a man might make, and her tales were not of battles or feats of strength, or of any matters which were more fittingly immortalised by a man; but there was an element in them, all the same, which some of the more sober-minded women of the tribe deplored. To the men she was like a faintly pricking thorn in the foot which they could not discover. For she was mischievously wary, telling her tales only to groups of enraptured children, singing her songs only to circles of women, whose eyes, bright with a mocking, ageless knowledge, met the suspicious glances of their menfolk and silenced the uneasy protests on their lips. It was more dignified, they decided, to ignore her, to pretend that she was doing no more than most women did—making a lullaby or some such trifle—but in their hearts they could not help knowing that there was more to it than that. Why, they asked each other irritably, should she want to make new songs at all? Were there not already innumerable tales for children, hallowed by centuries of use? Were there not lullabies that had been sung to their grandfathers and their great-grandfathers? What other songs should a woman need? What tales were these that she whispered to the dyins, which made them shake with suppressed laughter and dart sideways glances at the sullen men? What was the magic in her words which sometimes darkened their eyes with a strange ecstasy, so that though their bodies lay acquiescent to the dominance of their husbands, they seemed yet far away, withdrawn behind some barrier against which a man felt his rapacious strength as futile as the lashing of stormy surf upon the cliffs?

No, she was an unsatisfactory creature—wayward, all mockery and sparkle—a creature who stirred a man's blood with a warm glance and then chilled it with derision; a creature who, with one sly gesture, one whispered word, could strip his superiority from him and leave him smarting like a sulky child.

The young warriors of the tribe looked at her and swung restlessly between resentment and desire, for she was small and slender and gracefully built, and she had a way of looking up from beneath her hair and of smiling which plucked at a man's nerves. Kuurin wanted her, and so did By-gone, Bennilong's inseparable friend and companion, but she only laughed at them, and took refuge behind the fact that two of the elders of the tribe were also arguing which should have her for a second wife. In the end, these two fought for her, and one was so badly wounded that he had no more need of wives, and the old wife of the other, adroitly insulted by Warreweer, caused such a disturbance that he decided that peace was even more desirable than the prize of his victory. And then Warreweer began, quite shamelessly, to make eyes at Ballederry.

Ballederry was one of the handsomest young warriors of the tribe, and everyone thought that now Warreweer would be content, and settle down to respectable wifehood and motherhood. But no, she teased and tormented Ballederry until he grew fierce and short-tempered and took another wife instead; and Warreweer, scolded by the older women, rebuked by the older men, envied by the young wives and adored by the children, laughed, and made more tales, funnier and wickeder than ever.

But though the older women listened, and though they could not help laughing, they would shake their bony fingers at her warningly.

"Wait!" they would say. "One day Wirrawilberoo, the Whirlwind, will overtake you and leave a baby spirit in your body! That is the fate of young girls who will not marry and become good wives, as all women should!"

But still Warreweer only laughed, and though Wirrawilberoo did come one day, and the unmarried girls fled, screaming, for shelter, it was not in Warreweer's body that he placed the baby-spirit, but in that of poor OOnah who was fat and placid and good-tempered and very plain, and was unmarried only because, so far, no man had wanted her for a wife.

So Warreweer remained unpunished. But soon it began to be whispered among the young women that she was not always as merry as she appeared, and that sometimes when she was out in her canoe she neglected her line and let her fire go out, and squatted motionless on her heels, singing to herself a song which was not one of those commonly chanted by the women while fishing. And then it was whispered that her eyes were often upon Arabanoo, and this was indeed food for gossip, for Arabanoo had two wives already and two sons, and it was considered that he would be the last to approve of Warreweer and her flighty ways. That she should look upon him, of all men! Arabanoo, the calm, the kindly, the quiet-voiced; Arabanoo, who laughed seldom but smiled often. Arabanoo, to whom children came to have their toys mended; Arabanoo, who was so gentle and so patient that he hardly ever beat his wives, and so wise that even the old men were willing to listen when he spoke! No, no, they said, putting their heads together while they shredded bark for their fishing lines and rolled it against their thighs, or wove their grass baskets, or chipped their fishhooks from hard shells and rubbed them patiently to a shining smoothness—no, no, the wilful Warreweer was to be humbled now, for Arabanoo would never look at her.

They were right. Arabanoo did not seem to see her glances; he was soberly busy with his own affairs, his hunting and fishing, his two fine boys, his tribal duties and responsibilities. So Warreweer got married at last—to Weeruwee, who was quite old and needed a wife to care for him now that his two former ones were both dead. Continually he exhorted her to go and seek a baby spirit, and she obeyed him in this, docilely enough, spending long hours on the great outcrop of rock from which no fewer than three of the women had recently acquired sons; but still no child moved in her body, and Weeruwee grew peevish and beat her when he could catch her, which was not often, for he was lame from an old spear wound in the leg.

1788

IN THIS land where time was only the unvarying cycle of nature, the seasons, like the trees and the animals and the men, were born, and waxed to their full strength, and faded, and were eternally replaced. They added strength and maturity to Bennilong's tough body, but failed to quell the ebullience of his spirits. Wunbula's skill in hunting was his, and Wunbula's eloquence. And sometimes, still, when he saw the ocean from the cliffs, its blue patched with green and purple and spangled with the silver glitter of the sun, Wunbula's dream was his also, and for a second a white cloud on the horizon would bring his heart into his mouth with a strange emotion which was half longing and half dread.

So that when in the dusk of one cloudy summer day a messenger from the Gweagal arrived in haste, bursting with the importance of his news, Bennilong, joining the excited group which gathered to listen, felt his spirit melt into a strange receptiveness, as though all about him, from the trees, from the earth, from the air, voices were saying, "It is here." He knew, before the words came which confirmed his knowledge, that the magic boat had returned. He listened avidly, his eyes glittering and his muscles taut with excitement.

Indeed it was so. When the sun was a little past its height, the messenger told them, a winged boat such as Wunbula's corroboree of the Bereewolgal described had entered between Bunnabee and Gwea, the headlands of their bay, and had come to rest there. From it a smaller boat had appeared, bearing strange beings such as those who so long ago had come to the same shore.

Two canoes, the tale went on, lay upon the beach where their owners had left them when they returned from fishing earlier in the day, and the strangers had landed so close to them that Wileemaring and others, fearing that they meant to steal them, had sprung to their feet with menacing cries and gestures. Upon this one of the visitors, who seemed to be a person of authority, had held up some strange and very beautiful objects, and, handing them to one of his companions, had directed that they should be placed upon one of the canoes. The tribe, astonished but

33

reassured by this obviously friendly gesture, had ceased its brandishing of spears and awaited events. By a pantomime which the messenger faithfully imitated, the strangers had then made it known that they required water, and the black men had indicated to them where it might be found. It was impossible to say with certainty, the spellbound audience was informed, whether these beings were men, for their faces were hairless, and their bodies hidden by strange coverings. But when they had landed, that same one who had caused the gift to be placed upon the canoe, laid down an object which the tribesmen took to be a weapon, since all were similarly equipped, and advanced alone toward them, holding out more gifts, and making unmistakable signs of goodwill.

Booloomir, one of the elders who remembered the coming of the other winged boat so many years ago and who had spoken with the people who came on it, had then called for silence, and had expressed his opinion that these were similar beings, and would prove to be as harmless. They would remain a few days, occupying themselves mysteriously, and would then disappear again in their magic boat; for had not this always happened, as was well known from the legends of their forefathers? In the meantime, as they had shown themselves friendly, it would be obviously unbecoming to attack them. Thereupon all had laid down their spears and advanced a little, warily, still mindful of the fact that these might after all be spirits with magic at command.

Separated only by a few feet from the one who proffered the gifts, they had halted again. Now the messenger, summoning all his eloquence, chilled the blood of his hearers, for he made it known that these strangers, at close quarters, were repellent and hideous to a quite remarkable degree. Their white, naked faces, their pale eyes, their pinched noses, looked incredibly evil and malign, and they exhaled a peculiar and unpleasant odour, so that the black men, their nostrils twitching, looked at each other uneasily, smelling danger as an animal smells it, mistrusting the unknown.

Again it was Booloomir who took the initiative. He could not bring himself to go nearer, but he greatly desired, as did they all, to handle and examine the glittering ornaments which were being offered to them, so he made signs that they should be laid upon the ground, and when this was done, and the giver had retreated a few steps, he had advanced and picked them up.

Now, indeed, the tongue of Wunbula was needed to describe the beauty of these things. They were smooth and hard as pebbles polished in the creek bed, and round as the glistening eggs which spiders leave beneath the stones; all the colours of the flowers were in them, and the colour of the sky at noon, and the colour of the sun itself. Nor was this all. Dazzled by the beauty of these things, Booloomir had at last nerved himself to approach near enough to examine the coverings which these people wore, and had himself been adorned with a long strip of the self-same substance, which was soft to the touch, and brilliant in colour as the tall flower I-see-you-from-afar. . . .

Bennilong turned abruptly and flung away from the group, his face heavy and sullen. It was his boat—his and his father's, Wunbula's. Had they not gone day after day to the cliffs to watch for it, while others laughed at them? And was it just that now it should appear not to him but to others? That it should bring gifts to the Gweagal and none to him, Bennilong, who all the years of his life had (so it seemed to him now) faithfully awaited it? Should the withered neck of an old man like Booloomir flaunt the gorgeous decorations which belonged by right, and would lie so magnificently about his own broad shoulders? Like a child he sulked, walking alone through the darkening bush, longing to return with the messenger, as several men of the tribe were doing, to see for himself, but pretending perversely that he did not care, it was nothing to him, others might marvel at this thing, but he, Bennilong, son of Wunbula, the great youara-gurrugin, had known all about it for so long that it held no interest for him now. It was very late when he returned to the camp, and Barangaroo scolded because he roused her roughly to make room for him on the 'possum skins; so he gave her a blow or two, and she reviled him, and it ended, as such incidents usually did, in his lying with her under the sketchy shelter of the mia-mia, finding sleep and solace in her arms.

* * *

But his pique was not proof against the astonishing news which fol-lowed. More winged boats arrived—and more still! In all, the messenger demonstrated, one for each of his ten fingers, and then one more! This was too much for Bennilong's curiosity. He went and looked—from a distance. He watched the coming and going of the small boats as they landed parties and returned to their ships. He particularly admired the gorgeous coverings of the men who most commonly carried the weapons, and the appearance of a red coat was enough to draw his attention from any other sight. He examined the gifts which the white men had bestowed upon the Gweagal, and agreed that, though beautiful, they were useless things and not suitable possessions for a warrior. But still he could not bring himself to go down to the shore.

He did not think about his mood—merely obeyed it. He was aware, as his father had been aware so long ago, of an invisible thread of destiny which held him to these strangers, drew him towards them; and like all primitive creatures under the threat of coercion, he resisted nervously, wild and mistrustful, jealous of his spiritual liberty. It was as if something warned him not to go forward to meet the hour which would inevitably come upon him. All his life it had been approaching, all his life he had watched for it, and now that it was so close he would not stir a step or lift a finger to hasten a climax which would find him in its appointed time. So when, a few days later, home again with his own people, they saw from the cliffs of Burrawarra three of the small boats making for the entrance of their harbour, he was not surprised.

He saw dark looks on the faces of his countrymen, for there were many who felt that the strangers had already stayed long enough, and this fresh intrusion into their own particular domain was resented. On the opposite headland of Boree, warriors of the Cammeraygal appeared, brandishing their spears, and shouting fiercely: "Whurra! Whurra!" Bennilong's companions took up the cry. He joined in it, but, before his natural excitability drowned other sensations, he was fleetingly conscious of a dreamlike knowledge that all this commotion meant nothing. The time was not yet for the invaders to be gone.

Nevertheless, he rushed down the hillside with the others, shaking his spear aloft, yelling his defiance, keeping the boats well under observation as they rounded the south headland and made in for a crescent of sandy beach.

While the white men landed they watched from the hillside, their dark bodies camouflaged in the shadow of a rocky outcrop. The strangers, too, they thought, seemed excited. They stood on the beach and pointed this way and that, but always at the harbour. Bennilong and others recognised among them the man who seemed to be their leader; he looked pleased, and spoke rapidly, and they heard him summon one of his companions by calling, "Hunter!" Once there was a little outburst of laughter, and once one of the men gave vent to his obvious good spirits with a comical gesture and a few dancing steps in the sand, at which the black men smiled in spite of themselves.

Suddenly looking up the hillside, the leader saw them, and said something which made all the white men turn, too, lifting their weapons as if in preparation for attack. About him Bennilong felt the tenseness of his fellows, saw hands close more tightly about the shafts of spears, saw feet shift on the ground, gripping more firmly, heard a mutter of defiance run ominously into silence.

Then the leader of the white men moved. He said over his shoulder something which made his men lower their weapons. He laid his own down upon the sand, and, holding his empty hands outstretched before him, began to walk slowly up the beach. Now another murmur arose in the group of blacks, but this time of approval. This white man was no coward. Tirrawuul laid down his spears and stepped forward to meet him. They studied each other curiously.

Tirrawuul saw a smallish man, quite incredibly ugly, with a pale face and a very large nose. He was covered from head to foot, and, though his coverings were not as splendid as those of the men with the weapons, Tirrawuul, himself a leader, could recognise in him a confidence and authority which required no outward trappings.

Phillip saw an elderly savage, with greying, tangled hair, and alert dark eyes. He was stark naked, and strangely ornamented with raised scars across his body and upper arms. But he stood very erect, and wore his air of leadership with unconscious dignity. For the present, at all events, they assured each other wordlessly, there need be no bloodshed.

Some of the more belligerent young warriors among the blacks were at first disappointed that they were to be cheated of their battle. But it was not in the nature of these sons of the race of Murri to harbour resentment for long. They were quick to observe and to learn, full of curiosity and intelligence, but above all, gay and light-hearted. Their martial ardour could be swiftly roused, and physical courage was a virtue drilled into them from babyhood by precept, example, and bitter tests; but it was more natural to them to be friendly, and they were devoid of malice or suspicion. In these white intruders they saw as yet only dimly and intermittently a menace to their peace. It had been their happy habit for thousands of years to live each day as it came, secure in the knowledge that their land would provide for their tomorrows; and it was pleasanter to think of the white men, not as foes but as quaint beings who would provide them with intriguing gifts, and material for endless gossip, conjecture, and mimicry.

So they moved forward, clustering round Tirrawuul, and the white men near the boats came forward, too, and there was a great deal of talk and merriment and mutual misunderstanding. But Bennilong, usually in the forefront of any enterprise, hung back. He stood motionless and almost invisible in the dark shadow of the rock, staring at the white man who, later, he was to call Be-anga, Father, and he felt the thread of his destiny strung so tensely that he was afraid. More than a few days' wonder, a few days' amusement had come into his life. Here was something which was to draw him into an alien world and hold him there even after death, a lonely, comical, tragic and immortal figure; something which was to bring him knowledge, that heady draught with the after-taste of bitterness; something whose promise and menace he felt already with the perceptiveness of his race, and, with its fatalism, accepted.

Unnoticed, he slipped away. He did not see the strange thing of which his companions told him later—the manner in which the white men had heated water and cooked food in it. Several times during the three days the strangers spent in exploring the harbour in their boats, he crept close to their camping place, listened to their voices, studied their actions. He heard of their visit to the beach of Cannae beyond Boree the northern headland, where only a narrow neck of low-lying land divides harbour and sea. Here many of the Cammeraygal had assembled to watch them land, and some had waded out into the water to meet the boats; the white men and the black had mingled freely until suddenly a disturbing thing had happened. The white men's leader, rising, had summoned his people about him, and drawn round them in the sand a vast circle which he had given the blacks to understand they must not cross.

This, plainly, was magic. Subdued, and more than a little suspicious, the Cammeraygal had withdrawn, for it was well known that marks upon the ground were sometimes sinister and dangerous. But no hostile magic had followed. From within the circle the white men had attempted to converse. Already in his tenacious memory Bennilong had stored away new words: "Hat," "Coat," "Shoe"—strange-sounding words, he thought, as sharp as the cracking of a twig. These, he knew, partly from his own aloof observation, and partly from the gossip of his companions, were the names of different parts of their coverings; but there was a substance which they ate which was called "verygood," and a kind of a coolamon from which they drank which its owner had referred to as a "that."

At Cannae, he learned, not only the white men but the blacks had been teachers. The strangers, pointing to the sky, the water, the sand, and to various parts of their own bodies, had been faithfully instructed, and though their tongues had stumbled clumsily there had been no laughter, for it is not courteous to mock at one who seeks for knowledge.

Bennilong, however, whose ebullient spirits soon overcame his uneasiness when he was out of sight of the invaders, became famous for his mimicry of the white men's speech; capering about with a bit of bark balanced upon his head, and crying "Hat! Hat!", he reduced his friends and the children of the camp to gales of appreciative laughter. But at night, lying wakeful on his 'possum skins, he saw an aspect of such preposterous speech which was not comical, but, to Wunbula's son, very serious indeed. How could songs be made in such a tongue? It had no resonance, no dignity, no rich roll of syllables. "Hat," "Coat," "Shoe!" With a contemptuous grunt, he rolled over and composed himself for sleep.

* * *

When the three boats left the harbour again and journeyed back down the coast to join the fleet of winged ships, Tirrawuul was relieved. But Bennilong, gloomy and bad-tempered, felt a sense of anti-climax. Was this indeed the end? Was it possible that Wunbula's words were never to be fulfilled—that he was never to see a winged ship pass from the ocean into their quiet waters between the gateways, Burrawarra and Boree?

* * *

It was coming. It had been so long expected, so long watched for, so strongly welded into that part of Bennilong's mind where legends dwelt, and so lately and so bitterly despaired of, that now, watching from the cliffs, kneeling on the same rock where Wunbula had stood so many years ago, he was overcome and silenced by the strangeness of his sensations. The two worlds which indeed never seemed very sharply separated, were now confusingly intermingled, huge with portents, swelling unbearably towards some monstrous climax. The shadow world of dreams and spells and spirits had become real, ratified by a white sail against the blue water; and the real world grew misty, dimmed by a miracle, shaken by magic made visible.

To the others, clustering vociferously about him, it was merely one of the winged ships—wonderful, exciting and a little awesome. But upon Bennilong whose childhood had been haunted by it, whose earliest recollections were of long vigils on these selfsame cliffs, it had a deep and confusing emotional effect. His memories were so vivid and so sharply defined, that now, in the dreamlike merging of the spiritual and material worlds, he could see Wunbula, erect and motionless, staring out at the empty horizon; and he could feel as he had felt then, with his alert and receptive child-mind attuned to his father's mood, the longing, at once hopeful and despairing, with which that great youara-gurrugin had watched for one more glimpse of a thing whose beauty had so stirred his heart.

Now it was here. Was not Wunbula here, too? The one did not seem to Bennilong less certain than the other. He was small again, sleepy and cross, and, suddenly, frightened. He did not remember the image of Kuurang which he had made; that, long ago, had faded with other unimportant things from his memory. But now, emotionally transported back to that far-away morning, he found fear there—a freezing, choking fear of some uncomprehended peril, and his flesh crept and his hands grew damp about his spear, and into the eyes which never moved from the approaching sail there crept a dreadful apprehension.

Steadily it came nearer. Sometimes, dipping in the swell, its wings swung and turned golden in the afternoon sunlight, like the wings of the gulls which swooped about them. Its beauty, Bennilong thought, struggling hazily with his fear, was like the beauty of some of the songs which Wunbula had made, filling one with an exquisite melancholy, and its movement over the water was graceful and serene.

Tirrawuul, frowning beneath his bushy eyebrows, watched it sombrely. Not only in his tribe, but among the Gweagal, too, the presence of the white men was beginning to be regarded with a certain resentment. There were too many of them. One ship, which remained in the same spot—a few men who pottered about harmlessly examining shrubs and shells— there had been nothing in this to excite alarm. But here were eleven ships, and many, many white men. There was an air of purpose about their activities, which was not less disturbing because it was mysterious. Now the earlier visitation was seen in a new light. Wunbula's magic boat had returned to its own far-off home, and the voyagers had told their white brothers of this land, and now here they were. What did they want? Why should they send so many boats—so many men? It was true that they seemed willing enough to be friendly, but was that enough? It was not the kind of friendliness which Tirrawuul understood, and he had felt anger stir in him, watching these men who came as strangers to a land, and yet trod its soil as if it were their own. His perceptiveness was lively, subtle and aware. There was a note in the white men's voices which he did not like, a look in their eyes which was not less offensive for being puzzling. No man, he thought, had ever before looked upon him, upon his tribe, with patronage and contempt. These were emotions unknown among his people, except as they might be directed at some individual who, by cravenness, by discourtesy, by meanness or disloyalty, had justly earned the scorn of his fellows. Against their enemies in battle they loosed their anger and their hatred, according them, all the same, the respect of free warriors to others as free and as valiant as themselves. But these men had looked at him—at him, Tirrawuul!—as if . . .

His brows drew sharply together, and he made a convulsive movement of anger. For he had realised that the look these men cast upon him and his tribe was just such a look as he himself might cast upon a group of chattering women—a look not unkindly, but only half attentive, a look which said plainly: "These are inferior creatures . . ."

He stood up and turned his back on the ocean and the ship, looking up the long winding reaches of the harbour to where it faded away in the saffron glow of afternoon. He had been, for many years now, the man to whom his tribe turned for counsel. He had earned that place, they thought, mainly by the strength of his arm in his younger days, and by his intrepidity in battle. But he knew himself that he had earned it rather because, when others were full of excitement, he was calm; when others raged and argued, he was silent and pondered; and when at last all had exhausted their words, and turned, at a loss, to him, he spoke.

Soon he would have to speak again. In all his long life no such problem had ever confronted him as this which he now saw advancing up the coast with the sun gilding its white sails. The resentment which stirred in him said fiercely: "Resist, kill, drive out these invaders!" But he had not grown old without learning to mistrust the counsels of anger, and he stood apart from the rest, thinking as he watched, turning over and over in his mind the facts and details which had been gathered concerning the white men and their habits and accoutrements. One account in particular which had come from the Gweagal perturbed him. Many of the white men carried objects which were clearly weapons, for it was their custom to lay them down for a sign of friendliness, as a man might lay down his spears. These weapons were said to make a loud, sharp, and terrifying noise, but the manner in which they were effective was still a mystery. Nevertheless they had another kind of weapon, small, quite short, but obviously fashioned upon the same principle as the larger one, and this certain members of the Gweagal had seen actually in use. It was related that a white man had borrowed a bark shield and set it up against a tree, and then, standing at six spears' lengths, and pointing his weapon at the bark, he had caused it to make its noise, which was not unlike the noise which some stones make when they fly apart in the heat of the fire but much louder. The tribesmen had been startled by the report, but had advanced as invited to examine the shield. And there was a hole through the middle of it.

Suddenly silent they had looked at it and at each other, sharply aware that if this small weapon could make a hole through a sheet of bark at such a distance it could also make a hole through a man's body. They had retreated backwards towards their own weapons which they had left lying on the beach, but the white men had made renewed overtures of friendship and the incident had ended quietly.

But Tirrawuul remembered it. If the small weapon were so deadly might not the larger one be more potent still? Moreover, what kind of a weapon was it which, merely by remaining in its owner's hand, could fling death so far? Was he, Tirrawuul, to engage his tribe in a battle with wielders of magical power? Was it not the counsel of wisdom to wait, and to watch, and to restrain? For though these people showed no intention of immediate departure, they must, of course, depart some day, and return to their own mysterious land, and there was no sense, therefore, in losing, by means of hostile magic, valuable warriors who were needed for the protection of the tribe.

He looked round at his companions. It would not be difficult, he thought, to guide them in this matter. They were all talking and pointing and exclaiming, and a few were shaking their spears and shouting, "Whurra! Whurra!" as they had shouted on the earlier visit of the strangers, but he read excitement rather than anger in their faces. They had resented the coming of the smaller boats into their harbour a few days ago, but their various friendly encounters with the white men had cooled resentment and whetted curiosity, and now they were already eager for more gifts and more entertainment.

Good. Let the white men come, and, in their own time, depart unharmed. Tirrawuul, with a little sigh, for he was growing old and sometimes felt a weariness in his legs, laid his spears and his wommerah on the ground and squatted beside them in the shade of a rock. The winged boat was almost beneath them now, riding gracefully into the harbour between Burrawarra and Boree.

Moving to some subtly communicated rhythm, without words exchanged or orders given, the black men began to withdraw. No man hid, but no man was more visible than the flickering shadow of a tree. No man hurried, but within the space of a few minutes the cliffs were deserted, and once away from the vicinity they travelled fast. Bennilong began to relieve the tenseness of his mood by talking loudly and showing off, reminding them of the legend of his father, Wunbula, and that he alone had expected the winged boat to return, he alone of all the tribe had never ceased to prophesy its reappearance. They laughed at him good-naturedly, calling him Kon-kon-taallin, loud-mouth, boaster, but kindly, because, for all his boasting, he was a warrior and a worthy member of the tribe.

* * *

The *Supply* had come to anchor in a little bay some miles from the entrance of the harbour. She lay there now in the gathering darkness with her sails furled, and yellow fingers of radiance from her still lights reached out tremblingly across the black water.

The land engulfed her in the majestic silence of its antiquity. Governor Phillip stood on the deck watching the twilight sink into night, and struggled with an illusion. There was no sense of Time here. Tonight— was it Now, or a thousand years ago? What was it in the life of a man which gave him that reassuring sense of the passage of Time? On his little journey from the cradle to the grave, how comforting to feel that Time moves forward with him—how chilling, how strange, how awesome, to feel, as one felt here, that Time was static, a vast, eternal, unmoving empti- ness through which the tiny pathway of one's life ran from darkness into darkness, and was lost!

It was the silence, he thought, which stretched one's nerves. A man should feel about him the stir of his own restless spirit; he should see the fruits of his energy and his inventiveness, he should hear the sounds of his multifarious activities. If there were but a native village to be seen, it would be something to which one could anchor one's drifting sense of human dignity and pride. It would be Man established and securely rooted, Man dominant, and Nature, however slightly, subdued.

But there was nothing. Nature, undisturbed and unchallenged for countless centuries, had here reached a might, a stature which made man feel less than pigmy size. This ship upon which one stood, its achieve- ment, its workmanship, the many ingenious devices by which the ocean had been conquered—why did they suddenly seem less than nothing, so that for a nightmarish second one wondered if one had dreamed them— if one had dreamed oneself—if there were, indeed, any such place as England, any such man as Arthur Phillip, any such creed and code as those by which one had lived faithfully for nearly fifty years?

He sighed and shivered slightly, for the evening was cool after the heat of the midsummer day. All about the ship the water lay inky dark, re- flecting unfamiliar stars; the shores were nothing but an outline, black shapes of tree-tops silhouetted against an indigo sky. No sound from them. No hostility, from man or beast. Nothing to grapple with. No call to action. Only this darkness which kept the senses painfully alert, this silence which tautened the nerves, and this devilish illusion of arrested time. "Tomorrow," he said briskly to himself, but the word was empty. The ageless land had drained it of its meaning and its promise. There was nothing but oneself, a tiny spark of consciousness, alone and aghast in this unconquerable silence.

* * *

But the darkness hid its own people, and the silence did not rebuke their voices. The women and the children and the young boys not yet initiated were left alone in the camp, and it was the men alone who assembled at the Bora ground to discuss and decide upon their attitude to the interlopers. Here was an occasion for conclave and the judgment of the elders of the tribe, and to join them came warriors from the Gweagal, the Wanngal, the Wallumedegal, and the Cammeraygal, for the towris of all were affected by this unprecedented invasion. It was Colbee who first voiced the doubt which lay uneasily at the back of every mind.

Who could say, after all, what manner of beings these were, who were so pale and strangely hideous? Was it not true that their forefathers had told tales of such beings, having the semblance of men; was there not this legend, and that legend . . . And his hearers nodded, looking at each other uneasily with the memory heavy upon them that many of the legends proclaimed such visitors to be the spirits of long-departed tribesmen seeking their homes again. If this were true, deference must be shown to them.

Suddenly and noisily, there was a dissentient voice—Bennilong's. He had in reality no strong views upon the subject. The day, to him, had been one of intense nervous stress, in which he had undergone a psychological reversion to a childhood dominated by two emotions—his admiration for Colbee, and his desire to see the winged boat. Both had been dimmed by the years which had brought him manhood and some consequence in his tribe, but the one, revived so vividly by the coming of the ship, had awakened the other, and both drove him now, as they had then, to a reckless display of self-assertiveness. He did not know what he thought or what he wanted. He was like a child, rising on a crest of bewilderment and unhappiness to heights of intoxicating naughtiness, and he proclaimed loudly, drunk with excitement, that he did not believe that the newcomers were spirits but men like themselves, and if they proved hostile they must

be overpowered and their winged boats taken from them, and he, Bennilong, son of Wunbula, who, after all, knew more about it than any of
them, would journey with a few chosen comrades across the sea . . .

At this there was a great stir, and Tirrawuul said testily that in the
days of his youth it had not been customary for a young man so to thrust
himself forward in the conclaves of the tribe, and Bennilong scowled, and
Arabanoo, quiet voiced and calm, intervened. If these were indeed men,
he said, would they not observe the normal etiquette of a tribe advancing
peacefully into the territory of another tribe? Would they not send an
emissary with the customary message-stick, and if they did not do so
might it not be interpreted as a sign of hostility?

Many agreed to this, but Colbee reminded them of the gifts which the
strangers had bestowed, and suggested that in a tribe so outlandish and
obviously given to peculiar customs, gifts might be supposed to take the
place of message-sticks. Soberly at last they all agreed to this, and Tirrawuul, who was still angry with Bennilong, reiterated, looking fixedly at
him, that failing evidence of hostility on the part of the new arrivals they
were not to be harmed. Bennilong, who did not really want to harm
anyone, recovered his good temper, and shook his spear aloft ferociously,
teasing Tirrawuul with such gay audacity that the proceedings broke up
in disorder, amidst merriment from the younger men, and outraged head-
shaking from the elders.

But at daybreak the whole camp was astir. Bennilong and his friend,
By-gone, travelled together. Sheltered by the trees, they crept close to the
cove called Warrung where the winged ship had at last come to anchor,
and there, presently joined by others, they lay and watched and marvelled,
whispering to each other. Bennilong was trembling all over as an animal
trembles, not with fear but with excitement and leashed alertness. Now
that it was here, larger and more beautiful than he had ever imagined, it
seemed to him that he had never really stopped waiting for it—never
really doubted that it would come, and he beat softly on the rock with his
hand, saying over and over again to himself, "Wonta-kal bara? Wonta-kal
bara?" From what land do they come? And elaborating, without thought,
from the inner urgency of his wonder: "From what land do they come in
a boat which flies like a bird, in a boat lovely and swift as the eagle—what
men are they who fear not Turong, and who come with Wirri, the sun,
from his sleeping place beneath the sea?" And his companions, unstirring,
never moving their eyes from the vessel anchored in the cove, muttered
softly at intervals: "Manyero, I know not, manyero, manyero . . ."

The word beat beneath Bennilong's exaltation of excitement, an ominous undertone, an obeisance to the only thing a man might fear, the unknown. His chant faltered on his lips, and By-gone, still muttering, "Manyero," stretched his hand out instinctively and closed it over his spear.

Presently, to stand beside Tirrawuul, came Colbee, and other members of the Cadigal. It was evident, they agreed, that these people had several leaders, for there were those who gave orders, and those who obeyed, but it was clear that the supreme ruler was the same man of slight stature whom they had encountered before; already, among themselves, he bore his title, "Be-anga," the name which they gave not only to their real fathers, but to such members of their tribes as showed unmistakable powers of leadership. To him even the other leaders deferred, but was not this also a very strange thing, for there were many who were of far greater size and strength, and of far more commanding presence? There were those, for instance, who wore the gorgeous blood-red coverings, marked across the breast with white bands such as they themselves sometimes painted with clay upon their own dark skins, and who carried the long weapons. But the Be-anga bore neither these, nor shield, nor spear, nor anything else with which he might force obedience upon his followers. It was Colbee, serious and observant, who presently offered a solution to this puzzle. Did not the other leaders, upon approaching this man, make a ritual sign with their hands to their foreheads, and was it not likely, therefore, that he was no ordinary man, but a sorcerer, who, having magic at his command, had no need of weapons?

There were divided opinions upon this point, but another problem soon distracted them from it. There were among these people some of a kind which had not, until now, been visible. They were so obviously inferior to the rest, so herded and driven, so harshly ordered from place to place, so drably covered in comparison with the others, that it could only be concluded that they were members of a different tribe altogether.

And if so, why had they not all been slain honourably in the great battle which must have taken place before men would so surrender their manhood? They looked again at Colbee, but he could only shake his head.

It appeared that the main preoccupation of this astonishing people, upon making camp, was not to build mia-mias or to cook food, but to fell trees. For this purpose they used implements which were, obviously, hatchets, but which gleamed in the sun, and bit deeply into the wood at each stroke so that the splinters flew and the trees crashed with incredible rapidity.

All the morning their strange activities continued. What was their purpose? While the sun climbed up the sky they toiled, and the black men could see no result emerging from their labours. There began to be a few pointed comments and some derisive laughter for the inefficiency of a tribe which took so long to establish its camp; but when a row of shelters sprang into being which were not made of bark or boughs, but of some whitish substance which the strangers unloaded from their boats, a silence of astonishment fell.

Bennilong was particularly interested in the doings of a small group of men who were carrying a tall, slender sapling down to the eastern shore of the cove. Here they set it upright, embedding it firmly in a deep hole in the ground which had been made ready to receive it, packing stones and earth about it so that it stood at last as if rooted. Could there, By-gone demanded, be wisdom in the minds of people who felled a tree for the express purpose of setting it up in a different place? But suddenly there fluttered out from its top an object so bright and beautiful that Bennilong, who dearly loved splendour and gay colours, felt his heart lift and turn in an anguish of admiration and covetousness. A rapt silence fell upon the watchers. They had never seen anything half so beautiful as this thing which was red as blood, and white as a cloud, and blue as the sky above it; they could not tear their eyes away from its brilliance, the lovely way shadows ran and coiled along it as it flapped in the afternoon sunlight, the gaiety and cheerfulness of its fluttering corners.

They were not at all surprised when they saw that it was to be worshipped. All the people assembled beneath it, those who were armed and brightly clad upon one side, and upon the other the enslaved tribe. They all looked up at it, and it seemed to fill them, as well it might, with excitement and enthusiasm. Drinking vessels were brought; the Be-anga cried out loudly a few words which were repeated by the others; they all drank, lifting their hands as if in salutation—and then, suddenly, a noise shattered the silence.

Bennilong and his friends never knew how it happened, but they, who a moment ago had been lying or sitting on the ground, were now on their feet, strung to a desperate tension, quivering with shock and horror. By-gone muttered with a dry throat: "Morungle . . ." but no one took any notice of him, for the sun was shining brightly and there was not a cloud in the sky. But still, far down the harbour, curling round the distant headlands and away into the hills, went the echo of that appalling sound, and above the strange weapons of the invaders a little smoke hung, and then vanished.

Colbee saw it. He said slowly: "It is the weapon of the white man. It roars like thunder and flashes like lightning, and it can make a hole through a shield at fifty paces . . ."

From the group of white men there came three loud cries. From the winged ship there floated across the water like an echo three more, and then there was silence. Their nerves still taut, their breath still quickened, the black men watched again.

* * *

Captain-Lieutenant Watkin Tench of the Marines sat in his cabin on the transport *Charlotte,* scribbling in his journal. It was not, on this momentous and very perfect day, exactly what he wanted to do, for the cabin was hot, and he himself, as he admitted with some amusement, not a little excited; but he was a young man who regarded it as a duty to preserve at all times an unruffled air, and he liked to see himself seated here at his table searching fastidiously for *le mot juste* while everyone else was on deck scanning the coastline.

But there was more to it than that. He was not only capable of creating a conception of himself and standing back to admire it. His Celtic ancestry enabled him also to perform the feat of retreating another step still and grinning at his own admiration. Nor had he any intention of missing the fun altogether for the sake of observing himself in a favourable light. His pen flew over the paper a little faster than usual, and he promised himself, as he wrote, that when he had finished this one paragraph he would go on deck and see what there was to be seen, for the afternoon was fading, and by now, surely, they must be nearly abreast of this fabulous Port Jackson to which the Commodore had summoned them.

He was writing at this moment of their brief (but still too long) sojourn in that God-forsaken Botany Bay to which Phillip had returned to lift their steadily declining spirits with news of removal, and he paused, wrinkling his brows for the hundredth time, with wonder that Cook should have spoken so highly of the place—a dreary waste of swamp and sandhills, a barren and inhospitable shoreline! It had been odd and amusing, certainly, to meet and talk with the Indians, and it was of one such meeting that he was writing now, when he had gone ashore with a little seven-year-old boy, the son of one of the marines, and had met a party of savages, led by a hideous old man, who had all been greatly amazed at the child's clothes, and his white skin.

"I bade my little charge not to be afraid," he scribbled "and introduced him to the acquaintance of this uncouth personage. The Indian, with great gentleness, laid his hand on the child's hat and afterwards felt his cloathes, muttering to himself all the while."

That would do. Captain Tench yawned, stretched, and threw down his pen. He would bring his notes up-to-date, revise and polish them, at some more convenient time. But he had learned during the interminable voyage how one day faded into another just like it, how idleness and apathy grew upon one, how easy it was to allow the finished day to slide away, unrecorded into the past. As he gathered his papers together and stood up, his eye caught a paragraph which he had penned not so very many days ago, and he reread it, smiling rather wryly to himself:

"Joy sparkled on every countenance, and congratulations issued from every mouth. Ithaca itself was scarcely more longed for by Ulysses than Botany Bay by the adventurers who had traversed so many thousand miles to take possession of it. . . ."

Alas for their high hopes! He would not soon forget, he thought, even without his journal to remind him, the deepening depression, the sense of anti-climax which had grown upon them during their brief stay in that desolate spot. Indeed, if it had not been for the arrival of the French ships which, towards the end, had created an agreeable diversion, God alone knew what quarrels and unpleasantness might not have resulted from their frayed nerves and their bitter disappointment. He was enjoying, as he went up on deck, the remembered flavour of that affair. There had been a touch of comedy in it—such comedy as he approved, suave, polished, the hint delicately conveyed and as delicately accepted. The Governor had already left for Port Jackson in the *Supply,* but Hunter had proved very equal to the occasion. He had been, from the first, when he had despatched a boat with Ball in command to meet and escort the French ships into the Bay, the perfect host. There must be no misunderstanding upon that point, and Hunter had made the position beautifully and courteously clear. M. le Comte de la Perouse was indeed welcome to this land upon which they themselves had first set eyes exactly six days earlier. M. le Comte was invited to help himself to wood and water: Captain Clonard was received with ceremony on board the *Sirius,* and presto!—the Frenchmen were the honoured guests of His British Majesty's Government (not yet established) in New Holland.

Now, as he stepped out into the afternoon sunlight and the strong, fresh breeze, Captain Tench found himself hoping fervently that this new site which the Governor had chosen would come up to the glowing expectations which his description had aroused in them. For himself, he believed

that it would, not only because he was, by nature, light-hearted and optimistic, but because his respect for Phillip's judgment was profound. The
journey up the coast had taken only a few hours, and now, shading his
eyes against the declining sun, he could see the vessels ahead of them
making in for the entrance which Phillip had described, a wide entrance
between sheer cliffs which, shadowed now, and assailed by the white,
high-tossing surf, formed a forbidding gateway to the tranquil haven
they were seeking.

Tench was suddenly filled with a furious impatience. He was sick to
death of this wallowing *Charlotte,* which had been his home for eight
months; it was just his luck, he thought, that he should have had to
travel on the most decrepit of all these decrepit vessels, on the one which
was, even in this grotesque fleet of antiquated tubs, the slowest and most
antiquated of all. He was sick of the food, the everlasting salt beef, sick
of the cramped quarters, sick of the uncertainty, longing for dry land and
some alleviation of their present discomforts.

Lieutenant Creswell was on deck, too, and Tench, feeling his ebullient
spirits bubbling towards that point where they must find outlet in speech,
went and stood beside him, whistling *Malbrouck* softly to himself, and
trying to decide whether a movement, a flicker which he had caught
silhouetted on the skyline, were natives, or merely shrubs tossing in the
breeze.

"Well," said Lieutenant Creswell, holding his hat to shield his eyes
from the sun, "we have arrived. Let us hope we're not to be disappointed
again."

Tench shook his head. They were between the headlands now; the
low, thickly wooded hills ahead sloped down to meet still, blue water
which was opening out to right and left of them, and he answered confidently:

"The Governor spoke well of it; he is not a man to exaggerate."

Creswell shrugged.

"We need more than calm water. Heaven only knows what blunders
and privations you may yet have to record in that everlasting journal of
yours."

Tench turned away abruptly. He did not, in his present mood, like
the bitter tone, and he did not like the word "blunders." The voyage had
been hard; they had all suffered. Eight months and the whole width of
the world separated them from their homes, and their first glimpse of the
new land had been anything but encouraging. And Creswell, like many
of the others, had had much to endure from a stomach which resented the

monotonous and not too wholesome diet of the long voyage; allowances must be made for a man with indigestion. It was natural, perhaps, that there should be occasional murmurs, discontent, criticism. . . .

All the same, Tench reflected, there were many things which were natural and, at the same time, damned bad form. One should live and die with an air. To hold firmly to the small graces of behaviour was a duty doubly imperative when few other graces remained. And if there had been blunders they had been made before the Fleet sailed, not since, and not by the Governor.

For the first time, now that their permanent destination was so close, and the hour for adjustment and construction so nearly upon them, he thought of the future with a trace of anxiety clearly defined by their unfortunate experience at Botany Bay. On the high seas it had been impossible to shepherd one's thoughts of this fabulous, almost mythical country into any clear pattern either of hope or of despondency. It was too vague, too utterly unknown. One's mind still held images of the other landfalls of the voyage. The rocky, mist-bound slopes of Teneriffe and the cheerful white town of Santa Cruz had seemed, if unfamiliar, still in their own world, but once across the equator life had become a little unreal, and the extravagant, theatrical beauty of Rio had remained in the memory, not to be dislodged, as a kind of embodiment of all that was bizarre, fertile, languorous, opulent. One remembered the little boats of the fruit sellers swarming around the vessels, one remembered the fruit itself, the colour of the piled oranges against the blue water, legendary tales of gold and diamonds, the still air imprisoned by the mountains. And one remembered Table Bay, and a certain savagery in its landscape, which, he thought, had accorded well with the harsh manners of its Dutch inhabitants; a windy, dusty, thirsty place, oppressed and dominated by its mountain.

But this . . .

This was quite different again. One had been prepared, of course, he acknowledged, faintly troubled, for that. But the recorded descriptions of Cook and others had had singularly little life. He himself, Tench thought with a parenthetical flash of his normal buoyancy, could render a far more spirited account, and would do so in good time. But there had been no visual precedent in one's mind to establish an image of this kind of difference. . . .

And instantly his quick brain, leaping between a word and its association, found a description of the difference by adding a syllable to it. Its difference was indifference. This place did not welcome you, like Rio;

it did not look particularly fertile, and it was certainly not languorous. Nor did it repel you, like Table Bay; it offered no enmity, no resistance. It simply waited.

And he found himself thinking of the meagre rations which they carried, and of their numbers, a mere fifteen hundred, of whom half were felons, desperate characters not to be relied upon; and he wondered about the Indians, and how numerous they were, and whether they could be actually as peaceable as they had appeared at Botany Bay, and what lay between this day and the end of their strange adventure.

The end? He reminded himself sharply that for some of them there would be no end. He, when his term had expired, would return to England, the richer by a tale which would open lovely eyes, and cause soft "Oh's!" of astonishment, and, if he could trust his wit (and he thought he could), silvery bursts of merriment. But many of the wretches below would never see their birthplace again—would never leave this remote and enigmatic land. It was to be their home, the home of their children and their grandchildren . . .

Captain Tench was a young man who lived vigorously and with enjoyment in the present. Excursions into the past bored, and excursions into the future disturbed, him, but in the moment that it took him to shake himself free of his involuntary lapse into imagination, he found himself staring round at the harbour with a kind of astonishment, conceiving it , as a scene not merely visited, but inhabited by white men.

Safe again in the comfortable span of his own lifetime, he wrinkled his nose with a very proper disgust. His morality was the morality of his times; his sense of justice, if not his natural humanity, was dominated by its conventions. He was an officer and a gentleman, and it was not his business to concern himself with the making or the administration of the law. It merely occurred to him, therefore, to be devoutly thankful that he himself would be returning to a more congenial world, and to reflect with distaste upon the kind of community which one might expect to evolve from this most unsavoury beginning.

Now they were rounding a low and densely wooded point, and ahead of them the water stretched away westward as far as the eye could follow it. Everywhere the vegetation seemed the same—a dullish, neutral tint, incredibly monotonous. Little crescent-shaped beaches alternated with rocky headlands; and on these parties of Indians appeared from time to time, waving their spears and talking excitedly. Now and then, with a rainbow flash among the trees, birds which Tench took to be a species of parraquet darted from shadow into sunlight and were gone again. They had passed two small islands and were now coming abreast of a larger one, and ahead was yet a fourth, the last rays of the dying sun gilding its rocky pinnacle.

Lieutenant Creswell, behind him, said:

"Listen!"

For a moment Tench heard nothing but the beat of a gull's wings as it swooped past. Then, coming apparently from round the next point, he heard the unmistakable sound of axe blows, and knew they had arrived.

* * *

The sun was almost gone before the last of the winged ships came to anchor in the cove; by that time most of the black men had gone off to hunt their supper, for their bellies must be filled, white men or no white men. Just before dusk fell Barangaroo arrived. She had had a successful day's fishing, and her basket was full of fish and grubs and oysters, so Bennilong, grunting approval, settled himself to watch a little longer. He noticed that the lovely object which had fluttered from the sapling was now being taken down, and he found this wise and understandable, for so rare and precious a thing obviously should not be left to the mischievous whims of the spirits who come with darkness.

One fire blazed on the shore near the row of shelters, but most of the white people were returning to their ships. The little cove looked strange, with a strangeness which chilled Barangaroo's heart. She did not like the fallen trees, the scattered belongings of the white men, the row of strange dwellings they had erected. From their boats, now lying with furled wings upon the darkening water of the cove, there came the still glimmer of mysterious lights which were not fires. She shut her eyes and opened them again rapidly, half believing that they would see the blackly shining water stretching unbroken from shore to shore as it had always been; but there they still were, the strange boats, so many of them, so large, so hedged about with mystery!

She peered at Bennilong. There was an intentness in his watching which frightened her. Life, quite suddenly, was bereft of its simplicity; there was danger here. She felt it, smelt it, heard it in the alien tones of voices which carried with eerie distinctness across the water, saw it in the devastation down there by the shore, knew in a flash that already it had laid its finger upon Bennilong. . . .

She said nothing, squatting motionless on the rock behind him, knowing that the terrors of a woman are to be nursed in her own heart. For it is the function of man to be fearless, and what man could face a woman's knowledge and remain undaunted? So she kept quite still, her face impassive and her dark eyes melancholy, feeling the life of her race stir within her body, and knowing its movement for the throes not of birth, but of death.

*   *   *

Captain Tench, coming on deck for a breath of air before retiring, glanced up at the starry sky, so much denser, softer, nearer than the night firmament of his homeland, and down at the darkly shining water, and about him at the dark and silent and interminable trees. Far away on a height of the northern shore he saw the glimmer of a fire, and immediately he felt that the darkness was inhabited, the silence pregnant with sound, the weight of some age-old alliance between this land and its people not resisting but passively obstructing them. He thought, puzzled, "I have never felt more an intruder in my life!" And then, laughing at himself, shrugged, and went down to bed.

*   *   *

Andrew Prentice was the first on the deck of the *Scarborough* upon that Sunday morning when the landing of the convicts began. He stood against the rail blinking in the strong sunlight, scratching his verminous body mechanically, staring at the shore. He heard the muttered comments of his companions behind him, but he said nothing himself. The dry earth —any earth—was what he wanted, and the country to which they had come was, at this moment, not a prison, but a goal. His first consciousness of it was its sharp impact on his senses; it was a cloudy day with gleams of sunlight now and then, but there was a glare from the water which dazzled his eyes; scents came to him which were alien, unidentifiable; a sound, high, piercing—an ear-splitting sound—shrilled from the unfamiliar green which clothed the slopping shores.

He felt himself baulk as if he had breasted some invisible barrier, and, since all his life he had met obstacles with fury and a tigerish vindictiveness, hatred of this land sprang to life in him, ready-made. The water, a still, glittering sheet, stretched away into the distance. The trees were tall and their leaves glittered, too, so that they seemed more silver than green, and their trunks were skeleton-white. No ocean was visible. They lay here in this unknown, landlocked harbour, and on the shore there waited some kind of life of which Prentice could know nothing save that it would be ugly, harsh, and cruel. He did not resent or fear that knowledge. Ugliness and cruelty had been his daily fare all his life and he had toughened morally and spiritually to cope with them, so that now no human misery and no human depravity had power to penetrate the self-protective insensitiveness of his spirit. But for a second something had penetrated it, and he resented that flash of perception in himself all the more fiercely because it was something he could not name or account for, and because it had startled him for a split second and then vanished leaving him nothing but the flavour of an emotion. He stared at the shore, turning his red head slowly, lowered, looking up beneath his brows. There was nothing forbidding about the landscape; no towering cliffs, no barren sand dunes, no majestic skyline, and Prentice gave back to its impassivity a sullen and contemptuous glare. Already from a couple of the other transports boatloads of convicts were putting out, and, with a sudden stirring of excitement, he wondered how soon it would be before the women were disembarked. He had thought of Ellen during the voyage with hatred, because it was her fault that they were here. Since the child had been ill she had been more and more reckless in her thefts; shrewish, too, dangerous and malevolent when he had grudged her her perilously won spoils which she always wanted to spend on the blasted child, who was sure to die anyhow. But now, at the end of the journey, and at the beginning of a new communal life, he felt his long-starved desire begin to stir and rage. On this transport only male convicts had been carried, herded in semi-darkness, in filth and idleness and the morale-destroying boredom of an eight months' voyage, and they had endured the natural penalty of that unnatural segregation. Prentice had come through it all right. His nerves were blunted, and he had long forgotten what it was to feel ashamed of anything. In the world which he knew, life was not enriched but made more base by every fresh experience, and he had learned, as, in defence of their sanity such men must learn, to regard morals and ethics as luxuries not available to the poor.

Now, watching the boatloads of stores and convicts going ashore, his thought of Ellen held no kindliness—indeed no personal quality at all. She was merely a female body which would be available when they were both landed, and beyond physical assuagement his mind did not care to seek. He more or less presumed that his son would have died on the voyage, but beyond that gave him no thought. No one, indeed, had thought of *him* when he was four years old, except desultorily, to toss him a scrap of food from time to time, and as often as not to let him steal or forage for himself, and he knew that those days had been his training for life. Sharp wits, alertness, mistrust, an inspired capacity for lying and deceit, a deep-rooted habit of expecting always the worst, the ugliest and the most hopeless—these things were his equipment, and he cherished them, girding himself in them as in an armour, and brandishing a resentful hatred of more fortunate human beings as a well-tried sword.

Well, the voyage was over. They had arrived. Where? There was none among them who had any clear idea of the geographical position of this New Holland to which they had come. It had been, at home, a fabulous-sounding name, if it had been even that; a place on the other side of the earth, inhabited by black savages. It might be a large island, or it might be a small one. It might be, for all they knew, part of Asia. But at all events, it was land. There would be fresh water, there would be animals one could kill for fresh meat, there would be some kinds of fruit growing. And there would be daylight, sun, clean air to breathe.

Yes, already there were these last things. The drab, shuffling group on the deck stood in them, looking at the shore. From there the sharp double crack of axe blow and echo came to them across the water. Boats from the storeships were rowing backward and forward; already a patch of ground had been cleared and tents erected—the nucleus of a strange community on the fringe of an ominously quiet, implacably waiting continent.

Obedient to a word of command, the convicts began to move forward. Accustomed by now to being herded, accustomed to being acquiescent, they walked heavily along the deck, feeling the press of other acquiescent, suffering, unwashed and repellent bodies about them. In the boats they sat silent, a little stupefied by the unaccustomed fresh air and bright light, and by the sense of space about them which gave a ghostly illusion of freedom.

* * *

The Governor was ashore. A slight, straight figure in his blue coat, he stood in the shade of a tall tree, wiping his hot forehead with a handkerchief and holding his three-cornered hat under his arm while he talked to Zachary Clark, the Assistant Commissary. Prentice, to whom it was second nature to ferret out and absorb information against a time when it might be useful to him, watched his gestures, thinking sharply behind his expressionless eyes that in the confusion of the next few days it should not be impossible to help oneself to a few extra rations when the stores were partially established.

Already, in his mind, he was turning this confusion to account. He saw that it was not going to be easy for authority to build order from such chaos. Escape, he thought, with dawning excitement, was, surely, not so desperate a gamble here? The woods came down to the shore, they were dense, and what could be easier than to slip away some evening when dusk was falling, and not return? Impossible, here, to set unfailing guard over them; tools must be given to them to build and dig with, a musket could be stolen, somewhere in the woods there must be food, else how did the natives live? And somewhere, if one could keep going long enough, there must be civilization—a port—ships sailing . . .

A thought of Ellen touched his consciousness and was instantly discarded. A man could travel better alone, or perhaps with another man. And if the child still lived she would not leave it, so let her stay, and rot. His excitement mounted. Here was a situation he could enjoy. Here was authority in difficulties, authority working not with the whole might and power of its established sovereignty behind it, but isolated, in disorder, hampered by lack of all that social machinery by which it oppressed such people as himself. He saw, in the eyes of many of his fellows, a dawning appreciation of this fact. Passing and repassing each other in the course of the day's work, they grew almost light-hearted with the knowledge that Fate had given them an opportunity at least to hinder and obstruct, if not openly to rebel.

All day the boats went backward and forward between the ships and the shore, unloading men and animals and stores. All day the work went on, but the confusion increased rather than lessened, and the cleared land at the end of the cove soon wore an air of elaborate insanity which Captain Tench, busy as he was, found time to contemplate with a good deal of amusement.

"Business now sat on every brow," he recorded jauntily that night in his journal, "and the scene, to an indifferent spectator at leisure to contemplate it, would have been highly picturesque and amusing. In one place a party cutting down the woods; a second setting up of a blacksmith's forge; a third dragging along a load of stones or provisions; here an officer pitching his marquee, with a detachment of troops parading on one side of him, and a cook's fire blazing up on the other."

His eyebrows went up a trifle when he saw the Governor's portable canvas house being erected on the east side of the cove, but he confessed to himslf with satisfaction that if any man lived who could invest so makeshift a dwelling with the dignity proper to the seat of government, that man was Arthur Phillip.

All day the trees crashed, and the clearing crept back from the shore. Phillip the seaman, who liked everything shipshape, who betrayed in his person and his habits an almost pernickety tidiness, moved in the heart of this chaos, and never by a flicker of expression or by a tone of voice

betrayed the almost revolted exasperation with which he surveyed it.
Seamen, marines, officers, convicts; pigs, sheep, fowls, cattle; bedding,
boxes, ropes, tools, bits of furniture, loads of foodstuffs—this, he thought,
wore rather the air of an emergency evacuation than of a planned settlement!

He knew, long before the day was out, what faced him. He had not
enough tools, and those he had were of inferior quality. Not enough clothing for the convicts, many of whom were already in rags. Not enough
artisans—carpenters, stonemasons, blacksmiths. Not enough farmers.
Only once during the day he paused to think about it. Then, standing on
a little rise to the east of the cove he looked down at his community, and
realised that he would have to bully it into surviving. He was nothing if
not a realist. He knew that nine-tenths of the convicts would go near to
starving rather than work, and because he was essentially fairminded he
was even able to comprehend their twisted logic. "We are prisoners. Why
should we help to build our gaol?" Suddenly he looked up; the swarm
of humanity and its destructive activity was lost, and he saw only the
country and felt a strange stirring of excitement in his heart. There was
more than a gaol here; he would make it more. He would travel inland,
find good country for pasture and for farming, send for settlers, build up
a free community . . .

"For," he thought, remembering and repeating a phrase he had used
even before leaving England, "I would not wish convicts to lay the foundations of an empire . . ."

It was a thought which had sprung from a deep conviction then. Now,
even as he re-formed it, he found that its validity was being assailed. He
did not know why it no longer seemed important, and because he could
find no reason he reasserted it with a certain obstinacy. One *would* not
wish convicts to lay the foundations of an empire. But again he had the
uneasy sense of having made a false step—lost his bearings—left himself
vulnerable to some force which he named a danger only because it was
more powerful than himself, who, by virtue of his commission from the
King, should have been omnipotent. It was as if the land, watching
indifferently, had said to him: "What does it matter? The lives of these
miserable men will be over in the blink of an eye, and their children will
be mine—not yours."

Phillip half shut his eyes, dazzled by the sun and by something which
had been near enough to an hallucination. He had seen a city on these
shores. He had seen wharves crowded with shipping. He had seen wide
streets and lofty buildings, and the homes of a free and happy people,

and he was startled by his own inability to dismiss so fanciful a vision with incredulity or at least with scepticism. Deep within him, hopeful and undismayed, something said stubbornly, "Why not?"

It was high time, he thought grimly, beginning to walk down the hill again, that he got back to work.

* * *

The blacks were moving camp. It had become quite evident from the behaviour of the white men that they had no intention of immediate departure. Though they had not so far shown any sign of hostility, many of the blacks, and especially the older men, were uneasy, and it was upon their insistence that the camp was being deserted, and the tribe moving away from the vicinity of the cove which the invaders had occupied.

Bennilong quite openly resented this move. It was becoming more and more plain to him, and to many of the younger men, that benefits were to be derived from the presence of the white strangers, for there was no end to the beauty and the efficiency of their possessions, and already they had been generous with gifts.

Leaning on his spear, and watching Barangaroo sulkily as she collected their belongings for the march, he was thinking that it was a sad thing to grow old and lose one's enterprise like Tirrawuul and other elders of the tribe; to be unable to see how desirable it was that some young man of courage and address, some young man of imagination and quick wit, some young man, in short, like himself, should go among these people and observe their ways.

He scowled, watching Barangaroo as she loaded herself with their belongings—baskets and water-carriers, a flat, smooth pounding stone, a bundle of kangaroo sinews for sewing, a woven receptacle full of white and red and yellow clay, a precious supply of whale grease wrapped in ti-tree bark, a bundle of 'possum skins, and an assortment of Bennilong's spare weapons. Her movements were quick and supple, and high lights slid along her limbs and breasts as she stooped and straightened. She was glad that they were moving camp, and she was not at all impressed by Bennilong's bad temper, though she was careful to move outside the reach of his arm. She feared and mistrusted the strangers, though she hoped that some day she, too, might be given such ornaments as those which Colbee's wife, Daringha, so proudly wore. But there was no sense, she felt, in remaining too near such beings. Her blood chilled a little, and her flesh crept merely to think of them; her womanhood revolted from the sexlessness of their appearance—their bodies hidden away, their faces beardless—and she stole a glance at Bennilong for comfort, and unwarily dropped her package of whale grease on the still hot embers of their fire.

Bennilong's bad temper erupted. He dropped his spear and shield and began to belabour her about the head and shoulders with his wommerah, shouting revilements upon her carelessness which were almost drowned by her shrill cries. It was a domestic wrangle, ended as abruptly as it began. Bennilong, feeling better for his outburst, grunted and picked up his spear and shield again, and Barangaroo, rubbing a lump on the side of her head, and setting to work to gather up her scattered belongings, continued her meditations where they had been interrupted.

Indeed, she reflected, the fate of the women of these white newcomers must be a sad and dreadful one. Could a woman find joy or pride in lying with such beings? At first (so Daringha had told her sister, Peeka, and Peeka, whispering, had told Barangaroo) it had been suspected that all the strangers were women, but one of their number had furnished most positive proof that they were men. Yet might not some of them be women? Barangaroo snatched up the last of her burdens, driven by an obscure urge to put as much distance as possible between herself and these people as speedily as might be. For a man was a man, strong and bearded and virile, and a woman was a woman, built for service and endurance, and it was an ugly thought, and one which frightened her, that they should be indistinguishable from each other. Troubled, seeing confusedly as one sees in dreams, she had a vision of some age-old stability undermined, some ancestral security disturbed. Not her mind, but her blood denied these pale intruders, not her reason, but her body revolted, as if, already, they had threatened rape. She stole another glance at Bennilong.

He was still standing moodily leaning on his spear and watching the preparations for departure. The mia-mias were all dismantled and the fires out; the children had gathered up their playthings and the dogs were running about excitedly, snapping at each other, eager to be away. The women were nearly ready, loaded with young babies and camp gear, so that the warriors preceding them should be unencumbered for battle or for hunting, if opportunities presented themselves.

It was, he thought peevishly, a foolish and fruitless thing which they were doing, for even their new camp would be within easy walking distance of the white men's cove, and he, for one, would return often to watch them and their ships and their doings from the shelter of the hillside. Curiosity burned in him consumingly. Acquisitiveness drove him. To know, to have. Here, into their life, had come something new, rich in marvels. He longed to plunge into it and draw that richness out for himself. Already in his mind there was a song stirring about these people, a song of their coming, of their appearance, of their strange activities and their stranger implements. In this alone there was material for a fine corroboree, but secretly there was more, much more, that would never pass his lips. For almost unconsciously, in the ecstasy of composition, he had gone beyond the tale of things which had happened, into the realm, to him not very different, of things which might happen; and his song had become a saga of the prowess of Bennilong, son of Wunbula, who was great not only in his own tribe but in the tribe of the white man, sharing their councils, versed in their customs, speaking their tongue, voyaging in their winged ship where no other man of his race had gone . . .

It was foolish, he thought, to withdraw like this. It was true that since the coming of the white men fish had become scarce in the vicinity of their cove—but that, after all, was a small matter. It was all very well for Tirrawuul to warn that their friendliness might be assumed. Were there not many great warriors in the tribe to defend it, and would not the Gweagal and the Wanngal and the Wallumedegal and the Cammeraygal come to their assistance if need arose, and would not the shores be black with them, as bristling with their spears as the back of Piggiebillah with his spikes?

Soon the white men would be gone, and perhaps never again in his own lifetime would a winged ship visit their shores. Never again would this chance come to handle and examine strange things, to fill one's eager eyes with marvels, and one's hungry brain with rich material for thought. One morning he would go down to the cove and it would be deserted. The winged ships would be gone, the rows of white mia-mias would be gone, the lovely thing on the top of the sapling no longer fluttering against the sky. Slowly, while he grew old with waiting, the bush would claim the cove again, the felled trees would rot away, from standing stumps the pink and crimson leaves would shoot, and undergrowth would clothe the trampled ground. Nothing would be left of the white men but his own song of them, his own corroboree, so that his children and his children's children would know, and wait perhaps, as he had waited, for them to come again.

Tramping through the bush with the other warriors, he was sullenly silent, and none spoke to him, not even By-gone, knowing the darkness of his mood. That night he sat for a long time before the embers of his fire, thinking gloomily of the red and black pattern which he had made with such care and pride upon his shield, and how much finer it would look if it could have such a pattern as that which decorated the lovely fluttering thing which the white men worshipped.

* * *

But the next day his confidence was shaken. The white men, not content, it seemed, with the cove they had inhabited, came up the harbour in two of their small boats; far up, so that the blacks, coming down to the rocks opposite their new camp were just in time to see them making in for the shore. This was too much. Did not the black men themselves, in their own land, keep to the towris of their own tribes? Had they not conceded to these white men a towri of their own, and must they now thrust themselves in this unmannerly fashion, and, without so much as the civility of a message-stick to announce their arrival, into the towri of a tribe which had purposely withdrawn from them?

Tirrawuul was furious. He made no attempt to restrain his companions as they rushed down to the water's edge, brandishing their spears. From mouth to mouth, back through bush their cry went: "Coo-ee! Coo-ee!" and the rocks of the shore became thronged with dark and menacing figures.

Captain Hunter, standing in the bow of the six-oared boat, ceased his pacific gesturing and turned to Bradley.

"They seem hostile. And we have not seen them before in such numbers." He called across to the other boat. "It were wiser not to land, I think, Mr. Keltie."

The master of the *Sirius* agreed. On a previous expedition a day or two before, in the lower part of the harbour, they had met and fraternised with a party of natives, and Mr. Keltie had no wish for too close an acquaintance with spears such as he had then examined. Hunter, judging their small company of sixteen souls with three muskets between them as being quite inadequate for an encounter, and, mindful of the Governor's order that the natives were not to be fired upon except in case of dire necessity, gave orders to draw away from the shore.

Tirrawuul watched them vanish down the harbour. He had been angry, but not too angry to notice Hunter's friendly gestures of farewell, and he was puzzled by the complexity of a situation which seemed governed by no rules with which he was familiar. As his resentment faded he was aware again of the uneasiness which he felt in all his thoughts of these people. Here, for the first time in his life, he saw men who made him afraid. It was not themselves he feared. Old as he was, there was not one among them against whom, armed like himself with spear and shield, he would have hesitated to fight. But he was aware of a knowledge in them which he could only conceive as magical; of powers which they wielded against which no power of his own or of his countrymen could prevail. He shook his grey head wearily, alone on the deserted rocks, for all the others had scattered through the bush to near-by hilltops to watch the boats safely out of their domain. He shook his head, knowing that again he must counsel patience to his people, calm their anger, hold them with words of wisdom until their blood cooled. Soon the white men would depart, and their magic with them; the land would wipe out the traces of their passing and be at peace again.

* * *

The Governor, hurrying across to his canvas house, glanced up at the sky. Blue-black and menacing, it seemed to hang low over the settlement. The trees had lost their glitter, their leaves were still, and their colour matched the glassy, leaden hue of the water. He thought, "It only needed this!"

Inside, alone for a moment, he paused. Sometimes during these chaotic days of disembarkation, he had found such brief intervals of solitude necessary, not only to marshal his thoughts and to make his decisions, but to search himself for reserves of fortitude which so far he had never failed to find. He pulled a seat up to his table and sat down to think. There was this business of Norfolk Island; that must be attended to at once. His instructions, which he could have almost repeated by heart, allowed no delay in the acquisition of that little Pacific Island which "being represented as a spot which may hereafter become useful, you are, as soon as circumstances will admit of it, to send a small establishment thither to secure the same to us, and prevent it being occupied by the subjects of any other European power. . . ."

Lieutenant King of the *Sirius,* he thought, was undoubtedly the man for that task. A very dependable young officer, King, steady and reliable; he could be trusted to see such an undertaking through with credit. He should be summoned today, immediately, and given his instructions, and the *Supply* should sail as soon as possible.

That point settled, Phillip turned his thoughts to the Reverend Mr. Johnson, who was clamouring for religious observances. Very right and proper, the Governor reflected a little wearily, and he should have them soon—the day after tomorrow, in fact—but, in the meantime, the most pressing problem was the disembarking of the women.

Wrestling with it, the Governor's hand crept to his side and stayed there, pressing a little, as if in admonishment of the faint pain which thrust up to his consciousness now and then, and the two lines between his brows deepened sharply, half in response to its importunity, and half for the anxiety of his thoughts.

For there could be no doubt at all what would happen once the female convicts came ashore. Two hundred and fifty women, and eight hundred sex-starved men. And not only the convicts, either. He sighed, drumming on the table with his fingers, thinking that there might be times when discipline would defeat itself, times when wisdom would turn a blind eye upon excesses which ignorance or callousness have invited. Nature, he thought, brings her own cure for such excesses, a surer cure, a more effective one than any he could devise. But he was still troubled, wondering if among those depraved and unfortunate women there might not still be some who were virtuous.

One thing was certain—here, again, there could be no question of delay. In his heart he was thankful for that, feeling that after the long, enforced idleness of the voyage, activity was the medicine they all needed; it had been his first care to provide incessant physical labour for all who were capable of it. Now and then, from the depth of his preoccupations, he had felt a glow less of pride than of deep and satisfying contentment in what he had already achieved. It was no mean feat to have brought the whole fleet safely to its destination, and the knowledge that he had done so helped him to face a future whose dangers and difficulties he was too sane to ignore.

He baulked at the word "dangers" but could not dismiss it. Here were no dangers of any kind he had known before. His mind flickered back to the actions he had fought—that first one off Minorca when he was eighteen, and Quiberon Bay a few years later, and the bombardment of Port Royal; and to other perils—the epidemic on the *Pilar* which had left him without sufficient hands to navigate his ship, and that wild and stormy voyage on the *Europe* from St. Helen's to Santiago, and the fire which broke out on board during another voyage to Madras. Those were dangers. The ordinary dangers of the profession he had chosen. But here "danger" had another meaning, and he was not sure that he had grasped it yet. He had caught a glimpse of it upon that first day, but its nature still eluded him. He was only conscious of its power. He stared through the open doorway, his fingers beating their soft tattoo on the tabletop, and he felt this danger, not challenging him as danger had so often done before, but standing quietly at his side waiting for him to move unwarily. With deliberation he called it by its names, saying them over to himself slowly, lingering on each one to consider it.

Lawlessness and insubordination he had met before, but he was already aware that here he would meet them in a new guise. Armed mutiny, he thought wryly, was least to be feared—there were other and subtler forms of rebellion, and he knew by now that they would come not only from the convicts. Already it was clear to him that from his Lieutenant-Governor, Commandant of the Marine Battalion, he would be able to exact only a grudging service. A strange man, Major Ross—a difficult man, touchy, envious, suspicious. There was nothing, he thought, that you could do with such a man but avoid him, treating him, of course, with scrupulous courtesy, but confiding in him as little as possible, and relying on him not at all. With the marine officers—soldiers now to be unwillingly pressed into unspectacular civilian duties—difficulties might well be expected to arise. They were all good enough men, he told himself worriedly, but were they capable of the enormous effort of imaginative readjustment which this enterprise was certainly going to demand of them? He found himself making a mental inventory of them. Shea, bulky and good-natured, with a touch of the buffoon; Meredith, languid and inclined to be supercilious; Campbell, hand-in-glove with Major Ross and, therefore, not likely to be well disposed towards himself; Tench, first and foremost a young man of the world, cultured, quick-witted, imperturbably good-humoured; Dawes, studious, intelligent, and self-contained. A bunch of lieutenants—Kellow, quiet and unassuming, a born follower; Morrison, Faddy, Timins, Poulden, all unremarkable young men; William Collins —Was there, perhaps, latent in him, some of the quality of his elder brother, David? Ralph Clark, a rather hysterical youth, fickle and unpredictable; George Johnston, Creswell, Shairp, Davey, all adequate for their own jobs, all men who, occupying their appointed niches in a firmly established society, would acquit themselves well enough. But had they that extra moral force which was needed to make them useful in the building of a new community? Of them all, he thought, with a sigh, Tench and Dawes seemed the only ones who had anything beyond their routine military training to contribute; and Tench's qualities—the easy graces of manner and conversation, the lively humour, the sophisticated wit—were ones which would shine oddly, but not ungratefully, in the grim and dingy struggle for survival which was before them.

Of his naval officers he thought more hopefully, not only by reason of their own worth, but because, comparatively isolated on their ships, coming and going upon those voyages which would be necessary for the establishment of the colony at Norfolk Island, they would be a little apart from the disastrous psychological stresses which bear down the morale of a crowded and isolated community. Intrigues, quarrels and discontents would touch them less. He found himself envying them, thinking with a flash of nostalgia that he, too, was a sailor, and his place the sea.

Hunter and King, he thought, shaking this momentary dissatisfaction from him, were men to be relied upon, towers of strength. Ball and Bradley were efficient and intelligent. No, there was not likely to be trouble there, or not, he amended wryly, trouble of man's making. That blue ocean they had crossed was not always blue—not always pacific . . .

He swung his thoughts back to his inventory, searching now amongst what might be called the civilian population of his miniature state. There was Brewer, of course, officially Provost Marshall, but actually that useful being, a man of many trades. An old friend, Brewer, many times tried. His early training as a carpenter, his smattering of agricultural knowledge, might here, oddly enough, be turned to useful account at last, and he would be able to make drawings, too, of flowers and plants to send to Sir Joseph Banks. . . .

Then there was White, the surgeon, an indefatigable young man with an explosive and uncompromising temper, but with a genuine devotion to his work, and there were his assistants, Arndell and Balmain. And David Collins, the Judge-Advocate, whose calm, judicial outlook would, no doubt, see him through the difficulties and pitfalls of a function for which he was, after all, rather young, and quite untrained.

And the Reverend Mr. Johnson . . .

He stood up impatiently. What was the use? These men would all perform their appointed work faithfully enough, and according to the light which was in them. Something subtler was at the root of his uneasiness. It was not the men whom he was doubting, it was . . . the place . . .

Why? He found quick, clear reasons and paraded them smartly before an inner eye which still watched them unsatisfied. They were too isolated. Conventions, customs, morals, the intangible things by which human society ordered its communal life, had already become strangely ghostly here. The sharp outline of accepted standards was already wavering. It was his business to redraw it, blacker, clearer, more uncompromising than ever. And he would do it. For that, after all, he was here—to plant in a remote and barbaric land the seed of his own land's glorious tradition. . . . With a faint uneasy chill he seemed to feel the danger at his side stir a little, as though, again, he had made a false move.

Impatiently his thoughts shifted from vague apprehensions to the practical matters in which he always found himself at home. Hunger. His eyes, still blindly focussed on the dull green trees outside, became seeing and anxious. What, in Heaven's name, did this country afford in the way of foodstuffs? They had caught some fish, and one of the men had shot a bird which was said to be fair eating; kangaroos did not seem to be plentiful, and so far no edible fruits or berries had been discovered. If the promised storeships with fresh supplies should be delayed—or lost . . .

But he shook this thought away, too, annoyed with himself that he should be brooding on imagined troubles when such present and immediate ones clamoured for his attention. The natives, for instance. What was to be apprehended from them? They seemed to be peaceable enough, but their bearing was alert and resolute, and there might be any number of them. They might be, at the least, a constant harassment, and, at the worst, a definite menace. In one corner of his mind, awaiting the moment when he should have leisure to put it into execution, he stored a plan for winning their confidence. It was a plan in which the practical good sense of the man clashed strangely with the unimaginative habit of his time. He saw no difficulty in the way of forming an acquaintance with these savages. If none presented themselves at the camp voluntarily, it would be a simple matter to capture one or two of them, and to show them, in their captivity, such marks of consideration as would make it apparent to them that they had nothing to fear. So he thought, sitting at his table, his mind more sharply whetted, more richly stored than the minds of the natives, but his sensitiveness so blunted by the constant sight of men in chains, men imprisoned, men humiliated, that he failed to see what every black child knew without teaching—that the only restraint which a man can support without loss of dignity is that which he imposes on himself.

He rose, his hand still pressed absently against his side, and went to the doorway to send for King. Standing there, he beckoned to a convict who was working near by, and when the man had gone on his errand the Governor still stood staring at a scene whose desolation was emphasised by the lowering sky. The twigs and branches of felled trees littered the ground, the tents and improvised shelters had a makeshift air, the scattered implements and contrivances of civilisation seemed incongruous and even a little unreal, like things seen in dreams. The whole place, he thought, looked like a fresh wound; and when he lifted his head and turned it, searching with troubled eyes the sky, the hills, the water, his thoughts were not only of the threatening storm.

* * *

During those first days, encouraged by a confusion which increased rather than abated, Prentice became more and more optimistic. The whole scheme, he told himself jubilantly, was going to collapse before very long. The Governor had as much chance of building a permanent community here as he had of flying. Fiercely, fed not only from his own experience but bred in him by generations of ancestors who had lived hardly and died bitterly for the benefit of their betters, he rejoiced at what he saw as the inevitable downfall of at least one small section of the class he hated. Outnumbered, ill-equipped, divided against itself (for he had kept his ears alert, and it was an open secret that the Governor and the Lieutenant-Governor were at loggerheads), what chance would they have against a well-planned rebellion, once the transports and their crews had left? Contemptuously he refused to be one of the many who, during that first week, deserted, and, making their way through the forest to Botany Bay, tried to persuade the Frenchmen to take them back to Europe. Fools! Prentice grinned at them sourly as they straggled back to the settlement, ragged, weary and despairing.

But, after a few days, he felt a restlessness. The mere fact of release from the airless, verminous, and crowded quarters of the transport was something to which many of the convicts already felt their bodies responding. At night they still returned there, for huts were not yet ready for more than a few, but during the day they moved in sunlight, in air which was hot and close with threatening storms, but fresh and cleanly-smelling, and there was space about them, and distances to look at, and movement for muscles slackened by disuse. They began to feel hungry, ravenous, and they watched the livestock being landed with avid, calculating eyes.

One evening, a youth called Barrett said to Prentice:

"I could fancy a bit o' fresh meat. Shouldn't be hard . . . one night? Eh?"

Prentice gave him a sideways glance and a non-committal nod. He knew that Barrett, in spite of his youth, was an enterprising fellow. His skill and audacity in manufacturing counterfeit coins from spoons and buttons and buckles during the voyage had earned for him the admiration and respect of his fellows, and had fed an always lively sense of his own superiority. But Prentice had been nursing his own ambition, and, tight as his belt lay across his hollow stomach, his schemes went deeper than the stealing of a fowl or a few pounds of flour. Since coming to this place he had found himself remembering that he was country-bred. The ugly years of hand-to-mouth existence in London had so filled his consciousness that not until he had found himself treading the bare ground and looking up at the sky through the leaves of trees, had he remembered that his boyhood had been passed among people who won subsistence from the earth. So he replied shortly:

"Time enough for that. I got other plans."

He did not expound them, suspecting shrewdly that they would not appeal to Barrett to whom an audience was the first necessity. Barrett did not press him. He liked the centre of the stage for himself, and he had no use for men who made plans independently. To secure for himself small alleviations from time to time was the minor reason for his ceaseless campaign against authority. What drove him was the need for drama, the excitement of plotting and intrigue, the illusion of a freely functioning will.

Prentice left him and slouched away down to the water's edge. He stood on a rock watching the silver line of the water lapping around it, and thinking. It was a gun he wanted, and a spade, and a supply of grain, things for sustenance and self-defence, things for a free man. If these damned savages, he thought, spitting contemptuously into the clear water, could live from the land, so could he, for a time. He would be satisfied now with nothing but freedom. Not freedom in ten years' time, when his sentence was expired, but soon, here, in this drab, silent and accursed country, which had set up its impalpable resistances against him the first moment he looked at it. His aggressiveness, always aflame against authority, was now turned, too, upon a place which he felt had tried to intimidate him, and he saw escape and survival as a double victory—over his gaolers and his gaol.

Good behaviour, he thought. That was the ticket. Orderly, civil, prompt in obedience, free with his "Sirs" and "Your Honours." Watching all the time. There would be small privileges, a little less surveillance for such men. An opportunity would come. He must have a good cache somewhere in the woods, to be furnished by degrees with tools, food, a gun and ammunition, so that when the moment arrived he could slip away unburdened. . . .

A movement behind him made him turn so sharply that he almost overbalanced from his rock. He had been so deeply absorbed in his thoughts that it had seemed as if they must be apparent to an eavesdropper as they were to himself, and his eyes, as he turned, were murderous. A child of about four, clad in nondescript garments, stared back at him, frightened, but hostile.

If it hadn't been for the red hair, Prentice thought, so like his own, and the sharp, dark eyes, he might not have known his son. In the year since their arrest had separated him from his wife, the child had not so much grown as altered. He seemed not exactly bigger, but longer, thinner, sharper, less baby and more boy. They stared at each other, without affection on the man's part, or recognition on the child's, and Prentice said at last in a voice which sounded threatening, because he was still startled:

"Where's your mother?"

The child pointed across the water to one of the ships. His father noticed that when he was scared he still sucked furiously at his thumb.

He asked:

"Who brought you ashore, then?"

Again the child pointed, turning this time to indicate two women, wives of marines, who were gossiping with a couple of men near the Governor's house. But his eyes swung back at once, fascinated and fearful, to the head of this terrifying man. He had been so teased on the ship about the colour of his hair that it had become, to his mind, inseparable from his own individuality, and now here was a man with a lowering, unkindly face, who had just such hair as his own, and who stirred in him dim recollections which were ugly and unwelcome. His months on a convict transport had still further enlarged a vocabulary already rich beyond his years in profanity; suddenly he removed his thumb, and with shrill bravado spat out a stream of blasphemous invective.

Prentice glared at him, feeling a red flush of temper darken his face. It was because of this brat, after all, that he was here. He got down from the rock and bent over the child, glancing up and about as he did so to see that they were not being watched. He said, low and with menace:

"I'm y' father, see? And little boys that speak uncivil to their fathers die and go to hell and get burnt up by flames. And when you get back to that ship you tell y' mother how you saw me, and you tell her if she's been up to any tricks like some of the women I'll skin her alive, see? And you, too!"

The child sucked even more furiously at his thumb. His eyes widened and darkened and his face paled, but he did not budge. It was Prentice who, edging round him and swearing under his breath, walked heavily away.

* * *

It was very hot, even in the shade of the trees, though indeed this shade was not like English shade, dense and dark and cool. The high, sparse leaves only filtered the fierce sunlight, spilling it in flickering coins of light on the bark and twig besprinkled ground. Mr. Johnson's voice rose and fell in a monotonous chant, and Captain Tench stifled a yawn and blinked tears from his eyes, thinking that, in their present situation, "What shall I render to the Lord for all His benefits toward me?" was perhaps as unsuitable a text as that worthy gentleman could have chosen.

Nevertheless, he admitted, looking round with benign approval, nearly everyone was listening with a praiseworthy semblance of attention. It would be impossible to swear, for instance, from the Governor's decorously impassive face that he was wrestling mentally with the thousand problems which beset him; or from the far-away stare of Dawes that he was engrossed in calculations; or from the dark and handsomely saturnine countenance of Hunter that he was still speculating about the natives, whose manners and customs had so intrigued his attention. Nor was the scowl on Major Ross' face to be necessarily attributed to regrets for his five fine sheep killed yesterday by lightning, for a scowl was, nowadays, his normal expression. All one could be certain of, Tench decided, allowing his gaze to rest for a distasteful moment on the slightly open mouth and the glazing eyes of Lieutenant Clark, was that that young man's thoughts were certainly with his wife Betsey, tales of whose peerless loveliness and impregnable virtue Captain Tench found extremely tedious.

Several of the convicts were nodding. As the service progressed and the sun beat down still more fiercely, steam rose from the ground sodden by the fierce thunderstorms of the previous two days. The Reverend Mr. Johnson, gasping in the humid air, strove manfully with his enumeration of the benefits which the Lord had rendered them, while on the western hillside Bennilong and his companions lay hidden, watching him with awe and wonder.

Was there, they marvelled, no end to the eccentricities of this tribe? For now it would appear that not the slender man in the blue coat was the leader, but this other with the round pale face like Yenandah, the moon, for all bowed their heads before him and muttered spells to avert his anger. Yet it could be seen that sometimes he lifted his face toward the sky as if in supplication, and once, his voice growing stern, he pointed, warningly, heavenward. Was it possible, Kuurin whispered to Bennilong, that this tribe also knew of Baiame, the good spirit, who dwells in the heavens? Might it be that the moon-faced one was aware of the visits which Baiame sometimes paid to the earth, bringing gifts to the good and meting out punishment to the wicked, and might he, perhaps, be warning his people of such a coming, bidding them search their hearts that they might be ready to meet the judgment of the Maker-of-all?

Indeed, had his words been comprehensible to them, they might have understood him to be saying exactly that. But the convicts, to whom his exhortation was mainly addressed, were not really listening. They heard his voice only as a familiar noise, long since shorn of any meaning or of any true bearing upon their lives. "Be just," religion said to them, sheltering in the skirts of the society which meted out injustice. "Steal not," leaving them to a life in which not to steal was not to eat. "Be temperate, be continent," it said to them whose harsh existence was only made endurable by spells of black oblivion.

So they had long ago ceased to listen. They did not listen now but stood, a shuffling, ill-smelling crowd, soporific in the moist heat, thinking vaguely of scenes whose squalor stank against the primitive cleanliness of their present surroundings. Thinking of crowded city slums, of thatched hovels in the country, of a land which had repudiated them, but to which, because it was familiar, their thoughts returned with a hopeless longing. Under this torrent of hot, golden light they stood bemused, and dreamed of a gently tinted landscape. The apparent passivity of the country had not prepared them for the fury of the storm which it had loosed on them in the height of their disembarkation. The rain had come down, not in drops but solidly; they staggered under it. It lashed their faces, ran in rivers round their ankles, soaked their ragged clothes, beat their tents and their miserable mud huts to the ground. Their nerves still remembered the horrifying sound of a great tree splintering to fragments, their eyes were wearied by the glare of lightning, their eardrums battered to exhaustion by the crash of thunder. So now, lulled by Mr. Johnson's voice, they searched their memories for rain which fell softly, soaking into green fields, splashing on stone pavements, blurring the hard edges of buildings, dimming the distant hills. These images were not thoughts; for all their thoughts were bitter, twisted away from beauty, hardened against hope. They were no more than a shield unconsciously set up between themselves and an alien environment, a respite from the effort of adjustment.

It was that word "adjustment" which was in the Governor's mind. Looking over the ranks of convicts, he felt a bitter indignation stir in him. He had asked for men who had some training or some knowledge which would make them useful in the establishment of a colony; at the very least, he had urged, let him have sound men, healthy men. Never, by one word, spoken or written, would he criticise His Majesty's Government, but in his heart he knew that its first concern had been to rid itself as expeditiously as possible of human beings whose utter uselessness would make them, in any community, an expensive embarrassment, a well-nigh insoluble problem.

There they were. Old, sick, idle, depraved, ignorant. His material. On that treacherous foundaton he must, somehow, build solidly. It seemed possible to him. Calm and unemotional as he was, he could see visions. It was this quality in him, perhaps, which so antagonised Major Ross, who could see little but grievances. In the lean years still mercifully hidden from them, it was a quality which was to sustain not only himself but the whole community.

After the storms of the last day or two, his anxiety was chiefly for shelter. But already he had received unfavorable accounts of the timber, and among all the convicts he had only been able to muster twelve carpenters, several of whom were unfit for work. From the ships, he planned, deaf to Mr. Johnson's eloquence, he would hire a few more, and, lacking proper overseers, the marines would have to be pressed into service as supervisors. The tools and implements which had been sent out satisfied him neither in quantity nor in quality, but they must be made to do. The reserve of clothing provided for the convicts was inferior and mostly too small; the crease between his eyes deepened as he thought of the coming winter. He decided, too, that he must protest again in his despatches, as he had protested before their departure from England, against the incredible folly of sending convicts and stores in different ships. In spite of the heat, he felt a cold pricking of his skin at the thought of their plight now, had one of their store-ships been lost on the voyage.

For it was pretty clear, already, that the country was not going to help them to food any more than to shelter. There seemed to be no edible fruits, few berries, and very little game. Fish were sometimes fairly plentiful and sometimes very scarce. The soil, too, looked less promising for cultivation than he had hoped, and he had been concerned to find himself even poorer in agriculturists than in carpenters. In all the colony, there seemed to be not even a trained and intelligent gardener.

In a momentary retreat from the mounting burden of his anxieties, he thought of the land itself. Even in the turmoil of these first days he had been conscious of a thousand new things—strange plants, flowers, trees, seeds—things which he had handled, examined, wondered over, wishing himself a botanist, or that he had someone with him to take an expert and knowledgeable interest in this treasure trove. Sir Joseph Banks, he reflected, must see specimens of all these things. In the course of those expeditions inland, which he was already impatient to begin, he would make a collection to send to his friend at the first opportunity. For himself, he realised, they could be only symbols of the country. In their unfamiliar shapes and textures they embodied for him the thing which he felt set against him—the almost terrifying differentness of the land. He was conscious of this, but not of his own reaction to it, and still less of the hidden significance of that reaction. For his thoughts were again of adjustment. Mr. Johnson was already adjusting himself to Divine Service beneath a tree instead of a roof. Major Ross and his marines must adjust themselves to the idea of performing duties not normally a part of their routine. The convicts, bred to see themselves as enemies of society, must be taught differently. He himself must be all the time alert to catch the mood of changing time and circumstance. He thought of it as a voluntary adjustment, not conscious of it as the first moulding process of the land.

* * *

Three days later the women came ashore. Ellen Prentice, with Johnny on her knee, sat in the bow of one of the boats, and looked back at the transport almost with regret. She had been born in a city slum; in all her life she had never trodden on the unpaved earth. The horrors of the ship she knew, but the horrors of life on shore were only to be guessed. Her guesses had been garnished by rumour and by hints from the seamen until now her eyes, turning toward the land, were round and stupid with alarm.

It was not her husband whom she feared. It was not the knowledge which she shared with the other women, the awareness of a starved and uncontrollable lust awaiting them. They could meet and match that; their lives had not taught them fastidiousness. Ellen was pregnant again, but this did not disturb her in spite of her husband's message, which Johnny had faithfully transmitted, for she knew her value in a community where women were so outnumbered.

It was the place which frightened her. She had never lived so close to trees before. Nor were there proper houses for them to go to—only tents and a few rudely constructed huts of boughs plastered over with mud. And there were blacks. Naked savages, almost certainly cannibals according to the seamen, bloodthirsty and ferocious, would prowl, armed with spears, about the settlement at night. Having no God and no religion, thought Ellen, with simplicity, what was to deter them from wanton slaying? She clutched Johnny closer, measuring their distance from the shore with her eyes, telling herself despairingly that she would almost as soon jump out of the boat and drown as set foot on that gloomy, unfamiliar shore.

Long before they landed she saw her husband. His red head always made him conspicuous in any crowd, and now, with the morning sunlight touching it, it was like a flame. A few of the women were sullen, but most were laughing shrilly. New slops had been issued to them the day before, and all had made some attempt at tidiness—some even at adornment. They were all nervously conscious of a tension, as if some magnetic attraction were drawing them toward the moving, muttering crowd upon the shore. Ellen, feeling herself caught by it, too, responded to the crude witticism of a girl beside her, with a high, unreal giggle, so that Johnny, very still upon her knee, looked up into her face, and then quickly down again at the water.

Ellen had always been dull-witted, but the normal instincts of her sex were strong in her. Promiscuity held no particular appeal to her, but she would always take the line of least resistance. She wanted a man, and would have been quite content with one, but almost any one would do. Nevertheless, she had spent her life in an environment which had taught her to use what power she had on her own behalf, and she was conscious today of her youth, and her still neat figure, her bright eyes, and her mass of long, dark hair. Her love for Johnny was fierce and possessive, but entirely unimaginative. She had stolen recklessly to feed him, but now, feeling him tremble in her arms, she thought his fear was for the deep water which he was watching over the side of the boat, and was quite incapable of realising that a child might be sensitive to a mass emotion which could be made only more terrifying by its incomprehensibility.

When they landed, she set him down on the ground beside her, and, almost instantly, he was in the centre of a crowd. He could see nothing at all but the raggedly clad legs of men and the drab coloured skirts of women; they pressed about him, continually moving, and from above his head there came a sudden clamour of voices in which his own feeble, protesting cry was drowned. He was clutching his mother's skirt, and, unsteady as he was from long confinement and inadequate food, it was only this frantic grip which kept him on his feet at all. Suddenly he realised that all the skirts were alike, and panic seized him. *Was* this his mother? Or that? Or this other one behind him? He peered up, trying to catch a glimpse of her face, but the suffocating press of bodies was too close about him, and, although he hardly ever wept, he felt tears gather in his eyes now and let out a wail which still passed unnoticed in the uproar.

This could not be his mother who let his cry go unheeded. He released the skirt, and grabbed another, tugging at it urgently, but an unfamiliar face glared down at him, flushed and angry, and an impatient hand whisked it from his grasp. Utterly confused now he clutched first at one and then at another, staggering and frightened, the hard knees of men bruising him, his small feet continually trampled, until, anchoring himself to another skirt, he was borne at last to the edge of the crowd, and there, glancing upward only to find himself still motherless, he abandoned himself to an overwhelming despair.

He made no outcry about it, but stood quite still, sucking his thumb and looking at the ground. This, he had long ago discovered, was the safest thing to do in moments of doubt or misery. To look about one was to see bewildering and frightening things. To look at the faces of grown-up people was worst of all. So he kept his head well down, and, suddenly, at his feet, as if to reward him, he saw something comforting and lovely.

He bent and picked it up, glancing round with the furtiveness of habit. It was a short, grey twig, and on the end of it were three little wooden cups. They were so small that he could not even put the tip of his little finger into them, but they were exquisitely round and perfect, and delicately divided inside into four neat compartments. To whom did it belong, this lovely and exciting small thing? His eyes became sharp and sly, and he held it against his body with both hands to conceal it, for he was not going to give it up—no, not for anything, not even if he was whipped for stealing, not even if they told him again about the flames and torments which were in store for thieves.

It would be best to run away and hide with it. He looked about, and noticed the stream, thinking how entrancing it would be to fill the little cups with water and drink from them. He edged away slowly, still staring very hard at the ground, as if by not looking at any grown-ups he could make himself invisible to them.

Away from the clearing and into the patchy shadow of the trees, he stopped and sat down on the ground behind a log to examine his treasure. His tautly strung nerves slackened, and he slid with the merciful ease of childhood into a timeless world, too rarely visited, where he was happy and at peace. He gathered up a little of the sandy earth and filled the cups with it; then he poured it out and found tiny pinkish pebbles which would go in instead. After a while he broke the cups from the twig and turned them upside down, when they became caps, and he himself small enough to wear them, small enough to walk hidden in the coarse grass, to hide under a brown leaf, to go about his own affairs unnoticed, undisturbed.

To be alone, free from restriction and exhortation, was so strange and heady a luxury that he became a little drunk with it. In the cramped quarters on the transport which he had inhabited for so long, he had all but forgotten any other kind of environment; now it seemed that there was no limit to where one might walk. He could remember London vaguely; there one could go a long way in the streets, but if one ventured into invitingly open doorways one was apt to be hustled out again and beaten or, at least, scolded. No dream which he had ever dreamed had suggested such spaciousness as this. Nor was it an alarming spaciousness, for it was all the same; one became accustomed to it as one walked. It confronted one with no shocks, but was, instead, one long series of pleasant small surprises.

He moved slowly, stopping now and then to examine some leaf or stone or low growing flower. He found that there were shrubs which pricked, and learned to edge round them, and once a huge insect, whirring its papery wings on a near-by branch, startled him into an upward glance. But mostly he stuck to his rule of watching the ground. It was near to him, and friendly, and almost every step rewarded him with a new find. He climbed a hill without noticing that it was a hill, but by the time he reached the top he was very hot and rather tired, so he sat down in the shade of an overhanging rock and began to play with his wooden cups again. While he sat there, clouds obscured the sun, and thunder grumbled distantly. He was afraid and thought of returning, but a sharp, heavy downpour of rain kept him crouching in the shelter of his rock, and by the time the sun came out again and the threatening storm passed over, he forgot his fears and became absorbed in his game once more.

It was the sound of footsteps which made him look up, expecting, re-signedly, to see his mother or someone from the settlement come to take him back and punish him for running away. But it was a black man, standing not ten paces from him, and Johnny felt his limbs, all his body, go weak and watery with terror.

He had not believed that there were black people. He had often been told to behave or a black man would get him, but he had not behaved, and no black man had come, so he had thought that it was only another of the lies which grown-up people so frequently told. Now he knew that retribution was upon him; he had stolen the little cups, and here was the black man come to punish him.

This alarming person wore no clothes at all; he was standing quite still leaning on a long stick, and looking steadily away over the tree-tops. Obeying, from habit, his ostrichlike instinct, Johnny bent his head, sucked his thumb, and stared fixedly at the ground between his thin, outstretched legs.

But the movement was his undoing. It brought his red head from shadow to sunlight, and Arabanoo's quick eye caught its metallic gleam. He uttered an exclamation of astonishment and took two steps toward the child, who lifted his head and opened his mouth to scream. The black man and the white child stared at each other for a long moment, and the scream, halted on Johnny's lips, found its way out eventually as a rather absent-minded sob. For the man looked quite friendly. After a sharp, quick look around, as if to discover whether any more white people were about, he had turned again to Johnny and was smiling, saying something which, though it was incomprehensible, did not sound threatening. His long stick was pointed at one end, and looked as if it could kill a person very easily, but he seemed to have no hostile intention, for he leaned it against a tree trunk and squatted beside Johnny patting him on the back in the most reassuring way. Now and then, uttering what sounded like exclamations of surprise, but always smiling, he fingered the child's clothes; it was the thatch of brilliant hair, however, which most intrigued him. He could keep neither his eyes nor his hands away from it, and seemed to invite comparison with his own by bending his head and guiding Johnny's hand to his own dark and tangled locks.

But Johnny's fist was tightly clenched and would not open, so presently, with one large black forefinger, the stranger touched it enquiringly. Johnny jumped. Was he, after all, to be punished for his theft? Was this the rightful owner of the little wooden cups? The black man, laughing and talking, tried very gently to force the child's fingers up, and, at last, mistrustful and despairing, Johnny slowly yielded and showed the contents of his small, grubby palm.

The black man laughed quite loudly now, and pointed upward to the trees. Johnny stared at him solemnly, content not to understand so long as he might close his fingers again over his treasure. But suddenly the black man jumped up and went to the foot of a tall tree, and before Johnny's round and unbelieving eyes, walked straight up the slender trunk and disappeared. If Johnny had looked up he could have watched, but his habit was too strong. Down his head went; while strange things were afoot it was safer so. He did not look up even when he knew the black man was beside him again, for he was frightened of a being who could walk up trees.

A black hand was thrust under his eyes; he stared at it incredulously. It was *full* of little cups—many, many of them, so many that his own hands could not hold them all. He looked up into a widely grinning face, and slowly, almost painfully, he smiled.

Now they were friends. When Arabanoo, pointing down the other side of the hill, made signs to Johnny to accompany him, the child scrambled to his feet willingly enough, stowing his playthings in a pocket in the skirt of his clumsy smock. Arabanoo, looking down at him, marvelled at the unsteadiness of his legs, and at the inexpert way in which he set his feet down, so that stones slipped and twigs rolled beneath them, and he was in constant danger of falling. This birrahlee, he decided, would take all day to reach the side of the gully where his wife and his son and a couple of other children were hunting for witchetty grubs in the great rotting logs, so he bent and swung Johnny to his shoulders.

After the first convulsive moment of fear, the child clutched Arabanoo's thick hair and accepted the new arrangement. Presently, as he began to adjust himself to the swinging rhythm of the black man's movements, he found that he enjoyed being so high up in the air. He could still see nothing but trees—the whole world, it seemed, held nothing else. From the deck of the transport he had seen trees on the shore at Rio and the Cape, but they had not seemed real to him; they were a scene, a picture, at which he had looked from afar. In the part of London where he had lived there had been no trees at all, though he had a hazy memory of having seen some somewhere in that dead and vanished life. These were the first he had ever touched, and sometimes, lifting one hand cautiously, he was able to grab a leaf or two as they passed. They felt cool and smooth in his hot palms, and he was conscious of a strange but rather pleasant smell which came from them.

Presently they reached the bottom of the hill and paused at the edge of a little stream, running briskly after the heavy rain of the last few days. Arabanoo swung Johnny from his shoulders and set him down on his feet on a flat rock beside the water, and, immediately, wild with joy and excitement behind his solemn face and unsmiling eyes, Johnny realised that now he could fill his little cups and drink from them. He squatted on the rock and emptied his pocket carefully. He heard Arabanoo call out something—a strange call, first long drawn out and then sharp and short: "Coo-oo-oo-ee!" But he was too busy to pay much attention. He took one of the wooden cups and dipped it in the water; it held so little that when he tilted it to his mouth it yielded no more than a moisture on his lips, but it was cool and delicious, and he proceeded methodically, laying the cups from which he had drunk to one side, and taking new ones from the other.

A shrill babel of voices made him look up, impatient of being disturbed. On the opposite side of the stream, staring at him, pointing and gesticulating delightedly were a black woman and two, no, three, black children. Johnny's mouth, open in readiness for the next cup, remained open in sheer astonishment. It had never occurred to him that there would be black children. There were a boy and a girl of about his own age, and an older boy. None of them wore any clothes. They seemed to be having an argument about him, for the woman and the two boys kept on crying out: "Wongerra!" while the little girl shrilly insisted: "Werowey!"

He let them chatter, saying nothing himself, for this, also, he had found, was safest. When they splashed through the stream and clustered round him he stood up and allowed them to examine his clothes and his hair as the man had done; now he did not look at the ground, but returned their stare with solemn and unblinking eyes. He wondered why they had no clothes, and their obvious admiration of his own single rough garment gave him, for a moment, a little thrill of superiority—the first he had ever known. But when he saw how the children waded in the deeper pools, how they splashed each other and pushed each other over, to arise again, spluttering and squealing with laughter, he decided that perhaps it would be pleasanter to be naked, and he dragged at his ill-fitting smock until something gave way, and he struggled out of it.

There was a smitten silence. The black people stared, fascinated, at his thin, milk-white body, and the children came closer, and the younger boy, awed, stretched out a forefinger to touch his skin. Suddenly the little girl began to wail. "Wongerra!" she sobbed heartbrokenly, "wongerra! wongerra!" She sat down with a bump in the shallow water, her fat legs sticking out in front of her, and wept inconsolably. The boys snatched the word and made a gleeful chant of it. "Wongerra! wongerra!" they exulted, capering triumphantly about him.

But Arabanoo's wife, Milba, was disturbed. What kind of a mother had this birrahlee, who allowed him to starve so that his little bones showed through his white skin? She picked up her grass-woven basket and rummaged in it. Their search for witchetty grubs had been a successful one today—a couple of handfuls squirmed in the bottom of her basket, white and fat and succulent. She took two in her palm and squatted beside the white child, offering them, asking cajolingly: "Yuroo? Yuroo?"

Johnny looked down at the grubs with interest. He touched them with his finger, but drew it away quickly when they moved. The boys urged him reassuringly. Arabanoo himself nodded encouragement and repeated many times: "Boodjerree." Even the little girl stopped weeping and came nearer to watch. It did not occur to Johnny that these things were being offered him for food, so he merely stared. The woman, surprised and shocked by his ignorance, bade one of the boys demonstrate their excellence, which he did more than willingly, while the others looked on with eyes so full of envy that Johnny, who was not yet old enough to have acquired very firmly rooted prejudices, at last accepted one and bit a piece off it, tentatively.

He did not like it much, and in any case he was not as hungry as Milba imagined. He had never known what it was to feed well, and his body had come to accept a meagre diet as natural. So he handed the other half back, and sat down on the rock again to continue his play.

The sun was almost set before the game broke up. Arabanoo and his wife left them early in the afternoon for there was the evening meal to be sought. It had been a strange kind of game, for in Johnny there was an unchildlike tenacity of purpose which was almost grim; he had decided that he was going to fill the little cups and drink from them, and he did so, solemnly and interminably, setting down one and picking up another with an awful and unvarying regularity. The black children could not beguile him from it. Their movements about him were like the wayward hoverings of butterflies. Their interest flickered from one thing to another, bright and transient as sunlight. While he squatted immovably in one spot, they were everywhere—a hundred yards up the stream, a hundred yards down it; this side, that side, scrambling up a boulder, running like 'possums along a fallen log. Now and then they joined him. Clustered round him, incessantly chattering, his silence surprised, but did not damp them; indeed they had soon decided among themselves that he could not speak. When he put his smock on again, they watched him with awe. It was back to front, but that worried neither them nor him.

When the shadows were long, Arabanoo returned. He had sent his wife home to camp with the evening meal, and he swung Johnny on to his shoulder again and set off with him up the hill. The black children stood beside the stream and called after him shrilly, waving their arms. Johnny clutched Arabanoo's hair and wondered where he was to be taken now. He had been happy all day though he scarcely knew it, and active happiness was so wearying an emotion that he felt sleepy now, and his thoughts turned to his mother, having no image of home.

It was almost dusk when Arabanoo set him on the ground and pointed down the hill to lights showing between the trees. There were more lights than usual tonight, and much more noise; the black man decided that the white tribes were holding a corroboree, and was benevolently pleased that his small charge should be back in time to enjoy such festivities as might be thought proper for him.

Johnny stood dumbly, feeling a strange heaviness settle on his spirits again. He understood that this was where his mother was, for he could see the ships moored in the cove, so he looked once at Arabanoo, and then set off obediently, though without enthusiasm, for his mind retained a memory of some fear which had assailed him in this place.

Whatever it was, he could still feel it there, and more strongly than ever. It was growing dark when he came out from the trees into the clearing, and cooking fires were alight before the huts and tents. Through their shifting red glare figures moved wildly, and huge shadows were thrown so that it looked as if giants were reeling and capering about. There was a great deal of shouting and cursing, bursts of singing, drunken laughter, savage quarrelling, and once a long, shrill scream. Johnny halted. Remembering the red-headed man's threat, he knew then that his mother was being skinned alive, and that in a little while, most likely, his own turn would come. Like an insect feigning death, he froze into immobility, his head bent, staring at the ground, sucking furiously at his thumb.

*   *   *

Lightning was flickering far away over the low hilltops, and there was a distant grumble of thunder. Sailors had come ashore from some of the transports bringing rum, and in the rows of tents and huts, and in the shadows of trees and rocks, there was a wild uprising of too long frustrated desire, an orgy of emotional release. Drunk, not only with the hot, strong spirits, the convicts challenged the unforgiving grimness of their lives; the raucous blasphemies and obscenities which they uttered were flung up, distorted, from some still unbroken defiance of the shapeless and nameless power which held them captive. Here were a few hours which they could snatch from the dreary procession of todays and tomorrows; in the dark blue velvet of the night, close and still with the threat of the rising storm, they snatched and drained them, wringing from them their last ounce of ecstasy, finding in an instinctive retreat into primitive emotion a symbol of spiritual potency, a shadowy reminder of lost human power.

The Governor was nowhere to be seen—in fact, all the officers were conspicuous by their invisibility. It was tacitly admitted that, though Authority had sown a wind, it was not prepared to reap the whirlwind. So Johnny, motionless, shapeless as a small dark shrub in the gathering night, stood unnoticed and alone. He stood for so long that he almost fell asleep on his feet, and was roused, his heart thumping madly with shock, by a clap of thunder almost overhead. Rain began to fall in large, slow drops, and lightning lit the world luridly. It was a world in which Johnny could see no nook or corner for himself, and he stared almost longingly at his ship, moored far out across the black water where he could not reach it.

At last, with a resignation terrible in its maturity, he began to walk slowly towards the tents. It was raining heavily now, and nervous as he was of the noise, and the dark, firelit figures, he was still more frightened of the lonely menace of the night. Near the first hut, as he sidled up to it in the shadows, a woman, half-clad and more than half drunk, saw him and called something which might have been a curse or an endearment, but he eluded her waveringly outstretched hand, and slid through the low entrance into the hut behind her. He stumbled over a prostrate body, and a man, invisible, swore at him, and flung him off. A woman's voice let out a wild yell of laughter which was so suddenly quenched that the silence after it seemed shaking. Johnny edged away into a corner and sat quite still. After a while, his eyes grew accustomed to the darkness, but what he saw filled him with such a dreary sense of fear and hopelessness and bewilderment that he took refuge in his tried technique, and kept his head down and his eyes on the ground. He remembered that he had had no supper and pressed his hands over his stomach, wishing that he had eaten all of the white wriggling grub which the black woman had offered him. The rain was pelting down now, and two other people had squeezed into the hut. Johnny was afraid they might throw him out, so he lay down and buried himself under some stale-smelling garments which were lying about, and partly because he was too small to take up much room, and partly because they were too drunk to notice him, the other occupants of the hut let him lie undisturbed. After a while he fell asleep, and dreamed horribly.

* * *

Captain Tench sat long over his journal that night, but wrote little. He was nothing if not a man of the world, and yet he had seen things that day which stirred an uneasiness in him. He had come early to his quarters on the *Charlotte,* seeking quiet and fulfilling the Governor's instructions that officers were to turn a blind eye and a deaf ear upon the orgy which would inevitably take place after the landing of the women.

But quiet was not to be had that night. The hardly endurable heat of the day had culminated again in a storm, and even to a less lively imagination than Tench's it might have seemed that all the evil of earth and heaven was let loose, and some reckless spirit of self-destruction in the settlement was lifting itself in challenge to the destroying sky. Almost simultaneously with the thin, purplish glare of the lightning came thunder; bursting suddenly in a crack which seemed to shake the ship, it alternated with the distant sounds of singing and shouting from the shore, and from the other vessels in the cove.

It was still very hot. Captain Tench played with his pen and looked at his virgin page thinking, with unwonted soberness, that it would be easy to dismiss this business as being merely a demonstration of the incorrigible depravity of a set of hopeless rogues. It would be easy, and perhaps comforting to oneself, to be able to regard the Saturnalia which was going on ashore with the unmitigated horror and disgust with which, for instance, Mr. Johnson regarded it. It might even be easy to hate all the convicts, and particularly the women, as Lieutenant Clark did, with a hatred so viperish and sadistic as to suggest to Captain Tench a condition of mind which would have been far from acceptable to the pure and spotless Betsey.

What was hard for a young man who had always found the ethical rules laid down for him by custom quite adequate to any situation which he had met before, was to be confronted by a disturbing suspicion that rogues and roguery might arise otherwise than from an innate disposition towards evil.

He wiped his fingers, sticky with heat, on his handkerchief, and settled himself with determination to write. His notes of these first few days had not been as full as he could have wished. There had been so much to do. He turned back to glance at what he had last written:

"But as severity alone was known to be inadequate at once to chastise and reform, no opportunity was omitted to assure the convicts that by their good behaviour and submissive deportment, every claim to present distinction and future favour was to be earned."

Well, he thought, there was surely no fault to be found with that. A sound statement, well enough expressed, though not, perhaps, in his happiest style. He wrote on slowly, listening to a burst of shouting from the shore:

"That this caution was not attended with all the good effects which were hoped from it, I have only to lament; that it operated in some circumstances is indisputable; nor will a candid and humane mind . . ."

his pen moved faster now, "fail to consider and allow for the situation these unfortunate beings so peculiarly stood in. While they were kept on board ship, the two sexes had been kept most rigorously apart; but when landed their separation became impracticable, and would have been, perhaps, wrong. Licentiousness was the unavoidable consequence. . . ."

A crash of thunder shook the ship, so that the light from the lamp above shivered on his page. He flung his pen down, his nerves on edge. There was much to write still before he should have brought his narrative up-to-date, but tonight was not the time for it. He was suddenly acutely aware of their fearful isolation. He saw in imagination, as if he were God, the thousands of miles of coastline stretching north and south, dark, storm-swept, and in all its length only this one small, tortured fragment of another world, an alien people. One must cling tightly, he thought, under the impact of such a vision, to one's long established confidence, one's comforting awareness of superiority and dominion. One must remember England . . .

He was on his feet. He had seen too many storms to be easily disturbed by them, but that last clap of thunder, he thought ruefully, had seemed especially intended for his defenceless head. How was one to think of England in a country which bombarded one with reminders of itself in the shape of thunderbolts?

*   *   *

It was a sullen crowd of convicts which assembled next morning by the Governor's orders to hear his Commission read, and to witness the formal establishment of the colony. They were all by now suffering the natural reaction from their night of excess and carousal, and in the strong morning light they slouched exhaustedly, their sallow faces lined with fatigue and privation, their brows drawn sharply together, and their eyes half closed against the glare. There was a breeze blowing. It flapped the colours gaily and ruffled the surface of the water, but could not freshen the sullen and oppressive atmosphere. There were still storms about, threatening the already desperate confusion of the settlement with still greater chaos.

Among the women Ellen Prentice stood apathetically, stupid with weariness, too wrapped in the misery of her own physical distress to take even a desultory interest in the preparations for the coming ceremony. She nearly always felt this sickness in the mornings now, and today there was added to it the aftermath of drunkenness and lust, and a spiritual malaise more complicated, less easy to define.

When she had missed Johnny the day before she had felt, at first, nothing but the blind irritation of checked desire. She had told herself and others, impatiently, that he could not be far away, and she had searched for him crossly, with one ear for the angry jeers of her husband and the coarsely jesting allusions of other men. She did not know when it was that she had begun to be afraid, and too look over her shoulder, furtively, at the trees. Each time she found herself doing that she had turned away furiously, to search with the rapid thoroughness of panic among huts and tents and piles of stores and implements, thrusting into groups of people, clambering about rocks near the shore, peering behind the dying foliage of felled trees. She had called him, angrily: "Johnny! Johnny! Come out or I'll lam the 'ide off y'!" But when he still did not answer she had found herself looking at the trees again. The heat and her exertions had combined with the feverish excitement of her mood to reduce her to a queer state in which her thoughts came with the hazy inaccuracy of dreams. She did not think of seeking help in her search; she knew that Johnny was important to no one but herself. When she began walking towards the trees her fear increased at every step, so that she seemed moving in a nightmare with weights upon her feet, her brain tormented by a phantasmagoria of naked savages, enormous snakes, wild animals which she could only picture as lions or tigers. All that she remembered of it now was stifling heat, strange smells, shrubs which tore her hands and clothes, sounds which had brought her to a terrified standstill, staring wildly about for a visible danger which would have been almost a relief from the constant menace of invisible malignity which she felt surrounding her.

One moment detached itself. She had stood under a huge tree, and, feeling the nausea of her pregnancy threaten to overwhelm her, she had put out her hand to the great white trunk for support. It was cool and smooth; she had moved nearer and leaned her hot forehead against it gratefully.

Perhaps she had fainted then. Or very nearly, for what came afterward was no more than the dark chaos of dreaming. People about her—men and women—shouting and laughter—the hot, sweet, maddening liquor running through her body like a reviving flame. The black tide of desire rising to sweep away everything in its possessing flood, and her own wild laughter coming up out of the depths of it as from one who was glad to drown . . .

Now she was exhausted. Like the others she had spent herself physically and emotionally, maddened by the illusion of joy, until she had no sensation left. When Johnny had been discovered, flushed and feverish under his pile of rags in a corner of one of the huts, she had felt nothing but a dull ache of resentment. She had found enough physical strength to give him the few crude attentions which circumstances allowed—a drink of water, a makeshift bed in the shade, a mouthful or two of stale bread and salt pork which he had instantly vomited up again—and then she had sat beside him with her head in her hands while her soul retreated into dark labyrinths too tortuous for her ill-functioning brain to dare.

Her resentment was for a poverty in herself which she felt and knew to be unjust. She was being cheated. By the nine months when she had carried Johnny in her womb, and by the agony in which she had borne him, she had fairly earned of life a wealth which it was now denying her. Confusedly aware that the griefs and anxieties of motherhood are not less enriching than its joys, she searched her heart sullenly for ecstasy at Johnny's safety, nerve-stretching dread of his illness—and could find neither. Her life had somehow robbed her of her human birthright of sharp sensations. There was a murky twilight in her being which would no longer admit those electrifying streaks and flashes and explosions which mean pain or rapture, agony or ardour to less exhausted souls. She could not trace this bitterness to its source, but she felt it as a last injustice, a final unendurable addition to the burden of her life, and, standing now morosely among the other women, she did not even trouble to guess what new misery this assembly, with its noisy display of officialdom, was about to inflict on her.

When the order came for the convicts to sit on the ground she felt her knees give way, as if they had been merely awaiting the permission of authority. With her head bent, and her eyes closed, leaning heavily against the shoulder of the woman next to her, she sank into a torpor hardly stirred even by the drums and fifes which heralded the arrival of the marine battalion.

*   *   *

Phillip, watching with Captain Collins, the Judge-Advocate, from the door of his canvas house, was looking a little grim. He judged that this was the moment for a display of authority. The majestically unvarying law of nature which decrees that excess shall be followed by satiation had reduced this sorry crowd to a state in which they would be incapable of moral resistance to that other law which he represented. In a little while, when they had time to recover, they might remember the absence of restriction which they had enjoyed last night; now was the time to make it clear to them that authority was about to reassert itself.

Again the words of his Instructions were unequivocal:

". . . and being arrived, to take upon you the execution of the trust we have reposed in you, as soon as conveniently may be . . ."

He looked down at the marines who were now marching on to the ground, with a martial beat of drums and a gay fluttering of flags, and he felt an involuntary stiffening in himself, as if he were bracing himself to an ordeal not properly begun until now.

". . . with all due solemnity to cause our Commission under our Great Seal of Great Britain constituting you our Governor and Commander-in-Chief as aforesaid to be read and published."

With all due solemnity. He looked critically at the scene, vaguely dissatisfied with it, and yet unable to see how he could have added to its impressiveness. The marines, under arms, were now drawn up in a circle round the convicts, their scarlet coats contrasting bravely with the wayward blue of the water and the steadfast blue of the sky. The principal officers were grouped round the small camp table which had been set up to receive the red leather cases containing the documents which it would be the Judge-Advocate's task to read. Officers from the ships had come ashore to attend; the wives of the marines were all in their best; even Mrs. Johnson, by adding a white collar to her sober gown, had managed to convey her appreciation of the importance of this official occasion.

What was wanting? Why did it all look a little unreal, a little—even —yes—ridiculous? The Governor stared so hard that the scene performed that trick which so often results from a fixed gaze which becomes absent-minded and unfocussed. It receded; it became a queer little view through the wrong end of a telescope, a puppet-show very far away, a parade of mannikins—not even mannikins, but toy soldiers . . .

For one second, Phillip felt a most peculiar and agonising stab of shame. Not since he had been a very small child had he known that guilty sense of having made himself so ridiculous that there was nothing left for it but to die. In that second he saw, with wide-open, startled eyes, the truth which lay behind this childish display in which he was about to take his part. He saw this proclamation of ownership, with its pathetic bravado of pomp and ceremony, as a piece of infantile impertinence, of presumption so colossal and grotesque as to be worthy of nothing but the aloof indifference with which the land was treating it.

His whole conscious being, outraged, leapt to check and strangle this preposterous idea. He girded himself in his authority and in the prides and traditions in which he had been fostered. His moment of revelation had come and gone so swiftly that he was aware of nothing save that he had felt a momentary uneasiness which was now past. He said briefly:

"Time we went down, I think, Captain Collins."

They moved forward to take their places. Standing before that unimpressive table, watching Collins as he unfastened the cases and extracted the documents, Phillip's mind was fixed tenaciously upon the present. He saw himself above all and beyond all as a practical man, and mistrusted a little the perceptiveness which shot now and then like a disturbing ray across his well-disciplined thoughts and neatly ordered convictions. Here was a place and an occasion, he told himself, for keeping a cool head; he ignored the streak of warm irrationality which assured him that the seed of some future greatness lay in this dismal beginning. He narrowed his vision grimly and deliberately, like a man crossing treacherous marshland, who must keep his eyes for the next precarious foothold. One step at a time, but each step firm—and forward. At the moment his most pressing business was to recover moral ascendancy, to make unequivocally clear, not only to the convicts but to the whole community, his position of authority, and his inflexible determination to use it for the best interest of the settlement as a whole. This meant isolation. It meant an austere and lonely reliance upon himself. He looked round at the silently waiting ranks of people, seeing them in his mind as his care, his responsibility; recognising and accepting his years of spiritual solitude.

The Judge-Advocate cleared his throat and began:

"George the Third by the Grace of God, King of Great Britain, France and Ireland, Defender of the Faith . . ."

Andrew Prentice, conspicuous in the forefront of the convict-herd, watched and listened with attention. His enormous physical vitality enabled him to bear the consequences of his orgy better than most of his companions, and though he was tired and contemptuous and resentful he had not forgotten his resolve. An alert and intelligent appearance whenever authority spoke would serve him well, so he leaned a little forward and fixed his eyes on the Judge-Advocate's face. His interest, however, was not all simulated. He was curious to know just how this affair was to be managed, and exactly what powers had been given to the Governor, and, though he was vague as to the nature of the documents which Collins was preparing to read, he suspected that in them, or in the Governor's address which was to follow, there would be matter worth attention. There had been a good deal of argument among the prisoners on the subject of the death penalty. He himself did not believe that Phillip had power to order capital punishment; nor was he sure whether the Governor might pardon and remit sentences. These things were important.

The Judge-Advocate's voice carried clearly:

"To our trusty and well-beloved Arthur Phillip Esquire:

"We, reposing especial trust and confidence in the prudence courage and loyalty of you the said Arthur Phillip of our especial grace certain knowledge and meer motion have thought it fit to constitute and appoint and by these presents do constitute and appoint you the said Phillip to be our Captain General and Governor in Chief in and over our territory called New South Wales extending from the Northern Cape or extremity of the coast called Cape York in the latitude of ten degrees thirty-seven minutes south to the southern extremity of the said territory of New South Wales or South Cape in the latitude of forty-three degrees thirty-nine minutes south and of all the country inland westward so far as the one hundred and thirty-fifth degree of east longitude reckoning from the meridian of Greenwich including all the islands adjacent in the Pacific Ocean within the latitudes aforesaid of ten degrees thirty-seven minutes north and forty-three degrees and thirty-nine minutes south and of all towns garrisons castles forts and all other fortifications or other military works which may be hereafter erected upon the said territory or any of the said islands. . . ."

Prentice's gaze became a little fixed. He did not lack shrewdness and cunning, but the intricacies of formal language confused him, and he scowled, contemptuous of elaborate and sonorous phrases which he found it difficult to follow. His attention wavered and became spasmodic. There was a great deal about oaths which seemed to him both boring and superfluous, and a stipulation about No Popery to which he accorded a second's vague approval for no particular reason, having no formal religion of his own. He fell into a waking trance, unequal to the effort of mental concentration, until he was again aroused by words which touched his interest:

"And we do hereby give and grant unto you full power and authority where you shall see cause or shall judge any offender or offenders in criminal matters or for any fine or fines or forfeitures due unto us fit objects of our mercy to pardon all such offenders and to remit all such offences fines and forfeitures treason and wilful murder only excepted in which cases you shall likewise have power upon extraordinary occasions to grant reprieves to the offenders untill and to the intent our royal pleasure may be known therein."

After that Prentice heard no more for a time.

"To pardon all such offenders . . ."

that was clear enough.

"Treason or wilful murder only excepted . . ."

He had no fault to find with that, having no intention of turning murderer, and being possessed of sufficient sense to keep treasonable thoughts to himself. Collins' voice, growing a little weary now, went on:

". . . pirates and rebels both at sea and land . . . to vanquish apprehend and take and being so taken according to law to put to death or keep and preserve alive at your discretion . . ."

Close behind him, Prentice heard the negro convict, Black Caesar, spit contemptuously.

*   *   *

Major Ross, standing stiffly near the Governor, could feel the sweat trickling between his shoulder blades. The resentment, which he was not even trying to suppress, mingled with his physical discomfort to form a mood whose sneering bitterness was written plainly on his face. Had there ever been such powers vested in one man as belonged to this undersized shrimp standing just in front of him, with his hat under his arm, and his beak of a nose already showing the effect of its week's exposure to the fierce, if intermittent, sunshine?

One thing, Ross decided, was very certain. He was not going to allow the dignity and consequence of the military, which he represented, to be belittled and insulted by this naval captain. Already there had been indications. Were his men to be turned into carpenters and bricklayers? Or, worse, into gaolers, overseers of such scum as these convicts? Captain-Lieutenant Tench, he thought sourly, looking across at that gentleman's hot but still genial countenance, might find such a situation amusing;

for himself it remained an outrage, and one against which he should on the first occasion, offer an indignant protest.

He craned his head to see how much more of this harangue they must endure. Collins seemed to be nearing the end, but there were other documents to follow, and then, no doubt, His Excellency would honour them with a speech. From it, Ross told himself, his sense of injury finding vent in sarcasm, he, Robert Ross, Commanding Officer of the Marines, Lieutenant-Governor of the colony now in process of being proclaimed, might learn, if he listened with humble attention, some of the aims, plans and intentions with which the Governor had never seen fit to acquaint him personally. For Phillip's uncommunicativeness rankled. Conscious as he was of the fundamental incompatibility of their characters, of the spark of hostility always alight and ready to be fanned by the smallest misunderstanding into a blaze, he was yet incapable of the detached common sense which told Phillip that when two people cannot agree they had best keep apart as much as possible.

Thrown by unlucky chance into a material environment in which, quite soon, the small dignities of life were to be dwarfed by the crude necessity for struggling to remain alive, he recognised in others an inner freedom unattainable by him. He saw it in Phillip, maddeningly aware of some far-away consummation which gave point and significance to a sordidly depressing task. He saw it in Hunter, coming and going in his sober and thorough brain as contentedly as he would come and go in his ship during the long exile ahead of them, and in Collins secure and peaceful in his integrity. Even Mr. Johnson had it, resigning himself with Christian meekness, and Lieutenant Clark, escaping happily into a roseate world of romance, and Captain Tench, perversely finding comedy in this unlikely situation. Lieutenant Dawes, perhaps, was spiritually freer than any of them, in a mind capable of contemplating guns, stars, and humanity with equal detachment and serenity.

The very convicts had their emotional release of hatred. They could rebel openly; nothing was expected of them. But for himself, he thought, turning for comfort helplessly to the one who had never failed to give it, there could be only stern discipline and unremitting duty. The duty which he owed, not to Phillip, that little antipodean tyrant, but to the King (God bless him!) he would perform faithfully; nor would his men ever find him wanting in his task of upholding their rights and privileges as soldiers. Had he not, even before the Fleet sailed from Portsmouth, been vigorous and insistent in his efforts on their behalf? He was reminded comfortingly of the dignified phrases of the letter in which he had protested against the disposal of his men in the *Alexander,* and the lack of food for the children of marines. His parting letter to Nepean, too, was now remembered with melancholy satisfaction. It had been the letter of a devoted husband, a tender father, about to leave, at the call of duty, all that he held dear. But its closing paragraph had shown that here was one who was, first and last, a soldier, able to forget his natural and manly emotions in his concern for the honour and advancement of his corps.

He straightened his shoulders, assuring himself that he would (God helping him) continue to follow that hard path of duty in the face of sneers and slights and jealous underminings of his authority; calmed and fortified by these reflections, he held his chin a little higher still and composed his face into lines of patient and dignified endurance.

*   *   *

Now the Governor was to speak. As he faced the convicts his eyes were not those of a visionary, but of a disciplinarian. His voice was crisp, his words unambiguous to the point of brutality. He was speaking to people hardened in an anti-social mould. In their malleable childhood circumstances had shaped them to an ugly pattern; life and the years had set them in it too firmly for any sudden remoulding—too firmly, in many cases, for any remoulding at all. The hope which Phillip felt was for the future, and the harshness which coloured his words was inspired by his one overmastering determination—that there should be a future, and that it must spring from this precarious present.

He knew very well to what a state of physical and spiritual exhaustion they were reduced this morning, and he judged the moment a good one for allowing them a glimpse of his own inflexible purpose. It was more than a glimpse they had. Not only the convicts but the whole assemblage became aware, as he spoke, of immense, inexhaustible reserves of fortitude in this slight and unimpressive figure. It became apparent to them that the queer enterprise in which they found themselves engaged was more than an episode in their lives, to be lived through somehow, and then forgotten. For the first time they were forced to see it as actual and permanent. They had never been able to believe that before, and later, when the impact of Phillip's personality had faded, they would again cease to believe it, sharing as they did, down to the humblest convict, the unshakable faith of the Englishman that no other land than England is quite real.

He informed them, coldly and lucidly, that he had tried being lenient with them, and had found that it did not work. In future, severity would be his method. He would have no more such behaviour as last night's, and any man attempting to invade the women's huts would be promptly fired upon. He told them with dispassionate contempt that they were lazy and shiftless, and that he would not have the many idle supported by the industrious few. He took some time to explain to them the sacredness of their small supply of livestock. "In England," he said, "thieving poultry is not punished with death, in consequence of their being so easily supplied, but here a fowl is of the utmost consequence to the settlement, as well as every other species of stock as they are reserved for breed; therefore, stealing the most trifling article of stock or provisions shall be punished with death."

He allowed a pause after this word. He wanted them to remember the documents which the Judge-Advocate had just read to them—documents investing him with an awful and absolute power, which it was imperative that they should realise he would not hesitate to use.

After the pause his voice dropped a semitone, and he offered them, as an antidote to that ugly last word, a few sentences of reassurance—even of encouragement. Their work, he told them, would never be beyond their abilities, but he was determined that every man should contribute his share towards making himself and the rest of the community happy and comfortable as soon as might be.

There were a few nudges and sardonic grins among the convicts at this point. Happy and comfortable! It was no function of any government which they had ever known to care for their happiness and comfort. So far they had received at its hands neither adequate food, clothing nor shelter, and they were not such fools as to suppose that Phillip, its representative, could conjure such things for them out of the thin air. His Excellency, so went their unspoken and unanimous thought, was making a great mistake if he imagined that, having been haled to this place in ignominy and suffering, they were now going to fall over themselves in their eagerness to make their gaol more efficient. There was nothing complicated about their plans. They would do here as they had always done—live from hand to mouth, and from day to day. Some of them would survive and some of them would die, and every one of them would scheme for his own advantage and the confusion and embarrassment of an authority which existed only to oppress them. They saw no future—here or anywhere. Today had always been enough for them to contend with, and they would snatch such respite as it offered, how and when they could.

They watched the Governor passing up and down reviewing the companies of marines and receiving their salutes; they scrambled heavily to their feet when the band played *God Save the King,* bringing the ceremonies to a close; they obeyed the command which dismissed them. The only thing which touched them with a flicker of interest was the fact that Phillip had proclaimed the rest of the day a holiday. They straggled off to their huts or into the woods to make the most of it, each after his own fashion.

* * *

Phillip invited his officers to a cold luncheon. He was determined to round off the ceremonies properly, and it was, at all events outwardly, a cheerful gathering at which the obvious toasts were drunk and acclaimed. But that night, when thunder and lightning were again grumbling and flickering round the settlement, Lieutenant Clark wrote sadly in his diary: ". . . the mutton which had been killed yesterday was full of maggots, nothing will keep 24 hours in this country. . . ."

The land was determined, it appeared, to make all this pomp and circumstance look rather silly.

* * *

Now that the formalities were over, Phillip settled down in earnest to his task. It was a task which, seen from a distance, and as a whole, looked colossal, epic, a task for a giant or a hero. In fact, as he soon discovered when he came to grapple with it, it resolved itself into a series of petty incidents, a wearisome routine. The weather was not the least of their trials. Ever since they landed it had been ominous, breaking out now and then in a thunderstorm whose elemental violence, terrifying as it was, seemed almost a relief from the sultry oppressiveness of the air. Day after day there had appeared in Lieutenant Bradley's faithful record a tale of cloudy skies, thunder squalls, heavy rain; night after night lightning had flickered and thunder grumbled about the settlement; red and black ants swarmed over everything.

Now, for a while in a week or two of rather precarious clear weather there was a perceptible brightening of spirits and lifting of morale. Under the blue sky the land seemed kinder and invited expeditions. Not only the English at Port Jackson, but the French, still at anchor in Botany Bay, felt it, and there was a little outbreak of sociable hospitality. Life became shaped by routine and fell into a kind of untidy pattern. They had all been so long at sea, so long anticipating this arrival as a climax, that it was queerly disconcerting to realise that life must still go on, and that there was now no climax ahead, nothing to look forward to but the day upon which they would reembark for England, a day so far distant and so obscured by all the chances which might befall it as to seem beyond rational thought at all. Days slid past and were gone, and each one, adding an incident to the mounting tale, helped to shape the queer pattern into which their communal life was falling.

A sailor was caught in the women's tents and drummed out of camp with his hands tied behind him, and a band playing the "Rogue's March." The first Criminal Court assembled and dealt with three convict offenders. Captain Shea shot a kangaroo. Captain Marshall gave a birthday party on the *Scarborough*. Lieutenant King sailed for Norfolk Island on the *Supply*, taking with him some of the less recalcitrant convicts and a few women. The Governor explored the upper reaches of the harbour. A convict woman was flogged at the cart's tail for stealing. The negro cook of the *Prince of Wales* transport was drowned. . . .

Phillip found his eyes turning continually westward to where, against the horizon, an irregular line of blue faded enigmatically into the sky. He wanted to explore. He climbed often to the nearer hilltops and surveyed the endless trees, their dull olive green deepening to purple in the folded gullies, lightening to gold on the sunny ridges, and returned to his still chaotic settlement with a sense of depression and frustration.

For the present he must organise, he must construct, and there were moments in those first weeks when he came near to despair. It was not the magnitude of his task which appalled him, but the petty triviality of the obstructions which he found constantly in his way. Here in this rough clearing by the harbour shore it would have been hard enough, even with efficient overseers, to maintain watch and discipline over eight hundred convicts; without them it was impossible. Debased and outlawed by a society which now, magnificently ignoring the law of cause and effect, demanded their cooperation, they strayed into the woods and came back without their tools, pleased that they had thus provided themselves with an excuse for idleness. Bored, ignorant, having none of those inner resources which only culture can bestow, they sought excitement as an antidote to despair, and found it in quarrels, drunkenness, debauchery, and petty thieving, and at last, inevitably, in the sport of baiting such natives as they encountered in the woods or on the shore. They clashed constantly with the seamen who came to the camp to seek diversion in the women's tents; there were brawls, followed by the inevitable punishments. There were hidden discontents and muttered grievances. There were protests, appeals, denunciations, and all found their way, eventually, to

Phillip. He dealt with them sharply and decisively, pleasing some and offending many, and none more than his Lieutenant-Governor, Major Ross. There was a neglect of military exercises which that gentleman found nothing short of outrageous, and he could not see eye to eye with Phillip who judged that, for the moment, parades must give way to the more soberly utilitarian business of providing shelter for the winter, and that barracks and storehouses were more important than the fortifications for which Major Ross' martial spirit longed. It became necessary for the Lieutenant-Governor's self-respect that he should envisage some situation in which he, as Commander of the Marines, would come into his own, and he warned Phillip peevishly that the natives were less peaceable than they seemed, and would undoubtedly descend on the settlement in force some night and wipe it out. Phillip listened courteously and went on building storehouses. Major Ross, disgruntled, returned to his quarters on the other side of the stream, with a sour glance for Captain Tench who was superintending the work of a party of marines and wearing that expression which never failed to infuriate his superior officer—an expression which suggested that he was quietly enjoying some very good joke which others were too dense to see.

He was, indeed, savouring the quaintness of a situation in which, as he was to write later, "the possession of a spade, a wheelbarrow or a dunghill was more coveted than the most refulgent arms in which heroism ever dazzled."

* * *

Captain David Collins, walking one evening round the shore near the land already set apart by the Governor for a farm, watched the clouds banking up over the tree-tops, and knew that another storm was brewing. Against the pale flicker of still distant lightning on the water the pinnacle of a little island stood out starkly, and Collins found himself thinking of the convict whom his own Criminal Court had sentenced, only this morning, to eight days in irons, and upon bread and water, on that barren and solitary rock. He felt himself under no necessity to commiserate with this man, nor with his fellow miscreant who had been sentenced to one hundred and fifty lashes; his was a judicial mind, and though the years were to mellow it, it had that knack, so comforting to its owner, of seeing an incident isolated from its context in the lives of those whom it concerned. His sincerity, his sense of justice, his natural kindliness, was thus undisturbed by questions which might have tormented a more imaginative man. Crime must be punished. He saw it as simply as that, not searching backward for first causes, not asking himself, "Whose crime?", not racking himself with questions which can never be answered by any one man, but which must be, eventually, answered by mankind. His only thought, watching the dark outline of the rock which the blacks called Mattewaya, and the convicts, with sardonic humour, were soon to rechristen "Pinch-gut," was that such lenient treatment might well encourage, rather than suppress, the natural insubordination of the convicts.

Feeling a drop of rain upon his cheek he turned and retraced his steps towards the settlement, intending to visit his brother, William; but as he approached the Governor's house where a light was burning, he saw Phillip come to the doorway and glance up at the swollen sky. Peering through the dark and recognising his Judge-Advocate, he beckoned:

"We are to have another deluge presently, Captain Collins. Come in and drink a glass of wine with me."

Collins, brushing raindrops from his sleeve, followed him inside and was no sooner seated than the storm broke. It was impossible, at first, to talk, with the thunder bursting in cannonades overhead, and the rain pelting down on the canvas roof and finding its way in trickles into the room. They sat one on each side of the table, sipping their wine and holding themselves with unconscious tautness; to remain quite still, to ignore the horrifying and intimidating din outside gave them a pleasing illusion of invulnerability. A drip splashed on to some papers on the table and Phillip moved them aside. Collins realised that with every flash of lightning he was listening for that sound which they had already heard once, of a great tree being torn to pieces like paper; then, he thought, only some sheep and pigs had been killed—the next time . . .

Phillip, in the enforced silence, was studying his guest. He liked this serious young man whose calm, almost placid, eyes surveyed the ugly chaos of their present life with reassuring steadiness. Such a man, he thought, was invaluable to a community like this, and he asked abruptly, his voice high and sharp over the diminishing sound of rain on the stretched canvas:

"What do you make of this country, Captain Collins?"

Collins, as was his habit, considered the question carefully before he answered.

"It is hard to say, Sir, as yet. Beyond a harbour as good as one could hope to find, there seems to be little to recommend it."

Phillip agreed thoughtfully:

"There seems to be very little. No food, no timber, no rivers . . ." He stood up and began walking to and fro in the restricted space, his hands behind his back. "But, after all, what do we know of it yet? When things go more smoothly here—quite soon, I hope—I shall make some expeditions into the country. That line of hills . . ." he jerked his head toward the west, "I should like to know what lies on the other side of them." Frowning, intent on his thoughts, he looked at Collins without seeing him, speaking almost to himself. "It shouldn't be difficult. They don't look to be more than thirty miles away. . . ."

Rather dubiously, Collins said:

"I cannot think, Sir, that if there were any very fertile country so close, the natives would remain in such numbers here."

"The natives! They are the most important question of all." Phillip came back to his seat and took up his glass again. "It is a little strange, don't you think, that none have come about the camp, except for the two old men who turned up the other day? And they would not have come so near if I had not gone to them and persuaded them. I should have thought that they would come—for more gifts, if not from mere curiosity. What keeps them away?"

Collins suggested:

"Fear?"

The Governor shook his head, impatiently.

"They are not a cowardly people. And they come about the boats freely enough when our men haul the seine down the harbour. It's the settlement they avoid."

"Does it matter, Sir, so long as they remain peaceably inclined?"

Phillip finished his wine and sat turning the stem of his glass between his fingers.

"It matters very much. I want to know more of this country, and as quickly as may be. Who should tell me but its natives? I want to learn enough of their language to ask them of its rivers, its mountains, its lakes, its animals, its climate and rainfall. . . ."

Collins, listening to the steady drumming on the roof, suppressed the dry comment which rose to his lips, and said:

"It should not be difficult to entice one of them here—with gifts, or promises of gifts. He would soon learn that he had nothing to fear from us, and eventually others would follow."

"In the meantime," Phillip answered grimly, "the convicts stray into the woods. Sooner or later there will be trouble between them and the natives—and I doubt if it will be the natives who provoke it. Have you noticed, Captain Collins, how they leave their belongings lying about?

Half a dozen times, walking along the shore, I have come on their bags and lines and swords and other implements scattered on the rocks—their canoes beached and left unattended. It would appear that there may be fewer thieves in their ranks than in ours."

"If," Collins suggested, "you would be pleased to make an order, Sir, prohibiting our people from interfering with their things—setting out punishments for infringing such a rule . . ."

Phillip nodded.

"That shall be done, of course. But it must be faced that we have a set of the most depraved and infamous wretches on our hands. I have never found that orders, or punishments either, seem to check their villainies very much. I have greater hope in constant employment—though what with illness and lack of tools that is not always possible either. I understand that already our people have been collecting these native weapons and selling them to the men on the transports as curiosities to be sent home to England. That will have to stop." He was silent for a moment, and then asked abruptly: "The man who was sent to the island this morning—was he in good health?"

Surprised, Collins answered:

"He seemed so, Sir."

"Mr. White tells me there is a great deal of scurvy among the convicts. We shall have to push along with preparing the ground for vegetables. Have you any knowledge of farming, Captain Collins?"

Collins who had joined the Marines at fourteen, replied gravely:

"No, Sir."

"There is worse employment," Phillip said, "than farming. I have had some small experience."

Collins thought that his voice sounded suddenly a little depressed, and that the alertness of his eyes was clouded. He remained silent while Phillip, watching the lamplight shift on the bowl of his wine glass as he turned and turned it, went back in his thoughts to the town of Lyndhurst in the New Forest where once, for a time, he had escaped from the solitariness of his nature and known an interval of brittle happiness. Now, in his memory, it was again a refuge. It was to him what this land, which he found alien and hostile, was to its black inhabitants; secure, mellowed for its people by their long unity with it. The thousands of miles of ocean which held his body from his homeland were spanned by a single leap of his mind, and he walked again in summer under the dense shadow of oaks and beeches, saw the brilliant berries of the holly, felt the keen air of winter on his cheeks, remembered the way the little shaggy Forest ponies had stared at him with their bright, unfrightened eyes. . . .

How simple it had been, and how unreal it seemed now, that leisurely, rural life! The eye of his memory watched from afar, with an indulgent sadness, that self who had once passed days in the quiet, respectable occupations of a gentleman farmer, the small duties of his local office as Overseer of the Poor, and long, peaceful evenings, reading or writing or keeping accounts, while Margaret sat opposite, bending her graceful neck over her needlework, the firelight on her hands. . . .

Farming. That brought words to him—names: Vernals, Glasshayes, Blackacres. And pictures of a deep soil, and a smooth countryside, sleek with long cultivation, lush with the soft, moist climate, sleepily, acquiescently fertile with the faithful tillage of hundreds of years. It was strange, he thought, that he should have torn that chapter from his life to find another, a kind of caricature of it, confronting him so many years later, in so distant a land. Here the spade jarred in one's hand against the unyielding earth, the sun burned and the storms flayed, and the vast trees shed tough bark upon the ground instead of soft, swiftly rotting leaves.

Farming would be different here. . . .

The rain ceased. Phillip, with a little start, looked up, flung back again into the arduous, solitary and responsible life which was his destiny, to find Collins, risen, facing him across the table.

"The rain has stopped—if you will excuse me, Sir . . . ?"

Phillip nodded.

"Yes. And I have work to do."

He looked with distaste at the pile of papers on his table, hating the endless duty of writing, writing, writing, which kept him from the action which far better suited him. Orders, pardons, letters, proclamations, notes for his first despatch . . . He glanced at Collins and thought: "That's a trustworthy young fellow. Intelligent, too, and loyal. Perhaps—later. . . ."

He left his thought half-formed, and said aloud, with a touch of the dry humour which sometimes flickered under his rather prim manner:

"Farming will come to be a much regarded accomplishment in this community, Captain Collins. Our greatest honour, mark my words, will be for the man who grows the finest cabbages."

At the door they said good-night. There was no sound outside but the running of water in little gutters, and the drip of it from trees, and the brisk gurgle of the stream. Collins, as he picked his way towards his own quarters through the mud, was still pondering the Governor's last words.

It had not been a joke, but the mask of one spread over the grim face of reality.

*   *   *

Lieutenant Clark, with a scarf wrapped round his head, looked up irritably as Lieutenant Timins came blundering into the marquee which they shared with Tom Davey. He had a toothache which seemed to be splitting his head in half, and, upon a shooting expedition up the harbour the previous afternoon, he had so blistered the palms of his hands in his first attempt at rowing, that he doubted if he would be able to hold the pen to inscribe the day's doings in his journal.

Lieutenant Timins, seating himself on an upturned box, said blithely: "I say, Ralph, Will Collins and Meredith have got some punch brewed, and they want us to go over and . . ."

Clark, extracting his journal from its place in his brassbound chest, and holding it gingerly between the tips of his fingers, answered through the scarf with muffled austerity that he must beg to be excused. Meredith, Timins, William Collins and the rest, he thought, though officers and gentlemen and his very good friends, lacked that refinement of soul which is bestowed on a man by the ennobling influence of a pure woman. There were moments, and this was one, when a man should be left alone with his spiritual and physical anguish. He seated himself with some ostentation at his table, and hoped that Timins would take the hint. Timins, however, was in no hurry. He volunteered affably:

"There's great commotion in the women's camp, so Tom Davey tells me. One of them swears she saw the alligator again, not ten yards from her hut, the same that Surgeon Bowes saw a few days ago. She says . . ."

Lieutenant Clark replied vindictively that they were a pack of lying sluts, and he would not give a farthing for any of their tales. Most likely, he continued, becoming vehement as he always did upon the subject of the women convicts, what she had seen was one of her paramours crawling on his belly towards her hut, for they were all alike, a set of damned whores and a disgrace to their sex.

Timins agreed amiably, and instanced, in corroboration, the woman who had been flogged at the cart's tail only two days before for stealing from one of the others.

"For myself," he declared, settling himself more comfortably, "I think 'em far worse than the men. D'you know, Ralph, Bowes told me that when Mr. Shortland and his clerk and the Commissary went on the *Lady Penhryn* to issue slops to the women there was one—Ann Smith, her name was—that had been a most insubordinate hussy all the voyage, and when Mr. Miller was good enough to take some notice of her, telling her how little she deserved the slops after having behaved so ill, and how grateful she ought to be for them, damned if she didn't take them and fling them down on the deck and refuse to have any part of them, and all the time using the most abandoned language." He yawned, and finished rather indistinctly from between his stretched jaws: "I like a woman to have dignity."

Lieutenant Clark thawed to a congenial theme. He almost forgot his toothache and quite forgot his smarting hands in the discussion which followed, upon the charms and virtues of the ideal woman; and if they sketched in the virtues rather hastily, they made amends by the loving detail in which they lingered over the charms, until, overcome by their own eloquence, they returned feverishly to the present and sought assuagement each in his own way—Lieutenant Timins by plunging out into the night in search of the punch to which he had been invited, and Lieutenant Clark by drawing from his bosom his Betsey's picture, upon which, for a bemused quarter of an hour, he feasted his imagination no less than his eyes. At last, sighing heavily, and seeking an illusion of closer union with the image which stared back so unresponsively into his ardent eyes, he opened his journal and wrote:

"This being the Lord's Day got up early and kissed your dear sweet image as usual on this day. Major Ross sent down to ask if I would be so good as to let the Governor have our marquee to take the Sacrament in, which I could not refuse and I am happy that it had so much honour, oh my God, my God, I wish that I was fit to take the Lord's Supper, when it pleases Him that I return home the first thing that I shall do will be to take it with you my dear Betsey, I will keep this table also as long as I live for it is the first table that ever the Lord's Supper was eaten from in this country. . . ." *

But it was no use. Neither piety nor the exaltation of spiritual communion with the beloved could ease the agonising, red-hot pain of his aching tooth, or the smarting of his blistered hands, or the torment of that other need of which he could only speak obliquely to his virtuous wife; throwing his cloak about his shoulders, he stepped out into the clear, starlit night to follow Lieutenant Timins in his quest for punch.

* * *

---

* From the original in the Mitchell Library, Sydney, Australia.

A few days later, the Governor, who, up till now, had slept aboard the *Sirius,* moved ashore. With his coming the little colony seemed finally to take root in the grudging soil of this inhospitable land, and by degrees, as officers selected the spots for their makeshift dwellings, and brought to them with their possessions some small air of comfort and permanence, the feeling grew up that this was, for the time being, and little as they might like it, their home.

To most of them it seemed a dreary prospect. Its main effect upon the convicts was to make them feel that now, being settled, they must resume normal life, which meant that they must fend for themselves in any way which offered, snatching unlawful pleasures in the women's huts, unlawful idleness in the sheltering woods, and, inevitably, adding unlawfully to their meagre rations by pilfering from the stores. This was, at first, comparatively easy. Storehouses were not yet completed, and discipline not fully organised or established. Andrew Prentice, though he was sorely tempted several times, refrained from joining the small conspiracies which were hatched among the convicts, and congratulated himself grimly when, towards the end of February, four men were brought before the Criminal Court at its first session for stealing food, and three of them were sentenced to death. The subterranean hatred and resentment always smouldering among desperate and degraded people now woke to a fierce and glowing heat. Sullen, menacing, it became an almost visible emanation from their sorry ranks, and Phillip, tightening his mouth stubbornly, gave orders for the whole battalion of marines to turn out under arms at the execution, in case of an uprising. Nor did he allow time for the situation to develop; with a stern and terrifying promptness he ordered that the sentence was to be carried out immediately, the same afternoon.

All that day, wherever a group of convicts worked, chopping trees or dragging logs across the ground, cutting rushes down the harbour or labouring in the saw pits about the settlement, a dark undercurrent of shackled power ran dangerously, gathering the accumulated bitterness of past generations, fortifying it with new resentments, to hand it on, a little fiercer, a little stronger, to the hour when it would become at last omnipotent and destroying.

That hour was not yet. The land was to delay it here, the wide land which was to offer to their descendants a richness of opportunity which they themselves had never known. They were to die as they had lived, full of hatred and frustration, but hope waited for their children. That was something which they could not know. All they could see as they herded back to the settlement to watch authority win another round in the endless battle between them, was an array of red coats, an array of muskets, a noosed rope hanging from the branch of a dripping tree.

* * *

Bennilong, passing through the woods, skirting behind the settlement, had become aware that something was afoot. He had, like his companions, avoided the settlement itself, obeying the aboriginal law of courtesy which does not permit the casual intrusion of a member of one tribe into the camp of another; but several times he had followed the high ridge of land on the western shore and from a rocky outcrop on its summit observed what he could of the doings of the white men. He had seen, for instance, a woman being very terribly beaten, and he had been horrified, not by the punishment, but by the thought of the enormity of the crime she must have committed to be so fiercely chastised. She was, obviously, one of the subject tribe, for whom, already, the black men had conceived a strong mistrust and contempt, for it was always these people who stole their spears and other implements; and whereas the Be-anga and his tribe were invariably friendly, these others when they encountered the blacks in the bush had only evil looks for them, and words which sounded heavy with insult. Bennilong, therefore, had felt no pity for the woman, but he had wondered why she had been so held up to the execration of the whole tribe instead of being privately beaten by her husband in the normal way.

Today, aware of unusual activities among the mia-mias of the white men, he followed the ridge to his point of vantage, and there settled himself under an overhanging ledge to watch. It had been raining at intervals all day, and in the failing light of late afternoon the settlement looked sodden, squalid, infinitely dejected. So much labour, thought Bennilong, puzzled, so much destruction, for so strangely unprepossessing a result! But now his attention was captured by the appearance of a group of the red-coated men with the weapons, and, feasting his eyes on their splendour, he was disappointed when arriving at a certain spot under a large tree, they merely stood still, instead of performing as he had expected, some ceremonial dance or ritual. Then he perceived that they were all looking at something, and for the first time he noticed a rope hanging from the branch of the tree, and he wondered if this were another object of worship and felt that if it were it compared but poorly with the one which now hung, limp and soaking, from its pole on the opposite side of the stream.

Next, the subordinate tribe appeared. Indeed, Bennilong thought disdainfully, the Be-anga and his people might well hold them in contempt.

For whereas the red-coated men walked swiftly, holding themselves erect as men should, these others shuffled along as if they were old or infirm, and stood with their shoulders bowed and hands hanging slackly by their sides. Then, from a near-by tent there came another small procession. Here were more red-coats, and among them, walking clumsily with their arms pinioned to their sides, three men of the inferior tribe. One of them hung back; once he stopped altogether, and struggled to free himself, and cried aloud some words in such a tone of mingled fury and despair that Bennilong had no need to know their meaning. But he was urged forward like his companions by the red-coated ones who prodded him in the back with their weapons. Beside them walked one whom Bennilong presently recognised by his clothing as the man with the round, pale face like Yenandah, the moon, carrying in his hands that same small object which he had used upon the day when the black men had watched him exhorting his companions, and receiving their homage.

Bennilong felt his blood leap with excitement and anticipation. Now, without doubt, there would be a battle. No tribe, however base, however cowardly, would stand by and see its members so mishandled without offering some show of resistance. He waited tensely. There was, indeed, a stir among the grey company; he saw a movement pass over it like the shadow of a cloud over water, and a pale shifting of colour as faces turned simultaneously in one direction. A sound went up from it—not the fierce, grunting, hiccoughing noise which, swelling in crescendo of defiant yells, marked the awakening belligerence of his own people, but a confused murmur, incoherent, stifled, frustrated, dying away into a shameful silence. . . .

Was it possible? Bennilong stared incredulously, feeling a strange and alien sensation creep over him, rising in a wave so that his breath quickened; for he, who could not understand the words of the white man, understood very well that primitive sound in which anger, defiance and hatred had been strangled by fear; and that silence, burdened with a humiliation which, because they were men like himself, was his humiliation, too. . . .

He put his hands flat against his breast in an unconscious gesture, as if he felt that the life which dwelt there were being assailed, as if he wanted to reassure himself that *here* behind this fortress of bone and skin and flesh there still dwelt Bennilong, son of Wunbula, in whose creed men might slay each other but never shame the manhood which was their common heritage. Peering through the gathering dusk, there was a crease of uneasy bewilderment between his brows.

*   *   *

Barrett was carrying it off well. There was something in his swaggering and truculent hardihood upon which his companions leaned desperately, something in his youth which had shamed them, up till now, into a poor imitation of his unconcern. But he was sustained by something which they did not share; they could not understand that to him no situation was wholly unendurable so long as he was the centre of it, no fate altogether terrifying if it held an element of drama. He was a man who could meet big moments, but not little ones. Dullness, monotony, the unspectacular routine of life, were all that he feared. On the stage he might have passed for a genius; in the gutter he was a villain, and the gallows his inevitable end.

He would not sit, like the others, while they waited for the summons, but stood where he could look out through the door of the Guard Tent at the grey, damp landscape. He was in the grip of that spiritual excitement which dulls realisation, and his awareness of himself was so strong, his consciousness of his own vitality so deep-rooted that he had not yet been able to understand fully that he was to die. His dramatic interpretation of a condemned man was so faithful, so full of fire and integrity that he was carried away by it himself, and when the time came for them to march out surrounded by an armed guard, all apprehension was swallowed up in the concentration which he brought to bear upon giving a performance which was flawless and inspired.

His companions were less fortunate. Hall, a shipmate of Barrett's and like him an Exeter man, had a mind which worked slowly but with a relentless matter-of-factness. He had never in his life seen anything save with his physical eyes, but what he saw with them he saw very clearly, without imagination, philosophy, religion, or any other device by which men commonly soften the stark outlines of reality. He moved forward now automatically, with a queer jerkiness because his knees were weak with fear. When the Reverend Mr. Johnson, paler than ever with distress and repugnance for his task, muttered a conventional word or two in his ear, he stared at him so blankly that the worthy gentleman fell back in confusion, and addressed himself instead to Lovell.

Lovell, who lived mainly in his physical sensations, was entirely occupied with the one thought that the breath was presently to be choked from his body. He cared not a rap for the spirit which would then, according to Mr. Johnson, ascend to Heaven or descend to Hell. Nothing that he had ever heard of Hell seemed worse than a hundred things which life had shown him; but, on the other hand, this same life which could be so terrible could also yield, upon occasions made only more precious by

their rarity, pleasures beside which the promised bliss of Heaven faded
into nothingness. So he glared like a captured animal, turned aside the
pious phrases of Mr. Johnson with curses, the vital spark in him so soon to
be extinguished, flaring upward madly like a rocket before it falls in
darkness.

.When they reached the tree it was almost dusk, for the heavy, rain-laden
clouds obscured the evening light. The convict who had been appointed
hangman was giving trouble. Grey-faced, defiant, with more than a touch
of hysteria in his voice, he swore that he would not perform his part, and
a wave of emotional excitement spread dangerously from him through
the crowd. Into this moment, ugly with potential frenzy, there came a
message and a document for the Lieutenant-Governor. There was an
avid silence while Ross, still flushed and angry from his passage with the
recalcitrant executioner, unfolded it, and read. In the failing light hundreds of eyes watched him peeringly, and when he announced that Lovell
and Hall had been granted a twenty-four-hour reprieve, the sound which
ran through the crowd was a phantom sound, rustling, sibilant, the release of breath held in an agony of suspense.

Now, for the first time, Barrett seemed to falter, but only for the
moment in which it took him to see that his solitude lent him even greater
drama. The trouble with the hangman began again, and continued agon-
isingly until Ross, nervous and furious, cut it short by threatening the
man that he would order the marines to shoot him unless he performed
his duty forthwith. Then, silent, defeated, shaking, he took up his position, and Barrett was ordered to mount the ladder. He did so, very pale,
but still sustained by his sense of drama, and when Mr. Johnson, his voice
quavering with earnestness and emotion, began to pray aloud, the condemned man, seeing him as a subsidiary player in his tremendous scene,
took his cue, joining fervently in the prayer.

The sound of his own voice, quite clear, far steadier than the Chaplain's,
so stimulated him that he went on talking when the prayer was over,
speaking not from any inner conviction, but reciting the conventional
lines which he saw as appropriate to the situation, lamenting the evil of
his past life, exhorting his fellows to take a warning from his miserable
fate. But when he felt himself nearing the end of what it was fitting for
him to say he began to be aware of the empty anticlimax which an actor
feels when the last words of a successful play are spoken, and the curtain
falls, and the illusion dies. Dimly, as if through a breaking mist, he began
to see the grey wet trees, and he was overcome by a forlorn astonishment.
"Why am I here?" The awareness of his exile was like a pain twisting in

his heart, and a sudden nostalgia clamoured in him that it was not here that he should die. He felt the relentlessness of time, as if the second of his death was travelling towards him, would overtake him, and pass on, dropping his bones indifferently in this foreign earth. . . .

Stop it, stop it! There must be some way to halt that inexorable and overwhelming force. Delay it, push it back for a minute, a second even, and— Who knows?—some cataclysm may yet wrench you from this web of circumstance which has trapped you like a fly—you may yet see yourself again as a living man watching life stretch away into a kindly obscurity, instead of as an aching consciousness, already disembodied, alone, aghast. . . .

He asked, dry-throated, if he might speak to a man—one of the convicts; and when the permission was given and the man, unwilling, with sidelong looks as at one already dead, approached, Barrett bent and whispered to him, but was not conscious of his own words, only that he had halted the enemy for a few seconds. He looked round wildly. Nothing was happening. His brain felt numb, his inventiveness and quick wit paralysed. He asked, clumsily, if he might speak to a woman, and was curtly refused. Suddenly he felt a weight against his back and knew that the moment had caught up with him, merciless and irresistible, bearing him forward, forward, over the edge of a chasm into death. . . .

* * *

It was almost dark now. The swinging shape under the tree was all but invisible, and lights were appearing here and there among the tents, and on the ships moored in the cove. Everything was very quiet. Bennilong was frightened. He had seen many men die, he had slain many himself, but he had never thought of death as a shameful thing before. It was a thing which came to all men, and sometimes in a terrifying guise; to fall in battle was a fitting end for a warrior, but even the stoutest heart might quail with the knowledge that sorcery had been invoked—that somewhere, for instance, an enemy was working an evil magic upon one's footprint in the sand; or that the pains inflicted vindictively upon an image of oneself would presently pass into one's real body, gnawing at one's vitals; or that the bone was being pointed, and one's death "sung" from afar. Yes, such death was terrible indeed, but here was a different kind of terror. He moved uneasily, glancing over his shoulder, the whites of his eyes showing, the hairs on the back of his neck pricking like a dog's. For this man had gone out of life in a dreadful silence. Where were his family, his womenfolk, who should have been about him, beating their breasts and tearing their faces with their nails till the blood ran down? Where was the wailing, the grief which was not so much for the death of one man as for the defeat of mankind by the great enemy? "Our brother we shall not see again. . . ." Where was the frenzy of the living who have seen a fragment of life annihilated, and who must express, in yells of fury, in fierce threats and savage maledictions their hatred of the unseen power which can snatch a man from his fellows, and make him no more than the dust upon the ground?

Here there was only silence—and in it Bennilong heard the ghostly approach of all the evil in the world which his own people were so careful to keep at bay with their spirited defiance. What manner of people were these who could not hear, or did not heed the clamour of malignant powers rushing to inhabit the empty gulf of silence which they had created round the passing of a man's spirit?

The man, obviously, had been a malefactor, a transgressor of some law, and his strange death, no doubt, was justly imposed upon him. But surely and effortlessly the black man saw to the heart of the problem, knew that while execution may be lawful, serving the only good which is the welfare of the group, humiliation and indignity will recoil upon the heads of those who inflict them, warping and flawing their image of themselves. For a man, looking into the eyes of another man, sees himself therein; to Bennilong that was more than a matter of reflection—it was a symbol of the truth.

Would they, he thought nervously, do *nothing* to avert the evil which to him seemed an almost visible pall hanging over the settlement? Would they not noisily destroy the belongings of the dead man, tear down his dwelling, carry his body far away, walking erratically, zig-zag, through the trees, building smoky fires across the path, that his spirit might not find its way back, unrestful and malignant, to their camp?

He stood up and took his spears from where he had set them, carefully upright, against the rock. There was a sickness, he thought, uneasily, in the hearts of the white men. He felt that it was hatred—not the swift flaring and swift fading hostility of enemies in battle, but a slow hatred that never died, a dull, sullen hatred like a poison, a self-hatred, perverted and obscene. . . .

He turned his back sharply on the settlement, and immediately it was not. Before him there was nothing but his land as he had always known it, the still ranks of trees in diminishing perspective dying from view in the darkness, the underside of the downward peeling bark made rich vermilion by the rain, the aromatic scents of the bush coming up strongly from the wet earth, and ahead, out of sight but clearly visible to the keen eye of his imagination, his camp, his people, his laws.

He set off swiftly. His mind was the mind of his race—quick, subtle, eager, volatile. No single emotion could dominate it for very long, and already, in his unconscious wisdom, he was exorcising with images of the normal routine of his life, the uneasiness which the white men's actions had roused in him. Already the scene which he had witnessed was losing its clarity of outline as a hard object does under water, already his imagination was moulding it, bedecking it, already in his mind he was far, far away—generations away with his great-great-grandchildren who would sit about their fire and hear the tale which Bennilong, the famous youara-gurrugin, had made, about the white men who had come and killed one of their number strangely and in silence, and departed again to their own land.

* * *

This time, Phillip thought, wrapping himself in his cloak and holding out his hands to the comforting blaze of the fire, they would surely achieve something. It was their third expedition, and it had begun badly enough, but they had seven days' provisions with them, and should be able to penetrate many miles farther into the country than they had done before. He would not admit, even to himself, the depression which he felt tonight. He glanced round in the circle of firelight at his companions. Ball and George Johnston were talking to each other. White was scribbling something in a little book, leaning so close to the fire to see that his cheeks were crimson with heat. Creswell was sitting against a fallen log, making some small adjustment to his haversack and whistling softly to himself, and David Collins was lying on his back with his head on his clasped hands, staring serenely at the tree-tops. At the sight of their young faces, fitfully illumined by the leaping flames, Phillip was sharply aware of the gap in age which separated him from even the eldest of them, and of the faint nagging pain in his side which he was trying to ignore.

To all his other anxieties there was added now an infuriating doubt of his own physical health and endurance. His body had become to him one more troublesome, obstructing, stupidly recalcitrant element to be bullied into playing its part, and so far he had bullied it successfully. The epidemic of dysentery which had swept the camp early in March had not spared him; nevertheless, before he had fully recovered he had set out upon his first expedition to Broken Bay. There, during a week of almost incessant rain, he had slept on the wet ground, lived continually in damp clothes— and failed to find the river mouth which he had sought. He had returned to find the community in Port Jackson still struggling with sickness. William Collins, pale as a ghost and thin as a skeleton, was emerging into a hard won convalescence. Ralph Clark was better, but still greenish and inclined to be querulous. Mr. Johnson and his wife, both of whom had been prostrated, were up and about again. But in Surgeon White's inadequate hospital some two hundred convicts still lay in rows beneath their scanty covering, their bones watery with weakness, their faces smeared with pallor.

Now, sitting wearily before the campfire, Phillip's mind went back over the six weeks since that first disheartening return. So much effort, he thought, and so little actual achievement. He had set men to work immediately upon a new hospital for the sick, and barracks for the marines, who were still under canvas. He had begun to manufacture bricks. The *Supply* had returned from Norfolk Island, bringing not only news of King and his little settlement there, but a welcome cargo of turtle from another small island which they had discovered and named after Lord Howe.

And then trouble. The kind of trouble which he had almost come to think of as synonymous with the name of his Lieutenant-Governor. A private had struck another private, and the officers comprising the subsequent court-martial had passed a sentence of which Major Ross disapproved. He had ordered them to assemble again and reconsider the sentence; they did so, and saw no occasion to alter it. Phillip, staring into the fire, found himself reflecting on the waste of time which is brought about by the conflicting of incompatible temperaments. In this particular business he saw the overbearing and choleric Major up against the courteous immovability of the urbane Captain Tench, who had acted upon this occasion as president of the court-martial. He even smiled faintly to himself thinking of the way in which temper, frayed nerves, hostility, a hundred human emotions, somehow broke through the careful phraseology of official communications. Behind the brief postscript to the account of the original proceedings, he seemed to see Captain Tench, amused but determined, conducting himself in this passage at arms with his superior officer with all his accustomed sang-froid, and yet not without a certain schoolboyish glee.

"The court having met a second time, by order of the commanding officer, to reconsider the nature and extent of the crime laid to the prisoner's charge . . . do not in deliberation among themselves see any cause to rescind the sentence they have already given."

Phillip had sighed when he read that. Now the war was on. Now he was drawn into it. The first sentences of Major Ross' communication to himself had fairly trembled with rage:

". . . finding that the court-martial seemed determined to wrest all power from the commanding officer . . ."

How unsure of himself must a man be, Phillip thought, who was so perpetually concerned for his dignity and power!

". . . from their determined obstinacy I had no alternative left but the mortifying and disagreeable one of suspending the President and members that composed the court-martial from all duty, by putting them under an arrest . . ."

Under an arrest! Four captains and twelve lieutenants in the whole detachment, and Major Ross must put one captain and four lieutenants out of action! Phillip picked up a billet of wood and flung it on the fire a little harder than was necessary, so that a cloud of crimson sparks shot up into the darkness. He had tried reason, but you could not reason with an angry man. The court-martial which he demanded was not possible. The whole thing was a confounded nuisance, and he had settled it at last with a general order whose crisp final sentence reflected his impatience:

"The officers now under arrest to return to their duty."

Since then things had been quiet enough. But with the end of March there had come a coolness in the nights, and a nip in the early morning air. Autumn was upon them, and still the building went on too slowly, and of those who were not too ill to work many were too old, and many more too idle. Phillip moved restlessly, drawing his cloak more closely about him and turning a little so that the heat of the fire fell on his side where the threat of pain still lay, never quite fading from his consciousness. This was the second of two expeditions, separated only by a few days at the settlement, and he was beginning to wonder if he had demanded too much of his body.

On that first trip they had found nothing of importance, though several things of interest—a black swan, a rock decorated with rude carvings, a wood of immense trees—and a sight, nearer and yet still tantalisingly distant, of the inland range of mountains, larkspur coloured against a pale blue sky.

Somewhere in the heart of those hills a river must rise. Phillip stared at the ground, pushing pebbles about idly with a twig, and thinking of the effort it had cost them to make the few miles of their previous journeys. He had seen many different kinds of country, but never anything to equal this for sheer stubborn difficulty. The stony ground demanded tough feet and tougher footgear—indeed, on the previous excursion two of his men had collapsed entirely, their shoes in ribbons, and had had to be sent back with Ball by boat to the settlement. In this country, he thought, you could walk for miles through dense undergrowth which dragged at your thighs and hid the ground so that your feet stumbled blindly; you could struggle for an hour through a wood of tiny saplings no thicker than your wrist, but so closely growing that they dragged the haversack from your shoulders as you pushed between them. You could meet creeks and marshes which twisted so deviously that at last you waded them, up to your waist, rather than spend irritating hours in skirting them. You could come upon the giant trunk of a fallen tree, sprawling down the hillside in a tangle of its branches, and stand for a moment panting with exertion, hating it, measuring the comparative effort required for clambering over it or going around it. Or you could come, as they had come that morning, upon brushwood and undergrowth so thick that it was literally impenetrable, driving them back, exhausted, almost to the point of their morning's departure. And all the time, ears, eyes, must be alert. For this was, after all, a strange country . . .

His thoughts checked on a shadowy emotion which he now recognised and resented. He had meant a foreign country, an unfamiliar country, but now the word echoed in his mind with a different meaning and he lifted his head and glanced round trying to pierce the darkness which lay outside the circle of firelight, and up at the fringe of flame-reddened tree-tops overhead. A strange country. A queer country. The antipodes . . . the other side of the world. . . .

Suddenly he felt it. Things happened differently here. Seasons were reversed, the earth, the soil itself seemed another kind of substance, the very pattern of the stars overhead was unfamiliar. Everything which lived in it, everything which grew in it, was stamped unmistakably with its character. What happened, then, to men transplanted? Had he not felt, already, the necessity to adjust, to compromise? Acknowledging it, he felt himself stiffening against the thought which inevitably followed. Moral adjustment? Moral compromises? Different standards, different habits of thought, truths for which their fathers would have died become no longer truths, the clear-drawn pattern of the social structure they had known blurring, fading, growing unreal and unimportant, and some new conception arising, born out of their union with the land. . . .

No, no! In his annoyance he rose abruptly. These were not the kind of thoughts which his mind, even in its idle moments, was accustomed to spin. They were indeed so foreign to his mental habit that they afforded one more disquieting indication of an influence working more potently than he cared to acknowledge. Discipline, however, was something in which he could believe sincerely, and he summoned it now to marshal his thoughts into orderly and accepted grooves. By the time the fire had burned low and he and his companions, wrapped in their cloaks or Scotch plaids, had settled themselves in their tents for the night, he had recovered his moral confidence, but his body, more than ever, was betraying him.

He slept for a while—a restless sleep with sharp, uneasy half-awakenings. He was so tired that even after the threat of pain became a reality, some corner of his fitful consciousness denied it, thrust it back with his uneasy dreams where it became a thing visible and tangible but continually changing, drawing into itself all the anxieties, all the dangers, all the difficulties which had confronted him. Sometimes it was dark and surging and endless like the ocean; sometimes it stabbed rhythmically and became an axe biting into the rotten heart of a tree; sometimes it was close, impenetrable, exhausting, like the thickets which had repelled them this morning; sometimes, with a flash of agony, it was lightning; sometimes it looked at him with many faces, sullen, pallid, brutish; sometimes with only one—the face of Tirrawuul, dimming and fading, and then leaping forward again, unendurably, as the face of Major Ross.

So long as it was outside himself he could cling to the fringe of sleep. Between waking and delirium he fought to hold it away, denying it its place in his body where it would become real, part of himself, Arthur Phillip, lying cold and ill in a tent in the sombre woods of New Holland. But it was a losing fight. He woke to the sound of his own groan, and to a clap of thunder which seemed like a blow upon his body. He struggled to his elbow, pressing his other arm across his eyes for a moment to subdue the swimming of his head. The dying firelight was a pinkish flush against the side of the tent, and he could hear the sharp hiss of glowing logs as a light rain began to patter on them. A shadow loomed over him; David Collins, crouching on one knee, asked, anxiously:

"Are you ill, Sir?"

Phillip lay back again and shut his eyes.

"Yes." He added almost mechanically: "It's nothing—it will pass. We shall be able to push forward in the morning."

He wondered if the pain would be easier lying on his side, and tried to turn, but the effort brought another groan from his lips. He heard Collins say: "I called Mr. White, Sir . . ."

In the darkness Phillip, with astonishment, felt the muscles of his mouth twitch, but the impulse of amusement could not compete with the pain and his smile was stillborn. He hardly knew what had inspired it—the earnest whispering of Collins, or the tousled hair of White, or the cocoon-like silhouette of George Johnston sitting up wrapped in his cloak and peering sleepily across at them. Whatever it had been, its failure left him feeling unutterably depressed. He said rather impatiently to White:

"It's my old complaint—it will pass if I keep still." Filled with the dread of the invalid for the long night, and his unreasoning belief that the daylight hours must inevitably bring ease, he added a question: "What time is it?"

Collins answered:

"It's only a little after eleven, Sir."

Phillip shut his eyes again. A little after eleven. He had been hoping for three o'clock—or even four o'clock—for through his semi-consciousness he had seemed to be aware of time passing interminably. White was lifting his head and holding a cup to his lips, so he drank, thinking that whatever it was it would do but little good. What he wanted was warmth. Warmth and a soft bed, and sleep, but above all, warmth. He felt an extra covering laid over him and opened his eyes again for a moment; Collins was still there, his head lifted and turned away, listening to the rain coming down heavily now on the canvas, and his profile, showing sharply as a flash of lightning lit the sky, seemed to Phillip almost saintly in its calm. He said wearily, shutting his eyes again:

"I shall do very well now, Collins. Go and get some sleep. We shall have to be away early in the morning."

He lay very still, carefully still, even breathing with cautious regularity. He began to feel warmer; it was Collins' plaid, he suspected, which lay over him. By degrees the pain slackened and subsided into a dull aching. His attention never left it; he watched its retreat as he would have watched the possibly treacherous manoeuvrings of an enemy, but as the long hours passed he knew it routed for the time being, knew with unutterable relief that when the daylight came he would indeed be able to go on. Through the narrow opening of the tent he saw the dark sky paling to a grey, wet dawn, and inside the huddled forms of his companions changed from black mounds to recognisable men. White, lying on his back with his mouth slightly open, sleeping like a child. Johnston looking flushed and rather babyish, with his cheek pillowed on his hand, and Collins face downward with his head on his folded arms. Phillip moved his stiff, cramped body apprehensively. He felt bruised all over, as if someone had been belabouring him with a club, but he was warm now, almost free of pain, and intensely sleepy.

Collins, wakened later by a gleam of watery sunlight, looked across at the Governor and saw him sleeping exhaustedly, his face sallow and pinched in the cold morning light, a furrow of pain ploughed deeply between his brows.

* * *

They let him sleep while he could. It was not long, for the sun came out brightly and loraquets flew over the camp screeching, and a giant kingfisher far up in one of the highest branches overhead burst out into his harsh, wild travesty of laughter. White reached for his gun—but as if the bird recognised it he was gone, and far away in the woods his mirth died into chuckles and then into silence.

When the Governor emerged from his tent there was but little to be said. To their inquiries he replied, with a courteous finality which forbade insistence, that he was greatly refreshed by his sleep, and ready to go on. Behind his back they exchanged glances which were worried, but resigned. They had known their commander long enough now to recognise a determination which was almost stubbornness, a tenacity of purpose which allowed no obstacle as insuperable, a disregard of his own personal comfort which bordered on asceticism. Now, his skin leaden, his eyes ringed with fatigue, he outlined their day's program while they ate, and led the way an hour later when, having assembled their gear, they set out.

This time they skirted the thicket which had repelled them the previous day. It was a tedious business. George Johnston, mopping his forehead with his handkerchief, and switching flies from his face with a leafy twig, beguiled the hours with memories of a more congenial life and scene. They blazed the tree trunks as they went. And very necessary, Creswell thought, looking round him at the undulating country when they halted once for breath on the top of a hill. The incredible monotony of the landscape depressed him. He looked with wondering dislike at the trees, finding them all the same, and all scraggy. He missed the denseness of foliage and the moist greenness which he associated with woods, and he noticed that even this morning, after heavy rain in the night, the dampness of the ground was only a surface dampness, sending up to one's nostrils not the rich smell or thickly fallen leaves, perpetually moist, but a warm, queer, stimulating fragrance. It was all wrong. Woods should not be stimulating, but restful. In them one should instinctively loiter, not only physically, but mentally, one's feet cushioned on softly springing ground, one's thoughts cushioned on senses lulled by peacefulness. These woods were hot, and dry and exhausting; the senses, far from being lulled, were strung to a painful alertness. The smells were too strong and heady; the sun was too bright and the shadows too dark; the silence was too intense, and the noises which broke it too harsh and violent; the ground was too hard underfoot, and the undergrowth too woody, and unfairly armed with hidden prickles. He began to be sorry that he had joined this third expedition, and for a moment he felt a qualm of uneasiness, understanding why several of the convicts had missed their way in these nightmare woods and vanished, never to be seen again; and how it had come about that Dr. Arndell and his companion had been lost for two nights much closer to the settlement than this . . .

White walked with his eyes in the tree-tops. He was interested in the birds, and not only as food, though his musket brought down two crows and a white cockatoo during the day. It was nearly noon when they found themselves confronted by yet another arm of the ubiquitous Port Jackson. They followed it, still westward, but the Governor's pace was slow now, and when a few miles farther up they came upon a small fresh water stream, they were not surprised when he called a halt. Now, for an hour or so, after the exertion of the day, it was pleasant to rest in the shade, sipping the cold water, bathing hot faces, hands and feet, enjoying the savoury smell which came from the kettle in which White's crows and cockatoo were being transformed into soup.

By evening blue-black clouds were banking up. The air was heavy, motionless, and almost tangible substance. That night their sleep was again broken by the drumming of rain on their tents and the white glare of lightning through the canvas, but in the morning the sun came out uncertainly through breaking clouds and they turned their backs on it and made for the west once more. On the banks of this narrowing arm of the harbour the walking was easier, and their spirits rose as they went. For here the country really did seem better. They walked, at times, waist high in grass along flattish ground and between vast trees growing well apart. The water was shallower, and the opposite bank closing in, so that they walked beside what was little more than a broad stream. It was after midday when they came upon the end of it, and they were conscious of a sense of excitement and climax. From their first arrival the sea had been always with them, the salt smell never out of their nostrils. No matter where they had trudged through the woods they had been halted by some arm of it lying before them, blue and placid, reminding them that they had not yet forsaken the coast, not yet penetrated beyond the outer edge of their new domain. Now, above the broad belt of rounded stones and boulders which spanned the stream where they stood, it was no longer tidal; the water which trickled down over and among them was fresh water. They looked at each other with a feeling of achievement. This was the end of the coastal and the beginning of the inland stage.

A new zest filled them. Suddenly the expedition became rather jolly and full of interest. They saw ducks and teal, and promised themselves a banquet that night. There were cheerful congratulations for good marksmanship, and some friendly badinage for failures. When late in the afternoon the sky became overcast again, they halted and made camp, and their ducks, stuffed with slices of salt pork, and roasted over the fire, provided a feast which changed their high spirits to a replete and silent contentment. Even the weather relented. The clouds passed over; a clear evening sky of gold and lilac faded into starlit darkness, and for the first time they felt themselves at peace in the land, their nerves relaxed almost as if they were at home.

But between waking and sleeping that night Phillip started up in his tent, listening. He saw his companions listening, too, with lifted heads. George Johnston said in an undertone:

"What was it?"

Phillip made no reply, his ears straining for a repetition of the noise which had startled them all. Collins sat up.

"It sounded like a voice . . ."

"Indians?" Creswell, on his elbow, peered anxiously through the open slit of the tent.

White suggested: "A bird, perhaps?"

Phillip got up and went outside. The night was dark blue and utterly silent. He stood by the tent, listening, straining his eyes. Nothing moved, not even a leaf on the trees, not even the red embers of the dying fire. White came out and stood beside him and from the other tent one of the marines emerged, head and shoulders, and blinked at them inquiringly.

Their mood of confidence and well-being was destroyed. Again the land was enigmatic and they themselves aliens in it, having no right, no place in its intimidating immensity of silence.

Phillip said, abruptly:

"It was nothing. Some bird or animal . . ."

He turned back into the tent, and White followed him. George Johnston said doubtfully:

"It *sounded* like a voice . . ."

No one answered him.

*   *   *

The next day was tedious and exhausting. They left the stream and walking became difficult, the country sullen and monotonous. They passed a number of deserted native huts, and several times they saw kangaroos lift startled heads, their black noses and their sensitive ears twitching with alarm. Muskets were raised, but without success; the animals were gone so swiftly in their great swinging bounds, their bodies merging so confusingly with the shadowy undergrowth, that, as White ruefully remarked, one half wondered if they had been there at all.

By the middle of the afternoon they all confessed themselves tired. But they had carried no water that day, and the prospect of a dry camp was unattractive, so they went on for another hour and found a pool in a creek bed otherwise dry. They set to work wearily to pitch their tents, but the ground, in spite of recent rains, was dry and hard as iron, and the men swore as they tried to hammer the tent pegs into it. The trees were full of birds, mostly lorikeet and paroquets; as they went about their preparations for the night they paused now and then to stare up at the vivid flash of wings, blue, green, crimson, in the sunlight above the high tree-tops, and when they spoke they were forced to shout to make themselves heard above the din of the birds' incessant chattering.

They brought down several for their cooking-pot. A few gorgeous feathers were examined and preserved, to find their way, in letters, across the sea to England, and the rest lay on the ground to be pointed at next day by the natives as proof of the potency of the white men's weapons.

By that time Phillip and his party had made another half-dozen miles to the westward, and were standing moodily on the edge of what White described that night in his journal as a "chasm," but which was merely the deep bed of a watercourse. They were tired of these watercourses. They appeared to follow no given direction, but simply lay there across one's path, steep, rocky gutters, anything from six to sixty feet deep, demanding of footsore and heavily laden men an effort which seemed entirely disproportionate to the amount of distance which one gained in crossing them. They had followed a few up, skirting them at the head of their gully, but this wasted time, and time was precious.

So they sighed, adjusting the straps of their haversacks on their stiff shoulders, and began to follow the Governor who was already scrambling down the slope. In the creek bed they paused to drink from a pool, and then scaled the opposite bank. Creswell muttered peevishly to Johnston: "We might go on like this for days."

"Weeks."

"This is the most God-forsaken country on earth. I don't believe it has any rivers."

Johnston shrugged.

"What does it matter? It's a convict colony. It serves very well for that without rivers—for the present at least."

They trudged along blindly, in the grip of that sullen mood which comes with fatigue and discomfort. Uphill, now. Stones and twigs slid beneath their feet, and through the scrub no summit was visible upon which they could fix their eyes and their hopes. Their pace became slower; every now and then they halted, panting and sweating, to rest for a few moments. After a time the undergrowth thinned; the trees became larger and grew more sparsely as they ascended, and at last, coming out on the top, they dropped their burdens and allowed their haversacks to slip from their shoulders down their arms and thence to the ground.

Phillip, standing on the highest point of the hilltop and staring westward, took his hat off and ran a rather grimy handkerchief over his forehead and round the back of his neck. It was about midday. Before them the same undulating hills and valleys stretched away, broken here and there by drifts of smoke which might be native fires or burning trees such as two which they had passed, and had concluded to have been struck by lightning. But the Governor's eyes swept over these impatiently to fasten on the hills which lay along the horizon, nearer now, but still surprisingly far away. Upon their previous expedition, about fifteen miles from the coast, he had seen them clearly for the first time. Before, they had been only a blue shadow, their height and shape confused by cloud and distance, by the misty light of morning, or the golden haze of afternoon. Now they stood sharply outlined, a flat, purple range running north and south, a barrier which might hide anything—or nothing. . . .

He felt at once a hope, an uprising of confidence, and a deep, almost childish disappointment. The first emotion was impersonal. It was the

Governor of New Holland who felt that he was looking at the future
of his territory; it was Arthur Phillip, fifty years old and conscious of
illness and fatigue, who, measuring the miles they had come and the miles
which yet lay between them and that rampart of hills, suspected that it
was not for him to cross them—perhaps not even to reach them. . . .

Collins asked:

"How far distant would you say they are, Sir? Twenty miles?"

"Nearer to thirty, I should judge. This country is deceptive. From the
settlement I had thought them not more than fifty, and we must have
come—how far should you say, Mr. White? Thirty miles?"

"At least thirty, I should think, Sir. Most likely a little more."

Phillip looked dubious. Already he had begun to realise that in this
country one's conception of distance, like everything else, must be revised.
A hundred yards, he thought, if it includes a "chasm," may leave a smarting impression upon the memory which will transform it into a mile,
and he was inclined to suspect that their progress might have been less
than it should have been for the enormous effort expended upon it. He
sighed and sat down to rest with his back against a rock and his eyes
still on the distant hills. In the centre was the slightly higher peak which
he had named Richmond Hill, and to the north and south of it the ranges
faded away into the distance as far as the eye could see. "Those," he said,
pointing northward, "are the ones I called Carmarthen Hills, and
those . . ."

A thought slid across his mind uneasily: "Why should I have named
them? They must have their names already . . ."

They had had their names, he realised, and their names had been old
when the Roman legions were invading Britain, bringing to the land
of a conquered race, as he was bringing now, names from their own
homeland. Something warned him to disturb the antiquity of this place
as little as might be, and, irritated by the persistent recurrence of what
seemed an emotion of foolish superstition, he finished briskly, "Those to
the south are the Lansdown Hills. Shall we go on, gentlemen?"

It was necessary, he thought, to name landmarks as they were discovered. It made identification simpler—set up finger-posts, as it were, for
future explorers. Watching his companions as they clambered reluctantly
to their feet again and shouldered their loads, he felt confident, serene in
the immediate business of conducting his expedition.

But he realised before evening that they could go no farther. Their
provisions were running very low, and so far they had been able to supplement them only with occasional birds. And yet natives lived in the

neighbourhood. How? Not a day had passed without their seeing some trace of their presence—huts, burnt out fires, notched trees, a fragment of chewed fern root—and only once, in a few fish bones and fragments of mussel shells had there been any evidence of their having brought food with them from the coast. Apparently they were able to hunt more successfully with their primitive weapons than the white men with their firearms. Phillip, bitterly disappointed, gave the order to return.

It was an exhausting march. In the evening a few lorikeet and two crows flavoured their remaining bread, but the next day saw their food quite exhausted, and a long, tedious walk between them and the upper reaches of the harbour where boats had been ordered to come daily to wait for them. The blazed trees, at all events, relieved them of the need for thought. It was necessary now to hurry, and they trudged doggedly all through the heat of the day, walking heavily even with their lightened loads, silent, concentrating on the mere effort of setting one foot before the other. Phillip, ahead, suddenly found himself treading in space, and pitched forward into a hollow in the ground which had been hidden by long grass. He lay winded and shaken for the second or two which it took Johnston and White to reach him, but scrambled to his feet, refusing help, and set off again. Immediately, as if the jarring shock of his fall had been a signal, the pain in his side had stirred. He walked stiffly now, leaning over a little, narrowing his whole consciousness to the ground under his feet and eyes, so that it was not until he heard Collins call out, "There's the water!" that he realised they had reached the harbour again. By now it was late afternoon; he stood looking at the narrow arm of water and knew that he could go no farther—and yet if the boats left the appointed rendezvous before they were able to reach it, they would all go supperless that night. He glanced round at the ring of tired, grimy faces and decided that the youngsters, Johnston and Creswell, looked fittest.

"We shall halt here for the night." He straightened his back with an effort. "Two or three had best go on ahead to meet the boats and bring us back provisions. You and Creswell, Mr. Johnston—and take one of the men with you. Tell the boats to come for us in the morning."

He watched them go. His body cried out for rest and warmth. The evening was chilly though it had been hot all day, and low, wreathing mists stirred over the glassy water. When a fire was made he sat near it, turning so that its warmth fell upon his side, and reviewed the expedition now virtually ended.

Again they had achieved nothing of importance. But no, that was not quite true. He was so anxious to reach the hills—had been so disappointed at their failure to do so—that he had almost forgotten that they had, at least, discovered what looked like a patch of really fertile country here at the head of the harbour. And standing on the hilltop yesterday, studying the convolutions of the hills, he had imagined that he saw a gap in them —the kind of gap through which a great river might flow and wind at the foot of the mountains till it reached the sea.

He moved so that his back had the support of a tree trunk, wondering if he would get through the night without another attack such as he had had during the first night of their trip, and watching the men as they lighted another fire for themselves farther along the bank. He noticed that there was very little talk, and no laughter. They were tired, but it was hunger which made them restless and short-tempered. They drew their belts tightly over their empty stomachs and sat round the fire with their knees drawn up. Phillip, watching them still, hoped that they were not remembering the eerie, mournful sound, still unexplained, which had twice disturbed their sleep, for he knew how dangerously superstition might work in cold and tired and hungry men.

Johnston and Creswell, blundering back noisily through the woods towards the light of their fires, were greeted with acclamation which was a little too frenzied for the importance of the occasion. Phillip was a practical psychologist; his life had taught him to know men and to judge their mood from just such indications as this. While the suddenly eager and vociferous group drank rum and ate heartily of bread and beef, he made a mental note of a potential crisis avoided, a situation with the germ of danger in it made normal again by food.

Food. All through another tortured night his thoughts returned to that word. Food, food, food. The stores would not hold out forever, and none knew better than himself the dangers of the wide ocean which ships must cross to bring them more. And what, he thought, moving with painful stealth in the darkness of the tent, if the Government sent him another batch of convicts before he had had time to build a more stable environment for those already here? "If they had given me some useful men!" he thought for the thousandth time. "Carpenters, bricklayers, tradesmen of all kinds, farmers, farmers, farmers. . . ."

As before, it was dawn before he slept, and full daylight when he wakened. By the time the boats joined them he was as weary as if he had done a long day's march, but his curiosity, his restless determination to know his territory, would not allow him to return to the settlement without exploring the coves of this hitherto unknown section of the harbour.

And it was, after all, a day spent far from unpleasantly. He sat in the stern of the boat with his hat pulled forward over his eyes to screen them from the flickering dazzle of the water, and enjoyed the warmth of the sunshine on his aching back, and the pleasant sound of dipping oars and water slapping on the gunwales. They landed at midday and lunched idly, lounging on sunny rocks by the water's edge, feeling themselves a compact and firmly welded little group, united by an experience which, though it had brought them no danger and but little excitement, had yet set them apart as the only white men to have penetrated beyond the coastal regions of the land.

During the afternoon natives appeared in canoes and paddled alongside the boats to receive the gifts which the Governor pressed upon them. They had been puzzled by this expedition. Unobtrusively, passing the duty from one group to another, they had kept track of the party's progress. Every night, beyond the circle of light made by the white men's absurd huge fires, black bodies had merged with black shadows, and dark, star-bright eyes had watched. For what were the white men seeking? Why had the Be-anga stood upon the hilltop staring westward at the high country which they themselves had never visited? Why had his followers found it necessary to scar the bark of the trees as they went in order to find their way back? Was it possible that they could be blind to the tale of their passing which was written so plainly on the ground? Why did they travel so absurdly burdened, carrying shelter when shelter was so easily to be made, food when food was all about them for the seeking? At first it had seemed sinister—this womanless march. Thus warriors set out on a raiding expedition, travelling fast, leaving their womenfolk, their aged, and their young behind. But it became clear that this was no raid. Why then had they not taken some of their women with them to carry their burdens and prepare their food?

There were no answers to these questions—and unanswered questions are mysteries, and mysteries are magic, and magic lay across the black men's hearts like an uneasy spell. They took gifts from the hands of the Be-anga, staring into his face with the sharp curiosity of children, handling the things which he gave them with puzzled wonder, as if somewhere in their lovely and glittering uselessness there might lie the explanation of so much unnatural behaviour.

It was late afternoon when the boats vanished down the harbour. Collins, looking back, found himself regretting their return, and the passing of this enchanted day which had seemed almost unreal in its leisure, its brilliance, its glassy purity. The canoes of the natives showed like black specks against water which reflected a sunset of flaunting gold and crimson. When the boats rounded the point of their own cove the day was done, and in the sad, purplish twilight of the autumn evening the settlement lay before them, straggling across its desecrated shores, ugly, lonely, squalid and forlorn.

* * *

Bennilong was lying across his canoe on his belly, his feet touching the water on one side, his face submerged on the other so that he could watch the darting of the fish deep under the ruffled surface. He was holding his four-pronged spear poised, ready to drive it down upon his quarry, when he heard a noise, a confused mingling of shouts and cries, and he lifted his head and swung himself back into his canoe, staring at the near-by shore.

He had come with a party of his fellow tribesmen to fish, and in several of the canoes dotted about the bay startled men and women were turning their heads, shouting excitedly to each other across the intervening water. Not far from him he could see Barangaroo winding in her line, and he called to ask her what had happened that the group on the beach were so excited and enraged, but she had been intent upon her fishing and replied crossly that she knew no more than himself. He began to paddle rapidly for the shore, but before he jumped out into the shallow water he had seen one white man lying on the beach with three spears in his body, and another on his knees with his arms upflung to ward off the blow of a raised club.

Bennilong felt the hairs all over his body rise and prickle with hatred, for, by their clothes, he could see that these were members of the despised and inferior white tribe. He was exultant that one of them had been slain, and he ran as fast as he could in the soft beach sand so that he should not be too late to see the blow which would despatch the other. He thrust a way through the press of naked bodies, and saw the second white man, a youth, sag over and sprawl face downward on the sand. Good! The sound which went up from the throats of the natives was a spontaneous sound of satisfaction and approval. Bennilong turned to look at the other body, standing over it very much as he had stood, years ago, over the slain Kuurang, pleased that death had been dealt so expertly. He had not, so far, learned the cause of this execution, but in such matters he trusted his skin, which warned him that snakes and convicts alike were his enemies. Towards the other white men—towards the Be-anga and his followers—his instinct taught him to feel differently. His thought processes were too simple to analyse the obvious fact that they were worthy of the name of man, while these others by merely wearing the appearance of humanity offered a subtle insult to the principles of manhood as he understood them. In the uncomplicated logic of his mind he was content to feel that these were degraded human beings, and to know a fierce resentment that such a thing could be. In his experience inferiority came only from within, and was then deserving of contempt. He had not yet begun to realise the poisoned fact of civilised life which was to disrupt his integrity in later years—that merit might be measured by possessions, and that this inferior tribe had become inferior not because it was unworthy but because it was dispossessed. Happy still in his unassailed beliefs, he stared down at the dead man with the unsentimental satisfaction of a doctor who sees an infection exterminated. He noticed with approval that the spear in the breast had been driven straight and true; not he, himself, Bennilong, son of Wunbula, could have dealt a better blow. He glanced round the ring of intent faces.

"Gan-to bon bunkulla tetti kulwun?"

Wurrawunnah, lean and wiry, still trembling with fury and excitement, answered him with fierce pride:

"Gatoa bon tura."

Bennilong nodded his congratulations. From the vociferous descriptions of half a dozen of his friends he now learned the whole story. The slain men, coming to cut rushes for the roofing of their shelters, as the Duggerigai often did, had been recognised by Wurrawunnah as the two who, a few days previously, had stolen his canoe from this same beach. There was no man, Wurrawunnah cried, striking his breast and rolling his eyes with still unabated fury, who could thus wrong him and flee fast enough to escape his vengeance, though these, miserable creatures that they were, had tried. There they lay, and thus would lie any other of this despicable race who in future should tamper with his belongings.

Leaving the slain lying there, the tribesmen set out for their camp, some by water and others through the bush, still arguing about the occurrence as they went. Because the majority were still angry, still excited by the sight of bloodshed, there was much talk of violence. The white Be-anga and his men they would not harm. Those of the red-coats, the magic-wielders, were best avoided. But these others, these good-for-nothing travesties of manhood, they would slay without hesitation wherever they should meet them. Bennilong, striding ahead, talked louder, more bloodthirstily than the rest.

When they reached the camp it was dark. After they had eaten, the elders called a council, and more than three hundred warriors assembled at the Bora ground that night.

The whole business, they agreed passionately, was becoming too serious to be ignored. This was not the first time they had been forced to assert themselves against insult and theft. More than two moons had come and gone since, in conclave, they had decided that if these people stole their possessions they would retaliate in kind. They had chosen one of the islands in the harbour for this first protest, for here a small party of the despised ones worked alone, guarded by a couple of the men in the brightly coloured coats. Here they came with their strange implements to make holes in the ground and to turn the earth up so that it looked as if a thousand wombats had been burrowing there, and here several of the tribesmen had crept upon them and snatched up their tools and made off to their canoes again. It had puzzled them a little that the men in the red coats should have been so irate, and that they should have entered into pursuit, and caused their fire-breathing weapons to sting the bare legs of the retreating maurauders. For it was plain enough that they had no love for the inferior tribe; why, then, should they be so swift to defend them and their belongings?

But the thefts of their own possessions went on. Not now could a man beach his canoe and be sure of finding it unharmed on his return. Not now could he stand his spears against a rock or a tree trunk and leave them there. Only the knowledge that the white Be-anga himself lent no countenance to these depredations had so far curbed their resentment. They had seen him berate one of his followers for even lifting a fish-spear left lying on the rocks, to examine it. Many times he had come among them on the harbour shores in friendliness and confidence, asking to be allowed to see their weapons, showing by gesture and expression his admiration of them, handling them with care and returning them with civility; these things they remembered, for in their category of virtues courtesy held a high place.

Therefore they agreed that it was not the Be-anga's fault. They looked at each other uncertainly. What bewildered them—what made it impossible for them to formulate plans or theories—was their ignorance of the rules by which these Bereewolgal governed their behaviour. What was their Law? For all their watching, for all their discussion and conjecture, the black men had been able to observe nothing which seemed to indicate that the strangers understood or followed any comprehensible rules of conduct. Indeed, their actions were wildly inconsistent. Had not Bennilong himself seen them inflict a most terrible and shameful punishment upon one of their women? And yet, when the Be-anga had one day observed a tribesman give his wife a few disciplinary and well-deserved blows on the head and shoulders, had he not seemed greatly shocked and shown signs of intense disapproval?

And who was in authority over them? Surely the Be-anga, who showed himself in his fearlessness so worthy a leader? But if so, why, upon certain days, did they all, even the Be-anga, bow down before the moon-faced one? And why, upon other occasions, had the moon-faced one, with all the others, been observed paying homage to the thing which they called the "flag"? To whom, or to what, ultimately, did the Duggeri-gai owe allegiance?

To this important, this vital, question, they had as yet found no answer. For themselves, they lived by the Law—a law incredibly complicated, and with ramifications bewildering to any but a tribesman born to it as an age-old heritage. But it was a law not vested in any single man. It was common property, it dwelt in every man's heart, and the young children before they could walk were aware of it. It was a terrible law, full of fear and magic, but they trusted it because it worked; they lived by it because for thousands of years it had preserved them, assuring them of those things which are man's fundamental needs, providing for their hunger, lending them zest for life, courage in battle, and resignation in the face of death. There was no step which they took, from birth to burial, but was dictated by the Law, no thought which crossed their minds but was coloured by it, no conceivable deed which they might commit which did not bear, clearly and irrefutably, in their own minds, its sanction or its condemnation. It was absolute and it was terrible, but it was real, it was bedrock, it left them no possible evasion.

Now, for the first time they were conscious of a confusion in their thoughts and were troubled by a situation not provided for in their Law. Centuries of security had failed to breed in them the persistent aggressiveness of their brethren in other lands; they knew only the swift flaring rage which served them for their tribal battles. They were the children of the human family, having the gaiety, the monkey-like inquisitiveness, the monkey-like lack of application of the very young. They had, as children have, a deeply rooted sense of justice; like children they were generous, devoid of rancour or suspicion, driven by the impulse of the moment, vain, inveterate actors and mimics. Troubled by their instinctive awareness of qualities in the white man which must keep him always a stranger, they were still incapable of even guessing at the workings of his mind—the mind which had travelled so far from their primitive wisdom in its search for knowledge that it was already astray in the labyrinths of its own psychological chaos. It was a mind which had gained subtlety and lost simplicity, a mind which explored the universe, but had long, long ago lost sight of itself. It was a mind which, finding its activities incompatible with its faith, had gradually substituted for that faith a system of mechanical worship by which it was enabled to believe that it might simultaneously serve God and Mammon. It was a mind which had become so active, so ingenious, so tough, so flexible, so tortuous, that it was able to make a show of holding apart the indivisible forces of man's soul. It was able to say devoutly in one section, "Thou shalt not kill," while from another it invented plausible justifications for massacre. It was able to proclaim, "Blessed are the poor in spirit," and bend all its energies to the building of power and dominion. It was able to extol mercy and be merciless, to preach kindness and be brutal, to praise truth and practise deceit. And it was still able to regard itself with sincere complacency. Here were mysteries forever beyond the understanding of the race of Murri.

They only knew that these were indeed strangers—not because they came from a distant land, not because their skins were white instead of black, but for a deeper reason which they could not analyse, though they felt it with increasing apprehension. A weapon such as the gooroobeera of the white man was a terrible one but was not to be dreaded any more than a spear in the hands of men who lived by some law which they could understand. A weapon, however terrible, could deal no more than death —but who could tell, who could even guess, what was in the heart of its wielder, having no knowledge of the rules by which he lived?

Tirrawuul, returning to his mia-mia when the conclave was over, squatted a long time by his dying fire, his thin legs crossed and his grey head bent. There was an uneasiness abroad among his people. More than an uneasiness—a kind of tense and alert defiance, dangerous because no enemy resisted; an anticipation of peril, demoralising because the peril was shapeless, unseen, unnamed. They could react to it only as they reacted to other, more normal perils, with noisy threats, and ferocious declarations of their intrepidity. Tirrawuul had not even attempted to dissuade them from their fiercely reiterated intention of slaying at sight any of the inferior white men whom they might meet in the woods. Indeed he had agreed that it must be so. No warrior should endure insult and injustice. He had even agreed to the suggestion of an elder of the proud and haughty Cammeraygal, that they must assemble in force and let themselves be seen thus, armed and resolute, by the white Be-anga, so that he should know that he had warriors to deal with.

Nevertheless, in his heart he was still troubled. Not by the thought of a few deaths, either among the white men or the black; death was a thing which came to the individual, and he knew that it was the tribe which mattered. The thought which was bending his head and keeping him sleepless from his 'possum rug and the warm body of his young bride was the dreadful thought that perhaps the tribe was not immortal, after all. Such a thought had never visited him before, and he was afraid of it. There had been, indeed (the legends told of them), instances in which all the men of a tribe had been exterminated in battle, and the women and children absorbed into the tribe of the victors, but his thought had been different—vaguer—more dreadful than that. For he perceived that there were other ways in which a man might die than in losing the breath out of his body; there was another way in which a tribe might die—by violating its laws, forsaking its customs, forgetting its legends, dying from within—within!

He smote his gnarled hands against his breast in the agony of this thought. He looked round fearfully at the silent camp, shaken by the closeness of the evil which had come upon their land with the coming of the Bereewolgal. The superstitious dread of his race clutched him by the throat, and he stared, almost expecting to see the familiar scene become an empty gulf of nothingness, like the harbour on those early mornings when it lay enshrouded in a white fog, and a coo-ee from the opposite shore echoed eerily like the cry of a spirit from another world. But nothing happened; everything was as usual; all save himself were peacefully asleep. Before a dozen mia-mias red embers were still glowing, and close beside them the dogs lay, their ears pricking and their bodies twitching, whining softly sometimes in their uneasy slumber. In one of the mia-mias a baby woke and wailed, and he heard the soft, rebuking voice of the mother cajoling it, and the grunt of the father, disturbed, turning over again to sleep. It seemed to him that he saw it not only with his own eyes, but with the eyes of his ancestors who had watched scenes no different from this for a thousand years, and, feeling a little comforted, he looked up at the sky and drew further reassurance from the everlasting stars. There was Baiame's grove; there was Berai-berai, that young scapegrace burul winungailun miai-miai whom the Maker-of-all had caught up to the Heavens and placed near the seven maidens, and there were the seven maidens themselves, six of them twinkling boldly, and one, the modest one, hiding herself shyly from Berai-berai's too ardent eyes . . .

Tirrawuul yawned. He blinked sleepily and stood up, not bothering to disguise the stiffness of his bones as there was no one there to watch.

All was well; everything was unchanged; soon the white men would depart. He must indeed be growing old, troubled with the sick fancies of
the aged. The heavens and the earth and the race of Murri—these things
were immortal. He stood for a moment scratching his shoulder and warming his feet over the embers, and then, crawling into his mia-mia, pushed
his wife aside and settled himself comfortably in the rugs, still warm from
her youthful body.

*   *   *

Lieutenant Kellow woke, shivering in the grey dawn. He was lying
nearest to the tent opening so he rolled over, keeping his coat still well
huddled about his shoulders, and, thrusting an unkempt head out,
scanned with disfavour the deserted beach and sandhills of Botany Bay.

It was something to be thankful for, he thought, his eyes watering in
the sharp air, that the settlement had not been made here; miserable as
their situation was at Port Jackson, they were at least spared the daily
contemplation of this barren and depressing scene.

The great fires which they had made last night on either side of their
tents in an effort to combat the bitter cold had burned away to fine grey
ash which the dawn wind was lifting and stirring in little clouds over the
beach sand. The rank grass clothing those undulating slopes which Captain Cook had so optimistically called "meadows" was white with frost,
and a few wind-tortured trees stood out bleakly against the steel-coloured
sky.

It was the first day of June. Lieutenant Kellow drew his head back
sharply into the semi-obscurity of the tent, and, dropping his face on to
his improvised pillow, curled himself together with a shudder of cold.
June! The month of roses! Summer! He shut his eyes, voluptuously imagining it. Grass that was smoothly shaven, close and firm and springing,
an emerald carpet! Trees—real trees, leafy trees, with low spreading
branches! Long, long evenings, hours of languid, enchanted twilight, the
day over, the night not yet begun! Gardens full of scent and colour, lovely
not only for that—not even mainly for that—but because they were established, accepted; because they were there with the benign consent and
cooperation of the land, thrusting their roots into her hospitable soil, lifting their leaves and blossoms and tendrils to her beneficent sunshine and
her gentle rains . . .

June! He dozed and dreamed of it, and woke again, stiff in every limb,
to find the camp rousing for the day.

The Governor was out already. White, emerging into the pallid morning sunlight, saw him returning along the beach, and went down to meet him. The surgeon walked with less than his usual vigour, feeling liverish and depressed, not only as the result of a cold and mostly sleepless night. He already loathed this land in which he knew himself utterly out of his element—a sociable young man in a community devoid of social life, something of a ladies' man in an environment whose only "ladies" were convicts and black dyins and a few respectable married women—and nothing but his well-developed sense of professional responsibility and his physical energy saved him from utter melancholy.

He was continually conscious, too, of the frustration which any medical man of conscience must feel upon being forced to practise his craft with inadequate tools and resources, and upon hopeless human material. So many of his patients had been doomed before he ever set eyes upon them. They had no reserves, moral or physical. They lay there in his hospital tent staring at the roof and waiting to die, and he could do nothing. The fresh food he needed for them was not available; even now he felt, like a new wound, the despairing disappointment which had filled him a few days ago when the *Supply* had returned from Lord Howe Island without the turtle which he had been so anxiously expecting. He had gone back to his patients with what amounted to a death warrant, and they had recognised it as such. He had seen that, looking down at their emaciated bodies, their pale mouths where the teeth were loosened in bleeding gums, their expressionless eyes which stared up at his face and read his helplessness there . . .

He had welcomed the chance to join this brief expedition of the Governor's, glad to get away from the settlement even if only for a couple of days, leaving Arndell and Balmain in charge of the sick. He did not feel as strongly as the Governor did in the matter of discovering the native murderers of the two rush-cutters whose bodies had been brought to his hospital two days ago. To him the expedition was merely a walk, a respite, an antidote of physical exertion to the disheartening futility of his daily routine.

As he plodded towards the Governor through the loose sand he was thinking that it looked very much as if the natives had guessed the object of their journey, and were purposely avoiding them. All yesterday, from the time of their landing in the rush-cutters' bay, during the long walk through the woods to this spot, they had seen not a single black. When they had arrived, about sunset, there had been none on the shore, though there were some twenty canoes scattered about on the glassy surface of the great bay, their occupants busy with their fishing, and a thin blue spiral of smoke going up from the fires which they kept burning on flat stones in the bottoms of their canoes. They had taken no notice of calls and signs; from the fact that nearly all were using lines, and not spears, it had seemed likely that they were women, though they were too far distant from the shore to be certain in the failing light. They had paddled to the far side of the bay and landed there after dusk, when it would have been useless to attempt to follow them.

No, White thought, the task of discovering which, among the hundreds of natives who inhabited the neighbourhood, had killed the two convicts was an impossible one. He had thought so from the moment when the Governor, not ordinarily squeamish, had turned his eyes rather hurriedly from what was left of William Okey.

"We must find out who did this, Mr. White."

Whoever did it, White had thought, studying the injuries with professional detachment, had done it savagely, in rage. Three spears, one driven clean through the breastbone. The head beaten in with such force that the brains oozed through the shattered skull. Clotted blood welling in eyeless sockets . . .

"I wonder," Phillip had said, "if that is one of their customs—to gouge out the eyes?"

"That might have been birds, Sir. The other man has very few marks of violence on him."

Phillip had walked up and down the tent with his hands clasped under his coat tails as he often did when he was disturbed.

"I shall go myself—at once. Tomorrow. I don't believe this was an unprovoked attack. There will be some explanation—I must find it. This kind of thing is becoming too frequent, Mr. White. There was Ayres wounded a little while ago, and that other convict, Peter Burn, and now these two killed. We shall have serious trouble if we don't come to some understanding with these people."

White had found himself cynically wondering how one came to an understanding with people whose speech was incomprehensible, but he said nothing, content to leave so tough a problem to the Governor. Now it seemed that they were not even to see the natives, far less speak to them. As he came up to Phillip he noticed the leaden pallor of the Governor's skin, and the brownish smudges of sleeplessness beneath his eyes. Phillip said briskly as the surgeon turned and they fell into step together:

"Good morning, Mr. White. I have been reconnoitering. There are some fifty canoes drawn up on the beach just round that next headland. There must be natives somewhere in the vicinity."

"Fifty?" White was astonished. "We have never seen so many together before, I think."

"No."

Phillip walked in silence then, frowning at the sand. Fifty canoes assembled. No natives. He found this puzzling and slightly ominous. Why should they, who had hitherto met him with such goodwill, suddenly withdraw themselves like this—if it were not that the friendly spirit which he had tried so hard to foster had changed to one of suspicion and hostility?

He was still silent while they ate a hasty meal beside their dismantled tents and gear. He was silent later, standing with uncovered head before the grave of Pere Receveur, whose death had cast a gloom over the last few days of the French explorers on this melancholy shore. It was a strange resting-place, he thought, for a man of learning and culture. The low mound had already lost its form, and the sand had blown over and about it, so that if it had not been for the rough headstone and the copper plate which he himself had ordered to be fixed to a near-by tree, in place of the board which the natives had torn down, one might have passed it without knowing that the bones of a man lay there. He read the inscription absently, wondering in a detached way if he, too, would end like this, giving his body to disintegration in a hard, unfriendly earth.

Hic Jacet
Le Receveur
Ex F. F. Minoribus Gallia Sacerdos
Physicus in Circumnavigatione Mundi
Duce de La Peyrouse
Obit Die 17th Febr. Anno 1788

He turned away, and his companions followed, pulling on their hats again, silent in the face of a fate which they could not but know might be theirs also. Phillip said soberly:

"I shall see that there is a suitable headstone placed later on. We might as well return to the settlement at once—it doesn't look as if the natives mean to show themselves, and we could search all day and never find them if they meant to evade us. There is no object in remaining here."

Lieutenant Johnston, rubbing his cold finger-tips together, said:

"I expect we shall never discover the culprits after all."

Phillip said shortly:

"I doubt if they were the culprits. We have no reason to believe that they murder wantonly, unprovoked." Behind his back Johnston, unabashed, sketched a shrug and a faint grimace.

*　　*　　*

They set out, glad to be on the move, following the coastal path which the natives used in their journeys between Port Jackson and Botany Bay. They walked in single file, feeling the blood quicken in their half-frozen limbs, and enjoying the increasing warmth of the sun. White, walking ahead, found his eyes turning continually to the ocean, scanning the horizon with a ridiculous and barely acknowledged hope. He did not expect to see a ship, but there remained in his mind, all the same, the teasing thought that at any moment a sail *might* appear. If it did it could mean nothing to him. It would not take him back to his homeland, it might not even come from his homeland, but it would be visible and material proof that there still existed a world which, in this remote, secret, self-enclosed land sometimes seemed as shadowy as a half-remembered dream.

Suddenly he found himself listening. The sea made a low, continuous background of noise, and the tramp of their own feet rang on the frosty ground, but he had heard something else. Voices? Many voices? He stopped dead, the warm glow which exercise had aroused in his body quenched by an icy spasm of shock. A bend in the path had brought them round a great face of rock into a little cove, and it was swarming with armed natives. There must be, he rapidly calculated, as his companions came up with him and stood staring, over two hundred men, nearly a hundred women and children. And there could be no doubt of their temper . . .

Taken as much by surprise as were the intruders, they sprang angrily to their feet, snatching up weapons or brandishing those which they already held. An elderly man, in a group not ten yards from the little party of white men, advanced towards them, making fierce signs to them to retreat, and a mutter of resentment rose and swelled to an uproar as his fellows saw the six marines draw close together and hold their fire-breathing sticks in readiness. They knew very well why the white Be-anga had come. It was no secret from them that he had gone to the bay where they had slain his people, and, failing to find the slayers there, had journeyed to the towri of the Gweagal in search of them. Now they were assembling in force as they had planned, to assert themselves. They did not doubt, staring past him with hatred at the six red-coated ones, that presently from each of the gooroobeera fire would shoot forth to destroy them, and their rage was intensified when they saw that not only these, but two of the despised white tribe were thus armed with magic against which they could pit nothing but their defiance.

The Be-anga had stolen a march on them. They were not ready yet to meet him. Tirrawuul, Bennilong, Caruey, Colbee, and many other warriors both of their own tribe and those of the Gweagal, and the Cammeraygal were away, summoning all to the great meeting, but as the Be-anga was here . . .

Suddenly the air above their heads bristled with raised spears.

White, Johnston and Kellow exchanged rapid glances of alarm. There could be only one outcome to this, if it came to open hostilities. They had not stirred since the Governor, in that first startled moment of encounter, had, with a word and a gesture, bidden them halt. Perhaps six seconds passed, heavily unreal, like time dreamed, while the twelve men felt life lift and concentrate in them, gathering its resources to perform whatsoever should be demanded of it to outwit death.

In black men and white alike, hungry, insistent, and unscrupulous, threatened life worked feverishly in those poised seconds. They became, in every nerve, muscle and thought, mere laboratories for the chemistry of that first human instinct, self-preservation. Fear, the threat of extinction, poured into them like a flood, changed by the addition of pride into a fierce hostility. Boiling, fed by a mounting excitement, it generated a hatred which spread like poison gas, invisible and deadly.

Into this disastrous brew the serene and fearless humanity of the Governor dropped like a neutralising agent. He passed his musket to White, and holding his empty hands out in front of him as he had done before, advanced towards the muttering crowd. Their attention thus deflected from the hated red coats, the black men watched him doubtfully, half expecting that lightnings would shoot from his eyes to slay them. But his eyes were calm, and his voice, though it spoke incomprehensible words, was the voice of friendship. They stared at him, their minds halted, their thoughts suspended, their rage subsiding, allowing counsel to flow to them through their nerves, alert to catch and hold the message of their delicately tuned perceptions, feeling his sincerity pass like a cool breeze through an atmosphere white-hot and quivering with calamity. They stared, wrestling in their hearts with the mystery of their unity with him; here, among these strangers, these not-to-be-comprehended beings, was a brother; here was one whose mind seemed revealed to them, though his words were meaningless. Slowly, in the tranced way of children who obey an inner compulsion, they reacted to his confidence in them. Spears were lowered, weapons dropped; they gathered round him, their mood changing with wayward suddenness, finding outlet from tension in noisy talk and laughter. How pleasant it was to have the burden of rage and hatred lifted from the heart! They laughed and laughed, crowding round him, even crowding round the soldiers, only edging away with sidelong looks of mistrust and aversion from the two convicts.

Phillip produced presents—beads, fishhooks, a mirror. They accepted them, recognising this, by now, as the white man's ceremonial of friendship. Except for the fishhooks, they were not really very useful things and were presently discarded, and a few womenfolk were allowed to come forward and receive objects obviously more suitable for them than for men and warriors. Then Phillip began to speak to them. They listened, curiously, delighted with the sound of new words, trying them over on their agile parrot tongues, incredibly and rather comically successful in their imitation of his clear, clipped speech. He seemed, they thought, to be asking them something, and now and then, for a little while, spasmodically, they tried to understand. But mental effort was tiresome and unnecessary. Why should they understand the words of the Be-anga if his heart was known to them? Once he took one of their spears and made a motion as if to drive it into his breast, looking at them inquiringly, and they cried out in protestation, shaking their heads—no, no, they would not do that, they would not slay him—he was their friend!

When at last they turned to go, the old man who had first threatened hurried to escort them. There were warriors assembled in the next cove, he explained to their uncomprehending ears, who must be assured that the Be-anga came in peace, or trouble might ensue. He led the way, taking them a little off the path to show them a fine stream of fresh water, drinking from it himself and smacking his lips to show that it was good. He saw Kellow stoop to pluck a toadstool, and made anxious signs to him to throw it away, holding his hands over his belly, and contorting his features in an agonised grimace of pain; but when White picked some green low growing herb he was all smiles, and chewed a leaf or two himself to show that it was harmless. For he knew that these white people, for all their magic, were quite pitifully ignorant in the matter of food. A hundred times upon that strange excursion of theirs they had passed a feast not knowing that it was there—honey in the wild bees' nest, grubs in the rotting logs, tasty fern roots in abundance, crayfish in the fresh-water pools—he jabbered and gesticulated, trying to tell them so, but they did not understand. At the top of a hill, looking down into the next cove, he stood and called to his countrymen below. His lifted hands told them that these white men who were about to pass were friends, and then, his mission ended, he stood aside and watched them go.

They said little on the long walk, and paused only once. The Governor, reaching the top of a small crest, stopped and pointed to the far-off Lansdown Hills.

"Look!"

They could all see it—a thin, blue column of smoke rising straight as a shaft in the still, wintry air, losing itself in the forget-me-not sky. Kellow said eagerly:

"Natives, Sir? You think the mountains are inhabited, then?"

White was feeling cross. He had had enough of natives for one day. He said sourly:

"It might be only another lightning struck tree."

Phillip looked at him and then back at the smoke. He said composedly:

"Well—we shall know some day. . . ."

* * *

Andrew Prentice slipped unostentatiously back into the settlement late one night, well pleased with his day's work. It was the fourth of June, the birthday of His Majesty the King, and the celebrations which had marked the occasion had given him opportunities not to be neglected for the supplementing of his fast growing cache in the woods. A holiday had been proclaimed, and the always sketchy supervision of the convicts had been relaxed to enable officers to attend the Governor's dinner party. The *Sirius* and the *Supply* had fired royal salutes, the harbour foreshores had thundered echoes to the volleys fired by the marine battalion and by the transports still remaining in the cove; the band had played; there had been toasting and cheering and speechmaking.

Prentice, dutifully and conspicuously in the forefront of the convict throng, had lifted his voice in vociferous and enthusiastic loyalty, but he had kept his eyes, ears, and wits alert. While the officers were being entertained by His Excellency, he reasoned, it would be simple to enter and ransack their tents. He would slip away at once, then, with his spoil, returning in the evening when bonfires were to be lit and a half-pint of grog issued all round so that the convicts might drink to the health of their Sovereign. The difficulty, he realised, would not be to evade the eye of authority. It was the dislike of his fellows which threatened him. He was unpopular, and knew it. It pleased him so long as it did not menace his plans, for he felt a growing contempt for that impulsive, bungling, reckless form of insubordination which always ended in detection and punishment. His motto was to work alone, trusting no one. To work slowly, patiently, laying a firm foundation for escape. Every time a convict disappeared, to return or be found days later ragged, exhausted, and starving, he smiled grimly, swearing to himself that not thus would his own adventure end.

It had never been particularly difficult in this perforce loosely organised settlement to slip away, to absent oneself for a few hours and return in time for the muster—and no one any the wiser. Lately, thanks to his determined pose of respectful obedience, it had become easier still. Authority, so desperately hard-pressed for reliable overseers, had been forced to find them among the ranks of the convicts themselves—and who more suitable for a position of some responsibility than Prentice, always prompt, assiduous, civil and conscientious?

First he had searched for his hiding place, his base, from which, well equipped, well supplied with clothes and provisions, he would make his bid for freedom. It had taken him weeks to find it; more than once he had known a chill of fear, believing himself lost. Once he had been out all night, returning in the morning, haggard and exhausted, with a tale of having strayed from his working party and missed his way. That experience had damped his enthusiasm for a little while. He had known the panic of looking round at a country which, as far as the eye could see in every direction, was the same, an endless repetition of hills and gullies and the melancholy monotony of dull-green trees, and he had spent a nerve-racked night crouched beneath an overhanging rock, afraid to light a fire for fear it might betray him to the blacks. Once back at the settlement, however, his determination had revived, and the next opportunity had found him even farther afield than before, still searching. It was a business which took patience, and he was not a patient man. It took self-control, and he was a man of savage and ungovernable temper. He grew silent, secretive, suspicious, dangerous with dammed-back energy and smothered hatred, but he held to his course with the bitter obstinacy of a man who knows that without his aim, his one solitary idea, life would become hideous and intolerable.

Freedom. He thought of it incessantly. In the spring, he thought, as soon as the nights begin to be warm again. Let them feed and shelter me here through the winter, and in the spring—in the spring—in the spring . . . He had no plans save that he would make westward, and no reason for making westward save that the enigmatic line of blue hills beckoned him very much as they beckoned Phillip. Anything might lie behind hills. Fertile country teeming with game, broad rivers full of fish and haunted by wild ducks. His imagination painted him pictures of a life of ease and plenty, and he lived upon them spiritually while he tramped the rough ridges and scoured the tangled gullies, searching and searching . . .

At last he found it. He reckoned that it was some six or seven miles from the settlement—a wall of rock, honeycombed, like so many of the sandstone cliffs of the neighbourhood, with rounded, weather-worn holes. Under an overhanging ledge and hidden by a dense mass of prickly scrub, he had discovered one large enough to crawl into, and here, on the fine sand of the floor, dry in all weather, he had, by degrees, bestowed his hazardously acquired possessions. The spade and the axe and the small hatchet had been easy, for the convicts were continually discarding these in the dense undergrowth of the woods in order to evade their work. The nails had been more difficult, for an insufficient supply had been sent out, and they were issued sparingly, and a close watch kept upon their disposal. Half a dozen here and a dozen there had been the safest way, building up his supply gradually. The seamen, bringing their grog ashore to carouse with the women convicts, had several times proved easy prey; he had stolen a useful looking knife from one, and a small compass from another. He had purloined a haversack belonging to one of the marines, and, in the early days, helping to unload the stores, he had managed to coil and dispose of fifty feet of strong light rope which he had afterwards retrieved. A musket had been harder. The marine from whom he had stolen it had been savage, anticipating the wrath of his hot-tempered. Major, and had organised so thorough a search that it had almost been discovered where Prentice had hidden it, standing upright in the burnt-out centre of a hollow tree. Only his own good character, and his quickness in getting to the tree first and denying that it was there, had averted that disaster. Ammunition had been his problem—until today. From the officers' deserted tents, and from the marines' barracks, he had made a pretty haul; the thought of it lying securely hidden there against his day of need had sustained him through his cold, exhausting struggle back to the settlement.

He had taken a pair of shoes, too, from Captain Tench's tent, and a blanket from Lieutenant Clark's. Altogether it had been a good day. For the first time, he thought with a sardonic grin, the King had been his friend! When he had stowed everything away to his satisfaction, and rolled a boulder into place in the opening of the tiny cave to secure it against the intrusion of animals, he had crawled out through the under-growth and stood upright against the rock wall, breathing heavily with his exertions. But on an impulse, instead of setting out directly on his long march back, he had clambered up the twenty-foot cliff and found himself on a rocky plateau from which the ground fell away steeply to the west.

He was not used to beauty. Coming upon it suddenly like this it had startled him, and he had stared at it warily, mistrusting it because its lavish and breath-taking splendour seemed spread out there for no eyes but his. Neither man, nor God, nor Nature, had ever given him anything for nothing. There had always been a bargain, with the worst of it for him. The God who was preached to him offered him a nebulous salvation for a life of ignoble subservience. Nature had more than once exacted penalties from him in payment for such pleasures as he understood. Now, in front of his sharp, antagonistic eyes an immense serenity of space and colour stretched to the horizon; there the blue mountains were darken-ing to violet while he watched, and the sun, already half-hidden behind them, was laying bars of crimson between the saffron clouds. The miles of undulating tree-tops were no longer sombre green, but rosy gold; in the gullies hyacinth shadows lay as if painted, and a wintry bloom crept up from them to merge with the pale austerity of the fading sky. The air was sharp and pure, the silence ancient.

He had been painfully aware of a new significance in his plans for escape, a new element in his concept of freedom. For a second or two of spiritual struggle and resistance he saw himself as not only escaping from something, but as escaping to something—something which he could not but identify with the aloof and uncontaminated splendour upon which his eyes were fixed. Into *that,* his awakened nerves had told him, he was going; and he had felt a momentary turmoil in himself, a belated and heroic effort of his malformed spirit to rid itself of the accumulated ugli-ness of his life, a wild impulse of response to a glory offered too late.

He had looked away from it uneasily, down at his clumsy hands, and watched the rosy light fade, leaving them leaden-coloured and dirty, with broken nails, and a sprinkling of red hairs. He had felt angry and sullen because he had been shaken by an emotion which was unfamiliar to him, and during his walk back to the settlement he had taken refuge from it behind his defences of hatred and contempt.

*   *   *

The bonfires were blazing and there was a good deal of shouting and merriment going on when he returned. He stared from the shelter of the trees, his brows contracted over his small, quick-glancing eyes, his mouth a downward arc of scorn. Fools! A holiday, a bonfire, and half a pint of spirits could make them forget that this was hell on earth, could it? It could make them forget that they were outcasts, subject to hardship, torment, indignity or death—slaves in all but name! That was something, he swore, standing motionless in the shadow of a tree trunk, which he would never forget. Or accept. His only weapons, all his life, had been cunning and hatred, but he would use those two against "them" while he had breath in his body. He was not to be taken in by the Governor's pose of humanity. His Excellency was one of "them"—not to be trusted, an inveterate and hereditary enemy. Prentice lifted his head and looked across the clearing, across the stream to the opposite hillside where a light shone in Phillip's house, and there was a gleam of triumph in his eyes. He was not to be fooled! He knew "them"! He knew their cool air of authority, the assurance of their manner, their condescending kindliness, their bleak, detached anger! He knew that however human any one of them might seem to be, taken together they were as implacable as death. He knew that so long as they could use their power to hold a man on his knees to serve them, they would never let him get to his feet. But they knew, too, that even a man on his knees must have, occasionally, his illusions of joy and freedom, his moments of admittance to his heritage, his ration of emotional release. He must be allowed—even encouraged, now and then—to lift a tankard to the King, a cheer for England, a shining eye to the triumphant flag. And he would not remember, in that heady illusion of fraternity with his betters, that his King and his country and his flag had all combined to destroy, and then to disown him, for he is a fool, not resolute enough in hatred, made happy by the blaze of a bonfire and a half-pint of grog!

Quietly, skirting the clearing, he chose his place to emerge, grinning to himself because it was all too absurdly easy. Outside the glare of the bonfires the darkness was sooty; a few men nudged each other and glanced across at him, sitting where there had been no one a moment or two before, the firelight glinting on his thick, red eyebrows and his carrotty thatch of hair.

* * *

In her hut, Ellen was writhing and groaning in labour. The woman who tended her was more than a little drunk, and impatient to join in the revelry again, and Ellen's screams went unheeded by anyone but Johnny who sat outside the door where he had been hurriedly thrust to get him out of the way. A good many jokes had been made about the convict brat who had chosen the same birthday as His Majesty's, and Johnny was wondering if His Majesty's mother also had screamed thus when he was born.

* * *

By the time the last transports were ready to leave it was midwinter. The days were short and sunsets flared extravagantly behind the purple line of the western hills, leaving a cold, misty twilight which faded rapidly into night. An aching depression descended upon the white community. A thousand small things combined to make them feel themselves forsaken and forlorn. The Governor's cattle—two bulls and four cows—had strayed off into the woods and been lost owing to the negligence of their convict keeper. There had been a slight earthquake shock; the fish had vanished from the harbour; the transports were going home; it was cold; rations were insufficient; there was a long, long list of sick. It was as if a voiceless complaint, an inarticulate protest, went up perpetually from the ugly, muddled little settlement. Why are we here? Oh, why are we here, who should be in England? England! The word was spoken more and more frequently, with a greater and greater longing as the days passed, and the impending departure of the transports brought home with bitter poignancy the hard facts of their exile and their isolation. Suddenly there was an outbreak of letter-writing; homesickness found relief in it. Among the officers and the marines pens flew fast and lights burned late. But what was there to say? Their lives were hemmed in by this accursed country—they must write of it, and of their miserable situation in it, for there was nothing else.

On board the *Supply,* its master, David Blackburn, penned rather laboriously a letter to his friend, Mr. Richard Knight:

"With Respect to this Country . . ." he wrote, and then paused. He was a conscientious man, and he had no desire to paint a picture which was either too bright or too gloomy. It was not for him, a seaman, to measure the possibilities or the disadvantages of an enterprise conceived and sanctioned by his betters, so he continued with careful moderation:

". . . I am really at a loss, my Friend, what to say 'tis true we know but Little of it. But I believe it is the General Opinion that it will be a Number of Years before the Mother Country can Derive Any Advantage from it. . . ."

From outside he could hear the seamen calling to a party of natives passing in their canoes; women amongst them evidently, he thought, judging by the ribald tones and the bursts of laughter which accompanied words fortunately incomprehensible to the black charmers.

". . . We are certainly at present situated on the outskirts of the Country on account of the Convenience of so Good a Harbour—But we have seen on a Clear Day a Ridge of very high land, I suppose 30 or 40 Miles Distant—Our Parties have never Yet been so far. But I am informed the Governor intends Going with a Strong Party Very Early this Spring, and I think there is reason to suppose he will find much better land there. . . ."

The native girls, paddling round the ship, managing their clumsy bark canoes with astonishing dexterity, were not blind to the ardent glances of the men who hung over the rails. When they encountered the Duggerigai ashore, their own menfolk kept them well in the background, but here, from the safety of their canoes, their bright, dark eyes were mischievously provocative, and the shrill sound of their voices and their excited laughter floated across the water to the tent of Lieutenant Ralph Clark, where he sat reading over a letter which he had begun two days earlier:

". . . you must not expect to have a minute account of the Country and our situation here from me. . . ."

He sighed and fidgeted, tapping his teeth with his pen, half his attention on the cheerful sounds of badinage and merriment from outside; then suddenly he began to scribble with glib ferocity:

"I shall only tell you that this is the poorest country in the world, which its inhabitants show, they are the most miserable set of wretches under the sun. . . ."

How they laughed! What had they, naked heathen savages, to be so happy about? The women hideous—revolting to eyes which had feasted on the beauty of the incomparable Betsey. Why did one dream so much? Dreams, dreams, night after night one's sleep was made restless by them, and one wakened feverish and unrefreshed . . .

He rubbed his hand over his eyes and went on writing:

". . . there is no other river or spring in the country that we have been able to find or meet with, all the fresh water comes out of large swamps, which the country abounds with, the country is overrun with large trees, not one acre of clear ground to be seen, nor is there one tree out of fifty but what is burnt with the lightning, nor nothing in it fit for the substance of man, what with earthquakes, thunder and lightning, it is to be sure a sweet country, the thunder and lightning is the most terrible I ever heard, it is the opinion of everybody here that Government will remove the Settlement to some other place for if it remains here the country will not be able to maintain itself in one hundred years. . . ."

His fingers were numb with cold, and he paused to chafe some warmth into them, frustration and homesickness swelling in him to an unbearable pitch of self-pity.

". . . I am sorry to say that Major Ross and the Governor are not on the best of terms, nor is the former with several of us, he is, without exception the most disagreeable commanding officer I ever knew. . . ."

There was no sound of voices from outside now. He glanced through the doorway and saw that a fine, drizzling rain had begun to fall. The dreary cheerlessness of the place stirred in him a hatred which could find no outlet but in his written words:

"My God, I would not stay longer than I could help in this Country if they would give me a Capt's Commission."

Now that the sky was so overcast the light was bad. Huddled in his cloak he bent low over his paper, rationalising into contempt and dislike a fear which sometimes came near to panic—a feverish longing for escape.

* * *

Surgeon White wrote hastily to Lord Sydney, leaning on a makeshift table, still wearing the greatcoat in which he had just returned through the rain from the hospital. His hair was disordered and his mouth was truculent, and he wasted no words in preamble:

"My Lord,
"The prevalance of disease among the troops and convicts who on landing were tainted with the scurvy, and the likelyhood of its continuance from the food (salt provisions) on which they are from necessity obliged to live, has made the consumption of medicines so very great that the inclosed supply will be very much wanted before any ships can possibly arrive here from England.
"The distress among the troops, their wives and children, as well as among the convicts, for want to necessaries to aid the operation of medicines has been great."

A heavier downpour of rain made him look up. He glared at it, exasperated, regarding it as an enemy, another of the many enemies arrayed against him in his losing fight with sickness. How can you make men well, he thought furiously, when you cannot even feed them, when you cannot even keep them warm? He hated this country—not with the nervous, querulous hatred of Lieutenant Clark, but heartily and savagely. So it was going to rain hard now, was it? All right; in a moment he would go and huddle his patients still closer together in the tent to avoid the places which leaked, and he would rummage about for some extra coverings, and give them some soup, well watered down, but at least hot. And they would die just the same. He gave a snort which was half rage and half defiance, and dipped his pen in the ink again:

"What are included under the head of necessaries?"

He scribbled angrily:

"I take the liberty to enumerate, which are sugar, sago, oatmeal, barley, rice, currants, different spices, vinegar and portable soup. Indeed our situation, not having any fresh animal food, nor being able to make a change in the diet, which has and must be salt meat, makes these things more necessary here than, perhaps, in any quarter of the globe. However, the necessity of having these things sent out by the first opportunity will no doubt be strongly recommended to your Lordship's notice by His Excellency Governor Phillip. I have mentioned them lest they should escape him through the multiplicity of matters all new settlements afford. I have to entreat your Lordship will be pleased to cause the medicines to be sent from Apothecaries' Hall, where they are sure to be genuine and fresh, a circumstance, considering the immense distance we are off, and the length of time it will take before we can receive them, that cannot be too much attended to. Care in the putting them up and having them placed in a dry place where no wet can come at them during the voyage, is another circumstance equally to be attended to."

He thought grimly, "Well, I have asked. I can't do more." He signed his name hurriedly, "John White, Surgeon," and threw his pen down as if it were the sum of his irksome responsibilities which he was violently discarding.

* * *

The Reverend Richard Johnson, having arranged his writing materials with nicety, drew his chair up to his table and seated himself, but did not immediately take up his pen. He had, in fact, already dealt with his correspondence, and there was no one else to whom he really needed to write; but it was necessary that he should make some show of being busy in order to justify to himself the fact that he was not plodding through the rain to carry the consolations of religion to the sick. Later, of course, he would go. At present, his home, poor as it was, had a certain cosiness which he was loth to abandon. His wife, excellent woman, was mending his best shirt, seated near the doorway where the light fell upon her work; there was a fire burning, and from the next room a pleasing odour of cooking made his nostrils twitch with anticipatory content. He would write, he decided, to Mr. Evan Nepean, Under Secretary of State. Very pleasant and friendly Mr. Nepean had been to him when he had called with his letter of introduction from Sir Charles Middleton. It would not do to seem ungrateful or forgetful of his civility. The writing of sermons had lent to all literary composition, in Mr. Johnson's mind, a flavour of sanctity, and it was with a certain dignified importance that he dipped his pen in the ink and wrote a careful superscription:

"Port Jackson in the County of Cumberland
"New South Wales, July 12th, 1788

"Hon'd Sir,
"Though I have nothing particular to mention to you, I cannot think of letting the Fleet return to England without dropping you a single line to inform you of my health and welfare. It would be unnecessary for me, Sir, to give you any account of the various circumstances or incidences respecting the Fleet during our late passage from England to this distant part of the globe, as, no doubt, you will receive ample information respecting these matters, together with a description of this country as to climate natives, etc., etc., from his Excellency Arthur Phillip Esq., our Governour, and others. Everything here is as yet (as you may easily suppose) very unsettled, but hope in time our situation may be rendered more comfortable, and even now, all things considered, thank God, I have no reason to complain."

He paused to allow himself a moment's self-congratulation upon this example of lofty forbearance. For indeed he had very ample reason to complain. Was it fitting that the Governor should push on so determinedly with the erection of profane buildings, while the Word of God was still preached under the open sky or in an unfinished storehouse? Less concern was shown for religion than he could have wished, and this in a place which, surely, stood more in need of spiritual guidance than any other spot on earth.

Nevertheless he would be patient. He composed himself to write again, firmly subduing a faint anxiety, a nagging sense of inadequacy which had often troubled him since the beginning of this adventure. Sin, crime, human wickedness and depravity seemed more than life-size here, painted against the sombre, unrelenting background of an unknown land; there were moments when he suspected that he had strayed into some way of life which was too big for him, moments when he wondered if it might not have been better if he had never heard the call of duty which had led him here. Suddenly a drip found its way through the palm thatched roof and splashed on to the floor. *Drip, drip, drip,* it went, until Mrs. Johnson, rising fetched a tin basin to place beneath it, and then its note changed. *Plonk, plonk, plonk,* over and over again with enraging monotony. Mr. Johnson gave a hunted glance around the room, but there was no escape; of course not. He sighed and dipped his pen in the ink again. Its faint scratching across the paper was a pleasant sound, civilised, scholarly. He tried to listen to it and to ignore that other sound which so relentlessly reminded him of exile.

* * *

Major Ross, too, had written a letter to Mr. Evan Nepean, but he had finished it some days ago, and this evening he was reading it over before sealing it, and reading with a considerable satisfaction for it seemed to him that it put the whole preposterous situation clearly and bluntly, as a soldier's letter should, without mincing words. It would make plain to Mr. Nepean that there was one man in this marooned community who would not submit tamely to the absurd, tyrannical moods of its Governor. There would be one letter at least (but he suspected that there would be many more) telling the unvarnished truth about this hopeless, barren and unprofitable land.

"Camp, Sydney Cove, New South Wales,
"10th July, 1788

"My Dear Sir,

"I know not whether the Secretary of State expects I am to write to him or not, but I suppose rather not, for as I came out without any orders or instructions from your office with respect to the intentions of Government, so am I still ignorant of it, for the Governor has never told me, neither has he ever advised or consulted with me on the subject, and I believe everybody else are in the dark as well as myself. Should his Lordship expect letters from me, I hope you will think the above a sufficient excuse, for I cannot see how I could write without informing him of the manner in which the Governor treats me as Lieut. Governor; and as to the detachment they have just the same cause for complaint that I have. This you will see cannot be done without my letter coming in the manner of a complaint, which I by no means wish to be the case at this stage of the business; but I will not answer for what may be the case hereafter, for, take my word for it, there is not a man in this place but wishes to return home, and indeed they have no less than cause, for I believe there never was a set of people so much upon the parrish as this garrison is, and what little we want, even to a single nail, we must not send to the Commissary for it, but must apply to his Excellency, and when we do he allways sayes there is but little come out, and of course it is but little we get, and what we are obliged to take as a mark of favor.

"If you want a true description of this country it is only to be found amongst many of the private letters sent home; however, I will, in confidence, venture to assure YOU that this country will never answer to settle in, for altho' I think corn will grow here, yet I am convinced that if ever it is able to maintain the people here it cannot be in less time than probably a hundred years hence. I therefore think it will be cheaper to feed the convicts on turtle and venison at the London Tavern than be at the expence of sending them here.

"I have now only to add my hope that yourself, Mrs. Nepean, and the family are well, and to assure you that it is not possible you can be better than you are wished to be by James Campbell, as well as by, my dear sir,
"Yours &c.,
R. Ross"

*　　*　　*

The Governor sat down at his writing table reluctantly. It was covered with papers—not littered, for he was a man of orderly habits, but neatly stacked—and he looked at them with distaste, for sometimes it seemed that he did nothing but write and dictate. It was inevitable, of course, that the authorities at home must be kept informed, and seeing this as a part of his duty he performed it faithfully, describing the land, the climate, the natives, and all the conditions and activities of the settlement with a wealth of conscientious detail. Now, with a sigh, he drew towards him the formidable pile of papers which the transports were to take back to England. He turned them over, his brows wrinkled in concentration. Was there anything of importance which he had left unsaid? Any vital necessities he had forgotten to ask for, any useful information he had neglected to give? Here was his first despatch to Lord Sydney—some eight thousand words of careful description—here were the enclosures appointing King as Commandant of Norfolk Island, and his instructions for the conduct of that office. Here was the official account of that unfortunate court-martial which had stirred up so much trouble. Here was a letter to Mr. Nepean, mostly about food, and here another despatch to

Lord Sydney with an enclosure about the livestock of the colony; here was another long private letter to Mr. Nepean, enclosing a list of articles badly needed in the settlement. This, to Lord Sydney again, told of the good land near the head of the harbour, and this . . .

He threw them down. There they all were, and he was heartily sick of them. Many were in duplicate or in triplicate, and some of the public letters even in quadruplicate, to cheat the mischances of a long and perilous voyage. And yet he must write one more. Upon the letters which these ships carried back to England might depend the fate of his colony; he thought of it thus, possessively, jealous for its welfare and advancement. Not only his own letters, but others—those of Major Ross, for instance—would be read and debated by men who had it in their power to wrest him, by a word, from this enterprise in which he had somehow acquired so deep-rooted a faith.

He drew a sheet of paper before him and began to write:

"My Lord,
"The publick letters to your Lordship will show the situation of this settlement, and the little difficultys we have met with, which time, an additional force, and proper people for cultivating the land will remove; and your Lordship may be assured that anxious to render a very essential service to my country, by the establishment of a colony, which from its situation must hereafter be a valuable acquisition to Great Britain, no perseverence will be wanting on my part, and which consideration alone could make amends for the being surrounded by the most infamous of mankind, it is to your Lordship and to Nepean only that I make a declaration of this kind. Time will remove all difficultys, and with a few familys who have been used to the cultivation of lands, this country will wear a more pleasing aspect, and those who are to come out, knowing what the country really is will be less disappointed. As to myself I am satisfied to remain so long as my services are wanted: I am serving my country and serving the cause of humanity. I flatter myself that by the return of the ships that brought us out provisions, and on which is placed our sole dependence, I shall be able to give your Lordship a more satisfactory account of this country."

He paused, rereading that last sentence. "By the return of the ships . . ." For a moment his mind became nothing but memory—memory of shrieking winds and groaning timbers and vast seas, mountain-high, and the fragility and the awful loneliness of a ship alone in a storm-tormented ocean. Soberly he underlined the words, *"and on which is placed our sole dependence."*

When he had written another paragraph praising King and asking for his promotion as a reward of merit, he closed the letter and stood up thankfully. Now there was practical business to be set afoot, for the *Supply* must be made ready for a journey to Norfolk Island with stores —those stores for which King was depending on him just as he was depending on the authorities at home. He was half way to the door when he stopped with a sharp exclamation of annoyance and returned to his table.

"My dear Sir,"

he wrote hastily to Nepean, for the afternoon was nearly over and the light was fading,

"To the articles which I have mentioned as more immediately wanted the following, tho' so very necessary, have escaped my memory till this moment. Leather for soals for the men's shooes, and the materials for mending them. Shooes here last but a very short time, and the want of these materials, and thread to mend the cloathing, will render it impossible to make them serve more than half the time for which they were intended. This country requires warm cloathing in the winter: the rains are frequent and the nights very cold.

"You will excuse the repetition of our wants; they will, I hope, be less in future.

"I have &c.,
"A. Phillip."

He added yet another afterthought:

"Vinegar will be very acceptable; it is very much wanted."

How early and how suddenly the twilight closed in on these wet winter evenings! He stood up, rubbing his cold fingers together and blinking eyes tired from straining in the half-light. He put on his hat and greatcoat and went out into the rain, walking fast to restore the circulation in his chilled body. There were lights just being lit on the transports in the cove, and he stared across at them as he walked, thinking wryly that he was probably the only man in the settlement who did not long to be on board them when they sailed.

* * *

It had been a hard winter for the black men; not only physically but spiritually they had suffered. Their minds, once occupied only with the clearly defined concerns of their own elaborately organised communal life, had been constantly jolted into confused and painful activity by the presence of the Duggerigai. Now they were no longer carefree. Now they were no longer in tune with their lives, moving easily to the rhythm of their age-old customs, facing each day with confidence, knowing that the Law would guide them in any emergency which might arise.

Now they awoke to a faint uneasiness, perplexing because it was not altogether unpleasant. Now they were conscious of a faintly exciting division in their own hearts, so that they scarcely knew if they admired the white men or despised them. Now they were torn between awe and contempt, between friendliness and resentment; they were no longer whole, there was a poison at work.

They all felt it. Here were beings who, without wounding or slaying them, were yet working them a mischief so deadly that even the most intrepid warrior was sometimes visited by a pang of superstitious fear. And yet it would take more than a few months to eradicate or even to modify the characteristics which centuries had rooted so firmly in them. They could resent, but not for long; they could think, and think clearly with a sharp flash of logic and good sense, but their brains were not trained to the long chain of reasoning, the patient exploration of cause and effect, the tenacious pursuit of an idea, the cold, final pinning down of a conclusion. They could only swing between their natural reactions, meeting friendliness with delight and injustice with fierce resentment.

And was it not injustice that the Bereewolgal should, with their great canoes and their great nets, go hauling up and down the harbour so that there were no fish left for the black men to spear or for the black women to catch on their lines? Many times they themselves had helped to drag in those nets, and had been given some of the catch, and had accepted them as a friendly gift; but when fish were no longer plentiful, and the women and children grew thin, and the warriors bound strong cord tightly about their bellies to allay the pangs of hunger, was it right that the Bereewolgal should still feast while they, to whom the land belonged, came near to starving? The white men had brought much of their own food with them—why, then, did they not eat it, and leave the black man's food to him?

One day a group of the Cammeraygal had descended upon the fishing boats of the invaders and taken half the catch by force, but after that there were always red-coated ones in the boats, with their magical fire-breathing weapons, and it was better, after all, to hunger a little than to die.

Not only the fish but the kangaroos and other smaller game had become scarce since the advent of the white men. The noise they made, the continual banging of their gooroobeera, their incessant tramping about through the bush, the strange, evil emanation which seemed to spread from them, polluting the very air, these things had made the animals nervous and sent them far afield, so that now it was seldom indeed that a kangaroo was brought back to camp for the evening meal.

And yet it was not possible to hate all these people. It was not possible to hate the Be-anga, friendly and fearless, or him whom they called Collins, who was so often with him, or the large young man who was a mighty carrahdy, and who had, one day, cut off all the round golden ornaments from his coat and tied them laughingly round the waist of Weenoora, so that she was the envy of all the other women in the tribe. It was even becoming difficult now to remember all the time that these were strangers in the land. They had been here so long now, so very, very long, that already their coming seemed almost as lost in the mists of the past as the coming of Mommon and Yaburog. It was necessary to make an effort of memory to see the cove of Weerong as it had been before, and to remember the harbour in times when there had been no winged ships coming and going, and no smaller boats crawling about like many legged insects on its calm, blue water.

* * *

Bennilong still watched the settlement sometimes from his vantage-point on the hillside. He was, for a time, deeply interested in the stones which the white men shaped for building their dwellings—smooth sided, regularly shaped stones which they fashioned of clay and dried with fire so that they became as hard as any rock. But when he saw the labour which went into the building of their houses, and the way in which two of them collapsed after heavy rain, he laughed and decided that a bark shelter or an overhanging ledge was quite as efficient and must less trouble.

During the winter he had a good deal of trouble with Barangaroo. It was not in Bennilong to be constant; he had a roving and amorous eye, and an inexhaustible physical zest which drove him ever on to fresh conquests; nor was it in Barangaroo to be patient and uncomplaining. His faithlessness she could have borne, but her own continued childlessness soured her temper so that she welcomed any excuse to rail at him. She had visited the places where the baby spirits waited, and she had performed certain rites known only to women, and now she was becoming sullen and shrewish, and her head and shoulders were often bruised and bleeding from her husband's exasperated correction. Nevertheless there existed between them a fierce and stormy attachment. Even in the worst times of that hard winter Barangaroo never failed to have a supper cooked which would at least take the edge from Bennilong's voracious appetite. No matter how he beat and scolded her, it was to her that he always returned for consolation when his impulsive nature and violent actions brought down trouble upon his head.

During the winter Weeruwee, the elderly husband of Bennilong's sister, Warreweer, had died, and Warreweer was now married again to a much younger man called Gnungagnunga Murremurgan, a gentle and kindhearted fellow who, so Bennilong considered, made no real attempt to discipline her unbecoming audacity and light-heartedness. She, skimming about in her bark canoe and darting round the transports at anchor in the cove like a waterbeetle round a stranded log, had become so friendly with the seamen who gathered at the rails to talk and laugh with her, that she had learned many of their words and could call to them, flashing her teeth and her bright, dark eyes: "Good day!" and "Good-bye!" and "God save the King!"

But the first excitement which the appearance of the white men had brought into the lives of the tribespeople had long since faded. Now there was only this general restlessness, this uneasy awareness of time and change, this queer stimulation of thought, this necessity to puzzle over things which had always seemed simple before.

Tirrawuul died of it. He was too old to grapple with the disturbing thoughts which came to him, too old to endure even the first faint forewarning shadow of change which he felt in the spiritual restlessness of his people, once so serenely confident in a faith which never had been challenged. So the desire for life went out of him, and he lay down in his mia-mia and died, and there was a terrible wailing in the camp.

Now the winter was over. The Cammeraygal were holding a corroboree, and Bennilong with many of his fellow tribesmen, including his inseparable companion By-gone, Ballederry the fleet-footed, and the kindly and popular Arabanoo, had gone to be present at the festivities. The day was hot and many warriors of both tribes had gone down to the beach, but they had no sooner arrived than two of the white men's boats were seen making in for the shore. They watched them come, standing motionless, the old uneasy doubts falling like a shadow over the carefree gaiety of their holiday mood. What did the Duggerigai want now? Why were there red-coated ones in the boats with their fire-breathing weapons in their hands? Was not that one—the one standing in the bow of the first boat—he whom they called by an unpronounceable name, to which the nearest they could come was Dyon-ton? Was he not constantly to be seen with the Be-anga, and had he not accompanied him upon at least one of his incomprehensible journeys? They nodded agreement among themselves. See, as usual, he was making signs of reassurance and goodwill. Their tenseness slackened, their taut grip on their spears relaxed; well, they thought resignedly, he was the Be-anga's friend, and therefore theirs, and they would accept with becoming civility some more of the rather foolish gifts which were the white man's ceremonial of friendship. They laid their weapons on the sand and walked down to the water's edge, the little harbour surf breaking pleasantly about their feet, and the soft sand sliding away from beneath their insteps with each receding wave.

But as the boats beached and the Bereewolgal jumped out on to the sand, the black men began to look at each other nervously, feeling that familiar prickle of the skin, that lifting of the hairs of the body, that faint quickening of the heartbeats which were their primitive reaction to the sensed presence of danger. For they were not civilised enough to be unaware of evil when it was near them, and to them evil was peril, terrible and destroying, an enemy of the inner life, just as hunger and wounds were enemies of the physical life; they needed nothing but their sharply tuned senses to tell them that it was here, close to them, threatening and malign.

But where? The voice of Dyon-ton was friendly; he smiled. His followers smiled too. The gifts they offered were the same kind of gifts which the Be-anga had often distributed among them. Why, then, was it as if a mist swam between them and the Bereewolgal, through which they saw each other move like phantoms instead of as fellow men? It must be, they thought nervously, yet another magic of the white men, an invisible magic, more deadly than the gooroobeera, striking not at the body, but at the spirit. . . .

Ai-ye! Ki-yah! Ki-yah! The evil was suddenly let loose! The Duggerigai, their faces no longer smiling, but fierce and vengeful, were rushing on them, the air was torn with the shouts of Dyon-ton and his companions and with their own startled yells. Magic was invoked against them, an evil magic the more terrible because it was invisible, and no man could tell or even guess whence or how it came. There was nothing for it but to flee, to reach the shelter of the trees where the white men travelled so slowly and so clumsily, and they scattered, racing up the beach and into the shadowy bush where they were halted, smitten, fast breathing, by the cries of two of their number who had not escaped. From among the trees they peered out on to the sun-drenched, golden beach; two black, naked bodies were writhing and struggling in the grip of several of the white men; others remained by the boats, ready to push off, and still others, holding their gooroobeera in readiness, stood staring towards the trees in case of an attempted rescue. One of the captives was Arabanoo. Already, with a rope about his neck and his hands and feet bound, he was being dragged to one of the boats, yelling with fury and defiance, fighting and struggling so desperately that another man rushed to aid those who were already bundling him into the boat. The other captive, a powerful and active young man called Meerung, had succeeded in dragging the man who held him into the water. Here, unencumbered by clothing or weapon, he had the advantage, and when the white man could no longer feel the sand beneath his feet, he let go, and Meerung, with a shout of triumph, dived, and swam beneath the water to safety.

Now in the hearts of the tribesmen fury took the place of fear. Treachery so black was indeed evil, but it was not magic. Rage flamed in them, a rage which dried up their dread of the gooroobeera as a bush fire dries the last trickle of water in a creek. They broke out again in a body from among the trees and rushed down on to the beach, snatching up scattered spears as they went, shouting encouragement to Arabanoo and revilements upon the duplicity of the white men.

But it was too late. Already the boat to whose thwarts Arabanoo lay bound had put out from the shore, and the other was close behind it. Over the heads of the white men, pulling desperately at their oars, spears began to fly, and Lieutenant Johnston, watching one glance from the side of his boat, ordered his men to fire over the heads of the natives. Ball, in the other boat, mopped his forehead with his handkerchief and called out: "That will soon send them to cover."

On the beach the natives began to retreat. The boats now were out of range of their spears, and Arabanoo was gone. They did not doubt that he would be instantly slain; already, in their hearts they were mourning him as one dead.

And Johnston, looking down at his captive, still struggling with his bonds and shouting hoarsely to his companions on the shore, said rather petulantly:

"Well, my friend, I hope you were worth it!"

* * *

Arabanoo was silent now. He, like his friends, took it for granted that he was to be killed—for what other reason could he have been taken?

That was bad enough; it was like seeing darkness come at noon, but worse, filling him with panic and agony, was this nightmare of being bound. When Dyon-ton directed that his hands and feet were to be freed he hardly cared that it was probably the signal for his end. But he was not released from the rope which bound him to the boat, and he crouched on his knees and dragged at it incessantly, not so much because he hoped to loosen it as because some part of him was still incredulous of it; death he could understand, but not captivity.

He wondered how they would kill him. Would he die by the magic of the gooroobeera? Would they plunge their long bright knives into his body? Would they—he made a convulsive movement of terror and stared round him with wild, desperate eyes—would they slay him as Bennilong had seen them slay one of their own people—would his body hang by its neck in the twilight, swinging from the branch of a high tree—alone, quite alone, without the friendly clamour of his mourning friends to speed his outward rushing spirit on its way?

He started violently at a touch on his arm, and looked up to find one of the white men offering him some cooked fish. He stared at the watching faces about him, his thoughts labouring and confused. They were not, now, inimical faces. Several of them were grinning at him, friendly, none looked fierce enough to slay him. He saw no hatred in the eyes that watched him, no vengefulness; only curiosity and a mild amusement. Why had they taken him? Were they friends or foes? If they meant to slay him why should they feed him first?

There was no answer to such questions. There was no answer to any question about the white men. Their ways were incomprehensible ways. With a momentary flash of inspiration he wondered if they were less comprehensible to him than to themselves, knew a stab of wondering pity for creatures so abandoned to the powers of evil as to have no ruling Law to shelter them and hold their actions fast and secure in rigid rules of conduct. In the meantime it was foolish not to eat when food was offered, so he took the fish and ate it silently, staring out across the bright water with dark and melancholy eyes.

* * *

Lieutenant Dawes and his friend Captain Tench were walking on the hill by the Observatory when the boats came in. Captain Tench, as usual, was doing all the talking; a mobile face and a pair of expressive hands aided his fluent tongue, but still his lively humour and his quick wit ran ahead of them, so that he was no sooner finished with one sentence than he was embarked upon another, no sooner at the end of one theme than another opened alluringly before him.

This suited Lieutenant Dawes very well. He was content to listen and not overfond of talking, and he strolled contentedly with his hands clasped behind his back and his eyes on the winding reaches of the harbour.

"We should do famously," Tench was saying, "in collaboration. The taste for authorship has grown upon me, Dawes. Upon my word, I don't know how I should have endured my leisure if I had not had my journals and my Narrative to keep me employed. A work upon the language of these natives would be very well received, I should think. If the Governor is successful in getting some of them to live amongst us it should not be difficult to . . ."

"Well," Dawes said, shading his eyes with his hat and staring down the harbour, "we shall know quite soon. There are the two boats coming up now. Can you see if there are any Indians in them?"

"Not yet." Tench turned away from the glare of the water blinking dazzled eyes. "They are not near enough. I tell you, Dawes, I'm glad the Governor did not pitch on me for that task. I should not have enjoyed it, should you?"

"I think," Dawes replied calmly, "that I should have refused it."

Tench stared.

"Refused? But my dear fellow . . ."

He stopped, realising alertly that this was not a subject for discussion. There was a fanatic buried somewhere in this quiet, efficient, and well liked young lieutenant. All his diligence, his irreproachable discipline, and his cheerful courtesy could not quite hide that his ultimate allegiance was to some inner self which would stand like granite, if occasion arose, against orders and entreaties alike. To this undivided soul Tench, whose personality had as many facets as a diamond, could offer a genuine respect, while still hoping, with a shrug, that it would not too often find itself at odds with an imperfect world. He turned again to watch the boats.

They were past the little island with its rocky pinnacle now, and as he watched through eyes half shut against the strong sunlight, Tench found his attention wandering from them, and his senses taking charge. How strong the colours were! The blues—so many blues—were streaked near the shores with green which turned almost golden over shallow-covered sand. The trees were dense and dark, but flickering with the sparkle of their sunlit leaves. The sunshine was so strong that one almost seemed to see through a haze of golden dust. Its heat burned. He could feel it on his hands and his face, for he had acquired the habit of going hatless and his skin had already darkened to brown. There was no sound but the splash of little waves against the rocks on the shore and occasional voices from the settlement, and the faint, dry rustle of leaves overhead. The breeze which stirred them came in from the ocean, and its strong, salty smell was mingled with the scent of a white flowering shrub at his side. He picked a spray of it, and held it against his nostrils, remembering that in his Narrative he had likened it to the English May, and then, in his excitement, he dropped it, for the boats were making in to the cove, and there was, quite unmistakably, a black man in the first of them.

Dawes said, dryly:

"It looks as if Johnston has been successful. Can you see if there is another in Ball's boat?"

Tench shook his head.

"No. Only one. Come along, Dawes, let's go down to the landing to meet them. This promises to be interesting."

They hurried along the hillside, passing Lieutenant Ball's garden, passing the hospital and a dreary cluster of convicts' huts, passing the marines' camp and crossing the parade ground, and all the time they could see the news spreading from mouth to mouth, and from every corner of the settlement men, women, and children began to converge upon the little wharf on the east side of the cove.

It was a large and motley crowd which greeted Arabanoo when the boat touched and he was hustled out, still bound, upon the landing. Convicts, marines, officers, women, children, and dogs crowded about him, and the subtly offensive smell which his people had so often noticed before touched his nerves with panic so that he shrank back from them as from an evil sorcery.

But there was no escape. He had accepted that fact now. The quiet fatalism of his race, joined to his own gentle and patient nature, forbade what seemed to him an obviously useless resistance, and he moved forward with his escort, the crowd thronging about him, the men and women laughing and pointing, the children prodding him with daring forefingers, the strange dogs of the white people, so unlike the dingo pups which were their own pets and companions, sniffing at his heels and yelping excitedly. His eyes moved nervously from them to the people; he saw more and more coming to look at him. There, walking as fast as he could with dignity, came the round-faced one, and his woman with him; there came another of the many leaders of these people, a stern visaged man walking stiffly erect and staring about him with a haughtiness which was also to be seen among those overbearing and powerful warriors, the Cammeraygal. Here were two young men, laughing and shouldering their way through the crowd. And here, in a group about his feet, were children . . .

Arabanoo paused. Some of the wildness faded from his eyes as he looked at them. His instinct, primitive and unerring, made a leap which brought him the comfort denied by his labouring brain. Here, before his eyes, was the proof of the common humanity which he shared with these people—why had he feared? But how ugly they were, these little ones of the Bereewolgal! How pale their hair and eyes, how pale and how thin their faces! And what affliction was this which so ate away the teeth in the mouths grinning excitedly up at him? He bent to them, smiling his compassion, shaking his head protestingly when they drew away from him in alarm. He had a sudden sense of security and relief. Here was the root of all things—the perpetuation of all tribes, white or black. Every deed, every emotion, was bound up with the children by whom the immortality of the tribe was assured. In the hearts of the white men, he thought, there must be feelings as tender as those which he knew in looking at his sons. And then he found himself confronted by the peaked, white face, and dark, inscrutable eyes of Johnny Prentice.

He cried out delightedly. Johnny, wary and mistrustful, tried to edge away. Arabanoo, laughing and cajoling, lifted the cap which covered his red hair and fingered a lock of it, demanding eagerly of the crowd: "Ganumba noa unni yinal?"

They smiled at him uncomprehendingly, puzzled by his obvious preference for Johnny. And Johnny, who had only one rule of life which was to remain as inconspicuous and incommunicative as possible, edged away from the captive's outstretched hand and escaped.

It was a long time now since that enchanted day he had spent in the woods with the black man and his family, but he had not forgotten it. He had never tried to repeat it because, in some dim way, he associated it with the terrors and miseries of the night which had followed it, and with the long days when he lay ill and gasping in his mother's hut; but fear had hit him like a lightning stroke when he had looked up and recognised the black face upon which the eyes of the whole settlement had been fixed.

His fears were all nebulous. For the actual hardships of his life, hunger, cold, beatings, unkindness, contempt, he was not conscious of dread. It was the cumulative effect of them, by which the world was made malign and insecure, which obsessed his mind and governed all his actions. Why was his friend, the black man, here among his mortal enemies, the grown-ups? Was the black man, perhaps, not his friend after all? Had he come to reveal the secret which Johnny had hoarded all that long year—the secret of a whole day spent happily, a whole day unrebuked, a whole day of playtime?

Johnny never doubted that it had been a sinful day. He lived and breathed an atmosphere of guilt and punishment. In his heart he felt that it was wicked of him to be alive at all; to enjoy being alive was a height of depravity which he had achieved only once—and now he was to be betrayed . . .

From the outskirts of the crowd he stole a backward glance. Arabanoo was being hurried away towards the Governor's house. Presently he was lost to Johnny's sight in the throng of people who surrounded him.

* * *

Arabanoo dined with the Governor, and was unconscious of being honoured. He sat at a small table close to that at which the Be-anga and his friends ate, and looked soberly at the food which was set before him. There was fish, and duck; both smelt good, but when he picked a piece up in his fingers he found it so hot that he put it down again hurriedly and stared in surprise at the white people who were so unconcernedly eating it. One of the young men whom he had noticed near the landing place now passed him something else—a powdery substance which looked like pure white sand. Arabanoo sniffed it dubiously and shook his head, pushing the offering away.

He twisted and turned to examine the seat upon which he sat. It was pleasantly soft—much softer than rock or earth—and it had very beautiful markings on it, coloured markings, which he traced admiringly with his forefinger, but it had a disturbing way of moving when he moved, as if it were alive. Nor was it really comfortable, in spite of being soft. He longed to take his food and squat on the floor with it, for it was awkward and inconvenient to eat thus, up in the air, with one's legs hanging foolishly in front of one. Nevertheless his quick instinctive courtesy taught him that here, in his own tribe, it was the Be-anga's right to dictate its customs, so he only fidgeted, looking about him at many unfamiliar things, and feeling his food with his finger now and then to see if it was cool enough to eat.

Presently the Be-anga offered him a drinking vessel containing a dark liquid. He was thirsty, so he took it and smelt it warily, but his nostrils wrinkled in distaste, and he shook his head and continued to shake it obstinately even when the Be-anga himself drank from it and urged it upon him again, saying several times, "Good! Good!"

Good. Arabanoo repeated the word. Good. He would remember the name of this dark liquid with the unpleasant smell. "Good weeree," he said earnestly, pushing it away. "Bado boodjerree," he continued, pointing at a large pitcher on the table, "ngai-ri bado."

They laughed, understanding his gesture, and poured him water which he drank thirstily. He was conscious of a strange weariness—a weariness of fatigue and mental effort. There was an exhausting unrestfulness about these white people. It was not that they talked more than his own countrymen but that there was a queer urgency about their speech. They fired incomprehensible words at him and then waited, with an unrelenting question in their eyes. They kept his brain at a tension to which it was unaccustomed, seeming to demand something of him; but it was no material thing. He sighed and yawned, looking down at his fingers, greasy with food, and began to wipe them absently on the soft covering of his seat.

But apparently this was forbidden by the customs of the Bereewolgal. They made signs to him, shaking their heads, so he desisted, and used, instead, something which they handed to him which was like the stuff of which their garments were made, but white as a cloud. It seemed to him that his fingers made a more conspicuous mark upon this than they would have made upon the chair, but that, after all, was the Be-anga's business.

When the meal was over they took him into another room, and here some of his apprehension returned, for at last they appeared to have some mysterious designs on his person, touching his thick, tangled hair, making certain preparations and producing certain implements whose use he could not even guess.

He pulled away from their restraining hands, gesturing his rejection of their entreaties, and backed against the wall, saying: "Bee-all! Bee-all! Unijerunbi minku?" But they only laughed and renewed their urging. Then the smiling young man took up an implement which shone wonderfully in the shaft of sunlight through the window and whose movement was like the legs of a man walking, and he summoned one of his fellows, calling upon Arabanoo to watch. Holding a lock of the man's hair he lifted the implement to it; there was a sharp little sound, and behold, the lock lay in his hand, severed! Arabanoo became interested. There could be no doubt that the Bereewolgal had their own kind of cleverness, though they were so ignorant of essentials. This process, to which they appeared to want him to submit, was doubtless a tribal ceremony—perhaps a part of their initiation, comparable to the tooth-knocking, scarring, and other operations of his own people. Was it not, then, an indication that, far from wishing to harm him, they desired to do him honour by admitting him to the rites of their Law? He stared doubtfully, struggling to reconcile this thought with the memory of his capture, resigning himself at last to bewilderment, falling back on his senses, which warned him to see the whole of the ceremonial performed on someone else before he submitted to it himself.

They seemed to understand the gestures by which he sought to tell them this. The man who was appointed for demonstration smiled so broadly, and there was so much laughter and good humour, that Arabanoo found himself smiling too, and leaning forward to watch the whole proceeding with a sharp intentness. Now, at last, the mystery of the naked faces of the Bereewolgal was solved, for it seemed that before their beards had time to grow long they were scraped from their face, leaving the skin smooth and shining, and soft to the touch as a woman's! And their hair was severed so that it lay short about their heads, and smoothed with another implement until it was as neat and shining as the newly-preened feathers of a bird. By the time it was all finished Arabanoo was quite reassured. There was nothing sinister in this amusing ceremony. Nor could it be an initiation which was treated with such hilarity. It must be simply a game, a pastime, and he had never yet refused to join a game. He laughed while they cut his hair, and cried encouragement to them in their hunt for the vermin which dwelt in it until the room rang with merriment; it was with difficulty that they persuaded him to restrain his mirth while they shaved the thick, dark stubble from his chin.

Captain Tench, standing back with his head on one side, exclaimed: "Upon my word, gentlemen, this is a very personable young fellow! A bath, now, and some clothes, and we shall make a dandy of him yet!"

The bath was unpleasant. Arabanoo was no longer uneasy, but he was tired of being handled, and he did not like the feel of hot water on his skin. His patience was strained to the breaking point while the smiling young man whom they called Tench, with his shirt sleeves rolled above his elbows and his hair slightly ruffled with his exertions, bent over the tub of soapy water and scrubbed vigorously, seeking to discover, under the layers of grease and dirt, the true colour of their prisoner.

But deprived of those comfortable and protective coatings, Arabanoo felt cold and unhappy. Even the summery air slid with a chill feeling over his naked skin, and he shivered, moving into the shaft of sunlight, looking unwillingly at the clothes which they brought for him, and wishing that they would weary, as he had, of the game. When they insisted, however, he allowed himself to be dressed; he moved awkwardly, wondering how a man could endure such restriction of his body, how he could run, leap, hunt, fight, with his limbs hampered and the delicate sensations of his body blunted and smothered under these clumsy coverings.

He was glad when the evening came. They had let him cook his own meal, but he had not enjoyed it because of the heavy thing about his wrist which they had tried to tell him was a Ben-ga-dee, but which he had soon discovered was obviously intended to keep him in captivity. That had made him angry, sullen, and miserable. Now he was exhausted, not physically but emotionally. It was no use trying to understand people who mixed friendliness with treachery; it was no use looking in their faces, for their faces were all alike, and told you nothing; it was no use talking to them, for they did not understand.

He wished that they had let him sleep alone, or at least outside, under the sky. In the tiny room with a convict for guard, he moved restlessly about, fumbling with the fetter on his wrist, looking up at the roof and about him at the walls with the nervous ranging movements of a caged animal, skirting the lighted lamp mistrustfully, longing for the star-pricked darkness, and the 'possum rugs in his mia-mia, and the warm bodies of his wife and children.

It was a little better when the magic light was quenched. Then he lay quietly in the darkness, with his eyes shut and his manacled wrist outflung, and went back on the sure wings of his unfettered spirit to the campfires of his tribe.

* * *

The captive slept more soundly that night than the Governor. Phillip lay awake, his light still burning by his bedside, his tired mind wrestling with a thousand cares. This was the last day of the year. They had been here for eleven months, and for all his dauntless optimism he could not pretend to himself that they had made as much progress as he had hoped.

Building still went on with infinite slowness. During the winter all labour had been held up by heavy rains, and much of what had already been accomplished was ruined. The brick kiln had fallen in, the walls of the house being built for himself had collapsed, the convicts' dwellings were in a condition to beggar description. He had become increasingly conscious of an impatient irritation, not only at the inadequacy of the settlement but at its squalid ugliness. It was not possible, he thought, pushing his blanket back restlessly, to visit the other coves, or to explore the other great harbours which lay to the north and the south, without feeling the poignancy of their wild and uncontaminated loveliness. It was not possible to return here, to walk the muddy, trampled ground, to see the rows of miserable huts, the sorry patches of garden begun and abandoned, the heaps of stacked bricks and firewood, the sullen, hopeless, planless ugliness of the place, without an uneasy sense of desecration.

There was only one refuge from such a feeling—only one path by which one could climb from the irrational emotion of guilt to the height of a serene and confident intellectual conception. One must see not the present, but the future. One must plan ahead—and plan boldly, nobly, magnificently, not for a convict settlement, a prison for degraded outcasts, but for a city, the headquarters of a nation of free men. It might sound chimerical, but it was necessary. He felt that so deeply and with such certainty that he had no need to elaborate or to explain it to himself. It was a conviction imposed upon him by that innermost core of his character, not fully recognised by himself, but instantly apparent to the black men, and making him alone, of all the invaders, at least partly comprehensible to them—his indestructible faith in human dignity and worth.

Such a place as this, then, must be seen as temporary—a difficult and unsavory stage in an upward struggle. To be content to see it alone, isolated, without that ghostly dawn of promise behind it, would have seemed to him a weakness and a betrayal.

He had accepted the loneliness which this entailed. He made no effort to convert his followers to an idea which seemed to them fantastically optimistic. He did not demand that they should share his dream of the future, but he did expect their cooperation in the present. He wondered now, lying sleepless through the hot, summer night, if the one did not, perhaps, imply the other? Was it because it all seemed so pointless to them, because they could not see it save as a dismal setting for a fragment of their own existence, that they served it less than whole-heartedly?

This tense atmosphere of strain and hostility, this obstinate, stupid, sulky obstructionism, these incessant quarrels! White and Lieutenant Long at daggers drawn; Ross and Campbell, once firm friends, now passing each other haughtily, without speaking; Ross and Tench at odds over the removal of some timber from the saw pits; Ross complaining of Lieutenant Furzer; White quarrelling with Balmain and going out in the dead of night to settle it with pistols!

So much time, he thought, and so much nervous energy was wasted on follies like these! And yet it was not possible to blame the men overmuch.

It was only just, indeed, to give to most of them due credit for much loyalty, much willing devotion to duty, much more or less cheerful adjustment to circumstances. And to feel grateful that one's own task, arduous, solitary and harassing as it was, should be lightened, as theirs was not, by a sustaining confidence in the future.

One thing in the present, at least, was making better progress than even his most sanguine moments had led him to expect. Norfolk Island, that tiny outpost of his dominion, was flourishing. The transport *Golden Grove*, returning from a voyage carrying provisions and more settlers to King and his little colony there, had brought reports of its soil and possibilities which were cheering. Perhaps before long that fertile earth might yield, not only for the island itself, but for the main settlement, the vegetables and fruits which the soil of Sydney Cove had so far grown so grudgingly.

Food. His thoughts could never stray very far from this vital, this alarmingly urgent problem. It was nearly three months now since, despairing of the arrival of the long expected storeships from England, he had sent Hunter in the *Sirius* to fetch supplies from Capetown. Where was he now? Battling with storms, endangered by icebergs, hampered by the sickness of an almost certainly scurvy-ridden crew? Anchored safely in Table Bay? Or lying somewhere at the bottom of the ocean never to be seen again?

Phillip sat up in bed, oppressed by the heat and by his own insistent anxieties. He rested his head in his hands and turned his thoughts with grim determination to Rose Hill. Here, at the head of the harbour, on that fertile patch of land which they had discovered during their autumn expedition, he had, two months ago, founded yet another embryo settlement. In that gently undulating country where the soil was rich and dark, really good progress might, in time, be made with farming. But that part of his life, during which he had himself turned farmer, harassed him with reminders of the serene and leisurely processes of Nature. It was no use trying to hurry the cycle of the seasons, the productiveness of seed which would germinate in its own good time, the sweetening of clods turned upward to the gradual alchemy of sun and rain and air. Here there could be no such farming as his thorough and painstaking nature would approve; again he was driven by necessity into the muddling and the makeshifts which his orderly spirit loathed. Trees were felled and burned, but there was no time for the enormous labour of grubbing out stumps. Nor was it in his power to give to this earth what that of his own land had fed upon for centuries—the patient, persistent, knowledgeable husbandry of men born for generations to the cultivation of the soil. Here it must be turned by exhausted and insufficiently nourished convicts, sown sullenly and inexpertly, tended grudgingly and despairingly, while the fierce sun baked it hard as rock, and the savage rains made a bog of it, and all the time the horror of famine came nearer. . . .

What was the truth about this land? What virtue had it, what wealth? There had been much wild talk of mines—iron, tin, silver. Even gold. There had been that unhappy wretch, Daley, only this month executed for robbery, who had got himself into trouble earlier in the year for manufacturing a specimen of "gold" most ingeniously from a brass buckle, and setting the whole place by the ears with talk of his discovery of a mine. Mines! In these desperate straits, Phillip thought impatiently, cut off from their homeland, faced with starvation, he, for one, would feel but little enthusiasm for the richest of gold mines. He was, as he had written not so long ago to Sir Joseph Banks, at an age when three or four years were of some value, and were to be better employed than in looking for gold mines. Farmers were what he wanted. Strong, capable, industrious farmers. Mines could wait. There might, of course, be fabulous wealth waiting somewhere beyond those blue hills. There might be anything . . .

What was it which kept burning in him this flame of faith in a land of which, after all, he knew next to nothing? More than once he had found himself writing words in his despatches which had surprised himself. He remembered a letter to Lord Sydney: ". . . nor do I doubt that this country will prove the most valuable acquisition Great Britain ever made." Even at the time he had felt a faint astonishment at his own conviction, and he felt it again now, and threw the bedclothes back restlessly and got out of bed. ". . . nor do I doubt . . ." Why such certainty? On what was it based? He went across to the doorway and outside into the clear night and looked up at the sky. He felt again the sense which had so often troubled him before, of the utter strangeness of this land in which he found himself, and he remembered the name given to it by earlier explorers, and said under his breath, looking at the gaunt, still branches of a gum tree outlined against the sky: *"Terra Australis incognita"*—incognita, indeed! What did he know of it? A little of a seemingly endless coastline, a fringe of an apparently endless interior, a glimpse of those blue mountains which he had called the Carmarthen Hills. Beyond them? Beyond them the *terra Australis incognita!* And he had written: ". . . nor do I doubt . . ."

There came over him as he stood there, with an influence sobering and steadying rather than alarming, a sense of deep responsibility. To whom, to what? But, of course, to his country, his homeland, that far, green island on the other side of the world. Those words of his—had they been, perhaps, misleading? He had no grounds for so high, so extravagant a claim. Had he not—he to whom they looked for faithful intelligence of this new venture—painted a picture more cheerfully coloured than the facts of their present existence warranted?

He breathed deeply. There was something rather refreshing, he thought, in the smell of these queer forests. Looking over the settlement with eyes now growing accustomed to the darkness, he could see the lines of the convicts' huts, and his mind, the mind of the administrator, began to consider their occupants with intentness and detachment. It had been his habit, all his life, to perform such tasks as lay to his hand, thinking not overmuch of them and saying less; but he had not been able to subdue the gnawing sense of dissatisfaction which, from the beginning of their sojourn in this place, had gone hand in hand with his rigid performance of duty. The seed of it lay there, in those convict huts. This was no place for them; they were the product of a different world from this . . .

Suddenly illumination came to him, and a deep relief. Here, buried in him and unsuspected till now, was the knowledge which had lent him that seemingly irrational confidence. He was a practical man, a stranger to all mysticism and introspection. He believed, as all good Englishmen did, that his race was Heaven-favoured, Heaven-guided, sent to be a builder in strange lands and a teacher of strange peoples. But now he felt a power which was even stronger than the power of his race, an influence from the land itself—the strange land, the *terra incognita*—which human folly and human brutality could not harm, could not even touch. He saw now that they had delivered themselves up to it, that no word or deed or authority of his could stay its quiet, unhurried processes of envelopment and absorption. *"Acquisition!"* The ageless silence swallowed the presumptuous word. What had been thrust upon it as shame and degradation and hypocrisy became merely human life; the overlying, man-made creeds and customs and conceptions fell from it, leaving it nakedly reborn.

Here indeed was value, here indeed was wealth, and hope, and rich justification for confidence! Phillip's sigh was half weariness and half relief for an uneasiness allayed. ". . . nor do I doubt . . ." They had been the right words after all. He went slowly back to bed, walking with less than his usual alertness, for he was very tired.

*　　*　　*

Two other people in the settlement were wakeful that night. Mrs. Johnson, smothering her head beneath the bedclothes that she might not disturb her husband, wept for her stillborn child. And Andrew Prentice, wary, tense, crawling on all fours with infinite caution, slipped past the watch and vanished into the black silence of the trees.

1789

DAYBREAK—the first dawn of the year 1789—found Andrew Prentice crouched against a wind-tortured tree on a rocky crest, bullying himself out of his fear. For he had not travelled more than a couple of hours last night before he knew himself lost. He had never set out from the cove in darkness before, but he would have sworn that his route was, by now, so firmly in his mind that he could almost have followed it blindfolded. Peering about in the grey morning light he could see no landmark which was familiar. Or rather—so damnably and eerily confusing was this monotonous landscape—there was not a shrub, a tree, a rock, a hill slope, a curving creek bed, which he did not seem to have seen a thousand times, but always differently arranged. It was like a nightmare in which the familiar, madly and horribly distorted and confused, becomes even stranger than the unfamiliar. The warning of panic which he had felt before made him curse uneasily, half aloud, and then glance round him fearfully, shocked by the sound of his own voice in this spectral early morning silence.

On his shoulders he had a knapsack of food, partly stolen last night from the meagre rations of his fellow convicts, and partly purchased from a sailor as the price of his convenient absence from Ellen's hut. With what was already hidden, he had reckoned that he had enough to keep him going for six weeks—without it, perhaps sufficient for two. He clambered stiffly to his feet and stared at the eastern sky, where glowing streaks were heralding the sunrise. He would have been in a less perilous position, he thought, if he had dared to stop at once last night when first he knew himself astray. But so near the settlement it was not safe to halt, and he had pushed on blindly through the night, slipping and stumbling down gullies which seemed twice their depth, clambering out again on his hands and knees, struggling and sweating through sudden thickets of prickly undergrowth until exhaustion had stopped him, and he had fallen face downward on the ground and snatched an hour or two of terror-haunted sleep.

Now he had only one thought—he must find his cave. Without it he was done. He had nothing with him but food and a knife—a useless sort of weapon against the long, barbed spears of the natives; and, moreover, he was ill. Lack of fresh food, insufficiency of even what there was, had sapped his strength so that in the spring, when he had meant to abscond, he was lying in the hospital with an attack of dysentery which had left his great frame emaciated and his powerful muscles little stronger than Johnny's. It was only in these last few weeks that he had felt his vigour returning and his determination hardening again into the old obsession which had sustained him for so long. But the effort of the night had told on him; he knew it, and stared at the wild tangle of hills and gullies with a sinking heart.

To reach his cache from the cove it was necessary, he knew, to travel south for a couple of miles in order to skirt an arm of the harbour, and then to turn abruptly and bear slightly north of west. Had he made this turn correctly in the darkness, or had he come farther south still? To continue in his first direction would, he knew, bring him to the northern arm of Botany Bay, and staring southward he believed that he could see indications of the creek which emptied itself into the waters of that ill-omened harbour.

He had, then, come too far south. Standing with his back to the breaking sunrise, he could see, to his right, deep, distant folds in the hills which might be the winding reaches of Port Jackson. To make northwest now, but not enough north to bring him to those sharply indented shores, should hold him approximately to the course he wanted. Distance was the trouble. He could make no estimate of how far he had come last night. It might have been five miles, or ten, and he could not even guess now how much farther he must go before he might expect to find his cave. It was, he had reckoned, some seven miles from the point where the turn was made, not more than nine altogether from the settlement itself. If he had been travelling almost south last night he must still have at least six or seven miles to go—probably more . . .

Fear gnawed at him while he hesitated, urging him to put as much distance as he could between himself and the place from which he was now a confessed fugitive and thief. To be taken would mean a flogging at the least; perhaps, as he had stolen food, it might mean death. If the other thefts, of which he had so far managed to remain unsuspected, were now to be attributed to him, it would certainly mean death . . .

The thought made him look round nervously and thrust himself between a rock and a thickly growing shrub for concealment. He must go on—and quickly. But first he must eat.

He took bread and salt beef from his knapsack and began to gnaw them ravenously, thinking of food. He had made what enquiries he could about what the natives ate, but few at the settlement were any wiser than himself. It was known that they chewed fern roots, and it was said that they had, upon one occasion, shown the Governor another plant which they used for food, but no one had been able to tell him what it was. There was the sweet-tea vine, of course, which made a not unpleasing infusion and was said by the doctors to be medicinally valuable. Apart from these there was nothing but what he carried, and such birds and animals as he might be able to secure. This thought, with its reminder of his utter dependence upon his musket, brought him to his feet in a fever to be away in search of it. He turned his back on the rising sun and set off down the hill, his clumsy shoes slipping on the loose stones and the dry, fallen leaves.

All through the morning he tramped doggedly. Twice, in the shadowy coolness of creek beds he paused to drink, and once a snake startled him, uncoiling itself swiftly from a flat rock beside a pool and vanishing soundlessly into the undergrowth. In the early afternoon he toiled up yet another hillside, and sat down on its summit, breathing heavily and wiping the sweat from his forehead with his hand. By now he was facing the possibility that he would never find his cave, turning over in his mind the thought of going back—throwing himself on the Governor's mercy, relying on the good record he had so painstakingly built up, lying his way out of the thefts somehow . . .

His eyes, staring desperately round a landscape which seemed no different from that at which he had looked six hours ago, became suddenly fixed, incredulous, wild with a dawning hope. That wall of rock with the sunlight striking its face—was it—was it not—*his* wall? But it was behind him. Three or four miles away at the very least, across two gullies. And not in the direction from which he had come at all. Beneath the drumming of his excited blood fear stirred in him again, reminding him how hopelessly wrong he had been, how easily this accursed land could fool him, swallow him, take him into its unknown fastnesses and there leave him to die and rot . . .

Perhaps he was wrong. Here one tree was like another tree, one view like another view— Why should not one rock face be like another? Supposing that he struggled back across those gullies, up those rough hills, only to find that it was not his hiding place, after all? The thought made his mouth go dry and his hands shake, for he knew himself almost at the end of his strength again. But there was nothing else for it. He dragged

himself to his feet and set off towards the cliff. As he descended the hill
he lost sight of it, and found it again much farther to the north than he
had thought, when he won to the top of the next ridge. He altered his
course and plunged downward once more. At the bottom of the hill he
paused to drink from a pool in a creek bed, and to swallow a few mouthfuls of bread before beginning the upward climb. It was the worst that
he had so far encountered. Almost immediately he found himself confronted by a line of cliffs—not high, but just high enough to halt him.
Fifteen feet here, twenty feet there, dropping back to twelve a little
farther along, but all vertical and quite unbroken. He skirted it, staring
upward in hatred and exasperation. Here and there he tried to climb it,
but there were never enough hand- and footholds. Twice the brittle sandstone broke beneath his feet when he put his weight on it, and he grazed
his hands and face as he slithered down the few feet to the ground. He
walked along it as an animal walks along the barred wall of its cage until
he came to a place where it was not more than fifteen feet, and shrubs
growing here and there promised assistance. Half way up he slipped and
grabbed wildly at a clump of long grass growing from a ledge. It held,
but when he dragged himself up beside it he found that it had cut the
palm of his hand like a razor, and blood was dripping on to the rock.
But he was up. Cursing, half-sobbing with weariness and pain, he clambered out on the top and set off up the hill again. By now it was late
afternoon; the sun was almost gone. When he reached the crest of the
ridge and climbed a rock to look about him, it had sunk behind the
western mountains, dusk was creeping up out of the valleys, and his wall
had vanished.

He broke down and raved aloud, rubbing his hands over his grimy face
so that it was streaked with blood from his lacerated palm. To have done
so much, schemed and stolen and lied so patiently, to have drilled himself
to silence, to have kept a civil tongue while his heart flamed with hatred,
and then, when he had thought it was all over, to encounter this! To have
gone to and fro so often, so confidently, and then, upon the final and
trimphant journey, to be so baffled and so cruelly tried! Not lost! Christ,
no, not lost! He knew where the cave was. He had seen it not an hour
ago. It was over there to the left—perhaps not quite so far—or perhaps . . .

He found that he was shivering, though the sweat of exertion still ran
down his temples. Perhaps it was not there at all. Perhaps it simply *was
not there* . . . anywhere. He had never heeded bogey tales; he was a
materialist, finding enough of grimness and horror in his daily life with-

out going in search of it through the realms of the supernatural. But he had spent his life among people who were ready enough to be credulous, and now he found himself remembering their whispered tales. What could you not believe of such a land as this? A land in which summer was winter, and trees kept their leaves all the year round, where the very air you breathed had an unfamiliar flavour and smell, where you had only to pause and be still at night and lift your face to the sky to know that there was Something here which no civilised land would tolerate. There had been queer tales brought back by some of those who had absconded only to return, starving and demoralised. Tales of creeks that were flowing when you left them at midday and bone dry when you returned at sunset. Tales of a Thing that drank at the pools at night, and had horns, and made an eerie, lowing sound. Tales of a witchcraft on the land, so that as you stood and looked to the right the woods were green, but to the left they were dead and cold, their trees like skeletons; but you could never see the line where the difference began. Tales of things that disappeared, hills, trees, streams—why not rock faces with caves in them?

He sat slackly, his hands hanging over his knees, his labouring breath subsiding to normality, and his panic subsiding with it. That was all fools' talk. This country was a Hell, but Hell did not frighten him—he had seen too much of it. After his rage, a kind of quietness came upon him—a stubborn, desperate calm. He stood up, holding his haversack by its straps, and looked about him. The land held him enfolded in a quietness which outmatched his own; he heard his own breathing in it. He felt himself obscurely angered, and breathed more softly till not the dusk itself was quieter. That was what seemed important now—to be as calm, as still, as noiseless as the twilight which surrounded him, and his muscles grew rigid and his nerves taut with the effort of immobility.

The land answered him with darkness. It came down like a blue-black fog, dense, impenetrable, emphasising its silence, now, with a thousand stealthy sounds. Prentice shut his teeth together and countered with his own bitter, nerve-stretched calm. He listened, holding himself ready for anything with which the night might seek to trick him into panic. He laid his haversack on the ground very gently, and sat down beside it with infinite slowness and caution. Nothing, he swore, should make him move. Here he would stay until the dawn showed him the way again. After a time he stretched himself on his back and fixed his eyes on a gap in the tree-tops, and watched the stars until he slept.

* * *

Arabanoo stood on the deck of the *Supply* and stared upward nervously at its unfurled sails. He had not wanted to come on board this nowee of the white man, but the Be-anga had persuaded him, and now he was mistrustful, haunted by a fear which grew stronger every minute that he was to be taken right away from his own country, across the sea, to the mysterious land from which the Bereewolgal came. It made him uneasy to see the spread wings, and when he felt the deck beneath his feet quiver, and saw the prow swing round till it pointed down the harbour, his fear became a panic-stricken certainty. He began to tremble. Now he understood why they had not slain him; now the kindness with which they had treated him was explained. They had saved him alive that they might take him in their nowee and show him to their countrymen across the sea; and he would never see his home or his people again.

He glanced round at the group of white men who stood talking near him, and the Be-anga, seeing his distress, laid a reassuring hand on his shoulder. But how, thought Arabanoo, should he be reassured when already the wind was filling the great white wings and the shores were slipping by, and all that was familiar was soon to be left behind? He stood still, twitching a little under his skin as a held dog does, waiting for release. He was watching a jutting headland come nearer, measuring its distance from the ship, not thinking at all, but holding himself in readiness to obey a compelling urge which was rising in him.

He felt no resentment now against the white men. He had lived among them for long enough to decide that they were, towards himself at least, a kindly people. From that first morning after his capture when they had taken him all round their camp, showing him many unfamiliar things, some beautiful, some obviously useful, and some merely incomprehensible, he had known that they meant him no harm—that they were, indeed, genuinely anxious for his welfare and contentment. Contentment! He had looked at them long and searchingly in those first days, trying to understand when they presented him with trifles, thinking to please him. It was as if one took away the sun from the heavens and offered a handful of glowworms as recompense! And yet they had seemed to understand his sorrow when he had stood on the point called Tulagulla, but for which they had a different name, and stared mournfully across the water at the smoke from one of the campfires of his countrymen. "Gwee-un," he had said sadly, pointing to it, and they had patted his back and tried to cheer him by showing him more of their possessions.

He had been bewildered by these at first. There were so many, their number and variety seemed endless. Was it not a great trouble, he asked, when the tribe wished to move its camp, to have so many things to carry with it? They had not understood him well enough to answer, but he had decided for himself that it was because of this they were forced to build such very large nowees, and he wondered if perhaps their own land was so small that they had been forced to leave it to find room for their possessions.

He had begun to realise quite soon that if they had a Law, this was the foundation of it. It was quite clear that the more possessions a man had, the nobler he was assumed to be, and the greater was the authority he wielded over his fellows. The Be-anga, for instance, had more possessions than anyone. His fine dwelling was full of them. Arabanoo had been taught their names, and could repeat them—chair, plate, fork, table, towel, paper, pen, coat, book—there seemed never to be an end. And yet these were not all. He had been given to understand that even the food, so carefully hidden away and so jealously guarded, belonged to the Be-anga. For a long time he had not believed this; it was so manifestly ridiculous that he thought it was a joke, and laughed merrily every time it was mentioned. But he had discovered that it was not a joke at all; men were punished for taking it. It did not matter that they were hungry—they must not touch the food, for it belonged not to the whole tribe, but to the Be-anga alone, and they might eat only what he gave them. It was fortunate, Arabanoo reflected, that the Be-anga was a good man.

And many other things—the wonderful implements (which, of all their belongings seemed to him the most admirable) for building their houses and digging up the ground and felling trees and cutting the trunks into small pieces—these, too, were the Be-anga's. Yet, for all his wisdom and kindliness, the Be-anga was not a powerful man. Almost any of the others—Dyon-ton, for instance, or the smiling young man called Tench, or the carrahdy, White, could have overpowered him in an instant.

The despised ones, on the other hand, had almost no possessions. Their coverings were miserable, their dwellings inferior, and it appeared that even the things they drank from and the plates upon which they took their food were not theirs, but merely lent to them by the Be-anga. They had no weapons at all. How was a man a man without weapons? The red-coated ones, it appeared, were the only warriors. It was their duty to defend all the rest, even those worthless ones who, surely, were of no value to any tribe.

Yes, it was clear that the Be-anga, because he had many possessions, might command, and the others, because they had few, or none, must obey. And the less they had the more harshly were they ordered, and the more continuously they toiled. But how, in the first place, had the Be-anga acquired such wealth? Had he slain many other leaders and taken their possessions from them? Arabanoo had many times abandoned the problem in perplexity when he reached this point. It was a mystery hidden in that far-off land from which the strangers had come, but he was not sufficiently interested in its solution to wish to journey so far in search of it. The Bereewolgal were welcome to their Law, whatever it was; he was content with his own.

He longed for it. Standing on the deck of the winged nowee, cold at heart with the threat of exile, he knew how desperately, how passionately, he had missed it in the long, long time he had spent with these strangers. There was nothing but the Law which could keep a man's heart at peace— Was that the reason why the white men were so full of unrest? For there was no peace in their camp, no lasting joyousness. It was as though, being of one tribe, they were yet enemies—not for a moment or two, settling their dispute as men should with weapons or a trial of strength, but obsessed by a veiled mistrust of each other. There was an element of confusion somewhere; there was a deep and terrible sense of unhappiness. Many times when he had sat with them at their table, sharing their food, he had been conscious of it. It was as if every man were two men, one smiling and confident, and the other imprisoned behind those smiles and that confidence, haunted, despairing, as a man might be who knew that the bone was being pointed at him and that he was doomed to die.

No, fine as their possessions were, Arabanoo had no wish to share them any longer. He could feel the joy which was his heritage being squeezed out of him by the intolerable awareness of their misery. He waited, watching the headland come nearer, motionless, intent, and when they were abreast of it he broke from among the group, ran to the rails, and dived overboard.

The shock of the water roused him to a tremendous exhilaration and excitement, but it was followed instantly by fear. They would point their gooroobeera at him, and slay him as he swam, so he must dive and swim under the water as long as he could—only thus might he escape. But when he tried he found that he could not dive; he had forgotten that he was encumbered by the clothing of the white men. Panic-stricken, he struggled desperately; he got his head under the water, but the folds of his coat billowed about him, buoying him up, impeding his movements, and he began to gasp for breath, rolling and struggling clumsily—he, Arabanoo, known as one of the fastest swimmers and most expert divers of his tribe!

He glanced over his shoulder. They had lowered a small boat, and already they were pursuing him. He tried to unfasten his coat, but the buttons defied him. He floundered on, his heart pounding, horrified by the clumsy helplessness of legs and arms which had never failed him before. Now his clothes were becoming sodden, weighing him down; now if he dived perhaps he would never be able to come up again. The shore seemed hardly nearer than when he had first dived, and behind him he could hear the rhythmic creak and splash of the white's men's paddles. He made a last violent effort, but in his heart he knew that it was hopeless. Nevertheless, when they came abreast of him and leaned over to grab his shoulders, he fought savagely and insanely so that the boat rocked. He had no breath for the wild words of protest which clamoured in him, but they would not have heeded them anyhow. He was dragged over the side of the boat and held by two men. Soaking, wild-eyed, his breath still labouring in his chest, he found himself on board the winged nowee again, and the Be-anga stooping over him, talking to him in tones of not unkindly rebuke.

He made no response. He licked the salt taste from his lips, rubbed at a bruise on his shin, and kept his head sullenly bent. After a time they left him alone.

And then, suddenly, everything was changed; he sat up, his eyes bright with an almost incredulous joy and relief. A boat was being lowered, the Be-anga and his followers were about to go down into it, and they were calling him!

"Arabanoo! Come! Come!"

Come! That was one of the first words they had taught him, and he sprang to his feet, the sullenness vanished from his face, his dark eyes alight. They laughed at him teasingly as he sprang down into the boat, laughed still more when he waved the *Supply* away with a dismissing motion of his hands, crying out: "Go! Go! Go!" and urging the oarsmen to pull faster, as if he could not too soon put a great stretch of water between himself and the ship which had so nearly taken him from his home. Phillip tried to explain to him. They had never meant to take him away. They were only going to bid adieu to their friends. It was weeree that Arabanoo should try to escape, and he must not do it again.

Arabanoo hardly listened, except to shake his head gaily when he heard the word weeree. Nothing was weeree now! All the horror was forgotten. Happiness was so radiant a thing that anger and resentment vanished in its blinding light. He talked cheerfully all the way back to the cove, while the *Supply* slipped out of the harbour, and set her course for Norfolk Island.

But happiness could not endure very long in the camp of the Bereewolgal. It became a thing to be pursued and courted, instead of a thing dwelling always in one's heart. Arabanoo was only really happy when he played with the white children, and then the screams of merriment which went up from the group surrounding him often brought smiles to the faces of the older people, going so seriously, so heavily, about their occupations. He taught the children many words of his own tongue, and learned much from them. Almost any morning he was to be seen in the centre of a noisy circle, pointing from one thing to another, while their shrill, excited voices named each one in triumph. There in the sky, round and blazing and golden, was . . . "Wirri!" they yelled. And there, white and soft, floating lazily across the blue sky . . . "Kurru!" And there, stretching in a blue arc from horizon to horizon . . . "Dulka! Dulka!" Arabanoo laughed delightedly, talking to them rapidly in his own soft, liquid tongue. Ah, but those were easy! Let us now learn some new ones! See, when I stretch my arms wide, wide, like this, it is murrai —murrai—murrai. Their eyes were solemn, intent, not yet understanding. But look, with my fingers close together, very close, it is murruwulung. Not yet? Such foolish little ones! See, here is a pebble—look close or you will not see it at all. Murruwulung. Murruwulung. His voice, thin and high as the whisper of wind through reeds, sang the minuteness of it. But here is a rock upon which we all sit, and many more might sit, too. Murrai! He flung his arms wide, his voice booming: "Murrai! Murrai!"

A little girl, shaking dirty flaxen curls back from her face, squealed excitedly: "Big! Big! He means big! Murrai! Big!"

They learned faster than their elders. While Phillip was still struggling to make himself understood to his guest with a few dozen words, Johnny Prentice and several other children were chattering with him fluently in a queer mixture of his tongue and their own. Johnny remained his favourite. To him he sang the song of the wild dog hunt:

> "Dinga dinga burula
> Murringa dibura . . ."

To him he explained how Wirri, the sun, was a woman, in love with Yenandah, the moon, but as Yenandah despised her she must always pursue him endlessly across the sky. It was the duty of Yenandah to make the girl babies and give them into the care of Wadahgudjaelwon, the birth-spirit, who would find suitable mothers for them. Sometimes Wahn, the crow, helped Yenandah, but the girl babies whom he made were noisy and quarrelsome, and grew up into scolding women. Such a one, he confided to Johnny, was Barangaroo, wife of Bennilong, a warrior of his tribe. She, undoubtedly, had been made by Wahn, the crow . . .

Johnny looked at him askance. There had been little privacy in the slum where he was born, less in the hold of a transport, and none at all in a convict hut. He had ears and eyes and the quick wits which a precarious life develops and he did not believe a word of this rigmarole. But he decided that as all grown-ups told lies upon this particular matter, the lies of Arabanoo were pleasanter lies than those of his own people. He was quite willing to hear more of them. He asked:

"Who makes the boys?"

Arabanoo was astonished at his ignorance. But, of course, the boys were made by Boomayahmayahmul, the wood-lizard, the quick and wise one. Did Johnny not know that? No? Did his mother not tell him stories? No? Did he not know, for instance, the story of why Goomble-gubbon, the bustard, lays only two eggs in a season, and why Dinewan, the emu, has no wings? Settled comfortably in the crook of Arabanoo's arm Johnny heard this tale so often that he was able to repeat it to himself at night before he slept, and Ellen often stared down at him with an irritated pucker between her brows, and a dim feeling that it was irreligious that he should be learning such gibberish.

"Dinewan boorool diggayah gillumnee . . ."

"Oh, for Christ's sake, Johnny . . ."

"Goomblegubbon numbardee boorool boolwarunnee. Dinewan numbardee. . . ."

"Shut y' mouth, d'y' hear me? No better than a heathen y'self, learnin' things off that savage . . ."

So Johnny kept quiet, and thought it to himself instead.

"Baiyan noo murruldundi gunnoonah burraybundi nurreebah burri bunnagullundi. . . ."

The things which one heard in Arabanoo's tongue, he thought, were pleasanter to remember just before sleep than the things one heard in one's own.

* * *

The hatred and unhappiness which Arabanoo felt so keenly in the camp of the white men was, to them, merely a heaviness of the spirit so familiar that they had long since ceased to notice it. Phillip and the officers would have said, if they had been pressed, that in such a situation, far removed from their friends and the amenities of civilised life, it was but natural that there should be mistrust, jealousies, grievances. As for the convicts— What was there to do but shrug, and punish? Such people were, by nature, violent, ignorant, and undisciplined, hereditary enemies of order. They would never have acknowledged what to their black captive seemed so clear as to allow of no question—that in thus admitting, even insisting upon the inferiority of their fellows, they were exposing themselves to a subtle and potent danger. How was it possible to maim and deface the image of manhood without injuring oneself? How was it possible to shame a man without sharing in his shame as one shared in his manhood? Arabanoo would watch the lines of convicts being herded off to their day's work, and he would feel a vague uneasiness, and his eyes, turning towards the Governor, would be melancholy, dark with a knowledge which he could never have expressed, even in his own tongue, for among his people certain laws were so clearly understood that it was not necessary to speak of them. All he could think was that there was danger here. For there was so much sorrow, and sorrow was evil, and evil was dangerous.

*   *   *

One windy day in March the danger showed its head. Suddenly in the brick kilns where the convicts were at work there was an emotional explosion, a psychological reaction to the slow degradation which they were suffering, a savage, blind determination to rid themselves of their own unendurable consciousness of subjection by passing on their humiliation to others, still lower, still more helpless than themselves.

That was not how they saw it. Their need was fundamental and desperate—a need for self-respect. They had been bred to a world in which the power to coerce alone was admirable, and they could see their own bid for human dignity only as a demonstration of physical force. Against whom could they hope to assert themselves? There was only one answer. Savages, naked, untaught, heathen, little better than beasts— here were human beings even lower than themselves!

Excitement swelled. It was so long since they had felt the exciting power of making a decision for themselves. So long since they had seen what in their inflamed imaginations they saw now—themselves dominant, triumphant, striking fear into the hearts of others. So long since they had felt the intoxication of making a gesture of defiance such as they made now, flinging down their tools, snatching them up again, not as tools, but as weapons. So long since they had marched as they marched now, in a ragged formation, but willingly, obeying not the harsh word or the threatened whip of an overseer, but the obscure urge of their own hearts.

The weather was still hot, though the summer was dying. Most of the wildflowers were over, and upon the shrubs where they had bloomed strange, woody seeds were forming. The shed bark and twigs were dry, and they made a noisy crackling beneath the feet of the convicts as they walked, drunk with excitement, brandishing their tools or the great cudgels which they had hacked from fallen trees. To Kuurin, watching them from an opposite hillside, this was one expedition which presented no mystery. This was a battle party. Save that their skins were white, and their bodies covered, and their weapons different, these might have been a group of his own countrymen upon a warlike march. The air of purpose, the fierce gladness, the grunted exclamations, the bursts of excited laughter . . . Kuurin stared, and thought, and vanished quietly among the trees.

As he travelled he thought contemptuously of these clumsy enemies who moved so slowly and inexpertly through the hot, spicy-scented bush. It was easy to outdistance them on his long, lean legs—the tireless legs which the nomadic habit of centuries had developed in his race. Now and then, as he went, he uttered the far-carrying rallying-cry of his people: "Coo-oo-oo-ee!" And for several miles around the hunters left their fishing or their emu-tracking and hastened through the bush to their camp. By the time Kuurin arrived with his news there was a fairly formidable party assembled—more than enough, they said disdainfully, to deal with the despised ones, and they set out towards the white settlement to meet the aggressors.

The convicts, suddenly confronted by a horde of black, naked figures, which leapt almost as if from the ground to confront them, were taken by surprise. Were these the quiet, peaceable people who were to have allowed themselves to be plundered? Had they fallen in with another tribe altogether? These were ferocious—yes, awe-inspiring figures. There was a quality of stark power in their lean, leaping bodies which identified them with the harshness and gauntness of the land itself. Poised for the attack, their faces contorted with rage, their lips moving incessantly to form the rhythmic, grunting battle noises of their ancestors, they seemed to gather into themselves all the mystery and wildness of their country, so that the convicts felt themselves arrayed not only against a human enemy but against a place-spirit, awful, invisible, and invulnerable.

With one accord they broke, scattered, fled for their lives, howling in terror, the spears of the black warriors singing through the air about them. One fell dead; seven were wounded. Several, fleeter-footed than the rest, arrived gasping for breath in the settlement and gave the alarm. Phillip, furious, sent an officer and a detachment of marines to the rescue, and waited grimly for their return.

When the dead man had been brought in and the wounded taken to the hospital, he questioned the remainder. His voice was sharp and hard, his eyes probed relentlessly. What had provoked this attack by the natives? Nothing, nothing indeed, they assured him, shuffling uneasily under his angry stare. They had been quietly picking sweet-tea—without a thought in the world, Your Excellency, for the Indians—when suddenly there they were all around, yelling and throwing spears . . .

Phillip barked out:

"Rubbish! They have never attacked without provocation." He looked round at the blank, dull faces with their furtive, watchful eyes. "Was any injury offered to them—or their belongings? Any insult?" There was a muttered chorus of denial, but Phillip's eyes, hawklike when he was angry, had noticed that a couple of the youngest, hardly more than boys, dropped their gaze to the floor and looked uneasy. He snapped at them.

"Come! You—and you—answer me! Why were you not at your work in the kilns? By whose permission were you straying in the woods at that time? I have not yet had the truth, and I mean to get it."

The contest was uneven. He spoke not only with the dynamic strength of his own personality, but he had behind him all the power and authority which had hounded and threatened them all their lives. He could have them flogged, imprisoned on the island, hanged. They had been conditioned all their lives to submission and obedience; only the shreds and remnants of moral strength remained to them. Almost immediately they succumbed to the threat in his last words; there was a clamour of confession and repentance, of promises and supplications. Tight-lipped, disgusted, Phillip ordered them all a flogging, and turned his back on them, as they were hustled away.

He stood at his table, drumming nervously on it with his finger-tips, the vertical creases deeper than ever between his brows. It was intolerable that his careful plans should be thus continually upset by ignorance and disobedience. How was he ever to gain the confidence, the cooperation of the Indians while such incidents occurred? At least, he thought, he might partially counter the ill effect of this particular occurrence by making Arabanoo understand that those who molested his people did not do so with impunity.

He called to Captain Collins who was writing in the next room, and gave an order. Arabanoo was to be present at the punishment of the convicts. He was to be informed of the reason for it. That was all.

* * *

When it was over Arabanoo went away by himself. He was as much alone as he was ever allowed to be. The guard detailed to attend him stood at a little distance, conversing with another man, glancing only occasionally at his charge—a grotesque figure in his ill-fitting European clothes and his bare feet, wearing a fetter on his ankle, and sitting on a rock by the water's edge wrestling with an overwhelming sense of shame and despair.

These were two emotions so foreign to him, and so agonising, that he wondered if he would, perhaps, die of them. Such a feeling in one's breast must be almost a death. And yet his body lived and moved, his breath came smoothly, he could feel the damp sand cool beneath his feet. He had seen blood and pain. That was nothing—nothing at all. His own people in their rites of initiation suffered far greater physical pain, shed far more blood. It was part of the lot of mankind and womankind that such things should be endured stoically, the spirit dominating the quailing flesh.

He squatted on his rock, rubbing his hands backward and forward along the coarse cloth of his trousers, his dark eyes fixed and opaque with the intensity of his thoughts. He had seen pain and blood, but it was not that which had aroused his every nerve to an agony of horror. It was that a man should be helpless while he suffered—that he should be bound, dragged, held up to contempt, humiliated in the eyes of his whole tribe. It was not that pain should be inflicted on him, but that it should be inflicted on him against his will; it was that he should struggle, and beseech, and beg for mercy . . .

Arabanoo lifted his head slowly and looked round at the cove and the settlement, now sinking into dusk. His eyes had a searching, puzzled look. His land had not seen such things before. In his closeness to it he seemed to feel its aloof untouchability, and he made, for the first time in his life, a conscious effort to join its spirit with his own, and share its inviolability.

This feeling of death within him. He had been shamed because he was a man and had seen another man suffering indignity. He had protested; he had cried out in horror. What did it matter what they had done? If they had attacked his tribe, were not its menfolk warriors who could avenge themselves? Could not the Bereewolgal see that this was an evil magic which they were spinning about themselves? Could they not see that for one man to shame another destroys them both? Let them release these men—let his own people meet them in battle . . .

But it was no use. They had not seemed to understand. They had stood quite calmly, watching. Could it be that they were . . .

Arabanoo jerked his head round like an animal cornered; the whites of his eyes shone in the twilight. For he, who had witnessed this thing only once, had the feeling of death in his heart. Could it be that they, who had witnessed it so often, were, indeed, not dying, but already dead within? Were they evil spirits—mawn—inhuman beings wearing the guise of humanity? Did this not explain everything—their weapons which could slay without touching, their miraculous power over fire, the super-human skill of their carrahdy, the strange wickedness which one could feel in them . . .

Ah, but it was not only wickedness. He sighed, tormented by the confusion of his thoughts; for he had felt goodness in them, too. Not only he but his fellow countrymen had felt the goodness in the Be-anga, the close firm bond of their common humanity. In many of the others he had felt it also—kindness, generosity, even sometimes the blessed spark of gaiety which was so precious to his people. And he had played with their children, fondled them, told them the tales which his own children loved to hear, joined in their games which his own children also played. . . .

No, they were men; but men terribly beset by an evil magic of unhappiness. Men without peace, men without serenity. Men without a Law. Bereewolgal, indeed, Arabanoo thought sadly, drawing marks in the wet sand with his toe, men come from afar, through strange torments of the spirit from some very, very distant time when they had been light-hearted like his own people. Yapallun! Yapallun! Bereewolgal! Men come from afar!

* * *

The *Supply* returned on the 24th of March. Now, a week or so later, Phillip sat alone at his table, surrounded as usual by papers, rereading King's despatches and thinking about freedom. How precious a thing it must be, how cherished a conception, how deeply-rooted a need, that men should strive and dare for it so madly! The account he read here, of a planned uprising by the convicts on Norfolk Island—an uprising, fortunately, he thought, discovered and suppressed in time—seemed to tell, between its calmly phrased lines, a tale of utter desperation. And yet there on that comparatively fertile island they were really better off than they would have been here, where starvation was coming daily nearer.

For Hunter had not returned with the *Sirius*. No ship had come from England. It was as if the world they had left had abandoned and forgotten them—they might as well be on the moon! If, he thought wearily, all the discontents and envies of that lost world could have been left behind in it, one might have endured the loss of its amenities more cheerfully; but the former grew and flourished. The latest trouble with Major Ross, which had begun with the death of Captain Shea in February, and the question of promotion to the vacancy thus caused, was still dragging on, gathering like a snowball. Already Campbell and Collins were mixed up in it—the whole battalion would be involved, most likely, before it was done with! Then there had been that unsavoury business of execution for robbery from the stores; and not convicts, this time, but marines. Six of them. In God's name why could they not understand how heinous a crime the stealing of food became in a community wholly dependent on its fast dwindling rations? Even more disturbing than their execution, had been the thought of how long their depredations had gone on —how much longer they might still have continued undetected if it had not been for their noisy carousals in the huts of the women convicts.

Pretty soon, Phillip thought, he must try to relieve the drain upon the food supply here by sending a few more people to Norfolk Island. King, too, had better have military reinforcements; another uprising might be attempted. In the meantime, there was nothing to be done here but continue to exist, continue to impose a pattern of order, continue to plan for things which might never happen. He had sent Blackburn, for instance, to survey one of the bays of the harbour so that foreign ships might anchor there. Even to himself it sounded fantastic. Foreign ships! The last foreign ships which they had seen—the *Boussole* and the *Astrolabe* —were like phantoms in the memory now: it was only with a conscious effort that one could imagine a sail upon the horizon which was not the sail of the little *Supply*, faithfully acting errand-boy between Norfolk Island and Port Jackson. No, it would be many a long day before the sails of foreign ships came down in Neutral Bay, but there was a certain grim and defiant satisfaction to be wrung out of preparing for them. For the moment there was only one sail he wanted to see, one for news of which he waited every day—the sail of the *Sirius,* safe, laden, bringing them at least a respite from starvation. . . .

Collins was standing in the doorway.

"If you are not busy, Sir . . ."

Phillip started out of his anxious abstraction.

"What is it, Captain Collins?"

Collins came in and stood on the opposite side of the table, looking worried.

"There seems to be some kind of illness, Sir, among the natives. Some of the men who have been fishing in the bays down the harbour say that there are numbers of them in great distress. And many dead. There's a family in the opposite cove—parents and two children—who appear to be dying."

Phillip stood up, pushing his papers away. He picked up his hat and went to the door.

"Tell them to man a boat and send one of the surgeons to me. I shall take Arabanoo as well—he may be able to help us understand each other. There he is, down by the store—never mind, Collins, I'll call him myself as I go down."

The group of children broke and backed away shyly as the Governor approached. His Excellency was grave faced, and seemed always to be deep in thought, and he held the power of life and death and punishment in his hands. They were in awe of him, and wondered that a black man should show no sign of uneasiness in so august a presence. Phillip said briefly:

"Come, Arabanoo. Come with me."

Arabanoo was going with His Excellency in a boat. The children stood solemnly, staring. When their black friend laughed and waved to them they did not respond, being a little shocked that he should behave with such freedom when the Governor was there.

*　　*　　*

They were lying on the sand under an overhanging rock—an elderly man, dying; a little girl, dead; a little boy of about ten, himself bright-eyed with fever, pouring water from a shell over his father's burning forehead. A few sticks were smouldering near by, for the cave was shadowed, and the air chilly.

Phillip, advancing towards them, thought that he had never seen such a picture of human misery. It shamed him that the glance the man turned on him was not one of hope, but of distrust, and of fear for the safety of his son; his movement not one of welcome, but of protection to the thin body of the child crouching at his side. The first thing, he thought, is to gain their confidence, and he motioned Arabanoo forward, hoping that the sight of their countryman might allay their fears.

Arabanoo hesitated. These were not members of his own tribe, but of the Wallumedegal; it was not for him, but for their own people to minister to them at death. Where were their own people? What sickness was this which caused sores to break out all over their bodies? He looked round uneasily, reading a story on the sandy floor of the cave. This was very strange. Many people had been here. Food had been eaten, and fires kindled. People had slept here. And then, suddenly, all had departed save these. Why? What evil had they seen that they should flee from their sick like this?

He looked at Phillip with a question and a doubt in his eyes. But the Be-anga's only answer was to beckon him forward from where he himself already knelt by the side of the old man. Ah, well, if the Be-anga had no fear of this evil, whatever it might be, neither would he, Arabanoo, fear it. He assured his countryman in a quick burst of words that neither he nor his child would suffer any harm at the hands of the Bereewolgal.

Phillip rose and began to look about. There had been talk of a woman, too. Behind a rock at a little distance he found her. Standing aghast over the emaciated corpse, covered with pustules, and already cold, he heard Arabanoo utter the word Be-anga several times, and with it another word whose now familiar meaning brought him again a sense of humility. "Boodjerree," Arabanoo was assuring the man, as he raised him gently under the shoulders and held water to his lips. "Boodjerree," he consoled the child, trembling under his hand and darting terrified glances at Phillip's motionless back.

"Boodjerree!" Was it "good" that he represented to this gay, fearless, primitive and friendly people? This was surely smallpox. The surgeon, coming to stand beside him and look down at the dreadful remains of a human being at his feet, confirmed his shocked suspicion, but his eyes matched Phillip's in bewilderment. Could they have brought this scourge to the land with them? They had never seen a native bearing traces of it. And yet, on the other hand, none of the white people had suffered from it since landing—the last case had been at the Cape, a full seventeen months before. How had it happened? Phillip shook the question away from him impatiently. No matter; there it was. He made a gesture toward the dead woman before he turned back to the cave.

"Don't show her to Arabanoo. Come—we must get the child and the man into the boat."

But Arabanoo would not go without burying the little girl. He made a grave in the sand and lined it carefully with grass, and when he had laid her in it he covered her, too, with grass so that her body should not touch the sand. He did not wail for her, or sing any of the customary songs of death. She was not of his tribe, and she was only a little girl, anyhow, not so very important. Her mother might have wailed, or her sisters, but where were they? He turned away from the mound he had raised, and carried the boy gently down to the boat.

In an unused hut near the hospital the old man lay uneasily, his filming eyes asking a perpetual question, his head painfully lifted from time to time to look at his son, to touch him lovingly on the breast, and to turn again to the white men as if praying them anxiously for the safety of his child. They bathed him, they made a fire for him, they gave him water and offered him food; he wondered why they took so much trouble, for he had known for a long time that death was upon him. The little boy, Nanbarree, wondered too. His father was an old man, and it was but natural that old men should die. When he saw that his breath was gone, and his eyelids closed for ever he called the carrahdy of the Beree-wolgal and pointed to the still body.

"Bo-ee," he said composedly. Then he lay back on the comfortable bed which they had provided for him, and addressed the whole of his young vitality to recovery.

* * *

The surgeon adopted him. Henceforward he was one of the white community. But now there were more and still more tales of death among the natives. All round the foreshores of the harbour they were dying. There was hardly a cove where bodies were not to be found, and many of those not yet afflicted, terrified by this unknown ill which even the greatest carrahdy of the Cammeraygal was unable to combat, fled from the coast inland, so that the shores were almost deserted, left to the dying and the dead.

The Governor's boat brought two more in to the settlement—a young man and a girl of about fourteen, called Booron. Arabanoo waited on them both with endless patience. When the young man died the girl crept to his side and lay close to him, wordless, soundless, tearless, until the cold of the autumn evening set her shivering, and she was coaxed back beneath her blankets. She was quiet and docile then—so quiet and so docile that Mrs. Johnson, nerving herself conscientiously to the duty of visiting the heathen, was sufficiently impressed to accept her into her own household, hoping to teach her, in time, the Christian virtues.

* * *

Then a happier circumstance lifted the sagging spirits of the whole community and sent a flood of relief through the Governor by which he measured, in some astonishment, the depths of anxiety in which he had passed the previous weeks.

For Hunter returned, bringing the *Sirius* safely into port again, laden with stores, after an arduous and eventful journey right round the globe. She slipped into the harbour one evening early in May, and her crew, crowding the rails, still a little gaunt from scurvy and a nerve-racking passage up the coast from Van Diemen's Land, found themselves looking at the still water, at the olive coloured shores, even at the settlement itself, with a surprising feeling that they had come home.

Hunter, going ashore to report to the Governor, felt himself suddenly in another world. He stood in the doorway, running his hand over his stiff, leathery, wind-bitten cheeks, startled, almost moved, by the sight of a cheery fire and a group of men quietly drinking tea about it. The loneliness of a ship on the ocean, dwarfed by gigantic ice-floes, battered by gales, assaulted by mountainous seas, was an impression still so fresh in his mind that he could not receive this picture of cosy domesticity without a shock.

It was pleasant to be so welcomed. It was pleasant to realise that one had brought at least a reprieve from disaster—thought it was no more than that. He had a year's provisions for his ship's crew on board, and enough for the settlement to stave off want for a few more months. It was something to have achieved and now it was pleasant to stretch one's feet to the fire, and lie back in a chair, and drink tea among one's friends. Nevertheless, the loneliness of his command, the solitude of long responsibility, still betrayed him now and then into abstracted silences. Yes, it was like a different world, he thought, watching them. Here was the Governor, leaning forward to poke at the fire so that its glow lent his sallow face a deceptive ruddiness. Here was Tench, somehow managing to appear immaculate in a worn and shabby uniform, the two long creases from his nose to the outer corners of his mouth looking deeper than ever in the firelight, so that even when he was silent his face seemed to be making some lightly ironical comment. Here was Collins, calm, observant and courteous, doing the honours with the teacups, and there in the shadows, silent, with his chin on his breast and his eyes on the leaping flames, was Lieutenant Dawes. But most strange of all, thought Hunter, was the spectacle of a black man—a not uncomely young fellow of thirty or thereabouts—clothed and combed and brushed, sitting up to the tea-table and managing his cup and saucer as to the manner born.

Phillip introduced him.

"This, Captain Hunter, is our friend Arabanoo."

Arabanoo's teeth and eyes flashed whitely in the firelight as he smiled. Hunter, he knew, was the owner of the great nowee which had been so long absent, and whose return this evening had occasioned so much rejoicing. He put his cup down and collected his thoughts for the effort of speech in a strange tongue.

"I," he began, laying his hand on his breast and regarding the returned hero earnestly, "I—go—you . . ." He stopped. He could not remember the word which they used for nowee. However, the Be-anga would understand, and help him. He brightened and repeated confidently: "I go you nowee?"

Phillip translated:

"He wants to go on your ship, Hunter."

"Ship," Arabanoo agreed. "I go you ship, Hun-ter?"

"Tomorrow," Hunter promised.

"Parrebuga," Tench supplied.

Arabanoo nodded his satisfaction and took up his cup again.

Now they spoke of other things. Hunter had soon exhausted such news of Europe as he had gleaned at the Cape. He told them then of his outward voyage, and of how, when they were scarcely clear of Port Jackson, the ship's carpenter had reported that she was leaking; he had told them of the distress of his crew from scurvy, and of how, arriving at the Cape, he had landed no less than forty sick, having just twelve men left in each watch, of whom half were too ill to go aloft. It was a tale of struggle and hardship and endless anxiety, told calmly and received without surprise. It was the tale of almost any long voyage, and when it was told it was Hunter's turn to ask for news.

"And Rose Hill? How do things progress there?"

Phillip handed his cup to Collins and stretched his feet towards the blaze.

"Pretty well. We have got a number of huts built, and a barracks. Some of the gardens have been successful, and we have a considerable amount of ground prepared for grain."

"And the people? Have any more strayed from the settlement or absconded?"

Tench shrugged his shoulders.

"A number, my dear Hunter, have simply vanished. I don't know if they stray deliberately or by accident, but they disappear. Two marines were reported missing from Rose Hill only a day or two ago. They set off to pick sweet-tea, and that was the end of them. Then there was that fellow Prentice, one of the convicts . . ."

Hunter nodded.

"I remember him. A civil sort of fellow, more useful than most."

"A red-headed rogue!" Tench contradicted warmly. "He vanished on New Year's Day—four months ago—and I suspect that my best pair of shoes vanished with him."

"I have had a path made." Phillip, sitting up to take his replenished cup from Collins, sounded slightly impatient. "It runs due south from the settlement, and stragglers who have missed their way may sometimes chance on it and so find their way home. It's all I can do. If they will stray beyond the known limits in country such as this they take their lives in their hands. Some more tea, Captain Hunter?"

"Thank you, Sir. And Norfolk Island? You have good news from King?"

"Good and bad. An uprising was planned and circumvented. Everything appears to be quiet now."

The Governor spoke rather wearily. For him, too, Hunter thought, this safe return of the *Sirius* was a slackening of enormous nervous strain. Now that he came to look at them closely they all—even Tench—looked rather depressed. And he found himself thinking that it might be easier to face the impersonal forces of nature, winds, storms, icebergs and uncharted rocks, than the subtle, nerve destroying atmosphere of this ill-omened settlement.

*   *   *

Before he entered the hut the Governor paused. He was astonished, even a little confused, that the suffering of an Indian could move him so deeply. He said to White, who had halted just behind him:

"I suppose there can be no hope of saving him, Mr. White? He's dying?"

White wore the angry, stubborn look which characterised him when he found his professional skill defeated.

"He's certainly dying, Sir."

Phillip nodded and stepped inside. Nothing since their coming, not even the thought of their own danger from starvation, had upset him as much as this disastrous epidemic which was still decimating the native population of the harbour, though the white people themselves seemed to be immune. Now that Arabanoo had contracted the disease his feeling of guilt amounted to a torment. He had thought several times, watching their captive's gentle ministrations to his countrymen, that "savage" was a strange word to apply to him. It worried him with its associations; he saw the stealthy ferocity of the tiger, the evil grace of a shark turning under the water the bared fangs of a chained and snarling dog. That had brought him a new association, and one from which he could find a measure of relief in action. Chained! Good God, why was Arabanoo still chained? He had given a peremptory order that the fetter was to be removed—he was to be no longer supervised—he was free. . . .

But he was not free now. He had known that himself, rubbing his chafed ankle as the fetter fell from it. They had bound him, these strange white people, with something which held him more firmly than their bonds. He had accepted them as his friends. And of what use, in any case, was freedom to him now? His tribe was broken and scattered. He had gone with the white men in their boats down the harbour to seek for his family and his friends, but he had found only corpses. Horror had filled him, searching the coves, once the haunt of fishing parties, the playground of shrill-voiced children. Now only bodies were there—many, many, bodies, most of them unrecognisable, heaped together, lying where they had fallen, sitting propped against rocks, loathsome and already putrid.

Not a living soul. What terror was it which had smitten his people during his absence from them? Why had they not buried or burned their dead? Where had they gone, and from what were they fleeing? He had groaned aloud, beating his breast in grief: "Bo-ee! Bo-ee!" and had returned silently with his white friends to their settlement. That was his home now, for his tribe had vanished, but still he felt himself an alien. He continued to tell tales to the white children, thinking sadly as he spoke of his own sons whom he would never see again. He dined with the Governor and his friends on board the nowee of Hunter, being anxious to show that he was ashamed of his fear upon that other occasion when he had thought that he was to be taken away over the sea. He was willing and friendly and cheerful, but quieter than before.

Then the evil came on him. It came quite suddenly, a burning in his body as if a fire were consuming him, a pain in his head so that for a time it was as if his sight were bewitched, and he saw everything in a haze, shifting, distorted and unreal. The Bereewolgal were like brothers to him. Their great carrahdy, White, tended him unceasingly. The Be-anga came often to see him, and spoke to him laboriously in his own tongue:

"Boodjerree, yagoona, Arabanoo?"

"Moo-laa-ly, Be-anga. Cardalung; n'gai-ri bado."

He drank from the cup which the Be-anga held to his lips, but his throat was so sore and swollen that it hurt him to swallow. Beside him were the bottles and basins and bandages and salves with which White had tried doggedly, first, to cure his disease, and finally to alleviate his sufferings. He had submitted with a touching faith, swallowing nauseous drugs and potions uncomplainingly, for he had too often seen these medicine men of the Bereewolgal perform miracles to wish to appear discourteously sceptical of their power. But he knew that he was going to die. Even the magic of the white men was powerless against this ill which had sprung from nowhere to afflict his people. It was a strange way of death. He had always imagined that either he would fall in battle, or, growing old and feeble, he would know, as Tirrawuul had known, that his time was come, and so, turning his face to the wall of his mia-mia, quietly await the end.

What he could never have imagined was the chilly, defeated silence in which death came to the dwellings of the white men. It was as though one were already dead and laid in one's grave to see the narrow walls and the low roof enclosing one from the tree-tops and the sky; to listen and listen, and hear nothing. It would have been comforting to see one's tribe about one, fierce wailing, beating their breasts, the women tearing their hair and scratching their faces with their nails, the whole urgent life of the community directed against his enemy, defying and reviling it, lending its strength to the failing spirit, supporting it with its human clamour to that very last moment when it must break free and journey on alone. . . .

He looked up at the two men standing motionless beside him, the Be-anga, the carrahdy, White. These were his friends, but they made no clamour for him. They only stood looking at him in silence, sadly, and the Be-anga, stooping, laid a kindly hand on his hot brow. Their ways were strange ways indeed, but he was too weary now to think of them more. They had left the door of the hut open; he could see past them to a patch of blue sky and a gum tree branch across it. He fixed his eyes on the flickering

sunlit leaves and lay motionless until his lids grew heavy. Then he closed
them, and died.

* * *

Prentice had been out for several months; he was not sure exactly
how long. He had tried at first to keep a count of the days as they passed,
but he knew that he had become confused during the time that he lay
ill and the blacks cared for him, and when he recovered he had not
troubled about it again. After those first two nights of horror when he
had thought that his hiding place was lost to him, he had only once, and
then for no more than a brief moment, despaired. It was on that second
night when he had resisted panic, held himself tautly in a desperate and
stubborn resistance to the unseen forces of the land which was waiting to
destroy him, that he had won his victory over doubt. For the next morning he had found his cave quite easily. It was as if, having tried him and
found him not less stubborn than itself, the land had grown less hostile.
He had knelt before the opening in the sandstone cliff peering in at his
neatly stacked treasures, and he had felt his life lying in the hollow
of his hand, the freedom he had won, his for ever. Such an emotion was as
the elixir of life to him. Success, achievement, triumph, the heady knowledge of worth within himself! His courage and his endurance and his determination grew and flowered under this rising sun of self-confidence,
tried and justified. A man had only to lay his plans, he thought vaingloriously, he had only to follow them, trusting nobody, confiding in nobody. In this mood he had planned again. There was too much gear to
carry all at once, but he would sacrifice not so much as a single nail.
They were all useful things; his common sense was able to justify a decision which had a more obscure and subtle origin. True to the Law
which Arabanoo had recognised, he saw his possessions as the measure of
his worth, and clung to them fiercely as symbols of his hard won freedom.
So he must go in stages, leaving one lot, returning for another—a long,
dreary, arduous business, but not too long for his inexhaustible patience,
not too arduous for his unlimited endurance! He had climbed to the top
of his rock to set himself a course by his compass, and before he came
down he had paused for a moment looking with grim, half-shut eyes at
the tangled hills between him and the distant mountains, as if challenging
them to assault the half-inspired optimism of his mood. They did not
assault it. They lay sleepily, golden-green in the sunlight, ignoring him.

Ten days. It had taken him that, returning on his tracks continually,
to reach the outskirts of Rose Hill. Here he had meant to lie in hiding

or a day or two, creeping near to the tiny settlement at night in the hope
that he might be able to steal some food, but he had felt reckless that
evening, and he had taken a more daring way. In the gathering twilight
he had walked into the settlement carrying his spade over his shoulder,
for most of the convicts at Rose Hill were engaged in preparing the
ground for crops. Slouching along with his red head bent and carefully
covered by a cap, he was like any other of the drab, anonymous figures
who had straggled back to their huts at the close of the day's work. Sit-
ing humped up beside a clump of bushes in the quick-falling darkness,
he looked as inanimate as they, and until nightfall remained as motionless.
Then he began to prowl. Twice he halted, frozen by approaching footsteps, approaching voices, the swinging beam of a lantern carried over the
uneven ground. When he crept away at last he carried the full weekly
ration of two convicts and a couple of fresh-water eels just caught from
the river by one of the soldiers.

He had eaten well that night, within sight of the lights of Rose Hill. It
was hot and he needed no fire, but would have lit one if he dared to keep
off the tormenting clouds of mosquitoes. There was a listening hush over
everything, a stillness. He had never known the woods so silent; not a leaf
moved, not a strip of bark rustled. Opening his eyes from snatches of
unrestful sleep he seemed to see the starry sky so close that he might
almost put up his hand and touch it, and he stirred uneasily, rising on his
elbow and peering about in the darkness, feeling that the earth was expecting something, and that he only was alien and ignorant.

He woke to daylight and a flash of panic, sitting up and staring wildly
about him, his heart still hammering with fright. Through his sleep he
had been aware of noise—a noise pitched in a key almost unendurable,
having a half-hidden rhythm beneath its nerve-racking continuity, a noise
whose vibrations seemed almost visible, shimmering in the fierce, unreal
sunlight. With steadying consciousness he knew that it was only those
blasted insects in the trees. He had thought himself accustomed to them
by now, but there was a terrible insistence, a maniacal shrillness, an incredible volume in their song today. It went with the queer colour of the
sunlight, the almost orange intensity of it. The stillness he had noticed
last night had become deathly; it was as if all material things, by their
very immobility, achieved a kind of non-existence, leaving the world to
that merciless sound and that cruel golden light.

He had walked all that day, his shoulders bowed under the weight of
his load. Towards evening he began to shiver. His head ached and his
sight blurred, and his thoughts began to slide away from him, making

patterns which he dimly knew to be insane. Why was everyone screaming
so? Everyone in London screaming at the tops of their voices. They were
after him, that was it. They were after him. He could distinguish the
words now. *"Sto-o-o-o-p thief! Sto-o-o-o-p thief!"* Rhythmically, without
mercy; shrill, inhuman voices. Faster, then. Only keep going, faster and
faster, and they will lose you in these narrow streets and dark alleys, and
the tormenting sound of their screaming will die away. There is a door
way—make a dash for it. No, no doorway. Farther on. Christ, you fool
what are you raving about? Doorways! You're Andrew Prentice, convict
escaping from Sydney Cove in New Holland. Escaping. Escaping. Well
that's what I said. They're after me, screaming. That isn't screaming—it'
the sound of heat. In English heat has no sound, but here things are dif
ferent. There's fog in London—grey, cool, dense as a blanket, not burning
your eyeballs like this molten sunshine. Here things are different. Winter
is summer, and summer screams and dances in the air, and the sunlight i
bright orange, and your shadow, stumbling ahead of you, is purple. Pur
ple. Not grey and soft like shadows in England, but purple . . .

Shadow?

A last remnant of reason brought him to a standstill, staring at hi
purple shadow, sobered by shock. For a second or two his brain cleared
and a monstrous fact stood out in it, overwhelming. Why was his shadow
in front of him, and not behind? It was late afternoon and he was trav
elling west. He turned slowly, hardly daring to look, and there was th
mountain range behind him. When had he turned? Dry-mouthed, hi
knees trembling, he faced them again, and took a few stumbling step
before he fell.

That was the gap in his knowledge. He did not know how long
he had lain there, but when he awoke beneath a rude bark shelter hi
body was like a skeleton, and he was so weak that he could not even
raise his hand to his mouth to eat. The black men had fed him; he sup
posed that if they had come upon him when he was well he would have
regarded them as enemies, feared and hated them, and probably fired
upon them. But when he opened his eyes in the camp and saw them al
about him he was too ill to care. Too ill to be very interested. When they
held water to his lips in large shells he drank. When they put food in hi
mouth he ate. When they spoke he stared at them incuriously and fell into
a swooning sleep again.

They left him where they had first placed him, in a bark mia-mia, and
went about their own affairs, taking only a casual interest in him, bu
supplying his needs as a matter of course. They were of the Boorooberon

al, a tribe which visited the coast only for corroborees and intertribal ceremonies, but they had heard of the coming of the white men and were mildly interested in this helpless being with the flaming hair and beard, who had chosen their towri in which to die. They were surprised when he did not die, but went on obstinately living, day after day. They had stared in perplexity and faint contempt at the vast load which he had been carrying when he fell. Had he no woman to carry his burdens that he might be prepared, as a man should always be, for hunting and battle? Was this object a weapon? They examined it curiously but made no attempt to tamper with it, and laid it beside his other belongings near the mia-mia to which they carried him. Days later, a woman and some children searching for roots in the ferny undergrowth some miles away came upon the rest of his gear hidden under a fallen tree, and brought it back to the camp. It was examined, commented upon, wondered over, and placed with the rest to await its owner's recovery or death.

Sometimes the children would creep to the opening of the mia-mia and stare in at the hideous, unkempt figure, but when he moved and muttered in delirium they fled, believing him possessed by a spirit. When the fever left him and he returned, slowly and with infinite reluctance to the life he had so nearly abandoned, he found himself already accepted, if not welcomed, by the tribe. Thoughts and memories came down on him like burdens, insupportable, and he returned to the prison of his own spirit to find his old gaolers awaiting him there. Distrust, suspicion, resentment. He stared at his black hosts from sullen watchful eyes, wondering what lay behind their attention and their casual courtesy, and hatred leapt up in him, vindictive and revengeful, when he remembered his belongings. He called, harshly:

"Here! You!"

Beereewan, the black man whom he had addressed, turned and regarded him. These were the first words the stranger had spoken since the spirit which had guided his tongue in sleep had left him. They might mean anything, but their tone was unpleasant. Beereewan approached the mia-mia and squatted down before it, inscrutably attentive. Prentice glared at him in hostile exasperation.

"Gun!" he said, urgently. "You take gun? Where?" He sketched the size and shape of his musket in the air. Beereewan continued to stare at him gravely. As the fuller realisation of what such a loss would mean came upon Prentice, he burst out into a savage torrent of words:

"Look, y' damned dirty heathen! My things! I carry—see? Like this I carry . . ." He made a movement to illustrate the burden he had borne upon his shoulders, and added with concentrated venom: "By Christ, i you bastards stole my . . ."

But Beereewan was walking away. Limp, exhausted by his rage, an the exertion of trying to make himself understood, Prentice fell back o the ground, sweating, half-fainting, and very near to tears of fury an frustration. Now he was done. Without his possessions his self-esteem failed him; he was nothing.

He opened his eyes wearily, feeling something pushed against him. Hi bundles of food, his musket, his spade, his axe, not only those thing which he had carried, but also those which he had left behind, wer lying at his side. Beereewan, meeting his eyes, said briefly, "N'ga!" an walked off again.

After that it had been merely a question of regaining strength. Wit his possessions beside him he felt himself already renewed. The foo which the natives gave him he ate ravenously, not asking or caring muc what it was. He noticed that they ate snakes, which the coastal tribe would never do, and he saw, too, how they made traps on the trees fo 'possums, and in the long grass for birds, and how they would sometime catch one of the small brown stingless bees of the country, and stick morsel of white fur to it, and thus follow it to its hive. One day he sav them spear a kangaroo, and joined in the feast which followed, but h took no part in the hunting himself, even when he was strong enough For why, he thought shrewdly, should he squander his energy and hi ammunition while these people would continue to feed him?

He wondered very often how long it was since he had left the settle ment. In this accursed country the foliage of the trees offered no calenda to his unaccustomed eye. It was growing so cold at night, however, tha he judged it to be near winter, and reckoned that it must be nearly fiv months since he had made his escape. He began to be restless. He realise with a faint surprise that he had not felt so well for years. For months h had slept out of doors, breathing the clean spicy-scented air of the woods for months he had drunk nothing but water; since his arrival at the cam he had lived entirely on the fresh food with which the blacks supplie him. It did not satisfy him; he was always hungry, but he could feel a energy and alertness in his body which he had not known since his boy hood in the English countryside. He had lost most of his fear of recap ture, and at night he slept soundly. One day he decided to leave the cam and make westward again to the river of which he had heard the blac men speak, and from which they often returned with ducks for thei supper.

But before he left he acquired another possession. He had lived among the natives long enough to observe their customs, and it occurred to him that one of their women would be useful to him. She would carry half his load, she would help him to find food, she would know something of the country, she would supply those needs for which, in his newly found health, his body was clamouring again. And if she proved a nuisance she could be easily discarded. He could see no flaw in the plan. A slave, a guide, a mistress, a beast of burden all in one—what could be better?

It was easy enough, by means of signs, to make his request to the elders of the tribe. They considered it gravely, and acknowledged his need. The first two young women whom he indicated were rather indignantly denied him; he gathered that they were already wives. At last Beereewan produced a girl called Cunnembeillee, and gave Prentice to understand that he might have her. He looked her over dubiously, reflecting that she was not, even according to the standards of these hideous people, a beauty. She stood bashfully on one skinny leg, with the other hooked behind it, and stared at him with bright, blank eyes. Like the rest, her thin body was plentifully besmeared with grease and ashes. Her hair, matted together with some gummy substance, and ornamented with kangaroo teeth, stuck out in wild spikes about her head, and her nose was even flatter than those of most of her countrywomen. Nevertheless she was young, and she looked strong, with that wiry, inexhaustible toughness which some small women have. He nodded his acceptance, and made a sign to her to follow him.

She hesitated only for a moment, and that pause was one of vague, unformed fear rather than of active unwillingness. Her husband-to-be, to whom she had been betrothed in childhood, had died in battle before she reached maturity, and it was her misfortune to be related to most of the marriageable men of her tribe in such a way that it would have been contrary to the Law for them to take her for wife. In time, no doubt, some arrangement would have been made for her, but in the meantime here was this stranger, this teeri-yeetchbeem who obviously needed a woman. She herself saw quite clearly the reasonableness of it. She was sorry for him. He had been weak and helpless, but now that he was well again it was apparent that he was a proper man, and it was unbecoming and ridiculous that he should be womanless. Beside the leanness of her countrymen he looked thickset and powerful. He had discarded, since he had lived with the tribe, all his clothing except a pair of ragged trousers and bursting shoes, and his red beard now mingled with the thatch of red hair on his wide chest. He was a man, and therefore to be followed and

obeyed; she saw that, but was conscious of a deep, hidden fear of him
She could conceive of no past which had held him, and she could imagine
no future which would receive him. She could only know that he was
different—deeply and fundamentally different from her own people, and
that no life with him could be like the life she would have led with a
husband of her own race. He came suddenly from nowhere. As suddenly
he was about to depart, and she with him . . .

He repeated sharply:

"Come!"

She would have to learn his words. Here was one she had learned
already, for his angry gesture left no doubt of his meaning. She hurried
to him, picked up the larger of his two bundles, and bending under its
weight, her eyes on the ground, followed him submissively into the un
known.

*   *   *

Captain Tench was as near to gloom as his sanguine temperament
would allow. Sydney Cove, he thought moodily, was dull enough, even
with the few opportunities it afforded for social intercourse and intelligent
conversation—even with the festivities which had marked the second
celebration of His Majesty's birthday in this distant land—even with the
introduction of the Drama!

But Rose Hill! To be saddled with the command of this desolate mili
tary outpost at any time would have been tedious, but now, with news just
arrived that the Governor was going exploring again, it was infuriating
it was heartbreaking, it was altogether damnable!

And it appeared that they had really discovered a river at last. This next
expedition was to explore it. According to the news which had arrived
from the cove, His Excellency was greatly encouraged by what he had
seen, and determined to set out again in about a fortnight's time.

Captain Tench, lighting his lamp and pulling his chair up to the table
sighed enviously. Collins, Johnston, Hunter, White, Worgan, Fowell—
What would he not give to be in the shoes of any one of them! Discon
solately, he pulled his journal towards him and breathed upon his fingers
to warm them before turning the pages. It was colder at Rose Hill than
down the harbour; the open country often showed white with frost in the
early mornings. From here the Blue Mountains seemed bluer than ever
and tantalisingly close. Somehow, Tench reflected, the title the Governor
had given them seemed to be but little used. Their name was already
made for them; they wore it, a mysterious mantle of colour, changing

with the changing light from purest azure to all the subtle shades of violet and amethyst, darkening with evening or the threat of evil weather, to a sombre indigo. It did not matter what name might be bestowed upon them; whenever the eyes of man rested on them his mind would name them, inevitably, the Blue Mountains. Now they were to be reached at last, for the river which had been discovered flowed at the very foot of them. And he, Watkin Tench, who so dearly loved to be in the thick of things, must mope in this dismal spot with nothing to do but record the activities of luckier men in his journal!

He turned his pages, reading glumly here and there, with only half his attention. Ah, yes, poor Arabanoo!

"His countenance was thoughtful but not animated: his fidelity and gratitude, particularly to his friend the Governor, were constant and undeviating, and deserve to be recorded. Although of a gentle and peacable temper, we early discovered that he was impatient of indignity, and allowed of no superiority on our part. He knew that he was in our power; but the independence of his mind never forsook him. If the slightest insult were offered to him he would return it with interest. At retaliation of merriment he was often happy; and frequently turned the laugh against his antagonist. . . ."

Yes, poor Arabanoo! And now they were again without anyone who could act as an interpreter, a go-between, bringing some measure of understanding between the black men and the white. It was unfortunate and disheartening for the Governor; Tench, flicking over another page, wondered idly if he would try the same tactics again, and reflected that he would be unlikely to find another protégé such as the gentle and kindly Arabanoo.

"The anniversary of His Majesty's birthday was celebrated as heretofore. . . ."

The usual ceremonies, the usual loyal toasts, the usual firing of salutes. But it had been, in two ways, an event. They had all dined, at the Governor's invitation, in his new house, lately finished. To be in a real house, after eighteen months of makeshift dwellings, had lent the flavour of a feast to a not very interesting meal. And the convicts' presentation, afterwards, of *The Recruiting Officer* had been an experience always to be remembered! For a little while, in that queer atmosphere of make-believe they had all escaped from the grim reality of their situation. They had been no longer the punishers and the punished. How great a relief it had been to forget that. . . .

"The exhilarating effect of a splendid theatre is well known; and I am not ashamed to confess that the proper distribution of three or four yards of stained paper, and a dozen farthing candles stuck around the mud walls of a convict hut, failed not to diffuse general complacency on the countenances of sixty people of various descriptions, who were assembled to applaud the presentation. . . ."

All the rest of his life, he thought, tilting his chair back and playing idly with his pen, he would look back on these few years as an astonishing interlude, so remote, so utterly divorced from what went before, or what would come after, as to seem rather like a dream. It was as well that he kept his journal—faithfully—as well that he had published his Narrative; otherwise he might in time have come to doubt that it had ever happened at all! At present, unfortunately, it was real enough. The fragment of life at Sydney Cove had already, like those lower forms of life which inhabit stagnant ponds, divided itself so that now three fragments existed, instead of one. It amused him to think of it thus—as primitive and embryonic life, splitting and splitting, spreading itself over this unknown portion of the globe; and of himself, incongruous in his sophistication, and yet blessedly able, by reason of that very sophistication, to savour and enjoy his own incongruousness!

He was glad that his duty as a subordinate demanded no more of him than to obey. Thus he could remain detached, observant, without suffering too much of mental stress. The Governor's was not a task to be envied. Perhaps for him, too, these parties of exploration were a respite as well as a duty. His latest disagreement with Major Ross had dragged on since April, and, Tench thought, with a wry and irreverent grimace for his superior officer, it must have been with a sigh of relief that Phillip had turned his back on the settlement to set out on his previous expedition earlier in the month.

And he had found his river. Tench, coming back to that tantalising fact, sighed, brought his chair down heavily on its four legs again, stabbed his pen into the ink, and wrote:

"Broken Bay, which was supposed to be completely explored, became again an object of research. On the sixth instant, the governor, accompanied by a large party in two boats, proceeded thither. Here they again wandered over piles of misshapen desolation, contemplating scenes of wild solitude, whose unvarying appearance renders them incapable of affording either novelty or gratification. But when they had given over the hope of farther discovery, by pursuing the windings of an inlet, which, from its appearance, was supposed to be a short creek, they suddenly found themselves at the entrance of a fresh water river up which they proceeded twenty miles in a westerly direction: and would have farther prosecuted their research, had not a failure of provisions obliged them to return. This river they described to be of considerable breadth and of great depth; but its banks had hitherto presented nothing better than a counterpart of the rocks and precipices which surround Broken Bay."

He stared disconsolately at his page; he was in no mood for writing to-night. He pushed his chair back and went outside. It was a cold, starlit night, and he could just see the mountains, a low black ridge against the sky. Visited suddenly by inspiration, his depression fell away from him; he would have an expedition of his own! Arndell was here, and Lowes of the *Sirius*—they would accompany him—and he would take a couple of marines and a convict or two, and supplies for three or four days. From here the mountains seemed so close as to be almost inviting them. There was a hill some five miles distant; they would make for that, and from its summit survey the surrounding country and decide upon their direction.

He felt quite cheerful again now and whistled as he went indoors, his footsteps ringing on the frosty ground.

*   *   *

Barangaroo, digging in the rotting wood of a fallen log for witchetty grubs, lifted her head with the movement of a startled wallaby, listening. She had grown so thin that all her bones showed, and she moved slowly, like an old woman, but she had not been afflicted by the evil sickness, and she was so thankful for this that she hardly noticed her own weakness. For Bennilong had been very ill indeed. The evil spirit which, no doubt, caused the malady, had taken possession of him so that for several nights it had raved incessantly in his voice, saying many incomprehensible things, shouting his name aloud—Bennilong, Bennilong, Bennilong—muttering about the Bereewolgal, muttering about a strange winged nowee which flew in the air like a bird, muttering about the Be-anga of the white men; until, crouching beside him and pouring water over his head, she had felt the tears of her own fright and weakness running down her cheeks.

Now she did not care any longer about his faithlessness. He was Bennilong. In her love for him she became humble, abasing herself because thus she could glorify him. She was only Barangaroo, bad-tempered and scolding, no longer very young; he was Bennilong, stronger and taller than almost any other of his tribe, magnificent, a hunter, a maker of corroborees, lovable, so that even his faults seemed endearing. How should such a man turn his eyes from all women save one, and that one herself? Patiently she fetched water for him and kindled fire; laboriously she hunted for food to keep him and herself alive. For the tribe was scattered now. Everyone had fled from the old towris when the evil came. There was a general suspicion that it was caused by a magic which the white men had cast upon the place, and there was nothing to do but to desert the old camping and hunting grounds and seek out a new refuge, untroubled by these white invaders.

Barangaroo paused, her head lifted. It was a sound she knew, and it sent a chill of terror to her heart. A rhythmic sound, a faint rattle, a faint splash. And then voices. She pushed through the undergrowth to a spot from which she could look down the precipitous slopes on to the arm of this northern harbour, lying green and glassy beneath the clear winter sun, and there she saw them—the boats of the Bereewolgal, pursuing them even here, come to spread their destroying magic in another towri, never to be eluded—never—never . . .

She sat down among the prickly bushes and wept weakly, her thin knees drawn up to her breast and her forehead resting on them. Where were they going now, and what did they want? They would not find Bennilong—he lay in a mia-mia far up the hillside, so she did not fear for him—but she wept and wept, weak from want of food, and from sleeplessness, and from misery, and from fear.

There had been no peace since these white people came. There had been quarrels and arguments in the tribe such as she had never known before, and Bennilong had been in the thick of every one. Did he like these Bereewolgal, or did he hate them? She did not know. No one knew Bennilong, himself, perhaps, did not know. Sometimes he was fierce in his denunciations, bloodthirsty in his threats. Sometimes he spoke wildly of them and of himself, almost as if he were of their tribe, and not of his own. Nothing but his strength, his prowess as a warrior, and the allowances which everyone made for his hot temper and his always extravagant speech, had saved him on these occasions from the wrath of his fellows.

For herself she had no doubts about them at all. They were evil people, upsetting the decent rhythm of life. In her heart she knew that it was her own sex which insisted upon the safety and stability which were given to a tribe by the Law. Without the close-woven structure of tribal custom,

ll would be chaos, the fierce destructive instincts of man would endanger
he life which woman produced. The first hint of its disintegration aroused
her to hatred and rebellion. They were treacherous people, too, these
woman-faced men! Had they not taken Arabanoo by guile, and who
knew, now, what had become of him, or of the boy, Nanbarree, and his
father, or of Booron and Burra-bu, all of whom had vanished into the
camp of the white men, never to be seen again?

Now, if the Bereewolgal were coming here, she thought, smearing the
tears away from her eyes with her arm, they might as well go back to
their own towri when Bennilong was strong enough to walk. It was
pleasanter there. In these steep gullies the narrow upper reaches of the
harbour lay winding sinuously like green snakes, in almost perpetual
shade. Only for a few hours at midday the sun shone down into these
gorges, and Barangaroo loved the sun. She rose and picked up her basket,
looking into it mournfully. She had found only four grubs and a lizard.
Farther up the river, where the water ran fresh and the steep banks flattened out, there were yams to be found by digging, but now that she had
seen the boats of the white men she was afraid to go there. It was a long
way to walk, and she was very tired. She knew where a few others of her
tribe were camped, and had tried to get Bennilong there, but the sickness
had come upon him too sharply, and she had been forced to build a mia-
mia over him where he fell. She wished she knew where By-gone was, or
Ballederry, or Kuurin, but they had all vanished, and she was too busy
seeking food to seek for them, too. Today, having so little in her basket,
she might go as far as the camp she knew, and tell them the news of the
coming of the white men, and if they had food themselves they would
give her some for Bennilong. All he needed now was to eat well, and
bring the strength back to his body; the madness and the burning had left
him, the sores were healing, leaving their imprint strangely, like tiny
hollows, on his skin. Now he was only weak, lying all day on his 'possum
skins, calling to her fretfully for water, for fire, for food, or for her mere
presence. But very often she could not be there, for it was necessary to go
far in search of food. It was not like living in a camp with one's tribe,
where, if one had had bad luck in the day's hunting, there was always
someone else whose luck had been good, and who would give one-half his
store. So she had to leave him often, and she never returned without fear.
If he would shout at her, she thought, strike her, berate her for the meagre-
ness of the provisions she brought, she would feel happier. It did not seem
as if this could be Bennilong, so limp and tired, and without curiosity.

But it was Bennilong. Only that knowledge had often kept her skinny legs moving; only that thought supported her now, slipping like a black wraith through the trees with her almost empty basket in her hand.

*   *   *

Captain Hunter looked down ruefully at his shoes whose worn soles were tied to their uppers with string, and then, even more ruefully at the densely wooded and precipitous slopes which climbed from the water's edge. This, he thought, was a dismal ending to a highly satisfactory expedition! Tramping back along the coast from Broken Bay, they had arrived the evening before upon the shores of the northwest arm of Port Jackson and camped there, firing muskets at intervals in the hope that someone at the settlement might hear and send a boat for them. Several times through the cold July night Hunter had awakened, and, lifting his head from his blanket, had seen the Governor sitting upright near the fire, his body turned so that its heat fell upon his side, and he had marvelled at the endurance which dwelt in that not particularly robust frame. For the expedition had been strenuous; he himself, strong as he was, had felt the strain of it. The others, he had thought, glancing at their huddled shapes, were young men, but for himself, fifty-two, and for the Governor only a year or so younger, there was no longer the resilience of youth to be counted upon, and sleep must be wooed, and then was not always won.

Nevertheless he was glad to have been one of the party which had discovered the Hawkesbury, as the Governor had named it; glad to have stood upon Richmond Hill and seen the mountains so near. While it was all still fresh in his mind, he resolved, he would write an account of it, for it had been full of incident. Their meetings with several groups of natives, for instance, and their impression that they had seen some of them before at Port Jackson. It was a mystery, he reflected, how they existed so far from the coast. At Richmond Hill, their farthest point, they must have been at least thirty miles in a direct line from the sea, and they had found little that a man might feed upon except a few small yams, not much larger than walnuts. Such natives as they had seen had looked, indeed, half-starved, and the ravages of smallpox were apparent.

This Hawkesbury seemed to be quite a considerable river—a river navigable for merchant ships almost as far as the fall which had halted their own boats near Richmond Hill. He himself had made careful observations of distance and latitude, of the depth of the water, and the height of the banks, and they had all been astonished by the indications which they saw of huge floods. What torrents they must be which poured down from the mountains, submerging the flat land on either side of the banks, tearing up trees by the roots, so that they lay like a field of corn beaten flat by a storm, wedging vast logs in the branches of any which were strong enough to remain standing, thirty—even forty feet above the normal level of the water! And that winding arm which they had first followed, curving away into the hills with rocky cliffs hemming it in on either side— where might it not lead the explorer in time? Perhaps, by following it, one might come right across the mountains, and find on the other side . . .

He had yawned, and checked his galloping thoughts. All in good time! An alluring task, but not, in any case, for him, John Hunter, naval captain, whose business was with the sea. And his thoughts had turned then to the *Sirius,* so badly damaged by her rough passage from the Cape, and dwelt there until his eyes, smarting from the smoke of the fire, closed, and he snatched another hour or so of sleep.

Breakfasting the next morning upon their few remaining scraps of food, they had all paused. Heads were lifted, hands strayed half way to mouths, glances were exchanged.

"One of the ships' guns," Hunter said.

"Someone must be lost." Phillip, chewing his stale mouthful of bread conscientiously but without relish, had wondered for the hundredth time at the persistent rashness with which, even after so many disappearances, seamen, convicts, and marines alike would wander from the settlement. He had said shortly:

"We had better fire muskets from time to time. He might hear them."

But for the present there was their own predicament to be considered. Earlier they had been filled with optimism by the discovery of a native canoe, but the first man to embark overturned it, and it sank, leaving him to swim ashore defeated. Then they had made a canoe of sorts for themselves—a monstrous object, thought Hunter wryly—but the wood of the country was too heavy, and it would not bear the weight of even one man. So now it was a question of walking round the head of this arm of the harbour, and crossing the rugged hills to the shore opposite Sydney Cove. Hunter, gazing dejectedly at his shoes, declined. Of all the foreshores this was the roughest, the most precipitous, intersected by creeks, densely timbered, sprawling and tumbling in a confusion of hills and gullies, and he did not relish the prospect of a barefooted march. Better, he thought, to retrace his steps to Broken Bay, and there rejoin the boats.

"Who will come with me?" He took off his hat and the sharp sea wind blew pleasantly on his hot forehead. "I've no wish to meet a party of the natives single-handed. You, Mr. White? Collins?"

David Collins pulled himself up from the ground where he had been resting with his back against a tree trunk, and agreed rather glumly. Even his serene temperament was ruffled by the thought of the useless exertion they had expended, and his thoughts, while he sat staring at the blue water, had been unusually pessimistic.

This post of his, Judge-Advocate to a penal settlement, was no sinecure; and since there had been added to it the duties of Secretary to the Governor, he had found himself with a load of responsibility upon his shoulders which might well have tried the patience and the courage of a much older man. Even now, weary and hungry and dirty as he was, he felt a reluctance to return to the settlement—to plunge again into an atmosphere thick with the resentments of Major Ross, and the open enmity of Captain Campbell; to his desk and his papers which piled about him like snowdrifts—protests, orders, writs, affidavits, summonses, petitions, letters . . .

"How far should you say it is, Collins?"

"How far . . . I'm sorry, Sir, I did not hear what you were saying."

Phillip pointed to the opposite shore.

"These two men propose to swim across. I should not think it more than four hundred yards, or thereabouts."

Hunter, in the act of hoisting his knapsack once more to his weary shoulders for the return march to Broken Bay, paused hopefully. The two marines who had volunteered for the swim were already stripping off their clothes. With bundles on their shoulders containing shoes, trousers, and a shirt each, and with a heartening dram of spirits in their bellies to keep out the cold, they waded into the water and struck out for the opposite shore. One, nearing it, was seen to flounder, drag his load from his shoulders and struggle on without it; but presently, to the intense relief of the watchers, both scrambled out on the rocks to lie prone for a few moments, recovering their breath. When at last they vanished into the trees on the far shore, one clad and one naked, there was nothing more to do but wait.

*   *   *

The Governor, just back from a journey of inspection to Rose Hill, drew a chair up to the fire and sat down wearily, with a sigh of relief. It was near the end of August, and, though at midday spring was in the air, the nights were still cold, and he held his fingers to the blaze and promised himself a few idle moments before turning to the accumulations of business which awaited him on his desk.

This pain in his side was beginning to alarm him; he did not want to feel that the task he had undertaken was beyond his physical strength. It had, indeed, become more to him than a task, and whenever he felt the pain threatening he resisted it resentfully, as if it were an enemy trying to dislodge him from a function which he regarded as peculiarly his own.

Nevertheless, he admitted, staring into the fire, he could not, at his age, expect to treat an ailment with contempt, and that was how he had been treating it in these last three strenuous months. The two expeditions to Broken Bay had tried his strength; he could not deny that when they had returned at last in the boats which had been sent for them, and with the addition to their party of the exhausted Peter White, sailmaker, who had been lost for four days, he had been ready to drop with fatigue. Ever since then the pain had been stirring. Not a fierce, definite pain, but a slyly nagging reminder, a malicious warning. He had set out reluctantly for Rose Hill. Here in his own house there was at least a bed, but in the hut of the worthy Henry Dodd, overseer of the convicts, he had slept upon bare boards, and the muttered threat of the pain had become a growl. He had noticed, too, that his always sallow skin had lately acquired a leaden tinge, and that there was a darkness like bruising round his eyes.

He roused himself wearily and stretched out his arm to the desk to pick up the pile of papers laid ready for his inspection by David Collins. The moment he saw the handwriting of Major Ross a little spasm of irritation shook him. He knew before he opened it what he should find, and he felt his patience stretched tensely in anticipation of the strain which was to be put upon it. What would the grievance be this time? He unfolded the paper and read:

> "Sydney Cove,
> "26th August 1789.

"Sir,

"Your Excellency's having so repeatedly told me that the working convicts, employed on the west side of the cove, were to be under the command and authority of the Lieut-Governor, so far that none of them should be removed from it by your Excellency without his knowledge, that it cannot have escaped your memory, it would be presumptuous in the extreme in me to suppose your Excellency not to know that when either duty, business or pleasure may at any time induce your Excellency to absent yourself from this cove, there cannot then remain in it any authority superior to that of the Lieut-Governor."

Phillip felt a flush rise to his cheeks; the angry blood drummed behind his eyes so that the writing blurred, and he paused, staring steadily at the wall until he could read more calmly.

"Pleasure!" There was venom in that word. It held just that fragment of truth which made its falseness the more cruel, though respite, rather than pleasure, was the only personal advantage he had gained from his arduous explorations. And the respite was from Ross himself, and from the atmosphere of discord which he created. As for this last absence at Rose Hill, nothing but the sternest sense of duty had induced him to undertake it. Major Ross, he reflected more calmly, was one of those strange individuals who, feeling themselves perpetually undervalued, seek to restore their self-esteem by wounding and belittling others. That word, so cleverly placed with a seeming casualness, had achieved its object. It had made him, for a moment, lose his temper. It had filled him with bitterness and hostility before he even knew what the letter was about. He read on:

"I shall proceed to acquaint your Excellency with an account of what I cannot but deem an insult offered to me . . ."

Yes, here it was! Had ever a man been so often insulted as Major Ross! Apparently, he found as he continued, this particular insult arose out of an order which he, Phillip, had given concerning a convict plasterer called Thady. Where, in Heaven's name, thought the Governor irritably, had Ross been able to discover an affront in that?

"However much I feel myself hurt by this impropriety of the manner in which the order came, I immediately determined with myself to give way to it. . . ."

Now, Phillip thought, not without a touch of grim amusement, there was to be a display of nobility!

". . . the terms upon which I am too well known to stand with you render it absolutely necessary for me, in justice to my own consequence . . ."

Phillip flung the letter down impatiently and leaned back in his chair. He would have to go into this. It meant more letters—how tired he was of composing letters and despatches! And a further waste, upon trivialities, of time and energy which might be more usefully employed. He called to Collins who was writing at his table in the next room:

"It seems that there has been some trouble with Major Ross about Thady. What happened while I was away?"

Collins appeared in the doorway, pen in hand.

"I sent Brewer to tell him to join Bloodsworth's gang, as you directed,

Sir, but I must confess I forgot about it until Monday evening. Then I was informed by Bloodsworth that the man had been working for Major Ross, so I gave directions, naturally, that he should finish what work he was engaged upon, as I was sure you had no knowledge of his being so employed when you ordered him to join Bloodsworth. What is Major Ross' complaint, Sir?"

Phillip sighed. He would have liked, at this moment, to let himself go, but in these eighteen months he had learned the value of silence and restraint in a small community. So he only said:

"He appears to feel himself slighted by my having left instructions with you. You had better write me a formal account of the incident, Captain Collins, and I shall send an answer to Major Ross in the morning. I'm going to bed now; good-night."

When he had gone Collins pulled a fresh sheet of paper before him and settled himself grimly to write:

"Sir:

"Your Excellency having this evening done me the favour to acquaint me that the Lieut-Governor had written to your Excellency complaining of some part of my conduct towards him while you were absent from the settlement, I beg leave to lay the following particulars before you; but in so doing I must request you not to understand that I seek either to justify or excuse what I have done, except in the instance I shall mention; for however seriously the Lieut-Governor may treat the circumstance, I can hardly deem it worth the discussion . . ."

He sat back to read and savour that phrase with no little satisfaction, and continued:

". . . and should not say a word on the subject were I not desirous of convincing your Excellency how little it was my wish to create a misunderstanding during your Excellency's temporary absence from the immediate seat of government."

That, he thought, was a fairly adequate preamble. It was true that the Governor was well enough acquainted with his contempt for Major Ross' bickering habit, but there was a certain comfort, nevertheless, in setting it upon record. Nor, he thought with contentment, was it necessary for him to assure Phillip of his own loyalty—but again there was virtue in the written word and the Governor was capable of reading sincerity into formal phrasing. He finished the letter rapidly, setting out the facts with his usual conscientious precision. He could not, in his closing sentence, resist a veiled jibe, but though he wrote:

". . . it has always been my wish to forward, not obstruct, the public service."

He did resist the temptation to underline the "my."

When it was finished and placed upon the Governor's table, he left the house and went outside. It was a clear, cold night; the stars winked distantly in a wintry sky, and a bleak little wind from the sea brought a salty smell to remind him of the thousands of miles of ocean which lay between him and his home.

He tried to think of England, but found his thoughts held as relentlessly as his body to this enterprise which now so completely absorbed his energies and his attention. He could not but be aware of his importance to its well-being, and its ultimate success; he could not but know that Phillip's appointment of him as his secretary was the measure of Phillip's reliance upon him, and there had been growing in him, with the growth of his responsibility, a feeling for this dismal little community which was almost affection—almost, even, pride!

The glimmer of a lantern and the tramp of feet on the opposite side of the stream attracted his attention, and he reflected with some surprise that the Watch was proving, on the whole, very satisfactory. It was a pity, of course, that it had been necessary to compose this first makeshift police patrol of convicts, but the best behaved men had been carefully selected, and the scheme seemed to be answering even better than he and Phillip had hoped when they formulated it. It was a strange thing, he mused, that it had been found impossible to impress upon many of the people the utter heinousness of theft in such a situation as theirs. Dependent as they all were upon the public stores for their sustenance, they seemed still unable to realise that their carefully husbanded food had now achieved a value which was almost sacredness, and its theft had become a sin rather than a crime.

He began to wonder how many of the convicts who made the claim had already served out their terms. It was a most unfortunate oversight that the papers from which this information could have been obtained had been left behind in England, and that the Governor, therefore, had no means of verifying the many assertions which had been made by convicts who claimed that their sentences had expired, and that they were now entitled to be treated as free men. One could hardly have imagined, he thought, picking his way carefully in the darkness towards his own house, the number of unforeseen difficulties which could arise in such a community. At home difficulties could always be met somehow—adjustments made, compromises reached—but here in this utter isolation a fact stared you starkly in the face and you realised with dismay that there was nothing you could do about it. Nothing at all.

The animals, for instance, which were being so carefully reserved for breeding purposes. Why were they producing such a disproportionate number of male offspring? Here was such a fact—and a disturbing one in a country which was expected by the home authorities to make itself self-supporting as rapidly as possible. Twelve piglets, and only three females! Seven kids, and six of them males! Was this a mere unfortunate accident, or was it another mysterious effect of a land in which Nature wore altogether so strange a face that no variation of the usual order seemed too freakish to accept? Timber was another of those disturbing and non-adjustable facts. Their experience here had been unhappy enough —but from King at Norfolk Island came discouraging reports of the great pine trees of whose usefulness he had at first held high hopes. They were no good for masts or yards, too brittle for oars, too porous for boats . . .

His thoughts were sharply interrupted as he passed the clergyman's house which stood close to his own by the sight of a shadowy figure in the doorway. He said in a sharp undertone:

"Who's there?"

The figure moved. He found himself looking down into a pair of brilliant black eyes whose whites shone in the starlight. He recognised the native girl whom Mrs. Johnson had taken into her household and said reprovingly:

"You should be indoors, Booron."

He could see from her unwinking stare that she did not understand, so he turned her to face the door, and pushed her gently towards it. She gave him one more glance and went obediently. Collins, turning away, walked on to his own dwelling with a new thought in his mind. Why did she stand there in the dark and the cold, that child in the shapeless smock with which Mrs. Johnson had covered her nakedness, staring at the trees? Could it be that she was not happy to be fed and clothed and decently housed, and taught the first principles of civilization? Could it be that she was homesick for her own kind of life, as he and all his compatriots were homesick for theirs? Did she wonder where her own people were, her relatives and her friends, so disastrously scattered by the epidemic? Was she nerving herself to escape in an effort to find them?

Until he slept that night his hands remembered the feel of her thin shoulders, and his mind held, uneasily, the image of her sad, unchildish eyes.

Slowly, as the epidemic spent its force, the almost deserted shores of Port Jackson became populous again. Gradually, with returning health and confidence, the tribes drifted back to their old towris; on the long stretch of the south shore, from Sydney Cove to Rose Hill, the campfires of the Wanngal glimmered at night, and were answered by those of the Wallumedegal on the other side. In their own wild and rocky territory upon the northwest arm, the proud and warlike Cammeraygal reassembled, and in the quiet sandy bays near the headland of Burrawarra the canoes of the Cadigal lay beached once more.

But there were not nearly so many canoes as formerly. Colbee, his face deeply pitted with the scars of the disease, his short, sturdy body as yet hardly restored to its normal strength, looked at them sadly. Now more than ever he was a leader in his tribe, for most of the old men had died, either from the sickness, or from starvation during the ensuing chaos, or from the spears of other tribes whose territory they had invaded and who feared for their own food supplies. He was a leader, but there was no need for him to tell his people what must now be done. There must be rest for a time, an abandoning of tired bodies to Nature, for her sure and benevolent renewal. It was enough now to eat and sleep, to lie long hours basking in the sun, feeling its warmth creep into the blood and course like a reviving stream through languid and weakened limbs. The daily search for food was, for the present, sufficient exertion; and it was only as the spring days lengthened that they began to feel their vigour returning and to take a desultory interest in the Bereewolgal once more.

There they still were in their ugly camp upon the shores of Warrung. They had built many more dwelling places—one of them tall and solid as a mighty rock—and they had made the most ridiculous tracks, far wider than a track need ever be, and they had begun a second camp far up at the head of the harbour, in the towri of the Wanngal. But the novelty of their presence had worn off. Their coming already belonged to the past and between it and the present lay the Sickness, a monstrous event by which time would be reckoned for many generations to come. The presence of the white men was already coming to be regarded not as a problem but as a fact. They had been here so long now—a long, long time indeed—so long that it was only with a tiresome mental effort that one's mind went back to a time when they had not been here. For when life goes on, serene and unchanging, for century after century, there is no need to look back—or forward. Today is enough; the human mind dwells securely in it, and yesterday is a dark curtain fallen for ever, and tomorrow one not yet drawn aside. There they were, the queer white people, labouring incessantly, achieving nothing but confusion. The natives were content to leave them alone. Now and then, up and down the two hundred miles of harbour shore, there were skirmishes. The white men intruded, the black men flung a spear or two, the white men replied with their gooroobeera, and the incident was closed. Already it was as if they were just another tribe—more disturbing perhaps than the other tribes, because more difficult to understand—but apparently willing enough to be left alone to their own strange activities. Hostility and mistrust flared up sporadically, fanned to a flame by some sudden appearance, by the report of a gun, by some sign of their presence or passing in a place where they had not been seen before. But this was no time for serious warfare. The tribes were weakened, many, many warriors had died, and in the panic-stricken flight weapons had been lost or abandoned; now there must be a time set apart for tribal reconstruction. The men must make new wommerahs and boomerangs, they must mark out new shields in the thick bark of the trees, digging deeply round the outline into the wood itself, driving wedges with care and patience to split the section neatly from the trunk, making a shield such as any warrior might be proud to bear. They must await the flowering of the grass tree to make fresh supplies of spears, both for hunting and fishing. The women must weave new nets and lines, and search for the shell from which fishhooks might be made, and they must also bear children to replenish the tribe. No, there was no time, just now, to bother about the Bereewolgal.

* * *

Bennilong had celebrated his regained health and his return to his own towri with an outburst of amorousness. He acquired a new spear wound on his head from an irate husband, another through his arm from a warrior upon whose bride his roving eye had rested too ardently, and he got his hand well bitten by a young woman of the Wallumedegal, called Odooroodah, whose resistance had been so spirited that he had been forced to beat her into insensibility. Never had he felt so well. Never had life pounded through his veins so exuberantly. It was as if his body, having known weakness for the first time, were now asserting its return to health with a gusto which hardly allowed him a moment's stillness. His movements had a spring in them, his appetite was insatiable, his grin flashed broadly, his rages erupted with explosive violence, and his vanity soared, bearing his spirit upward as if on wings, so that he felt larger than life, and wherever he went a tumult surrounded him. Argument, quarrelling, laughter. Upon any group which he left a silence fell; it was as if a shadow had crossed the sun, leaving the air chilly.

Barangaroo recovered more slowly. No matter how well she ate she did not seem to grow much fatter, and she no longer had the strength and energy which had made her so useful a wife. It was as if, in those long weeks when, half starving herself, she had tramped the unfamiliar ridges seeking the food to keep Bennilong alive, she had used up what remained of her youth, and was now nothing but a middle-aged woman with a sharp and shrewish tongue. Watching Bennilong as he strutted about, she thought that she too should assert her vitality in the way proper to women, and she went off by herself day after day to certain places well known to the dyins, hoping that Wadahgudjaelwon would look with a favourable eye upon her and entrust a baby spirit to her care.

* * *

It was about this time that Johnny Prentice, like his father, disappeared. He had been seen last upon the evening when his mother's third child was born, and he had told one of the other children that he was tired of the settlement and was going away to live with the Indians. No one believed this preposterous story except Ellen. The settlement was searched from end to end, a party was sent out into the woods hallooing and firing muskets, a somewhat desultory examination of the water round the foreshores of the cove was made, and then it was decided that he must have drowned himself somehow, or lost himself in the woods like so many other stragglers, and there was no more to be done about it.

Ellen had been very ill when this last baby was born. Her second child, conceived during the voyage, and born upon the King's birthday, was now fifteen months old, a fair-haired, wizen-faced little girl, bearing, by courtesy, the name of Maria Prentice, though her father was certainly not Andrew. The third, who now lay in Ellen's arms, worrying fretfully at her breast and keeping up a thin wail of frustrated hunger, wore the proof of his legitimacy in a thatch of red hair and a pair of bright dark eyes, but it was neither of him nor of Maria that Ellen was thinking, but of Johnny, lost for nearly a week now. Johnny, casually supposed dead by all but herself; Johnny, for whom she had stolen more recklessly than was safe, and for whom she cherished an inarticulate, possessive love which she had never felt for either of her other children.

No one else might believe it when he said that he was going to live with the Indians, but she believed it. She believed it bitterly, with a revival of the agonising jealousy which she had felt for Arabanoo. Johnny had never loved her as he had loved that heathen savage. When the black man died, she remembered, he had seemed to go almost insane with grief. He had wept and wept until he fell asleep with exhaustion, and woke to weep again. For days he had wept, refusing food, breaking out of his sobbing sometimes into loud wails of unchildish misery and despair. Ellen, at her wits' end, had tried bribes, threats, cajolery, scoldings, beatings, all to no avail; she had even begged the Reverend Mr. Johnson to help her, but he had only prayed, and that had seemed to make Johnny worse than ever. The other women convicts, coming to stare at him with avid awe, had assured Ellen ghoulishly that he was losing his mind, and she had just begun to believe that they were right when he stopped crying suddenly and slept like the dead for twenty-four hours.

But from that time he had been different. He was no longer the dumb and unobtrusive child he had been, moving silently, speaking seldom, accepting submissively such punishments and rebukes as were meted out to him. He became wild and malicious. A demon was in him, so that never a day passed when he was not the centre of a storm, cuffed and sworn at, but hitting and kicking back now, and cursing back, too, evilly and expertly, in his shrill voice. It seemed that he could not rest if he were not harming or plaguing someone. He meddled, he stole, he carried malicious tales, he pinched Maria, he put sand in the precious food, and once he even threw a stone at Mr. Johnson. Such conduct could not go unpunished, and life for Johnny became one endless series of scoldings, threats, and beatings. Grown-ups had always been his enemies, but now he was their enemy too, and he would declare no truce. Once, though he had never loved her, his mother had been a kind of refuge; to be by her side was all he knew of home. But she had not liked Arabanoo, his friend, his only friend, so he had come to look upon her, too, as hostile.

When Arabanoo died he had wished that he could die too. All his weeping had been because he could not—a fury of resentment at his helplessness. It had become unendurable that life could so buffet and torment one, and one could do nothing in retaliation, not even die. His brain had hovered, as the women said, on the verge of utter collapse, but he was not the son of Andrew Prentice for nothing. The sullen, mulish tenacity of purpose which sustained his father lived in Johnny too; he was not the kind to fall into that abject surrender, that ultimate acknowledgment of defeat. But he could no longer live submissively. He hated life, and he would fight it in the only way in which a small boy of six can fight—by being outrageously and incessantly rebellious.

He did not know why the birth of his brother should have set the final seal upon his determination to run away. He was not in the least jealous of the squirming creature in his mother's arms. It did occur to him that there would now be even less room in the hut than formerly, and that he would sometimes be told to watch the baby, or even hold it. And he disliked babies because they cried, and were sick, and made messes, and smelled bad, and altogether took up too much of everyone's time and attention.

There was no difficulty at all about running away. The children were more or less unsupervised most of the time, and Johnny had by now made himself so cordially detested by everyone that he was left a good deal to himself. Once away from the settlement, he decided, he would make down the harbour, keeping as close to the shore as he could, and soon he would fall in with some of Arabanoo's tribe, fishing in the bays. It did not occur to him now to be afraid of the black people, and he considered that he knew quite enough of their language to make them understand that he intended to live with them in future. He would explain to them, he planned, that he had been a friend of Arabanoo, and that he wished to be received into their tribe, and to learn to do all the things which their own little boys did; and he had not the smallest doubt but that they would greet him with open arms.

He was entirely right. He, an ignorant convict child, had found far less difficulty in understanding the race of Murri than had the conscientious and well-meaning Governor. Arabanoo and Arthur Phillip had talked to each other across a gulf; Arabanoo and Johnny Prentice had met confidently and happily upon the common ground of their unsophistication. By nightfall upon the day of his escape Johnny was sitting contentedly by the campfires of the Cadigal, eating a hearty meal of barely cooked fish, and drinking clear water from a shell.

His hosts, thinking at first that he had strayed from his own camp, offered to escort him back, but when he had made them understand that he wanted to remain they were amused and delighted, and summoned their own children to keep him company. There had been many exciting games, and a great deal of hilarity over Johnny's ignorance of the rules, and later, when it grew dark, one of the men had told him tales. The pink firelight chasing the shadows up the tree trunks, had led his gaze higher and higher to find the inky sky pricked with stars which now, for the first time, filled him with conscious wonder and delight. The black men, seeing his rapt, unmoving stare, lifted his arm to point from one constellation to another, and his voice began a quick, chanting recital of old legends. Johnny had listened breathlessly, understanding not everything, but enough. Heaven, he well knew, was the dwelling place of God the stern avenger who punished one for doing wrong—and that had been enough, in the past, to keep his eyes from it. But now it appeared that not only God dwelt there, but also someone called Baiame, of whom his new friend seemed greatly to approve. And instead of angels, who were really like lesser gods, and quite as unsympathetic, there were, he learned, many interesting people in the sky.

"Mirrabooka!"

The black man's lean forefinger pointed urgently toward a gap between the tree-tops, and then, in the dust beside the fire, made marks to show the position of the stars he meant, so that Johnny was able to see them quite clearly. There were four very bright ones, arranged something like a cross, and a fifth, dimmer and smaller, near by. Two of the bright ones, Johnny was told, were great warriors who had fought for a woman called Namirra, and wounded each other so badly that they both died; and the other two were their brothers, who had been so overcome by grief that they killed Namirra, who was now the fifth pale star, and then killed themselves too.

And from the stars the tales came down to earth, and told of birds and animals and children. And Johnny had shown off his knowledge of the tale which Arabanoo had told him about Goomblegubbon, and they had all exclaimed and clapped their hands and nodded their heads in congratulation, and Johnny had felt enormously clever and proud and happy. He had slept in a mia-mia in a tangled heap of other children, so he had not felt cold or lonely, and his last waking thought had been to wonder at his own foolishness in not coming here long, long ago.

* * *

It was not until more than a week later that the crew of a fishing boat noticed a white child playing among some black children on a beach near the mouth of the harbour. Dumbfounded, they drew in to the shore, and beheld Johnny, stark naked, deeply absorbed in some game which they were playing with the fine white sand. Suddenly one of the children looked up and saw the boat; there was a stir among them, and Johnny's red head jerked upward, flaming in the sun among the black locks of his companions. They stood staring, but Johnny was gone in a flash, darting like a rabbit for cover into the surrounding bush. The men, puzzled, rowed back to the settlement with their tale.

The Governor sent out a party to bring him back, with instructions to keep the proceedings friendly. They rowed to the same beach, landed, searched, but not a native was to be seen, and no sign of a camp was found. The next day, trying again, they came upon two native women and a group of children, Johnny amongst them, chipping oysters from the rocks with stone knives. Johnny fled again, but this time he was pursued and captured. He fought and bit and screamed and struggled; the black women stared and the children whispered, but made no effort to intervene.

"No! No!" yelled Johnny, and then, frantically, to his black friends: "Bee-all! Bee-all!" But the women only shook their heads at him, shocked by such recalcitrant behaviour. If the birrahlee chose to visit them, well and good, but of course his own tribe had the first claim upon him. No tribe, naturally, would wish to lose a fine boy who would, in time, grow to manhood and be a credit to it, a defender of its territory and its rights. So they only waved their hands and called after him: "Guioa, Dyonn-ee! Guioa!"

And the boat took him back to the settlement.

*   *   *

In September the supply of butter gave out. Phillip was again being tormented by anxiety about food. Rats had multiplied, and there was incessant warfare between them and the Commissary. Hunted by dogs from the storehouses, they fled to the gardens and devoured the Indian corn, and as the month of October passed the Governor realised that the already inadequate rations must be still more rigidly curtailed. For the women, already upon two-thirds of the men's allowance, he judged that there could be no further reduction.

The spring faded into summer again. Walking alone in the woods, making his way to a near-by hilltop from which he could see the settlement and the harbour and the far blue line of hills, Phillip reflected that in England the spring could never come and pass almost unnoticed, as it had done here. He paused to examine a tree trunk which one would have thought hopelessly destroyed by the fire which had raged about it last summer. But now, breaking out from it in seemingly haphazard fashion, all up and down its blackened stem and branches, tiny tufts of blood-red leaves caught the afternoon sunlight, and blazed like rubies. The woods, indeed, when one stood thus with the western sun behind their young leaves, gave almost the impression of another fire. Through half-closed eyes one saw rose and ruby and amber, stirred and tossed by the sea breeze until they looked like dancing flames.

Above and beyond them the Governor's eyes went again to the hills.

Nearly two years, now, and still they hid a mystery! Far up one shining arm of the harbour he could see a black shape which he knew to be the boat which carried provisions from Sydney to Rose Hill; the first boat built in the colony, named by the convicts the *Rose Hill Packet,* and later sardonically rechristened *The Lump.* A lump she looked indeed, he thought, wallowing along like some fabulous amphibian monster! The mere sight of her drove his anxiety about food back into his consciousness with a blow which seemed almost physical. Perhaps the *Supply,* just off again on another trip to Norfolk Island, might bring them back some turtle from Lord Howe. Perhaps the recent very good hauls of fish would continue. Perhaps—perhaps any day now, there might be a storeship from England. . . .

It was no use trying to teach many of the convicts to be provident. He had accepted that fact by now, resignedly, too busy with the present to go back in his imagination to the life which had made improvidence their inevitable philosophy. Weekly rations, issued on Saturday, were gone by Tuesday. That, he thought restlessly, might be considered their own affair if their labour were not so sorely needed; men starved for half the week were useless men.

He turned to look down the harbour towards the sea, and then abruptly faced the west again, annoyed because he had recognised a faint, irrational hope that a miracle might happen—that he might see a long-awaited sail rounding the point, and know that England had not forgotten him after all. But there was no sail. He must school himself to face the fact that there might be no sail for many months yet, and turning his back upon the ocean, facing the unknown hinterland of the continent, was a movement symbolic of his determination to put his faith not in miracles but in his own fortitude.

The mountains had an airy, insubstantial appearance in this light. Strain his eyes as he would, he could not quite determine where they ended and the low-lying clouds began. He must send out another expedition. Who knew but that relief and comfort for every one of them might lie behind those hills? The river which Tench had discovered upon that expedition of his from Rose Hill, and which he himself had named after Mr. Nepean, might well be an arm of the Hawkesbury which his own party had explored about the same time. This should be determined; and the mountains should be penetrated as far as possible. Another attempt must be made, but he could not himself leave the settlement at present, and there was not the same enthusiasm for exploring now which had been discernible at first among the younger officers. Those of them who had had a taste of it did not seem very anxious for more just yet. Perhaps when time had softened the memory of struggle and exertion, curiosity would arouse a zest once more. Dawes, perhaps . . . Yes, when it was last mentioned Dawes had seemed not unwilling . . .

The year was ending. Phillip, staring westward, felt impatiently that not enough had been achieved, and he found himself remembering Arabanoo, and that experiment so successfully maturing and so tragically brought to an end. For a long time he had thought that it might be repeated. Here was something which could be done at once—another step forward which might still be made before the end of the year. With the dying out of the smallpox the natives had returned, and now, Phillip thought, was the moment to lay a couple of them by the heels, and win them, as Arabanoo had been almost won, by kind treatment, and a life which, rough at it was, must surely be easier than that to which these miserable savages were accustomed. He walked briskly back to the settlement, making his plans. Lieutenant Bradley should go down the harbour with an armed boat and attend to the capture. And Dawes should be approached about the expedition. Perhaps before the New Year dawned there might be, after all, some new line of hope to follow.

* * *

So one bright day near the end of November, Lieutenant Bradley left the Governor's presence with a long face. It was an unpleasant task which had been allotted to him, and he said little and looked glum as he sat in the stern of the boat going down the harbour. Nevertheless orders were orders, and he kept his eyes alert, scanning the cresents of sand at the heads of the coves as the boat passed them, watching for a sign of their black inhabitants.

Walking on a beach near the South Head, he saw, at last, two of them, unarmed, and gave the word for the boat to draw in to the shore.

Colbee and Bennilong paused, shading their eyes with their hands and staring across the water at the antics of the white men, who were standing up in their boat, waving, calling out, holding up something, and beckoning.

Colbee, mystified, grunted: "Magra!"

Bennilong nodded eagerly. Yes, they were fish which the white men were waving in the air—fine big fish, which they seemed to be offering. He was, as usual, hungry, and quite willing to be saved the exertion of catching his supper, so he returneed their salutations genially, and asked Colbee:

"Yen-ou?"

Colbee assented. They walked down to the water's edge together, and stood where the wavelets broke about their ankles, and all the time the boat came nearer, and the white men continued to call out, and to wave the fish invitingly above their heads.

"Kia?" shouted Colbee. "N'gai-ri!" shouted Bennilong. "Fish!" shouted Lieutenant Bradley. "Here's some fish for you! What the deuce is their word for fish, Mr. Keltie? Good fish! Nice fish! Boodjerree! Boodjerree fish!"

The keel of the boat scraped the sand. Five of the white men jumped ashore, their hands full of fish, and presented them to Bennilong and Colbee, who received them with somewhat mystified willingness. Then there was a word from Lieutenant Bradley, a rush and a scuffle, the two natives were overwhelmed, their legs knocked from under them, their arms pinioned, and they were floundering in the bottom of the boat almost before they had let out their first yells of fury and astonishment.

From the trees dark figures appeared, running down the beach. But the gooroobeera of the white men were pointing at them, the invisible death which they dealt threatened already depleted ranks—and how should a tribe survive without enough warriors to protect it? The boat was well out from the shore by now, the wet oars gleaming as the men strained at them. Colbee and Bennilong! The tribesmen looked at each other in dismay, and then with a slowly dawning hope which changed swiftly to high-spirited optimism. Bennilong and Colbee! Here were no quiet and gentle souls such as Arabanoo had been! Not for very long would the Bereewolgal detain Colbee and Bennilong against their will! Shrugging their shoulders they returned to their camp, and the boat receded up the harbour, a vanishing speck against the golden glitter of the water.

* * *

Nanbarree and Booron were there to greet them when they stepped ashore. The children were shocked to see these respected warriors of their tribe helpless and in captivity, but their months in the camp of the white people had so confused their minds that they hardly knew whether to congratulate or condole. It was true that the Bereewolgal were kind. It was true that they bestowed sufficient food, and that in the cold season the mia-mias which they built were warmer than ones made of bark. These things they told their countrymen, looking nervously at Bennilong where he stood towering over Colbee, for they could see that he was in one of his famous rages, and when Bennilong was angry children hid

behind their mothers and peered at him in awe, as at lightning in the sky.
But when he shouted and gesticulated the white men only smiled. If
he had a spear, Booron whispered to Nanbarree, and if his hands were
not bound, they would not smile! Now they were being taken to the
house of the Be-anga. "Aie! But Bennilong is angry!" "Colbee also is
angry, but he says less than Bennilong." "What will become of the Be-anga
if Bennilong challenges him to battle?" "See, now they are entering . . ."
Whispering excitedly they watched the closed door, half expecting that
it would presently burst open, and that Bennilong and the Be-anga would
reel out, joined in mortal combat. But it remained shut, and there was not
even a sound of shouting from within.

*   *   *

Lieutenant Dawes paused in midstream to adjust his haversack, and to
stare upward at the steeply sloping hills before him. It was the tenth day
of December, and the sun, though not yet high, beat down hotly on his
head and shoulders and danced blindingly on the little rapids of the ford.
The water, running strongly, dragged at his knees, and he glanced up and
down stream, thinking that they had been fortunate indeed to find this
crossing, for elsewhere the water was smooth, hiding unknown depths.

The sergeant and the two marines were across already, and George
Johnston was just climbing out on the opposite bank. He dumped his load
on the ground, and knelt upon the bank, sluicing cold water over his face.
Evidently, Dawes thought, the look of those steep and rugged hills up
which they must presently toil, urged him to make the most of the river
while he could.

Lowes passed him while he stood there, moving slowly and cautiously,
feeling with his feet beneath the water for a firm foothold on the rounded,
slippery stones, leaning a little upstream against the force of the current.
Under the rushing water the stones were just visible, red and golden, their
colour borrowing light from the sun and fluidity from the clear water, so
that they seemed to move and sparkle.

Dawes began to move forward again. This Nepean, he thought, was a
pleasant spot, and for himself he would have wished for nothing better
than to loiter beside it for a day or two, examining the shrubs and flowers
to which, in their always pressing haste, they were able to give only a
cursory attention. But hidden from them now by those hilltops there lay
the Carmarthen Mountains, the definite objective which the Governor had
instructed him to reach if possible, and if they were to do so, and return
before their food gave out, there could be no delay.

Joining his companions on the opposite bank, he dropped his haversack and laid his musket beside it, and sat down to wash the sand out of his shoes and stockings. Round Hill, whose summit Phillip wished them to reach, might be, he reflected, some twenty-seven or twenty-eight miles in a straight line from where they sat. No great distance; it should be possible. He glanced up at the hills again and was suddenly impatient to be off. Shouldering their loads they turned their faces westward, and set off across the gently undulating slopes which led up to the foothills. Inside an hour they had begun to climb. They scrambled up a stony slope so steep that sometimes they must touch their fingers to the ground to maintain a balance. The sun climbed too, scorching the earth with its heat, and the shrubs and trees began to give out their strong, spicy odours, and the air began to throb with the cicada chorus. At the top of the slope they rested, wiping sweat from their brows and staring down at the river, already some seven hundred feet below them. Starry white flowers shone up from the surface of the rock upon which Dawes sat, a surface which seemed unbroken until, searching, he found the hair-thin crack through which persistent roots bored down to earth and hidden moisture. When they went on again they were walking on comparatively level ground; underfoot it was hard, and parched, and stony, and yet things grew in it. On the tall shrubs which had borne the bold red flowers which the natives called waratahs, long seed-pods were already forming, and here and there, from a scatter of lavender coloured blossoms, a faint smell of vanilla mingled rather incongruously with the stronger scent of eucalyptus, and the heady perfume of small plants bruised by their passing.

Dawes, counting paces mechanically, was aroused before another hour had passed by a call from Lowes:

"There it is!"

He glanced up, surprised; he had not expected to catch a glimpse of their goal so soon. They had emerged from the sparse, starved timber on to the rocky edge of a deep gully, and stood for a moment looking westward to where Round Hill had come into view, its domed top dark against the sky. Dawes, extracting his compass from his pocket, said hopefully:

"It doesn't look very far. Not much more than twenty miles I should have said."

Johnston was staring at the deep gully before them. He said gloomily:

"No great distance if the country were level. But if we are to descend and reascend some hundreds of feet in every mile or so we shall make slow progress."

They made a zig-zag course down the hill, their feet slipping on the loose stones, and climbed laboriously out upon the other side. The morning became a monotonous repetition of small gullies, separated by here a mile, and there a mere hundred yards or so of rough but level ground. From each new eminence as they won it they looked eagerly around them, and saw nothing, north, south, east or west, but tree-tops.

At midday, climbing to the summit of yet another ridge they halted, and dumped their gear thankfully upon the ground. They were too hot and too weary to talk; they looked at the bloomy, lavender shadows which lay between the hills, and saw them only as representing so many more exhausting obstacles to their advance. Recovering his breath, and refreshed a little by a faint breeze which played fitfully about this high place, Dawes began to study the rock which was his seat. It looked as if it had once been liquid—poured out while a gale was raging, so that it had hardened suddenly in curves and convolutions, ridges, ripples and crests, like those made in sand by an incoming wave. In places it appeared to have boiled, as porridge boils; some Gorgon force of nature had arrested it in the very act of bubbling, for here they were, bubbles in stone, some burst, some still intact . . .

Lowes was pointing down the hillside.

"There should be a run of water in that valley."

Dawes, shading his eyes with his hat, studied the backbone of the ridge on which they sat.

"We might save ourselves the trouble of climbing into it and out again," he said, "by skirting round it up there. What do you say, Lowes?"

Lowes, who had stretched himself at full length in a narrow strip of shade afforded by the rock, struggled unwillingly to one elbow. He agreed rather grudgingly:

"It *looks* unbroken."

Johnston said sourly:

"You can't trust your eyes in this country. Take my word for it, we shall find a chasm at our feet, and be forced to return."

He was almost right. For about an hour it was not unpleasant keeping to the crest of the ridge, for it was more open than others they had crossed, and walking was easier. Then Dawes, who was ahead, halted suddenly, and Johnston, coming up to him, looked, and said: "Ha!" not without a certain glum satisfaction. They stood on the brink of a line of cliff, some thirty to fifty feet high. Below them they could see the way clear on to the next ridge, but the cliff, perpendicular, and in some places overhung, offered no means of descent. Dawes began to walk along it in a northerly direction.

"You go the other way," he called to Johnston. "Not too far, and give a shout now and then. You wait here, Lowes, with the men. There must be a way down somewhere."

He found it twenty minutes later—a small diagonal cleft down which they might scramble with some difficulty, and plodded back to the meeting place to summon his companions. Johnston was still absent, but his voice answered their call from a distance, and he appeared at last, his fresh complexion crimson with heat and exertion, to report the cliff line quite unbroken as far as he had explored it.

It was late afternoon by the time they reached the bottom of Dawes' cleft, bruised and scratched and short of temper. Lowes sucked a finger which had been hit by a dislodged stone, and Johnston craned his head ruefully to observe a rent in the shoulder of his coat. Sunset found them on the crest of the ridge which they had observed from their halting place at midday, but they hardly paused to admire a scene magnificent in its lonely vastness, bathed in golden light, and splashed with cobalt shadow. They plunged down the next gully, wanting only to reach the stream which they expected to find at its foot, longing only to be rid of their loads, to light a fire, to eat and drink, and rest.

There was no stream—only the dry bed of one. They plodded up it dejectedly in the dusk, and Johnston found at last, by blundering into it in the gathering darkness, a little pool. They unslung their haversacks and dropped to the ground where they stood, too tired even for speech.

The next day was almost a repetition of the first, and the day after that was marked only by the fact that now the gullies were consistently deeper and more precipitous. Once they came upon an open valley where the soil, to judge by the size of the trees which grew in it, was comparatively good, but they were soon out of it again, struggling through dense undergrowth, over sandy, stony and unprofitable ground.

On the fourteenth of December, four days after leaving the Nepean, Dawes called a halt upon the summit of a little hill which rose from one of the ridges, and announced that they could go no further. There was Round Hill, rising stolidly from its wild chaos of lesser hills, not more, Dawes estimated, than twelve miles from where they stood. But between them and it the nightmare of hills and valleys persisted, and there was barely enough food in their knapsacks to see them back to Rose Hill.

Well, Dawes thought resignedly, if he could not reach it himself he could at least record what they had seen, for the benefit of some future explorer, and he pulled out the rough sketch map of their progress which he had been keeping and made a note on it.

"The country between . . ."

He reflected a moment, and then announced:

"I shall call this hill after our friend Captain Twiss."

Lowes was half asleep, and made no response. Johnston, glancing round, said sardonically: "A compliment, indeed!" and went on rummaging in his haversack for the shirt which he had washed in a pool the night before. Dawes, unruffled, continued to write in his small, neat hand:

"The country between Mount Twiss and Round Hill appeared not easy of access."

He studied the landscape carefully, a frown between his brows. How was one to describe such a scene? Trees, trees, trees. As far as the eye could see, only trees, clothing a tangled sea of hills and valleys. Nothing else. No landmarks to speak of, except the humped shape of Round Hill, and the long sprawl of Saddle Hill to the right of it, and a few lesser excrescences near them, hardly worthy to be named. In the space to the southwest of the dot beside which he had already neatly inscribed its new name, Mount Twiss, he wrote:

"All this country as far as the eye can reach from very high hills appears very mountainous and covered with trees."

To the north he wrote:

"This part of the country bearing from Mount Twiss in the direction of NNE, and NE has the appearance of steep rocky ridges of hills rising immediately one above another, and as the distance increases it continues to appear the same for Thirty miles."

He turned his eyes westward again. Alas for the Governor's high hopes! Not yet, at all events, were they in sight of the kinder country, the richer soil which he had hoped to find! He sighed, and wrote carefully in the space beyond Round Hill:

"What is to be seen of the Country in this direction through the intervals in the Carmarthen Mountains, appears to be exactly similar to what is already described in the South West."

He folded his paper and sat down to stow it away in his haversack.

"We shall make for Rose Hill again," he said. "There's no more to be seen here than what we have seen already. The next party must come prepared for a much longer march."

Lowes said: "Not even the natives can live here. We have seen no sign of them but a few shells the first day, and the remains of an old fire. What benefit can there be for us in a country which is too poor even to support those miserable wretches? We have seen nothing for four days but stones and sand and starved trees."

George Johnston had rolled down his stockings, and was examining long scratches on his legs, made by the prickly scrub, and already rising in white and irritable weals. He said peevishly without looking up:

"If you were to march for a month you would find nothing else. There *is* nothing else. Let us leave the abominable land to its own abominable people, I say." He adjusted his stockings and scrambled to his feet. "If we set out at once we might reach that stream we passed this morning before nightfall. Come along—let us be off."

* * *

Many years ago, Bennilong thought, I saw this thing. Many, many years ago, when I was but a birrahlee, all this was known to me. When I have slept my Doowee has seen it. In the heart of my father, Wunbula, there was a knowledge that I should come at last to the camp of the Bereewolgal. . . .

He glanced at Colbee, sitting moodily in the doorway of the hut. During their detention in the white men's camp the casual deference which he normally paid to the older man had been strangely reinforced by a recurrence of his childish awe. It was as if there were left over in him from his childhood two emotions, inextricably interwoven; as if it were not possible to arouse the one without stirring the other also into life. He hardly knew if he were happy here or not. It was pleasant and gratifying to his vanity to be so much the centre of interest. It was an opportunity such as he seldom had to show off to an audience which seemed to hang upon his every word. And it was surely cause for self-congratulation that he had been able to learn, so very rapidly, not only the tongue of the white men but their manners and customs also.

He was determined to match them in everything. He ate their foods, and after a time began to enjoy them. He even drank their magic liquid which ran down the throat like fire, and was proud when they applauded him, and teased Colbee, who would not touch it. There could be no doubt that there was magic in it, for after one had drunk there came a glowing warmth into one's heart and mind; one felt larger than before, more confident, richer in strength and daring. It was like the feeling which came while one was making a corroboree, but even more potent. It was an expanding of one's spirit, so that the whole world became one's own, and there was nothing too difficult for accomplishment, and no power which one could not overthrow.

It might very well be, he had reflected, the whole secret of the white men's knowledge. He himself, after he had drunk, seemed to be aware of things he had never known before. He saw them, as yet, but dimly; he could never tell exactly what they were, but only that he was conscious of them—vast ideas, formless but magnificent, colossal, undefined ambitions, an intoxicating appreciation of potentialities within himself. Now when they offered him this miracle-working drink, he accepted it eagerly, and called loudly for more. He was proud, too, that he could eat five times the amount that any white man ate. He was proud to wear the clothes they gave him, and walked often in the sunshine so that he might admire his shadow, which was now the same as the shadow of a white man.

He sang many of his songs for them, and performed sections of a corroboree which he had made. He suspected, with some chagrin, that they did not know he was a notable youara-gurrugin, and the son of Wunbula, the greatest of them all. He told them many times, but they did not seem to understand, though they applauded his performances enthusiastically enough.

His ear was quick to pick up sounds, his tongue agile in repeating them, his memory tenacious. Quite soon he could speak fluently in their language, though there was always one sound which baffled him. Colbee could not, or would not, learn half so fast. Sitting in the lamplight when the evening meal was over, and the cloth removed, with a circle of white men about him, cheering him on, encouraging him with smiles and nods, Bennilong indulged in orgies of boastfulness. He recounted his prowess both in war and in love. With rich and graphic gestures, when words failed him, he suggested the opulent charms of the maiden who had bitten his hands, and described the manner of his conquest in terms which brought delighted roars of laughter from his hearers.

But now, looking at Colbee sitting dejectedly in the doorway of the hut, a shudder of uneasiness passed over him. Indeed, there was much in this life which was good . . . Why was it not possible to be completely at ease? Colbee was not happy here. The reserved compliance which he showed masked an inflexible resolve which no friendliness of the white men, no gifts, no easy living, no flattery, could move. Bennilong knew of it; sometimes he shared it, and always in his heart he understood the emotion which fed it, and strove against it because it warred with the excitement which he felt in this new kind of life. Somewhere, beneath all this friendliness, there was insult; somewhere beneath the kindness there was treachery. He could not deny this conviction, but he fought against it, and was torn by the strife. Colbee did not fight it; instead he nursed it grimly in his heart, and was whole. He would not agree to what Bennilong sometimes asserted—that the shackles on their legs, these ropes attached to them, these men holding the ropes and leading them about as they led some of their animals, might be merely another of the strange customs of an inexplicable people. It was not so. Bennilong knew it as surely as Colbee, and had no need to form his knowledge into words, or even into coherent thought, for it was a knowledge born in him and in his forefathers for uncountable generations. Tribal customs might differ, but the eternal relationship of man to man must remain inviolate. Freedom was the root of it, from which dignity and confidence and justice and all other noble qualities of man must grow; and now, for the first time in his life, he was not free. It was not to be denied. Watching Colbee, he no longer attempted to deny it.

It was nearly dark, but the candles had not yet been lit in the hut. The two men who guarded them were eating their supper, and he himself had been enjoying a banquet of fish and bread until there had come to him, from Colbee's motionless figure, silhouetted in the doorway, a kind of shock, a trembling awareness of crisis. With his hands half way to his open mouth, he stared. And in a moment Colbee made a swift movement, a twist, a violent wrench; the end of his rope was lying on the ground, and he himself was away, shadowlike in the dusk, over the paling fence which enclosed the hut—gone . . .

Bennilong, with a cry, leapt to his feet to follow. But the guards were afoot too, shouting, giving the alarm. They had him by the shoulders, and by the rope fastened to his leg, and there was no hope of escape now. He did not struggle, but stood tense like an animal, sweating and trembling with excitement. Not now. No, not now, but soon, he would go back to his own people. For a little while still he would remain, until the suspicions of the Bereewolgal were allayed, and their alertness slackened once again. Then he would do as his countryman had done; for, from childhood he had known that the ways of Colbee were good ways to follow.

1790

Cunnembeillee was unhappy, exhausted, and afraid. Life with the red-headed one was very hard. She had never imagined that any human being could be so consistently and savagely bad-tempered. He never laughed at all; he never made a joke. Once, when she had tried to amuse him and make him less heavy-hearted by performing a little dance which was one of the most popular comedies of her tribe, he had snarled at her, and struck her with a stick. Even when he summoned her to share his bed of ferns and the harsh, prickly coverings which he called blankets, she was forlornly aware that there was no real joy in his embrace. There must be a great sorrow in his heart, she thought, or he must have an enemy who is singing ill to him from some distant place, for it is not natural that a man should never laugh . . .

She had little to laugh about herself. Hardship, weariness, beatings, cold and hunger—these were all things which women must expect to endure sometimes. She was prepared for these. But loneliness was something which she had never imagined, and it was a continual weight of misery on her spirit. No matter what other trials a woman had to support, there would always be, so she had thought, the excitement of communal life about her, the coming and going of the warriors, the preparations for ceremonies and festivities, the delightful gossiping over camp matters with the other women, a new baby to be seen and admired, a death to mourn, a marriage to discuss.

But with her strange white husband it was not so. At first a few members of her tribe, upon hunting expeditions to the part of the river where she dwelt, would hail her and paddle across in their canoes for a few minutes' conversation, and then it was as if a weight of years fell from her shoulders, and she could not speak fast enough to say all that was in her thoughts, or laugh loudly enough to release the unbearable flood of joy in her heart. But her husband scowled at her people and spoke to them in a way which affronted them. He did not want them in his camp—that was clear. Cunnembeillee, heavy-hearted, knew that they would not come again. What a strange man was this An-droo, who kept

239

his whole life locked behind his sullen eyes, hoarding it to himself, as if life were not a gift which one shared with all one's fellow men, anguish and joy alike! Did he never rejoice? Did he know no songs? Sometimes he muttered to himself, but this could not be singing, she decided, for it was a bitter, angry sound, as if he were reviling someone, and his eyes looked frightened, as if he were seeing dreadful things.

If he had let her people visit her, she thought sadly, it would not have been so hard; they would have shared the spoil of their hunt when they found that there was so little in the white man's camp. For he did not seem to be very good at hunting himself, and mostly she had had to feed them both, and be beaten when there was not enough. Sometimes he killed birds by magic from his gooroobeera, but it was one of the many strange things about him that he did not appear to be a very successful sorcerer, for quite often when he pointed his weapon his prey escaped unharmed. Even when he was successful he seemed frightened of the noise it made. It was a very loud and startling noise, certainly, but Cunnembeillee could not understand, all the same, why, every time it shattered the silence he stared nervously about him, sometimes hiding and compelling her to hide with him for a long time afterwards.

But as the days passed he had seemed to grow bolder, and quite soon he was more successful, too. He had no less than three of the magic weapons now, for one day when she had gone farther afield than usual, following a wild bee to its hive, she had come upon two dead men. They were Bereewolgal and they wore very fine coverings of bright red; one was lying face downward with his gooroobeera beside him, and the other was half sitting against a rock, nursing his weapon across his knees. They were both very, very thin, and had a heavy growth of beard on their faces, but they had not been dead for many days, and it was cold weather, so Prentice, hastily summoned by Cunnembeillee, had been able to strip the bodies and take possession of the weapons. He had given one of the red coverings to Cunnembeillee. She had accepted it with awe, for it was more magnificent than anything she had ever seen, but she did not often wear it, for it was not comfortable and hampered her movements. Nevertheless, she guarded it with an almost passionate jealousy, and often she would sit with it across her bony knees, stroking it, fingering its buttons, admiring its rich colour, wondering how it had been fashioned. The red-headed one had made no attempt to bury or burn the bodies of his countrymen. That had astonished and shocked Cunnembeillee a good deal, but she knew better than to comment.

All through the cold weather they had lived on the banks of the river, and she had had to work very hard indeed to keep them both alive. She did not dare to criticise the inscrutable ways of her master, but she sometimes thought that they might have got on better if he had had no gooroobeera at all. The noise of it so frightened the ducks that they grew more and more shy; she had often felt tears smarting in her eyes, and pressed her fingers hard over her hollow stomach, watching them rise with a whirring of wings and disappear from sight; and she would wonder how it came about that a man did not know that quiet was needed to catch ducks—stealthy, patient movement to the river bank, practised swimming under water, a rise for breath now and then, so softly that the water hardly rippled about one's head, bound craftily with reeds and grasses . . .

Many times she had been just about to seize one when from around the next bend came that sharp and heart-stopping sound, and up went her prey almost from her hands, and she must swim back to the bank and return to be beaten for coming empty-handed.

But as his skill with the fire-breathing weapon increased, the red-headed one had grown less ill-tempered. Since the miracle of the beasts he had sometimes been almost jovial. That had been the most astonishing and the most terrifying thing which had ever happened to Cunnembeillee. One morning, when he was dozing in the sun and she was digging for roots by the river banks, she had heard an extraordinary noise, and had leapt to her feet, ready to run, her heart pounding with fear of the unknown. No bird or beast which she knew made such a sound as this low, mournful moaning which came from somewhere on the opposite bank. Then she had seen them—beasts which, to her one horrified glance, seemed larger than the largest kangaroo; beasts which went on all fours like a dingo, but which bore white, naked bones, curving upon their heads, and whose moaning noise now seemed a savage roaring which filled her ears like thunder.

She had dropped her basket with a yell and fled up the hillside to her protector. She cowered behind him, sobbing and chattering that evil spirits had come to destroy them. He was so quiet that at last her own terror calmed in wonder, so still that she took her hands away from her face and peered up at him. That look in his eyes! An exultation which hardly dared, yet, to own itself—an unbelieving joy—a dark, almost savage triumph!

Cattle, by God! Prentice could hear his heart thudding. The Governor's cattle which had been lost eighteen months earlier! Didn't he know them like his own hand, hadn't he tended them more than once before that fool had let them stray? Fool? He called down blessings on the head of the fool, and stared at the beasts hungrily as they stood in the reedy slush at the river bank, drinking thirstily. Two bulls, four cows, and four lusty calves, three of them heifers!

Then, through his elation, his wits had begun to work. These beasts were not starving; their sides were round and sleek, their coats glossy. Somewhere they had found good country. His first thought had been slaughter, and even now he felt the saliva rise in his mouth— How many years was it since he had tasted a red and juicy steak? That was the reaction of the habit which his life had fastened upon him—to grab while there was something within reach, never to deny himself an immediate respite, an immediate satisfaction of the senses; for who knew when another opportunity might come?

But, surprisingly, he had found himself checking that first lust of meat-hunger. He had become aware of something so strange that at first he was almost afraid to think of it. Now there was a future. The fact startled and blinded him; his brain began to grope painfully after its implications. When there was a future one must prepare for it, build for it, exert oneself for it. When there was a future, life became larger, the horizon receded, and one looked at it instead of at the patch of ground at one's feet, which had been all-sufficient before. When there was a future, hardship and struggle and endurance seemed not only to be bearable but even to arouse a queer, bitter exhilaration, and the transient pleasures, once so avidly sought and snatched, seemed unimportant.

He looked at the cattle and from them up and down the river, and behind him at the hills, climbing westward, and slowly he began to link this discovery of a future to the land. He was not, by that time, very apprehensive of recapture. Too many convicts had strayed, never to return, and there was no time for elaborate search parties. It would be assumed that he had perished of hunger, or been murdered by the blacks, and his name would be forgotten in the settlement. So he was free. And this was his country.

He did not like it any better than he had liked it before, but now he thought of it as no longer necessarily a gaol. He looked at the cattle and nodded his head slowly to himself. Two bulls, four cows, four fine calves, and—somewhere—a good pasture land. That was the beginning of his future.

They had followed the cattle, ambling idly and leisurely along the grassy flats. Cunnembeillee had been so frightened at first that she had several times tried to run away, so Prentice had tied a rope round her neck and driven her along in front of him, and in time she had lost some of her fear, so long as the beasts did not come too close. They were wild at first; even Prentice dared not approach them. The bulls lowered their heads and pawed the ground, the cows lifted mistrustful eyes, and the calves kept close to their mothers, nuzzling their warm flanks. But Prentice was patient. Where the cattle were, there was he, there was Cunnembeillee, there was the smoke of their fire and the smell of their human presence. After a time the animals hardly lifted their heads from feeding when the man passed, coming a little nearer each time.

* * *

Now Cunnembeillee had to confess that An-droo had been wiser than she, for there was good hunting in this place to which the beasts had led them. The grass grew green and high on the flats beside the river, and there were many ducks upon its surface, and many fish in its deeper pools, and many kangaroos in the surrounding hills. When they had arrived and she had realised that they were to make a camp here she had almost wept with joy, for the journey had been very hard. She was used to burdens, like all the women of her race, but the burdens which she had had to carry for the white man had worn the skin from her shoulders and bent her back so that it was agony to straighten it again. Now, she thought, at last, at last, there would be rest!

But no. All day there was work to do. All day the great, sharp hatchet gleamed in the sunlight, swung by the white man's powerful arm, and trees crashed, and their branches were hewn from them, and in a shaded hollow, buried among the frondy leaves of a wattle grove, a shelter grew up at which she stared sometimes, heavy-eyed and exhausted, wondering why a good bark mia-mia would not have served as well. Yet it was a very fine dwelling. Even the red-headed one himself could stand upright in it, and it withstood the fiercest wind, and when it rained not more than a few trickles found their way inside. Sometimes when she was not too tired and the man was out of sight, she would spend a few moments opening and shutting the door, and peering in at all the treasures which, with such labour, they had carried to the spot. For except at night when he called her, she was not allowed to go inside. She had her own bark mia-mia with its tiny fire burning before it, and the red coat of the dead soldier for its only furnishing.

When the hut was finished, there was still no rest. More trees were felled, more logs hewn. Now it was even harder, for sometimes they had to be dragged quite a long way, and the white man made a kind of

harness with his rope, and all day Cunnembeillee toiled. It was a yard
which he was making. She had learned many of his words by now.
It was a yard in which he might place the beasts while he slept, so that
they could not stray, and at last it was finished. Now, surely, there would
be rest.

But no again. The ground must be broken and turned over. By now
it was summer, and all day as Cunnembeillee worked she wondered at
the joyless life of this white man who was not content to have found a
pleasant towri, rich with food, but must toil and toil in the burning heat,
and make her toil, too, until she feared for the new life which was moving
in her body. For the birth-spirit had favoured her, and before the summer
died she would have borne her son.

*   *   *

There was only one thought in the minds of the colonists now, only
one topic of conversation wherever they gathered—in the Governor's
house, in the officers' quarters, in the marines' barracks or in the convicts'
huts— When would ships arrive from England with supplies? Down at
the outpost which Captain Hunter had established on South Head to
signal the arrival of ships to the anxiously waiting community, young
Daniel Southwell, lonely and bored, divided the endless days between
working in his garden and watching the ocean longingly for a sail.
Sometimes, with beating heart, he would stare at a white speck on the
horizon, straining his eyes, hoping against hope, only to recognise it at
last as a cloud, and turn back miserably to his digging.

Almost every day, at the cove, there were wild rumours, false alarms
which roused a delirium of excitement from which the exiles, disappointed yet again, sank back deeper than ever into despair. There was
only one walk which anyone ever bothered to take now, and it led along
the high ridge from Sydney Cove to South Head, and commanded many
fine views of the ocean. Here the Governor himself often walked with
Bennilong as his companion; there was a dreamlike strangeness, Bennilong thought sometimes, in this repetition in his life. Not even Wunbula,
his real father, had looked for a winged boat with greater longing and
persistence than did this other man to whom, also, he gave the title
Be-anga.

But no sail appeared. Once indeed, early in February, the flag ran
up, and there was a shock of joy in the settlement, quickly damped when
it was realised that it had only heralded the return of the *Supply* from
Norfolk Island. Phillip, who had sent home no less than seven separate

and urgent requests for at least two years' provisions, began to fear the almost unthinkable—that ships had indeed been sent, and had been lost. He realised then that he must take strong measures if his colony was to survive at all. The flour which they had brought with them from England was quite exhausted; they had now only that which Hunter had secured at the Cape—sufficient to last them for a few more months at most. Everyone in the settlement, including himself, was on short rations and he had been forced to halve the allowance of spirits. Starvation was an ugly thought, but even uglier, to the Governor, was the threat of panic and despair which he began to read in the eyes of his people. With the growing sense of being irrevocably cut off from the civilisation which had produced them, the veneer of discipline began to crack. The scanty produce of the gardens was more and more recklessly plundered. Lieutenant Clark, visiting his island down the harbour, found that thieves had dug up his potatoes. "I wish they were in hell for their kindness!" he wrote querulously in his journal, his belt drawn tighter than it had ever been before, and his Betsey momentarily forgotten in a sensuous longing for food.

There was nothing to be done, Phillip realised, but to divide forces. Norfolk Island, with its fertile soil, its vegetables, its abundance of birds, would support many more than it now held, and the resources of Sydney Cove might be thus husbanded for those who remained. Two companies of marines should go, he decided, and some two hundred convicts, men, women and children.

And Major Ross should take them. He weighed the pros and cons of this step with even more than his usual conscientious detachment, recognising the personal sense of liberation which would come to him with the removal of his Lieutenant-Governor. He made his decision without consulting any one, and announced it calmly, giving as his reason that he wished King to return to England to lay the whole position before the authorities. Then, having decided, he relaxed, allowing himself to savour his relief. For the Major had chosen this peculiarly difficult time in which to find himself insulted again. The old grievance about Collins and the convict, Thady, which everyone had thought finished with six months before, had been revived, and Phillip had felt his patience stretched to breaking point. His pain had been worrying him a good deal, the inadequate food ration was still further undermining his health, and he was becoming anxiously aware that there were moments when his own nerve was shaken, his own confidence wavering, his own serenity threatened. That was serious, even if no one suspected it but himself. Quite as a matter of course, he had accepted it as part of his leadership that the rest of the community should lean morally on him, and he knew what the result would be if his fortitude failed him, if he lost his temper and flayed Major Ross with the bitter words which had been so often boiling behind his tight-shut lips. He took stock of his strength, physical and mental, and realised with his usual good sense that the one must depend to a great extent upon the other. His physical condition he could do little to improve, but at least he could relieve his quite sufficiently harassed nerves of the continual additional wear and tear which was imposed upon them by his second-in-command.

As in the first February of their arrival, this February, too, was made miserable by continuous deluges of rain. The rough roads and tracks of the settlement became running gutters, the clear water of the cove was muddied, the houses of the officers leaked, the huts of the convicts collapsed, and White's surgical instruments rusted in their cases. "God help us," Ralph Clark wrote dejectedly, "if some ships don't arrive I don't know what we will do."

In this state of misery and despair the preparations went forward for the sailing of the *Sirius* and the *Supply*. The *Sirius,* it was decided, having landed her passengers at Norfolk Island, was to return post haste to Port Jackson, and then, if in the meantime no ships had yet arrived from England, she was to set out again upon another voyage to bring back stores from Batavia or Canton. When at last the two ships sailed early in March not much more than half the population remained, and depression settled down upon the hearts of the people. Tension, eased in some directions, had become intensified in others; friendships had been broken up, the communal life which had in those two long years welded itself laboriously into some kind of working order, was rudely disturbed. They had no heart for anything. They were exiled, forgotten, facing another winter, and always hungry. In the whole settlement, only Bennilong ate well (though not nearly well enough to satisfy himself), for Phillip feared to let him know the desperate straits to which the white people were reduced. March passed, the days growing cooler and the rain still pelting down. Phillip tried to rally the convicts to work upon the building of a new storehouse, but he was forced to realise that men half starved cannot work. And still the rations dwindled, and still no ships appeared.

In April the Governor made what he felt must be a last effort at conserving the food supply. Everyone must now live on less than half of a ration which had never been generous. Four pounds of flour a week, two and a half of salt pork, one and a half of rice. He met David Collins' eyes as he gave the order. Nothing was said; they both knew that now it was only a question of waiting for ships or for starvation.

* * *

There were rumours that the flag was flying on South Head. The people looked at each other warily, hiding their own faint glimmer of hope, but searching for it hungrily in the eyes of their companions. They said to each other with careful calm: "It's only the *Sirius,* or the *Supply.*" "About now they should be returning." "There's no cause for excitement." Nevertheless, such work as was in progress stopped; silently, under a mask of indifference, the settlement held its breath and waited.

Captain Tench hurried to Dawes' observatory on Point Maskelyne. Peering through the telescope he saw that the flag was indeed flying, but only one human being was to be seen—not leaping in the air with excitement as he would certainly have been if an unknown ship had been sighted, but strolling about near the flagstaff with every sign of unconcern. Tench, turning away with a sigh and a shrug, walked back to the head of the cove to report his observations to the Governor.

Phillip gave no sign of disappointment. If it was the *Sirius,* he thought, which was most likely, she must set out again almost immediately for China. He felt a stab of envy for Hunter, wishing that it could be his own lot to act instead of waiting here endlessly, schooling himself to present a calm face and an imperturbable air.

He said to Tench:

"Have them man my boat, if you please, Captain. I shall go down the harbour to meet them."

"May I go with you, Sir?"

Tench, carefully maintaining the attitude of one without a care in the world, understood and shared a mood in which action, even if it were only a brief excursion in a rowing-boat, seemed an alleviation of this dismal anti-climax. Fate, he felt, was behaving with a crude, an almost vulgar, animosity, against which the best defence a gentleman might set up was an unruffled serenity. As the seaman strained at their oars and the breeze whipped little white crests on the blue water, he clutched his hat brim and spoke cheerfully of King's return, and of the changes he would see when he landed in the settlement which he had left two years ago. Nevertheless, as they rounded the point which had hidden the lower reaches of the harbour from their view, he spoke again, and this time there was a sharp note of anxiety in his voice:

"Sir, prepare yourself for bad news . . ."

For a boat from the *Supply* was rowing towards them, and from his place in the bow Captain Ball was making gestures which could mean only disaster. . . .

The boats came together. The Governor saw nothing but Ball's face, puckered with distress and agitation; he gripped the gunwales hard and waited for the words he knew must come. For there could be only one calamity to bring the *Supply* back alone, to paint such misery on Ball's face, to hold the moment unendurably suspended thus, like a sword before it crashed upon one's head.

Ball stammered:

"The *Sirius,* Sir . . . I very much regret to report . . . wrecked . . . no loss of life, Sir . . . off Norfolk Island on the nineteenth, Sir . . ."

* * *

Now there was only the *Supply*. That was the thought in the mind of every officer who attended the council which Phillip called that evening in his house. A ship of one hundred and seventy-two tons was now their only link with the outside world; King, sitting next to the Governor, thought gloomily that she was a very insubstantial link—an ill-sailing little vessel, far too small ever to have been sent upon so long and hazardous a voyage. He was tired. His thoughts were still obsessed by Norfolk Island, and by the memories of those last days of consternation, struggle and confusion. There had been such joy on the morning when the two ships were sighted; he himself had been awakened by the sound of cheering, and he had dressed and hurried out with the one thought in his mind that at last vessels must have arrived at Port Jackson from England, at last news was to reach them, after nearly three years without a word from their native land.

The shock of his disappointment was still fresh in his memory. He had stood reading Phillip's letters which Ball had handed to him, and he had known that the news was flying from mouth to mouth, that all over the island men were saying to each other in apprehension and dismay: "No ships from home yet." "The Governor has sent over more people." "They're near starving at Sydney Cove." "We're to have Major Ross in command."

Five days of hard work landing stores and people—and then disaster. Hunter had toiled desperately to save his ship. King's memory still held a picture of his face just after he had been dragged ashore on the "traveller" through the surf; bruised, dazed, half-drowned, he had pushed aside the hands of those who sought to support him and stared with a kind of incredulity at what remained of the *Sirius,* pounding on the reef.

King shielded his eyes from the lamplight with his hand, only half listening to the grave voices of his brother officers. He was still seeing pictures—martial law on the island, marines patrolling the beach to guard such stores as were washed in, anxious conclaves between himself, Ross, Hunter, and Ball. Two convicts going out to the wreck to fling the livestock overboard. Lieutenant Clark hysterically belabouring a convict with a stick. Smoke going up from the *Sirius*—"Look! They've set her afire!" The young convict carpenter, Arscott, struggling heroically out through the surf to extinguish the flames . . .

He rubbed his hand over his eyes and sat up, trying to fix his mind upon what Phillip was saying. It was Major Ross' duty now to worry about Norfolk Island; that fact made him feel unaccountably forlorn. He looked round the room. He had been, as Tench had foretold, deeply interested in the changes which had taken place here at Sydney Cove since he had left it two years ago. The thick forest which had clothed the shores down to the water's edge had retreated, and a township had sprung up, dominated by the Governor's house. The soldiers were in barracks, and the sick in a temporary hospital building. Many of the officers had quite good houses made of bricks from the local kilns, or of plastered logs, and there was even a pottery . . .

With an effort he fixed his mind on the serious matters which were being discussed. The Governor, looking even sallower and slighter than when King had last seen him, was leaning forward over the table playing with a pen, and keeping his eyes on it as he outlined their position.

"On our present ration, then, gentlemen, the stores contain sufficient salt meat to serve us until the 2nd July. We shall have flour until about the twentieth of August, and rice or peas until October. I need not tell you, for we all know it too well, that the quality of this food is no more satisfactory than its quantity. . . ."

He broke off, glanced up, and then down again at his pen, unable to meet the eyes of these men whose worn uniforms already hung upon them loosely. Pork between three and four years old, he thought; rice which literally crawled . . .

He went on briskly:

"Nevertheless, we can and must supplement this food with fish, and for that purpose I propose that all boats, both public and private, be engaged in fishing. Also that the best marksmen among us must be employed in hunting kangaroos, which, when secured, must be delivered to the Commissary."

He paused again, and then said, slowly:

"And we shall have to reduce the ration still farther. I propose to order that in future two pounds of pork, two and a half of flour, two of rice or a quart of peas shall be issued every week to every grown person in the settlement, and to every child over the age of eighteen months." In the dead silence which followed, he turned to look at Ball, sitting with his hands in his pockets and his chin on his breast. "And you, Lieutenant Ball, must make the *Supply* ready to leave as soon as possible for Batavia."

"Yes, Sir."

There seemed no more to be said. The land held them as in a vice, helpless. If succour were to come, it must come from over the sea, for the land, aloof and dispassionate, would yield them nothing. It would watch them die and take their bones into its earth, and reclothe their deserted settlement with its quiet, gaunt trees, and remain undisturbed in its ancient tranquillity.

Soberly, in subdued voices, avoiding each other's eyes, they bade the Governor good-night, and left him.

* * *

A week or so later, when the *Supply* was almost ready to sail, Phillip settled down to his correspondence. It was like living his troubles over again to record them in such detail; he chafed at the necessity, wishing that he could put them behind him, wipe them from his mind, conserving his mental energy to meet the critical and perhaps tragic future.

From where he sat with his papers spread about him, he could see the *Supply* lying at anchor in the cove, and for days, during pauses in the writing or dictation of his letters, he found his eyes drawn to her anxiously, his fears for her forming a background to his written words.

"I have had the honour of informing your Lordship that the *Sirius* and the *Supply* sailed the 6th March. The *Supply* returned to this port the 5th April, when I received the following account from Captain Hunter respecting the loss of His Majesty's ship *Sirius*. . . ."

So long as a vessel lay there in the cove, one had an irrational feeling of security. It was when the harbour was empty that the feeling of being marooned oppressed the settlement. Before, when the *Supply* had been absent at Norfolk Island, and the *Sirius* on her way to the Cape, and the cove had been left for the first time deserted, there had been a continual uneasiness among the people lest accident should befall both vessels. Now, with only one left, and that one the little *Supply,* anxiety would be redoubled, confidence even harder to maintain. . . .

"Dear Nepean,
    "Lieutenant King will give you this letter, and can inform you particularly of the situation in which he leaves us.
    "Two years' good conduct and perseverance, exerted for the public good, will, I hope, give him a step in the Navy; and if ever you want to employ an officer where patience and exemplary conduct is requisite you will thank me for pointing him out."

Patience and exemplary conduct. That applied, thank Heaven, not only to King, but to Ball, in command of the *Supply*—to Ball, on whom, now, all their hopes must be concentrated. . . .

"The Commissary who was appointed for this colony through your friendship has acted so unlike the Commissary that he has lost his health, and in three years has never made three shillings. . . . I warmly recommend him to your interest with Lord Sydney for some stipend however small. If he lives to reach England I hope he will meet with your countenance. . . ."

He felt a superstitious chill, and checked it sternly. It was of Andrew Miller's health he had been thinking, but now, staring through the window at the *Supply,* he realised that there might be another reason for his not living to reach England. . . .

"My Lord,
    "Tho' I seldom have an opportunity of assuring your Lordship of my respects, when it offers I embrace it with pleasure. . . . As the settlement is now fixed, whenever His Majesty's service permits, I shall be glad to return to England, where I have reason to suppose my private affairs may make my presence necessary; but which I do not ask in any publick letters, nor should I mention a desire of leaving this country at this moment, but that more than a year must pass before it can possibly take place. . . ."

Much more than a year, probably. And in the meantime the pain grew worse, the attacks more frequent. Now they were endurable; now he could still carry on his work—but by then . . .

"Dear Nepean,
    "The *Supply* will sail immediately, and the necessity of sending to Batavia for provisions will, I presume, be obvious; I do it more from being

persuaded that some accident must have prevented the ships arriving.
. . . I have exprest a wish to return to England when the service permits,
a request I should not have made at this moment but that the inconveniences under which the colony now labours will be done away long
before my letters can reach England, and more than a year must pass before I can have any answer. . . . I should have no objection to return
here . . . but to come to England for a twelve month is what I wish, for
many reasons . . .

"Dismal accounts will, I make no doubt, be sent to England, but we
shall not starve, though seven-eighth of the colony deserves nothing better. . . ."

Phillip smiled to himself rather grimly. All over the settlement at this
moment, here and at Rose Hill and at the South Head outpost pens must
be busy. It was not difficult to imagine the tenor of the letters which the
Supply would bear away across the ocean!

"The inclosed account will shew the provisions remaining in the settlement, and the time for which the different species will last. . . . I have
thought it necessary to be thus particular, . . . as I think it probable that
report may make our situation more unpleasant than it really is. . . ."

Not if he could prevent it would all this effort and endurance be
wasted! Not if words of his could influence them should the authorities
uproot this sickly offshoot of their country, struggling for survival in an
inhospitable earth! He had sown the seed, he had tended and cherished
the plant, and he believed with all his heart that it would live to reach
maturity. Let him but keep sap running in it, and the seeds which fell
from it would fall not on alien, but on native soil.

*   *   *

Surgeon White had no such belief. In his energetic and intensely practical brain, facts alone were welcomed, and such facts as he had observed
during his sojourn at Port Jackson had served only to convince him that
no more God-forsaken spot existed upon the whole face of the globe.
He condemned it officially, and hated it privately; sitting in his house
a day or two before the *Supply* was to sail, he recorded his feelings and
convictions with characteristic and uncompromising vigour:

". . . a country and place," he wrote, emphatically, "so forbidding and
so hateful as only to merit execration and curses, for it has been a source
of expence to the mother country and of evil and misfortune to us, with-

out there ever being the smallest likelihood of its repaying or recompencing either. From what we have already seen we may conclude that there is not a single article in the whole country that in the nature of things could prove of the smallest use or advantage to the mother country or the commercial world. In the name of Heaven what has the Ministry been about? Surely they have quite forgotten or neglected us otherwise they would have sent to see what had become of us, and to know how we were likely to succeed. However, they must soon know from the heavy bills which will be presented to them, and the misfortunes and losses which have already happened to us, how necessary it becomes to relinquish a scheme that in the nature of things can never answer. It would be wise by the first step to withdraw the settlement . . ."

He paused, laying down his pen and opening and shutting his hand to ease his fingers, cramped by long and rapid writing. His indignation had mounted as he wrote; in this mood he could have faced the Secretary of State, the Lords Commissioners of the Treasury, and the Lords of the Admiralty, all in a body, and poured his scorn upon them for thus wasting the public moneys. Botany Bay! Swamps and sandhills! Port Jackson! Picturesque enough, indeed, but can men fill their bellies with scenery? Norfolk Island! A place, as the French Commanders had said, "only fit for angels and eagles to reside in."

"The *Supply* tender sails to-morrow for Batavia, in hopes that the Dutch may be able to send in time to save us; should any accident happen to her, Lord have mercy upon us. . . ."

His brain made sharp professional pictures for him as he wrote. The food would dwindle and dwindle; one man after another would collapse, one woman after another would be borne into his hospital, needing nothing that his skill could give her. Children, huge-eyed and skeleton limbed, would stare up at him and die. There would come a time when he could make not even a pretence of helping them. There would come a time when none was even strong enough to bury the dead, and they would lie under this blue, bright sky with the living beside them, and you would scarce be able to tell which . . .

Yes, he thought, throwing his pen down, his face dark with anger, Lord have mercy on us then!

* * *

Bennilong was hungry. For a long time now he had not had what he considered to be an adequate meal. He stared in astonishment at the meagre rations which the white men ate, and wondered if perhaps they were coming to the end of the Be-anga's store of food. There could be no doubt, he thought, observing them curiously, that they were anxious, for everyone went fishing these days, even the leaders of the tribe, Collins, whom he regarded now as a particular friend, and Tench, the smiling one, and White, and those others who also had the power of healing; yes, even the moon-faced one who conducted the weekly corroboree (a very inferior corroboree, dull, spiritless, always drearily the same), and many of the warriors in the red coats. All the boats were out every day and often at night, too, and many watched for their return, pleased by a good catch or disheartened by a poor one.

Also they sent out hunting parties. Bennilong was not sure whether it was because they were very poor hunters or because their weapons were inadequate that they returned so often emptyhanded. Indeed, in more ways than these, there seemed to be changes in the life of the Bereewolgal. It seemed that not only their food but their supply of clothes was becoming exhausted. The red-coated ones, who had at first been so resplendent, now looked shabby and faded, and when they gathered to perform their own peculiar corroboree there were many of them who went barefooted. Among the inferior tribe (whose members, Bennilong had learned by now, were malefactors who had violated the laws of their tribe) many were half naked, and every day their women were to be seen sitting outside their huts sewing at their garments so that they should not fall in pieces.

Nor did they work any longer as they had worked before. It was as if they were all ill, and Bennilong wondered sometimes if they were about to be smitten with some sickness, such as that which had wrought such havoc among his own people. But they showed none of the signs of that particular evil. They only sat about looking miserable. They seemed to have no heart even for talking any more. They were like . . .

A thought came to Bennilong now which disturbed him considerably. They were like men at whom the bone is being pointed. Among his own people this dreadful thing happened now and then. An enemy afar held the bone pointed in the direction of him whose death he desired, singing a malevolent magic, and slowly and quite inevitably the victim died. He grew dull and listless, even as these people were growing. He lost his zest for life and the light went out of his eyes, and after a time he lay down quietly in his mia-mia and turned his face away, and the life went out of his body.

Was it possible that a whole tribe might die thus? Was it to escape some malignant foe that they had left their own land, and were they now being pursued by his evil machinations from across the ocean itself? Bennilong walked uneasily among the dwellings of the white men, torn between his vanity which was so flattered by the consequence which he enjoyed here, and the heavy sense of doom which to his sharp perceptions seemed to hang like a thundercloud above the place.

More and more he felt it, and looked with bewilderment at the Be-anga who still moved among his afflicted people with every appearance of tranquillity. One day, standing near the storehouse while the ration was being issued, he saw a man come out, staggering. His clothes were tattered, his feet bare, his eyes glaring wildly in a face whose skin was stretched tightly over the bones, and he was clutching his food as if he feared that someone was about to wrest it from him. Bennilong stared at him, and Captain Tench, who was passing, stopped, too, arrested by the man's desperate appearance. Surely, thought Bennilong, death is very near to this unhappy man! Yes! He took a few paces and fell, sprawling face downward, his precious burden spilled by his side. Called by Captain Tench, a couple of men hurried up and carried him off to the hospital, where Bennilong, overcome by curiosity, followed. The man, he heard presently, was indeed dead. Later, listening to a conversation between Tench and White, he learned that White had opened the man's body and found his stomach to be completely empty.

Bennilong went away shaking his head. What was the good of all the white men's magic if it could not fill their bellies? What was the good of all their possessions, all their knowledge, if they were going to die because their stomachs were empty? He was worried. Here were a people to whom he had accorded an admiration not less fervent for being mixed with some envy and some hostility, and it looked very much as if they were going to fail ignominiously in the only true test of tribal virility—survival. Were these a people to respect? Were they a tribe with which a notable warrior, a renowed hunter might fraternise? And, even more serious, might he not starve himself if he did not soon make his escape and return to his own tribe, in which such matters were so much more sensibly arranged?

Yes, he was hungry—and not only for food. All his being seemed one vast hunger which nothing in the camp of the Duggerigai could assuage. He was hungry for the companionship of his own people, hungry for laughter, hungry for the excitement of the hunt, hungry for the rich spiritual fulfilment of the corroboree. He was hungry for love, too, and his thoughts turned continually to Odooroodah, who had bitten his hand, and sometimes even to Barangaroo. Above all, he was hungry for freedom and he began to sink into a melancholy periodically ripped and shattered by violent outbursts of rage.

Escape was not easy. He slept in the Be-anga's house, and an attendant always slept with him, and the window was too far from the ground for a leap, in any case. He thought the whole matter over carefully, and one cold morning in the autumn, long before the dawn began to lighten the sky, he awakened his gaoler with groans.

"Weeree!" he moaned, clutching his stomach and rolling his eyes wildly. "In belly bad! Yapallun! Yapallun!"

The white man grunted irritably and pulled his blankets closer about him. Bennilong lifted his voice in vociferous lamentation:

"Come! Come! Bennilong moo-la-ly—in belly bad, bad! Out go! Kai kai karakai!"

His attendant, cursing, stumbled sleepily to his feet, shivering and clutching his blanket about his shoulders. The damned Indian, he thought angrily, would awaken the Governor with his clamour. . . .

"All right, all right, blast ye for a black heathen! Hold y' noise for Gawd's sake or you'll have 'is Excellency wantin' to know what for. Come on and be damned to ye! Hurry up!"

They stole down the stair and out into the velvety darkness, Bennilong warily alert, but remembering to emit, now and then, a blood-curdling groan; the white man still half asleep and growling sullenly to him to make haste.

It was done in a moment. He was gone almost before his startled keeper had time to force his sagging eyelids open. He was over the low fence, running, running, his eyes on the friendly darkness of the bush, his ears full of the shouts which were announcing his escape. Once among the trees he felt safer; it was as if his land were opening sheltering and protecting arms to him, and before he had gone far he paused to drag off his clothes. He stood in the darkness stretching his naked body, enjoying the sharp cold of the air on his skin, and the unrestricted movement of his limbs. He was grinning to himself, thinking how he had outwitted his guard, and what a fine story it would make to tell the tribe, and how well he would recount it, and how greatly they would all admire him. He rehearsed the tale as he went, carrying his bundle of discarded clothes under his arm, trying his words over and over as a good youara-gurrugin should, stretching graphic pictures with his hands, feeling care and uneasiness fall from his spirit as the clothes had fallen from his body. Wau! The Bereewolgal might be clever, but they were no match for Bennilong!

Phillip only shrugged when he heard of it. A few months ago he would have been disappointed, now the subtraction from the colony of one who could eat the share of six at a meal and still remain unsatisfied, might not be regarded as altogether a misfortune. All his attention and all his energy were directed towards a last desperate effort to hold the colony together, to keep alive a glimmer of hope, and with it a semblance of discipline. Convicts scratching feebly at the soil in a half-hearted effort to prepare the ground for crops which they would probably never live to sow, saw his slight, straight figure moving about among them, planning and directing as if it were life which lay ahead rather than a miserable and lingering death. Rats and crows—even dogs—went into the cooking pot these days. The supply of salt failed, and two large iron boilers were set up on the eastern point of the cove to supply the deficiency from the sea water. Fishing lines wore out; profiting by a knowledge he had picked up from his native captives, Phillip set a convict rope-maker to fashioning new ones from the bark of a tree. Once two hundred pounds of fish were caught; once, through carelessness or the ineptitude of weakness and despair, half of a good haul was lost. Every day the weather grew colder, and every day the defeat which he read in the faces of his people struck a new chill to the Governor's heart. Three hundredweight of flour, which was his own personal property, he had given into the general store, and at his own table no more was served than in the convicts' huts.

May, that month so lovely and so lauded in their homeland, dragged to a miserable end, and June came in tempestuously with wind and rain and a menacing foretaste of winter. Huddled under the grey veil of the rain, the settlement looked deserted, for no one stirred from such shelter as he had. The Governor, in his house, sat with one hand to his side and made notes for his next despatch with the other. David Collins wrote up his journal and wondered what would become of it when he was dead. Mrs. Johnson held her three-months-old daughter in her arms and prayed, but not very hopefully. Surgeon White fidgeted about his hospital doing unnecessary things because inactivity drove him to fury. In the barracks soldiers swore and quarrelled and pulled their belts tighter. In her hut Ellen Prentice looked apathetically at Maria and wondered if she was going to die, and Johnny watched his chance and stole a piece of bread while her back was turned.

Then, on the third day of June, to Captain Tench, sitting alone and wondering ruefully if he was, after all, not to live to recount his adventures, there came the sound of shouting. He leapt to his feet, his heart thudding with excitement. Had he heard aright? Was it his longing for just those words which had inspired his imagination to believe he heard them? He rushed to his doorway and looked out; the street was alive with people, stumbling madly about in the rain. Women were sobbing hysterically, hugging babies in their arms, raining kisses on their heads. Ankle deep in mud the children capered unrebuked, and from every mouth the same jubilant cry was heard: "The flag's up!" "The flag's up."

Captain Tench did not even wait to snatch up his hat. He ran as he had never run before, the rain beating on his bare head and streaming down his face, the mud splashing from his feet on to his flying coat tails. On the hill near the observatory he took out his pocket glass with hands that shook, and peered through it. It was true. On South Head the flag was flying. He became aware that Dawes was beside him. They stood wringing each other by the hand, speechless, laughing, choking, the wind whipping their hair and the rain streaming down their faces so that it did not matter if a tear or two went with it.

* * *

When the *Lady Juliana,* as forerunner of the Second Fleet, arrived in Port Jackson in June 1790, Patrick Mannion was six years old. He did not know why his parents should have chosen to leave the big, tree-shaded home in Ireland which he quite clearly remembered, but he was glad, on the whole, that they had done so. He had occasionally (but not often) felt bored by the seeming endlessness of the ocean, and for a time he had been ill. His mother had not seemed to like the voyage at all. She had wept, and he had heard her say to his father: "I cannot endure it, Stephen," in a strange voice which frightened him at the time, though now it was only an uncomfortable memory. He did not know what "endure" meant, and he supposed that, whatever it was, his father or one of the officers had done it for her. Ladies, as he knew, were not very strong. Men had to carry chairs for them, and fetch sunshades, and open doors, and he did not find it strange or alarming when, as they neared the end of the voyage, his mother was permanently confined to her cabin, and only appeared on deck, looking pale and tremulous, upon that rapturously exciting day when the ship at last sailed between the two vast, rocky headlands of the harbour, and he knew that they had arrived.

It was a wild, wet afternoon, and Patrick stood on a sheltered portion of the deck with his parents, well muffled in his little greatcoat, and peered through the rain at the high cliffs between which the captain was cautiously working his way into the harbour. The surf was breaking against them, high and white and feathery. The canvas flapped and bellied in the wind, the rigging strained and creaked. The great swell of the slate-coloured water rose like hills and sank away like valleys before the bow of the ship, and once, peering down into it, Patrick saw a vast shadowy shape swim up out of the depths, and a black triangle cut the surface for a moment, and his father pointed at it and said it was a shark.

Up on one of the headlands a flag was flying, but there was no other sign of human habitation. The dark foreshores of the harbour were dimmed by rain, and the gulls, wheeling and swooping over the rigging kept up a harsh, wild, plaintive crying which, forever afterwards, Patrick was to associate with that day and scene.

Suddenly they saw a boat. It came into sight round one of the headlands of the harbour, and instantly the rails were crowded, and Patrick felt a queer, ashamed sense of relief, because, hidden deeply in his mind, there had been the faintest shadow of a suspicion that they must have come to the wrong place, for indeed it did not look as if anyone lived here at all.

The boat they had seen was presently joined by another, but after a time this second one disappeared round the headland again, and the first began to pull strongly towards them. Patrick was a warm-hearted and sociable little boy, and when it approached near enough for him to see the people in it he was delighted to observe the wild excitement with which they hailed the ship.

"They seem very glad to see us, Papa," he said, happily, waving his hand in response to the frantic salutations of a young man who was standing in the stern, flourishing his hat above his head, and exhorting the oarsmen to still greater efforts.

"Pull away, my lads!" Patrick heard him call out, "She is from Old England! A few strokes more and we shall be on board."

A wild cheer went up, echoed by the people, who lined the rails of the ship, and another voice from the boat shouted: "Hurrah for a bellyful, and news from our friends!"

It was very delightful indeed, Patrick thought, to be so welcomed. When the men came on board it seemed that they could not talk fast enough to get out all the questions which they wanted answered. The excitement of the passengers at having reached their destination was as nothing to the excitement of the inhabitants in greeting them.

After they had spoken for a time with the Captain, the young man who had waved his hat, and another gentleman who had been with him in the boat, were introduced to Patrick's parents as Captain Tench of the marines, and Captain Collins, secretary to the Governor. By that time, Tench had recovered something of his sang-froid. He bowed very gallantly over Mrs. Mannion's hand, and assured her that her charming presence would go far towards enlivening the society of Sydney Cove. She smiled at him and asked a little apprehensively:

"But is it, then, so dull, Captain?"

Tench made a faint, but comical grimace.

"It has been worse than dull, my dear Mrs. Mannion. But all that will be changed now." He turned to her husband. "You bring us much-needed relief, Sir; we have been—in sight of starvation."

Patrick was horrified. Starvation? Not enough to eat? He stared up incredulously at the lean young man in the faded uniform, beneath whose irreproachable manners a queer, primitive excitement still seemed to be bubbling. These were gentlemen—gentlemen *always* had enough to eat. Poor people, sometimes, did not, and then, if they were what was called "deserving," one's mother sent them soup and blankets and flannel petticoats, and one's father gave them money from time to time. Perhaps he had not heard correctly, or had not understood; he edged closer to listen. His father was speaking of the *Guardian* now—the store-ship which had struck the ice, and had been disabled. Patrick had heard all about this when they lay at the Cape of Good Hope, but he had not realised before that she had been bringing food to this place when it happened.

"Two years' provisions, I understand, Captain," his father was saying, "clothing, of course, medicines, blankets, fifteen casks of wine, and a large quantity of tools and implements. She should have reached you in February. Nothing could have been more unfortunate."

Patrick thought that Captain Tench looked at his father a little queerly, but he only agreed politely:

"Nothing, indeed."

"We heard, also, that there was a good number of animals on board— horses, cows, goats, deer, I believe, too . . . you have hunting here, Captain, no doubt? Is the sport good?"

Captain Tench replied rather shortly:

"We have hunted only for food, Sir, and then it has been too serious to be amusing. You were saying . . . About the livestock on the *Guardian* . . ."

"Ah, yes. Of course, they had to be destroyed when the ship struck. It was a miracle that Lieutenant Riou was able to get the vessel safe to the Cape. It appears that the convicts he was carrying behaved uncommonly well—no doubt the rascals realised it was their only hope. . . ."

"I understand you were able to bring some of her stores, however, Mr. Mannion?"

"Some, yes. But I should not suppose, Captain, that such as we bring could do more than lessen your want for a time, for we carry some two hundred and twenty female convicts ourselves. . . ."

Patrick, his bright, observant eyes on Captain Tench's face, felt a little disturbed. It was a pity, when he had been so very glad to see them, that every word his father uttered should seem to strike a little more of the joy from his face.

". . . and I am told," Stephen Mannion went on, "that a thousand more convicts were despatched towards the end of last year. I should imagine that their arrival was imminent. No doubt you have, by now, been able to make suitable arrangements for receiving them. They would, of course, bring their own stores . . ."

"Of course," agreed Captain Tench. He looked quite expressionless now, and, as he seemed to have nothing further to say, Patrick pulled shyly at his sleeve.

"Would you show me, Sir, where the town is?"

Captain Tench looked at him for a moment as if he were blind, or perhaps thinking very hard about something else. Then he bent down and pointed up the harbour.

"It is not a very large town," he explained, "and it is hidden from view in one of the bays on the southern shore up there. I hope you will not be disappointed when you see it, Patrick."

"I'm sure I shall not, Sir," Patrick said politely.

* * *

The Governor went away alone and shut himself into his room to read his first despatch from England:

"His Majesty is graciously pleased to approve of your conduct. . . ."

His eyes hurried over the opening phrases. It was not approval he wanted, but help.

"The unfortunate women on board the *Lady Juliana* . . . you will cause them to be employed in such a manner as may be conducive to the advantage of the settlement. . . . You will see by the enclosed invoice and bill of lading . . ."

Ah, here was the kind of news he wanted!

". . . the several tools and implements, articles of clothing, provisions, etc., which have been put on board the *Lady Juliana*. That ship will be followed in about a fortnight by His Majesty's ship the *Guardian*. . . ."

Phillip's tongue clicked on his palate in a sharp, involuntary sound of nervous irritation. The *Guardian,* beached at Table Bay! He read on, his fingers tapping on the table beside him:

"By the last-mentioned ship you will receive a farther supply equal to about three times the quantity embarked on board the former . . . as these stores and provisions have been procured at a very considerable expense, it is to be hoped that you will appropriate them to the best possible advantage."

There was, for a second, the shadow of a wry smile about the Governor's mouth as he read this plaintive sentence. How little, he thought, was understood of their plight at home, if it were imagined that food might be wasted at Sydney Cove! But the next paragraph wiped the smile from his lips, and left them grim:

"In the course of the autumn I expect that about 1000 more convicts of both sexes will be embarked from the several gaols and despatched to Port Jackson . . . you should make arrangements for their accommodation, as well as for their employment, on their arrival."

The little tattoo, which the Governor's fingers were still beating on the table, ceased. He sat back in his chair and looked out the window towards the cove, where the *Lady Juliana* with her freight of "unfortunate women" lay at anchor. Accommodation, when even now the shelter which they had for those who had arrived with the First Fleet was inadequate! Employment, when many of the women were either too ill or too old to work!

He skimmed the rest of the letter hastily, the spectre of those useless hordes which were soon to invade his settlement standing dark and mountain-high behind all his thoughts. For the first time, in the sudden relaxation from strain which the arrival of the *Lady Juliana* had caused, he was stabbed by doubt and despair. He saw his colony, for a few agonising moments, not as the beginning of a human achievement, but as the climax and culmination of human degradation. His imagination, sharpened by distress, showed it to him developing as the years went by into a squalid, crime-infested seaport whose name stank in the nostrils of every decent seafaring man, a vice-ridden community of thieves and criminals, a refuse-heap on to which the civilised nations of the world would fling their outcasts.

For he himself, he knew now, could not hold out much longer. Lately he had been hardly ever free of pain. When he was, it was a doubtful freedom for it was during these respites that his body became aware of its exhaustion, and forced him to realise that he could not for long remain equal to his task. And if the task were to be thus continuously and mercilessly multiplied, allowing him no breathing space . . .

There was no hope now. None. He could not keep pace with such a deluge of useless humanity. He could not build from it. As fast as he built, imposing his pattern of order and integrity, shiftlessness, ignorance and vice would appear like cracks in his edifice, threatening destruction. He threw the letter down and went across to the window, looking not at the cove, stirred suddenly like an ant-heap to seething activity, but beyond it to the opposite hillside. Unconsciously, he was seeking reassurance where he had found it before, and unconsciously he absorbed it again from the quiet serenity of a land which had never been in a hurry over its evolutionary processes. It rebuked, with its silence and its calm, his feverish impatiences. When he turned away from the window again his moment of despair was over.

*   *   *

Patrick was not exactly disappointed in the town. He saw the habitations of the strange community to which he had come with the uncritical, accepting eyes of sheltered childhood. It did occur to him, surveying the hillside which sloped up from the bay, that it was indeed a very small town—more like a village, really—and he did glance once at his mother (who looked alarmingly frail after the long voyage, and leaned heavily upon his father's arm), and wonder if she would like being here as well as in Ireland. There was, so far as he could see, only one house which looked really like a house, and that was the Governor's. It stood in a clearing on the eastern side of the cove, and the woods pressed in upon it from behind in a dark semicircle. It had a patch of garden in front of it, but there did not seem to be much growing there. It was surrounded by a fence, a straight path ran down from it to the water's edge, a little landing jutted out into the water, and there was a flagstaff before it with a flag hanging dejectedly, its challenging red and its royal blue faded by the sun to ghosts of their former glory. Patrick, who was to remain all his life very susceptible to visual impressions and very apt to be plunged by them into sharp and surprising emotions, felt, in the five minutes which he spent staring at the Governor's house, something which was partly excitement and partly grief.

It was such a very plain house; its straight lines, its two symmetrical chimneys, its five upstairs windows arranged with soldierly precision, gave it a certain dignity which was instantly overwhelmed by the greater dignity of the dark and silent trees behind it. There was grief in this scene somewhere, though Patrick, like a sensible child, was content to feel without understanding it. He was aware of a conflict already begun in which the house and all it stood for would be, inevitably, not vanquished, but absorbed; and he was aware, too, of excitement—and awful exhilaration that the House should dare to challenge the Trees, and should thus, square and solid, await and even invite a destiny which they and not it would shape.

The other houses, to which he next turned his attention, were, for the most part, merely huts. Their ugliness and their squalor did not shock or even surprise him, for he had been accustomed, in Ireland, to hovels quite as bad as these. It seemed natural to him that poor people should live in such places and go hungry, but he did find it hard to realise that here not only in the huts, but in the house of the Governor himself there had not been, for months past, enough to eat.

The settlement, so he heard Captain Collins telling his mother, had just come through the most bitter period of its whole precarious existence, and indeed there was not one of its inhabitants who did not bear traces of anxiety and privation. The Governor was thin; his complexion, under the tan which his outdoor life had lent it, had a toxic pallor, and there were deep lines between his brows for which worry and intermittent physical pain were equally responsible. The Reverend Mr. Johnson wore a permanent expression of vaguely astonished resentment, as if, though trained to Christian fortitude, he had never really expected to be forced to practise it. Young Mr. Southwell, whom duty at the lonely flagstaff had recently debarred from even such poor amusements as the settlement afforded, looked like a sulky and undernourished child, and even the debonair Captain Tench was a little subdued.

Patrick, an attentive if disregarded listener, learned that heavy rains had done much to damage the mud-plastered houses; that shooting parties went out hunting animals called kangaroos, which hopped instead of ran; that all the officers, even Mr. Johnson, helped with the fishing; that the Governor had given up his private store of flour so that all might share alike; and that the elegant Captain Tench, toasting his bit of three-year-old salt pork over the fire, always took great pains to catch the precious drops of fat which fell from it upon a piece of bread. He learned also that at the height of their misery a very dreadful thing had happened—a ship called the *Sirius* had been wrecked at a place called Norfolk Island. He was not quite clear why this was such a disaster, particularly as it seemed that no one had been drowned, but he realised from his father's head-shakings and his mother's little shocked exclamations, that it must have been very serious indeed.

He was considerably puzzled to learn that the country afforded next to nothing in the way of foodstuffs, for this did not seem to fit with what he had already been told about a native called Bennilong who had been living with the Governor, but who had become so distressed by the shortage of food in the settlement that he had left it and returned to the woods, where, presumably, he was able to satisfy his hunger.

It was to receive news, however, rather than to give it, that the colonists besieged the newcomers, and Patrick was soon confirmed in his suspicion that their tidings were not as welcome as themselves. They had not only to report the loss of the storeship *Guardian,* but the impending arrival of a great many more convicts. Patrick, who was standing near Captain Collins when he received this news and, gazing up at his tarnished epaulettes, saw his mouth tighten and his brows draw together; and he saw Mr. White, the surgeon, turn away abruptly with a lift of his shoulder, and say something under his breath to Captain Tench which caused that gentleman to raise his eyebrows and throw out his hands with a despairing gesture.

It seemed, Patrick decided seriously, that nobody really wanted the convicts; and for the first time he began to think of them and to wonder why, if they were so wicked, and such a trouble to feed and look after, they had been brought at all? He had been told during the voyage that the strange looking women whom he occasionally saw, but to whom he was never allowed to speak, were convicts, which meant wicked people. But were they really people? Patrick began to have serious doubts about this when, a few weeks later, the Second Fleet arrived, and he saw some of them disembarking.

On the 20th of June the storeship *Justinian* had cast anchor in the cove; with its coming, and the restoration of full rations, the settlement became, for a little while, almost a jolly place, and Patrick had been just about to decide that he might come to like being here when the *Neptune,* the *Scarborough* and the *Surprise* arrived.

That altered things. It was because there were so many convicts on board, and nobody wanted them. Patrick found himself left a good deal to his own resources, for his mother was often ill and kept to her room in the Governor's house where they were lodged, and his father was mostly too occupied to attend to him, so he roamed about talking to anyone who would listen and listening to anyone who would talk, and acquiring a good deal of very strange and rather frightening information. The result of it all was to make him doubt very seriously the humanity of convicts.

They certainly had arms and legs and heads, and most of them had clothes of a sort, though some were practically naked, but they were obviously a different *kind* of people, and he could well believe what he had been told of them, that they were very evil. Indeed it was apparent that they must be, for he knew that God caused good people to prosper and infallibly meted out punishment to wrongdoers. Now, deeply impressed, he was an eye-witness of the varied retributions which Heaven visited upon them. Hundreds were so sick that they could not stand, and so thin that the bones seemed about to pierce their skin, and Mr. Johnson, who went on board the *Surprise* to see them, came back looking green and holding his handkerchief to his face, and said that they smelt so bad that he could not bear it. When they were being taken from the ships they had to be pushed and thrown about like sacks, hoisted and lowered like bales, and some of them died while the boats were bringing them ashore. Some had died on the ships, too, and their bodies were thrown overboard. Patrick himself saw one lying naked on the rocks where the tide had left it, for clothes were too valuable to be wasted on a corpse.

How unspeakably and incomprehensibly dreadful their wickedness must have been, to have provoked God to such awful punishments! In a world which he had already found to be full of mysterious taboos, his parents' pronouncement that the convicts were to be avoided seemed eminently reasonable.

There were busy days in the settlement after the arrival of this dreadful cargo. Phillip, having roundly told the captains of the transports that he considered them little better than murderers, and that a full report of their infamous conduct would be sent to the home authorities, locked the rest of his indignation behind tight-shut lips, and went grimly about his work. He looked so quietly and blackly angry, however, that no one spoke more to him than was necessary for the receiving of orders and the giving of reports. He had never been more solitary than now when his settlement was suddenly crowded to bursting point; he had never been as near to despair when starvation faced them as he was now with such evidence of human bungling and brutality before him.

There was no eluding it. The evidences of it were all about him. Cold facts, figures, measurements, supported it. Three ships had carried, in addition to their crews, over a thousand convicts, over a hundred soldiers of the newly formed New South Wales Corps which was to supplant the marines, and some thirty-odd of their wives and children. He himself had seen the dens which were described as quarters for the convicts, dens in which each man, during that interminable voyage, had lived—or died—in some thirty-seven cubic feet of air-space, wearing the same shackles which had been used by slave-traders on the Guinea coast. He had spoken with Captain Hill of the New South Wales Corps, heard the note of horror in his voice, watched his hands moving nervously in the torment of his memories.

"Your Excellency, I shall never be able to forget what I have seen on this voyage. The *Surprise,* Sir, was of course quite unfitted for such a passage; even in the slightest sea she shipped so much water that the unhappy convicts were often over their waists. And the stench which came from their dungeons when the hatches were opened . . . The results, well, Sir, you have seen them. Of nine hundred male convicts embarked three hundred and seventy are dead—four hundred and fifty so ill and emaciated that I should suppose they will never regain their health. I tell you, Sir, the slave-trade is merciful compared with what I have seen in this fleet . . ."

Words such as these haunted him at night when he was trying to sleep. He faced the ugly truth that it was to the advantage of these captains and contractors that their charges should die—and the earlier in the voyage the better. They were paid not for convicts landed but for convicts shipped, and the more deaths there were the fewer mouths to feed, and the greater their profit. Were those who had died the fortunate ones? Those who had drawn their last breath in filth and darkness, who had had the clothes torn from their bodies before they were cold, even the plugs of tobacco they had been chewing stolen from their mouths as they lay dead, their deaths concealed for days so that their ration might continue to come to their neighbours. . . .

Were they more fortunate, perhaps, than the scarcely human creatures whom he had seen unloaded from the ships like so much worthless merchandise, half naked, their faces brutish and their eyes dull with suffering, crawling on their hands and knees because they were too weak to stand, dying of starvation, confinement, scurvy, dysentery, and the horrible diseases of debauchery? What was there for them now that they had preserved their bare lives through so much horror and degradation? He was almost impatient with himself because the insistent gleam of optimism, which had so far sustained him, seemed proof against even such ghastliness as this. They were alive, he thought. They *were* alive.

That spark of life, useless to themselves, was, nevertheless, a kind of immortality which this land would take and shape to its own ends. It's out of our hands now, he found himself thinking with a kind of inspired and fanatical fatalism. It's life we have brought here. The lamp may be dirty and untended, but the flame is pure. We can't harm that. There's hope still—not *for* them but *from* them . . .

Almost angrily he turned from such thoughts to others, more welcome to him because more immediately practical. What was he, in the meantime, to do with them? From a colonising point of view most of them were worse than useless. Where were the farmers he had asked for? The carpenters, the bricklayers, the healthy, work-hungry men who were to have helped him build his dream into a reality? He had been sleeping badly enough before; now, with a dark anger beating in him like a drum, he often lay awake till dawn, grappling with a situation which seemed more like a nightmare than anything he had ever seen in sleep.

Before this coming of the Second Fleet he had at least built some kind of organisation in his community. Now it was plunged back into a confusion far worse than that with which he had been faced two and a half years ago. White reported that of the newly arrived convicts more than a hundred could never, by reason of old age or disease, be anything but a burden to the community. The portable hospital which the *Justinian* had brought hardly began to shelter the sick; tents were pitched for them, but still they had nothing to lie on save the bare ground, soaked by recent rains, and one blanket between four of them to resist the winter cold.

To crown everything, Mr. Mannion and the officers of the New South Wales Corps were more than a little disgruntled at not finding comforts and conveniences which they considered they had a right to expect awaiting their arrival. They had been led to suppose, Lieutenant Macarthur said with some hauteur, that the settlement was well established. How was it, asked Mr. Mannion, that after two and a half years more had not been accomplished than this?

The Government was far too busy to listen to complaints. Mr. Mannion, he thought absent-mindedly, seemed to be rather a supercilious person, and Lieutenant Macarthur had already acquired a reputation for quarrelsomeness, but he had no time now for social intercourse, and when his eye rested upon any of the new arrivals his first, indeed his only, thought was, "Will he prove useful?" "Has he qualities which I can turn to the advantage of the settlements?" Such a one, he was inclined to think, was another Irishman, the young d'Arcy Wentworth who had made the voyage in the *Neptune* as assistant surgeon.

Patrick was beginning to be a good deal bored. Everyone at Government House was too busy to talk to him. Captain Collins and Captain Tench, and Mr. White, the surgeon, who, at first, had always had time for a word with him, now passed him with grave, preoccupied faces, or, at most, with a hurried pat on the head. His mother was still not well enough to go out, but he was taken once by his father for an outing to Rose Hill where a great deal of work was being done, building and digging and cutting down trees and burning stumps, and from the boat which took them up they had seen black men on the shore, and Patrick had felt a little nervous though he tried not to show it.

It might have been more fun, he thought forlornly, if there were not so many things one was not allowed to do. One must not stray beyond the clearing into the woods, and one must not play by the water, and one must not go near the convicts' huts or the marines' barracks or the sick tents or the hospital. It was all very lonely. There were plenty of other children in the settlement, but he was not allowed to play with them, and Mrs. Macarthur's little boy and Mrs. Johnson's little girl were, of course, far too small to be of any use at all to a boy who had turned six. For a time there had been some interest in burials, but one grew tired of these— there were so many of them. Mr. White and his assistants spent most of their time in the hospital and the sick tents, but it seemed that they could not stay the wrath of God, for the convicts just kept on dying. They had no beds to lie on, so the Governor sent out parties to cut grass and bracken, and sometimes Patrick was allowed to join these expeditions on condition that he stayed close to the responsible person in whose charge he was placed. He enjoyed these excursions very much, and flushed with pleasure upon one occasion when Mr. Dawes, seeing him return panting with his exertions, complimented him upon his load, and said: "We shall make a fine colonist of you in time, Patrick!"

Upon the next occasion when he went there was another little boy of about his own age in the party. Patrick watched him out of the corner of his eye, for he knew that he was a convict child, and, therefore, according to the rules, probably a wicked little boy; and indeed his behaviour seemed to confirm this supposition, for he was continually being impertinent to his elders, which shocked Patrick very much, and playing all kinds of pranks to annoy them. It was not the first time Patrick had seen him, for he was a conspicuous child, gnomelike with his thin legs and his wild thatch of red hair, and lit by some flame of devilment which had more than once attracted astonished stares from a little boy whose life had not taught him to be other than sweet-tempered.

Towards the end of the day Patrick found himself close enough to this child to speak, and as they were separated a little from the rest of the party, his natural craving for companionship, and a dash of healthy curiosity prompted him to break through the taboo.

"What's your name?"

The boy, gathering an armful of bracken from the ground, looked up at him sharply, his eyes bright and dark in his surprisingly dirty face. His reply, brief and withering, held words which Patrick did not understand, for he had never heard them before, but he knew from the tone, and from the malicious smile which went with it, and from some current of animosity which his quick Celtic perception instantly registered, that they were offensive. He went red and became angry, and as the boy straightened up with his arms full of ferns, gave him a push which made him stagger. The next instant they were fighting. Patrick had never fought anyone before; he hit wildly and aimlessly with wide-swinging arms, and he would have had very much the worst of the encounter if his opponent had not suddenly stopped fighting and begun to squeal and hop, slapping frantically at his bare feet and legs. Patrick, panting with rage and exertion, watched him with his mouth open. Incautiously he advanced a step, and the next moment he was squealing and hopping too. He screamed in terror: "It's snakes! It's snakes!" having the Irish child's almost superstitious fear of the reptiles which its patron saint had driven from his own country. But already the convict child was quiet; his face was wrinkled with pain and quite pale beneath its dirt. He said gaspingly, but with scorn: "Snakes! It's soldiers! Git away from the nest, you . . ."

This time Patrick did not resent the incomprehensible word. He took one horrified look at the seething mound at his feet, and fled. Only one ant had stung him, but the pain of it was red-hot, throbbing and shooting up his leg, and by the time the rest of the party, startled by their screams, had reached them, he was sitting on the ground with his stocking pushed down, rubbing at the spot and trying not to cry.

When they had roughly comforted him, laughed at him a little, warned him to keep away from soldier-ants' nests, and gone back to their work, he still sat rubbing his leg and looking sideways at the other child. No one had comforted him. No one had even realised that he had been stung too. He sat on a fallen log at a little distance with his head turned away, leaning forward and gripping the calves of his bare legs with his hands. After a few moments Patrick got up and went to him.

"How many bites did *you* get?"

"Nigh on ten, I reckon."

Patrick was silent, humiliated, bitterly ashamed of his one paltry sting. One! He looked down at the still figure, now ringed invincibly with glory by virtue of his greater pain, and for one giddy moment he toyed with the idea of going back to the nest, and acquiring not ten stings, but twenty. Then the convict boy shot a quick upward glance at him and put all such thoughts from his head, for there was a wet streak down one grimy cheek. Patrick looked away quickly, and said:

"The sting is very painful. My mother has a salve which she puts on sore places. Has your mother?"

The boy seemed to consider for a moment, and when he answered it was obliquely.

"You don't need any salves or such. The pain gets better by itself."

"Mine," said Patrick cheerfully, "is getting better already. Is yours?"

He looked down at the bare legs, and then, troubled, at the averted head. For instead of the one small lump which was the result of his own sting, the convict child's legs seemed to be a mass of raised white weals of puffy, reddened flesh, and there was another tear sliding down his cheek. Patrick said anxiously:

"Perhaps after all, my mother's salve . . ."

The boy made a scornful sound and got up from the log. He walked off without looking at Patrick, moving stiffly. Patrick followed. At the bottom of a little gully they came to a stream, a mere trickle of water between rocky pools, and here the boy sat down and began scraping mud from the banks with his fingers. Wetting it, he spread it all over his legs, patting and smoothing it, while Patrick, to whom mud was a forbidden joy, looked on in awe and envy.

"Why do you do that?"

"It's better than your salves. It's what the Indians do when soldiers bite them."

"How do you know?"

The boy gave him a dark, scornful glance.

"I seen them."

Patrick's eyes opened very widely.

"Do you . . . do you *know* some Indians?"

"I ran away and lived with them for a week. The Governor, he sent out a party to bring me back. But I'll go again some day."

Patrick was, for a moment or two, quite speechless. He had been told about the black people during the voyage. One of the sailors had said that they were cannibals, and when he had asked what that meant, and had been told, with a wealth of detail, he had had a bad nightmare, and the thought of them had been like a shadow across his bright anticipation of the new country. Since landing his fear had quieted a little, for everyone seemed to take them very much for granted, and those whom he had seen did not look at all fierce; but the thought of living with them, of running away from one's own family to do so, of having to be brought back by force, opened up such a confusion of new ideas that he could only stand staring, trying to reconcile them with his own. He ventured at last, thinking that perhaps he had not properly understood:

"Didn't you *want* to come home?"

Again that queer, unfathomable, experienced glance. The answer was a mere "No," unemphasised by anything except its tone, but it frightened Patrick. His fear was not of the boy, but of his own first dim comprehension of human suffering, the first faint crack in his armour of detachment. He did not dare to ask why this strange boy, whose superior knowledge and wisdom encircled him like an aura, did not like his home. Already, in a few moments, he was beginning to understand. His child's brain, still poignantly defenceless against the limpid clarity of its logic, still unversed in the saving adult art of rapid rationalisation, showed him a terrible answer to that unspoken question in a series of vivid, if chaotic pictures. He saw the miserable huts in the cove, built of interlaced branches and daubed with mud, he saw the grey, slow-moving line of convicts setting out for their day's work at the brick fields, he heard the sounds of brawling and drunken laughter that came from their quarters at night. He remembered the convict women on the ship, and realised for the first time that they were really women like his mother, and could have little boys of their own like himself. He remembered something which was only an impression because Mr. Dawes had suddenly seen him, and whisked him away—an impression of a naked back, and blood, and a sound he had never heard before, a man's voice crying out in pain . . .

He had seen these things, heard them, and remained insulated from them by his upbringing. The world in which they happened and the world in which he lived were separated by a barrier none the less strong for being invisible. Now, for the first time, his spirit broke through it, and stood aghast, not only at the horrors confronting it, but at its own overwhelming reaction of humility. For he had been taught by his mother that he should pity the unfortunate, but his unerring sensitiveness taught him that pity, here, was mere impertinence. He had no thoughts, and needed none. His perceptions alone led him to the knowledge that this convict child had earned the right to scorn him, and he sat down clasping his arms round his knees and asked humbly for enlightenment.

"Tell me about the Indians."

The boy went on patting the mud about his legs, his face intent, as if considering. Then he said:

"I heard 'em call you Patrick."

"That's my name. Patrick John Francis Mannion."

"My name's John too, but most calls me Johnny."

"What's your other name?"

"Prentice."

"How long have you been here?"

For a moment Johnny looked uncertain. He had, as a matter of fact, forgotten that he had ever been anywhere else. He said shortly:

"Oh—a long time—since I was only little."

"Shall you be glad," Patrick asked, "to go home again?"

Home? Again that shadow of surprise and doubt. Home? England? He had forgotten it. It had never occurred to him that he might go there some day. He was not at all sure that he wanted to. He rinsed the mud from his hands in the stream and said carelessly:

"I reckon this is my home. I reckon I'll stay here."

Patrick was staggered. He looked round him at the silent, shadowy place where they sat and tried to imagine a lifetime spent in it. Such a thing was inconceivable. No one, surely, *lived* here? For ever? Except, of course, the Indians. That reminded him of an even more intriguing subject than this difficult one in which each sentence uttered by one seemed a riddle before which the other stood baffled and uncomprehending.

"Tell me about when you lived with the Indians?"

Johnny picked up some dead leaves and began to float them one by one down the stream. Some of the tenseness faded from his face as he began to speak. Patrick, enthralled, learned that the black people, far from being terrifying ogres were very fond of children, and very kind to them. There was always plenty to eat in their camp, and they could spear fish in the most marvellous manner (only the men, of course—the women caught theirs with lines), and they made a most delicious sweet drink with water and honey which they took from bees' nests in the woods. The black children, Johnny assured him, played hide-and-seek just like white children, only they called it by a different name, and they had balls made out of kangaroo skin, and the little girls had wooden dolls. If he had not been brought back, Johnny continued with pride, he was to have been allowed to go with some of the black children for a foodless march. Two days they would have walked through the woods without a bite to eat. . . .

"But," protested Patrick, "why?" For he could not reconcile this with the tale of abundant food, nor could he understand why Johnny should speak with resentment as though he had missed a treat, when one of the sorest trials of the white settlement from which he had escaped was its lack of food. Johnny said fiercely:

"It's a . . . a sort of lesson. All the black children must learn it. It's to make them . . . so that . . ." he floundered, lacking words, and finished angrily, "It's what all the black children do. But I would have been the youngest. And I wouldn't have cried, or taken too much when we came back to the camp. . . ."

He threw his leaves away, obscurely discontented because he could not make this other boy see what seemed so obvious to him. He did not know how to explain that though enforced hunger was ugly, voluntary hunger, undertaken as the black children undertook it, to prove their hardihood and their self-control, was a matter for pride and great endeavour. He did not know how to describe the difference which he felt so strongly between the two environments which he had known in this land. He was sufficiently enslaved by the prejudices of his race to accept it as a fact that white people were immeasurably superior to black people; that to have clothes, even though they were only the ragged slops of convicts, was better than to go naked; that to live in a hut, even of wattle and daub, was better than to live in a bark shelter; that to wrap oneself in a blanket, even swarming with vermin, was better than to sleep upon the skins of 'possums. Yet in the native camp there had been happiness such as he had never known before. Gaiety, laughter, games and joking were not sporadic, tainted with bitterness and cruelty, or ugly with obscenity as he had always known them, but constant, warm and spontaneous, as if life were one long delight. Sometimes, as he had gathered even during his short sojourn among them, there was pain and privation to be borne, but he knew, though his knowledge became confusion when he tried to speak of it, that there these things were not a succession of brutal humiliations, but opportunities for endurance, tests of strength. He had seen death there, too, as he had seen it at the settlement—death by violence, for a breaker of the law. He had been present on the outskirts of the crowd, a solemn-eyed child of four, when Barrett was hanged, and his memory still thrust at him sometimes a picture of men, grey-faced with fear, their arms bound behind them, dragged to the tree like animals to slaughter. He did not know why his nerves shrank from this memory and not from the memory of a black man, also surrounded by implacable hostility, condemned but not humiliated, erect, unfettered, his shield on his arm, defending his body with skill and courage from the spears of his executioners, falling at last as he might have fallen in battle. . . .

Patrick was saying:

"But are they not . . . my mother has told me, and I have heard Mr. Johnson, too . . . are they not heathens?"

Johnny, scowling, gathered up some more leaves. The scraps of theology which he had picked up from Mr. Johnson's not very illuminating addresses, warred with an inner conviction. He had sat at night in the crook of an old black man's arm, he and Bangaree who was a little bigger than himself, and they had pointed at the stars and told him their names and many strange stories about them, laughing at his ignorance, but kindly, so that he did not mind. They had pointed at the place where there was a kind of luminous pathway across the sky, and explained that there Baiame dwelt, Baiame, Maker-of-all, the Builder. And they had explained that when the good men died their spirits left them and went above to join Baiame—"There, there!" they cried, pointing to the broad white path across the dark sky; there was Baiame's dwelling place, where the good walked with him beside his never failing stream . . .

Johnny, balancing a leaf upon the trickle of water, was forced to admit, sullenly, that they were heathens. It was no use trying to justify even to himself, his preference for such inferior people. He only knew that among them, for the first time in his brief life, he had learned to be care-free, had forgotten to be wary and mistrustful, had shed the aching sense of his own worthlessness; and overcome by an emotion which was half nostalgia for that lost happiness, and half delayed reaction to his pain, he flung himself face downward on the ground and wept.

Patrick sat very still, his eyes round with consternation. It was not for him to offer comfort to one who had lived with the Indians and suffered ten soldier-ant bites all at once. But the light was fading, and he could no longer hear the voices of the others calling to each other, and when he looked about him he felt vaguely afraid. There was a queer rustling noise which he could not account for until he looked up the pinkish trunk of the tree at whose bole he sat, up and up and up till his head was craned back as far as it would go, and then he saw a long festoon of bark swinging in the breeze, scraping and whispering. . . . He looked past it, up and up again, till the trunk lost itself in a sparse tracery of glittering leaves which seemed to vanish and reappear again against the pale gold, glittering sky. Patrick picked up a fallen leaf and turned it over and over in his fingers. It was not like other leaves which he knew, whose memory carried him back to the woods near his home in Ireland. Those were soft, and slightly hairy, and of an irregular shape, and you could see the light through them; but this one was slender and curved like a blade, smooth-edged, cool and slippery to the touch, and of a dull, opague green like the sea on a stormy day. Patrick dropped it and looked anxiously at Johnny's still heaving shoulders. He had suddenly remembered that in this country there was no long twilight, as there was at home. Night sprang at you treacherously as soon as the sun had set; already the shadows were lengthening, and there was a chill in the air. He said:

"I think it must be time for us to go back."

Johnny's head came up with a jerk. He listened, but there was no sound of voices. He sprang to his feet, smearing his arm impatiently across his tear-stained face, and called roughly to Patrick:

"Come on, hurry—they've gone!"

Patrick followed him. He found it difficult to keep up, but he did it, struggling through dense and prickly undergrowth, scrambling over fallen logs, his heart thudding, and not only with exertion. He was afraid of this place. It all looked alike. You could run and run, and still the same trees were about you, the same rough ground underfoot, the same quietness, the same rustlings. He knew quite well that if Johnny had not been with him he could never have found his way back to the settlement, and his mouth felt dry when he thought of being here alone at night, with snakes creeping about him in the darkness and no bed to sleep in.

They were just in sight of the settlement when they overtook some of the party who greeted them with astonishment, having believed them to be with others who had returned earlier. Patrick's father who had come out to look for him met them as they emerged into the clearing, and took him by the hand, asking him questions so that he had no time, even if he had had the breath, to say good-bye to Johnny. And indeed, when he turned to look, the convict child had already disappeared.

* * *

Stephen Mannion stood on the high cliffs of Burrawarra and watched the sails of the *Justinian* vanishing over the horizon. It was the end of July, cold and windy; he kept his hands thrust into the pockets of his greatcoat, its collar turned up about his chin, and cursed the idiotic whim which had led him to this place. He could not now even remember when the mad idea had first entered his head; it must have been, he thought wryly, upon some hilarious evening when he and his friends had been pursuing their usual custom of drinking too much and talking too wildly.

Many of his more insane undertakings had started thus—with a jest, a boast, a challenge . . .

He began to pick up small stones and fling them idly over the cliff. He hated this trait in himself which, all his life, had driven him into doing things he did not really want to do; indeed, he sometimes suspected that it was not, properly speaking, a trait of his own character at all, but that a family legend had imposed upon him a kind of spurious recklessness which was quite foreign to his nature. Everyone expected the Mannions to be imprudent; they always had been. Everyone expected them to do mad, rash things; and they always did. It had been almost a point of honour in the family for generations past that its head, before he finally settled down to hunting, drinking, and gout, should do something over which his acquaintances could fling up their hands and exclaim: "Those Mannions! Mad! Quite mad!"

But somehow, Stephen reflected, for at least several generations back, their madness had seemed to take a rather stereotyped form—almost as if they, like himself, had not really been driven by that picturesque irresponsibility whose first ingredient is a lively imagination, but had been hounded as he sometimes felt he himself was being hounded by a tyrannical legend.

It was Hugh, his great-great-grandfather, who had begun a kind of tradition in colonial escapades, for in 1615, only a couple of years after his marriage, he had gone to Virginia, and there had been unpleasantly slain by Indians. His son, Michael, a friend of Henry Cromwell, had journeyed to America in charge of a shipload of his countrymen who were being transported thither as political prisoners. Charles, son of Michael, had improved upon this strange tradition by not merely going to the colonies, but remaining there, in South Carolina, for no less than fifteen years, and returning at last with an American wife who became the mother of Patrick, Stephen's father. Patrick, in his turn, reading with indignation of the hostilities between the French and the English, not only in Europe but in the land of his mother's birth, had embarked for America when Stephen was about three, and had ingloriously died of dysentery during the siege of Louisburg.

But now the American colonies were colonies no longer. Instead, there was this barren, useless land. Stephen turned slowly, searching conscientiously for anything which might make him feel that there was a modicum of sense, not only in his own presence here, but in the existence of the colony itself. To the east, ocean; to the north, rocky headlands, cliffs, hillsides clothed with slatey-green trees; to the west the harbour, winding, deeply indented with bays, scattered with islands, vanishing out of sight between those same dull-green shores; to the south only a rising ground, harsh and stony and sandy as this one on which he stood, shutting from his view a waste of those same undulating hills, that same interminable monotony of trees . . .

Why had he come? What was he doing here? The incredible folly of it! Had his Great-great-grandfather Hugh felt himself stabbed by the same thought when he realised that he would never see his home again? Had his father, Patrick, before he died cursed himself for a fool as his son was doing now? Why—*why* had he come? For no other reason than that when he had first mentioned it his mother and his sisters and his uncle and his two aunts had all exclaimed in shocked unison: "Preposterous! You cannot be serious, Stephen!" Up to that moment he had not been serious; and after it he was not so much serious as mysteriously and irrevocably committed. Why had he not laughed it off? "Of course I'm not serious!" How easy—and how impossible!

He began to pace about, kicking at the stones and pebbles, all the threads of his thoughts tangled into a painful knot when they led to his wife, Harriet.

It was bad enough that he should have committed this incredible folly himself, but a thousand times worse that he should have involved her in its miserable consequences. He could still hear voices rising in a crescendo of disapproval. "You would not, *of course,* subject your wife to such an ordeal?" "Naturally you do not for one instant entertain the idea of taking dearest Harriet?"

Up to that moment he had not entertained any such idea; after it, it had been inevitable that dearest Harriet should go. She was very willing. "It will be," he had said gaily, "quite an adventure for us, will it not, Patrick?"

"Patrick? *Patrick?*" The air had become electric with what was almost an ecstasy of horror. "You would never take the child on such a voyage, Stephen? Think of the dangers, Harriet! Think of the associations! Think of the cannibals!"

She had said, serenely: "Stephen will take care of us."

And that was all. She had had no conception of what she was undertaking. Indeed he had to admit that he had had but little himself. Their passage through the tropics had been an experience which even now he shuddered to remember. From their cramped cabin they had been able to hear through the thin dividing walls the screams and curses and quarrelling of the convict women, their groans when they lay ill, the obscene and ribald jesting of their gaolers. In that stifling atmosphere every breath they drew had seemed heavy with infection, for fever raged among the women, and Harriet, waxy pale, had lain day after day with closed eyes as if the very effort of drawing breath were almost beyond her strength. Once, when a more than usually violent outburst of hysterical raving from the other side of the wall had penetrated to their cabin, she had opened eyes which were almost frantic with horror, and stooping over her he had felt her clutch his neck as if she were drowning, and whisper: "Oh, God help them! God help them!" He had tried to soothe her. These women were not like herself. They did not suffer as she did from inconveniences and discomforts. They were hardened, abandoned, infamous creatures, and she must not distress herself about them. How strangely she had looked at him then!

There had been but little he could do for her. Only to keep Patrick on deck as much as possible, and to assure her from time to time of his wellbeing. It had been that helplessness which tortured him. He had never been helpless before. All his life, wherever he went, money and influence had smoothed his path for him, and he had not really supposed that things would be different during the voyage, and at Botany Bay. It had not occurred to him that in a British colony, fully two years founded, there could still exist such squalor and confusion as they had found here.

Long before they had landed their only thought had been of a speedy return. They had been ten months on the voyage, and before two of them had passed Harriet had known herself pregnant again. If he had only acceded, Stephen thought, his pace quickening in his agitation, to her timid suggestion that they should leave the ship at Table Bay and return home! Might he not have done so if it had not been for the presence there of the shattered *Guardian*? Had he not been influenced by the thought of unbearable comments: "No, no, they did not reach Botany Bay after all. A store-ship struck the ice upon the same voyage, and Stephen was so disturbed by this that he abandoned the whole project. So prudent of him, was it not?"

Prudent! Unthinkable that a Mannion should be accused of prudence! He stopped dead and stared out towards the horizon but the sail was gone, and the ocean lay vast and empty, and behind him in that miserable settlement Harriet was ill, too ill to be moved, almost too ill to speak to him, dying, perhaps . . .

The *Lady Juliana* was to leave in a few days, and the *Neptune,* the *Surprise* and the *Scarborough* still lay at anchor in the harbour. If only the child might be born, if only Harriet might recover sufficiently for them to embark on one or the other of these ships! Even now, perhaps . . .

what was he idling about here for . . . He leapt to his feet and began to walk back towards the settlement, his heart heavy with dread.

*   *   *

The next day Patrick went with his father and Mr. Dawes for a walk. Papa would not go very far from the settlement, for he said that Mamma was ill and might wish to see him, so they set out along the shore. The wind had dropped and the sky was blue, and though in the shade the air was chilly the sun had a delightful warmth, so that Patrick was allowed to play in the rock pools which the high tide had filled, and to collect shells which lay on the wet sand. After a time they left the shore and climbed to the top of a ridge, and on the way Patrick found so many intriguing things to fill his hands and his pockets that he was glad when they halted at the top and he was able to spread them out for examination on a flat rock. When they returned to the settlement, he planned, he would find Johnny Prentice, and show them to him, and ask him several things which he wanted to know about them.

There was a strange kind of seed-pod, hard, woody, black, splitting open to display a reddish-brown interior with a tiny winged seed lying snugly in it; there was a leaf such as the one he had studied on that afternoon when he had talked to Johnny, but covered with little red lumps; there was a feather, soft and fluffy, grey, with a rosy tip; there was a tiny dead crab; there were several smooth pink pebbles, and many beautiful shells. But best of all there was something which he had broken from a prickly bush—could it be a seed? It was like a little head with a pointed animal face, and pricked ears—or were they horns? It looked impish, impertinent, slightly wicked. Two broken twigs stuck up on either side of it like raised arms.

He glanced up meaning to ask Papa or Mr. Dawes what it was, but the question died unspoken, and he turned instead to stare where his father was staring. He saw nothing but more woods. There was no change or variation in their colour, an unbroken, billowing sea of grey-green, and for the first time Patrick found his attention deflected from the small things which children love and fastened upon the aspect of the country as a whole. He stared at it soberly, puzzled by its unfamiliarity.

His father gave a short laugh and said suddenly:

"And this is winter!"

Winter? Patrick was astonished. He knew that it was July, but no one had so far thought of explaining to him that he was now in the Southern Hemisphere. It took him only a moment to accept as a fact that in this country where everything was different, July was no longer July, but December. The thought of December, however, gave him pause, for December meant Christmas, and how could Christmas be other than cold, with snow, perhaps, and big fires and holly berries behind the pictures, and a dark, dark morning when you wakened early and peered at the foot of the bed and saw your stocking bulging with promise in the half light?

He asked doubtfully:

"What is it like in the summer, Papa?"

His father laughed again, and even Patrick heard the undercurrent of bitterness. He waved an arm at the view and said:

"Just like this, Patrick—just like this—only hotter! Ask Mr. Dawes—he will tell you all about it."

But Mr. Dawes was silent. He was not, Patrick reflected, a very talkative man—not like Captain Tench who always had a laugh in his eyes and a flavour to his words which made other people's conversation seem rather dull. Mr. Dawes, with his chin on his hand and tapping his boot with a twig, sighed and said at last:

"There is a certain monotony about the landscape. One misses the spring. There is, properly speaking, no spring in this country."

Stephen Mannion burst out:

"No spring, no food, no society, no decent lodging, no amenities—nothing! I was a fool to come! And, I tell you, Mr. Dawes, I can see no future for it. It passes my comprehension how the Governor can be so sanguine! Look at it!" His outflung arm denounced the silent, unresponsive, waiting land. "The soil, as you all know by now, to your cost, is wretched. It provides nothing to speak of in the way of foodstuffs. The timber is worthless. You yourself have travelled inland a full fifty miles and found nothing better than what confronts us here. Indeed, you said, did you not, that it was considerably wilder and rougher than the coastal regions? It is a barbarous, God-forsaken country, only fit for the savages who inhabit it!"

Startled, Patrick stared at it. He did not know what "barbarous" meant; he thought it sounded like thorns, and there were certainly plenty of those. But "God-forsaken" was clear enough, and he stared with some awe at the land which was so worthless that even God did not want to have anything to do with it. The fear, the sense of strangeness which had assailed him before when he was alone with Johnny in the darkening woods, seemed to support, from his own experience, his all-wise and infallible father's condemnation. He said with a quaver in his voice:

"When shall we be going home, Papa?"

His father looked down at him. Patrick knew that all the Mannions had blue eyes; it was simply something which inevitably happened in the family. But he had never seen his father's eyes look as blue as they did now—or was it that he had gone rather pale? He said slowly:

"When your mother is well enough to undertake the voyage, Patrick, and when we can secure a passage . . ."

His voice trailed off into a silence which was broken almost immediately by a rush of angry words not addressed to Patrick, perhaps not to Mr. Dawes either, perhaps mainly to the rolling hills, secret and impassive in their monotone of green:

"It must be soon—before—it is *unthinkable* that she should, here of all places on earth—here in this accursed land . . ."

He rubbed his hand across his eyes. Mr. Dawes said nothing. Patrick, now thoroughly alarmed, felt the monstrous country holding them all like a prison, and that thought frightened him afresh because he knew that for the convicts it *was* a prison, and he felt confusedly that he and his parents had strayed somehow into a place which was essentially malevolent, and from which not even his father really knew how to escape. Anxiously he tried to help. France, too, was across the sea from Ireland, and he knew that his mother had often been there and had loved it, so he ventured:

"Papa."

"Yes, Patrick?"

"Could we not go—not on the sea, but in coaches, or on horseback—to —to some other country? To—to France . . ."

His father smiled. Mr. Dawes smiled. Patrick blushed hotly, realising that he had been foolish and not helpful at all. His father explained in a queer, flat voice:

"This country is an island, Patrick. A very large island, much, much larger than Ireland or England. And it has no roads that coaches could travel on, and there are no towns in it and no cities; only the settlement where you live, and Rose Hill. All the rest is . . ."

Again that wide movement of his arm, bitter and contemptuous. Again to Patrick, staring at what it indicated, a tight, suffocating awareness of isolation. A country with no roads! No cities! A country so big that no one knew its end, and all bewitched with silence! It was like bad dreams he had sometimes, nebulous dreams of a dreadful captivity from which only waking could release you. He felt his mouth twisting, and tried hard to control it, but his misery dragged its corners down in spite of him and filled his eyes with a scalding moisture. It was Mr. Dawes' quiet, rather slow voice which rescued him on the edge of an ignominious flood of tears:

"After all, Mr. Mannion, we do not really know yet. What is fifty miles in a country of this size? For myself," he shrugged, "I have no very great hopes. But over there, beyond those hills, there may be—something."

Patrick blinked his eyes clear and looked across the dull green landscape which his father's gestures had condemned, following Mr. Dawes' pointing finger. Far, far away on the horizon there was a blue line of hills. There were little clouds in the sky, and it was hard to tell what was mountain and what was cloud, but he stared, wrinkling his eyes against the sunlight, and his mind fastened wonderingly on to Mr. Dawes' last word.

Something.

He hardly knew whether to be excited or alarmed by such vagueness. He had never realised until he came here that there could be anything which grown-up people did not know. But since . . . !

He found himself remembering all sorts of questions which he had asked of different people.

"Mamma, are there truly birds here as tall as horses?"

"I do not know, my dear."

"Captain Tench, how many Indians do you suppose there are?"

"Indeed I wish I knew, Patrick."

"Mr. Johnson, will you kindly tell me what sort of animal these little bones were?"

"I have no idea, my little man."

Even the Governor himself:

"Are there lakes here, Sir, like the Lakes of Killarney?"

"That is something we have yet to discover, Patrick."

And now Mr. Dawes. Even Mr. Dawes who was so learned, who knew so much about the stars, and who was always writing figures down in a little book! Even Mr. Dawes did not know what was over there beyond that line of blue!

"Papa."

"Yes, Patrick?"

"What do you *think* might be over the other side of the hills? What do you *think*, Papa?"

His father's answer came slowly, not so much an answer to himself, Patrick felt, as a thinking aloud.

"I think it is all like this. And why? Because of its inhabitants. Consider, Mr. Dawes. Were there ever more miserable creatures? I maintain that they provide the key—there is no need to seek further. None but a barren and worthless land could produce such savages. They practise not even the most primitive sort of husbandry, they have no tools worthy of the name, their manners and customs are revolting, they are hardly higher than the apes. In no other land upon the globe has man so utterly failed to raise himself. I tell you I shudder to look at them and call them human."

Patrick darted a quick glance at his father's face. He was thinking of the convicts he had seen being disembarked from the Second Fleet, and of how he himself had wondered if they were really people; he thought it strange that his father should shudder at the blacks and not at them. He said earnestly:

"The Indians are very kind, Papa. Johnny Prentice told me . . ."

His father said sharply:

"What is this? Who is Johnny Prentice?"

"He is a—a boy, Papa, about as old as me, and he was with us one day when we were gathering grass and bracken. He lived with the Indians, Papa, in their camp. He liked it there, and he said that they do have tools, Papa, axes made of stone, and needles made out of bones, and fire-sticks to make fire with, and twine, and fishhooks, and they make warm rugs, Papa, out of skins of—of—some animal, I forget its name, and they have baskets and bags to carry their things in, and . . ."

He stopped. Papa was angry. He turned his back upon Patrick and said in a low, furious voice:

"Who is this child, Mr. Dawes? Do you know?"

Mr. Dawes glanced at Patrick with a little crease between his brows.

"He is the child of one of the convict women—a rather troublesome child, I believe, but . . ."

"What is this about his having lived with the Indians?"

"He—absconded from the settlement a year or so ago. We had some trouble in locating and recovering him. He is a high-spirited lad—wilful perhaps, and somewhat rough in his manner, but I think there is no real harm in him."

Patrick stood up very quietly and began edging away. His father called him sharply. He was hearing those accusing, ghostly voices again: *"You would never take the child . . . Think of the associations!"* He said harshly:

"Come here!"

Patrick stood before him.

"Now; I am seriously displeased with you, Patrick. You have been bidden to have no dealings with the convicts. Such a child is no fit companion for you. Understand, it is not to occur again."

Patrick's lips, from sheer habit, began to form, obediently, the words: "Yes, Papa." But suddenly he remembered the soldier-ant stings, the grim and astounding fortitude of the convict child, the magic of the tales he had told beside the trickling stream, and the confidence with which he had led the way home in the gathering dusk, and he felt that for once there was something which he understood better even than Papa. So he said:

"Indeed, Papa, he is much cleverer than I am. And—I think he may be braver, too, for he had ten . . ."

"Patrick!"

"Yes, Papa?"

"Do you dare to argue with me? I have told you you are to have no further converse with this child. That is enough. Well, Mr. Dawes, is it not time that we set out for home? Gather your things together, Patrick; we are going."

But Patrick left his treasures lying upon the rock, and carried home with him instead a queer feeling of resentment and rebellion in his heart. But before he turned to follow the two men, he looked back, shading his eyes, at the distant line of hills.

*　*　*

The *Lady Juliana* had sailed. The *Surprise* had sailed. The *Scarborough* had sailed. Now there was only the *Neptune* left, and Patrick, coming to visit his mother in her room and tell her the exciting news that this ship also was about to leave, was denied admittance. Papa, looking queer and pale, came to the door and explained that Mamma was not well enough to talk to him just now, so he must run away and amuse himself quietly, and perhaps later he might be allowed to come in. Patrick was puzzled and alarmed; he hung about the passage and saw the surgeon go in, and several women hurried to and fro carrying basins and towels and jugs of water, and after a while his father came out again. Patrick clutched at his coat as he hurried past.

"Papa!" He could feel tears welling in his eyes. "Papa, where are you going? What is the matter with Mamma?" His father's face, looking down at him, seemed so unfamiliar that his uneasiness increased to terror, and he wailed suddenly:

"I don't like it here, Papa! Why can't we go home? Why can't we go in the *Neptune*? Why can't we, Papa?"

His father stopped and bent down to him. His voice did not sound right, though his words were comforting.

"Mamma is not well enough for a long voyage, Patrick. We shall go home soon."

Patrick asked nervously:

"When will she be well enough?"

"I don't know, Patrick. Soon. Soon. Have you had your supper?"

"No, Papa."

"Well, have it, like a good child, and I will come and tell you later if you may go in."

But Patrick was in bed before his father returned. He sat down on a chair beside the cot and said as if he were very tired:

"You have a little brother, Patrick."

Patrick was thunderstruck.

"A brother, Papa? How? Where did he come from?"

"God sent him."

Patrick stared. Questions burned upon his lips. How had God sent him? Surely He would not have dropped him down from the sky, for that would have broken all his bones. Had He sent an angel to bring him? Then it was not fair—not fair at all—that Patrick had not been allowed to see this heavenly visitor. Or had He, perhaps, just waved a wand like the Little People do on Midsummer Eve, and there was the baby? This seemed the most likely, but still very strange. Patrick, longing for enlightenment, decided all the same not to ask Papa, for he had found that questions about God were apt to be very confusingly and unsatisfactorily answered. So he only said rather wistfully:

"Is Mamma well enough to see me now, Papa?"

"No—no, not yet, Patrick."

"When will she be better, Papa?"

"Soon."

"Tomorrow."

"I—don't know, Patrick. Perhaps not tomorrow. But quite soon, I hope."

"Where is he—my little brother?"

"He is with Mamma."

Patrick flushed. He saw no reason why his new brother should be thus favoured. Was Mamma, then, not going to care about him any more now that she had another little boy? He burst out:

"I don't like him! I won't have him for a brother! I wish God hadn't sent him . . ."

"*Patrick!*"

This was not the usual tone of rebuke. It was so unfamiliar that Patrick stared at his father in astonishment. How terribly unhappy he looked! How—yes—*frightened*! What an abominable country was this in which everyone was either miserable or afraid! Except the black people. A fierce tide of rebellion surged up in Patrick. He was tired of being good and having no one to play with, and if Mamma was going to have another little boy instead of him, he might as well . . .

"I'll go away like Johnny, and live with the Indians!"

The moment he had uttered this monstrous threat he was horrified at himself. In one's thoughts it seemed valorous and exciting but the sound of the spoken words made it terrifying, and he blinked up at his father apprehensively, awaiting the thunder of his wrath. But Papa did not even rebuke him. He said wearily:

"Go to sleep now, Patrick, like a good boy, and in the morning perhaps you may be able to see Mamma."

But in the morning Harriet Mannion was dead.

Patrick learned one fact from his mother's death; his family was not the most important thing on earth. He was surprised to discover this, but, on the whole, relieved. He had imagined that everyone would be thrown into the same despair as that which now gripped his father, the same uncertain, aching misery which kept himself, for several days, trembling on the verge of tears. But it was not so. The Governor and all the officers were courteously sympathetic, and Mrs. Johnson and Mrs. Macarthur and Mrs. Abbott and several other ladies were full of rather tearful condolences, and there was a funeral as impressive as circumstances allowed. But then it seemed as if life was to go on as before, and Patrick felt his confidence returning as it became apparent that the bottom had not fallen out of the world after all.

Patrick's new little brother, who was called Miles, was an ugly, purplish, wriggling object only to be regarded with a certain hostile curiosity, but he had to be nursed and cared for. Papa was desperate. Mrs. Johnson, who felt that her own increasing family quite sufficiently occupied her attention, offered vague sympathy, but no permanent assistance. Mrs. Macarthur, who was very young, and enjoying a small social success among the gentlemen of the garrison, could spare no time from her pretty dallying with the sciences of botany and astronomy, and from her preoccupation with her own fragile infant, Edward, to do more for Miles than nurse him now and then, and address him as "poor, motherless babe."

It was Mrs. Abbott, in the end, who made the suggestion which Stephen

Mannion first rejected with horror, then unwillingly considered, and finally, in despair, accepted.

There was a woman among the convicts, it appeared, whose infant, born on the same day as Miles, had died shortly after birth. She was not, of course, a respectable person; not at all the kind of person naturally, whom Mr. Mannion would, in happier circumstances, have engaged as foster-mother for his child. But she was young, and seemed healthy—was not that a great consideration? She would assure Miles during his first months, of abundant nourishment, ". . . and indeed, Mr. Mannion, I do not see how otherwise the child is to thrive. Consider the food available in this place . . ."

So Ellen Prentice was summoned. She stood before Mr. Mannion sullenly, hating him for the contempt and aversion which she read in his eyes. The two and a half years which she had spent in the settlement had altered her; she was only twenty-six, but she looked ten years older. She was thin, and her shoulders stooped, and her thick dark hair was dirty and unkempt, but she returned his stare so boldly that he stood up, queerly disconcerted, and addressed her over his shoulder:

"Your name?"

"Ellen Prentice, Sir."

"Prentice?" The name seemed familiar, but he had forgotten that it belonged to the little boy with whom Patrick had so disobediently associated. He went on sharply:

"Your husband, I am told, absconded from the settlement. How long ago?"

He had been told that, too, but he wanted to shame her. However, she only answered laconically, keeping her black eyes on him:

"Eighteen months—a bit more."

"You have children—how many?"

"Three, Sir."

"Their ages?"

"There's Johnny, he's goin' on seven, and Maria, she's two, and Andy's near thirteen months."

He looked at her, but in another spasm of distaste turned his back once more and went over to the window. The *Neptune* still lay at anchor, the last of the transports, but tomorrow would see her gone. He almost regretted his decision not to sail in her, but found an obscure comfort in thus expiating his criminal folly by condemning himself to a further sojourn in this horrible place. He felt, too, confusedly, that it would somehow be callous—faithless—to abandon so soon a land whose earth still lay freshly over the grave of his wife. She had been frail and timid and obedient, trusting always to his superior wisdom—and how wickedly he had failed her! *"Stephen will take care of us."* He had remembered those words so often and so poignantly that now he could bear to remember them no more, and he swung round to face Ellen again with a harshness which was partly the result of his own unendurable self-accusation:

"I wish to engage you as nurse for my child. Mrs. Johnson will—provide you with suitable clothing. That is all—for the present. You may go."

Much that he had meant to say remained unsaid; he had found the interview disturbing. The woman's cool self-possession had infuriated him. It was as if she knew very well that she had, in her swollen breasts, that which made her very much mistress of the situation. He uttered a sound of disgust, pacing up and down the room. Harriet's child—his child —a Mannion—to be nursed by such a creature! It had seemed bad enough that the baby should have been born in such a place, but that he should have as foster-mother a woman so obviously immoral and abandoned as Ellen Prentice, was a blow to Stephen Mannion's pride from which he felt that he could never recover.

He shared, in a degree, Patrick's astonishment at finding that his wife's death had caused hardly a ripple in the life of the settlement. There had been so many deaths. Since the arrival of the Second Fleet Mr. Johnson had performed nearly a hundred burials, and though the wife of Phillip Mannion was not, in her lifetime, to be for one moment placed in the same category as convicts, the outrageous fact remained that death seemed to make little distinction. She, like them, was hardly dead before she was forgotten, for it was life which was important here.

* * *

The other convict women, enviously sardonic, made ribald remarks to Ellen Prentice when they heard of her promotion. Now her ladyship was to wear a fine gown, and have shoes upon her feet—but let her not think that she was anything more than a convict woman, for all that! The only difference, they jeered, was that her next child would be blue-eyed—and blue-blooded!

Ellen only shrugged. What did it matter? The bestowal of her favours had always been the only coin in which she could pay for any small alleviations in her life, and if she must pay thus for her new comforts—well, it was a small price for a larger benefit than she had ever won before. Her position was officially that of nurse to the infant Miles, but it was taken for granted that she would also assume the duties of housekeeper; not only in the convict huts was that title accepted as a polite euphemism for another less respectable function.

Listening undisturbed to hints and jibes, Ellen remembered, but saw no reason to mention, the aversion with which her future master had looked at her. The recollection only made her smile cynically; she had too often seen aversion conquered by desire. Clad in the decent black gown which Mrs. Johnson had given her, carrying Andy on one arm, and dragging Maria by the hand, she set out to take up her abode in the house of Mr. Stephen Mannion.

* * *

The Governor, for the next month or so, was very busy. He was sending the healthiest of the convicts to Rose Hill, where an almost feverish activity now prevailed, for it was more urgent than ever that more land should be speedily prepared for crops. He planned new buildings for the township; he laid out a fine main street, two hundred feet wide, and a mile long, with a small house for himself standing on a pleasant hillside at its end. He was severely hampered by the lack of competent tradesmen, and of all the losses which the wreck of the *Guardian* had caused to the settlement, he felt most keenly the loss of the carpenters, stonemasons and bricklayers, who had been stranded at the Cape.

He was aware, too, in the midst of his multitude of anxieties, of increasing discontents among his people, and of criticism aimed at himself. Before, when the colony had consisted of only those whom his own Fleet had brought out, there had been less incentive to gossip about the grievances and discomforts which all knew and shared. Now, with newcomers in whom to confide, the temptation became strong in many to paint past trials in lurid colours, and to hint at even worse hardships to come. The new arrivals were sympathetic, expressed horror at such mismanagement, hinted obliquely, and then less obliquely, that the blame for it must lie somewhere—and where more justly than at the door of His Excellency?

Phillip could not but be aware of these subterranean murmurs, but was not greatly disturbed by them. He had been cheered by news from Tench, and Dawes, who had undertaken further explorations southwest and northwest of Rose Hill, and who had reported that to the south they had discovered land which seemed promising for cultivation. With the winter behind him, and the promise of spring in the air, he felt too hopeful to be concerned with whisperings and jealousies. Only to his friend, Sir Joseph Banks, did he write, with a shade of bitterness, a word in his own defence:

". . . As to my Conduct, if ever I have erred or consulted my own conveniency or interest, there will soon be those at home who will not lose an opportunity of pointing it out, but I have never to my knowledge swerved from the line of Conduct which I laid down for myself the day I embarked, and which had the good of the Service on which I am employed for its object."

* * *

There was a whale in the harbour; for weeks past its great humped back had been seen rising above the water. The natives observed that the Bereewolgal several times set out in pursuit of it in their boats, armed with weapons which they used like spears, but they were unsuccessful, and the monster continued to be seen at intervals swimming up and down in search of the opening through which it had blundered in from the sea. It was at this season that whales always passed, making up the coast, forsaking the cold southern ocean with its drifting polar ice for those tropical waters which lapped the northern shores of the continent; but it was not often that one found its way into the harbour, and the black men watched it hungrily, for whale flesh was a delicacy they seldom had an opportunity of tasting.

Barangaroo and her sister-in-law, Warreweer, and Colbee's wife, Daringha, gossiping on the rocks by the water's edge one crisp day towards the end of July, had been witnesses of a disaster which it caused. Four of the white men were fishing from a small boat at some distance from the shore, and Warreweer was making up quite scandalous stories about them, and the others were shrieking with laughter at the comical things she said, when suddenly the black back of the whale broke the surface quite near the boat. Warreweer stopped in the middle of an unflattering description of the person of the young midshipman who sat in the stern, and Barangaroo dropped the shell from which she had been making a fishhook, and Daringha, who was a soft-hearted person, uttered a little squeal of fright and anxiety. The men had seized the oars and were now rowing furiously, but the next moment the monster rose again, and this time so near that waves broke into the boat, half-filling it with water. The white men baled frantically and began again to row away from the spot where the creature had vanished. Moments passed; the water remained blue and unbroken. The women relaxed, and were just beginning to chatter excitedly about the narrow escape from death of these Duggerigai, when suddenly the whale rose like a mountain directly beneath the boat. Up and up he bore it, while Daringha screamed and hid her eyes; for an amazing second Barangaroo and Warreweer watched it poised there, and then it slid down the vast, slippery side of the monster and crashed into the water, and at the same moment the whale plunged again. Two of the white men disappeared instantly into the whirlpool made by the suction of its huge body; the other two struck out for the shore, but before they had gone more than half way the head of one vanished, and the other at last scrambled out upon the rocks alone.

This incident had caused some consternation in the camps of the black men when the news of it went round, for it was obviously perilous for the women to go out fishing in their frail bark canoes with such a monster about, and for a time most of the fishing was done from the rocks by the men with their spears.

In the early days of the spring, however, their apprehensions were changed to the most extravagant rejoicings, for the whale stranded on a beach in the towri of the Cammeraygal, and a messenger was immediately sent to all the neighbouring tribes, inviting them to a feast such as seldom came their way. From the bay of Gwea, down the coast where the winged ships of the white men had first anchored, came the Gweagal; from the most western reaches of the harbour came the Wanngal in their canoes, and from the opposite shore the Wallumedegal hurried on foot through the bush which was now sweet with the honey scent of wattle, and warm with the first breath of spring. Colbee, Bennilong, Kuurin, By-gone, Ballederry, and many others of their tribe embarked from the little beach below the cliffs of Burrawarra, and paddled across the entrance of the harbour, where the great swell from the ocean lifted their light canoes like corks, and Bennilong shouted cheerfully to the others, as they went, of the great repast which awaited them.

When they reached the beach where the whale lay stranded and already decomposing, their eyes glistened with anticipation. Aie! It was a long time since there had been such plenty! It was a long time since their bellies, accustomed to enforced periods of frugal living, had been stretched to bursting point as they were now to be stretched! Here was so much food that it was no longer unlawful to give one's hunger-lust full play. Now one might eat and eat until one's stomach rebelled and flung up the unaccustomed excess; now one might relax the tight rein upon which one was forced to ride one's hunger, and enjoy a superabundance; one might know the pleasure of unrestrained greed, and the exhaustion of satiety . . .

Fires were lit high on the beach, and great slabs of flesh hacked from the whale with stone knives. The feast was well in train when one of the boats of the Bereewolgal was seen approaching, and a ripple of uneasiness passed through the black throng. Were they never to be left in peace by these white invaders? What was their purpose now in breaking in, uninvited, upon this momentous feast? Had they designs upon the carcass of the whale themselves? It was remembered that they had hunted it, so it was not unreasonable to suppose that they placed some value upon it, and it was also remembered, and emphasised by Bennilong, that there had been want in their camp when he left it, and that the whale, therefore, might be coveted by them as food. But they should not have it! The warriors snatched up their scattered spears from the sand, and watched the approach of the boat with hostile eyes.

Surgeon White, with his adopted protégé, the black boy, Nanbarree, beside him said to Captain Nepean:

"We had best not land till we find out their temper. I don't like those spears. Speak to them, Nanbarree. Say we good, boodjerree, not hurt anyone. Say friends."

Nanbarree stood up obediently in the boat and called to his countrymen. He explained that the white men wanted nothing of them, but were merely bent upon one of their aimless expeditions up the coast. He assured them, in answer to their suspicious questioning, that the Bereewolgal had not known of the stranded whale, and did not want it. He informed them that there was now plenty of food in the camp at Syd-ney, for the winged nowees had brought it from a far-off land. He asked, on his own account, rather wistfully, if the whale flesh was good.

This was all quite satisfactory as far as it went; but upon two former occasions when white men had appeared and approached in their boats with protestations of friendship, there had been treachery, and the black men, though mollified, were still on their guard. Bennilong, hearing White call out his name, stepped forward from the throng, not ill-pleased at the opportunity for showing off his knowledge of their language. At first they did not seem to know him. He was thin, for food had been scarce lately, and his beard had grown longer than was convenient; it occurred to him that here was a chance of ridding himself of it and impressing his countrymen at the same time, so he entered into conversation affably enough:

"Good day! You call? What you want?"

White shouted:

"Bennilong? You Bennilong?"

"Here Bennilong, carrahdy. Where Be-anga? Be-anga Bennilong friend. Collin Bennilong friend. Where Collin?"

White said to Nepean: "It's Bennilong all right." He called out:

"Be-anga not far away, Bennilong." He pointed towards South Head where Phillip had gone that morning to inspect a landmark which was being erected for the guidance of ships, and Bennilong nodded eagerly. He wanted to be convinced that the white men had no intention of attempting a raid upon their feast, but he was very willing to share it with his friend the Be-anga.

"I go look for Be-anga," he stated. "I tell come, na-lau-ra . . ." Struck by a sudden thought, he forgot his hospitable intentions, and asked hopefully: "You bring mogo today? Give Bennilong mogo?"

White shook his head.

"No hatchets today, Bennilong. Another day bring hatchets."

Colbee now emerged from the crowd, and, looking grimly, but without malice at the white men, pointed to his ankle. "There," his gesture said, "you placed a fetter—but it is gone. I am free again."

The boat drew in to the shore, and the exploring party disembarked. Though they had no hatchets to satisfy Bennilong's importunity, a few shirts, handkerchiefs and knives were presented and accepted, and Bennilong immediately began to struggle into one of the shirts. His countrymen watched with interest, but Bennilong found it a more difficult matter than he had expected. He squirmed and writhed, his head half hidden, his arms contorted and flailing the air in his efforts, and White, grinning, signed to one of his men to assist. The man was the Governor's gamekeeper, McEntire; Bennilong had had a brush with him during his stay at the settlement, and had no love for him. Seeing him approach, and feeling the construction of the garment, now more or less on, the memory of captivity surged over him, making him shake with rage and defiance. He cried out in his own tongue, fiercely: "Do not come near me! Keep away!" Though the words were incomprehensible, his tone, gestures and expression made his meaning clear enough, and McEntire halted with a shrug of his shoulders, while White hastened to smooth over an awkward moment with a tactful compliment.

"You grow fine long beard, Bennilong."

Bennilong said sulkily:

"No good. Bennilong want take off—you take off?"

White shook his head.

"No razor, Bennilong. You come Sydney get razor. Here scissors."

Bennilong brightened. He had become quite skilled in the use of this implement during his stay with the white men, and he welcomed the chance of showing off before his friends. He stepped forward eagerly.

"Give Bennilong . . ." He shook his head impatiently. This was one of their impossible words; his tongue would not make it. It was a preposterous sound. He said shortly:

"Give."

The scissors were handed to him. In an attentive and respectful silence he arranged his fingers in them carefully, and began to cut his hair and beard, watched solemnly by scores of intent dark eyes. It was a satisfying moment for him, and when he was finished he was again in an excellent temper. White, pointing to the women and children who stood at a distance, asked:

"Which one your woman, Bennilong? Which one Barangaroo?"

Bennilong glanced at him slyly. He had won great admiration and applause in their camp by his accounts of his amorous adventures, his fickleness, and his irresistible attraction for women, and now he was in the mood for a little joke at their expense. He said airily:

"Barangaroo, she belong Colbee now. Me, Bennilong, not want any more. Me, Bennilong, have bulla murrai dyin." He rolled his eyes wickedly and sketched in the air with lascivious gestures an outline of abundant charms which sent his hearers, both white and black, into roars of laughter. It was increased among his own countrymen when White pointed to the scars of two new wounds, one through his arm and the other above his left eye, for it was well known in all the tribes that they were the result of an encounter with Odooroodah's husband, in which Bennilong had come off second best.

Bennilong, his self-esteem rudely shaken, retired, grumbling darkly, and White directed his coxswain to push off and land those members of the party who were bound for Broken Bay a little farther up the beach. This done, he gave orders that the boat should go immediately in search of Phillip, so that he might know of their encounter with Bennilong, but before they pulled out a party of natives came down with odoriferous slabs of whale flesh which they loaded into the boat with urgent requests that they should be presented to the Be-anga as a gift from his friend, Bennilong.

The feast then continued. The sun climbed up the sky and the whale stank, and the natives gorged happily. Flies swarmed about the vast carcass, and children scrambled for bits, or fell asleep curled up on the warm sand, their little bellies round and tight with plenty. Bennilong ate and ate until his very eyeballs seemed bursting. By degrees the party broke up, and the natives scattered into the woods to sleep off the effects of their orgy. By the time the Governor's boat was seen rounding the headland not more than a score or so remained about the carcass of the whale.

* * *

They ceased eating when they saw the boat, and began to comment among themselves. That one in the stern, said Bennilong, pointing authoritatively, was the Be-anga of the Bereewolgal, and an intimate friend of himself, Bennilong. He was a very great leader. None in his camp dared to oppose him, for he owned all the food, and could bestow or withhold it at will. Why, asked Wileemaring of the Gweagal, was he coming here? No doubt, said Bennilong loftily, he was coming to visit his friend Bennilong, Wolarawaree, whom he esteemed very highly, and whose counsel he had often asked. No doubt he was coming to beg of him to return to the camp which they called Syd-ney. Was it, Wileemaring demanded pertinently, necessary for him to beg? When he had desired Bennilong's company before had he not sent men in a boat who had approached with fair words and assurances of friendship, and then taken him by force? Might he not be bound upon another such errand now? For himself, Wileemaring concluded, he would take care to keep away from these Bereewolgal; he would see to it that no treacherous white men approached within arm's length of *him*!

Bennilong kicked sullenly at the sand. There was truth and reason in the words of Wileemaring, but it was unwelcome truth. He did not want to be captured again by the white men, but he did want to talk to them. He did want to receive any gifts which they might offer, especially hatchets, and he did want to display his familiarity with their words and customs before his countrymen. And in his heart there was a deep, almost uneasy veneration for the white Be-anga—a confused, superstitious tendency to link him with his own father, Wunbula, an aching awareness of tangled motives and desires within himself. Nevertheless Wileemaring's words had made an impression, and not only upon Bennilong. It was agreed that no matter how fair and friendly might be the words of the Bereewolgal, their intentions must remain suspect. Silently, watchfully they waited, while Phillip stood up in the boat and called:

"Waw Bennilong?"

Bennilong himself responded promptly by stepping forward, and the Governor called again:

"I am the Governor—Be-anga." He said to Collins, seated beside him:

"Stay in the boat, Collins, and you too, Lieutenant Waterhouse. Keep her on her oars, and have the muskets ready. I'm going ashore."

When the keel grated on the sand he stepped out and called again for Bennilong. Now that his mind was less harassed by anxiety he had found his thoughts turning often to that cheerful young savage who had dwelt beneath his roof, and when the news had reached him of the whale feast he had lost no time in setting out for Manly Cove, hoping to establish friendly relations with him again.

Bennilong, stepping forward, answered the Governor's greetings, but, with the words of Wileemaring still fresh in his mind, he backed away when Phillip attempted to approach. The Governor followed, holding out both his hands in his customary gesture of amity, until, among the trees which fringed the beach, the natives halted and entered into conversation with him. This was a prearranged strategy; sheltered by the trees, at some distance from the boat, and with the Be-anga alone among them, they were no longer unwilling to give him their hands. Bennilong's heart warmed to his white friend as they talked, and he was disappointed when Phillip, after a short conversation, returned down the beach to his boat. But he did not embark. Instead, closely watched from the trees, he was seen procuring bundles which he directed one of his people to carry, and came walking back across the sand towards them. Bennilong's eyes glistened as they approached, for he could see that one of the objects which the man was carrying was a bottle of wine. It was a very strange thing about this magical drink that the memory of it stayed with one, teasing, beckoning, alluring. Water one drank and forgot. Not so with this lovely, blood-red fluid. Many, many times since his return to his own people he had found himself remembering the caressing taste of it upon one's tongue, the sharp, warm feel of it sliding down one's throat, the rich, mellow glow which suffused one's being after drinking it. He called eagerly: "Wine! Wine!" but when it was given him he courteously remembered, even in his haste, to observe the ceremonial which the white men had taught him. Holding the glass up before him, after their custom, he cried loudly: "The King!" and swallowed the contents in two thirsty gulps.

Other presents were distributed among the natives, including several jackets, two of which Bennilong promptly put on over his shirt, and the Governor then returned again to the boat and brought Captain Collins back with him, instructing Waterhouse still to remain where he was.

Lieutenant Waterhouse was uneasy. To his right, from the shelter of the woods, a voice called out continually to Bennilong. He could not understand more than a word here and there, of which "nowee," often repeated, was one, but he suspected that Bennilong was being very efficiently informed of the movements of the boat's crew. It might well appear suspicious to them, he thought worriedly, that the boat was being kept so carefully afloat, as if ready for a hurried departure. Just so had their two previous raids been conducted, when first Arabanoo and then Bennilong and Colbee had been carried off. Was it likely that the natives had forgotten this? Was it likely that they would not be hostile? Was His Excellency not being just a little foolhardy? Waterhouse was relieved when a messenger from the Governor came down to the boat and desired him to join them. When he went up the beach he found Phillip talking to Colbee and Bennilong; Bennilong cut an odd figure with his shirt tails and his coat tails flapping about his naked legs, but he was in high spirits, for his fellows had seemed suitably impressed by his wine drinking, and by his fluent conversation in the tongue of the Bereewolgal. It pleased him, too, that he had been able to put on his jackets quite easily, while Colbee still held his over his arm, and was obliged to request Lieutenant Waterhouse, as he came up, to put it on for him. He could hear the warning calls from the native who was watching the boat, and he knew that it was possible that the Bereewolgal again intended treachery, but he was not much disturbed by the thought, for this time his people were prepared. There were many, many of them about him—far more than the white men could see—all on the alert, and all armed. He knew that for every one visible there were two or three invisible among the trees, and he laughed at Wileemaring's tense expression, and began to show off even more blatantly than before.

He remembered many of his white friends, and enquired of the Be-anga how they did. With a mischievous twinkle in his eye he stepped up to the astonished Lieutenant Waterhouse and kissed him soundly on the cheek, mentioning, as he did so, the name of a white woman upon whom he had once audaciously bestowed the same salute, and laughing heartily to see the fair skin of the young man burn with embarrassment. He was just beginning to get into his stride, taking the centre of the stage with all his usual gusto, when Phillip, noticing his scars, pointed to them and asked:

"How you hurt, Bennilong?"

A little ripple of amusement passed through the ranks of the black men; Bennilong was a notable warrior, an asset to any tribe, but they were not unwilling to see his inordinate vanity occasionally brought low, and they nudged each other, grinning, as his high spirits collapsed, and he replied with sullen arrogance:

"I hurt fight, Bot-any Bay."

He would say no more. He looked moodily at the ground and ignored the overtures of Phillip and David Collins. When the Governor, observing a particularly fine spear which he carried, asked to be allowed to examine it, he eyed him darkly and took it away to some distance where he laid it deliberately on the grass near the feet of Wileemaring.

Phillip looked at him, puzzled. Something had disturbed the harmony. Or had there ever been any harmony? He realised suddenly that behind the affability of Bennilong, behind all the politeness of the other natives, there had been mistrust. There was something in the air which seemed to spell danger. These natives were not exactly hostile, nor were they really friendly. They were simply watchful. He had had that thought before, but in a different connection. What was it? He looked past them at the tree-clothed hillside, and knew what it was. The land itself! Yes, he had felt that in the land, and now he felt it again in its people. Neither welcoming nor repelling. Neither genial nor inimical. Only watching out of some colossal past in whose arms they had rested so securely for so many ages that no change seemed possible. That no change *was* possible . . .

Nonsense, nonsense, and again nonsense! Already there were changes. Already the mark of civilisation lay upon the land. In fifty years, in a hundred years . . .

The watchful land, the watchful dark eyes made his hundred years seem the hundredth part of a second. Millions of years lay over the quiet trees; thousands of years dwelt undisturbed in the hearts and minds of these people. What happens—in the end? Which wins—man or the earth? From some storehouse of memory words were flung up to his consciousness, the words of an ancient inscription seen somewhere and forgotten till this moment:

> "The Earth walks on the Earth, glistening with gold,
> The Earth goes to the Earth sooner than it was wold,
> The Earth builds on the Earth Temples and Towers,
> The Earth says to the Earth: All will be ours."

Phillip was still staring at the hillside, but he was no longer seeing it. "All will be ours." His brain groped. Why had those words come to him like an illumination, and why did they seem so irrevocably bound up with the dark-skinned throng which surrounded him? "All will be ours."

There was an ominous ring to them which he resented, because their veiled threat seemed aimed at his own dominant race, passing lightly over the heads of these untutored savages. He looked at them, frowning, and found himself staring into the searching eyes of a black man whom he did not remember having seen before. He looked round sharply, wrenched back with a shock into the practical and urgent present, and realised that these people, under their seeming casualness, had been all the time alert; that their strategy had met and outmatched his own at every turn. He saw that they had, with apparent carelessness, arranged that this interview should be conducted among the trees where they had ample cover, and not on the beach where their bodies would be easy targets for the muskets of his men. Even now they stood in a crescent round the little group of white men, cutting off their retreat; and some of them—he was looking at Wileemaring again—seemed queerly tense, as if awaiting a signal . . .

He said to Collins in an undertone:

"I think we'll withdraw, Collins. I don't feel sure of them." To Bennilong he said: "I go now, Bennilong. I come back two days, bring you clothes, bring two hatchets, one for Bennilong, one for Colbee."

Bennilong nodded vehemently.

"Be-anga come two day. Bring hatchet Bennilong."

Phillip made a gesture of agreement and turned away. There was a sharp exchange of words between Bennilong and some of his fellows. "What did the Be-anga say?" "He says that he will bring me a hatchet." "I also want a hatchet." "And I!" "And I!" "Say to the Be-anga that we also wish for hatchets!" Bennilong, nothing loth, called:

"Be-anga!"

Phillip halted, turned.

Bennilong, indicating his countrymen, named them, and was about to interpret their wishes, when Phillip, misunderstanding, advanced towards Wileemaring, the last named, with his hand outstretched. The native did not move, but his eyes glittered queerly. Here at last was the treachery he had been expecting. The white man thought to approach him? To lay hands upon him? Never! His eyes flickered for one instant from Phillip's face to Bennilong's spear, lying in the grass at his feet.

Phillip, thinking to reassure him, took a dirk which he wore at his side, and flung it down upon the ground. With the rattle of its fall the tension exploded. What was this action? What power had the gleaming thing which lay between them? It looked like a weapon, and if one weapon could kill from afar, why not another? Like a flash, Wileemaring stooped to the spear, fixed it in his throwing stick, and stood poised.

Phillip felt a cold shock of fear lift the hairs upon his body, but he did not halt. To retreat now, he thought, would be disastrous. It might bring a hail of spears about them. He shook his head rebukingly, saying, "Weeree! Weeree!" but even as he spoke he knew, looking into the wild dark eyes of Wileemaring, that this time he could not stay the consequences of the panic which he read there.

Wileemaring's weight went back on to his right foot, his arm swung, the spear shot through the air. Phillip staggered. It was like a violent blow upon his right shoulder, and the force of it spun him round facing the beach. For a moment or two he was conscious of nothing but agony and uproar—a confusion of shouts and yells. As Collins dashed out on to the beach to call up men from the boat with their muskets, the thought flashed through his mind that it was fortunate the natives did not know that only two of them would fire. He began to stumble down the beach, trying to hold up the end of the spear, whose point protruded three inches from his back, and whose twelve-foot long shaft continually caught in the sand and halted him. He said faintly to Waterhouse:

"For God's sake, get this thing out. I can't run . . ."

Waterhouse stared at it in dismay. He could not draw it out without once more tearing the flesh with its inch long barb. Spears were still flying from the trees; Collins was shouting to the boat's crew to have her ready to push off, and the Governor, grey-faced with pain, was swaying where he stood. Waterhouse, distracted, seized the end of the spear and attempted to break it, but it was too tough. He swore and strained, glancing apprehensively over his shoulder, while Phillip tried weakly to pull a pistol from his pocket. Suddenly a spear whirred between them, and Lieutenant Waterhouse found himself staring in stupefaction at his thumb and forefinger from which the skin had been stripped, and blood was oozing. This frightened him so much that his next effort to break the spear was successful, and again they began to run down the beach towards the boat. A spear fell at Captain Collins' feet. Phillip moved drunkenly, but he was still fumbling for his pistol. By now, he was thinking hazily, they must have realised that only two of the firearms were effective; it was as well to let them know that there was another. He dragged it out, fired it in the air, and then knew hardly anything more than that Waterhouse was bundling him into the boat with more haste than gentleness, and that Collins and the rest of the crew, acting as rearguard, were running towards them with the heavy stumbling gait of men hurrying in soft sand.

The yells died away, the turmoil subsided, the soft swaying of the boat blended with the unsteadiness of his sight and of his queerly crowding

thoughts. He lay peacefully staring up at the cornflower blue sky and
thinking of Le Receveur's lonely grave. *"Hic jacet Arthur Phillip."* The
sand blew so thickly that it would soon cover the mound. He must have
a headstone erected. No, no, it was his own grave; he could not. But it
did not really matter that it would be hidden, buried, forgotten in an alien
country. He had never been other than solitary in his life, and his bones
would rest quietly enough in this soil which he had come near to loving.
Yes, that was a thought he had never had before, a realisation which came
vagrantly like—or with—a breath of sea wind across his face. He did not
feel so very alien now. It was hard to live, but easy enough to die in this
silent land with its air of timelessness, eternity . . . "The Earth says to
the Earth: All will be ours."

Collins looked down anxiously at his drawn, pallid face and his closed
eyes. He said:

"Pull your hardest, men."

The crew strained on their oars till the sweat ran down their faces and
their backs. The west wind was heavy with the scents of spring, and the
harbour was as blue as the sky. The beauty of the day seemed suddenly
cruel to Lieutenant Waterhouse, who was, after all, only eighteen, and he
turned his head away and jammed his hat down over his eyes so that no
one should see that they were wet with tears.

*   *   *

Phillip, his shoulder swathed in bandages, looked up from his papers as
Lieutenant Dawes entered. It was a week since he had been wounded,
and it seemed a month. To be rendered helpless now, when there was so
much to be done, irked him almost beyond endurance, and he continually
summoned officers to his bedside to report to him the progress of affairs
both at Sydney Cove and at Rose Hill.

The attack upon himself had disturbed him profoundly. There was not
time, he thought impatiently, for hostilities! He saw all the efforts, which
he had made in the past, to win the confidence of the natives, brought to
nothing in a moment. He saw his cherished plans for the construction of
an orderly civil life thrown into chaos by the necessity for military activities and precautions. He might, after all, have to abandon the building of
barracks, houses, stores, for the building of fortifications. He might have
to withdraw men from their agricultural pursuits and train them to bear
arms in defence of the settlement. These things were the acknowledged
cause of the persistence with which he asked his officers insatiably for
news of the natives. Had any been seen in the neighbourhood? Did they

seem friendly or otherwise? Were they armed? How many were there? But in his heart he had another reason for dismay. He did not want to fight these people, but he would not admit, even to himself, that the genuine humanitarianism of his motive was queerly mixed with another, superstitious and absurd. That unknown danger lurking at his side! What was it? This was a strange land, and who should know its mysteries but its own strange people? A conviction too fanciful to be consciously entertained, persisted in him, finding outlet in his actions. There was much to learn here. There was wisdom in these primitive communities; there was a dignity not to be hidden or overlaid by antics which seemed merely comical to sophisticated eyes, and the thought of destroying it stirred not only regret in him but actual fear.

He had tossed restlessly on his bed during those first days after his wounding, thinking of these things. They had been vaguely in his mind ever since it had happened, and he had been feverishly worried, believing himself about to die, because they were not things which he could explain, pass on to those who must take up his responsibilities when he was gone. It had been so easy to insist upon setting his papers in order before allowing Balmain to extract the spear; so easy to send Lieutenant Long after White and his party to warn them of possible attack. Practical matters were manageable. But there were other matters, no less important, which one saw as through a glass, darkly, and of which one could not even speak.

It had cheered him a little to learn from White when he had returned on the following day, that a party of natives whom they had encountered in Manly Cove had seemed friendly, and that Bennilong and Colbee, who were among them, had expressed great indignation against the man who had flung the spear. But from that time no one had seen any of the natives at sufficiently close quarters to converse with them until today—when news had come to him that Dawes, out in a boat with Mr. Johnson and Booron, had had a long conversation with two natives, and desired permission to wait upon the Governor with an account of what had passed.

He motioned Dawes to a chair with his left hand.

"Sit down, Dawes. You have some news of the natives for me?"

"Yes, Sir." Dawes drew his chair up to the bedside and laid his hat down on the floor beside him, with the thought in his mind that the Governor looked very ill indeed. "We encountered two men. They came up alongside our boat in their canoe, and asked how you did. They seemed pleased when we informed them that you were recovering."

"Did you know them—remember having seen them before?"

"No, Sir. They said they came from the Rose Hill district—Parramatta, as they call it. That's another thing I wanted to mention. They spoke with some indignation of our settlement there, Sir. So far as I could understand them, they said it was their territory, and that the presence of our people was driving the kangaroos away and spoiling their hunting grounds."

Phillip sighed, but he only said:

"I shall send up reinforcements to the garrison there tomorrow. It might be necessary. Did you gain any other information?"

"Yes, Sir. They said that the name of the native who wounded you was Wileemaring. He belongs to a Botany Bay tribe, I gathered. I tried to make them understand that it was a reprehensible action, Sir, and they seemed very willing to agree, saying 'Weeree!' many times, and showing signs of great disapproval."

Phillip nodded.

"You have not seen Bennilong?" To this question he added rather hurriedly: "Or Colbee?" He was surprised by his own eagerness to know that Bennilong was not entirely indifferent to his well-being. There had crept into his feeling for this young savage who called him "father" some of the half irritated affection which a true father might have felt for a headstrong and irresponsible son. There was a frankness, an open-hearted gusto, a total absence of any sort of inhibition about Bennilong which appealed to Phillip's inarticulate and rigidly reserved temperament, and he was conscious of a faint sadness when Dawes replied briefly:

"No, Sir."

"Ah, well!" The Governor lay back on his pillows. The room seemed dingy and chilly now that the sun had left its windows. The only bright things in it, he thought, were a great bunch of the fluffy, honey-scented, yellow flowers which Mrs. Macarthur had sent to him that morning, and the healthily sunburned countenance of Lieutenant Dawes. He was tired. Talking tired him still, for he had lost a great deal of blood; he said wearily:

"Thank you, Dawes. Will you send Captain Collins to me? I must give orders for the reinforcements for Rose Hill."

When Dawes had gone he half stretched his left hand towards his papers, and then let it fall again. Not now, not now.

*   *   *

Bennilong stood on the shore opposite Sydney Cove and pointed excitedly at the boats of the white men rowing across the water to them. This was a meeting which had been prearranged the same morning, and the natives were pleased to find that the Bereewolgal bore them no malice for the unfortunate wounding of their Be-anga. It was a foolish thing which Wileemaring had done, but it was no more than was to be expected, after all, when men of different tribes met and had no law and no language to show each other what was in their hearts. Wileemaring had been foolish, but not really culpable, his fellows decided, though Bennilong, in the first flood of his rage, had fallen upon him, and might have killed him if he had not been rescued by members of his own tribe.

Now friendly relations with the white men were about to be established once more, and here were their boats coming to prove it, bringing, no doubt, presents, among which there might be one or two useful things such as hatchets. A group of children, standing at a little distance, watched with bright-eyed curiosity, but the women were not to be seen. They were near by, however. Barangaroo, sullen and suspicious, stood behind a tree peering round its pinkish bole, never taking her eyes from Bennilong. Her heart was full of a jealous and resentful possessiveness. Bennilong was hers—hers! She thought it fiercely during most of her waking hours nowadays, for lately events seemed to be more and more denying it. He was now hopelessly enamoured of the beautiful young Odooroodah of the Bidegal, and he was continually getting himself into trouble over her. He had had many, many fights about her, and one day he would be killed. And now, not content with that, he was full of a feverish desire to renew his familiarity with the Bereewolgal. How unutterably foolish, she thought disdainfully, was the vanity of menfolk in general, and of Bennilong in particular! To satisfy it—to win a few amazed and admiring stares from his companions, he would venture again and again into the ill-omened society of the white men! They were a dangerous people. Ill fortune and disaster followed them. Misery dwelt in their camp. Why could he not leave them alone, she wondered resentfully, and devote himself to the affairs of his tribe?

Many of the other men were now almost as bad. They talked incessantly of the possessions and the accomplishments of the white people. They coveted their hatchets. Well, Barangaroo admitted sulkily, they were undoubtedly good hatchets. But were they not too good? It was true that they could fell quite a large tree with incredible rapidity, but why should one fell trees? A bit of their bark for shields and shelters, a few of their shed boughs for fires, a green branch or two to shroud the warrior prepared for burial—these were all they had ever asked of the trees, and why should they now wish to hew them down? Barangaroo watched with an uneasy hostility. She did not know why this new pastime stirred fear in her heart, but fear was there. For the first time in the history of her race, so she dimly felt, its easy brotherhood with the earth was being disturbed; for the first time her people were taking more than it offered; for the first time she became actively conscious of her land, of its omnipotence, of its quiet, waiting, watching might, and was afraid of it.

Now the white men, accompanied by Nanbarree and Booron, were landing. Aie! How ugly they were! They were coming forward, nodding, smiling, holding out their gifts as usual, and Bennilong was, also as usual, growing noisy and assertive in his excitement.

Barangaroo thrust her lower lip out and made a contemptuous noise. It was food which they were offering, and there was some of the strange drink, too, which Bennilong was always talking about. It was a magic drink, he said, which brought men strength and wisdom and ecstasy, and he had told her that he believed it to be by virtue of this drink alone that the Bereewolgal acquired their power. Barangaroo was prepared to believe anything of the white men, but she was not prepared to admit that her own people needed any greater strength than was already theirs, any deeper wisdom than that which their ancestors had bequeathed to them in their Law, any sweeter ecstasies than those provided by their tribal rites, by courtship and mating, by parenthood, by life itself.

Upon that occasion when Be-anga had been speared Bennilong had drunk some of this magic fluid. Barangaroo's own opinion was that it had not made him strong, but only noisy and quarrelsome; not wise, but distinctly more foolish than usual; and as for ecstasy, she had, for the first time, repulsed him savagely that night, for there was a smell upon his breath which she did not like. Now, watching him advance with enthusiasm upon the bottle which Tench was holding out to him, she grunted scornfully, and turned her back.

Bennilong quaffed the wine, and loudly demanded bread and beef. He offered portions to his friends who stood about him, and they tasted the meat dubiously, but refused the bread. It was odd looking stuff, they said to each other, eying it with aversion and squeezing it between their thumbs and forefingers—rather like fungus, pallid, spongy, and unwholesome. Bennilong, gulping down his last morsel with a greater display of relish than he really felt, demanded of Tench:

"You cut hair, beard today?"

Tench had brought not only a razor, but a barber, and Bennilong, seating himself upon a log, indicated with a lordly gesture that he was ready to be shaved. From her tree trunk Barangaroo watched the operation with smouldering eyes. She did not want her man to display naked, womanlike cheeks, like those of the Bereewolgal. When the throng of men surrounding her husband, edging nearer and nearer to watch more closely, hid him at last from her view, she squatted cross-legged on the ground, struggling with a sense of oppression from which she was only aroused by the sound of her own name.

Booron was standing a few yards away, grinning shyly, and twisting the skirt of her straight blue garment between her fingers, nervous and ill at ease, but filled with a trembling sense of happiness. Here was a woman of her own race, the first she had spoken to for eighteen months. She stared wistfully, eagerly, as if in the dark, sullen eyes of Barangaroo she might find a solution of all the fears and desires which had tormented her in that long, long time.

They were quite kind people, the Bereewolgal, and her docile and affectionate nature had taught her to respect and obey them. Was it possible that one so great as Mr. Dyon-ton, before whom even the Be-anga sometimes bowed his head, whose dignified gait and solemn mien marked him as apart from his fellows, who was obviously the chief sorcerer of the whole tribe, the leader of their weekly corroboree and the expounder of their Law, should speak other than the truth? She could not believe it possible. She listened attentively when he spoke, stored his words in her retentive memory, repeated them glibly when so instructed. At first, learning to understand their tongue, she had been astonished and delighted to find that new words may clothe an old, familiar story. For she found that these people were trying to teach her of the Maker-of-all, though they called him by a different name, and they pointed, as her own people did, to the Heavens as his dwelling place. Eagerly she had nodded her comprehension when Mrs. Johnson was instructing her. The Law of the white tribe, she had thought cheerfully, was evidently very much the same as her own Law, so she would get along very well with them. But no. It was the same, and yet not the same. There were incredible things in it. She repeated them dutifully, and tried to understand them, but could not. This heavenly Being of theirs, it seemed, expected that one should love one's enemies, which was, obviously, nonsense. The white people themselves considered it nonsense, for they were always quarrelling. Booron had never seen so much hatred and vindictiveness as she saw in their camp. Immanuel said that if someone stole one's coat one should give him one's cloak also—another absurd saying which the white men never thought of heeding, for if any member of their tribe stole so much as a handkerchief, let alone a coat, he was promptly flogged or put to death. Immanuel said that if a man smote you upon one cheek you should turn the other so that he might smite you again, and this was surely a shameful saying which would enrage any warrior worthy of the name. She could understand why the white people ignored these ridiculous commands, but she could not understand why they went on repeating them. A Law, if it was anything at all, was surely something to live by, something to which one might anchor one's spiritual life. Among her own people it was exactly that. It made hard, but not impossible, demands upon their courage and their self-control. It was so intricately interwoven not only with their own physical and spiritual needs, but with the peculiarities of the land itself, that all three became one, a mystical trinity functioning in harmony—the Law, the Land, the People.

But among these Bereewolgal what division! What conflicts! A Law endlessly repeated and endlessly disobeyed! Booron grew quite melancholy in her bewilderment. They were kind to her, they were clever beyond words; surely they must also be good? And yet, being clever, why were they so afraid? For they were afraid. Life itself seemed to terrify them. There were, for instance, certain simple matters the very mention of which seemed to throw them into a panic. There had been that extraordinary incident of the mirror. Mrs. Johnson had a mirror, a magical, shining, silvery thing in which one might see the image of oneself as one did in a still pool, only much more clearly, and it had been to Booron, once she got over her first vague uneasiness, a perpetual delight. When she had been brought to the settlement she was just ceasing to be a child, just becoming aware of her body and her gently swelling breasts, and she had, very naturally, wanted to observe her charms. Alone in the room with the mirror she had dragged off her frock and strutted delightedly, turning this way and that, practising those movements in which she had already received some instruction from the old women of her tribe, and which were some day to enhance her desirableness in the eyes of her husband. When Mrs. Johnson entered she had turned happily, proudly confident that this mature and experienced woman would commend and encourage her. But she saw only a stare of blank horror and disgust. What was the matter? With a chill of fear she turned back to the mirror. Was there some blemish—some deformity? Had she, in her still imperfect knowledge, done something amiss, offended against some mysterious taboo?

She never discovered. She only knew that Mrs. Johnson was terrified. Her face was as red as a sunset, her hands trembled, her voice trembled. She hustled Booron into her dress again. She scolded violently in a voice which sounded shrill and unnatural. It was wicked, wicked, this thing that Booron had done! It was immodest and disgraceful! "Weeree,

weeree!" she kept on saying, that being, at the time, almost the only native word she knew.

Booron had wept. She did not know why it was weeree, and she could not find out. Mrs. Johnson had taken the tears as a sign of repentance, and the incident had closed; but in Booron's mind it remained as a symbol of the inexplicable fear which haunted these people. It was a fear which affected her very nearly, for in those eighteen months she had changed from a child to a young woman, and she had had to do it quite alone. Things were not managed thus among her own people. When a girl neared marriageable age she was carefully watched and instructed. There were rites and ceremonies. Womanhood did not creep upon her silently and shamefully, shaking her with wild desires which must not be mentioned, strange ecstasies which must not be betrayed. It was welcomed, discussed, suitably dealt with, and made an occasion for pride, rejoicing and congratulation.

Now, standing shyly before Barangaroo, Booron smiled, but she was in a quandary. She had been sent to bring Bennilong's wife forward so that the white men might make her acquaintance—but would they not be offended by her nakedness? She understood quite well by now that it was considered shameful among them to go unclad. Barangaroo snapped at her:

"Unijerunbi minku?"

Booron jerked her head towards the group of men. Barangaroo pretended not to understand. She hitched her basket forward from where it was slung on her hip, and began to rummage in it busily, to show that she was not interested in the white people. Booron persisted:

"Kai, kai, karakai!"

Barangaroo glanced at her scornfully.

"Wutta?"

Again Booron pointed. The white men, she explained, wanted to see Barangaroo, the wife of Bennilong. They would give her presents. Bennilong also wanted her to come. But—but first she must cover herself with a garment, for the Bereewolgal considered it shameful to be naked. Barangaroo stared at her. Secretly she was impressed by Booron's blue dress. Her fingers had been itching to touch it, and she was not at all unwilling to wear one like it if it was to be obtained. Nevertheless, her old dislike of the white people persisted, and her old mistrust held her back. It was not until Bennilong himself came to find her, full of laughter and blandishments, that she allowed herself to be persuaded, and stepped gingerly into a white garment which Booron mysteriously produced from beneath her blue one, and fastened about her waist. Preceded by her husband and followed by Booron, she emerged from the trees and stood hesitating, eying the group of invaders from beneath her tangle of hair.

They laughed and took her by the hand and made strange extravagant gestures. They seemed very amused by her single garment, and, to Booron's dumbfounded astonishment, joined with Bennilong in urging her to dispense with it. Barangaroo, puzzled, but rather relieved, complied. She did not like the feel of it about her waist and legs, and it was not, in any case, nearly as beautiful as the blue one which Booron wore. She dropped it round her feet, stepped out of it, and immediately felt more at ease. At Bennilong's request they combed and cut her hair; when it was done she stood feeling it, and smiling in spite of herself because of the pride and pleasure which she saw in her husband's eyes. They offered her some of the magic drink, but she would not touch it. She noticed that he whom they called Tench seemed to speak of her often to his comrades, and to nod his head towards Booron at the same time, so she was not altogether surprised when Booron took her aside and explained that the white men wished her to pay a visit to their camp. They had thought, so Booron confided, that if she could be persuaded to go to the settlement, Bennilong and others might go too. Barangaroo listened sceptically, eying the white men askance. A visit! Did they imagine that she would trust them to let her go again once she was in their power? Or Bennilong either? She had not forgotten how he and Colbee had been held there. She said fiercely to Booron that she would not go—nor should Bennilong! And if Booron were wise she would not return with them either, but would slip away quietly, here and now, and return to her own people and her own ways. She looked the girl up and down with angry accusing eyes, and asked her questions which made Booron hang her head and dig up the earth with her bare toes in an agony of shame. What instruction had she received in the camp of the white people? In what ways had they prepared her for marriage? Had they taught her to do thus, and thus? No? What kind of a woman would she be? What man would ever desire such a one? Let her leave them quickly and return to her own tribe before it was too late, for her ignorance was shameful, and a disgrace to her womanhood.

Booron's face wrinkled in misery and indecision. When the white men called to her that they were leaving, and beckoned to her to join them, she hung back. And yet it did not matter which way she looked, there was fear and insecurity. Among her own people now, she would seem a stranger. All the young girls with whom, as a child, she had played, would feel an uneasiness in her company because she had not shared in the rites which had taught them those things which all women must learn. She had missed something; it was gone, irrevocably, and she could never make good the spiritual loss which it entailed. The mystical life of her people meant so much to them that this lack in her was as definite as a physical deformity, and she felt despair rise in her as she realised that now she belonged with them hardly more than with the Bereewolgal. . . .

Captain Tench was calling:

"Come, Booron! Come quickly!"

She took a few steps towards him and hesitated again. Barangaroo said nothing, but her eyes smouldered. In the house of Mr. Dyon-ton, thought Booron, there were lovely things, shining things, soft things. There were the little children whom she tended, and to whom she had given an ardent and unstinted love. It did not matter there if one had not performed all those rites which a young girl should perform. Nothing mattered there except to keep one's body covered, to speak softly, to be obedient . . .

"Booron!" Captain Tench sounded impatient and rather stern now. "Come at once, Booron—we are waiting for you!"

Obedience! Yes, that was a virtue in women, even among her own people. It could not be wrong, surely, to obey. She walked past the men with her head bent and got into the boat, but as they rowed back across the harbour to the settlement no one could persuade her to speak, and her eyes remained fixed upon the darkening shore which they had left.

* * *

This encounter, however, was the beginning of more cordial relations, for a time, between the white men and the black. Led and encouraged by Bennilong they began to frequent the settlement with a confidence which rapidly increased as they found that they might leave, as they had come, at will. Bennilong, however, had a good deal of domestic trouble with Barangaroo over the matter. She besought him not to trust the Bereewolgal; she insisted passionately that they were evil and treacherous, and would make him captive again; when arguments failed, she tried feminine wiles. Still unsuccessful, her never very large stock of patience was exhausted. She wept with rage and misery, she screamed vitupera-tions, she stamped on the ground, tore her hair, and finally eased her feel-ings by smashing her husband's favourite fishing spear. She suffered agonies of fear and anxiety until his return, but when he did return she was sullen. She responded neither to his anger nor his caresses, so he went off to Botany Bay in search of Odooroodah. Very often, now, there was discord in the mia-mia of Bennilong and Barangaroo.

* * *

Patrick soon decided that he liked their new living arrangements. The Mannions were no longer His Excellency's guests, but had a little house of their own well up on the hillside on the west side of the stream, not far from the Lieutenant-Governor's house. It was a queer sort of home, Patrick often thought, and he could not quite imagine Mamma in it, but for himself he liked it. It was built of the rather rough looking bricks which were made in the settlement, and roofed with shingles. When you entered by the main door you were in a room which ran the whole breadth of the house, and behind it, on either side of a narrow passage, there were two other smaller rooms, one of which was Papa's and the other the room which Patrick himself shared with his baby brother. At the back there was a kind of lean-to where the cooking was done, and a tiny room opening off this sheltered Ellen Prentice and her family. Behind this again there was a low paling fence; and then only a stretch of rough, scrubby grass, littered with the dead twigs and branches of the trees which had once stood there, separated the house from the woods. There were several sawn-off stumps of felled trees, and one of these became Patrick's throne and lookout post. From it he could gaze down over the settlement and away across the nearest low headland, and see the blue harbour winding out of sight towards the sea. He had a splendid view of the Governor's house, and of the road leading to it, and of the patches of garden beyond it, and of the ships lying at anchor in the cove. He could see the dark, small specks on the water far away which were the natives' canoes, and, with Johnny at his side to prompt him, he could imagine their strange alluring life, and follow them in his thoughts to some awesome ceremony, or thrilling chase, or wild, barbaric feast. All that he had ever heard of the dark-skinned races merged in his mind to form a tapestry of incredible brilliance and complication. When he invented games the natives always figured in them as apochryphal beings, part human, part giant, part Red Indian, part African Negro. The truth was that his mind dealt with them very much as theirs dealt with the spirits in which they so firmly believed. They were real, and yet not real. Neither the child mind nor the primitive mind boggled over that; reality became so often faded and distorted, unreality shone out so often with a poignant clarity, that they did not attempt to draw a line between them. Where should it be drawn? Was the stab of an emotion less real than the stab of a spear? At what stage of the savage initiation ceremony did physical agony become spiritual ecstasy? Patrick would have agreed with them that such questions were fruitless. For himself, to be dragged from a game to his dinner or his bed, was to be dragged from a world of brilliant actuality into one which was often far less real than dreams.

Papa had not wanted Ellen to have her children with her in his house—particularly not Johnny, but he had agreed at last on condition that Patrick was not to talk or play with them. By degrees, however, this rule was forgotten or ignored. Patrick thought it palpably foolish to have so interesting a companion as Johnny living in the same house with him and not enjoy his company. At first he disobeyed tentatively, with one eye upon Papa. But Papa was preoccupied, and did not seem to notice. Ever since Mamma's death he had been queer. He spent most of his time reading or writing in his own room, or going down to the foot of the hill to visit Captain and Mrs. Macarthur, or the Johnsons, and when he was in the house he seemed ill at ease, and anxious to get away as soon as possible to the seclusion of his own room. Once or twice he reprimanded Patrick for his association with the convict child, but Patrick, though he listened respectfully enough, was, for the first time in his life, consciously rebellious.

Far worse than Papa's displeasure were the snubs which he received from Johnny himself. Two confusing and contradictory facts now became apparent to Patrick. Papa did not consider Johnny good enough to associate with him. Johnny considered himself too good. On the whole Patrick agreed with Johnny. Johnny was far more accomplished and, in the things that mattered, far better informed than himself. He could not read or write, certainly, and he said no prayers, and could not ever remember having seen a real town, with proper roads and carriages and shops, but all the same Patrick was continually made aware of his own ignorance, his own inadequacy for coping with the life in which they found themselves. Johnny was excitingly, almost terrifyingly, sufficient unto himself. He never asked permission or advice. If he hurt himself—even quite bad cuts—he never ran to his mother for help or comfort. He disappeared for a whole day at a time, and no one cared. He came back late at night, long after Patrick was in bed, and no questions were asked. His mother talked to him as if he were a grown man, though when he angered her she would slap him on the side of the head fast enough. When this happened he did not cry but swore.

He treated Patrick, for the most part, with a laconic contempt. Many were the mornings when Patrick, alone on his tree-stump, enviously watched the ragged figure, the flying bare legs of Johnny, off down the hill towards the convicts' huts, to a spacious and exciting life from which he was for ever debarred. It was by accident that he discovered, one day, a great secret of Johnny's. Exploring the burnt-out hollow of a tree trunk, he had found a little box. It was heavy, and it jingled as he turned it over. Inside, to his intense awe and astonishment, he had found a handful of Spanish dollars. There was not an ounce of secretiveness in his nature; it was only by chance that when he told Johnny of this amazing find they were alone. Johnny's dark eyes snapped with fury, his face went pale under its freckles so that his hair seemed redder than ever by contrasts. He moved towards the startled Patrick slowly and evilly, with clenched fists and lowered head, and an expression of almost inhuman hatred and malice.

"Them's mine! Don't you touch 'em! Don't you tell nobody you've seen 'em, or I'll kill you! I'll get the knife out of me mother's kitchen, and I'll kill you while you're asleep!"

Patrick stared, his breath coming fast and his mouth dry. But he was indignant, too. He said rather breathlessly:

"Of course I won't touch them if they're yours. I didn't know they were. I don't want them, anyhow."

He saw the flicker of an expression in Johnny's eyes which he had often seen before. An instant's wavering before the impact of an incomprehensible idea. He felt suddenly sad because he knew that they had come again to one of those always recurring halts in their intercourse where they stood helplessly staring at each other from different worlds. But he felt, too, that it was not so hopeless as it had been at first. He was dimly aware that the mere fact of their association was building a bridge across the chasm which separated them. It was as if a filament of understanding blew out across the gulf from one towards the other, filmy and insubstantial as a spider's web, which catches the sun for an instant and then fades again into invisibility. So he knew now that it was incredible to Johnny that he should not covet money—and suddenly it seemed strange to himself, too. When he wanted money he asked Papa for it, and got it. But how did Johnny get it? Not from his mother, certainly. He said rather nervously:

"Where did you get them, Johnny?"

Johnny looked at him murderously without answering, and again Patrick felt the frail thread of his perception stretch and tauten between them. Johnny had stolen them! His heart thudded, and something of his horror must have shown in his eyes, for the convict child came a step nearer and the flame of his hostility seemed to scorch Patrick's face, for he put his hands to his cheeks and found them burning. No, it was blushing—that enraging habit which he had when he was embarrassed or ashamed. And yet it was not himself, surely, but Johnny who should be ashamed? But Johnny was not blushing. A thief. Papa was right. Convicts were wicked, even the children. He said, unhappily:

"Did you—steal them, Johnny?"

"I *took* 'em," said Johnny, very still, and full of potential violence.

"What for?" Patrick's voice was weak, and his blue eyes wavered uncomfortably away from Johnny's, bright and unmoving as the eyes of a snake.

"Because I wanted 'em. That's what for."

Patrick gave his head a little shake as if to clear his brain of its confusion. "But it's—it's wrong to steal. It's why so many of the convicts have been sent here. To punish them. Because it's wrong to steal. . . ."

He was stammering, incoherent, but convinced. Johnny was not going to argue about ethics. All he wanted was to know his secret safe and, as he watched Patrick's troubled face, some of the fear and fury faded from his eyes, leaving them shrewd and calculating. There was no doubt that this milksop of a child wanted to be his friend, and offers of friendship did not often come Johnny's way. Between himself and the other convict children there existed a kind of bandit freemasonry. They played together, schemed and stole together when they got the chance, but warily, keeping their eyes on each other and their wits alert, knowing that any one of them would betray the others in an instant if he saw in it a moment's advantage for himself. This was normal; it was life as they knew it—every child for himself, and the devil take the hindmost. But from Johnny, too, those spider-threads of perception drifted out sometimes towards this other child, and they told him now that here was a different creed.

Patrick might betray his secret, but not gleefully, for his own reward. If he betrayed it at all it would be unwillingly, in misery, because of some inner compulsion which Johnny had no wish to understand. But it should not be hard—indeed it should be very easy—to persuade him not to betray it at all. He said, slowly:

"I ain't like you. I ain't got any Pa to give me pennies just as I asks for 'em."

He glanced up to observe the effect of pathos. Patrick's brows were creased in worried concentration.

"And I never stole 'em all. Some was give to me for things I done for the officers. Messages, and such. And gettin' oysters from the rocks. I'm savin' up."

"What for?" Patrick looked up, puzzled. There were no shops here, full of children's toys. There was nothing, so far as he could see, upon which a child could spend money when he had acquired it. Johnny was hesitating. The truth burned his tongue. It was too enormous a secret, too stupendous an aim to keep bottled up inside oneself for ever. For months he had longed to tell someone, but his every instinct was for secrecy. He came closer to Patrick and whispered:

"Y' won't split on me?"

"Split . . . ?"

"Tell, y' ninny!"

"No," Patrick assured him seriously, "I won't tell. What *are* you saving up for?"

"For when I get grown up." Johnny's eyes gleamed. "I'm goin' to be gentry, like you."

Patrick flushed scarlet. He felt his skin crawl with embarrassment and did not know why. His mind raced and floundered. *Could* Johnny be gentry? Ever? Just by getting money? What did it mean—being "gentry"? Weren't you born so? Wasn't Papa born so, with money all ready for him, and the beautiful house in Ireland waiting, shrouded in its trees, and people there to serve him, and more people in the village to touch their caps when he rode by? Johnny? Johnny Prentice, the convict child? Oh, no, no, *no!*

He said awkwardly, helplessly:

"How?"

Johnny stared at him suspiciously.

"With me money, of course. I'm goin' to buy a house of me own, and land and horses and a carriage, and get servants and . . ."

"But," Patrick protested, "you can't—just by—it isn't only having money, Johnny. You—you have to *be* gentry. You have to be *born* so."

Johnny's eyes glinted belligerently.

"Y' don't! It's only money! All you got to do is to get enough money, and . . ."

"But not steal it!" Patrick's revelation left him no time for tact. "See, Johnny, if you steal the money it's no good, because the gentry don't steal, and stealing it would stop you from being gentry."

Johnny met this contemptuously with a dash of cold logic.

"I know the gentry doesn't steal—and why don't they? Because they 'aven't got to!"

This left Patrick speechless, drowning in a flood of disturbing thoughts. Was that, indeed, the only reason why gentry didn't steal? Because there was no need? Would Papa steal if he was poor? Oh, no, of course he wouldn't! If he was very, *very* poor, so that he was starving? N-no. No, he wouldn't. He would just starve. Would that be very sensible? Well, perhaps not sensible, but surely very right and noble? But wait a moment. What was God about all this time while Papa was starving? Ah, that made everything clear! God would not allow Papa to starve, for Papa, and everyone else, knew that God always came to the rescue of the good and the virtuous. But then . . . But then was there anything very noble after all in choosing to starve rather than steal if you knew all the time that God wouldn't *let* you starve?

Patrick sighed. He did not often miss Mamma, but he missed her now. It was one of those moments in which life and its problems seemed too large and overwhelming, and from which there had once been, but was now no more, the refuge of a soft lap and encircling arms and a loving voice.

One thing only was clear to him. If he told Papa about the dollars Johnny would be most dreadfully punished. Punishment! There was too much of it—everywhere, all the time! It made this place unhappy, it darkened the very sun! He said petulantly, on the edge of tears:

"You can keep your money. I don't care if you do steal! I don't care about anything!"

"If you tell . . ." began Johnny dangerously. Patrick wheeled on him in a fury.

"I'm not *going* to tell! I don't *care*! You can steal as much as you want to!" Misery taught him to wound. "But you're only an ig- an igerant convict, and you can't *ever* be gentry, no matter what you do! So there!"

Johnny hit out at him savagely. More by good luck than good management Patrick dodged a blow which would have made his nose bleed, and which would, inevitably, have been followed by worse if Ellen had not happened to come out at that moment with a bundle of washing over her arm. Johnny was dragged away; the sound of ringing slaps mingled with his shrill profanity and his mother's equally shrill abuse. Patrick bolted for the shelter of his stump, and crouched behind it, trembling, rubbing his knuckles into his eyes, wishing that Mamma had not died and that they were all back in Ireland where the pattern of life was clear and static, not shifting as it was here, terrible with the urgency of effort and adjustment.

* * *

Now the end of the year 1790 was in sight. The *Gorgon,* long expected, had not yet arrived. The floods of rain, which had so added to the miseries and discomforts of the settlers just before the arrival of the Second Fleet, seemed to have exhausted what the heavens had to send, for the latter half of the year was drought-stricken. Each day the sun came up over the edge of the ocean round and red as an orange, fierce already with the threat of its potential midday heat. The bare ground of the settlement, trodden by many feet, was thick with dust and the air swarmed with flies.

Hardly less annoying than the flies, by now, were the natives. By the middle of November Tench was writing of them in his journal:

"With the natives we are hand and glove. They throng the camp every day, and sometimes, by their clamour and importunity for bread and meat (of which they all now eat greedily) are become very troublesome. God knows we have little enough for ourselves!"

Little enough, indeed! Already the question of food was again an anxiety. Ball had returned on the 19th October, bringing the *Supply* safely back from Batavia, the first ship to circumnavigate the continent of New Holland, but such stores as she was able to carry could not go far among so many as the colony now harboured. He had, however, hired at Batavia, a Dutch snow, the *Waaksamheyd,* and, having loaded her with a store of rice and salt provisions, had left her under the command of a young lieutenant to follow him to Port Jackson.

"Full allowance," wrote Tench at this time, "(if eight pounds of flour, and either seven pounds of beef or four pounds of pork served alternately, per week, without either peas, oatmeal, spirits, butter or cheese, can be called so) is yet kept up; but if the Dutch snow does not arrive soon it must be shortened, as the casks in the storehouse, I observed yesterday, are woefully decreased."

Cultivation at Sydney Cove was now almost abandoned. The drought and the poor soil had combined to bring all efforts at the Government farm to nothing, and Phillip, at last despairing of it, now pressed on more grimly than ever with his agricultural experiments at Rose Hill. Here, during a brief visit in November, Tench, accompanied by Henry Dodd and the Reverend Mr. Johnson, made a tour of inspection. Mr. Johnson had discovered in himself unexpected capabilities as a farmer, and sometimes caught himself suspecting that his cultivation of melons and cucumbers was not only more interesting and rewarding but far more successful than his cultivation of souls. Looking at the fields of wheat, barley, oats and maize, Tench reflected that they, no less than human beings, must struggle to adapt themselves to new conditions. For they were struggling. Not here the rich and lush contentment of English fields. Except for one of maize which looked as flourishing as any he had ever seen and encouraged him to hope, there was a disheartened air about them. It was true, Henry Dodd confessed, that the ground had been, in their haste, inadequately prepared. Each convict had been expected to hoe sixteen rods a day, and in places, consequently, the surface had been merely disturbed. Stumps and roots of the great trees which had been felled still lay untidily about; their trunks and branches had been burned, and the ashes had been dug into the soil. Only in one place, upon the couple of acres belonging to James Ruse, freed convict, and now turned farmer, had there been a real battle with the soil. Here the hoeing had been deep and thorough; grass and weeds had been dug in to enrich it, and it had lain for a suitable period exposed to the air and the sun. Then, before the sowing of the seed, it had been again turned up, and after the reaping of the crop, Ruse told them, he would hoe and harrow it, and sow it with turnip seed to sweeten it for the coming year.

Looking at the man's drab and earth-stained figure, Tench felt his imagination stirred. He remembered the shock with which he had realised, on that first day of their arrival, nearly three years ago, that there were some among them who would never see their native land again. Here was one. Already his roots, so rudely torn up from Cornish soil, were establishing themselves in the new land; already he was drawing sustenance from it. Already he had found himself a wife, and from the chimney of the tiny hut near by the smoke of his hearth rose and faded into the clear air. To his children this land would be home, and England a name which their parents spoke sometimes when they had finished their long day's work and sat wearily on their doorstep to watch the stars come out. For a moment Tench saw the truth which Phillip had also seen, though with the difference that, being Tench, he saw it consciously, and, shaping it into epigram, lost some of its substance. "We don't build the future after all," he thought wryly "we only beget and bear it."

They left the little farm and its owner, and walked back to the township. Here, with a continent to dispose of, Phillip had been able to allow his instinct for spaciousness full play. The main street was to be a mile long; its breadth, as Tench wrote irrepressibly in his journal that night, would be such as to "make Pall Mall and Portland Place hide their diminished heads." Its buildings, unfortunately, could not yet be worthy of it.

They were called, by courtesy, houses, but they were no more than huts, some twenty-four feet by twelve, made of wattle-and-daub with thatched roofs, and divided inside into two rooms. Ten men were allotted to each, but twelve or fourteen were to be found in some. Already, beneath its film of dust, among all the débris of building, and the litter of human occupation, this township, too, wore the same air of poverty and squalor which lay like a blight on Sydney Cove.

Tench turned his back on it and looked westward towards his river. In that direction, he thought, their civilisation would expand; and he thought it serenely, with complacency, being, above all, a man who dwelt happily and zestfully in his own times, and found them good. Beginnings, he would have asserted cheerfully, whether of human beings or of nations, were bound to be unlovely. Pain and blood, sweat and labour, ugliness and indignity—thus men and nations must be born!

* * *

The Governor, having at last won the confidence of the natives was now finding their friendship embarrassing. The inhabitants of Sydney Cove, bored and eager for any kind of diversion, found it in the company of the black people, who, rapidly losing their mistrust when they found that they might come and go at will, began to invade the settlement in large numbers, no less intrigued by the white tribe than the white tribe by them. There was noise, confusion, hilarity, and, inevitably, quarrelling. Upon Bennilong, growing daily more conscious of his importance, fell the office of chief interpreter. He was made free of the Governor's house. He took it upon himself to conduct parties of his less enlightened countrymen about the settlement, teaching them the names of the objects which they saw, and his version of their uses. He had been given clothes, and was proud of them, though more often than not he went naked, and carried them slung across his shoulders in a net. The white people, with the same thoughtlessness which is so often displayed by an adult who encourages a child to show off for his own amusement, courted him one moment and at another, weary of him, snubbed him and waved him away. His vanity, thus alternately fed and affronted, made his always irascible temper more uncertain and more violent than ever. In the settlement he led one life; but away from it, by the campfires of his tribe, another awaited him. Here, restless and wakeful upon his 'possum rugs, he watched the stars till they faded, and wrestled with the chaos in his heart.

Once there had been only one Law; now there was another, the Law of the Bereewolgal, the law of personal power and personal possessions. Once there had been only Baiame, the Maker-of-all, who dwelt there among the stars, but now there were others who disputed the heavens with him. God, who was the especial friend and familiar of the moon-faced one; and his son, who had several names, and the King (although it was not yet clear to Bennilong whether this last great being dwelt always in the sky, or returned there only occasionally between his sojourns in the land beyond the sea, called England). Once—and this was the most disturbing thought of all—to be born a man was to be born to worth and dignity. Now it was not so simple. Now it was clear that men were not always warriors, but might be less free than the beasts, weaker than women, furtive-eyed, held in subjection by other men stronger and bolder than themselves. Behind the shock of such a knowledge there was a sweet, insidious excitement, and when he thought of it Bennilong felt his own strength clamouring in his body, his own aggressiveness swelling in his heart until it was a pain. To be powerful, like the Be-anga, to speak and be instantly obeyed, to frown and watch one's fellows quail! Such imaginings were like the drink of the Bereewolgal, a potent magic, a magic which made one feel larger than life, invulnerable, capable of anything! It was no longer enough to be merely Bennilong, son of Wunbula, a notable warrior and a notable youara-gurrugin. One must be a thousand times Bennilong, vast, feet upon the earth and head above the tree-tops, one's name a thunder in the ears of one's people, one's lightest saying more moving than a great corroboree, one's most trivial action a legend. . . .

If this had been one's only thinking! But it was not. In some secret and unassailable part of his being Bennilong was conscious of a voice which nothing, not even the magic drink of the Bereewolgal, could still. It was a cold, persistent voice which said that the white men were less men than the black. There was a pride in it which was not assertive, and against which his soaring vanities knew themselves diminished, a pride which even in the midst of his most slavish imitations of their ways flared up in him and seared the intruders with a flame of utter contempt.

In this misery of spiritual disunity he went to and fro between the camps of the white men and the black. Phillip, partly to please him and partly hoping that a headquarters of their own in the settlement might make the natives less of a nuisance, built him, at his request, a hut upon the end of the eastern headland of the cove. Here, in a house of his own—a white man's house, built of bricks and roofed with tiles—he spent more and more of his time, and here his people came to talk and laugh, to sing and dance and quarrel. From here, often accompanied by Barangaroo, who was slowly overcoming her suspicions of the white Be-anga's designs upon her husband, he swaggered into the settlement, full of good humour and self-importance. Warreweer, too, frequently paddled her canoe into the cove, and spent some time in exchanging badinage and pleasantries with the soldiers. A system of barter sprang up, the natives bringing fish which they traded with the white people for bread and other trifles. Booron, watching wistfully from the doorway of the Johnsons' house, grew restless. The sight of so many of her countrymen and women coming and going about the township roused in her a never wholly stifled longing for the life she had left, and she ran down to Warreweer one morning and begged to be taken away—begged with such earnestness that at last the Governor's permission was sought, and obtained. She wanted to be married, Booron explained earnestly to the Be-anga. She was now a woman, and it was fitting that she should return to her own people and find herself a mate. Phillip nodded his comprehension and let her go. She was away a fortnight and then reappeared, but only for a brief visit. She had been, she said, with Colbee. Yes, he had beaten her. But of course she would return—there was a young man of her tribe whose wife she was to be. And she vanished again.

Colbee, also, was a frequent visitor, sometimes bringing with him his wife, the gentle Daringha, now far advanced in pregnancy. The Governor noted with indignation that even this fact did not protect her from the corporal punishment which all native husbands seemed to inflict so casually.

It might be, he said once to Collins, a nuisance having them so continually about the settlement, but it was better than having them hostile. He summoned all his patience and his tact to deal with them; he made endless efforts to understand them; he pressed Bennilong constantly into service as interpreter. But still there were occasions when he told himself despairingly that the more one associated with them the less comprehensible they became.

He was awakened early one morning about the middle of November by a babel of voices in the yard adjoining his house, and turned swiftly, blinking at the brilliant square of blue sky which his window framed and sniffing the pleasant smell of burning wood and leaves. When he got out of bed and went across to his window, his first startled impression was that a whole tribe had moved into his back yard, but when he counted them there were only sixteen. They had made a fire, and were gathered about it cooking their breakfast. Bennilong was there, holding the centre of the stage as usual; two naked children were fighting with one of the native dogs for a piece of raw fish. Barangaroo was there, too, sitting a little apart from the others, her head resting on her thin, updrawn knees, and her hands clasped over it, tangled in her hair. She was taking no part, Phillip noticed, in the preparation of the meal, and when Bennilong offered her a piece of fish she lifted her head only for a moment to shake it, and then let it fall on her knees once more.

The Governor turned away from his window and began to dress. Evidently, he thought, Mistress Barangaroo had been in trouble with her husband again. She was a shrewish, ill-tempered woman; in his heart Phillip could not but feel that she must earn a good deal of the chastisement which was so often inflicted on her, but he resolved, all the same, as he went down the stairs and out into the early morning sunlight, to make one more effort to convince Bennilong that for a man to beat a woman was most exceedingly "weeree."

Bennilong laughed at him uproariously. He came eagerly at the Governor's call, holding a huge slab of greasy, half-cooked fish in both hands, and listened with puzzled indulgence to Phillip's grave rebuke. Not strike one's womenfolk? Not beat Barangaroo? But she had been bad— very bad. She had broken his throwing-stick and his best fish-spear. Of course he must beat her. He followed, nevertheless, willingly enough, when the Governor, beckoning to him, went to where Barangaroo still sat, her posture unaltered save that now her head lay sideways on her knees so that she could watch the Be-anga warily from beneath her hair. He bent over her, feeling her head, pointing accusingly to a fresh scalp wound, and to the contused marks of several large bruises on her shoulders. Bennilong nodded cheerfully. Yes, he had given her a good beating, for she had been very bad indeed. Now, however, she was good; he was entirely willing to share the Be-anga's sympathy for her, and laid his hand on her head in a caress which won him a swift upward glance of adoration from her dark eyes. When they had finished their breakfast, he explained to the Governor, he would take her, and another of the women who had also been chastised by her husband, to the hospital, where the great carradhy, White, would attend to their wounds. He smiled amiably, confident of the Be-anga's approval.

Phillip shrugged and gave it up. He went inside, leaving them to finish their meal, and, when his own breakfast was over, sat down as usual at his desk to deal with the day's affairs.

He often wondered afterwards what it could have been which so abruptly altered Bennilong's mood. Glancing up from his papers with some annoyance at so cavalier an interruption, he saw with surprise that the Bennilong who now entered with his customary freedom, was not the smiling and affable person of an hour or two ago. His face was dark and sullen; he sat down beside Phillip at the desk and began a long rambling tale from which the Governor gathered that his wife was again out of favour. He asked, puzzled:

"Barangaroo bad again?"

Bennilong shook his head impatiently. It was not Barangaroo, he explained, but another woman, whom he intended to beat with a hatchet, which he brandished ferociously as he talked. Phillip sighed. He had a great deal of work to attend to, and he was not in the mood for Bennilong's tempestuous presence. Nevertheless, he dared not dismiss him too summarily. He knew, by now, the touchy vanity of this young native, so he laid down his pen and said soothingly:

"No, no, Bennilong. Not beat woman."

Bennilong glared at him.

"Beat woman! Beat woman bad, bad! Kill!"

Phillip tried tactfully to divert his attention.

"Dinner soon, Bennilong. Good dinner, bread, meat, wine. Bennilong eat with Be-anga, drink wine . . ."

But Bennilong was not to be diverted. He sprang to his feet, and the implacable ferocity of his manner startled Phillip into the realisation that this was an urgent and immediate problem. Bennilong, striding angrily to the door, was stopped by the Governor's hand on his arm and found himself looking into eyes which were suddenly stern.

"I go with you, Bennilong. You not beat woman."

Bennilong snorted and wrenched himself free. Let the Be-anga come, then! Let him see how Bennilong avenged an insult! He stalked off, still flourishing his hatchet and muttering fiercely to himself, while Phillip, calling his orderly sergeant to accompany him, followed hurriedly. Leaving the house they met David Collins, who, on a few words of explanation, joined them, and they all walked along the shore towards Bennilong's hut on the point. Collins said in an undertone:

"Do you suppose he really means to kill the woman, Sir?"

Phillip frowned and shook his head.

"No, no. He's in one of his tempers. But I don't like that hatchet. If he attempts a beating with that it might well end fatally. I think I shall take it from him."

He said sharply to Bennilong:

"Give me that."

Bennilong, without as much as glancing at him, said angrily: "Bee-all!" Phillip was growing angry too, but he controlled himself and said:

"Give me the hatchet, Bennilong, and I give you this." He offered his cane, and at the same time laid hold of the weapon in Bennilong's hand. Bennilong, eying him with puzzled resentment, released it. Did this mean that the Be-anga no longer had any objection to his beating the beautiful but infamous Odooroodah? It did not matter in any case, for he would beat her whether the Be-anga approved or not. He shrugged, and began to walk on again, swishing the cane through the air, and describing in bloodcurdling detail the injuries which he proposed to inflict upon his victim.

There were some ten or eleven natives sitting about on the short grass before the hut, several women among them, and as they approached Phillip watched Bennilong closely to see which of these was to be the object of his rage. His pace had quickened as they neared the point, and his expression was so malevolent that the Governor thought better of allowing him even the cane, and, catching up with him, snatched it from his hand. He expected an outburst of fury, but Bennilong only grunted contemptuously. Lying about on the grass there were plenty of the weapons of his own people; one of those would serve his purpose better than the Be-anga's paltry stick. He snatched one up, and leapt suddenly at a young girl, who was lying huddled on the grass, inflicting on her, before the startled Governor could intervene, two such savage blows that she fell back and lay unconscious.

Phillip shouted to him peremptorily above the clamour which instantly arose.

"Stop, Bennilong! Stop! Put that down!"

But words were useless now; Bennilong looked as though he were bent on murder. Collins and the sergeant each grabbed him by an arm, and for a moment there was a struggle. The other natives watched excitedly, but made no attempt to interfere. Bennilong was an inveterate trouble-maker, and this was strictly a private affair of his own. Phillip, taking advantage of a momentary lull in which Bennilong substituted for his struggles an outburst of furious words, said sharply:

"Cover him with your musket, sergeant, and you, Collins, keep hold of his arm." He looked Bennilong grimly in the eyes and spoke with emphasis:

"Now understand me, Bennilong. You are not to beat this woman, or to harm her in any way." Glancing over his shoulder, he could see, to his relief, that Ball, watching the commotion from the *Supply,* had sent off an armed boat which was now rapidly approaching the shore. The other natives, upon seeing their companion menaced by one of the dreaded magic gooroobeera, had become excited, and were picking up their spears, showing signs of a hostility which Bennilong, loudly haranguing them, was obviously encouraging. Phillip, seeking to gain time, went on impressively, not troubling now to frame his sentence into words familiar to his protégé, but relying on his manner and gestures to make his meaning plain.

"I will not allow this, Bennilong. You are behaving very badly, and if you attempt any further violence I shall have to order my men to fire on you."

Pointing to the levelled musket of the sergeant, and then to the boat, now landing half a dozen armed seamen on the rocks, he waited confidently for the culprit to surrender. But Bennilong showed no sign whatever of being intimidated. Staring into the very barrel of the musket, his attitude of fiery truculence remained unchanged. The girl was his, he announced fiercely. By what right did the Be-anga interfere? Did he, Bennilong, attempt to hinder the Be-anga in the conduct of *his* tribal affairs? This woman now belonged to him, for he had stolen her from her tribe and had fought many battles and received many wounds on her account. He had fought with her husband, and when he had been on the ground, menaced by the spear of his antagonist, she had rushed in and struck him—him, Bennilong!—when he was all but helpless, and had almost cost him his life. Now that she was in his power nothing would induce him to forego his vengeance. He glared round him at the ring of muskets as if they were so many sticks, and made another threatening movement in the direction of the girl.

In that moment, in spite of exasperation, in spite of horror at what seemed an inhuman vindictiveness, Phillip almost loved him. Courage was a virtue he could admire. He ordered the armed men to close in and said quickly to Ball:

"Get her into the boat. Take her to the hospital and get Mr. White to attend to her." He turned again to Bennilong, now struggling madly in the grip of four brawny seamen.

"I take woman away, Bennilong. To hospital."

Bennilong said promptly:

"I go hospital, kill woman there."

"If you do," Phillip assured him, losing patience, "you will be shot." He regretted the words almost before they were out of his mouth—but they were said, and they had been understood: he must abide by them. He turned his back abruptly and set off along the shore with Collins, walking fast in his agitation, and tapping nervously on the palm of his left hand with his recovered cane. His affection for Bennilong was sincere, but it was not only that which filled him with alarm at the thought that he might have to make good his threat. To put Bennilong to death would be, he felt sure, not only to forfeit the goodwill of the native tribes, but to arouse their fierce hostility. Collins, dusting his hat and straightening his disordered collar, said ruefully:

"Did you ever know such a hot-headed rascal! What on earth was his object, Sir, in attacking that unfortunate girl?"

"Object!" Phillip switched irritably at the grasses with his cane. "He has no objects. He's a creature of impulse—as irresponsible as a child. I hope to God, Collins, that he behaves himself now—the last thing I should want would be to order his execution. What is he doing now?"

Collins glanced over his shoulder.

"The men are still holding him, Sir, and he doesn't look any calmer."

"Confound him!" said the Governor feelingly. And after a minute he added: "He took no more notice of those muskets than if they had been nosegays! The rogue has courage, Collins. I can't help but like him for it."

* * *

To the Governor's great relief, there was no sign of the culprit for two days. It was a relief which changed to utter bewilderment when at the end of that time he turned up at Government House with Barangaroo, blandly smiling, affable as ever, eager to assure the Be-anga that he was no longer angry with Odooroodah, and would not attempt again to beat her. Barangaroo, Phillip noticed, had a couple of fresh wounds on her head, but when he pointed accusingly at these Bennilong merely nodded cheerfully, and displayed a gash on his own shoulder which she had given him in return with one of his own clubs.

Phillip, resigned, abandoned the attempt to mediate in their domestic affairs; but wishing to test the sincerity of Bennilong's assurance that he bore no further animosity towards Odooroodah, he suggested that they go to the hospital to see her, when Mr. White could also take the opportunity of dressing their wounds. Bennilong complied, though without any great enthusiasm; but now a new aspect of the situation presented itself, for Bennilong, seeing his former victim, became so much the gallant and so little the avenger that it was Barangaroo's turn to grow vindictive.

She began to rail and rage; she grabbed a club and attempted to assault the girl; she flung off White's restraining hand and spat a torrent of native words at him before which he retreated, blinking. Bennilong stood by and grinned. White said angrily:

"Stop her, Bennilong! She'll kill the girl! Stop her! Good God, what a vixen!"

Bennilong, thus exhorted, caught his wife by the arm and gave her a ringing slap on the cheek, upon which she burst into a passion of wild weeping and rushed out of the room. All through the morning she created an uproar about the Governor's house, to which Odooroodah had been moved for greater security. She screamed insults and maledictions; she threw stones at Bennilong when he approached her; she scratched the face of a sentry who attempted to calm her; she took a plate of food which one of the Governor's servants brought as a peace offering and flung it in his face. Finally, discovering a bundle of her husband's spears leaning against the wall, she took possession of them, with noisy threats of how she would use them upon her rival. Phillip, exasperated by the clamour, came to the door and looked at her in despair.

"Put them down, Barangaroo. Weeree! Weeree!"

She shrilled a furious sentence at him in her own tongue, and raised a spear threateningly. Phillip said to the sentry:

"Take them from her."

The sentry, fingering his cheek, approached gingerly. Barangaroo glaring defiance, gathered the spears into a heap and sat down on them. The sentry glanced helplessly at the Governor, who was grimly subduing an impulse to tear his hair.

"Take them!" he ordered sharply, "Pull her off them, and take them right away from her."

The sentry, with a swift, flanking movement, got behind her and dragged her backwards with pinioned arms. As she lay sprawling he snatched the spears and retreated, breathing heavily. But now Bennilong was displeased. He did not like to see his spears in the possession of one of the red-coated ones, and loudly demanded their instant surrender. Phillip hesitated. A crowd of natives had by this time assembled, and he wanted, above all, to avert any situation in which Bennilong's turbulent temper might end in disaster for himself. He suggested a compromise:

"I take spears, Bennilong?"

Bennilong considered. The spears, he decided, and finally announced, must be given to him; but he himself would then deliver them into the care of the Be-anga. Phillip frowned at him doubtfully. An armed guard of soldiers, a crowd of excited natives, also armed, a wildcat of a woman, half-hysterical with jealousy—and Bennilong. If ever, he thought, there was a stage set for trouble, it was here; and, of all people, it was Bennilong, the firebrand, who would decide, once he had those spears, whether to precipitate it or not.

From his place on the step he looked down rather sadly at his young native friend. For a moment he forgot the crowd, forgot Barangaroo, forgot Odooroodah, and was conscious only of his feeling of unity with this turbulent young savage, and of his urgent desire to know that whatever differences of race and custom might hold them apart, there was still a personal confidence between them, a sense of mutual trust.

He asked slowly:

"You take spears, Bennilong, give spears to me?"

Bennilong nodded vigorously.

"I give kamai, Be-anga."

Phillip motioned an order to the soldier, who handed them over rather dubiously. It was very hot in the dusty yard, and suddenly very quiet while Bennilong examined his spears to see if their points had been injured. The natives watched him, the soldiers watched him, and Barangaroo, her face swollen with weeping, watched him too. Phillip, standing above them all on the step, looked away over their heads for a second or two at the blue harbour and the opposite shore, and it was only when he heard Bennilong's cheerful voice saying, "Here kamai, Be-anga," and saw the strong barbed points of them laid carefully against the wall beside him, that he realised how rigidly his muscles had been held.

* * *

Bennilong stayed to dinner, and Phillip, feeling rather exhausted after the noisy emotionalism of the morning, drew a breath of relaxation as he sat down to his meal. Odooroodah was safe. A young man who appeared to be her lover or her husband was with her. Bennilong was placated. Barangaroo had been sent away. The whole business was settled.

It was, therefore, with a sense of living in a nightmare that he was presently informed that Odooroodah was weeping and clamouring to be let out of the room where she was lodged, saying that she wished to go away with Bennilong.

"In the name of Heaven, Collins," he said in despair, "what do you make of that?"

Collins remarked dryly that even in their own society inconsistency was generally allowed to be a privilege of the female sex, and White, a ladies' man himself, winked genially at Bennilong across the table. Phillip shrugged, poured himself another drink, and ordered that the girl and the young man should be sent in. To the girl he said shortly:

"You want to go with Bennilong?"

She nodded tearfully, eagerly.

Phillip warned her irritably:

"Bennilong beat you."

She made no reply; her silence seemed to say that that was for Bennilong to decide. But that young man was in a sunny and benevolent mood. No, no, he assured the Be-anga indulgently, he would not beat her. He would not beat Barangaroo either. He would not beat anyone. Phillip turned back to the girl and tried again.

"Barangaroo beat you."

At this there was a clamour of denial. The young man, Bennilong, the girl herself, all combined in fervent assurances that Barangaroo would do nothing of the sort. She was no longer angry. She was good now.

The Governor pulled out his handkerchief and mopped his brow. White put his elbows on the table and took his head despairingly between his hands. Collins, preserving a judicial calm, asked reasonably:

"How do they know that?"

Phillip said impatiently:

"They can't know. They haven't seen the confounded shrew since she went off this morning. Or could that boy who came a while ago have brought them news?"

He looked searchingly at Bennilong, and was confronted by a countenance as guileless as a child's. He asked once more, with slow and impressive emphasis:

"You beat Odooroodah?"

There was not a shadow over Bennilong's beaming face. He laughed merrily.

"Bee-all! Bee-all! Not beat. Odooroodah good now."

"All right," said the Governor wearily. "All *right*! Let her go." He waved her away impatiently. "Go! Go!"

She went like a flash, running off in the direction of Bennilong's house. For a moment there was an exhausted silence at the table. Then White raised his glass solemnly.

"Your health, Bennilong!"

* * *

There was hardly anyone among the white men, with the exception of the Governor, who did not believe that the unfortunate Odooroodah would be promptly sacrificed. But Bennilong was as good as his word. He came next day to inform the Be-anga that he had sent her back to her own tribe; Phillip commended him, hoping devoutly that he would not find himself again involved in the amorous adventures of this native scapegrace.

Such disturbances, he decided philosophically, were, after all, but a small price to pay for the goodwill of a people who were essentially generous, and endlessly willing to be of service to those whom they liked and trusted. As instances of this generosity multiplied he became increasingly optimistic. The tale of a soldier, who had lost himself in the woods, added to his already high opinion of their integrity. Falling in with a party of natives and begging their assistance, this man had been informed that they would take him to the settlement if he would first give up his musket, which they would return to him upon arrival. With considerable misgivings, he had agreed. No sooner had he surrendered his weapon, however, than all the natives had laid their own upon the ground, and bidding him accompany them had escorted him to the settlement, returned him his gun, and bade him a friendly farewell.

Upon another occasion, seeing a boatload of white men overturn on the harbour, Bennilong and several of his friends had plunged to the rescue, and saved all the occupants. Not content with dragging them ashore, they had kindled a fire to dry their clothes, and finished by seeing them safely home.

Remembering such incidents, the Governor dared to hope more and more that this one of his many problems was solved. He was still far from believing that he understood this primitive race, but he felt that at least a hopeful stage had been reached, in which each was confident of the good intentions of the other.

It was, therefore, with a shock of utter dismay that he learned, early in December, that his game-keeper, McEntire, had been brought into the settlement with a spear through his body. The Governor was at Rose Hill when the news was brought to him, and he spent a sleepless night wondering what action he must take upon his return to Sydney Cove. Such an outrage could not be ignored, but he was loth to risk undoing, at a stroke, what it had taken him nearly three years to achieve, and he was continually haunted by the conviction that in all his dealings with the natives he was never able to find out more than half of the truth. This man, McEntire, he thought, had always been the object of their particular and consistent hatred. Why? Phillip had not forgotten that Bennilong, ordinarily so friendly and gregarious, could never be persuaded to speak to him or to approach him. He had not forgotten how the man had been shunned and repulsed by the natives upon that unlucky occasion when he himself had been attacked, and he could not avoid the suspicion that he might have earned his death. As a game-killer, he had been one of those authorised to carry a musket out into the woods in search of emus and kangaroos, and it was impossible to escape the knowledge that he might have used it not only in pursuit of game. Nevertheless, the natives could not be allowed to kill his men and escape unpunished. He told himself that he had tried indulgence and kindness, subduing, because he must, the itching suspicion that a little kindness cannot wipe out a great injustice, that land and liberty and livelihood cannot be paid for with a few fishhooks and beads, that the humiliation of captivity is not forgotten in the honour of a seat at His Excellency's table. . . .

The inward conflict, half unconscious, sharpened his temper and frayed his nerves. He sat alone upon his return from Rose Hill, wrestling with his problem and hating it as he had never hated any problem before. He was tired; in this relentless heat, these dry and drought-stricken days, the mere effort of forming a coherent thought seemed a labour, and he rested his forehead on his hands and then lifted it and snatched irritably at his handkerchief because his palms were wet with perspiration. He knew himself entangled with two irreconcilable ideas. Duty pushed him one way, and humanity the other, but it was an unequal contest; he had been bred to revere the former. He had lived all his life in a world which admitted no arguing with Orders. Orders, certainly, had bidden him treat the natives with indulgence. He had been told to "conciliate their affections." Had he not tried to do so? He had been instructed to see that his own people lived "in amity and kindness with them." This also he had attempted.

"And if any of our subjects shall wantonly destroy them, or give them any unnecessary interruption in the exercise of their several occupations, it is our will and pleasure that you do cause such offenders to be brought to punishment. . . ."

He pushed his chair back with a clatter and began to walk about the room. For the first time he felt a stirring of resentment that such impossible commands should have been laid upon him. No physical hardship, no material obstacle would have so roused him, but now he felt his inner self threatened by division, and was angered. Easy enough, he thought, to sit in London and pen humanitarian words! It was left to him to attempt the impossible—to find, in trying to obey them, that they rang hollow—hollow! "Unnecessary interruption"! Unnecessary—for whom? Am I to convince these people that it was "necessary" to steal their land from them? That it is "necessary," having stolen it, to hunt their game, to haul nets in their waters? That it is "necessary" now, to send an armed force against them? What is this "necessity"? The necessity for a distant gaol in which to herd our criminals! The necessity for another colonial possession! The necessity for empire and dominion, for power and glory . . .

Inevitably, those two words reframed themselves in a familiar context. He found his tired, stampeding brain repeating: "For Thine is the Kingdom, the Power and the Glory . . ." and turned back to his table and his chair, startled by the labyrinths into which his undisciplined thoughts were leading him. Deliberately he brought them back to order. Deliberately he refused to acknowledge that out of that large conception of his settlement which had sustained him, there had resulted a new and inevitable widening of his whole mental horizon. For a man cannot plan nobly and remain narrow; he cannot build for the future and remain mentally wedged in his little present; he cannot admit dreams of human advancement and exclude nightmares of human suffering; he cannot hold power, and wield it justly within limitations imposed upon him, without becoming ever more humble, more conscious of those limitations, more tortured by them, more rebelliously determined to break through them to some higher plane of conduct, unhampered by custom—by Orders—by Duty . . .

But these were impossible, incredible thoughts for a middle-aged naval captain, bred and set in the mould of his times, trained from childhood to see obedience to Authority as the first of all the virtues. What Authority? That was a question one did not need to ask, for the answer had been so often repeated that it rang in one's ears, deafening, shutting out all other sound. King and Country! King and Country! King and Country! Who could hear beyond that clarion call? Who would seek to do so?

Duty reared itself in his thoughts like a blank brick wall, and comforted him. You could put your back against that wall and fight till you died, seeing no enemies but those clearly enough defined for you by Authority, no cause but that which Authority handed to you ready-made, with your Instructions. Thus was life simplified. He sent for Tench, and sat down wearily at his table again.

Tench, facing him across it a few minutes later, wondered whether it were anxiety, anger, or physical pain which was making his pallor leaden and folding into deep grooves the two creases between his eyes. Phillip said abruptly:

"This business of McEntire . . ."

Tench thought with rueful but unsurprised apprehension, "So that's it!" There had been a good deal of conjecture as to how the Governor would deal with this latest assault, and Captain Tench, glancing out the window at the yellow blaze of sunlight, found himself suspecting cynically that a punitive expedition, if such were in His Excellency's mind, would probably turn out to be punishment for the avengers rather than the culprits. However, he only said, "Yes, Sir?" and waited attentively for the Governor to continue.

"I have decided," Phillip said slowly, "to send out a force against the tribe responsible. Colbee and other natives about the settlement seem agreed that the assailant was a man named Pemulwy, of the Bideegal. You are to assume this command, Captain Tench, choosing two subalterns to accompany you, and taking the sergeant and the two convicts who were with McEntire when the incident occurred, as guides. And about forty men."

He was sitting forward in his chair, staring at his clasped hands on the desk before him, so Tench permitted himself the shadow of a wry grimace while he answered again, dutifully:

"Yes, Sir."

"You will proceed," Phillip went on, "to the peninsula at the head of Botany Bay, which is, I understand, the headquarters of this tribe, and bring back two native prisoners . . ." Tench brightened a little, ". . . and put to death ten."

There was another pause. For two seconds Captain Tench's usually imperturbable countenance showed a flash of utter consternation. Ten! Put to death, in cold blood, ten of those poor devils, those cheerful, amusing, inoffensive creatures . . . He said again, mechanically, "Yes, Sir," but there was a different tone in his voice. Phillip heard it and looked up at him. Without words there passed between them a knowledge of the detestation with which they both regarded this task. Phillip went on grimly:

"You are to take them by surprise or by open force. In no circumstances are signs of friendship or invitation to be used. You are to destroy all weapons of war, but nothing else. You are not to burn huts or to injure women or children. I think—that's all."

For the fourth time Tench replied: "Yes, Sir." But as he turned to go the Governor stopped him. Since the arrival of the Second Fleet, and the influx of new personalities into his domain, Phillip had found himself relying more than ever upon the little group which had been with him from the beginning of this arduous adventure; and of them all, he felt none was more to be depended upon than this rather worldly young man, whose very worldliness, tempered as it was with humour and humanity, seemed to lend to all his judgments a balance, an indestructible good sense, which his commander had found useful upon more than one occasion. He said now:

"One moment, Captain Tench. Sit down."

"Thank you, Sir."

Phillip's voice became a little sharper, his manner a little primmer and more precise, as it always did when he spoke under the stress of an emotion.

"This is an unpleasant necessity, Captain. I regret it. It has always been my hope that no such measures would ever be needed. But since our arrival no fewer than seventeen of our people have been killed or wounded by the natives. Those that live on the north arm of Botany Bay—the Bideegal—have always seemed, I think, the most hostile, the most likely to prove troublesome. One sharp lesson may be enough to convince them that our people are not to be molested with impunity."

"No doubt you are right, Sir." Tench's tone was politely and beautifully calculated to convey a quite considerable doubt. Phillip stood up and walked across to the window.

"I have noticed this about them, Tench. As individuals they regard death lightly enough. But the strength of their tribes is of the utmost importance to them. Nothing seems to give them more concern than a prospect of the weakening of their numerical strength. That is why I think that the loss of ten warriors would be the sharpest form of penalty which I could inflict." He came back to his chair, but stood behind it, resting his hands on its carved back. "I have delayed this as long as I could. Now something must be done."

"You do not think, Sir," Tench suggested, "that they may have been—provoked—to their attack on McEntire?"

Phillip shook his head.

"No. On former occasions, yes. Sometimes they have retaliated upon our people for some injury or insult. Sometimes it has been—as in the case of my own wound—the result of a pure misapprehension. But this time there seems to have been no such reason. Our people were peacefully asleep in their tent, and were awakened to find natives creeping towards them with spears in their hands. McEntire himself, when he was speared, was doing no more than speak to them. I have questioned him . . ."

Tench's expressive eyebrows lifted a fraction of an inch. The Governor added emphatically:

". . . *and* the sergeant who was with him, of whose veracity I have the highest opinion, and the convicts. Their stories are short and simple and bear each other out in every detail."

Tench sighed.

"Did you not make some effort, Sir, to enlist the help of Bennilong and Colbee? Is nothing to be hoped for in that direction?"

Phillip made a little gesture of impatience.

"I don't understand them. They are utterly unreliable. Only yesterday they promised to go in search of the aggressor and bring him in, and went off, too, as if bent on that errand. But today—what I do find . . . ?"

Tench, who knew very well, lowered his eyes to hide their flicker of amusement, and answered:

"Colbee, certainly, is still about the settlement."

"He has been loitering round the lookout house all day. And Bennilong has gone across the harbour in his canoe to draw the teeth of some young men on the other side. I have never known a people with less stability of purpose."

"They might, all the same, Sir, give us some useful information about the culprit. There was some rumour that he was a man with a blemish in his left eye."

"I have no doubt of knowing the man once he is taken. The sergeant and the convicts all say they can identify him, and they all agree about his eye. But Bennilong—looking me in the face with the utmost assurance—swore that the man had a deformed foot, which is obviously a lie. No, we shall have to depend on ourselves in this matter. But . . ." he drew his chair out again and sat down wearily, ". . . if you can propose any alteration in my plan, Captain, which you would consider an improvement, let me hear it. I am most willing to listen."

Tench, thus encouraged, sat forward in his chair with a trace of eagerness.

"Thank you, Sir. If I might suggest—would it not answer the purpose equally well if, instead of putting ten to death, I were to capture six? Out of this number some—as many as Your Excellency thought proper—might be put to death and the rest set at liberty after having seen the fate of their companions."

Phillip reflected only for a moment, and then adopted this humaner proposition with an inward sigh of relief.

"Very well, Captain. If you can't capture six, shoot that number. If you can, I'll hang two of them and send the rest to Norfolk Island for a while, so that their companions will think they also have been killed. I shall make out an order, and you must be ready to march tomorrow morning, at daylight."

"Yes, Sir."

"And—Captain Tench . . ."

"Yes, Sir?"

"Don't forget—no signs of friendship are to be made to entice the natives near you."

"No, Sir, I won't forget."

He went out into the blazing heat, reflecting that after the method of capture which had been used in the case of Arabanoo, and later of Benni-long and Colbee, this admonition was, perhaps, a little belated.

*   *   *

But the representatives of His Majesty, sitting in conclave over the fate of the ignorant savages, had reckoned without their victims. By nightfall there was no man, woman or child in the neighbouring tribes who did not know all about the expedition. They looked at each other, puzzled, amused, even a little embarrassed by the stupidity of these white people. Let them come, tramping and crashing through the bush, laden with their gooroobeera and all their unwieldy gear, the noise of their progress waking the echoes for a mile around, the glare of their red coats ablaze through the tree trunks in the dappled light. What would they find? Quiet, bare feet would move lightly about them and they would hear nothing. Naked bodies, motionless, shadow-coloured, would lie near their path watching them pass, and they would not know. They would get very hot beneath all their coverings, very tired and bad-tempered beneath their loads, and they would not see a single black man all day long. It would be all very amusing, a source of much cheerfulness and merriment among the tribes. Indeed, yes—let them come!

*   *   *

Of the white men who had set out at four o'clock on that summer morning, only Tench (whose sense of comedy was equal to the trials of even such a day as this had been) preserved his equanimity by the time they made camp at night. Captain Hill of the New South Wales Corps had blistered heels. Lieutenant Poulden had a touch of the sun, and was taken with distressing shivering fits during his evening meal. Lieutenant Dawes had been sunk all day in the silence of a black mood from which nothing could rouse him. He had not liked this task. He had, actually, flatly refused to undertake it, and Captain Campbell had been forced to refer the matter to Phillip. Phillip, concerned for the future of this quiet young man with his vein of stubborn fanaticism, had tried to point out the consequences of what amounted to mutiny—the fatal effect of it upon a career promisingly begun. Dawes, respectful, but immovable under this line of argument, had at last sought the advice of Mr. Johnson, as his spiritual adviser, and had finally, rather grudgingly, capitulated. But he was not happy about it. He sat apart, grimly silent, and Tench, reflecting upon the limitations imposed by an inelastic conscience and an insufficiently developed sense of the ridiculous, shook his head ruefully, and left him alone.

For himself, he was beginning to feel hopeful.

"This terrific procession," as he described it later in his journal, consisting of four officers, two surgeons, three sergeants, three corporals, and forty privates, had marched all day, and had not set eyes upon a single native. "If we don't see them," Tench argued optimistically to himself, "we can't possibly be expected to capture them."

He slept as soundly as the mosquitoes allowed and wakened to another day of heat and exertion. Yesterday had been merely futile; today became embarrassing. They set out for a certain spot which Tench considered would be a good starting point for their operations and found themselves ignominiously lost. Emerging finally upon the sea-shore, they beheld five natives on the beach, whom they attempted to surround. The natives escaped quite easily while the soldiers panted after them heavily through the soft sand; once in the shelter of the bush they vanished as if swallowed up by it, leaving the white men at a standstill, cursing and mopping their streaming brows. Tench, between exasperation and amusement, next ordered an advance upon five huts which stood at some distance, but long before they were able to approach them their black occupants emerged, stared, leapt into their canoes and paddled away across the water, leaving the pursuers again discomfited.

There was nothing for it now, but to return to their baggage which they had left with a guard near the spot where their pursuit had begun. Nearing it, Tench halted, knitting his brows. Three hundred yards from the shore, waist-deep in the water, a single native stood unconcernedly fishing. What was to be done? Tench's vivid fancy pictured for him, not without relish, the spectacle of a score of his men floundering clumsily through the water to effect the capture of one naked savage, who, without doubt, would at the last moment dive expertly between their legs and elude them. "There are moments," he decided, "when blindness is undoubtedly a virtue." And he walked on with averted head, ignoring the solitary figure.

But the native had no intention of being ignored. As they passed he waved and shouted to them, calling them, to their surprise, by name, and finally beginning to wade toward the shore with the evident intention of joining them. Tench, at first, continued to ignore him, walking on more rapidly "for all the world," as he thought delightedly, "like a haughty and offended mistress, pursued by a too ardent lover!" But it was no use. The native, obviously, was not to be discouraged, and Tench at last resignedly called a halt to wait for him, making a mental resolution that no matter who he might turn out to be, he should leave them as freely as he came.

To their astonishment, it was Colbee, whom they had imagined to be at Sydney. Smiling broadly, he joined them, and Tench, in the faint hope that he might be able or willing to tell them something of the whereabouts of Pemulwy, began to question him. Colbee was all comprehension and helpfulness. Indeed, yes, he knew very well why the Be-anga had sent out this formidable party of warriors. He looked them over, and the warriors shuffled uneasily; was his smile just a little too broad for mere friendliness? It was to capture the slayer of their countryman, whose name, as everyone knew, was Pemulwy, of the Bideegal. But alas! Pemulwy was far from here—very, very far—many days' march! Colbee flung his arm out extravagantly towards the south, and smiled frankly into Captain Tench's sceptical eyes.

Tench glanced round at his little band. Most of them looked bored, sulky, and hot, though it was not yet ten o'clock in the morning. It was evident that the natives were too alert to allow themselves to be seen, far less captured. "Let us admit," Tench argued sensibly to himself, "that though we may be superior in force, we are no match for these people in strategy and finesse!" Briskly he ordered a return to their baggage, a rest, and food. Colbee, a self-invited guest, accompanied them, ate and drank largely of their provisions, and then settled himself comfortably among them for a sleep. At one o'clock they set out for home, and at three halted beside a soak of fresh water, where, during an interminable and suffocating night, they endured agonies from the bites of sandflies and mosquitoes.

It was a weary, bedraggled and unheroic force which reached the settlement next day. But when Captain Tench went to report his total and humiliating lack of success to the Governor, he looked less chastened than might have been expected.

Phillip, however, having made up his mind to punish, was not to be deflected by one failure. Another party, he decreed, must set out, and to Tench's dismay the command—"the painful pre-eminence," as he later wryly described it—was again to be his.

It was a smaller party this time. Lieutenant Abbott and Ensign Prentice of the New South Wales Corps replaced the officers of the previous expedition, and three sergeants, three corporals and thirty privates completed the force.

To take advantage of a full moon, and to avoid the extreme heat which had so exhausted them before, as well as in the hope of lending some secrecy to their movements, they decided to travel by night. The five huts which they had surprised before were again to be their objective, and a quarter past two in the morning found them sitting on the banks of the northern arm of Botany Bay waiting for the tide to ebb sufficiently to allow them to ford it. Tench, looking at the water, dark, mysterious, and malevolent in the light of the sitting moon, ordered his men to divest themselves of all that they carried save their arms and ammunition. A sergeant and six men were detailed to mount guard over the heap of baggage, and the rest, shivering a little in spite of the warmth of the night, clambered down the banks and waded into the water. Two arms of the harbour were thus crossed, and Tench was just beginning to congratulate himself upon having passed the worst obstacles, when they found themselves upon the bank of a creek some sixty yards wide. The tide was out and it looked dry, but Tench gave the word to advance with some misgivings. The moon was almost gone by now, but the first faint light of dawn lay like a smoke over the stark and melancholy scene. There were no big trees here—only stunted shrubs, black in the half light. "A perfect ambush," Tench thought, feeling his skin prickle, for a horde of armed savages! "A perfect moment," he thought, feeling the mud grip his ankles, "for an attack!" And it was getting deeper. All around him he could hear grunts and muttered curses, and the squelching sound of feet dragged by main force from a bog so thick, so viscid, that it gripped one's legs like glue. He took a few more steps, and the last one buried him almost to the waist in mud. To a dim figure beside him he said sharply:

"Is that you, Prentice?"

"Yes, Sir. Damnation! I can't move!"

To the right a sergeant called out:

"I'm stuck fast, Sir! I can't go forward or backward . . ."

As if his cry had released them there was a sudden clamour of voices: "Neither can I!" "I can't stir an inch!" "I'm sinking!" "Help!"

The voices stopped as abruptly as they had begun. Tench, with difficulty, craned his head towards the bank they had left. In the dim light he could see that the remainder of the party, warned by the plight of those in front, had scrambled back on to dry ground, and were now hurrying up the stream to cross it at its head. There was silence except for the noise they made, growing fainter, ceasing, and then increasing again as they hastened down upon the opposite side. The bogged men hardly spoke. Every movement only made them sink a little deeper, and Tench, resting his aching arms upon the top of his head, racked his brains for a method of escape. It was one of the soldiers who finally offered the solution, calling to those on the bank to cut boughs of trees and throw them; and while the pale dawn light strengthened they toiled and wallowed, swore and strove, dragged, pulled, pushed, and finally emerged, sorry figures, mud-be-plastered and exhausted.

But there was no time to rest. They scraped the mud from their persons as best they could, wiped it from their arms (quite half of which were now useless), and set out again. Just before sunrise they found themselves close to the huts, and Tench, dividing his forces into three, and ordering absolute silence, launched his attack. From three different directions they burst upon the tiny camp.

But no startled figures emerged; no hastily snatched spears greeted them; no screaming women and children cowered before this awesome display of the might of the dominant race. There was no one there.

The first slanting ray of sunlight, coming delicately through the trees, found them standing about rather foolishly, looking sheepish and bad-tempered. It flickered over them mercilessly, lingering on a square inch of unstained scarlet coat, a gleaming brass button, a bit of white pipeclay, a golden epaulette, as if ignoring, with a tact more deadly than any insult, the spectacle of their sweaty, mud-caked and bedraggled futility.

Captain Tench took off his hat, scratched his head, swore under his breath, and began to grin; but catching the austere eye of Abbott and the sulky eye of Prentice, he straightened his mouth again and addressed himself to the immemorial task of preserving the prestige of the forces. There was much virtue, he reflected, in silence. He might know, and every one of his men might know, that officers and soldiers of His Majesty had been made quite inconceivably ridiculous, but so long as no one admitted it there was no great harm done. What, indeed, could be more subversive of discipline than such solemn preparations, such elaborate precautions—and such an anti-climax? Officially he acknowledged, giving his orders with crisp matter-of-factness, it must be ignored out of existence. Privately he reserved the right to enjoy it.

* * *

Thus ended, ignominiously, His Excellency's first attempt at a punitive expedition. A second, undertaken shortly afterwards, during the last days of the year, ended less absurdly and more tragically. Two natives, seen robbing a potato patch belonging to the settlement, were reported to have flung a spear at a white man who attempted to stop them, and Phillip ordered a sergeant and a party of soldiers to go out after them and bring them in. The glimmer of a fire, long after dark, guided the pursuers when they had almost given up the chase, and in the excitement of closing in upon their quarry, one of the soldiers fired among the little group of dusky figures, startled from their meal. When they rushed in to take their prisoners they found only two women and a child, whom they secured; the two men had vanished, and the next day a trail of blood from the fire to the near-by shore showed that they had not escaped unharmed.

The natives who had been of late so amicably frequenting the settlement immediately became wary and mistrustful. One of the men, Bangai, they told the white people angrily, was mortally wounded; some said that he was dead. Phillip, hoping to undo the mischief, sent White with Nanbarree, and another native youth, Immerawanye, to find him, hoping that the surgeon's skill might save him and so restore the confidence of the natives.

But Bangai was undoubtedly dead. They found his body prepared for burial, covered with green boughs, and bearing on the shoulder the musket wound from which he had bled to death.

Bennilong, angry and aggressive, led a demonstration of protest. Were the white people, he demanded, to make free with the towris of his people, steal their fish, kill their kangaroos, endanger the whole food supply of the tribes, and begrudge in return a few roots out of the ground? At the head of a small party of his countrymen he descended upon one of the fishing boats of the white men and took back by force what he regarded as morally his own. For this act, the Be-anga, usually just and reasonable, but subject, like all the white men, to lapses into incomprehensible and indefensible conduct, had the impertinence to reproach him—to scold and berate him, as if he were a child or a disobedient woman! Furiously Bennilong turned upon him—he who alone of his people had sufficient knowledge of the language and customs of the white men to interpret so complicated a matter to them.

Had they not slain Bangai, he demanded, because he took a little of their food to fill his empty belly and the empty bellies of his dyins? If then, they were not to take the roots of the Bereewolgal, neither should the Bereewolgal take the fish from the waters which had belonged since time began to the black tribes. Let the Bereewolgal live upon the food which they had brought with them in their nowees. . . .

But his temper betrayed him. His uncontrollable excitability thickened his voice and dulled his memory. Moreover, he was not used to framing the subtleties of ethical conduct into words, even in his own language. Among his own people there was no need for such a thing. There was the Law, which all understood, and if one disobeyed it there were appointed penalties. His agile brain and his usually fluent tongue stumbled in the unaccustomed effort of self-expression. Of the tirade he poured forth, half in their language and half in his own, Phillip understood only a phrase here and there. Tired, discouraged and exasperated, he cut it short and left Bennilong standing there, shaking with rage, and boiling with still unspoken words.

1791

ANDREW PRENTICE had long ago lost count of time. If it had not been for his son, Bill (thus he had adapted the native name, Billalong, which Cunnembeillee had given to the infant) he would hardly have realised that it was passing at all. New Year's Day, the second anniversary of his escape, came and went unrecognised, but, lounging in the cool of the evening against the wall of his hut, he did glance at the child, who sat placidly in the doorway, and reckon that he must be nearly a year old by now.

From where Prentice sat he could see Cunnembeillee milking. It had been a shrewd move, he thought complacently, to provide himself with a native woman. Not only was she a good worker, a satisfactory mistress, and an unobtrusively obedient servant, but she had been able to make all kinds of small implements and utensils which had proved extremely useful. String, for instance. From the fur of 'possums, from the bark of trees, even from the hair of her own head, she had dexterously twisted and rubbed a twine which, when he examined it, he could hardly distinguish from that of his own people. The various vessels for holding water and food, which she had made from bark and wood, were scattered round the hut. Into one of them, the largest, the milk was even now spurting from the full udder of the cow, between her deft fingers. She had lost her fear of the cattle. Indeed, since the birth of the child she had become a less timorous creature altogether. During the winter she had invaded his hut which had always been forbidden to her before. Crouching before his fire with the baby in her arms, she had stared up at him with something which was not so much defiance as authority in her dark, unmoving eyes; he had grunted, and left her there, and from that time they had been less master and slave. He still struck her occasionally, but not very hard—merely to indicate his displeasure, and because it had become a habit; in any case it was what she expected and understood.

She had an inexhaustible endurance. Often from daybreak till sunset she had laboured beside him, the baby slung in a woven basket on her

347

back, and now Prentice, glancing about his domain, was able to feel the deep satisfaction of ownership and success. The cattle were safely yarded, and a fenced acre of land near the river had yielded passable crops. It had also yielded something less material which he recognised with a queer emotion of mingled astonishment and joy. He had rediscovered in it a fulfilment, a contentment long forgotten; he had rediscovered the earth. He had found that stores of knowledge from his country-bred boyhood had remained dormant in his mind, and as he brought up each fragment from where it had lain buried beneath the accumulations of later years, he had felt something of the elation of a prospector striking gold. It was a heady discovery, this unearthing of riches in himself, and though he found that many of his rules became invalid here, his self-respect was nourished by the mere fact of knowing them, of discarding them if they were useless, and framing new ones to suit a new environment. Holding a handful of earth in his palm, crumbling it between his fingers, he had realised that it was good, a rich, alluvial soil, a soil which would repay the work he was prepared to spend on it. All through that scorching, rainless summer, while the crops at Sydney Cove and Parramatta withered and died of drought, he toiled doggedly, and Cunnembeillee plodded to and fro between the gardens and the river, patiently pouring water round the roots of the strange plants which An-droo so inexplicably treasured. Later, with awed amazement, she had understood why. They had had melons, cucumbers, oats, maize, potatoes, and Indian corn. She had never eaten so well. Prentice had shot kangaroos, and once he had killed a calf. He did not use his musket more often than was necessary, partly because he was hoarding his ammunition, and partly because he feared that its report might betray his whereabouts to an exploring party. Cunnembeillee made traps for birds after the fashion of her people, and snared ducks on the river. Sometimes they had an eel or a fish for variety. There was milk in plenty, and honey from the wild bees' nests, which Cunnembeillee discovered in the bush.

As the months passed, and he became used to freedom, something in Prentice relaxed. He hardly ever feared recapture now, except in his dreams, and the bitter enmity with which he had faced a hostile world was starving in him for lack of sustenance. He was still taciturn, but now and then he smiled at the baby's antics, and allowed it to practise standing on its sturdy, bandy legs by holding on to his thumbs.

His eyes returned from their survey of his domain to rest upon his son, and remain there, a casual glance arrested, and becoming an attentive stare. The glance had seen a native child, but the stare discovered differences. Billalong's wavy hair was dark, but not so dark as Cunnembeillee's, and his skin, though tanned by exposure, was still much fairer than hers. Those things alone, however, Prentice reflected, would prove nothing, for the natives varied considerably in their colouring, and their young children, in any case, were usually fairer than adults. It was in the shape of the child's features, he decided, that his own blood showed. The nose was small and straight, and its nostrils not so spreading as those of the black people. The eyes were not so deeply sunk, and the brows not so jutting. . . .

He yawned, made sleepy by the heat after his day's work, and looked at Cunnembeillee again to see how she was progressing with her milking, his thoughts still playing idly about his son. He had often found himself watching curiously—and sometimes contemptuously—Cunnembeillee's methods of tending the infant, but he had never interfered. When it cried and would not be pacified, she built a fire, feeding it with twigs from one particular shrub, damping it to make a great smoke, and in this smoke she held the infant till its wails subsided. She had managed to convey to him that an evil spirit inhabited the child, and only thus could be dislodged; he watched cynically, and decided for himself that, in the instinctive effort to shut its mouth against the acrid smoke, the infant could not do otherwise than cease its yells. What matter? The operation had the desired effect, after all. He had watched her hasten to close the baby's mouth if it fell open during sleep, thus, she told him, the evil spirit entered. He had watched her rush to turn the child upon its left side when a parrot flew, screaming, over the camp, and upon its right side if the bird were a crow, but he had never been able to understand her explanation for these precautions. He was not really very interested. The child grew and thrived, and thus justified its mother's methods.

It was gnawing contentedly at a kangaroo bone, now, and staring in front of it with a fathomless, far-away gaze. Something in that rapt stare reminded its father suddenly of Johnny's babyhood, but he shied away violently from an unwelcome recollection. That life was gone. He would never return to it. He didn't care what had become of Ellen, or of Johnny either. Ellen was a slut. His black gin (he had picked up and corrupted a few of the native words by now) was worth half a dozen of her—hardworking, silent, obedient to his wishes, compliant to his desires, looking up to him as a woman should.

She had made no fuss at all, either, over the birth of the child. Never mentioned it. Kept on working as if there were nothing wrong, so that until the signs of maternity became unmistakable he had not even known that she was going to have a child. Catch Ellen, he thought sourly, catch any white woman, behaving like that! From the moment they knew they were pregnant they never let you forget it! They were martyrs, and you were the brute who was responsible for their martyrdom! He slapped at a mosquito, and gave a short laugh which merged into a muttered epithet. Cunnembeillee was different. It was almost as if she felt that it had noth-ing to do with him at all. It was her affair, and she kept it so. He had told himself that he was thankful for that—and yet, when the time for her labour came, he had felt uneasy, almost resentful, at her fierce insistence upon solitude. She would not allow him to approach her. She would not come into the hut, but built herself a mia-mia at some distance from it. Once, disturbed by her continued absence (for he had no wish to lose the services of so useful a person), he had gone in search of her. He had not found her, but he had stumbled upon some of her preparations, and had stood looking down with wrinkled brows at the bed she was making to receive his child. The ground had been carefully levelled and swept; not a twig, not a pebble, not a protruding root marred its smooth, sandy sur-face, and upon this foundation a carpet of leaves was in process of being laid. Each leaf had been separately placed, all the tips pointing one way, and each row overlapping the one next to it, so that the hard little stalks were covered. She must be gathering more leaves, he thought; and sud-denly, as the fresh, clean eucalyptus scent came up from the ground to his nostrils, he had turned without understanding his own impulse and blundered hurriedly away.

That night, unable to sleep, he had crept to a place from which he could see the tiny, winking light of her fire, and once he had heard her utter a strange sound—a cry which seemed half pain and half triumph. Returning to his hut, he had slept fitfully, haunted by that sound, aban-doned, between sleeping and waking, to a fear which would never have assailed him in his completely conscious moments. A tiny light in a vast darkness—a cry of pain and triumph! It was as if this land whose silence had always baffled him, had become articulate at last—and the sound of its voice was the oldest sound in the world. His sleep-befogged brain had recoiled from it in terror, knowing all the time that no recoil could save him. He was identified with it—helplessly, irrevocably. The land had taken him, used him, fashioned new life from him; his blood and his breath were now, even when he died, a part of it forever. His thoughts, sliding into sleep again, became atavistic nightmares. He saw it as a dark waste, all slime and ooze, with grass trees so tall that they speared the blood-red sky, inhabited by reptilian shapes which squirmed and spawned about his feet; and he called aloud in terror to Cunnembeillee, floundering after her through a murky twilight, afraid to lose sight of her, because, in such a place, only she could walk with confidence.

When the sunlight woke him he rose heavily and went to look for her. He found her squatting before her mia-mia with the baby in her arms. There was no trace of her ordeal. The ground in and about the mia-mia had been swept clean with a branch, and the fire was smoking. . . .

For the first time he saw her angry. She stared at him with an expression which made him shift awkwardly from one foot to the other, feeling that he had intruded unpardonably into some business which did not concern him in the least. She made a sharp movement of dismissal with one hand, saying peremptorily: "Go! Go!"

To his own surprise he had felt a desire to see the child, but it was lying in a curved piece of bark, held against her breast, and nothing of it was visible but one tiny foot. He had said surlily:

"Eat? Drink?"

She moved her head impatiently from side to side in negation, and repeated sharply: "Go!"

He had gone back to his hut feeling queerly chastened. More than a week had passed before she returned.

*   *   *

She had finished her milking now, and she walked up the hill rather slowly, carrying the brimming coolamon upon her hip. She put it down by the doorway of the hut, and then squatted on the ground beside the baby. He stretched his hands towards her, bouncing up and down in his excitement, and she gathered him into her arms and gave him her breast. How greedy he was, she thought proudly, and how strong! His small fists fought and kneaded in his impatience, his whole body arched and strove, and he sucked steadily, his hard round head warm against her flesh. She touched it gently with one forefinger. There were things which puzzled her about this child of hers, but she did not brood over them. They flickered across the gladness of her fulfilment as the thin shadows of the gum trees flickered over the sunlit ground. Whence did he come? Where was his spirit-place, from which Wadahgudjaelwon had brought him to lodge within her body? If An-droo had dreamed him he had never told her of it. Resting one day during a search for honey, she had laid her hand inadvertently upon a long, smooth stone, and bending to look at it she had found that it was hollow, and had known then that she would bear a child. But when he was born—when she had seen that his skin was pale, and his face somehow different from the faces of all the other babies she had known, she had remembered rather uneasily that once, alone near the hut, her curiosity had got the better of her, and she had crept inside and fingered her husband's strange possessions—and among them the long, hollow stem of his weapon. . . .

Yes, he was a strange child, unlike any other she had ever known. Once, soon after his birth, when she had seen from a thread of smoke farther up the river that a party of natives from that towri were coming to visit them, she had hastily rubbed the baby's body with charcoal to make it seem darker, for she feared the pity or the ridicule of the other women. But now that doubt and uneasiness was leaving her. He was so big and so strong that she could not help being proud of him. She was even beginning to be proud of his pale skin, and when the other dyins questioned her she answered them mysteriously, hinting that this was no ordinary child—and almost believing it herself.

Nor was she afraid of her husband any longer. She had been trained in the habit of obedience to her menfolk, and she was willing enough to obey still, but the fact that she had borne a son had added to her self-respect, her consciousness of her own value; her eyes, when they met his, were no longer timid. She was becoming reconciled to her life with him. She had begun to see that there was some object in his incessant labour; the warm milk from the cows was good for drinking, and she had become almost greedily fond of melons and potatoes. Moreover, she was not always lonely now. Occasionally a party of dyins from the tribe farther up the river came down to visit her, carrying their babies on their backs, surrounded by a horde of naked, noisy children, half a dozen dingo pups yelping at their heels. Then the little hut of Teeri-yeetchbeem, the Red-headed One, became the centre of much cheerful enjoyment. The dyins chattered and laughed and told Cunnembeillee the latest gossip of their tribe. The children played and quarrelled, and their screams mingled with the excited barking of the dogs. Upon the high, steeply sloping bank of the river they had made themselves a slide in the mud, and down this they shot in turn, entering the water with a terrific splash, and applauded by the delighted yells of their playmates. Billalong loved these occasions. All the women petted and admired him; all the other children played with him and carried him about. Cunnembeillee watched proudly. There was not another baby of his age among the black tribe who was any stronger, or any larger than hers.

*   *   *

His sucking had ceased from sheer exhaustion. Surfeited, he lay in her arms, his head heavily against her breast, his small, clenched fists thrown back, his eyes tightly shut, his breathing deep and regular. She glanced at Prentice. He was dozing, too, tired after the long, hot day, his chin sunk on his chest so that its thatch of red hair mingled with his beard, his ugly, work-scarred hands lying limply, with curled fingers, on his knee. Cunnembeillee, thus unobserved, stared from him to the child, and from the child back to him again. She felt suddenly a little lonely, and a little sad; with her thin legs stretched out straight before her, and her tangled black hair shadowing the melancholy of her eyes, she sat very still, so as not to disturb their sleep.

* * *

"Sydney, New South Wales,
"March 25th, 1791.

"Sir,
"It is not without concern that I find myself obliged to request his Majesty's permission to return to England.

"A complaint in the side, and from which, in more than two years, I have seldom been free has impaired my health, and at times puts it out of my power to attend to the charge with which His Majesty has been pleased to honour me in the manner I wish and the state of the colony requires.

"The settlement is now so fully established that the great labour may be said to be past; and it has, Sir, been attained under every possible disadvantage, though it is not in that situation in which I should wish to leave it, for it is not independent for the necessaries of life; and as I feel myself greatly interested in the good of a colony with the establishing of which I have been honoured, and to which I should wish to return, if the cause which now obliges me to desire permission to leave it, should be removed by the voyage, or by the assistance I may find in London, I therefore only request leave of absence from the Government."

Phillip signed his name and glanced at the clock on the mantelpiece. It was late, and he had had a tiring day, but he felt restless and disinclined for bed. The mere sight of his request set out in black and white seemed to give it a certain irrevocability, and to lend the day of his departure, still so far away, the urgent reality of tomorrow.

The weather was warm though the summer was nearly over, but now through an open window there came a breath of night air which was chilly, and reminded him that autumn was upon them again. He went

over to the window and closed it, and as he did so he saw the lights of the
Waaksamheyd which was to sail in a few days and bear his letter home.
He stood for a moment or two with his face close against the pane. Hunter
was returning to England in this ship with most of the crew of his ill-
fated *Sirius,* and Phillip knew very well that trouble was likely to brew
before the voyage was over between him and the dour Dutch captain of
the snow. Nevertheless, he thought, what else could he do? Who could
tell when the *Gorgon* would arrive, or if she would ever arrive at all?
Already he could see that recurring nightmare of famine creeping up
upon him again, and he stuck grimly to the obvious if rather crude fact
that a captain and a crew without a ship were so many mouths to feed,
and nothing else.

Hunter, he reflected, had looked nervy and hag-ridden upon his return,
at the end of February, from Norfolk Island. According to rumour the
atmosphere of hostility and discontent which Major Ross contrived to
create about him wherever he might be, had flourished evilly upon the
little island. Lieutenants Faddy and Kellow, it appeared, had carried their
brawling to the point of fighting a duel. There had been undignified and
acrimonious disputes about the disposal of the limited supply of liquor.
Bradley and Hunter had gone off to mess alone, and were, indeed, hardly
upon speaking terms with the Lieutenant-Governor. The whole community had divided itself into hostile camps, and the officers had quarrelled
continuously among themselves. He himself, Phillip knew, had come in
for a vast amount of blame. Why had he left them for so long without
relief? Without news? They could not forget their despair when, on short
rations, their salt provisions nearly exhausted, relying almost entirely
upon the vegetables they grew and the birds which flocked so thickly
about Mount Pitt, they had seen the sails of the *Lady Juliana* appear—and
pass without stopping.

Phillip felt no resentment at their animosity. He knew too well the
strain imposed upon the nerves of men marooned, half-starved, deprived
of their small comforts, and fretting continuously in the evil atmosphere
of uncongenial company. In such circumstances, he knew, the lack of a
glass of wine seems a martyrdom; a careless word is a deadly insult; it
becomes necessary to find some scapegoat whom one's disordered imagination may picture as an arch villain, and upon whom may be vented all
one's repressed irritations and disappointments. Hunter, gloomy and taciturn, might show distaste for the arrangements he had made for their
return; Bradley, more explosive, might treat him to glares of downright
animosity; that temperamental youth, Southwell, might look at him

askance from a sulky blue eye—but in their hearts they surely knew that he was doing what he must. The *Gorgon* was long, long overdue. The drought had meant a poor harvest. There were many to feed, and not much to feed them with. That was all.

He sighed and turned back to his table where the pile of letters which he had written in the preceding days lay ready for despatch. He had not the gift of popularity, and he knew it. But he was human enough to seek an antidote to the thoughts which had just been aching through his mind, and standing by his chair he leaned forward under the lamplight to re-read one paragraph of a page which lay uppermost. It was a letter from the officers who had been, three years ago, placed under arrest by Ross, and who had, in that invidious position, been performing their duties ever since.

"We cannot close this ungrateful subject," he read, "without requesting that your Excellency will deign to accept our warm and sincere thanks for the patience with which you have ever listened to our representations, in the course of those frequent and tiresome explanations which a cause long protracted necessarily occasions, and also for the numerous and repeated marks of kindness and attention which you have at all times been pleased to honour us with."

He turned his lamp low and straightened himself with an unwary movement. Instantly his hand went to his side, and a stab of pain dewed his forehead with sweat. In the half light, as he stood still, breathing carefully and waiting for it to pass, his mind echoed anxiously the words which, in his sharply pointed writing, lay beneath his unfocussed eyes:

"I only request leave of absence. I should wish to return. I should wish to return . . ."

A few days later the *Waaksamheyd* sailed. Phillip and most of the officers went down the harbour to see her off, and the shore of the cove was thronged with cheering and waving people. But another departure, the same evening, took place in stealth and darkness. William Bryant, convict, with his wife and two children, one a baby in arms, and seven other convicts, stole the Governor's boat and embarked upon an incredibly wild and desperate bid for freedom. Mary Bryant, holding the baby against her breast, dimly saw the towering cliffs of North Head against the starlit sky, and felt the little boat begin to lift and sink upon the ocean swell. She knew a shock of fear, and was to know many more, but she shut her teeth together grimly, and made no outcry about it. Huddling the children under her cloak, she slept fitfully through the long night while the coastline with its rocky cliffs and its crescent beaches slid by, and the men muttered excitedly to each other in the elation of escape.

* * *

The *Waaksamheyd* gone, the *Supply* once more despatched to Norfolk Island, Phillip turned his attention to home affairs, and the first thing he did, with a kind of grim resignation, was to reduce the ration again. There was no butter left, and no pease; neither the rice nor the pork was in a good state of preservation. And still the *Gorgon* did not come.

Again there began to creep over the settlement a sense of black depression; again Bennilong saw what he had so wonderingly seen before—an illness of the spirit descending upon the camp of the white men. It seemed that they were once more waiting for a boat to bring them food, and while they waited they lost such merriment and good humour as they had had, and became gloomy, silent and abstracted. The enmity between the Be-anga's people and the enslaved white tribe became more open and more violent, and many of the miserable creatures went about chained together, and some wore strange, heavy collars with spikes projecting outward from them.

Once Colbee's wife, the gentle Daringha, was the innocent cause of trouble. One of the despised white ones stole her fishing line, and was caught in the act. All the natives about the camp at the time were summoned to witness his punishment, and as they stood uneasily watching the lash coil over the naked, bloodstained back, their repugnance found expression in loud cries of horror and condemnation. Daringha wept bitterly, crouching on the ground with her head between her knees so that she need not see, but Barangaroo was furious. The primitive instincts of her sex taught her that a debased manhood was a peril to any tribe; it was an insult to that posterity which it was woman's business to produce. She snatched a heavy stick from the ground, and rushed at the man who wielded the lash, but she could not reach him. The red-coated ones closed round him to hold her back, and the horrible punishment went on. She shouted fiercely to him to stop, and her cry was echoed by her countrymen as they stood, a swaying black group, agitated, aghast, torn by anger and by pity, and by the fear of something which threatened to undermine their whole philosophy of life.

Out of this evil atmosphere of harshness and despair came the resentment, the rebelliousness which continued misery will always arouse in mankind. Captain Tench, observant, generous natured, and quick in his perceptions, felt it, and was moved to a rare outburst in his journal.

"I every day," he wrote, "see wretches pale with disease and wasted with famine, struggle against the horrors of their situation. How striking is the effect of subordination; how dreadful is the fear of punishment! The allotted task is still performed, even on the present reduced subsistence: the blacksmith sweats at his sultry forge; the sawyer labours pent-up in his pit, and the husbandman turns up the sterile glebe. . . ."

He sat thinking, his forehead on his hand, his eyes unusually sombre, scribbling aimlessly on a scrap of paper with his pen, and struggling with a thought whose obvious common sense was, even a century and a half later, to remain unappreciated. He wrote on slowly:

"But toil cannot be long supported without adequate refreshment. The first step in any community, which wishes to preserve honesty, should be to set the people above want."

He stopped again, staring in some astonishment at this revolutionary sentiment which he had penned. He had no idea at all how such a thing might be accomplished. With the accepting habit of his time he had already apologetically acknowledged his thoughts to be "ardent and generous, though hopeless and romantic," but now, with the picture of those pallid faces and those emaciated frames still freshly in his mind, he pursued, despite himself, a line of thought which his worldly brain could not but condemn as "chimerical."

"The throes of hunger," he wrote doggedly, "will ever prove too powerful for integrity to withstand."

He found himself worrying at the same question which had puzzled Patrick Mannion not long before. Would he himself, Watkin Tench, starve rather than steal? Steal? In such a community as this words challenged one to examination and analysis. He found himself thinking of the black people and their system in a land which gave them enough, but only just enough, for survival. Here, they said, was the land, and no man had a greater claim than his neighbour upon what it offered in the way of subsistence.

A shield, a spear, a canoe—these were things which one fashioned out of one's own skill, and which became, therefore, indubitably one's own personal property. But food—no! Food was the right of every man. One *took* it. The word "steal" had no meaning here . . .

Captain Tench shook his head impatiently. Impossible to compare the life and the laws of savages, he thought, with the life and the laws of civilised men. Property must remain sacred or the whole elaborate structure of the white man's world, its complicated social and economic system, its highly adaptable code of ethics, its triumphant culture, must collapse; and though he was capable of compassion he was far from conceiving that as anything but an appalling calamity. He went on writing, the fire gone out of him, his pen and his thoughts returning soberly to a recitation of gloomy facts:

"Hence arose a repetition of petty delinquencies which no vigilance could detect, no justice reach. Gardens were plundered; provisions pilfered; and the Indian corn stolen from the fields where it grew for public use."

It was inevitable. Life was so strangely precious that even those to whom it had become a burden refused to lie down tamely and die. Theft was the inevitable consequence of hunger; punishment was the inevitable consequence of theft; rebellion was the inevitable consequence of punishment; and so the vicious circle swung round to theft again. In it the inhabitants of Sydney Cove, from the Governor to the lowest of the convicts, moved as in a treadmill, captive, desperate, physically and spiritually exhausted, but still grimly alive.

* * *

Phillip was seized with a fit of restlessness. Within measurable time now he would be leaving the country—and what did he know of it? He had been so tied to his struggling little settlement, so incessantly occupied with the arduous business of keeping it going from month to month— almost from day to day—that he had forgotten, except at rare intervals, to lift his eyes from the soil of Sydney and Rose Hill to that far line of lavender coloured hills, and wonder what lay beyond them. He did not hope any longer that he himself would ever cross them. If three lusty young men such as Dawes, Johnston, and Lowes had found the travelling so hard, it was not for him, middle-aged and ill, to attempt it. But at least, he thought, he could get as far as the Nepean. He could follow it down and settle once and for all the still vexed question as to whether it were indeed the same river as the Hawkesbury.

He chose with care a strong party of twenty-one, including Collins, White, Dawes and Tench. Colbee, Bennilong and Ballederry getting wind of the expedition, and ascertaining by careful inquiry that plenty of food would be available, begged to be allowed to join it. The Governor, thinking that their knowledge of the country might be useful, was willing—but

Barangaroo was not. It was bad enough, she thought, that Bennilong should spend half his time in the camp of the Bereewolgal, mimicking their speech and their ways; she was not going to have him wandering off with them into unknown country. For the tribes seldom journeyed outside their own towris, and, contrary to Phillip's hopes and expectations, this would be an exploration no less for them than for him. So Barangaroo treated her husband to a domestic scene, the upshot of which was that a chastened Bennilong informed the Governor with such dignity as he could muster, that he had changed his mind and no longer wished to accompany them.

Early on the morning of Monday, April 11, 1791, the expedition set out from Rose Hill, every man carrying in his knapsack provisions for ten days. A gun, a blanket, a hatchet, a cooking kettle and a canteen completed a burden whose weight was approximately forty pounds. Why, asked Colbee of Ballederry, rolling his dark eyes in astonishment, did they not take a few of their idle, useless women along to carry these loads? Ballederry, with a shrug, expressed his view that in the serious matters of life these white people were entirely mad. Why should they wish to undertake such a journey at all? Why should the Be-anga elect to labour along in the burning heat when at Rose Hill he might have sat at his ease in the shade?

For themselves it was a holiday and an adventure; they walked tirelessly and cheerfully all day, cracking jokes between themselves, and laughing heartily when the white men stumbled. Before the first night's camp they were well out of their own towri, and into that (as they explained to Tench, in answer to his question) of the Boorooberongal.

"Boodjerree?" inquired Tench.

"Weeree!" replied Colbee with emphasis, for this tribe was, at the moment, none too friendly with the Cadigal, having recently stolen two women and three spears from them. Curiosity, however, was a far stronger emotion in the black men than hatred. Hatred was all very well on its appointed occasions, and serving its appointed purposes, but it was an uneasy emotion with which to burden the heart at other times. When, therefore, late that evening, Beereewan of the Boorooberongal, attracted by the glare of a campfire ten times the size of any he had ever seen before, crept through the trees with a few of his friends to investigate, he was deeply interested to observe men of his own race seated among the grotesque beings who surrounded the blaze.

These, he said to his companions, must be some of the tribe which had come from over the sea to dwell upon the coast. These must be the fellow tribesmen of Teeri-yeetchbeem, the Red-headed One, who had lived in their own camp for so long, and who had gone thence at last with Cunnembeillee. Their voices carried from the inky shadows to the circle of firelight, and heads were raised, listening. Collins said sharply to the Governor:

"Natives, Sir."

Phillip, who had been lying flat on his back, his head pillowed on a rolled up blanket, forgot his weariness and sat up alertly.

"Call them, Colbee," he commanded. "Say come. Say we give food."

Colbee cupped his hands round his mouth, and his summons went out eerily into the darkness.

"Coooooo—ee!"

Beereewan approached, carrying his glowing fire stick in his hand. Just outside the circle of firelight he halted to lay his spears on the ground, and then advanced, his head bent forward, and his eyes narrowed against the glare.

Colbee, with dignity and aplomb, appointed himself master of ceremonies.

"I am Colbee of the Cadigal," he announced.

Beereewan replied courteously:

"I am Beereewan of the Boorooberongal." And added: "What are these? Are they men, or women?"

Ballederry hastened to instruct him.

"They are men. They are Bereewolgal, men come from afar. They are our friends, and they will give you food as they have given it to us."

Beereewan hesitated, frowning. He had left no particular love or admiration for the only member of this tribe whom he had hitherto encountered, and the sight of these others did nothing to reassure him. The firelight, dancing upon their strange coverings, seemed to obscure their shape so that they hardly looked like human beings at all. On their pale faces it painted a reddish glare and dark flickering shadows, so that they seemed to grimace malevolently. All about them, piled in heaps lay bundles such as the Red-headed One had carried when he was found. Where were their womenfolk? No peaceful party travelled womanless.

Dubiously, he allowed himself to be led forward at last by Colbee, and learned with astonishment that the quiet, smallish man with the big nose was a great Be-anga, the leader and father of his tribe. Carefully he pronounced after Colbee the strange sounding names by which these people were introduced to him, and with slowly increasing confidence allowed his hand to be held by each in turn—a custom which he interpreted as a sign of friendship. When he departed, carrying with him some of the odd food of the white men (which, having smelt, he presently dropped in a thicket) he had decided that he must send a messenger up the river to the camp of the Red-headed One, who would surely be delighted to know that his friends were in the neighbourhood.

* * *

Sweating, panting, cursing luridly, the last stragglers of the party won to the top of the hill where the Governor was already standing bareheaded, with Tench and Collins at his side. They were staring gloomily at another distant hill with a cleft in it by which Phillip was able to proclaim it as the one they had been seeking by walking in an opposite direction.

There was nothing for it, he said briskly, but to go back the way they had come. That, certainly, was Richmond Hill. He glanced round at the hot and dirty faces of his followers. For two days they had stumbled over boulder strewn ground, struggled through dense undergrowth, slipped and slid on the wet ground of creek banks, sprawled on their noses with their feet entangled in vines and roots, rubbed at hands smarting with the sting of nettles, and chafed under the incessant raillery of their black companions, who suffered none of these mischances. And now the Governor said calmly that they must go back! They had been walking in the wrong direction! They swore and grumbled, mopping sweat and grime from their faces.

Phillip, studying the eminence on which they stood, noting its wild and rocky contours, the spiky sparseness of its vegetation, its whole air of arid and primitive uncouthness, was visited by one of his rare flashes of humour. He glanced at Tench, still contriving somehow to be an elegant figure in spite of a large rent in his trousers; still wearing his expression of slightly amused good humour beneath a smear of charcoal which decorated his cheek; still calm; still irreproachably well-mannered; still, even in this uncivilised wilderness, invincibly and imperturbably sophisticated.

"I think," Phillip said in his prim way, "that we shall call this hill after you, Captain Tench. Tench's Prospect Mount. It sounds well, does it not?"

Tench, taken by surprise, blinked round him at what he had just been deciding to describe in his journal as a "heap of desolation." Collins and Dawes were grinning at him, and White, suddenly struck by the full richness of the jest, let out a hearty guffaw which was echoed by Colbee and Ballederry, who did not understand, but liked to laugh whenever there seemed to be an excuse for it. Tench thought ruefully: "Good God, what a monument! The river, now—I wouldn't have minded having *that* named after me. I *did* discover it . . ." But he could not help appreciating so inspired an ineptitude, and the gravity of his voice was belied by the twinkle in his eye, and he bowed and said: "Thank you, Sir. I am indeed —greatly honoured."

* * *

Colbee and Ballederry were becoming very bored. They enlivened this dreary expedition to the best of their ability by singing and dancing and make fun of the flounderings of the white men, but they were impatient of a journey which seemed to them to have no object, and they began to demand plaintively and continuously: "Where's Rose Hill? Where? Where?" On the third day the river was reached again, and more natives of the Boorooberongal joined them to eat, sleep and converse. This relieved the tedium a little, for they were full of curiosity about the white men and their belongings, and Colbee and Ballederry were kept busy explaining about their weapons which slew by a magic fire, displaying their hatchets, their knapsacks, their cooking utensils, demonstrating the uses of buttons, buckles, and the small magical thing called Naa-moro, by which they were able to tell in which direction they should travel.

David Collins, stretched out before the fire, listened idly to their chatter, and watching with some amusement the indefatigable Tench busily scribbling down words of this different native dialect, and comparing them with those of the coastal tribes, found himself glancing from time to time at the Governor, who sat with his back against a tree trunk and his hands clasped round his knees. More than once during these days of severe exertion White had muttered to him in an exasperated undertone that His Excellency was mad to have undertaken such a trip. As early as the first day one of the party had collapsed from heat and fatigue; many others, at each halt, had dropped where they stood, to lie panting with closed eyes and thudding pulses until the word to move on was spoken. But the Governor was not one of these. During each period of rest he sat very still, and once or twice he had stretched himself out flat on his back with his hat over his face to cheat the flies and the sun; but he was always the first to move, and over the roughest ground and through the densest underbrush, his slight figure was always amongst the first half dozen. Collins could not see his face now, for it was in shadow, but he noted that the knuckles of the clasped hands showed bony-white, and by that strain and tenseness he knew that the Governor was fighting his pain once more. He had often heard Phillip say, he remembered, that it seemed to trouble him less when he was active; but White only grunted at that, and said that rest was essential to the cure of any ill.

What would happen to this place, Collins wondered, when Phillip was gone? Who was there to replace him in any true and adequate sense? His duties as Phillip's secretary had allowed him a closer intimacy than any of the others possessed, and he realised, without in the least understanding it, the strength which was given to the colony by the inexplicable fact of its Governor's unwavering, almost fanatical faith in it.

Things would be very different soon, he thought, watching the red sparks fly up from the fire and vanish in the darkness. The marines would go back to England on the *Gorgon;* King and Hunter were already gone; when Phillip went there would be only a handful left of those who had first raised the flag and drunk a toast to the King under the trees of Sydney Cove.

* * *

On the fifth day, within a few miles of their objective, Richmond Hill, they found their way again cut off by a creek flowing into the river. Drearily they tramped up it disheartened by the inexorable manner in which the land seemed determined to frustrate them at every move. The natives were like bored children, crying to go home. "Where's Rose Hill?" they wailed. "Where? Where?" They flung their hands up in the air and uttered a long, mournful, slowly diminishing cry which seemed to express immeasurable distance, looking at their white companions the while, with puzzled and imploring eyes. They were no longer willing and cooperative. When a duck was shot Ballederry refused to swim for it. Why, he demanded sullenly, should he? Many, many times he had swum for ducks, and never a share had he been given when they came, savoury-smelling, from the cooking pot. Crossly he told White to swim for it himself, and went away to sit alone upon a fallen log, and sulk.

After one more night Phillip gave the word to return. It had been a tiring, and in many ways a disappointing expedition, but not without its entertainment. Colbee and Ballederry were beside themselves with joy, and capered ahead of the party on the day's march which brought them back to Rose Hill. But the Governor, nearing the settlement, glanced back at the range of mountains, and said to Dawes, striding along beside him:

"Some of you younger men will have to make the next attempt, Mr. Dawes. I should be glad to have this question of the rivers settled once and for all."

Dawes nodded.

"A smaller party is best, I think, Sir. Four, perhaps. Not more than six. We might try again next month—Captain Tench and myself and a couple of men . . ."

He glanced inquiringly at Tench, who, humming to himself one of the plaintive airs of his Welsh forebears, made a nod serve for reply.

* * *

Ballederry, his face, breast and arms fiercely bedaubed with red clay, carrying his throwing stick and four spears with a menacing air of purpose, strode up the hill to the Governor's house at Rose Hill, and hammered on the closed door, calling loudly for the Be-anga. He was so angry that Phillip, coming out bareheaded into the sun to talk to him, was hardly able to follow his furiously incoherent story. With difficulty, grasping a word here and there, sometimes in the native tongue and sometimes in his own, he was able, at last to understand.

Ballederry had been taking fish to the huts, as he often did, to barter them with the convicts, and he had left his canoe hidden at some little distance. When he returned he had found it destroyed. Smashed to pieces. For this injury, he announced savagely, he would take his revenge upon the white tribe. . . .

Phillip, controlling his own surge of anger, spoke quietly:

"No, no, Ballederry. Very bad to break your nowee. Weeree, weeree! Be-anga angry, Be-anga punish. Ballederry not kill."

Ballederry interrupted him with a flood of native words.

Why should the Be-anga punish? It was not he who had been wronged, but himself, Ballederry, who was not a child or a woman that he must have his wrongs avenged for him. It was for him to deal with the offenders, and he would do so. He had come merely to inform the Be-anga of his intention. He would not wish the Be-anga to imagine that his followers were slain without cause. He would go out now and find them, and when he found them he would kill them.

He had turned to depart, and it had taken all Phillip's persuasion, the exercise of all the influence which he had gained, an outright appeal to that confidence and affection which he had won from the native mind, to stop him.

Let Ballederry wait, the Governor urged, let him only wait until the culprits should be discovered, and he should see them punished with his own eyes. Ballederry stared at him, puzzled and dissatisfied. What was the use of that, he asked impatiently. Did the Be-anga consider him incapable of defending his own honour? Phillip explained patiently that these people had offended not only against Ballederry, but against himself, their Be-anga, by disobeying his commands. Ballederry shrugged. In that case, of course, he acknowledged it was the Be-anga's right to punish them on his own account; he would defer his own revenge till later.

His shrug, his quieter manner, his air of acquiescence misled the Governor into imagining him placated, and upon this misunderstanding the matter rested. Phillip immediately set about having the culprits apprehended. It was not difficult; they had been seen in the act of destroying the canoe by a seaman, who described them, and Ballederry was summoned to witness their flogging. He watched with sullen uneasiness. It was incomprehensible to him that the Be-anga should feel his honour satisfied by an unpleasant ritual in which he took no part whatever—but it was, after all, his own business. Watching his expression, Phillip decided that he felt the punishment to be inadequate, and gave orders that he was to be informed that one of the offenders had been put to death. Ballederry scowled, turned his back on them all, and stalked off to await his own opportunity.

It came a few weeks later. The convict who staggered into the settlement wounded in two places by his spears, was not one of those who had destroyed the canoe, but to Ballederry that was of small importance. He belonged to their tribe. Blood had been shed. He was satisfied.

Phillip heard the news with dismay. Of all his native friends young Ballederry was, he thought, the most prepossessing. Less turbulent and less vain than Bennilong, less taciturn than Colbee, he had become, of late, such a favourite at Government House that Phillip had tentatively decided upon him as one of the two whom he hoped to take back with him to England when he departed. This was now out of the question. Grimly he gave orders that the young native was to be taken or shot; but he saw to it that the order was given in the presence of other natives, who could be trusted, he thought, to see that their countryman was warned.

He was. Promptly the word went out to Ballederry that the white Be-anga was very angry with him. He had directed the red-coated ones to slay him with their gooroobeera whenever or wherever they might encounter him. Ballederry stared, astonished, hurt, angry. Phillip's growing affection for him had been warmly returned. Day by day, meeting in the bush members of his tribe, he questioned them anxiously. Was the Be-anga still angry? Was it not yet safe for him to go to the white men's camp? Sometimes, recklessly, he went, hoping that the Be-anga would see and call to him. Once Nanbarree, hearing that he was in danger, stripped off his clothes and vanished into the bush to warn him. Once, seeing the Governor in his garden talking to Bennilong, he even paddled his canoe into the cove and called a greeting. But Bennilong shouted to him to flee quickly—the Be-anga was still angry, and had this moment given orders to a party of red-coated ones to set out in pursuit of him. Ballederry's canoe shot away again across the harbour, its owner bewildered and heavy hearted. Now he was a fugitive, even in his own towri, for the white men with their gooroobeera were everywhere. Now he was banished from the queer, exciting camp of the Bereewolgal; he would travel no more with the white Be-anga, nor sit at his table, nor see kindness and welcome in his eyes. . . .

Phillip, seeing him land, free and unharmed, upon the opposite shore, hid his relief behind a grim and unforgiving countenance.

Barangaroo was a less shrewish person nowadays. She still berated Bennilong when he displeased her, but almost absent-mindedly, as of more from habit than from any real anger. For the birth-spirit had favoured her at last. She was very happy, and inclined to be patronising towards Warreweer, who was still childless, and she spent most of her time with the gentle Daringha, Colbee's wife, who was also to bear a child, but much sooner than herself. Together they squatted by the hour outside Bennilong's hut on the eastern point of Sydney Cove, making twine and fishhooks and watching the incessant activity which went on in the camp of the Bereewolgal.

They were like bees or ants, these white people, Daringha said. They toiled and they swarmed, always moving, always going hurriedly from one place to another, always dragging things about, building, struggling, making a labour of their life.

At Parramatta, Barangaroo agreed, it was the same. She looked at the rows of huts, at the Governor's house, at the flag, feeling again the old aching sense of calamity which had tormented her upon the first arrival of these people. That was so long ago, and past emotions were no more real than dreams. She had come to accept their presence, and her fears had faded as her familiarity with them increased. She had learned to share her husband's confidence in the Be-anga; she had reason to respect the powers of the carrahdy, White, who had upon several occasions dressed her wounds. But now, laying her hands upon her body and feeling the movement of new life there, she was suddenly afraid again. Her child had a birthright—the land which had nurtured his forefathers for uncountable generations—but was not something happening to that land? Here, before her very eyes? Was it not being changed by the antlike industry of these white invaders? Was not their strange, unrestful influence reaching out more and more into the lives of her own people—even into the darkness of their mia-mias and the red light of their campfires? Had it not been felt among all the tribes like a dull uneasy pain, like the slow and implacable approach of death from a pointed bone, like the breathless heaviness which hangs upon the air, when, on a dark horizon, a distant fork of lighting cracks the sky?

Where was the danger? Where? Where? The passing centuries, going quietly over the heads of her ancestors, had evolved in their brains no machinery for the understanding of Change. And now, with Change beginning before their eyes, they stared at it with the detached curiosity of children watching a spectacle which could not touch their own lives, so quiet, so secure, so inviolable. . . .

But Barangaroo was nervous again. She looked with jealous suspicion upon the world which was to receive her child. Haunted by a dread which she could not name she turned her head away from the settlement and looked towards the northern shore whose trees still came down to the water's edge, and still climbed the hillsides as they had done ever since she could remember. Behind that hill, the eye of her mind saw more hills. Behind those hills more, and more still. Endless they were, the trees. Endless the land. And the camps of the Bereewolgal so small. She felt a little reassured, and was too wise to seek a reason. Comfort had come to her, and she would not seek its source, but was content to hold in her mind an image of the endless land. No man of her race knew its limits. She looked again, with a new serenity at the ugly, unhappy camp of the white men, and said placidly:

"They are not yet wise. They have a foolish law. No tribe can be happy whose law is so foolish. In time they will become wise . . ."

She nodded, indulgently maternal, and stretched herself full length on the dry, prickly grass. She was not young any longer, and this business of child-bearing did not come as easily as it had when she was a girl. She stared up at the blue sky, idly content because her body was functioning once more as a woman's body should, and because the heat of the sun upon it, and the movement of the child within it seemed but two parts of an intense and indestructible well-being.

* * *

This was the second time. Prentice, watching the natives disappear round the bend of the river, rubbed his hands absently against his thighs, his face darkening, falling again into its old lines of hatred and defiance.

What was he to do? He stood very still, thinking, his head lowered, his eyes shadowed by the wild thatch of his red hair, struggling between two instincts.

It was three months now since two members of the Boorooberongal had come to tell him that a large party of his own tribe was camped farther down the river. He had leapt to his feet, his heart hammering, the old, almost forgotten fear of life rushing back over him like a flood. "Where?" he had demanded fiercely, "How far?"

He had commanded Cunnembeillee to put out their fire lest its smoke betray them. He had yarded his cattle. He had taken his muskets and his store of ammunition from the hut. Then he had stared round his domain with eyes in which the hunger of possessiveness fought with his fear. The dread of losing all that he had made was like a foretaste of death. The laboriously turned earth within its strong fences, the sleek cattle in their yard, the hut, the few bits of clumsy furniture—these things were his, and he had never grown accustomed to the intoxicating sense of worth which that fact had bestowed on him. Now, feeling them menaced, and knowing his life endangered too, he hardly knew which threat terrified him more. That night they had slept a mile from the hut in a bark shelter of Cunnembeillee's making. Hidden in the underbrush it commanded a view of their own stretch of the river, and all night he had lain awake with his loaded musket beside him, tormented by the thought of losing all that he had so hardly won.

But there was no sign of the explorers. Towards evening of the next day, unable to endure uncertainty of their movements longer, he had set off down the river alone, keeping well away from the banks, and under cover.

Next morning he climbed to a hilltop from which a long stretch of the river was visible, but still he could see no sign of the hated red coats, nor even the smoke of a fire. Late that afternoon he fell in with a few women of the Boorooberongal, and he asked them about the white men. The women waved their arms towards the north, and then eastward. They had been there, much farther down the river, but now they were returning whence they had come. "Parramatta" one of the women repeated several times, and Prentice scowled in an effort of memory. The word was familiar—he had heard it at the settlement—but it was a moment or two before he remembered that it was the native name for Rose Hill. They had gone back, then! They had never really been near his part of the river at all!

His relief made him giddy; he sat down on the ground and rubbed his hand across his forehead, staring stupidly into the curious, amiable eyes of the dyins, and thinking vaguely and irrelevantly that they were like the eyes of a young wallaby he had caught once. In his brain hatred and fear had been mounting until they filled it like a heavy poison, and now, in its sudden ebb he realised that his head had felt tight, stuffed, a little mad. He had not known that he was tired, but now every bone in his body ached and every muscle was stiff with exhaustion. He was hungry, too. He pulled his haversack forward and rummaged in it, but there were only two small bits of kangaroo meat left, so he pointed to the dyins' baskets, and instantly a bird and a handful of yams were laid before him.

That had been the first alarm; here was another. Only a small party this time, the natives had informed him. Four of them. But nearer than before. This time Prentice took it more coolly. He set off down the river as before to investigate, and on the evening of the second day he was frozen in his tracks by the sound of a shot. It came from his own side of the river. Cautiously, still keeping himself well hidden, he advanced so that a long stretch of smooth water was visible, and saw a native canoe drawn up on the grassy bank. Near it a group of natives sat chattering and turning to point now and then towards a hill from whose direction the sound of the shot had come. Prentice stood watching them, and as he watched he felt himself invaded by an emotion which had never moved him before—compassion. It came flooding up to submerge the contempt which had always been his only feeling for a people who lacked the cunning and the hatred which were his own weapons; a people who were too stupid to realise the malevolence of life; a people who were willing to be trustful; a people who insisted on being light-hearted; a people so ignorant of the insatiable acquisitiveness of the white man that they were assisting with the utmost cheerfulness in their own undoing.

Suddenly from the bitterness of his own memories he saw their fate very clearly. His old hatred of "them"—the dominant class of his own race—was now aroused on behalf of that other race, whose blood mixed with his own in the veins of his infant son. "They" had flung him and his kind out of their own land, but that was not enough. "They" must have this land too, and make of it another hell on earth for the poor as they had made their own. And what was to prevent them?

He stared with almost incredulous fury at the naked figures on the bank. Acting ferryman for the red coats, were they, the poor fools! Didn't they know that they would be used just as long as they were useful and then annihilated as indifferently as if they were ants? Didn't they know yet that there was no mercy to be expected from "them"? Were they still being taken in by friendly words, beads, looking-glasses, smiles? The poor miserable ignorant savages! They didn't know of the might that reared itself behind His Excellency Arthur Phillip! They didn't know that thousands of miles away across the sea the law of the white men, the great law of Possession, was implacably at work stretching out greedy hands towards their continent.

"I could tell y' something!" he raged silently to the noisy group across the river. "I could tell y' what they do to their own kind—are they goin' to care about a crowd of naked heathens like you? So you *show* 'em your country, do y'? So y' take 'em here and there, and feed 'em when they're hungry, and guide 'em when they're lost, and care for 'em when they're sick, and ferry 'em across the river in your canoes! Y' poor, bloody bastards! I've 'eard y' laugh and sing! I've see y' playin' with y' brats and tellin' 'em tales! You wait! Soon y' won't 'ave no country—and y' won't *want* to sing. . . ."

He crouched among the undergrowth watching, and at last, as the twilight deepened, he saw the distant glimmer of a fire near the foot of the hill. Then he retreated and made camp for himself well out of sight and earshot. But early in the morning he was back again; he could see nothing of the white men, but he met some natives who told him that they had gone still farther westward. He cursed them vindictively, and settled down to wait, and while he waited he thought. Going westward. So they were beginning to push inland in earnest now. How much longer would he be safe, then? Would they not inevitably find him soon? Lately he had done some exploring westward himself; he had already discovered another valley and another river which joined this one, and he began to lay his plans for moving on. In the evening, dozing among the bracken, he was startled awake by the sound of voices. Peering out cautiously he saw them, his enemies, and felt his muscles tighten, and his breathing hurried with the intensity of his hatred. Again assisted by some half dozen natives, they were re-crossing the river about a hundred and fifty yards downstream. Two, whom he thought he recognised as Tench and Dawes, were standing naked on the opposite bank, clapping their arms about their bodies for warmth, and the other two were preparing for the crossing. A native, just bringing his canoe ashore, was handing out bundles of clothes, muskets, and knapsacks to the shivering figures on the other bank. Prentice stared grimly. There they stood, naked, disarmed, helpless, their tiny party split in two by the width of the river—and the poor black fools hadn't the sense to exterminate them! He had to shut his teeth tightly together to prevent himself from yelling directions to them. "Throw the muskets in the river! Throw everything in—clothes, food, everything!

There! Now you've got them! Let them see how hard and straight your spears can fly!" His fingers ached round his musket. Once he half lifted it, tempted almost beyond endurance. But some shred of caution, stronger even than his hatred, stayed his hand. He could only shoot one at a time; he couldn't be certain of getting them all. And then his whereabouts would be betrayed, armed parties would scour the river for him, he would be taken . . .

No, not that. He would end his own life sooner than go back to slavery after his taste of freedom. But that freedom was too precious to be jeopardised. So he commanded himself: "No, no." Before his tormented eyes the weapons and the bundles were handed back to their owners; the other two men were ferried safely across to join their companions. He watched them dress and gather up their gear, watched the natives pointing the way to them with vociferous friendliness, watched them march off eastward again in the direction of Rose Hill. Then he fell flat on his face among the bracken, sick with frustrated hatred and an agony of fear.

They had been twice, they would come again. There was no peace to be found anywhere in the world, no corner in which one could be safe from them. With a shapeless and incoherent bitterness he felt that what he now had he had earned. He had earned it by the long months of patience and planning, by the nightmare weeks of escape, by the fogs of delirium, the sweat of his toil, and by something else, still more valid, which he could not analyse. It was as if this independent freedom was his because he had come to value it so deeply. It was as if he valued it not only for what it gave him, but for what it made him, and his terror of losing it was becoming the terror of losing that something in himself which it had awakened. He tramped slowly back up the river at dawn the next morning, making his plans.

* * *

Now the Governor was worried not only about food, but about water. It was nearly June, and still no rain had fallen. Most of the little creeks about the cove had dried up, and the main stream which flowed through the settlement, and which had been one of his principal reasons for establishing it upon that spot, was now failing, too. He had long ago forbidden the cutting down of trees near its bank, so that by their shade the moisture might be conserved, but, walking up it one day towards the end of May with David Collins, he was alarmed to find it a mere trickle between a succession of boggy holes. He said soberly:

"A ship couldn't water at this, Collins. If we don't get rain soon . . ."

He left his sentence unfinished in words, and continued it in his thoughts. What steps should he—could he—take if he found his settlement waterless? Could the natives be pressed into service to help bring it from more distant streams? He thought not, remembering their volatility, their hatred of organised labour, the sacredness of their inter-tribal territories. Could the whole settlement be moved to Rose Hill? He corrected himself; Parramatta. He had decided that the native name should be officially restored to this place, and interrupted his own anxiety to make a mental note that an order must be given to that effect. Staring at the trickle in the creek bed, he remembered the broad, clear reaches of the Nepean, which Tench's latest expedition had finally identified as part of the Hawkesbury, and he wondered if he might be forced to move inland, abandoning Sydney Cove altogether, save as a port, and begin his settlement anew on the banks of that inexhaustible stream.

Water, food, food, water. The words tormented him all day and most of the night. How much longer could he keep the convicts working on their present ration? He saw them continually in his mind's eye, shambling about with the dragging gait of men who have no hope or interest left in life; he saw their faces, leaden coloured, with eyes which stared apathetically from dark hollows above their sunken cheeks; their feet, more often than not, were bare, and their ragged clothing flapped about their bodies emphasising rather than concealing their emaciation. They were in no fit state to work—and yet he dared not let them stop. He knew that if once he allowed idleness to grip the community they were all doomed. A show of purposefulness must be kept up. Some semblance of progress must be made. Unconsciously he was trying to counteract that poisonous belief which every convict held, and which came near enough to the truth. They had been sent here merely to be rid of them, and it mattered little if they lived or died. They were cumberers of the earth—but at least they need no longer cumber the soil of their native land.

Phillip knew of only one antidote to degradation, and he imposed it on them with a grim relentlessness which earned him nothing but hatred. They must work while they had strength to stand. They must feel that, however unwillingly, they were achieving something. They must be forced to realise that this place was not only a gaol, but the beginning of a colony where others would live after them, and for whom the way must be prepared. All through these last few weeks, feeling the autumn air grow crisper, he had watched the results of their slow, exhausted labours growing towards completion. The barracks at Parramatta was almost finished, and the N.S.W. Corps had moved in. The surveyor and the Reverend Mr.

Johnson were established in new houses. Cartloads of bricks were being brought in daily from the kilns on Brickfield Hill. From where he sat at this moment he could see men working over the stacks of posts and palings lower down the stream, with which they were to fence in this last precious reserve of water.

He felt suddenly exhausted himself. All this labour was his labour. There was not a brick carried, or a nail driven, or a post set upright in the ground, but was there by the effort of his will and the obstinacy of his faith. He had a mad, resentful feeling that the whole place existed only because he believed in it, and a wild impulse to annihilate it merely by denial, and so win some rest. He moved abruptly, seeking to vanquish nerves which more and more often lately betrayed him into such absurd fancies, by imposing upon himself a still more rigid attention to material detail, and still more Spartan physical effort. He said with sharp matter-of-factness:

"We may as well go back. A few more weeks—and then if no rain has fallen I shall have to think of dividing our forces yet again. Who was that, Collins?"

Collins, arrested as the Governor had been, by the sound of footsteps among the undergrowth on the opposite bank, said slowly:

"I think it was Mr. Mannion, Sir. He seemed—anxious to avoid us."

"Ah." Phillip's non-committal monosyllable indicated an indifference which was not assumed. He would have held no very high opinion of Mr. Mannion at any time, but here, in his only just surviving settlement, a man who contributed nothing whatever to its progress or maintenance was, in his eyes, as good as non-existent. Little which happened in his community failed to come to his ears sooner or later, and he was very well aware of the whispers which coupled the name of Stephen Mannion with that of his convict servant and nursemaid, Ellen Prentice. They were not particularly scandalised whispers. Men were men, and women were scarce, and that was all there was to be said about it. Most of the officers had, at one time or another, contracted such temporary alliances; it was taken for granted.

Busy already with plans for the suitable celebration, in a few days, of His Majesty's birthday, the Governor set off down the stream again towards the settlement, with Collins, thoughtfully silent, beside him.

* * *

Stephen Mannion tramped through the dry bush, his head bent, and his lips moving as if in a fierce concentration of thought. But he was not really thinking; he had long ago exhausted his thoughts. For months after the death of his wife his brain had worked with a febrile intensity, turning in upon itself in horrified self-examination, retreating before what it found there and finding refuge in excuses until, in a moment of revulsion, it recognised the excuses as false, and plunged again, deeper and more disastrously, into remorse.

At first his torments had been intermittent. He had maintained a certain amount of intercourse with those whom he was able to regard as his equals in the settlement. He had gone down in the evenings, sometimes, to drink a glass of wine with Captain Hill, he had visited the Abbotts, and sung duets with Mrs. Macarthur to an accompaniment upon Mr. Worgan's piano. He had dined occasionally with the Governor, and made several excursions to Rose Hill.

The *Gorgon* was expected. That would end his exile. While he could keep this thought before him he could endure the nights which tortured him with memories and accusations. But the *Gorgon* did not come. Day after day, and week after week, and month after month went by, and still she did not come. In the meantime Stephen Mannion began to know himself. The Celtic habit of introspection which easy and pleasant circumstances had never fostered, began, now that he was idle, uncomfortable, and unhappy, to take possession of him. He plunged deeper and deeper into a bog of self-accusation, and with a masochistic pleasure stripped himself of qualities which he had worn as easily as he wore his clothing, and as superficially. He began to perceive that whatever his ancestors had been, he, Stephen Mannion, was not picturesquely mad, but dully and fearfully sane; not adventurous, but cautious; not brilliant and indispensable, but useless and inefficient. He had no background here, and without it he was nothing. He began to lose his confidence, and was horrified by the spectacle of himself without it. He began to resent his isolation. Everyone else had something to do; everyone else, even the convicts, lived to some purpose. When he talked to the Governor, to Captain Collins, to Mr. Johnson, to Mr. White, he was uneasily conscious that they were occupying an idle moment from which they would presently return to their duties, but from which he could return only to the solitude of his room, the tyranny of his thought, and the awareness of Ellen Prentice.

He avoided his house, and, when he had to enter it, shut himself alone in his room. He began to dread seeing Ellen at her work, meeting the cool, impassive glance of her dark eyes, coming upon her accidentally seated with the baby—Harriet's baby—in her arms, the white curve of her breast showing above its flaxen head.

Through the heat of that drought-stricken summer he had lived from day to day in the hope of seeing the flag go up to announce the arrival of the *Gorgon*. Hemmed in his prison of introspection the happenings of the colony had hardly touched him until the arrival of the *Waaksamheyd* in December had aroused in him a fresh access of hope. But there was no prospect, so the Governor said, of an immediate departure for the Dutch snow, for she was to convey the crew of the *Sirius* to England, and they were still at Norfolk Island. The weeks dragged on, and the temperature mounted to 102°, to 103°, to 105°, so that Ellen kicked off her shoes and went barefooted about the house, and unfastened the collar of her sober black gown and smiled to herself when she saw Stephen Mannion's eyes upon her.

Once, when he wanted to drink, Mannion had gone down the hill to seek company. Now it was too hot to move. He sat alone in his room with a bottle at his elbow, coatless, beaten into lethargy by the sultry atmosphere, the enervation of idleness, and the dreary round of his thoughts. It had been upon one such evening, just before Christmas, that he had at last made Ellen his mistress. It was late, he had been half-dozing in his chair, drawn up to the open window to catch such sea breeze as there was from the harbour, when the silence was broken by Miles' fretful wailing. Mannion started awake, his nerves grinding with irritation. The child was normally quiet and contented, but lately the heat had brought out a rash on his body, and he whimpered continually, a thin, high persistent lamentation, which his father found unendurable. Now, jerking upright in his chair, he faced the open window and tried to shut his ears to the sounds from the other room. The few lights which still shone in the settlement seemed hardly larger or closer than the stars which spangled the dark blue sky. An upstairs window of the Governor's house was a narrow oblong of light, and Mannion stared at it, full of a dull resentment against a man who could live with serenity and purpose in an environment which was slowly driving himself insane. The high, rhythmic wail of the child continued. Mannion clenched his fists and hammered them against his temples.

Then he heard movements—the opening of a door, the murmur of Ellen's voice, a change in the sound of the child's lament, a slackening, a sleepiness, an almost mechanical note. He sat rigidly, listening. Suddenly there were no more thoughts in his mind at all. For the first time in the five months since Harriet's death, his brain felt free, empty and clean. The generations of civilised life which had gone to the building up of his sophisticated capacity for self-torture fell away from him, leaving him no less primitive than Bennilong—no less whole in his desire.

The child was silent now, and again a door opened softly. Without consciousness of moving he found himself across the room, standing by his own door, breathing lightly and quickly, listening. He opened it abruptly. Ellen, a guttering tallow candle in her hand, looked up, only momentarily startled. In the candlelight her face seemed softened, her eyes bright, and her long dark hair fell heavily about her bare shoulders. She made no movement of protest, or even of surprise when, with a gesture of his hand he motioned her into his room. She had known that this would have to happen sometime, so why not tonight?

It had meant no more to her than that; when it became known in the settlement no one was particularly censorious. No one, in fact, gave it a second thought, save Mannion himself. He had gone too far in his orgy of spiritual self-abasement, and now he could not rescue himself. The habit had grown upon him, like the habit of his solitary drinking, and he could no more forego the perverse pleasures of remorse and self-loathing than he could resist the promise of oblivion which only liquor had to offer him. He made of his connection with Ellen a new lash for self-flagellation. The cynical indifference with which she met him became the measure of her viciousness, and the proof of his own degradation. He began by trying to shame her, and when he found he could not, her shamelessness became one more goad with which he could stab his self-respect to death.

But masochism, like other drugs, must be taken in larger and still larger doses. By the end of the summer it was not enough to have killed one's wife, to have dishonoured her memory, debased oneself with a low convict woman. A new torment was needed, and it was discovered in the *Waaksamheyd*, preparing, towards the end of March, for her voyage.

Had he not, Mannion asked himself luxuriously, forfeited his right to his homeland? Was he, contaminated by long and shameful association with a depraved woman, to return to his gracious home among the trees in Ireland, to kiss the cheek of his mother, to pollute the pure air which his young sisters breathed? Botany Bay! The ill-omened name caused a fastidious wrinkling of delicate nostrils all over the civilised world—was he, who had lived among its infamies, shared its squalor and its sordidness, now fit for any better life?

This was a new theme, offering subtle variations. Not only could he wallow in abasement when he contemplated it, but he could see his decision to remain shining like a lantern in a bog—a last surviving spark of nobility—a renunciation!

It was, in fact, mostly the apathy of a complete moral collapse. He had sunk deeply already into that inertia, that paralysis of will, to which continual self-contemplation always leads. His life had found a groove, and squalid and uncomfortable as it was, he shrank from leaving it, for that would have involved mental and spiritual readjustments. He was no longer equal to those. So the *Waaksamheyd* sailed without the Mannions, and Patrick, waving farewell from the cliffs, decided that on the whole he was glad they were staying. Miles celebrated the day by cutting his first tooth.

From that time Stephen Mannion had made a vice of solitude. He began to write—a long, rambling and interminable document, half journal and half eulogy of the departed Harriet. He had no literary facility, but he had a memory for dates and detail, and nothing else to do, so the stack of pages on his desk grew higher and higher, and were finally turned over to be written on the other side, for paper was scarce in the settlement.

"This day," he wrote, "I stood and watched the departure of the *Waaksamheyd* which might, in happier circumstances have borne me and my dear children home. Home! What tender memories are evoked by that word! How it breathes of peace and innocence and the sweet joys to which I have now forever said farewell. It was with a heavy heart indeed that I retraced my steps to the settlement, loath to quit those lovely scenes in which my fevered imagination had so lately revelled, for the squalid miseries of this community, and the solitude and misery of my poor hut.

"Found that E. had provided nothing for my supper, but some very ill-prepared fish . . ."

And so on. These pages were now his confessional. He hardly ever visited the settlement. Hill and Abbott, with whom he had been on fairly familiar terms, had both gone to Norfolk Island. The Governor was civil, but preoccupied. Collins was courteous, but aloof. Tench was rather flippantly ceremonious, and Dawes was downright rude. Mannion knew little of what went on in the settlement, and cared less. He paid hardly any attention to Patrick, and none at all to Miles. With the first breath of winter he shut himself in his room with his papers spread before him, and his bottle at his elbow, and not even Ellen dared to disturb him. He emerged only for those aimless walks, in one of which Collins and the Governor had surprised him. He walked fast, as if he were being pursued, and he had begun to talk to himself.

* * *

Early in July there arrived not the long awaited *Gorgon,* but the transport, *Mary Anne,* after an amazing passage of only four months and twelve day. To the homesick and news-hungry colonists she was a bitter disappointment, for she brought no letters for anyone save the Governor. No newspapers, no magazines, no tidings of troubled Europe—only a cargo of a hundred and forty female convicts, and no one welcomed them.

The *Gorgon,* so they were informed, whose sailing had been so long delayed, should soon arrive; but not only the *Gorgon.* The *Mary Anne* was but the forerunner of a Third Fleet, whose vessels, during the next three months, arrived at intervals, unloading their freight of convicts upon the already congested settlement.

The Governor accommodated them as best he could. The women from the *Mary Anne,* who, thanks to the humanity of its captain, arrived in fairly good health and spirits, found shelter among the existing huts at the cove. Two tents, each a hundred feet long, thatched with grass, were the best he could do for those who, arriving by later transports, were sent to Parramatta. During these months of feverish organisation he drove himself mercilessly; he had settlers to provide for now as well as convicts, for some of those whose terms were expired had expressed a wish to remain as farmers. He spent long and tiring days inspecting the country about Parramatta and deciding upon suitable areas for them; twelve he settled about the foot of Prospect Hill, and fifteen others in a district known as The Ponds, some two miles north east of Parramatta. Returning from these excursions he found himself wondering more than once if his strength would last another year, for it must be, he knew, at least as long as that before he could be released.

His settlement, he realised, was becoming a town. Looking down upon it one evening from an upper window of his house, he felt a pulse of excitement stir beneath his exhaustion. The sudden influx of people from the Third Fleet had quickened the tempo of life in the community, and now it had some of the urgency, the dynamic activity, the hidden motives and impulses, the incalculable potentialities which meant civilisation as he knew it. Suddenly he knew that his part in it was finished. He might return after a stay in England; he might remain for many years; he might continue to guide and develop it. But the critical period which had demanded just that one quality which few men on earth besides himself could have given it—faith—was over. He had nursed it through an infancy during which, a dozen times, a breath could have killed it. He had fought its will to die with his own will for its survival. He had poured his own vitality into it, and now it was finally and indestructibly alive.

He stared at it while the night came down from the surrounding hills, and its lights glimmered out to challenge the darkness. It would go on now, he thought, but where? He was conscious of a faint chill of apprehension—almost of panic. What was it that he had started? What was this thing, this life which he had fostered, and which, suddenly, while he was too busy to notice, had leapt beyond his complete control? Now it was quite dark outside, and the windowpane, instead of revealing his township, showed him the pale reflection of his own face—a disembodied face. Sharp lines of pain, privation and anxiety were ploughed between its brows; below the beaklike nose the full mouth was set in the close, nervous and sensitive lines of spiritual solitude. A ghostly face. He looked at it for a startled second, feeling himself hurled forward into a future which would know him only thus—as a ghost, the ghost of the founder of Sydney Cove.

He turned sharply from the window to light his lamp, and in its clear yellow radiance the present claimed him again with its unrelenting round of duties.

* * *

In September the *Gorgon* arrived at last, and with its coming those duties became social as well as administrative. With a certain repressed and old-maidish courtesy Phillip dealt with these new demands upon his energy and his time. He was glad to welcome King, perhaps his closest friend, who returned on the *Gorgon,* bringing with him a newly-acquired wife; he greeted Mrs. Parker, wife of the *Gorgon's* captain, with genuine kindliness. There were dinner parties, music in the evenings, the sound of women's laughter, little boating expeditions upon the harbour. King and his wife were guests at Government House, and Mrs. Parker came ashore every day to join them. Mrs. Macarthur was back from Rose Hill, delighted at the prospect of congenial feminine companionship, and the Governor, working at his desk, was often conscious of their voices, and the soft swish of their petticoats passing his door.

It was all quite pleasant, but it increased his sense of withdrawal. So long as the business had been hard, harsh, precarious, he had felt that he belonged to it. So long as every moment of it had needed his strength, his strength had been there to sustain it. But women's laughter! Petticoats! Picnics on grassy headlands, with an awning spread to protect delicate complexions from the sun! Nosegays of wildflowers brought with exclamations of delight for him to sniff!

He bowed, he smiled, he attended to the needs of his guests; he acted host courteously at dinners and luncheons. He went soberly about his work, driving his protesting body. He wrote or dictated his orders sitting late at his desk in the pool of golden light which his lamp shed over his stacked papers. But all the time he was aware of that strange sensation, half loss and half relief, which a woman feels when her child has been delivered. His settlement had drawn its life from him, it had been part of him, but now that close personal identity was broken. Now it must grow up without him, guided by other influences, struggling towards a maturity which he would never see. In the meantime he must continue to do battle for even the smallest of its needs.

"The iron pots in the colony," he wrote patiently, "before the last 1800 convicts were landed amounted to no more than what were barely sufficient. The Commissary is directed to make a return of those articles most wanted in the colony . . ."

* * *

Nearly two thousand people, not including the military, had been added to the settlement by the arrival of the Third Fleet; upon the occasion of His Majesty's birthday some fifty officers accepted the Governor's invitation to dinner. Phillip, foreseeing the disturbances which might have resulted from such a sudden influx, had laid down, from the arrival of the *Mary Anne,* stringent port orders which he rigidly enforced. A certain discipline prevailed; but beneath the outward submissiveness of the convicts he was conscious of rebellion. It was not an active or a militant rebellion—they were in no condition for that—but rather a dumb, obstinate determination to be free. In those months of pitiless confinement in the dark and stinking quarters of the transports the desire to move about, the desire to feel space about them, the desire to stretch themselves at ease in the sun had assumed the qualities of an obsession. Now it was as if a kind of infectious madness broke out among them. Persistently, stupidly, they broke away and wandered off into the woods. Recaptured, punished, they presently repeated the performance. It was as if they were sleep-walking, as if some instinct against which neither fear nor reason could prevail, drove them from one insane and foredoomed attempt to another. Such "escapes" were too hopeless, too utterly unplanned to excite anything but annoyance and a wondering contempt in the minds of officers who had never known what it was to be chained in one spot for weeks on end. They shrugged their astonishment at the imbecility of human beings who would suffer cold, hunger, the peril of native attack, and the certainty of either death by starvation, or recapture and flogging, for the sake of a few dubious hours of liberty.

One attempt, indeed, was conceived on a more ambitious scale. Twenty male convicts and one female, armed with tomahawks and knives, carrying each a week's provisions, absconded from Parramatta and set out to walk to China. Questioning them after their recapture Phillip discovered that they believed China to be no more than a hundred and fifty miles distant; but they only stared apathetically when he told them that the land whose shore they so unwillingly inhabited was an island.

That apathy disturbed the Governor. It was, to him, the most foreign and incomprehensible of reactions. His own spiritual vitality was such that he could understand most emotions: rapture, love and hope, rage, hatred, despair, and even fear, all seemed natural and comprehensible to him, but apathy was a negation of all that he felt life to be, and this contact with it stirred him to uneasy pondering. What must a man endure, he asked himself, before he is brought to this condition, this living death? His own life had not been an easy one. He had known physical hardship, anxiety, unhappiness and ill-health. He had known what these men had never known—the exhausting burden of responsibility. And on that word he paused, feeling his way to an answer. Out of that responsibility, crushing and burdensome as it had often seemed, his own strength had come, and he began to see that the human being can support all torments but the one final torment of feeling himself useless. A man lacking responsibility, he thought, lacks everything; he is destitute.

He began to be worried by his own compassion. He was not conscious of it as that, but merely as an increasing unrestfulness, a sense of frustration, an assault on a mind whose serenity had once seemed unassailable. He had never before felt it necessary to spare more than a passing stab of pity to felons—a pity, he realised now, which had been comforting to himself if not to them, warming him with a pleasant little glow of humanitarianism. So grateful an emotion had only been possible so long as there had been in his mind no doubt of the justice and the inevitability of their fate. Now that conviction was shaken, and his pity became bleak and painful. He was almost resentfully aware that he could no longer look at their sufferings with detachment, as from another plane. This little world which he had founded and governed was too small; discomfort, exile, hunger and despair had welded into one community two classes which, in their own country had been the poles apart; looking at the convicts now he was forced to recognise a common humanity between himself and those defeated men; thinking of them, he struggled back through the impeding generations of his civilisation towards the knowledge which the black men held so effortlessly. Their defeat was his defeat.

He had no time to brood over these matters. They were no more than attacks of spiritual pain which, instinctively, he resisted as obstinately as he resisted the physical pain which was lately becoming worse and worse. He found, indeed, in the physical pain, a welcome excuse for most unwelcome doubts. This, he told himself, was the natural result of ill-health and overwork. It was a depression of the spirits, which would pass when his health was restored.

He went about his work with his customary efficiency. His letters and despatches maintained their clear, cold note of official detachment. He was still first and foremost an administrator, which meant, inevitably, a disciplinarian. In moments of bitterness he told himself that it meant, in this case, nothing more than a glorified gaoler, but such moments were rare and fleeting. Almost in spite of himself results of his new perceptiveness were evident now and then. Rather more often than before a friendly word followed a stern one. After a harsh sentence would come an admonition almost fatherly; after a threat, a promise. But there was no comfort for him now in these small efforts of compassion, and he saw in the dull, hostile, or sardonic eyes of the convicts that there was none for them.

Worried by the stubborn, aimless, stupid attempts at escape, and by the rumour of a plot which was being hatched to seize and rob the stores, he ordered the convicts to be assembled, and told them sharply that in future armed parties would be sent in pursuit of absconders, with orders to fire on them if necessary. Any who were brought back alive, he informed them grimly, would be chained together, or marooned upon one of the islands of the harbour. An attempt upon the stores would be useless, and those concerned in such an outrage would be instantly put to death. Then looking down at the blank, sallow faces, sullen with fatigue, sharp with hunger, his voice altered.

"There shall be no hardship," he said, "for those among you who perform your tasks faithfully. I advise you all to go cheerfully about your labours, and to abandon all ideas of escape, for I assure you that escape from this place is impossible. Your fate, if you attempt it, is likely to be worse than any you will meet with here. I am informed that certain alterations in the hours of work have been petitioned for, and this shall be granted . . ." He stopped, hating himself for his hollow words, and then added abruptly: "That is all; you may go."

He sat alone thinking of what he had said. You shall be chained, you shall be fired upon, you shall be marooned upon an island. For what? For your desire for liberty. I, too, have come to desire that. My friends, if I do put fetters on your wrists your hands will yet be not less free than mine . . .

* * *

From the window Ellen watched Stephen Mannion walking down the hill with the surgeon and Captain Tench. Behind her Miles rattled the latch of the door and repeated with an urgency which was just becoming tearful: "Gum in! Gum in!"

She crossed the room to open the door for him, and caught a glimpse of herself as she did so in the mirror which hung on the opposite wall. She did not need it to assure herself of her attractions—she had seen acknowledgment of them in the appraising eye of Mr. White, and the amusedly appreciative eye of Captain Tench—but it gave her a thrill of pleasure all the same. The high colour in her cheeks, and the brilliance of her eyes were signs of an intense inward elation, for an anxiety which had long been disturbing her was now lifted.

Since the coming of the *Gorgon* Mannion had gradually relaxed his morbid habit of solitude. He had taken to going down to the Governor's to offer himself as escort for the ladies when they wished to take a walk; he had joined their husbands now and then at a game of cards; he had made one of several boating parties, and he had even picked a nosegay of wildflowers to present to Mrs. Parker.

This change in his habits had filled Ellen with a sulky foreboding. In his moods of bitterness, ill-temper, lust, or depression she felt sure of him; when he was drunk he seemed familiar to her—a mere man, not very different from others she had known. Dressed with care, shaved, brushed and sober, he became a gentleman again, and a gulf opened between them. Many times she had watched him from behind the curtains, talking to Mrs. Parker or Mrs. Macarthur. Her eyes rested on the delicate frills and billowings of their frocks, the lacy flutterings of their handkerchiefs, the graceful flaunting of their coloured parasols; she saw him bow over their hands, lean towards them with attentive gallantry, and she knew that his own world was drawing him back to it.

In the two years she had spent with him better food and easier living conditions had changed her from a sullen convict slattern to a handsome young woman, very conscious of her power. Her fine dark eyes were still bold, but no longer aggressive, her colour was high, her black, luxuriant hair glossy and neat. To her own astonishment and unbounded relief no pregnancy had resulted from her association with Mannion. She had won security—she had even grown used to it—and the thought of losing it caused her as much anger as alarm. If he went back to Ireland she would be merely a convict again. She would, of course, soon find another protector; women were so much in a minority that one such as herself, still young and comely, could almost take her pick among the officers. Nevertheless, she would not again find one who could give her the advantages to which she had become accustomed as Stephen Mannion's mistress. During the last weeks she had been turning these matters over anxiously in her mind, wondering what he had decided to do. He gave her no inkling, and an instinctive wisdom kept her from asking. She was not without influence over him, and she knew it; but she knew also that the first hint from her that she knew it would be sufficient to destroy it for ever.

His arrogance filled her with a contempt which held little resentment. She recognised quite clearly that she was using him quite as much as he was using her, and she saw their relationship as a wary contest to see which could win the greater advantage from the other. Here a test had arisen. If he went he had won. If he stayed she was still in the fight—and he was going to stay.

Captain Tench, who was to sail on the *Gorgon,* had come up this afternoon accompanied by Mr. White to say good-bye. Bringing wine for them, and setting it on the table, she had listened to their conversation. The Captain, it appeared, had spent the earlier part of the month at Parramatta upon a tour of inspection, and as they drew up their chairs he was pursuing a subject which had evidently been discussed before.

"Every man to his taste," he said, shrugging. "For myself the country holds no attractions as a permanent residence. I regard its future as— doubtful, to say the least . . ."

"Doubtful!" The surgeon put his glass down on the table with a little bang, and scraped the legs of his chair noisily on the floor as he swung it round to face the Captain. "*I* have no doubts! No doubts whatever! It is no country for civilised men, nor ever will be. Take my advice, Mr. Mannion, and do not be beguiled by these rosy dreams of a fabulous future. In a year or two at most, Government will see that it has been pouring money into the ocean, and the settlement will be withdrawn. Mark my words!"

Ellen felt a little stir of excitement. Did this mean that Mannion had decided to remain? Decided finally, coldly, soberly? She moved very softly about the room, adjusting curtains, arranging and rearranging the crockery on the dresser, so that she might hear a little more of this momentous conversation. She was glad of Mr. White's wholesale condemnation, for she knew that Mannion regarded him with some antipathy, and would be likely to lend more favour to a plan if it were derided by the surgeon. Captain Tench, on the other hand, he approved. Ellen listened breathlessly to that gentleman's reply:

"Come, come, Mr. White, things are not so bad as that. Your colleague, Mr. Arndell, has hopes of his farm, and I must say that it looked tolerably promising. And see how well Ruse has done for himself—eleven and a half acres in cultivation, a good brick house, four breeding sows, and some thirty fowls. Then there are Ramsay, and Webb, and Scheffer, all of whom have made some progress and are sanguine of success. Consider how much better equipped Mr. Mannion would be than any of these men. What are they, after all? Arndell, a man of your own calling, a couple of seamen, and a soldier. Mr. Mannion is a landowner, accustomed to the management and supervision of estates." He sipped his wine, looking over the brim of his glass at Mannion's complacent face, and went on suavely:

"He has, no doubt, an excellent knowledge of husbandry. More than all else he is in a position to employ labour; to go about the business patiently and thoroughly; to till the ground as it should be tilled, and to supply it with suitable fertilizers. No, no, if anyone could succeed in this country it would be Mr. Mannion."

Ellen darted a quick glance at him. He was smiling, but not more than usual. Why was it that she had seemed to hear mockery in his words? Mr. White was scowling at the floor—he was not likely to notice anything, a man who spoke his mind bluntly without undertones and nuances. And Mannion was obviously pleased. Ellen's lashes dropped to shadow the scorn in her eyes. All men, she thought, were vain, but never one so vain as this! Flattery could always win him, and well the Captain knew it, smiling so pleasantly, and toying so elegantly with the stem of his wineglass! What was behind this? Captain Tench and Mannion had never been intimate. Ellen had long ago decided that the Captain admired her protector no more than she did herself. Was it mere impishness which was making him turn Mannion's head towards this thought of farming, as a skilful driver might turn the head of a nervous and refractory horse? Mannion himself spoke now.

"There's much truth in what you say, Captain. I may indeed claim to have some small knowledge of farming. My estates in Ireland are large, and, I may say without undue vanity, I think, that they are well ordered. But I should not, in any event, make this my permanent home. That was never my intention, I assure you. There are certain—amenities—without which a cultivated man cannot live forever. My purpose would be merely to take up some land and see it in a fair way to development before returning to Ireland."

"And what," demanded the surgeon, crudely, "if the settlement is withdrawn?"

Mannion waved the question aside.

"It will not be withdrawn. I have no doubts on that score—nor, I may say, has His Excellency. I am inclined to think that there may be some future here for a man interested in agricultural pursuits. The same idea, I understand, has occurred to Macarthur, though I imagine his thoughts turn rather in the direction of livestock. Ellen—some more wine for Mr. White! No, gentlemen, I assure you I shall go carefully into the matter before committing myself, but in the meantime I remain. You may leave us, Ellen. Some time soon I shall go up to Parramatta and make an inspection of the land. What district would you recommend, Captain, having just made so exhaustive a tour?"

Ellen closed the door carefully behind her, and, bending down, put her ear to the crack.

"I should think," the Captain's voice sounded rather bored now—"that somewhere in the vicinity of Prospect Hill would answer best. Were it not so far from Parramatta I should be tempted to consider the banks of the Nepean."

"The banks of the Nepean." Mannion's voice was reflective, and Ellen felt a little chill. She wanted him to remain in the colony, and she wanted to stay with him, but she had no desire to vanish into the interior—to this river which but few men and no women of their race had yet seen. Captain Tench said briskly:

"Too far, my dear sir, altogether too far—at present. Later, perhaps, when settlement extends in that direction—as it doubtless will. But for the time being Prospect Hill is the spot."

"The soil is good?"

"It is so good as anything we have yet found in this country. There are streams and rivulets in the neighbourhood—and it is within reasonable distance of the township at Parramatta." Ellen heard the sound of a chair being pushed back. "And now, Mr. Mannion, I must make my farewells; I have still some preparations . . ."

The rest of his sentence was lost to Ellen in the noise of their movement, but she had heard enough. At least for the present he was not going. For a year—two years—perhaps even three—she was still secure. She had nothing to do but continue to please him, and she felt confident of being able to do that. When she heard them leave the house she entered the room again, and went across to the window to watch them walking down the hill. Behind her Miles rattled the latch, and called persistently: "Gum in! Gum in!"

*   *   *

She picked him up, and held him on one arm while she cleared the bottles and wineglasses from the table. Feeling the grip of his small arm round her neck she acknowledged to herself with some surprise that there had been another element in her fear of the Mannions' departure. She had not wanted to part with Miles. He was a little over two now, plump, sturdy and affectionate; she had had more time, while he was her nursling, to make friends with him than she had ever had with her own children. His beauty had not only won her heart, but it had made life kinder in all directions. Already, under the infant roundness of his face the promise of fine features, boldly drawn, was discernible, and from beneath his straight brows, now delicate as a pencil mark, his dark-lashed eyes were almost incredibly blue. There was a quality in his beauty which made everyone who came near him feel benevolent, and even Ellen had found herself, sometimes, touched by and included in the warmth of this spontaneous kindliness. Officers, seamen, natives, convicts, all smiled when they saw him; some of the smile was left over when their eyes met Ellen's, and roused a response, tentative and uncertain, in hers. Once or twice even quite respectable women, pausing to bend over the child, had been betrayed into speaking to his convict nurse almost as if she were not a convict.

Ellen was a woman who lived by her senses and her emotions. She did not think about her feelings for Miles; she was only conscious that he was something in her life which she did not want to lose—something which increased her value, not only in the eyes of others, but in her own. Patrick, on the other hand, she did not like. He was civil enough, even friendly, but in his presence she became outcast again. She resented his well-made body, which emphasised Johnny's skinny awkwardness, and his flashes of wit and merriment, in contrast to which Johnny was made to appear doubly ignorant and sullen.

Johnny, now eight, was by this time far beyond her control. He earned a few pence here and there, and sometimes he was paid for his services in food or spirits. He caught fish, and collected oysters, and chopped wood; he ran messages for the officers, fetched and carried for the women, spied or stole for anyone who would make it worth his while. Sometimes he vanished for several days at a time, either to Parramatta or to one of the native camps, but neither his mother nor anyone else troubled about that now. He hated everyone, but no one quite as fiercely as Stephen Mannion. Towards Patrick his attitude of wary and contemptuous tolerance remained unchanged. Towards his small sister and brother, Maria and Andy, he was completely indifferent, but he sometimes stopped to play with Miles, and had even been known to bring him a shell from the beach, and whittle him a boat from the light wood of the grass tree stalk.

By the time Ellen had the table set for supper, Stephen's voice could be heard outside calling to Patrick to come in. They entered together, and, as Miles, struggling out of her arms, made for his father on hurried and unsteady legs, she was struck anew by their likeness to each other, and their utter unlikeness to herself. She felt annoyed, hostile, jealous of Miles, and suddenly robbed of her triumph. Mannion, in high spirits, called her back as she was leaving the room.

"Ellen!"

She turned, her eyes shadowed and impassive, waiting for him to speak. For a moment, stooping to lift Miles, he was silent, and then, as much to Patrick as to her, he said:

"We shall be leaving this house, I imagine, quite soon."

Patrick gasped, excitedly:

"Leaving, Papa? Where are we going? Back to Ireland?"

Mannion looked at his elder son with sudden attention.

"Should you like to go back to Ireland, Patrick?"

Patrick's hesitation was only momentary.

"No. No, Papa, I don't think so. I like it here now. Perhaps *some day* I should like to go back to Ireland, but not yet."

Mannion laughed.

"That is excellent. For that is exactly what I propose. I am to turn farmer, Ellen. What do you think of that?" He added quickly, as if annoyed at himself for having asked the opinion of a convict woman: "Eh, Patrick?"

Ellen was glad enough not to answer. Patrick burst into a volley of questions, and she left them, closing the door quietly behind her. For her one step at a time. She would not yet begin to concern herself with the possible drawbacks of the new kind of life.

*   *   *

There had been so many burials. Phillip, standing bareheaded in the sunlight, looked down at the grave which had been dug in his garden to receive the body of young Ballederry, and wondered why this one should move him so much more than any of the others had done. He shifted from one foot to the other, for he was tired, and the ceremony had been a long one, and glanced about him at the queer assemblage of whites and blacks who had gathered to watch it. David Collins was there sober and attentive, missing nothing, storing details in his memory which he would tonight inscribe in his journal. Ballederry's father was there, standing apart except when he was performing some appointed part in the ritual—an elderly man, silent, sorrowful, and dignified. Ballederry's little brother was there, too, a child of five, still rather round-eyed from the ordeal of being led forward to be presented to the corpse. Colbee and Bennilong were there, seriously busy, directing the proceedings. Bennilong had requested that drums might be sounded in honour of his dead friend, and their rhythmic beat throbbed hollowly as the body was laid upon grass in the grave, on its right side, so that the sun shone upon it.

When the grave was filled in the Governor turned away and walked back to his house alone. He was glad that he had relented at the news of Ballederry's illness, and that he had bidden Bennilong bring him to the hospital, and the care of Surgeon White. He remembered the burning hand which he had taken in his own when the young man was brought to him, and the dark eyes, brilliant with fever, which had stared anxiously into his own, changing their anxiety to delight when he had denied anger, denied punishment and pursuit, recklessly promised that once again, when he was well, Ballederry should sit at the table of the white Be-anga, and dwell in his house.

He threw his hat down on his table and wiped his forehead with his handkerchief. Coming in from the brilliant sunshine into this darkened room, he was, for a second or two, half blind, and stood still with his hand on the back of his chair, blinking the sight back to his eyes.

The *Gorgon* was preparing to sail. Major Ross and his marines were already embarked, with the exception of a few who were to await the arrival of the remainder of the New South Wales Corps, and a handful who had desired to take up land and settle in the new colony. With their going, he thought, that early stage of endeavour would seem more than ever remote. The final departure, about three weeks ago, of the little *Supply,* now no longer fit for the arduous services required of her, had had a curious poignancy. There had been moments of silence among the cheers which sped her, moments when waving hands were still and handkerchiefs ceased to flutter, and memories had been vivid, picturing despair-filled months when she had been their only hope, and when the sight of her sails had made red-letter days in a dreary routine of endurance and privation. Even Collins, usually so self-contained, had confessed an affection for her; the more mercurial Tench had proclaimed, unabashed, that he could shed a tear for the passing of so gallant a little ship; he himself, watching her turn to breast the ocean swell as she passed between the Heads, had felt a pang.

She was the last of that First Fleet which he had brought across the sea, and there remained, now, but few of the officers who had come to the country with it. Hunter was gone, King was at Norfolk Island, Ball, Blackburn and Creswell had left on the *Supply,* Ross, Tench, and Dawes were already on board the *Gorgon.* Collins, thank Heaven, remained, industrious and serene. White remained, equally industrious, but still consumed by a stubborn hatred of the colony, and an almost ghoulish conviction of its ultimate downfall. The Reverend Richard Johnson also remained. From his preoccupation with the material welfare of his people, the Governor sometimes spared a puzzled glance for the man who was responsible for the welfare of their souls. He was too sincere himself not to recognise in this rather pompous young man an equal sincerity which struggled through a perpetual, bewildered sense of outrage. The faith of Mr. Johnson, he thought now, was of a different brand from his own, and he had sometimes almost envied the clergyman, who need not search his heart, but only his Bible, his volumes of sermons, and the stored teachings of his vocation, to find a guidance which seemed to him equal for any occasion. Mr. Johnson, in fact, had brought his faith with him, but he, Phillip, had built his own here. It was a painful faith, but it was rewarding—perhaps more rewarding, if he could judge from Mr. Johnson's air of patient martyrdom, than that which the clergyman so earnestly, conscientiously, and dully preached every Sabbath, to a more or less conscripted congregation.

He drew his chair out and sat down, but he was in no mood for putting together the papers which he must send home by the *Gorgon.* He was too tired even for coherent reflection, and as he sat there with his legs outstretched under the table and his hands lying idle on the arms of his chair, a series of disconnected thoughts were all he could achieve— a confused sequence of incongruously varied incidents which had gone to the making of the year.

Worries about Norfolk Island held him for a few minutes. The last few months of Ross' regime had evidently been ugly and chaotic; there were unpleasant tales of quarrelling among the officers, of a perpetual stir of mutinous unrest among the convicts, of a discipline so harsh as to deserve the name of oppression, of barbarous and incessant floggings, of a whole community living savagely and mistrustfully, like a pack of wolves. Now that King had resumed command there, Phillip thought, things would probably improve again.

With an abruptness which startled him into a physical movement, he found his thoughts jerked back again to the newly filled grave outside his house; and from Ballederry they leapt freakishly, but not altogether illogically, to Lieutenant Dawes. There, he thought rather sadly, were two young men with whom he had failed in his personal relationship. He could not admit that he had acted unjustly, or even harshly, in either case, but he suspected that a man with a happier manner might have been equally severe, and at the same time less hurtful. Ballederry, indeed, had broken down the barrier between them at last with his illness, with his unself-conscious and childlike desire for reconciliation; but Dawes had met stiffness with stiffness, and what might have been a mutual liking had become an unhappy and unwilling hostility. There could be no doubt that he had earned his Governor's displeasure by bartering stores with the convicts, and over that business of the punitive expedition; to say emphatically—even violently—in the presence of a brother officer, that he regretted having obeyed an order, and that he certainly would obey no such order in future, was mutiny, and not to be passed over.

And yet the Governor was honest enough to admit that it was not the mutinousness of the protest which had most shocked him, but the implication that he, Phillip, had given an order which was over-severe—even brutal; an order which no humane man could obey with a quiet conscience. It had shocked him the more because he had not been entirely able to refute it. The unease of his mind when he thought of the black people was growing all the time, and by now it was a dark, ever-present background to all his other cares. It was a bewilderment which was foreign to his usual clear and practical habit of thought, haunting him with an accusation that this great enterprise of his was not only a beginning but an end.

There was nothing, he told himself impatiently, that he could do about it. But he found himself remembering how Bennilong had come to him, full of pride and importance, explaining that when Barangaroo's time came he would bring her to the Be-anga's house, so that she might be delivered there, in earnest of the great friendship which existed between them. His officers, Phillip remembered wryly, had found this suggestion very funny indeed, and he himself had, rather hastily, assured Bennilong that the hospital was a more suitable place for such an event. But he could not avoid the suspicion that there had been a clear purport and a simple symbolism behind Bennilong's idea. His child was to be born under the roof of the Be-anga; the Governor knew, uneasily, that that meant under his protection. He had been regarded, whether he liked it or not, as a kind of god-parent—and the thought left him less amused than abashed.

Well, the hospital had not held Barangaroo for long. Only a few hours after her confinement he had seen her pottering about picking up sticks for her fire, while the newborn child lay snugly in a soft bark cradle nearby. Dilboong, they had called her. What was to be the fate of Dilboong in the land which was hers no longer?

He looked up and found that the day had faded as he sat there, and the room was dark.

1792

EARLY in the New Year of 1792, when Billalong was nearly two, Prentice was invited by the natives to attend an initiation ceremony. He had recognised long ago that the goodwill of the tribes which, according to their nomadic habit, came and went casually about his camp, was valuable—even necessary—to him; but the relaxation of the hostile attitude with which he had first met them was less a result of cynical self-interest than part of a general spiritual relaxation which had increased with freedom and independence. There had been a time when everything —man or woman, beast, bird, or inanimate object—had been a potential enemy. He had been incapable of looking on anyone or anything without the hatred of suspicion; now he found it possible to realise that there were men (even if they were only inferior black savages) who were willing to meet him on terms of confidence and friendship, expecting no benefits from him, but, on the contrary, extremely willing to be of service. And they were of service. They had brought him news of the Governor's expeditions. They had learned, with astonishing rapidity, enough of his language to understand him, and to make themselves understood. He had made no very serious attempt to learn theirs; his tongue would not form their words, and his memory would not store them. In any case it seemed to him more fitting that they should be privileged to learn his speech than that he should jeopardize his white man's dignity by repeating their outlandish gibberish.

He had long ago conceived the idea of making them work for him, and was at first elated with the result. They were excitedly and vociferously willing to try their hands at swinging a mattock or an axe, digging with a spade, or driving nails with a hammer. But he was forced at last to realise with shocked astonishment that they regarded such activities as a pastime. When they grew bored, which was very soon, they threw down their tools and disappeared. When he tried to make them understand that they should toil for certain hours—say from noon till sunset—they stared, shook their heads, and laughed heartily. He began to realise, not without indignation, that they recognised only one call to work, and that was the call of an empty belly.

Slowly, aided by their cheerful affability, guided by the mediation and interpretation of Cunnembeillee, and at least no longer obstructed by his own surly mistrust, Prentice developed his alliance with them. He learned something of their bush lore, and was astounded by their uncanny skill in tracking. He was not yet able to grasp the subtleties of their tribal organisation, or to understand the incredible complication of their marriage system, but he began to realise that there *was* an organisation, there *was* a system; he knew now that where he had at first seen only chaos and promiscuity there was, in fact, a Law. He made friends with one of the tribesmen in particular, a man of about his own age, named Milbooroo. The friendship was, indeed, of Milbooroo's seeking, for he had become deeply interested in the cattle, and so inordinately fond of milk that he willingly gave valuable if erratic services in return for an occasional brimming coolamon. He dug and hoed when he was asked to do so, but his heart was with the cattle, and upon the day when Prentice taught him to milk he was like a child in his delighted pride. He learned quickly; Prentice had never ceased to be astonished by the manual dexterity of the dark people, and now that it was becoming necessary for him to think about looking for a new home, he realised that a man like Milbooroo to tend the cattle in his absence would be invaluable.

His anxiety to do nothing which might upset the harmony of his relations with this useful man had made him accept the invitation to a ceremony about which he felt not the smallest curiosity, and he set out for the appointed place one hot summer evening, feeling surly and disgruntled. He stumbled back towards home in the early morning, and found himself on the thickly wooded slope of a hillside from which he could see the pale ribbon of river winding between the hills and feel the cool wind of dawn on his face. He slumped to the ground beside a tree trunk, and leaned against it with his head in his hands, too exhausted to move. He realised that he felt rather the same as he had after his illness, as if his veins ran water and his bones were string; his brain was empty, incurious, strangely peaceful. He had gone to the ceremony indifferently, ready to be contemptuous. At the edge of a cleared circle, carpeted with plucked leaves, all of one sort, he had sat with his arms resting across his updrawn knees, and the light of the fire opposite flickering over his red hair and beard. There had been all kinds of dull preliminaries, and he had watched them with bored superiority; but with the first distant sound of the bull-roarer he had felt his nerves jump, and had become conscious of a prickling sensation up the back of his neck, and over his scalp. He had made a clutch, too late, at memory. He had deliberately turned to those hardships and those horrors which, for three years now, he had been trying to forget, in an attempt to arm himself against the anticipation of fear which was sliding like a chill over his body. He had grown insensitiveness over his human spirit protectively as he had grown callouses on the palms of his hands, and he told himself hardily that he had seen too much of real horror to be frightened by the antics of a crowd of savages, and the noises of their bits of wood and string.

Watching, this antagonism had become a breathless attentiveness, and attentiveness had merged imperceptibly into a half hypnotised fascination. The firelight became nothing but a shifting glare to his fixed gaze, and through it, unfocussed, tall as trees, moved ghastly figures, clay-bedaubed and decorated with feathers; to his ears, not clearly as separate sounds, but confusedly, like the mingled voices of sea and winds, birds and branches, animals and men, came voices chanting in some rhythm which found its echoes in his blood, and kept time with the pounding of his heart. He found himself beating, as his companions were doing, upon his thighs and buttocks, but he did not stop. He was under some compulsion which he no longer wanted to resist. The glare brightened so that he blinked his dazzled eyes, and the tempo quickened, and his hands beat faster and his pulses with them. When he saw what was to be done, waves of sickness and waves of excitement rushed over him so that when he leapt to his feet he staggered giddily, but the sickness passed and the excitement remained, mounting to a frenzy.

Now the whole of life seemed concentrated within this hot circle of elemental light, and outside it, in the darkness, the world was peopled with malign spirits which must at all costs be exorcised. He recognised this, and the civilization which had used him so ill fell away like an unfastened garment, and his body taught him what his mind would never grasp. Lust shook him from head to foot as a gale shakes a tree; sex lust and blood lust brought from his throat, as from those of his black companions, a great shout of exultation when the thing was accomplished, and one more man was made, whole, potent and virile, a symbol of the immortality of mankind. Triumph burned in him; outside the circle of firelight he was aware of the dark earth spinning and knew with an indescribable sense of victory that here the ground beneath his feet was stable, and that the blood which stained it made it so.

All that was gone now. He had come down from some crest of emotional release which he had never known before, and now he was numb, and calm, though he still had a feeling that the world about him was rocking quietly before settling back into equilibrium. The trees were coming, ghostlike, out of the dark, taking shape before his tired, accepting eyes; the grey river was turning silver, and the stars were gone. Somewhere on the opposite bank a magpie was trying over, tentatively in that fragile hush, a few notes of its matinal song. Prentice put his hand up and rubbed it over his face and eyes, and then held it before him, staring in vague surprise at the dried blood spattered upon its palm. He shivered a little, pulled himself to his feet and began to stumble down the hill towards the river. As he walked he talked to himself half aloud, searching a rich vocabulary for opprobrious epithets and obscene names for so savage, superstitious, and debased a people, but they came from his lips with a curious lack of emphasis, almost mechanically, and his eyes, blank and peaceful, were the eyes of a sleepwalker.

*   *   *

For a time the memory of it lay heavily in his mind, and when the blacks came to visit him again he found himself looking at them askance, trying to recognise in these good-tempered and light-hearted people the awe-inspiring figures of that night. He had seen them, he remembered uneasily, looking like devils from the Pit, leaping, crouching, contorting their bodies and their faces horribly; he had heard them making sounds to freeze the blood, grunting, yelling and chanting. He had thought himself hardened to any terror which life might show him, proof against surprise at any human evil or depravity, but these people had shattered his protective shell of cynicism and shocked him to the innermost core of his being. He could not understand why, despite his loathing, he could no longer scorn them. In his world there had been depravities in plenty, but he had been accustomed to glimpse them only through rents in the cloak of furtiveness and secrecy which custom draped about him. Here there was no suggestion either of secrecy or shame. In the quick, dark eyes which met his own so alertly he found nothing but the cheerful serenity of spiritual well-being. It was himself who looked awkwardly away.

By degrees he forgot about it. Ever since the preceding May when Tench's second expedition had startled him from a growing sense of security, he had been grimly busy. Now he was setting the finishing touches to the new abode to which he intended to remove his family, his cattle and his worldly goods. He was well satisfied with it. It would be years, probably, he thought, before white men found their way into the valley which his black friends called Burragorang, and whose wide green river was the Wollondilly. And, once there, they would follow the main stream and settle along its banks, leaving him still undisturbed in the little pocket among the hills in which one of its tributaries rose.

By the time the days began to grow cooler, he had already made great progress. His new hut had two rooms and a window with strong wooden shutters. It had a table and a stool, and one bunk, for Cunnembeillee had never learned to sit otherwise than native fashion, on the ground, with one leg tucked beneath her, and asked no better bed than her pile of 'possum skins. He planned two small yards only for the cattle; here where the pasture was restricted to a few square miles of valley, ringed about with high, barren sandstone hills, the animals would not stray far. He had decided not to bring all of them here; their numbers had increased so much that there would not be food in this small valley for so many. He would bring, at first, only what he needed for milk and fresh meat; and by degrees, helped by the natives, he would drive the rest into the great valley of Burragorang, and leave them there to increase and multiply—an inexhaustible supply from which he could help himself as the need arose.

*　　*　　*

There were often occasions now when the Governor felt a momentary recurrence of that chill with which he had first realised that his tiny settlement had become a township. As time passed he became more and more conscious that somewhere in his planning, and in the planning of the home authorities, there had been a flaw—a factor which had never been taken into account. He had felt it from the first, and though he had tried to ignore it out of existence it was still there, and growing more obvious every day. He did not, even now, attempt to analyse it; to do so would have been to bestow upon it an importance which he still stubbornly denied. He could only turn away sharply from the memory of moments which had stabbed him with warning—of that first day when he had recognised danger at his side, waiting for him to move, of a morning when a fitting display of ceremony had seemed suddenly embarrassing and ridiculous, of a night beside a campfire when he had felt the land threatening to impose its differentness upon the people he had brought to it.

And he struggled angrily, too, against another impression which brought his self-respect to the verge of downfall, and menaced his nervous and sensitive pride with unendurable humiliation. Such authority as he wielded was a delegated authority; he was the agent of His Majesty's Government, the deputy of the King himself, and these had always seemed to him to be honourable functions, to which a man might bring his whole heart. Now, with something like consternation, he realised that time and distance were blurring the outlines of Whitehall, and dimming the royal countenance. He missed the psychological background of his country, where habit and tradition acted as brakes upon rebellious spirits. He missed those outward symbols of power by which the ignorant were maintained in suitable docility—magnificent buildings, cathedral spires, great estates, carriages and liveries, the authoritative bearing of the nobility and gentry, the actual bodily presence of the Sovereign. Each year as it passed had made that world seem more unreal; each year had built this land more firmly into the consciousness of the exiles. And the Governor, upholding in such isolation an authority so distant, so nebulous, was sometimes visited by a nightmare feeling that he was lending himself to a rather foolish bit of mummery—acting deputy to ghosts.

Nor could he longer dismiss his own unrest as a nervous reaction to physical illness. He felt it because it was there. He felt it because everyone was feeling it, and because, in the convicts at least, it was producing effects. He became more and more conscious that to plant an old order in a new environment was a formidable task; there were moments—those moments of chill—when he suspected that it would prove to be impossible.

To build a new nation! That had been his dream, and to that end all his efforts had been directed. But he saw now that when he had said "nation" he had meant "England," and that in meaning England he had brought himself into conflict with the land. For the land was not England, and nothing could make it so. It was, indeed, as different from England as any land could conceivably be; it shared with that country not even its seasons or its stars. And now, with four years gone by, Phillip knew that it was quietly taking matters out of his hands. He, too, was becoming ghostlike, because his allegiance was elsewhere.

He followed his own way grimly and undeviatingly, because there was nothing else he could do. The problem was too big for him, too big for any one man, or for any single generation of men. The land, he felt wearily, would settle it in its own good time—and meanwhile he was still the faithful servant of His Majesty King George III.

*   *   *

It was his duty to punish the insubordinate, and in the early months of the year 1792 there were more of these than ever before. What was in the Governor a spiritual malaise, became in the convicts an obstinate and sullen dissatisfaction, an inarticulate resentment. Here was a new, wide land, and it awakened a fever of restlessness in their blood. They did not like it, and few of them would have remained in it from choice, but the mere fact of its existence impressed upon their minds a consciousness that life as they had known it in England was not the only conceivable kind of life. They had realised change, and they thought, "If place can be so different, why not circumstance?"

Their unrest expressed itself in the only way it could—in thefts, in escapes, and even in defiance. The miserable ration kept them almost at the point of starvation, and deaths were reported every day. Once a large number of them gathered at Parramatta in what Collins described as "an improper and tumultuous manner," and so desperate was their bearing that Phillip issued a hurried order forbidding them to assemble again in numbers for any reason whatever. Once, frenzied by hunger, they robbed the bakehouse of flour by climbing down a chimney. Punishment seemed powerless to restrain them. One man, about to be hanged for theft, clutched the rope to his throat as if he loved it, crying out that he longed for death. And still in the fields about Parramatta emaciated figures stooped over spades and hoes, turning the clods feebly, coughing as they worked, plodding back to their huts at nightfall to sleep or to die.

About the middle of February the *Pitt* came in. She brought, as well as some ninety convicts and seven free women, the last company of the New South Wales Corps, and Major Francis Grose, its Commandant, who was to succeed Major Ross as Lieutenant-Governor. It had been a miserable voyage; soldiers and seamen who had gone ashore at St. Jago had died as the result of a fever contracted there, and many of the convicts, on arrival at Port Jackson, were taken straight from the ship to the sick-tents, scurvy-ridden and ulcerous.

Sickness became a major problem again, and throughout the autumn the hospital and the tents were crowded. Undernourishment aggravated sickness, and sickness threatened starvation, for supplies were dwindling rapidly once more, and the Governor feared to relax his efforts at cultivation. Watching the men at work he knew they were unfit for labour, but dared not let them cease.

And yet life went on, he saw with a faintly surprised relief, even in such circumstances as these. Men could still bicker and quarrel over trifles, women could still gossip and spread malicious tales, children could still play, even if rather listlessly, with a bit of wood, or a scrap of rag . . .

He watched Major Grose and the new arrivals of the New South Wales Corps with an almost detached curiosity. Soon, his knowledge of men and of administration warned him, there would be trouble here. The officers, he decided, were, for the most part, not a very prepossessing company, and he looked askance at their prompt plunge into commercial activity. They were hardly disembarked before they began selling, at exorbitant prices, all kinds of articles which they had brought with them apparently for that purpose, and with the austere pride of his naval tradition Phillip looked on contemptuously at this sordid huckstering. He realised, without surprise, that they were as much wanting in private morals as in professional dignity. It was more or less to be expected that they would take mistresses from among the convict women; but before long they were joining not only the women but the men in drinking and gambling, eating in their huts, and continually causing brawls by attempting to entice their womenfolk away.

For the moment the Governor was too worried about food to do more than observe them. With the bitter experiences of four years behind him, he dared not concern himself only with the present, and his letters to England made, civilly but urgently, the same old requests. A regular supply of food was wanted; a ship for the colony was wanted; clothing and tools were wanted; livestock was wanted; farmers were wanted. He hammered doggedly on this note. Farmers, farmers, farmers.

"I have, Sir, in all my letters pointed out the great advantages which would attend our having a few intelligent farmers as settlers. They would do more for the colony than five hundred settlers from soldiers and convicts, very few of whom are calculated for the life they must necessarily lead in this country."

He penned an apology which acquired in the writing almost the flavour of a rebuke:

"If it should appear that I have too frequently adverted to our wants, my being probed by the wants of every individual, and what I feel still more, the knowing how much might have been done in the time I have been in this country, and in how very different a state it would have been had we been more fortunate in receiving the necessary supplies, and a few intelligent men . . . will, I hope, plead my excuse."

The end of March was in sight, and still the expected store-ship did not arrive. The sick list grew daily more formidable. Mr. White, blunt and emphatic, told him what he knew very well—that there was no cure for starvation but food. He wrote to Nepean:

"I am now, Sir, anxiously awaiting the arrival of those supplies, and what I expect by the *Atlantic* from Calcutta, for very little labour is to be got from men who are not amply supplied with food; still less when these men have not been used to regular labour, and are worn out by want and long confinement. . . ."

He threw his pen down and went over to close the window which was rattling in a fresh southerly breeze. Clouds were banking up, he noticed, and the day had darkened. He thought: "Rain. And autumn almost upon us again. Well, we have weathered storms before, and we have survived four winters. . . ."

*   *   *

Patrick, looking up surreptitiously from his copybook to peer out the window of Mr. Johnson's parlour at the golden sunshine, tried to console himself with the reflection that, although it was a thousand pities that Papa (who for so long had seemed gratifyingly unaware of his existence) should have suddenly remembered that he needed to have lessons, there was undoubtedly a pleasant side to his morning penance.

For Mr. Johnson had some books. Papa had very few, and those he had he kept shut up in his own room. Patrick could remember a room in his home in Ireland which had been completely filled with books, and he often thought of it rather wistfully now that he had begun to discover what exciting things books could be. In those far-off days in Ireland he had been too young to read anything but MAT and CAT; Mamma had begun to teach him bigger words on the voyage, but then she had died and life had become altogether different, and for a long time he had not thought of reading any more.

For several months now he had come down most mornings to Mr. Johnson's house, and here, seated on a chair with two books on it to make it higher, and with his tongue curling out of the corner of his mouth in the earnestness of his effort, he had laboured at his copybook, making his up strokes light and his down strokes heavy, pointing the pen over his shoulder, and being careful not to drop blots.

Mr. Johnson was not always present, for he sometimes had to go to Parramatta, or to one of the other tiny settlements which were springing up in the neighbourhood of that town, or among the huts in Sydney, visiting the sick. But upon such occasions he left instructions with Mrs. Johnson that Patrick was to read certain marked passages in books which were set out ready for him, and then copy them out neatly, after which he would know them by heart, and be able to repeat them the next day. This, Patrick found, did not always work according to plan. For often, close to the marked passages were others, not marked, which were much more interesting, and which he remembered long after the marked ones had slid painlessly from his memory. And sometimes—indeed often—those chosen by his tutor were so dull that Patrick could not understand why anyone should want to remember them anyhow. This morning, for instance, Mr. Johnson, being busy with the composition of a letter to His Excellency, had bidden his pupil copy out and learn:

> "The rose withers, the blossom blasteth,
> The flowers fade, the morning hasteth,
> The Sun sets, the Shadow flies,
> The Gourd consumes, and Man he dies."

There was only one conceivable point of interest in this dull recital of the obvious, and Patrick ventured to interrupt the scratching of his tutor's pen:

"Please, Sir, what is a gourd?"

Mr. Johnson lifted a face made sallow by headache, and gloomy by his ever-gnawing sense of belittlement.

"A gourd, Patrick, is the large and fleshy fruit of a certain . . ." he hesitated—Was it a vine, or a tree? ". . . plant, which, when dried and scraped out, was used by the ancients as a drinking vessel, and, I believe, is still so used in certain parts of the world."

He bent over his paper again and marshaled his interrupted thoughts. He had already made his complaints about a scanty allowance for his increasing family, and about the exorbitant prices of food, and he had begun upon the question of the four hundred acres measured out for Church ground two years ago, and still in its virgin state, without so much as a tree felled upon it.

"I cannot," he continued, "suppose Government meant for me to use axe and spade myself, but this I have done, day after day."

He spread his left hand out and looked at it, his inclination to see a grievance in its hard and roughened palm warring with the still small voice of honesty which reminded him that he had derived a strangely deep, spiritual satisfaction, as well as much material benefit, from his cultivation of the soil. His conscience told him that he was, in his heart, more interested in the welfare of his cucumbers, his melons, his seedling limes and oranges, his beans and peas and guavas, than in the welfare of the immortal souls committed to his care. He had even, he remembered guiltily, raised a little tobacco . . .

Patrick looked dubiously at his bent head. Dared he interrupt again? He had finished copying out the marked passage, and had discovered by just turning one page back, a much pleasanter rhyme with another puzzle at the end of it. Mr. Johnson was frowning and looking very busy, so Patrick decided to read it again for himself first:

> "Like to the Damask rose you see,
> Or like the blossom on the Tree
> Or like the dainty flower of May
> Or like the morning of the Day,
> Or like the Sun, or like the Shade,
> Or like the Gourd which Jonah made . . ."

It was no use; he must ask.

"Mr. Johnson?"

The clergyman looked round at him rather sharply.

"What is it now, Patrick?"

"If a gourd grows on a plant, Sir, how could Jonah make one?"

Mr. Johnson said "Tchk!" and pushed his chair back from the table impatiently. What was all this about gourds? He went across to Patrick and read over the child's shoulder. "The Gourd which Jonah made"! He searched his memory. The Lord had caused a gourd to come up out of the ground— Wasn't that it?—to cover Jonah from the sun. He said peevishly:

"That is not what you were bidden to read, Patrick."

"No, Sir," Patrick admitted cheerfully, "but I had finished the other, so I read this. And I do not understand, Sir, how Jonah could have made the gourd . . ."

"He did not *make* it, child! I have already told you that it grew. But if he hollowed it out in the manner I described, for a drinking vessel, that would be, in a sense you understand . . ."

He pressed his hand to his forehead and groped behind him on his table for his Bible. "Wait a moment. I shall find the passage for you and you shall copy it out."

"Oh." Patrick began to see that he had been over-zealous in his thirst for enlightenment. He took the open Bible which Mr. Johnson proffered, and bent mournfully over his copybook again. Mr. Johnson returned to his chair and took up his pen.

His thoughts went back across the four long years he had spent in this hopeless land, cut off from men of his own vocation, strengthened only by rare letters from his friend and mentor, the Reverend John Newton.

It had been hard to maintain faith in the face of the horrors and depravities he had witnessed in this place, and no man, surely, had ever preached the Word of God to a less receptive congregation, or in more disheartening circumstances. He rummaged among some papers for his friend's last letter, and read it through again, finding a melancholy and wistful comfort in its words of commendation:

". . . tho' your account of the state of things around you was very affecting, and awakened my sympathy and pity, yet I was comforted by observing . . . that neither the discouragements you had met with . . . nor the probability that your sufferings might still be increased, had led you to drop one expression of regret for leaving home, nor to wish yourself back again. . . ."

Back again! Back in England where there was comfort and security, where the devil, if he stalked abroad, stalked not so nakedly as here; where there was the society of virtuous women and the companionship of godly men, where a respectful congregation touched caps to you in the village streets, and the gentry bowed graciously from their passing carriages! He sighed, and skimmed a few more sentences of the letter in his hand:

"I have not been disheartened by your apparent want of success. I have been told that skilful gardeners will undertake to sow and raise a sallad for dinner in the short time while the meat is roasting. But no gardener can raise oaks with such expedition. You are sent to New Holland, not to sow sallad seeds, but to plant acorns. . . . You are, I trust, planting for the next Century. . . ."

Mr. Johnson put the letter down and took his head in both hands despondently. He could not quite bring himself to believe with any fervour in a hundred years passed in this land; four had already seemed an eternity. Once again he was dimly and dejectedly conscious of some limitation in himself which made him and kept him unequal to his task. What had he neglected? Had he not performed every duty of his office regularly and conscientiously? Was it his fault that he was unable to lend that dignity and impressiveness to his services which might touch the stubborn hearts of his flock to repentance? Was it not rather the fault of a Governor who was so concerned with worldly matters that he could spare no men and no bricks to build a house for God? With sudden indignation he snatched up his pen and wrote:

"I did not come out here as an overseer or as a farmer. I have other things more, much more important, to attend to. My duty as a clergyman fully takes up all my time. Neither will my constitution admit of it—this is much impaired since I came into this country, and at this very time I feel such rheumatic pains and weakness that I can scarcely go through the duties of my office. This brings me to mention another circumstance. I have to perform divine service at three different places, viz, at Sydney, Parramatta, and at a settlement about three miles to the westward of Parramatta, and at never a one of these three places is there to this day any place of worship erected, nor so much as talked of. The last time I preached at Sydney was in the open air. Next Sunday, if the weather will permit, we shall assemble in an old boat-house close by the water-side, the sides and ends quite open. I declare to you it is a place not fit or safe for a stable or a cow house, and I declare further, owing to the violent pain I this moment, and have all this day, felt in my temples &c., I dread Sunday coming, aware of the danger and the consequences I have to expect. By the grace of God, however, I am resolved . . ."

"But, Mr. Johnson, it says here that Jonah did *not* make the gourd. . . ."

Mr. Johnson clutched his aching head between his hands and bit back a malediction upon all gourds. He snapped, testily:

"Pray do not continue to interrupt me, Patrick!"

". . . to go on in the discharge of my duty till I can hold out no longer, and then I must give up and leave this miserable people to spend their Sabbaths in a manner wholly like heathens."

Stirred to excitement by his own ultimatum, he leapt to his feet and began to pace up and down the room, and Patrick, seeing him apparently unoccupied, risked another question:

"Please, Sir, what is a booth?"

Mr. Johnson came to an abrupt halt, and looked at Patrick rather queerly.

"A booth? A booth, Patrick, is a shelter. Jonah had a booth, had he not, to protect him from the heat of the sun? But I am given no booth to shelter me from either sun or wind or rain when I preach the Word of God . . ."

"If," suggested Patrick eagerly, "you were to pray, Mr. Johnson, would not the Lord prepare a gourd for you as He did for Jonah, to be a shelter over your head?"

Mr. Johnson did not answer. Instead, he began walking up and down again, but more slowly now. Patrick suddenly noticed with astonishment that he looked very sick and pale, and that his hands were shaking. Over his shoulder he said:

"You may go now, child, if you have finished your copy."

Patrick slid from his chair with surprised alacrity, and tiptoed to the door. He said, "Good-bye, Sir," before he went out, and as he passed the window he had a glimpse of Mr. Johnson kneeling by his chair, with his bowed head in his hands.

*   *   *

April came in stormily. Many of the wattle and daub huts at Parramatta became uninhabitable, and all of them leaked. The ground so laboriously cleared lay under water, and seed just sown was washed away. Corn not yet reaped lay flattened in the mud, and the threat of winter was in the air. "With a dreadful sick list," David Collins wrote soberly in his journal, "and death making rapid strides, April commenced." By the middle of the month Phillip had been forced to reduce the weekly ration; every man now had three pounds of flour, two of maize, and four of pork, and every woman three of flour, one of maize, and four of pork. To his relief the weather improved, and work, interrupted by the storms, went on again. Brick huts for the convicts slowly replaced the miserable hovels at Sydney, and at Parramatta the foundations of a hospital and town hall were laid. But the Governor, with one anxious eye on the hunger-drawn faces of his people, and the other on the fast emptying stores, could find no solace now in the thought of broad streets and solid buildings. He had twenty-four days' supply of flour left, and enough salt meat for three months; it was perhaps a good thing, he thought, with the ruthlessness of desperation, that so many had recently died . . .

He turned all his attention to the problem of eking out these miserable supplies. A sixth of the Indian corn had been stolen, or destroyed by the storms, but the remainder he ordered to be ground by hand mills, or laboriously pounded with wooden pestle and mortar, to supplement a flour ration now still farther reduced to a pound and a half. Hunting parties were sent out into the woods to shoot kangaroos, and such smaller game as might be secured, and every day from dawn till dusk the fishing boats were busy.

Not only the colonists but their black neighbours also suffered during this lean period, for the continual scouring of the neighbourhood by the white hunters and the loud reports of their muskets drove the shy, wild creatures farther and farther afield, so that the black men came back emptyhanded, and there were hollow bellies in the tribes. With unassailable logic the natives then argued that if the invaders plundered their food supply, they must, in turn, help themselves to what they could find in the settlements, and clashes occurred between irate white men who discovered their precious grain being carried off by parties of natives, and indignant black men who saw no reason why the stealing should be all on one side.

* * *

Bennilong had acquired a new wife. Gooroobarooboolo was a comely young woman of the Gweagal, and a great friend of Bennilong's elder sister, Carangarang, from whom she had heard many tales of the shrewish temper of Barangaroo. Her screams and struggles, therefore, as she was dragged off in triumph from her own towri, were dictated by a lively apprehension of her co-wife rather than by a maidenly reluctance to be captured. Captured she was, however, and there was nothing for it but to settle down as best she could beside the campfire of her new husband.

Barangaroo, she found with relief, though hostile and short-tempered, was not actually violent. The elder wife was, as a matter of fact, not altogether sorry to have an assistant in her daily fishing and collecting of firewood, for since the birth of Dilboong she had felt far less energetic than before, and it was a relief to be able to sit still sometimes and send a younger woman off to do the work.

Gooroobarooboolo felt very strange at first. Among her tribe it had not been fully realised what changes had been wrought in the life of the Port Jackson tribes by the presence of the white men, and she was puzzled and disturbed by certain departures from established custom. Some deep-rooted instinct in her was shocked and offended when, instead of setting out with his spears in the morning to hunt or fish, Bennilong constantly went off in his canoe to the camp of the white men, and returned in the evening with no more than a bit of bread to contribute to the family meal. She and Barangaroo had to fish and forage very hard indeed to satisfy his enormous appetite, and Barangaroo, though she would allow no one else to scold him, attacked him herself very lustily, not only with her tongue, but often with her digging stick as well. Upon these occasions, to revenge himself, Bennilong grew very ardent in his attentions to his new wife, and Gooroobarooboolo herself then became the object of Barangaroo's hostility.

She watched her new husband with bewilderment and increasing un-easiness, and was conscious that Barangaroo was watching him too. And not only Barangaroo, but the whole tribe. He spent far too much time, she thought, anxiously, in the camp of the Duggerigai, and there could be no doubt that he was frequently neglectful of his tribal duties. Once he even refused to attend an initiation ceremony. It was all very disturbing and humiliating to a young wife who desired to be proud of her husband.

And then one day he created a sensation by announcing boastfully that the Be-anga of the white men was going away soon, in one of his winged boats, to England, and that he, Bennilong, was going with him.

Barangaroo, suckling Dilboong by the fire, looked up, and Gooroobarooboolo held her breath, waiting for a storm to break about Bennilong's head. He was waiting for it, too, ready to return word for word, and blow for blow. But, most strangely, Barangaroo only looked at him—a long, long, searching look, and then, with a brief grunt, bent her head over the child again. Bennilong laughed loudly and began to boast. This voyage, he said, was one which he had always expected to make; his father, Wunbula, had also expected it, and had told him of it when he was but a child. No other of his race, he proclaimed, had ever been across the sea to England, and none but himself was great enough to go, and to see the King who dwelt there.

But now Colbee called out challengingly from his own fire; he, too, knew the white Be-anga; he, too, could understand the tongue of the white men. And Bennilong spoke falsely when he said that he alone was to go, for only today he, Colbee, had learned that Immerawanye also was to be taken.

Bennilong scowled. If Immerawanye was to go, he retorted, it was of no importance. He was but a boy. He was to be taken only because it was not fitting that one such as himself should go on a long journey unattended by one of his own race. Such was the custom of the Bereewolgal. Did not the Be-anga always have one of his followers at his side when he walked abroad?

There was a yell of derisive laughter at this. Barangaroo, looking up again, said sharply that it was a very strange thing that Bennilong should think more of the customs of the white men than of those of his own people, and Gooroobarooboolo twisted her fingers together and kept her eyes upon the ground in an agony of shame and embarrassment.

Many and many a night after that the question was argued over the campfires. Bennilong, Colbee said sternly, was needed here to perform his part in the tribal life. Immerawanye also. A fine, straight, promising young warrior was Immerawanye, and why should he leave his own people and his own land? Who knew, after all, where the great winged boats would take them?

"To England!" Bennilong interrupted impatiently. "To England, to see the King!"

Looking into the still, dark eyes which watched him across the flames, he read a rejoinder in them, and stirred restlessly. *England*. A word. *The*

King. A name. What might not be the meaning of this word, this name? Even after so long a time there were those among the tribes who held that the white men were not men, but spirits. Firmly planted in their minds by centuries-old legends, was the belief that across the sea there could be nothing but the mysterious spirit-land from which the ancestral heroes, Mommon and Yaburog, had come. Quiet as the night and dark as the sky, they sat and watched this revolutionary in their midst, and the fire-light shone on the whites of their watchful eyes.

Silence. Bennilong listened, startled. How seldom, now, was it so quiet! For the first time he realised how great a part silence played in the life of his own people, and how great a part sound played in the life of the Bereewolgal. In his own camp, if there was noise it was the noise of talk-ing and laughter and argument, or, within the corroboree ring, the awe-some and inspiring sounds of ritual. But often there was silence, as there was now, and in it one's spirit was freed, knowing no time, passing like the wind, belonging to the past and the future as surely as to the present . . .

But in the camp of the white men the air was filled and shaken by a perpetual torment of sound. There were shoutings and bangings and the noisy tramp of feet. There were clankings of chains, loud reports from the fire-breathing weapons, cries of pain, incessant hammerings, loud music . . .

Suddenly Bennilong knew that this silence was binding him as with ropes—drawing him back from his adventure into the poised, timeless, unchanging mysteries of his own race and land. No sound, no move-ment . . .

He made an angry gesture, and flung his shield down with a clatter on a pile of spears.

"In England the King dwells in a house bigger than the Be-anga's house!"

His voice had cracked that enclosing silence; he went on with loud defiance, splintering it with the sound of words:

"There are many such houses—as many as the stars in the sky! There men may not fight each other, for the King guards all. Thus the Be-anga has told me. There men need not hunt, for there is much food and much wine put away in great storehouses. There every man and woman wears clothes, and sleeps in a house of bricks, and all love each other and live at peace. I shall go to England and see these things, and I shall return, and thus also we shall live . . ."

By-gone interrupted, thoughtfully:

"The unworthy ones—did they not come from England?"

Bennilong glared at him.

"They!" His tone shivered with contempt. "They are men and women who did not obey their Law. They took that which belonged to the King."

"There was one," By-gone said, still in the same quiet tone of reflection, "who told me that in England he was hungry."

Bennilong said, loftily:

"He was a fool. He should have asked the King for food, for there the King owns all, as the Be-anga here."

By-gone shrugged his shoulders.

"Thus I said to him. He laughed. His words were that the King would not give him food, nor his woman, nor his children, so that one night he went out into the woods to hunt. And he caught a small animal, no larger than Piggiebillah, the prickly one, and took it home for his woman, and they cooked and ate it. And the King was angry, and put chains upon his wrists and ankles, and sent him here."

A little sound ran through the listening group, like a sigh. Bennilong shouted, furiously:

"His words were false!"

He stared round the circle of firelit faces. The silence descended again. Colbee's head was bent, and the flickering light showed pitted skin upon his cheeks where the mysterious sickness had marked him. Bennilong's heart swelled with misery and indecision. All his life he had been tormented by these two allegiances—to the old tribal life governed by its ancient Law, for which Colbee stood as the symbol, and to some adventurousness of the blood and spirit which ardently sought and welcomed change. He looked at his friends resentfully, dimly aware that the quality in himself which they applauded when it expressed itself in the making of corroborees, was the same which they mistrusted when it drew him irresistibly into the new and exciting life of the white invaders.

* * *

Not long after this it was whispered among the women that Barangaroo was ill. She grew thin and ate little, and her milk failed so that Dilboong had to be suckled by one of the other women, and Gooroobarooboolo had to do all the fishing and foraging alone. When she grew worse a woman's magic was performed by Daringha, who bound a cord about the patient's forehead, and rubbed her own lips with the other end, whereby the evil blood was brought out and passed along the cord, where it was plainly to be seen staining Daringha's mouth, and trickling down her chin. But still Barangaroo lay tired and listless in her mia-mia and even the magic of a great carrahdy of the Cammeraygal failed to rouse her.

One morning she did not waken, and the wails of Gooroobarooboolo told the camp that death had come to it in the night. It so happened that there was another whale ashore at the time, so the ceremonial throwing of spears which always followed a death was combined with a whale-feast for which many tribes had assembled, and Barangaroo's funeral contests were long remembered.

When the time came for the burning of her body not only all Bennilong's relations, but the white Be-anga and several of his friends were present.

Upon a carefully prepared pile of brushwood her body lay, and beside her were her baskets, and her fishing lines, her bone needles and her balls of twine, her yam-stick and her wooden coolamon. Carangarang had come from Botany Bay, and stood with two of her children beside her, and a third in her arms; Gooroobarooboolo squatted beside Colbee's wife, Daringha, who was too ill to stand, and sat with her baby on her knees, coughing every now and then, and holding over her breast hands which grew thinner every day. Warreweer stood alone, looking up from beneath her hair as usual, but without mockery now, without sparkle. She was pregnant at last, and near her time; she thought that she understood, now, why the waywardness of her brother had caused such sorrow in the heart of Barangaroo, and she kept her eyes on the brushwood, watching unblinkingly while Bennilong placed logs on the body, and summoned her husband, Gnungagnunga Murremurgan, to come forward with his fire stick. She watched as the small flames ran together, catching the logs and becoming huge flames. The fire roared, and from its centre came a black and billowing smoke. Carangarang, watching her sister curiously, noticed that her lips moved.

Carangarang was something of a gossip, and was always deeply interested in the affairs of other people. Turning from Warreweer, she eyed Daringha for a moment, deciding that it would not be long before she, too, was dead; and she studied Gooroobarooboolo and wondered if she had yet been entrusted with a baby spirit. Now that Barangaroo was dead the younger wife's life would probably be pleasanter, for there could be no doubt that though Barangaroo had been a good enough wife, diligent in all her duties, she had been also a sharp-tempered and quarrelsome creature, and her camp would be the quieter for her passing. No one knew why she had died. Perhaps, though she had borne her child easily enough, and had seemed none the worse for it for some time afterwards, she was too old for such a business. Perhaps it was as many of the women whispered—that the joy had gone out of her life when Bennilong brought the young Gooroobarooboolo to his mia-mia. They had all waited for storms when that happened. The wounds Bennilong had received when he captured his new wife from the Gweagal, they whispered, would be as nothing to those Barangaroo would inflict upon him when he brought her home! Let Gooroobarooboolo beware, they said to each other, for Barangaroo would surely scratch her eyes out, and tear her hair in handfuls from her head!

Well, Carangarang reflected, they had been wrong. Barangaroo had been irritable and snappish, certainly, and rumour had it that once when Gooroobarooboolo had gone to lift up the infant Dilboong, Barangaroo had flung a billet of wood and hit her on the side of the head, so that she fell to the ground. But she had made no serious disturbance, and Carangarang was inclined to think that neither the birth of her child nor the advent of Gooroobarooboolo had had anything to do with her death. Her own opinion, which she had several times expounded to the women of her tribe, was that it was all a part of the evil influence of the white men. Was it not well known that Barangaroo had felt great uneasiness as her husband became more and more familiar with them? Had she not grown very quiet and melancholy when she heard that he was to go away across the sea with the white Be-anga? Had she not told Daringha that the magic drink which the white men gave him had once caused a madness to come into his mind, and an unsteadiness to his legs and arms, so that he could no longer fling a spear truly, or even stand firmly upon his feet? Was it not enough? Already, in her sorrow, her heart was dead. And the other women had nodded soberly, knowing that the body cannot survive the death of the heart.

This kind of sorrow, thought Carangarang, seemed to threaten a good many of the women. Even Daringha had wept because Colbee often took his fish to the white men's camp and exchanged it for bread instead of bringing it home. Even Warreweer, once so disgracefully casual and light-hearted over serious matters, had expressed the opinion lately that it was not fitting that her husband should have taken the name of a white man, Collins, in token of friendship.

The fire was burning fiercely now, and everyone was preparing to leave and set about the day's business. The Be-anga was walking back to his house with his friends, and Bennilong was with them, explaining that, if he could not find a woman of his own race to nurse Dilboong, he would seek for one among the women of the Bereewolgal. Warreweer was hurrying down to the shore where her canoe was beached, and Daringha, holding the baby on her hip with one arm, and smearing tears from her cheeks with the other hand, was following more slowly. Carangarang sighed and gathered her children and her belongings together for departure, sorry that the excitement of the day was over. Tomorrow there would be another ceremony, when Bennilong would rake the ashes together and form them into a mound, and after that he would depart with his spears to find Wileemaring (who, though he was a carrahdy, had refused to come and minister to Barangaroo in her illness) and there would be a fight. In the meantime, however, there was nothing to do but go home.

* * *

That night the women gathered about their campfires and sang the song that Warreweer had made for Barangaroo:

> "She is gone from us; never as she was will she return,
> Never more as she once did will she chop honey;
> Never more with her gunnai dig yams,
> She has gone from us; never as she was to return.
>
> Mussels there are in the creek and plenty,
> But she who lies there will dig no more,
> We shall fish as of old for cod-fish,
> But she who lies there will beg no more oil,
> Oil for her hair she will want no more."

They sang softly, swaying their bodies a little in the firelight, and tiny reflected flames leapt in their dark eyes. It was a new camp, for the place where a death has occurred must be instantly abandoned. The children were quiet; the men ceased their talk and listened. The memory of Barangaroo was no longer the memory of a sharp-tongued shrew, but of a woman who had served her husband and her tribe faithfully. The sound of their singing went up with the blue smoke, climbing between the rustling leaves of the tree-tops, fading into the dark, vanishing into that mysterious sky in which the familiar and eternal stars alone spelled reassurance. There, plainly to be seen, was the bright path where Baiame walked, and why should not the smoke reach it—or the song—or Barangaroo? They sang quietly, reflectively, monotonously, until the flames sank, and the little fires were only heaps of glowing ash.

"She is gone from us; never as she was will she return. . . ."

Across the water the Governor, writing at his table by the open window, paused for a moment, and lifted his head to listen.

* * *

Mr. Mannion, accepting the Governor's invitation to be seated, looked round the room with some curiosity. He had never before visited Phillip's Parramatta residence, and he acknowledged that, paltry as the whole building was by the standards of the civilised world, this room, at least, with its high ceiling and fine windows, had a certain spacious dignity. The Governor himself seemed, by contrast, even more meagre and insignificant than usual. He had a bad cold, doubtless contracted during the shocking weather in the earlier part of the month, and the pallor of his face emphasised the redness of his beaklike nose.

In spite of the bright sunshine outside there was a fire burning in the grate, and Phillip, drawing his own chair closer to it, inquired civilly:

"You have come, I assume, Mr. Mannion, on the business which you mentioned in your letter?"

"I have, Sir. I hope to convince you that my proposal to take up land on the Nepean is one which is worthy of your approval and support."

The Governor blew his nose, and leaned forward to poke the fire.

"I agree that the district is well calculated for settlement. I said as much to the Under-Secretary in a letter some two years ago—just after you arrived in this country, Mr. Mannion. It was my opinion then that some time must elapse before such a thing became practicable."

"For the description of persons you had in mind, Sir," Mr. Mannion said, with some hauteur, "your objections were doubtless valid. For myself, and at the present time, I cannot see that they apply."

Phillip was silent for a moment, holding his hands out to the blaze. He said at last:

"I understand that you made a journey recently, to inspect the neighbourhood?"

"I did, Your Excellency. I myself, and the gentlemen who accompanied me, were impressed—I may say enthusiastic . . ."

"Yes, yes." The Governor cut him short rather brusquely. "The land is good. I know it. But at present it is isolated. The nearest settlement is at Toongabbee, a full thirteen or fourteen miles distant. You have doubtless considered the disadvantages of this?"

Mannion stirred impatiently.

"Naturally, Sir, I have fully considered them. I repeat that to one in my position, and commanding the resources which I am able to command, they offer no serious objection. To an emancipated convict, or to the description of free settler which is likely to come into the country in the next few years, such difficulties would, I admit, be almost insuperable. I, however," concluded Mr. Mannion superbly, "am neither a penniless emigrant, nor a freed convict."

The Governor acknowledged this incontrovertible fact with a testy wave of his hand.

"You would propose to live there yourself, Mr. Mannion? You would take your children, and your—housekeeper? And her children?"

Mr. Mannion looked pained.

"I must make it clear to Your Excellency, once and for all, that I have no intention of remaining permanently in this country. My position forbids it. The future of my sons would not permit of it. The land which I take up I shall regard as an investment, and I shall remain here only so long as is necessary to set it in proper train. No doubt I shall visit the colony every few years to inspect it. My immediate intentions, however, are these: I shall have a small house erected, and huts for such convict labour as I may have occasion to employ. I shall write to Ireland to have certain men from my own estates sent out as overseers, together with horses, livestock, and necessary tools and implements. In the meantime, I propose to reside here in Parramatta with my household, making such journeys to the river as may be necessary for the superintending of the work in progress there."

Mr. Mannion sat back in his chair and waited with an expression of patient martyrdom for the next objection.

"You would need," said the Governor, "to place a reliable overseer in charge of your convict labourers at once. Such men are not easily to be found in the colony, as I know to my cost."

"I have already—anticipating your Excellency's cooperation—engaged a very respectable sort of man who came out, I understand, as a seaman on the *Sirius,* but who preferred to remain in the colony and turn his attention to agriculture. I have had no difficulty in persuading him that he will best further his own interest by devoting himself to mine. Indeed, Sir," Mr. Mannion concluded, with some warmth, "I should have supposed that you, as Governor of the colony, might have been pleased to see some of its unproductive lands taken up and cultivated by a man of substance and integrity."

The Governor leaned back in his chair, and in the ray of sunlight which now fell across his shoulders Mr. Mannion noticed that his coat was shabby and threadbare.

"My concern," he said, slowly, "and my apparent reluctance have been dictated only by my apprehending that I am responsible for the safety and well-being of every inhabitant in these settlements, Mr. Mannion. Upon the banks of the Nepean you will be upon the outer fringe of the explored lands of this continent. You will be at the very foot of a mountainous country which, so far, we have been unable to cross. Mr. Dawes, who led an expedition into it, assured me that it is wild and barren, and unlikely to harbour large numbers of natives—but we cannot know for certain that this is so. We do know—for I have met and talked with them myself—that there is at least one large tribe, the Boorooberongal, in the neighbourhood of the river, and in the event of an attack upon your people there . . ."

He broke off, and then said abruptly:

"However, you must be fully aware of this danger. Are you also aware that we have seen indications of the river rising, in rainy seasons, to a very considerable height?"

Mannion nodded, impatiently.

"I observed these indications myself, Sir, when I was there recently. The land I propose to take up is on a gently rising ground, and has a hill upon which the house and the huts of the convicts would be, I should suppose, safe from any flood."

"Very well. You shall lead the way, Mr. Mannion. Doubtless you will have neighbours before long." Phillip, rising, stood for a moment motionless, staring out of the long window, and Mannion, who had risen, too, turned also to look, struck by the expression on the Governor's face, and by his curious stillness. At the bottom of the hill two men were going slowly up the road, carrying a third; from the careless way in which they handled him, and from the limpness of his hanging arms, it was obvious that he was dead.

Mr. Mannion said, briskly:

"Another death in the fields? The poor wretches have been going off like flies recently, I'm told. No doubt the inclemency of the weather . . ."

The Governor snapped: "Starvation." Mr. Mannion blinked, and then shrugged.

"I must not detain you, Sir, from your many duties. I may take it, then, that you approve of my proposals?"

Phillip looked at him, absently.

"Eh? Proposals . . . Oh, yes. Yes, Mr. Mannion, I think there need be no obstacles in your way. It will be some time before you can despatch your letter to Ireland, but, in the meantime, you can be employed in clearing your land and erecting your buildings. I wish you success in your venture."

Mr. Mannion, bowing and preparing to take his departure, was arrested by a sudden: "One moment, Sir!" The Governor's rather uninterested gaze had become suddenly penetrating. He said, slowly:

"I should like—as a matter of curiosity, you understand—to hear your own personal opinion of the future of this colony?"

Mr. Mannion looked at him in some astonishment.

"I am proposing to lay out large sums in developing a portion of it, Your Excellency," he replied, coldly. "I should have supposed that this would indicate the measure of my confidence in it as a source of revenue."

"Ah!" Phillip blew his nose again, still looking attentively at his guest over his handkerchief. "You regard it, then, simply as a source of revenue?"

"Naturally."

Suddenly the Governor laughed. It was a thing he did so rarely that at first Mannion was not sure whether the brief sound, between a cackle and a snort, were indeed an expression of mirth or a paroxysm caused by his cold. But as he lowered his handkerchief it became apparent that he was smiling rather oddly.

"You will permit me one further warning. You intend to exploit this land. Have a care, Sir, that it does not end by exploiting you!"

Mr. Mannion stared. He had never liked this dry, reserved little man, and, since that laugh, he liked him less than ever. He even wondered for a moment whether the hardships and privations of his exile had unhinged the Governor's mind. He bowed again, stiffly.

"I am honoured, Sir, by your solicitude. Good day."

He paused a moment as he emerged from the front door, and stood frowning, irritably conscious of uneasiness. What could the fellow have meant? *"Have a care . . ."* Preposterous! He shook the memory away from him, and recovered his complacency by reflecting that he had got what he wanted. He squared his shoulders and breathed deeply, his spirits mounting every moment. He looked about him upon a scene which, in any mood, he must have called pleasant, but which, in his increasing glow of satisfaction, seemed positively Arcadian. His Excellency, he decided, had chosen the spot for his residence well. On this gently sloping hillside it commanded a view not only of the main street of the township, but of the narrow tidal creek which formed the most inland arm of the harbour, and of a fine stretch of the surrounding countryside.

April was nearly gone; the day was blue and golden, very fresh after the rain, and with an invigorating crispness in the air which struck pleasantly through the sun's warmth. At the foot of the hill three young poplars had been planted by the side of the street, and Mr. Mannion looked at them with approval, thinking how favourably their slender shape and delicate foliage, already pale gold, contrasted with the untidy irregularity and the monotonous dull green of the native trees. Beyond them the convicts' huts bordered the street, but even these hovels, unlovely as they were, and badly damaged by the recent storms, seemed less drab than usual in the limpid brilliance of the day.

Yes, Mr. Mannion was well pleased with the interview he had just concluded, and he walked briskly down the hill in high good humour. Ahead of him he could see the two men turning into one of the huts with their melancholy burden, and as he came abreast of it and passed on he heard a wild outburst of weeping from within. It was odd, he reflected, and would never cease to be a matter of bewilderment to him, that the tenderer emotions of life did seem to survive—sometimes, even to flourish—among the lower classes. For it was, as he had told Harriet during the voyage, generally admitted that they were beings of a coarser fibre than those in his own walk of life, and if they were less sensitive to physical suffering they should surely be, also, less susceptible to the pleasanter emotions of love or aesthetic appreciation, or to the spiritual agonies of bereavement. That wild, almost animal cry of grief which he had heard both astonished and annoyed him. It was unseemly, he felt, that a sorrow which he, Stephen Mannion, had felt for the death of his wife, should be thus reproduced—almost, one might say, caricatured—in the sorrow of some convict drab for one who was, no doubt, her paramour.

He passed the stocks with a glance for the ragged figure which stood there. Its dirty and bony hands hung limply on either side of the leaden coloured face which protruded grotesquely through the board, and confirmed Mr. Mannion in his conviction that these people were indeed of another clay. The unfortunate wretch, he thought with distaste, looked more like an ape than a man; and, merciful Heaven, how he stank!

He walked on briskly towards the landing place where he was to join the boat which would take him back to Sydney. Now that he was to have an interest in the colony—to become, in fact, himself a colonist (he allowed himself a whimsical smile for this quaint idea) he found that he viewed the various activities of the two settlements with a more critical eye. His own lands, he determined, should be tilled in no such makeshift manner as had been customary here at Parramatta. These niggardly hand-to-mouth methods of the Governor's would never answer. They should see what could be achieved by a man with bold ideas and money in his pocket. There were no limits to the possibilities of profit from this land. He could see it now. Strange, the blindness of so many who lived with the potentialities of untold wealth within their grasp, and yet lacked the courage or the enterprise to wring it from the unwilling soil! In all the colony, he supposed, no one save himself had fully grasped the advantages which were waiting to be won. Himself—and, perhaps, Macarthur.

Warm with exercise and self-approval, he allowed his thoughts to turn with luxurious tenderness towards his sons. His sons—Harriet's sons—growing to manhood in their own lovely homeland, would live to bless the courage and audacity of their father. Harriet herself, perhaps, from some remote celestial sphere might well be watching and applauding his expiation of the folly which had ended in her death. And when his letter arrived in Ireland there would be much clicking of tongues, and much horrified raising of hands, and the immemorial cry would go round the countryside:

"Those Mannions! Mad—quite mad!"

* * *

By June, thanks to the fresh meat, and to a supply of vegetables, mostly from the Governor's garden, the numbers in the hospital decreased, and Mr. Johnson was not quite so frequently summoned to read the burial service. On the 20th, amid wild relief and rejoicing, the *Atlantic* store-ship arrived from Calcutta with a cargo of rice, soujee, and dholl. The first elation subsided a little when it was found that all this food was of poor quality, and unpalatable; and though the ration of grain might now be supplemented, the ration of pork must be still further reduced. Eight casks of pork had been sent on board the *Atlantic*—as an experiment rather than as an actual contribution to the food supply—but these, when opened, were found to be already putrid. For five more miserable weeks the colony survived, and then the *Britannia,* coming to anchor in the harbour towards the end of July, solved the food problem for another few months at least.

* * *

During the autumn and early winter of this year, the natives brought to Prentice more rumours of visitors to the river, and again he went down to investigate. The first time he saw nothing but a few trees whose bark had been hacked, as if to mark them for some purpose, and he returned to the preparation of his new refuge in the hills. But before long fresh

reports from the natives sent him hurrying down the river again, and this
time, from the shelter of the scrub, he looked across the broad stream and
saw ominous signs of activity. Already trees had been felled, and convicts
were hacking the branches from them and burning them in great heaps,
so that the air was full of blue and fragrant smoke. There was a tall man
—obviously a gentleman, and equally obviously not an officer—who was
giving directions, and Prentice was forced to realise that at last, instead of
intermittent visits to the neighbourhood, he must expect and prepare for
settlement.

Well, he thought, he had already begun to prepare—and none too
soon! No part of this river would be safe for much longer now. He would
push forward with his own plans for moving—but, in the meantime,
might he not wring an advantage from this unwelcome intrusion? He
made a temporary camp round the next bend of the river, and kept the
gang of convicts under continual observation, finding a certain sadistic
delight in watching them labour, gloating when he saw them eat their
miserable ration of bread and salt meat, grinning to himself at the harshness of the overseer, roused by the sight of their misery and captivity to
a new enjoyment of his own freedom.

He was curious to know how they were to be victualed, and soon found
that once a week they were marched off to Parramatta, returning in the
evening of the next day but one, laden with provisions for the ensuing
week. The first building which they erected was a strong wooden hut,
obviously intended as a storehouse and a repository for their tools. Prentice
grinned to himself. His own few tools were showing, by now, the effect
of three years' hard use, and he reflected that there would be many things
in that shed which might be of service to him. The overseer always carried
a musket, and it was not too much to hope that even a store of ammunition might be left somewhere inside. He awaited the next departure of
the gang, and an hour or so later was across the river, prowling round the
hut and fingering the large padlocks on the door. The whole thing had
been stoutly built; he could see no means of getting into it. He toyed with
the idea of setting it on fire, but feared not only betrayal by smoke, but
that some or all of the contents might be destroyed, if the fire grew beyond
his control. Then he looked up at the shingled roof and slapped his thigh
in satisfaction. He dragged a long branch which had been hacked from
a felled tree, leaned it against the hut and climbed up it. He had with
him no tool but the strong knife stolen years ago from a seaman, its blade
worn down now to a bare two inches, but with this he hacked and levered
until he had one shingle free. The others came more easily, and within

an hour he was peering down into the dim interior of the hut. He scrambled through the opening, hung by his hands for a moment, and dropped. In the semi-darkness he stood motionless for a moment or two waiting for his eyes to accustom themselves to it, and by degrees he saw axes, hoes, spades, shovels, hammers, pickaxes, several boxes of nails, one large saw, and another box which contained, as well as an assortment of smaller tools, a few locks and hinges. He stared almost unbelievingly at these riches. How much must the settlement have advanced, he thought, to be able to equip one lonely settler so lavishly! He well knew how scarce all these things had been during his own year there; in the whole colony, at that time, there had been no more than fifty pickaxes.

He became suddenly feverishly anxious to get away with his spoils. To be hemmed within four walls and a locked door roused a kind of panic in him, and the knowledge that he was, until he broke his way out, a prisoner again, roused him to an almost maddened activity. He seized an axe and swung it savagely at the wall till the sweat ran down his body and his heart laboured. When he had smashed a hole just big enough to creep through he wiped the perspiration from his forehead and looked about him more calmly. He made a careful selection of all that he needed most. An axe, a spade, a hatchet, a pickaxe, a hoe, a saw. He found a length of rope to tie these together in a bundle, and then turned to the smaller articles. He could find no ammunition. There was a large pail half hidden behind some boxes in a corner, and he took that with delight, for Cunnembeillee's wooden coolamons, though well enough for drinking, were a tedious means of watering his plants in dry weather. Into it he put a plane, a chisel, a couple of files for sharpening his saw, a few locks and hinges, and as many nails as he could carry. Then, dragging all his plunder to the hole, he squeezed through, and pulled it after him.

Thus heavily laden it took him two full days to reach home again, although on the second afternoon he fell in with some of his native friends who carried most of his load for the remainder of the way. He rested there one night, and set out the next morning for his hut in the hills.

Here with his new tools, he employed himself for a few days, and in his utter solitude and seclusion became conscious of an emotion so unfamiliar that he did not at first recognise it as happiness. It came to him in sudden, unexpected ways; a dozen times in the course of his work his hand was arrested in mid-movement, and his eyes went blank as he savoured it, wondered over it, felt it run through his spirit with the sharp, refreshing shock of cold water on the body. Once, resting on his hoe and wiping the sweat from his forehead, he heard a magpie's note, and for the first time realised that it was beautiful. Once, bending over the stream to dip a pailful of water, he noticed the red and golden mosaic of pebbles in the creek bed, and paused to look at them for a moment. Freed from fear and hunger, he had been growing slowly towards the awareness of another self dwelling within the body which had hitherto been his only preoccupation, and now he was ready for the first fumbling, awkward efforts of self-knowledge. Beneath a wary bewilderment, ready to retreat into scepticism and contempt, he found that they brought him a poignant and sometimes painful stab of revelation.

Alone, and yet never lonely, he dug and hoed, sawed logs, split shingles for his roof. He made a few extra bits of rude furniture. Moved by a sudden impulse he patiently enlarged a natural hollow in one of the rocks of the creek bed, seeing in his mind's eye the sturdy brown body of Billalong splashing there on hot summer days. Finally he rehung his door and his window on the hinges, and fitted them with bolts and locks. No moment in his life had been more rich in satisfaction than that in which he at last stood back to survey his finished handiwork, and to hang the key of his completed home about his neck.

Cunnembeillee, bringing him his coolamon full of fresh milk when he returned to the river, thought that she had never seen him look so well content; Bill, staggering across the floor to clutch him about the knees, was lifted high in the air, and tickled till he squealed with laughter.

Twice during the next month the storehouse in the new clearing down the river was robbed, and in his remote and securely locked hut Prentice hid his growing wealth. Life had suddenly become very good—better than it had ever been. Not only had he freedom, and more material possessions than ever before—not only did he feel that in his new retreat he would be safe almost indefinitely—but he had the deep satisfaction of continually outwitting the tall gentleman, whom, from the first moment of seeing him, he had most vindictively hated.

His expeditions down the river had almost the flavour of entertainments. He looked forward to them eagerly, but never relaxed his caution. It was made easier for him because, as he had expected, the natives were blamed for his robberies, and after the third, Prentice, holding his sides, and aching with silent laughter, watched elaborate preparations being made to apprehend them. An extra overseer had been brought, he noticed, and when the time came for the gang to leave upon its weekly return to Parramatta, ten convicts, two overseers and the tall gentleman went into the hut to put away the tools—but only ten convicts and one overseer emerged. Prentice watched them out of sight, a grey slow-moving file of men with chains about their ankles, and his mirth altered, freezing into an ugly and sardonic grin.

The tall gentleman, waiting with nerves alert for maurauding natives, would spend but an indifferent night! Cheered by this pleasant reflection, he returned to his own camp, and slept peacefully till daybreak.

*   *   *

Spring was coming again. Cunnembeillee smelt it in the air as she set off with her woven basket in her hand for the day's foraging. Bill, half asleep, and gnawing contentedly at a piece of kangaroo bone, was slung upon her back, so she walked rather slowly because he was growing heavy now. The thin wavering shadows closed over her as she stepped beneath the trees, and the quiet bush welcomed her with promises. Its subdued neutral colouring was gradually being lit here and there with shy flickers of colour which confirmed the evidence of her nostrils that the cold season was nearly over. The young leaves of the trees were rosy, moist, and very small, and their trunks where the bark was peeling away showed delicately green. Everywhere there were glimmers of yellow which shone and faded as the moving branches above shed sun or shadow on frothy balls of blossom, and the air was full of the honey-scent of spring, strong, sweet and tempting. The ground was hard, strewn with dead leaves and fallen twigs, but the little plants which thrust green leaves through the tangled débris thrived, and found it good.

Cunnembeillee trod it with confidence and tranquillity. It was not her own towri, but she had learned it pretty well by now. The red-headed one, her husband, had not seemed to understand why, at first, her contribution to the food supply had been smaller than when they were camped farther down the river in the territory of her own tribe. In one's own towri there was hardly a tree or a stone which was unfamiliar. Thus one knew exactly where to look for roots or berries; one grew accustomed to the habits of the birds, and observed where they were nesting; one knew where the rotting logs were which might harbour grubs, and the places where one would be likely to find a black snake baking in the sun. In a new country it was more difficult. It became necessary to acquire with a laborious consciousness the knowledge which in one's own domain had been developing unconsciously ever since the days when, as a toddling birrahlee, one went out every morning with the other women upon the daily search for food.

With the other women! That was the memory which filled Cunnembeillee's heart with sadness. For though the women of the neighbouring tribe came to visit her from time to time, they always set out with their baskets from their own camp, and it was seldom indeed that Cunnembeillee had any other companion than Bill to cheer the solitude of her own search.

By now she knew her environment well enough, and she never returned without something in her basket. An-droo was strange about food, and would eat little that she brought except honey. She had been wounded, even indignant about this at first, for it lowered her in her own esteem that her contribution to the food supply of the family should be thus ignored; but she decided in the end that just as she herself, at certain times, must refrain from eating certain things, so for this white man, altogether so mysterious, there must be certain permanently forbidden foods.

She had grown accustomed to the neighbourhood, but never to the loneliness of her expeditions. She always left the hut with a heavy heart, remembering other departures from a camp cheerfully clamorous with voices and laughter; remembering leisurely preparations, a hundred times interrupted by some tale or some argument, or by some sudden and exciting quarrel followed by a sudden and delightful reconciliation. There had been no sense of painful urgency in that life, and no hint of a secret fear, hidden and unexpressed, such as haunted the camp of the white man.

She knew that soon they were to go away from here to yet another place, and the knowledge darkened her spirits with a nervous apprehension. For though to the white men one tract of this country was very much like another, to the natives there was always one which was home. It had a threefold character, for in its total area, which was the territory of the whole tribe, it incorporated also the small and constantly shifting home which was the temporary camp site, and the sacred place—perhaps a pool, perhaps a tree, perhaps a pile of rocks—where one's spirit had lodged before birth. Within its boundaries were the increase sites, the clearing for the ceremonies and corroborees of the men, and far away in another direction that in which the secret dances and rituals of the women were performed. There were hills and rocks which held a totemic significance, immortalising tales of the ancestral heroes. And there was the deep spiritual comfort of a lifelong familiarity. To leave one's own place and to go away to that of one's husband, was a fate which must frequently befall a woman, and Cunnembeillee had become reconciled by now to that first uprooting. But the prospect of a second journey into another unknown place made her uneasy. Again she was oppressed by the strangeness of this white man, frightened in her heart of one who seemed to have no spiritual anchorage. For the inner life was bound up with the tribal territory, and to pass so casually from one place to another was to tear up the roots of that inner life, and to throw into chaos the intricate machinery of the only social organisation which she understood.

Terrible to her, too, was the white man's hatred of his own tribe. He had made her understand that they hated him, too, and would capture and kill him if they could. Her instinct taught her that a tribe so divided against itself was a tribe whose foundations shook, a tribe into which no woman could wish her children to be born. Her blood warned her that so fixed and implacable a hatred of man for man became, all too easily, hatred of man for life, hatred of man for himself, a terrible inner decay, spelling ruin and disaster.

She had seen very little of her husband lately. He went away for many days at a time, and she knew that he was at the new place, doing all over again the work which they had so laboriously done here when they first came. But she had heard also from her black neighbours that there were members of his tribe constantly about the river banks in the territory of her own people, and that he sometimes went there secretly to observe them from a hiding place upon the opposite bank.

Today, thinking of him there where she herself so longed to be, she was overcome by homesickness. Ever since she had left her own people she had never seen her mother or her sister, and when once she had explained to the red-headed one that she wished to go and visit them, he had been angry and told her there was too much work to do.

She had submitted then because she was by nature quiet and docile. But the slow indignation of the normally even-tempered was rising in her, and today, made miserable by loneliness, she was near to rebellion. A husband had rights among her people—but so had a wife. It was unheard of that she should be denied the occasional companionship of her own family, and outrageous that her child should never yet have been shown to his grandmother. She had performed all her wifely duties faithfully —and far more. Every day she gathered firewood, and every day she found food. From the top of a little hill she looked down the river, shading her eyes, towards the towri of her tribe, and to Bill, restlessly awake and clutching lustily at her hair, she murmured promises.

* * *

Johnny Prentice had almost made up his mind to run away again. Since they had removed to Parramatta his affairs had gone badly. In

Sydney he had formed a regular clientèle among the convicts and the soldiers, for there were many small illegal acts of bartering to be negotiated, many clandestine messages to be run, many little thefts to be committed, and a nimble-fingered and nimble-witted child had opportunities and advantages in such transactions which were denied to an adult. His payments varied. Sometimes a bit of bread or meat was his reward, sometimes a ragged garment; sometimes the fragments of knowledge which he acquired could be turned to account by a little perilous blackmail. Sometimes he got nothing for his pains but a blow and a volley of abuse.

But since coming to Parramatta all this had been changed. Mr. Mannion, who, now that he had become so busy himself, could not bear to see anyone else idle, suddenly realised that he had on his hands a convict child of eight years, who should, undoubtedly, be made useful. So Johnny, sullen and rebellious, was set to work in the little garden which Mr. Mannion was having made before his house, and in which he intended (so Johnny learned from Patrick) to grow trees and plants which might later be transferred to his property on the Nepean. Johnny weeded and raked and watered in a ferment of rebelliousness. Occasionally, when his father was away at the river, Patrick came and helped him, but at such times the work went forward even more slowly than usual, for there were so many things to talk about.

From here one could see the mountains much more plainly. On a clear day they looked quite close. Patrick and Johnny often talked of them, and planned that when they were at last established on the banks of the river they would set out together to cross them, and succeed where their faint-hearted elders had failed. For, although it had been explained to Patrick that in a year or two at most he was to go back to Ireland and learn to live like a gentleman again, he never attempted to imagine so far ahead as that. Here he was, and over there near the mountains was a river, and on the banks of the river Papa was cultivating land and building a house; of course, he would live there some day, and be the first to find a way across the mountains. No one had thought of explaining anything to Johnny. He simply took it for granted that if one owned land one lived upon it. So that when Patrick came to help there was less done than ever, and Johnny nearly always got into trouble when Mr. Mannion returned. One day Johnny said:

"Why don't y' ask y' Pa to take us to the river next time?"

Patrick's eye bulged.

"He wouldn't! It's too far."

Johnny snorted.

"It's no more'n about fifteen, sixteen mile."

"But there's coming back, too."

"Not till next day."

"You mean . . ." said Patrick, dumbfounded, ". . . we'd *sleep* there? All night?"

" 'Course!"

"But there's no house!"

"There's a store-hut, ain't there? If you *got* to 'ave a roof over y' 'ead!"

Patrick blushed. It was no use trying to pretend that he was not frightened of the dark. How many times, lying awake in his bed in the house at Sydney, had he not heard through the thin partitions the stealthy sounds of Johnny's midnight returns! How often had he not marvelled humbly that there should be a boy, not older than himself, for whom the black mysterious night with its rustling trees and its moving shadows and its immensity of starlit sky held no terrors! But there *was* the store-hut, though it would be queer to sleep without a proper bed. And Papa would be there. He said, recklessly:

"I'll ask him!"

That night, summoning his courage, he tried.

"Papa?"

"Yes, Patrick?"

"Could I . . . would you, please, Papa, take me with you next time you go to the river?" He thought it better not to mention Johnny just yet. His father looked at him in astonishment.

"Take you to the river? Ridiculous, child! You could never walk so far."

"I think I could, Papa. I would try . . ."

"Nonsense, Patrick! Impossible! When my horses arrive from Ireland I shall take you. There, it is a promise! It is preposterous that so long after its establishment there should still be no more than one stallion and one mare in the whole colony! But it is all in a line with the general mismanagement and inefficiency. Run along, child, and don't plague me any more. It is out of the question."

Patrick reported his failure mournfully to Johnny; so far as he was concerned, the matter was closed. But Johnny shut his lips together angrily, and kept his own counsel. He was tired of this place. He wanted to see the river which everyone talked about, and he would see it. He waited until the next departure of the gang and slipped away after them, his pockets well filled with food stolen from his mother's kitchen.

It was easy enough to follow, keeping just out of sight, but just within earshot of clanking chains and occasional voices. Johnny's bare feet were as hard as the feet of the natives by now, and his body had their wiry and inexhaustible endurance. It was growing dark by the time they arrived —a mild evening at the end of August, and the twilight was full of the scent of the fluffy yellow flowers which grew thickly on the river banks. Johnny, skirting the clearing, pushed his way through the undergrowth and stood at last with his bare toes in the mud, looking up and down the broad stretch of darkening water, and feeling his heart thud with joy.

Through the trees he could see in the clearing the distant flicker of fires over which the evening meal was being cooked, and they looked so cheerful that for a moment he regretted that he had no means of making one himself, and wondered if he might be able to manage it as the natives did, with sticks. But he was too hungry to waste time trying. He walked upstream a little way to put a bend of the river between himself and the clearing. From the bank, here, the bracken swept back into the trees, a green sea, almost shoulder high; Johnny stamped himself a nest in it and sat down to eat his bit of bread and cooked fish. When he had finished he lay back contentedly with the green protecting wall about him, and stared at the sky and the moving tree-tops till he fell asleep.

*　　*　　*

Prentice had just made his last haul. It was not a large one, for there was but little to be found in the hut, now, which he needed. The only thing which had made him return once more was the hope that he might find ammunition for his muskets; again disappointed in this, he had satisfied himself with a few bowls and platters, a cooking kettle, a new tinderbox, a clasp knife, and another large pail.

Safely back by mid-afternoon at his camp across the river, he had hidden his belongings behind some bushes at the foot of an overhanging rock, and decided to find something with which to supplement the food he had brought with him. A fish, he reflected, would do very well, and with one of Cunnembeillee's lines in his hand he set out for a deep pool about a mile up the river, where fish were always plentiful. But before he had gone half the distance, he fell in with a group of natives—three men and two women of the Boorooberongal, cooking a duck and a couple of large birds on their fire of glowing embers. They greeted him civilly with words learned from him and from other visitors to their river!

"Goo' day."

He grunted a response, and seated himself, uninvited, at their fire. They were not affronted by what would have been, in one of their own race, an act of gross discourtesy, for they had grown used to him and his ways by now, and even regarded him, by virtue of his marriage to Cunnembeillee, as a kind of relation.

A generous portion of the duck was instantly offered and accepted. Congratulating himself upon having thus solved the problem of supper without exerting himself, Prentice settled himself with his back against a tree to eat in comfort. He was soon aware that the natives were alert, even a little nervous. They spoke rapidly, and he heard them mention often the name of Gheeger-Gheeger, the cold west wind which blew from the mountains. He knew that there was some absurd story which they believed about this wind; Cunnembeillee had often tried to explain to him. It was supposed to live, or to be shut up in a hollow log, from which it sometimes escaped, to come roaring down over the plains, with the bite of snow in it. The log, so he had gathered, was supposed to be rotting away, and the natives lived in dread of the day when it would no longer restrain the violent Gheeger-Gheeger, who would then rage about the earth forever, destroying all living things.

Tearing the meat from a bone with his teeth, he watched the natives with faintly contemptuous curiosity. They talked rapidly and excitedly among themselves, pointing up at the sky, and making gestures towards the west. Questioning them, he was told that there was a great rain somewhere. He looked up at the sky. There were a few clouds, but they were high and thin, and there was no wind. He asked:

"Rain come?"

They nodded emphatically. He shrugged his shoulders.

"Rain come—all right. Rain good. Eh? Good?"

They broke into a clamour of denial. They pointed towards the river, and made long, sweeping gestures with their arms which he understood to represent the rushing of water. They said, laboriously:

"Water. Water go too much along. Big water."

They pointed behind them to where, against the trunks of trees, piled driftwood indicated the level of previous floods, and upward to the higher branches, nodding urgently, and saying: "Big water. Too much."

Prentice stared, looked round him at the quiet evening, belched, and scrambled to his feet, having finished his meal. He stood hesitating for a moment, scratching his head and looking doubtfully down at his dark companions. Was there anything in this tale of a flood? Did they mean that there was a flood coming, or were they only working themselves to a frenzy of excitement as they sometimes did, over something which had happened a hundred years ago? He was half-inclined to make upstream at once, to assure himself that his cattle, his crops, his son, and his woman were not in any danger; he put them in that order in his thoughts.

Then he looked at the calm sky again, and the clear evening sunlight, and grunted impatiently. His stolen hoard, he knew, would be safe from any flood, for he had made his camp well up the hillside; what drew him back to it was not the fear of losing it, but a desire so strong that it was almost a craving, to witness, just once more, the fury and the discomfiture of the tall gentleman when he discovered that his hut had been robbed again. He looked forward to this luxury of vindictiveness with an almost painful eagerness, for he had seen his whole life since his escape as a triumph over "them"—a triumph only marred by the fact that, in foiling them, he could not himself witness them being foiled.

He had noticed that it was the almost invariable custom of the tall gentleman to arrive alone, or with one or two of the officers from the settlement, upon the morning after the arrival of the convicts and their overseer. He would spend the day inspecting the work of the previous week and giving directions for the week to come, and depart again for Parramatta the following morning.

By now, Prentice thought, the convicts would have arrived, but he was not interested in their reactions to his thefts. He gave his hosts a cursory farewell, and walked back, keeping well up the hill among the timber, and, as he approached the bend which hid his own camp from the clearing, going cautiously and silently, for he had noticed how clearly sounds and voices carried across the river.

Tonight he was disinclined for sleep. He made himself a small fire, close beneath the overhang of a large outcrop of rock which intervened between it and the direction in which the clearing lay, and sat before it for a long time with his head bent and his hands hanging over his knees, thinking.

This was the end of one chapter in his freedom. Tomorrow another would begin. Already everything movable had been transferred to the new hut; tomorrow there would be nothing more to do than to set fire to the old one, and leave it. Within a year or two no trace of his habitation would remain which might not be attributed to natives by a white explorer. Now the little hidden gully in the hills above Burragorang was his refuge, his home—even, if necessary, his fortress. With the help of Milbooroo and a couple of other natives, a bull, three cows, and two calves had been driven there, and left grazing contentedly beside the creek. Cunnembeillee, leaving Bill with one of the native women, had twice made the journey with him, her shoulders bent beneath her load. The first time, as they approached the narrow, rocky gorge which formed a natural gateway to the little valley, and through which its creek emerged, Prentice had discovered in himself a strange, almost boyish eagerness for her approval. He was proud of his hut, and he wanted her to admire it; he had watched her from the corner of his eye as it came into view.

Now, seated in front of the red glow of his dying fire, he found himself remembering those moments. As she stepped out of the water—for it was necessary to wade for a hundred yards in the shallow creek where it ran through the gorge—she had looked up and seen the hut, and the yards, and the dug earth, and the grazing cattle, and she had paused for a second or two, staring, pushing her tangle of dark hair back from her eyes. It was not pleasure which Prentice had read in them, or admiration, or even surprise, but a sadness, a resignation, which had stabbed his heart with a sudden shock of pain. It was the first time he had ever sought any other contact with her than the physical contact of desire, and at the rebuff the eagerness had died out of him, leaving him sullen and angry. But in the same second when his eyes, retreating instinctively from the sight which had hurt him, left her face, hers turned to him; when he looked at her again, coldly, to order her forward, he found a different look in them. She rarely smiled at him. Quieter, more serious than most of her race, her laughter was seldom heard except among the women and children of her people. Seeing her smile now, Prentice had realised that it was a response to his own fleeting moment of emotion, and he was conscious of some spiritual goodness, kindliness, integrity in her which confronted him with an invitation—almost an appeal. "Good," she had said, nodding towards the hut, and smiling at him. He had felt his long dormant perceptiveness waken as if in answer to that summons from her. Because she had looked into his mind, he found himself able for a strange second or two to look into hers, and ever since, at intervals, he had come back in his thoughts to what he had found there, turning it over and over, wondering, doubting, as one might turn a bright stone, uncertain of its value.

He could not remember when anyone had had an affection for him before. He supposed that his mother had, but if so it had left him no memory that he might compare with this new possession. There had been nothing between himself and Ellen but an intermittent excitement of the senses. He had felt only irritation and resentment for Johnny—a speechless, sullen child who had learned early to dodge from an upraised hand. The thought of Johnny brought him to Bill, and he found himself remembering the hug of fat arms about his legs, the drumming of small heels against his chest, the clutch of fearless hands in his beard, and felt his thoughts thrust forward as if by an inner compulsion into a future which must be made and shaped for Billalong.

Even now his mind turned with hesitation to a future. Into that realm he could not yet venture without a kind of uneasy diffidence, and in it he could walk only with a halting and uncertain step. Not his emotions, but his still anger-driven brain asserted his right to wander there, and he trod the pleasant paths of hope as awkwardly as once, long ago in childhood, he had trodden the velvety lawn of a great house, bearing a message to the Squire.

Staring into the embers he grew drowsy at last. His nodding head lifted with a jerk, and he yawned, and glanced at the sky, where a few thin, high clouds raced across the stars, hardly dimming them as they passed. He dragged a couple of large logs on to the fire, rolled himself in his blanket, and lay down with his feet to the flames.

He slept fitfully, and wakened towards dawn to a sound of wind in the tree-tops. He sat up, blinking, and looked at his fire. The wind had lifted and swirled the grey ash over him as he slept; his blanket, his beard, his face, were all covered with it. He stood up and shook it away from him, and brushed it from his body. A few red sparks survived beneath a fragment of black log, so he gathered twigs and sticks and fed them till they burst into a flame. The sky, he noticed, was overcast now, but the wind was from the west, and he had noticed that the worst wet weather usually blew from the southeast. He glanced above him at the rock roof; there was shelter here if it should be needed. This, he thought, would be no more than a passing storm. He threw another log in his fire, and slept again.

* * *

Towards morning, Johnny felt cold and sat up, hugging himself and shivering. For a moment he was lonely and thought of Patrick, wishing that he had come, too. Then he forgot his cold, forgot his loneliness, scrambled to his feet and peered eagerly through the trees. On the other side of the river, well up the hillside, there was the glimmer of a fire. Natives! In the morning, he decided, when it was light enough to see, he would find some way to get across, and he would go and find them, and stay with them for always and not go back to Parramatta at all. Hugging his knees with his arms he sat down again watching the red glow, comforted because it was the fire of friends who would welcome him, the symbol of the security of home.

As soon as the first pale daylight showed him the shapes of the trees, he emerged cautiously from his bracken bed and set off up the river to find a crossing place. He hurried for he was really cold now, and there was a nip in the wind which was tossing the tree-tops above him. He walked and walked, but still the water stretched deep and unbroken, from bank to bank. It struck him that the stream looked less clear than it had on the previous evening, and also that it was flowing faster, but he supposed that in the dusk his eyes had deceived him. There was not much flat ground beside it now, and from time to time Johnny found himself forced up on to the hillside, scrambling among logs and boulders, and pushing his way through dense scrub. The river was narrower here than it was further down, but he could see no way of crossing it. He had almost given up hope when he saw a place where, on the opposite bank, a huge tree had fallen into the river. Its trunk was partly submerged, but its branches stuck up into the air, and on his own side a long, rocky spit of land ran out to meet it, leaving a gap of not more than ten to fifteen yards of water to be crossed.

Johnny hesitated. He could swim a little—that was one of the things he had learned from the black children in their camp—but so far he had done his rather inexpert dog-paddling well within his depth, or with groups of far from inexpert children. Moreover, though he was warm himself now from walking, the wind was bleak, and the water looked cold and uninviting. He walked out along the spit of land and stood on the end of it, measuring the distance with his eye, and slapping his body with his thin arms to keep warm. It was the sudden realisation of hunger which made up his mind for him. He had no food left but a small piece of bread, and he ate that hastily, thinking of the hearty welcome and the good, half-raw meat which he would find when he had swum that narrow but terrifying stretch of water.

He clambered down the rock till he stood submerged to his knees, and with a sudden, reckless courage, plunged forward.

What was the matter? In terror he realised that it was not so easy here as in the harbour water. His chin would not stay up, and he struggled madly, swallowing large mouthfuls, and gasping for breath, but the kicking of his legs did carry him forward, and the tree was undoubtedly nearer than it had been. He was moving across, but he was also moving down; the current was slow, but he had not thought of making allowance for it, and he saw with despair that he was being borne past the nearest branch, whose dying leaves fluttered and rustled not more than half a dozen yards beyond his reach.

Suddenly his foot touched something under the water, and then his hand, touching it, too, on a higher level, instinctively clutched and held. It was another branch, invisible beneath the water, and, slowly feeling his way with hands and feet, he dragged himself by it closer and closer to the trunk. When he reached it, he was too exhausted, and too terrified, to go on for a while, but huddled there with both arms clasped tightly round a branch, shivering with cold and sobbing with the reaction from his fear.

It began to rain. Johnny did not take much notice of it at first; he could get no wetter than he already was, and for the moment he could not bring himself to relax his frantic grip upon the large and pleasantly solid feeling branch to which he had anchored himself. But after a time he began to grow so cold that he remembered the fire again, and so lonely and unhappy that his thoughts turned longingly to the friendly black people who would most certainly dry him, and feed him, and restore to him his shattered confidence. So he began to move with infinite caution along the trunk, sometimes on his feet, holding on to the branches, sometimes on his hands and knees, and once, where there was a long stretch without any branches at all, wriggling on his stomach like a snake. Near the shore the trunk was so big that he could walk on it as easily as on a path, and by the time he jumped down from it to the ground he had forgotten everything except the necessity for finding the natives who had made the fire. On this side of the river the bank was flat, open, and grassy, so he set off at a run, suddenly afraid that they might have chosen this very morning to move to another camp. It was raining harder and harder; the water and the trees were dimmed by it, and the rocks shone wetly, and little streams and tiny waterfalls splashed down from the hillside and ran into the river.

*   *   *

On the bare earth floor in the middle of the old hut Billalong sat playing with the once scarlet coat which his father had taken from the body of the dead soldier over three years ago. It had been his toy for so long now that little of its resplendency remained. Its colour had been buried beneath accretions of dirt and grease and charcoal, and it was so tattered that it was by now hardly recognisable as a coat at all. Its buttons only Cunnembeillee had refused to surrender to Billalong's ardently destructive fingers; upon a string spun by her own fingers from her own hair they hung about her neck, and she never passed a still pool without pausing to admire them.

She stood in the doorway now, fingering them and staring round the denuded hut. Nothing had been left in it—nothing at all. Outside, the ground once so laboriously cultivated and now for many months neglected, was overgrown with weeds and grass. All the winter, instead of bringing in new firewood, Prentice had been burning the posts and rails of his cattle yard. Before they left, she knew, he would set fire to this hut which he had built, and no trace of him would remain where he had lived and toiled so long.

At present he was down the river, taking a final look at the new camp which the white men were establishing in the towri of her own tribe. She could not understand why, when he feared and hated them so much, he did not keep away from them. If he had taken his weapon and gone off to fight with them she would have found it comprehensible. If he had slain them from ambush, as he surely could have done with his fire-breathing weapon, she would not have wondered. When he came back laden with things which he had stolen from them she understood. But to go, as he so often did, merely to watch them fell trees and burn branches, seemed to her irresponsible and absurd.

She knew that this was the last time. He had said that when he returned, in a few days, she must be ready to depart with him for the new hut, so far away, so unfamiliar, so lonely. But she had made up her mind that she would not go until she had been back to her own towri to see her mother and her family, and to show Bill to his relations. She had tried to tell her husband this, but, as so often happened, she was not sure if he had understood her or not. He had a way of looking at her from beneath his frowning brows which suggested that he was trying to follow her meaning, but often it seemed in the end that he had not been listening at all. It made no difference. She had decided to go. Obedience to one's husband was no doubt desirable up to a point, but obedience to natural law and tribal custom was more important still. Cunnembeillee was a far less timorous person than she had been three years ago. The status of married woman had begun a development of self-confidence in her, which had been given fresh impetus by motherhood, and reached a peak only lately when, going with her husband to visit his new hut, she had read in his eyes that he desired her approval and valued her commendation.

She was very willing to give him both. He, also, had developed. From being a tyrant he had become, she acknowledged, a good husband. As a provider, he was unorthodox, but successful. As a lover he was satisfactory. As a father—but here she frowned. He was indulgent—sometimes even affectionate—but he did not seem to understand that he had duties to perform. So far, indeed, Bill's training had been in her hands, but even as early as this his father should have shown some signs of teaching him the rudiments of tracking and bush lore. The fact was, and it must be admitted, that he knew very little of such matters himself. Milbooroo, shaking his head gravely, had told her something of his surprising ignorance. And so there had arisen in Cunnembeillee's mind disturbing thoughts of the future. In only a few years, Bill's real education must begin, and who was to teach him if his father could not, and his mother's brothers were far away? He must learn to handle his little spears and shield, he must learn to hunt, he must learn to distinguish the call of one bird from that of another, and to know the tracks of different animals. And later, when the time came for him to take part in those rites and ceremonies which no woman may witness, how would he fare with so strange a father who knew nothing of the mysteries from which alone his inner life could derive stability and enrichment?

Nothing in her association with the white man had disturbed Cunnembeillee so much as his mysterious detachment. He was the first human being she had ever known who was isolated—a solitary individual, existing, incomprehensibly, without background or relations. Even his single name, An-droo, told her nothing, whereas, among her own people, a man's names were his testimonial, his letter of introduction, and his genealogical tree, all in one. Among them, relationship was the very essence of the social order. Her vocabulary was rich in names for the different kinds and degrees of kinship, and implicit in every name were functions and responsibilities and taboos, so that from birth one was secure, embedded in the pattern of tribal organisation, one's place ready-made, one's guardians appointed, one's duties clearly defined.

She was profoundly uneasy in her fear that her child might be deprived of this rich and reassuring background. Father's relations he had none; and mother's relations were, so far, denied to him. No longer, she was determined, should they be denied. Her brothers should see him. He should be given, even if only for a little while, now and then, his rightful place as a member of his mother's tribe.

She picked him up, kicking and protesting, and slung him on to her back. Coming out into the bright sunshine she gathered up her fire sticks, her bundle of 'possum skins and her coolamon of food, and then glanced up at the sky, noticing the high white clouds scudding across its deep and brilliant blue. She turned her face northward and set off briskly along the river, while Billalong, resigned, sucked one of the buttons of her necklace, and fell asleep.

*　*　*

That night she camped beneath an overhanging rock, for it seemed to her that there was a smell of rain in the air. Early the next morning the sound of it, and a spatter of drops on her foot, roused her, and she sat up, peering sleepily out at the dripping trees. Disturbed by her movement, Billalong wakened and wailed with hunger, so she gathered him into her arms and gave him her breast, huddling as far back as she could into her shelter, and peering between the trees at what was visible of the river. Its clear green was streaked with yellow, and she knew what that meant. Far away up in the mountains there had been a great rain, and its waters were pouring down the creeks of a hundred gullies and gorges, to join this great river which would carry them away into the sea. She yawned and moved Billalong to the other breast. When his hunger was satisfied they would go on, for there was a small creek, a tributary of the river, to be crossed just before one came into her own towri, and, though normally but a few steps, never more than knee-deep, were needed to cross it, she knew that in such weather as this an hour or two might make it difficult.

The rain pelted down steadily, and the promise of spring which she had welcomed only a week or so ago, was denied now by a last late assault of winter. Billalong whimpered as they emerged from their shelter, but his mother flung the 'possum skins over him, head and all, like a tent, and ignored his complaints. By the middle of the day at least she would be home again; long before nightfall she would have found her tribe.

As she walked she kept her eye on the river. It was flowing faster, and it had grown perceptibly broader. She was not at all disturbed by it, for she had only to keep well up the hillside to be safe. She walked fast and lightly, warmed by exercise, cheered by the thought of the welcome which awaited her, eager for the vociferous admiration with which Billalong's relations would be sure to greet him. She kept up a little crooning song of contentment as she walked, and Billalong surfeited, and lulled by the sound, drowsed again with his cheek against her neck.

* * *

By the time the rain began Prentice had finished his meagre breakfast, and was busy undoing his key from the loop of white man's string upon which he had previously worn it, and rethreading it, for greater security, upon a thong of dried kangaroo hide. He looked at the downpour with annoyance, but as he moved to mend his fire a glimpse of the river brought him to his feet in alarm, and out into the open where he could get a better view. He dropped his key on the ground, and clambered a little way down the hillside to where, from a flat rock, a stretch of the river was visible. There was no doubt at all that it had risen considerably in the night; it was flowing fast, and its surface was littered with the sticks and branches and logs which it had swept from its banks. For a moment he stood hesitating, almost inclined to gather his belongings together and set out for home at once. But the thought of the clearing held him. Could the river rise high enough to submerge it? High enough to destroy the store-hut? He hardly dared to hope so, but he was not going to miss even the slenderest chance of seeing so delectable an event. If the flood were, indeed, to be a great flood, who knew but that it might discourage settlement on the river altogether for a time?

He clambered up the hill again and pushed all his belongings out of sight beneath the rock where they would keep dry. The key, forgotten in his excitement, lay where he had dropped it on the floor of his shelter.

Less than half an hour brought him to the spot from which he was accustomed to watch his enemies. Hidden in the dense scrub he lay, heedless of the rain, and looked down with malevolent eagerness across the brownish water to the clearing. The tall gentleman, he thought, with grudging hostility, had chosen his spot well. The banks were high, and the ground rose from them in a steady incline. The hut, half way up the slope, looked as though no flood could ever reach it. The tall gentleman himself evidently thought so. He was standing near the bank with the overseer, watching the river, and Prentice could observe no sign in him of disturbance or alarm. The convicts, he noticed, grimly, were still working, despite the pouring rain, but as they dragged the sodden branches of trees across the ground to add them to the accumulating piles, they paused now and then to stare at the yellow stream, and point, and talk furtively among themselves.

Prentice thought of the natives he had seen last night. These people knew; they had means of knowing. They talked mysteriously to other tribes over long distances, making signals with the smoke of their fires. They had said that it would be a "big water." They had pointed high up into the branches of the trees. Prentice felt a pang of uneasiness thinking of his cattle, but he stilled it with reassurance. They would get up into the hills. Milbooroo was there; he would not let any harm befall them. Nor did it matter, now, if his fields were inundated, or even if his hut was swept away. All the better, indeed! He had no further use for it, and it must be destroyed by fire if not by flood. Cunnembeillee would be safe enough. These natives knew how to look after themselves.

Reason told him that there was no need for him to go. But he knew in his heart that nothing would have made him move from this spot while a chance still remained that he might see discomfiture overtake one of "them." Lying there in the rain, watching avidly, he almost prayed.

* * *

Johnny, too, had realised that the river was rising. He was, at first, rather alarmed by it, for he had heard Mr. Mannion speaking of great floods, so he left the bank and climbed up the hillside where he felt safer, but where the walking was much more difficult. From among the trees he watched the opposite bank so that he would recognise the place where he had spent last night when he came to it, for in this way he hoped to find the fire whose light he had seen, or at least the dead ashes to which natives might return at nightfall. But as he walked, seeing nothing that looked familiar, he began to feel uneasy, and then scared. Supposing he couldn't find the natives? Supposing he couldn't get back across the river? It was quite certain that even now he could not go back the way he had come— and what if there were no other way? He began to realise how hungry he was, and yet at the thought of food a queer feeling of sickness came over him. He walked on more slowly, a forlorn sense of solitude and friendlessness creeping up to overwhelm his hope.

Presently he recognised his camp of the previous night. He could tell it by the sea of bracken, and by a big, dead tree which had fallen and got caught in a fork of another tree. The clearing, then, must be just round the next bend of the river—and somewhere quite close to where he now stood the natives must have made that fire which he had seen shining so invitingly through the trees. But as he moved on, hesitating and obscurely afraid, he found that he was walking downhill, and saw with a sinking heart that there was another creek just below him, a swiftly rushing creek, flowing down at right angles to join the river.

He tried to tell himself that it was quite narrow, and that he could wade it easily, but the truth was that the thought of water now terrified him beyond any control of reason or determination. If it had been merely up to his ankles he would have forded it reluctantly, but it would be well above his waist. He began to pull nervously at a little shrub beside him, stripping the leaves from the twigs, fighting down a desire to call aloud for help. He had grown chilled again with his slower walking, and the sick feeling ran in little gooseflesh waves over his body. It was years, now, since he had asked help of anybody; the stubbornness which he had in- herited from his long-forgotten father kept his lips shut, and the unchild- like faculty for weighing a situation which his hard and precarious life had developed, warned him that a cry, in any case, would go unheard. He made his way down to the creek, and began to walk slowly up alongside it, his face pinched and sallow, his legs wavering with fatigue. He felt so sick and cold and unhappy that when, ten minutes later, he came upon a natural crossing of boulders where no more than an easy jump or two was needed, he felt no elation. Standing at last upon the other side, he began plodding up the hill almost mechanically, thinking of nothing but how bad he felt inside, and how strange it was not to be able to tell if you were hot or cold.

Then, in the midst of all the grey wetness, the silver-green leaves, streaming with rain, the grey-brown, sodden earth, the dark rocks, spilling little waterfalls upon the ground, he saw a point of glowing, vermilion light. He stared at it hazily, a tremble of excitement added to his chilled shivering. This was the fire he had seen last night—he had found it! He had hoped that there would be natives beside it, and there were not, but that seemed unimportant now. Fire meant warmth; in a moment he was beside it, crouching over it, holding his hands down to the few glowing embers which remained, and struggling with a new problem which instantly confronted him. Everything was soaking wet. How could he coax from these few remaining sparks a flame which would warm him? The fire, he saw, had been built beneath an overhanging ledge of rock, otherwise it would have been extinguished long ago, and lying about in this comparative shelter there were a few dry twigs and leaves, and a tussock of dead grass hung from a crevice in the rock a foot or two from the ground. Johnny remembered that he had seen the natives build fires in the rain with even less than this in the way of dry fuel, and, slowly, with numbed and shaking fingers he collected a handful of grass and laid it cautiously against the largest piece of glowing charcoal. When a flame burst from it he added a few tiny twigs, and then a few a little larger, and at last, having no more that were dry, began to lay small wet sticks carefully over them. They spluttered and hissed, but they burned, and as the flames mounted Johnny's shiverings subsided and he began to feel better and to look about him for signs of the natives.

There was a key lying upon the ground. It was partly hidden by a small stone, and he moved the stone away with his foot and stared in a kind of stupefaction. It was a key. He had to tell himself this over and over again, and still it made no sense. A key. Here, in the unexplored forests of New Holland, lying in the rain upon the ground, a key. Not an old key, either. A bright new key. A key threaded on a loop of hide, large enough to go round your neck . . .

What did it lock? What *could* it lock? Johnny stared about him rather vaguely, so bewildered and confused that he would not have been really surprised if a large building like Government House had suddenly sprung out of the earth before him. He got to his knees, keeping his eyes suspiciously upon the key, and reached out for it slowly as if he expected it to vanish as his hand approached it. He picked it up and turned it over in his hands. He wondered if one of the convicts from the clearing had absconded, and brought the key of the store-hut with him, but he thought that he would have heard about it if there had been an escape. He could not imagine what it was for, but his acquisitive instinct would not allow him to leave it lying there. It unlocked *something,* and, in Johnny's experience, all the good things of life lay hidden behind locked doors. He hung it round his neck and huddled himself again over his fire which was now roaring merrily. Its warmth was reflected back by the rock, and by degrees Johnny began to feel much better. The natives, he thought, hopefully, would soon return, and then he would have food. He curled up with his face to the wall, and the grateful heat of the fire on his back, and fell asleep.

* * *

Cunnembeillee, coming to the steep little gully down which the creek rushed to join the river, paused for a moment to look curiously at the blurred print of a small bare foot, and at a shrub beside it whose topmost branches had been stripped of all their leaves. That, she thought, was an odd thing to do! But the print had been too much defaced by rain to offer her the wealth of information which she might otherwise have read in it, so she only glanced and went on, for she was in a hurry to finish her journey.

She stood by the creek not twenty yards from its mouth, and chose her spot for crossing it. The water was rushing down very fast, but it would not be higher than her waist, and there was a great boulder in the middle which would steady her across the worst of it, so she wasted no further time in reconnoitering, but pulled Billalong from her shoulders and set him astride her left hip, gripping him firmly with one arm, and holding her other belongings in the same hand. With her right arm thus left free, she stepped carefully into the water and felt her way forward. The current dragged strongly, but she had accomplished many river crossings, and knew how to keep her balance. She reached the rock in half a dozen steps, and put up her hand to grip it.

Under her fingers something moved and writhed. A black snake, tempted from its winter sleep by the early warmth, had come out to bask, and, sluggish with the sudden cold, had remained undisturbed by her approach, not moving till her hand actually touched it. With a sharp exclamation of fear, Cunnembeillee snatched her hand away unhurt, but the shock had made her move her foot unwarily. It came down on the slippery moss-covered surface of a water-rounded stone, and slid from under her. The rushing water dragged her to her knees, and foamed up about Billalong's neck and shoulders. Terrified, he yelled and struggled. Foaming with the force of a cataract round the obstructing boulder, the stream dragged him from his mother's arms, and before Cunnembeillee could get to her feet again he had been borne out of her reach. She could see his wet, black head appearing and disappearing where the rapid torrent of the creek joined the slower-moving current of the river.

She plunged after him. Like all the natives she swam well and strongly, and she caught him before he was far out from the river bank, but when she tried to swim for the shore she found that she could make no headway against the current. She battled with it until exhaustion warned her to battle no longer, and she rested breathlessly, with only just enough strength left to hold Bill's head above the water, and to look about her frantically for a means of rescue. The river was full of débris, but there was nothing near enough for her to clutch. Behind her, moving down with a certain deliberate majesty, its large, bone-white branches spreading above the water, a huge dead tree was floating, turning this way and that as the eddies caught it, slowing for a moment in some backwater, and then torn free again by the current, continuing its voyage to the sea.

Cunnembeillee said, sharply, to Bill: "Be quiet! Be quiet!" He had been half-drowned when she caught him, dazed and buffeted by the water, but now he was recovering and beginning to struggle again. She, who had been so proud of his strength, was afraid of it now. His little arms were like iron, fighting her, his small, tight fists pounded her face in panic. She looked about her wildly, searching the banks for some sign of her people. Now she was in her own towri, and somewhere along the river bank they were sure to be, watching the flood and talking about it. She tried to call for help, but there was no breath left in her, and the knowledge of her isolation from her own kind bore down her will to live and her will to fight for life. Only her terror for Billalong kept her struggling, and when she looked again she saw that the tree was gaining on her, and felt a gleam of hope. She manoeuvred for a position where she might grasp a branch of it as it passed, and gave all her strength to fighting the current which was bearing her downstream. Once upon the trunk of the tree, she thought, she could rest and recover her breath, and then she could scream. Somewhere her people must be, to hear her call and answer it. Somewhere—for the first time she realised it—her husband must be . . .

But she gave no further thought to him. In this moment of crisis he seemed remote and unreal. She gathered her strength for an effort as the trunk of the tree swung past her, and reached out for a jagged branch. She would have caught it if Bill had not flung himself suddenly backward; she sobbed aloud as her finger-tips grazed its bark. A moment later another branch struck her on the back and bore her forward with it. She writhed round to face it, and now Bill's strength and panic came to her aid. His arms fastened about it instinctively, and, relieved for a second or two of his weight, she clutched it herself and hung over it, one arm about the child. Her head was swimming, and her heart thumped against the cold wet surface of the branch.

Thus she lay; she did not know where the tree was carrying her, or how fast. She did not look at the banks of the river, or at the river itself. She had no thought but to maintain her grip and to keep Bill in his position on the branch. Thus Mannion's overseer saw her as the tree came round the bend, and shouted aloud, pointing excitedly, and calling to his employer who had walked farther down to observe how fast the river was rising by watching a nearly submerged rock near the bank. Thus Prentice saw her, startled by the overseer's shout, and following the direction of his pointing finger.

A native woman! He stared, straining his eyes and wiping the rain from his face with the back of his hand. Was that a child with her? A child, little more than a baby! He felt a pang of pity, and wondered if his countrymen on the opposite side would attempt a rescue.

The tall gentleman had come running, and the convicts, leaving their work, had shambled down to the bank, and now stood staring with detached curiosity. The overseer, Prentice noticed, was sent running up to the hut, from which he returned with a large coil of rope over his arm. Prentice gave a brief and sceptical grunt. It was a chance, he thought, but a slender one, and it must succeed the first time or not at all. The noose might or might not catch over a branch; if it did, no doubt the whole gang could hold the tree—perhaps even pull it to the bank. The fellow knew, at all events, how to handle a rope. Prentice allowed him a sour moment of admiration as he watched the coils fly out and the loop reach for the nearest upright branch. But it fell short. He tried again, too hurriedly, for the tree was already past him, and, failing, shrugged his shoulders and slowly dragged the rope ashore.

Now, Prentice noticed, the current was carrying the tree towards his own side of the river, and he saw the woman, who had watched the attempted rescue in a curious stillness and silence, lift her head, and heard her call out something. In the same instant, as the swinging of the tree gave him a clearer view of her, he noticed with a shock which made his breath stop and the hairs rise on his body, that she had a necklace round her neck—a necklace of large, round objects—a necklace of buttons . . . Cunnembeillee—and Bill . . .

He did not move. His eyes narrowed and became wary. His instinct for self-preservation held him motionless, but his mind raced. He spent no time in wondering how she came to be there—there she was. What was to happen? It was obvious that there was no white man on the opposite bank who felt himself called upon to risk his life for a negligible black woman and her child. He kept very still, his eyes restless, his hands restless, his heart thumping with a slow, breath-taking violence.

Something was happening in the river. It was flowing so fast now that there were little crested waves on it, and there was a faint, roaring noise in the distance. Leaning forward, gripping the branches of his shrubs, Prentice saw that the tree was swinging inward towards the bank faster than ever now, and relief swept over him. The side here was steep and rocky, unlike the earth bank of the opposite shore, and it looked as if one of the larger branches would scrape it, and perhaps catch behind one of many jutting boulders. Cunnembeillee, he could see, was edging along her branch towards the trunk, dragging and lifting Bill as she went, trying to reach a spot as near as possible to the shore. Every time she moved the child she had to pry his hands loose. Prentice could hear his protesting yells of terror, and see him struggle and kick in her thin straining arms.

He looked uneasily up the river. There must have been a freshet, he thought, somewhere higher up, for the rapidity of the current had increased suddenly, and the faint roar he had heard was growing louder. If it had not been for that sudden quickening, he realised, with angry desperation, she would have been safe by now, for, though a branch had caught and anchored as he had hoped, it was a precarious anchorage, perpetually threatened by the weight of the trunk, swinging downstream, and tugging at it in the ever-increasing fury of the current.

Cunnembeillee had worked herself along until she was within a few yards of the rock behind which the caught branch swayed and dragged, but now she was still again, hanging over the trunk limply, her forehead resting on it, one arm still clutching Billalong. Prentice, craning his head, peered at her anxiously, and then at the rocks. "Go on!" he urged her, inwardly, "Go on!" He was feverishly impatient with her for succumbing to fatigue or despair when the way of escape was so close. He craned his head to peer anxiously at the rocks. They were perpendicular certainly, but they stood not more than six feet out of the water, and they were sandstone, which meant that their surfaces would be rough, scored and ridged with crevices and narrow ledges, normally as good as a staircase to Cunnembeillee's strong fingers and agile feet. What was the matter with her? These natives! He struck his fist against the ground in exasperation. They had a way of submitting suddenly to death; he had seen it happen more than once. They would fight, but not quite till the last moment—not quite to the final breath in which the more stubborn resistance of the white man sometimes won him victory. Was she submitting now? Had she despaired? Or was she injured? Or just too tired?

He realised suddenly that to climb the rocks alone would be a very different matter from climbing them with a heavy, kicking child in her arms. Perhaps she was only resting, gathering her strength for that difficult attempt. But at any moment the branch might pull free—or break . . .

His stillness became a rigid immobility, like the immobility of death. The eyes of his body never moved from the woman and child in the river, but the eyes of his mind were looking inward, watching, aghast, the frenzy of his first spiritual conflict. *Now,* something had said to him—as clearly and peremptorily as any order he had ever heard barked by a gaoler or an overseer—*you must decide.* And instantly there had arisen in him a frantic clamour of panic-stricken protest. Not only life, it shouted at him was endangered here, but freedom. At the first sight of him, inevitably betrayed by his flaming hair and beard, muskets would crack from across the river. An escaped convict! The robber of the hut! An outlaw, an enemy of that sacred, musket-guarded civilisation! At this distance, in the rain, they might well miss their target, but down by the river his chance would be slighter. Nevertheless, it was not fear of death which held him, but the threat of a subtler peril. The instinct for concealment, for secrecy, which had grown stronger through every day of his hardly won and jealously guarded liberty, now recoiled from exposure as flesh recoils from white-hot metal. Remember, this instinct warned him, the struggles and the privations and the dogged, unrelenting toil with which you have built your freedom; remember the risks you have taken to buttress and preserve it; remember the dread of recapture which has wakened you at night, starting up at a sound with sweat on your forehead, and your hand reaching out for your musket! Remember, too, that it has opened up strange paths of thought, and stranger paths of hope. Remember that there have been moments when you have felt yourself trembling on the verge of a discovery—discovery of yourself, Andrew Prentice, a man, a human being, full of mysterious strength, not only physical. Remember your hut in the hills, your cattle, your possessions, the visible signs of that inner worth which rejected slavery, defied captivity, built life here in a land which had offered only death. Be still, be still, it said; there are other women—and what is a child . . .

* * *

Cunnembeillee had roused herself again; she was not trying to move any more, but she was staring about her, first at one bank and then at the other. Several times her gaze seemed to sweep over the very spot where Prentice lay hidden, and sweat broke out anew on his forehead and ran down his face with the rain. And then, suddenly, she flung her head back, and, with a wild note of despair, the summoning call of her people shrilled out faintly above the noise of the river and the rain:

"Coo—ee—ee—ee!" (Come! Come to me!)

There rose in Prentice's throat and burst from his lips an answering yell. It was full of defiance, and a strange exultation. He leapt from his hiding place and began to scramble down the hill, and when he heard cries of astonishment from the men on the opposite bank he shouted answers at them with a kind of delirious triumph, not knowing what his words were, but full of an indescribable sense of conquest, a fierce and reckless joy. Now let them see, he thought, and let them shoot! Not until I chose did they find me, and not their cleverness discovered me, but my own free action! They have done me great wrong in the past, but this final wrong they shall not do to me—that for fear of them I should lie in hiding while my woman and my child drown before my eyes!

He heard the sharp report of a musket, and laughed, shouting an obscene taunt as he plunged on down the hill. He scrambled out on the rock and was suddenly quiet, kneeling on its edge and looking down into Cunnembeillee's dark, exhausted eyes. There were no more shots from the opposite bank. He climbed down the rock face into the water, feeling carefully for toeholds, and stood at last on a submerged ledge, with the water lapping about his chest. Holding on to the rock with one hand, he reached the other out towards her, and said, gently:

"Give me Bill."

He did not know whether it was pain or joy which stabbed him when he saw how willingly the child released his hold upon the branch this time, how eagerly his arms went out towards his father's outstretched hand. Cunnembeillee, edging nearer and nearer, pushed him at last within its grasp, and Prentice, releasing his hold upon the rock and bending forward precariously, swung the child to his shoulders where he clung like a 'possum.

The water dragged at the tree trunk, the branch swayed and scraped, Cunnembeillee let go, tried to swim, and then clutched again, wildly, at her support. She said, weakly: "Too much—tired." Prentice swore under his breath, trying to grab the branch. Suddenly the whole tree shifted, and the trunk swung in closer to the rock, so that he was able to fling one arm over it and grasp Cunnembeillee's hand. But for the moment he did no more than hold it, staring up the river with startled attention. What *was* that noise? He looked back at her, and said, sharply:

"Come quick!"

She struggled clumsily under the trunk and came up beside him, her teeth chattering and her eyes half-closed. Now that the tree was no longer needed he tried to push it away, but it had settled firmly, and would not move. She began to clamber up the rock beside him, and he heard her moan: "Tired, too much tired." He dragged Bill from his shoulder, and held him in one arm, and with the other made a step for her on the sheer side of the rock. He said, urgently:

"Put your foot there—now on my shoulder—now on my head. Quick!" He braced himself to take her momentary weight, and as it came on to his shoulder he saw a line of water coming down the river. It was unlike a wave, for it sloped backward, and it wore its line of foam not as a crest, but as a thin white streak, pushed ahead of it at its foot; behind it the whole river seemed to advance at a higher level, and it stretched quite solid and unbroken from bank to bank. And he saw a huge log being borne along in front of it, and coming straight towards the tree. He caught his breath, and Bill cried out in pain at the sudden tightening of his grip.

Cunnembeillee was up. She was lying flat on her stomach and reaching down for Bill. Prentice tried to turn, but the trunk was so close against him now that he could not. He lifted the child high above his head and felt him taken by his mother's hands, but all the time his eyes were on the log and the advancing wall of water. He tried to push the trunk away from his chest so that he could turn, but all his strength was nothing against the pressure of the current. He felt desperately behind him on the rock for handholds by which he could hoist himself up without turning; he heard Cunnembeillee scream, he heard a sound of shouting from the opposite bank, and he thought vaguely that the great black log which was bearing down on him was just like one which had lain for years on the bank where he went to fetch his water. He thought how strange it was that it should wear so friendly and familiar an appearance.

Then it struck the tree trunk, driving it against his chest, and his ribs splintered like eggshell. The wave went past with a roaring sound, wrenching the trunk free, and Prentice's body sagged down into the water; his red hair showed for a moment on the surface like a patch of russet seaweed, and then vanished.

* * *

Cunnembeillee's wild outcry came only faintly across the roaring of the river to the white men watching on the other bank, for they had retreated as the water began scouring out the earth bank on which they stood; now, across the ever-widening brown torrent, and through the grey veil of pelting rain, she was nothing but a dark heap lying prostrate on a rock, with another smaller heap beside her.

Mr. Mannion turned sharply away and walked up to the shelter of the hut, and his overseer watched him curiously as he went. He wondered if his master knew that the one shot he had fired, under orders, had been purposely wide of the mark. He wondered whether he would have fired again if another command had come. He wondered why it had not come, and remembered a queer, sick expression on Mannion's face as he had turned away. He glanced at the convicts rather furtively, and found his look returned. Some chord of memory had been touched by the sight of the man's flaming hair and beard, and hearing one of the convicts mutter to another the name "Prentice," he remembered. Prentice! A surly and unpopular rogue! Four years! It was possible, then, to escape and live! Possible to escape—and to give up life, give up a hard-won freedom . . . For a moment there was an interchange of thought and emotion between them all. For a moment the barriers of caste which held them apart went down, and without a word spoken a spark of unity woke, flickered, flamed, and died again.

* * *

Cunnembeillee dragged herself to her feet with Bill in her arms. Her man, the red-headed one, was dead, but her son lived, and must be tended. She looked down at him, dully. His soaked hair was dragged back from his forehead, and his face looked puckered, sunken, old. His eyes were closed, and his body twitched and shivered in her arms. She began to clamber painfully, and very slowly, up the slope, her own eyes dark and staring, her own body limp with fatigue and the shock of her grief. If she could meet with none of her own people quite soon, she thought rather hopelessly, she must find shelter and make a fire, and this would be a long, laborious process, for she had lost her fire sticks; the preparation of others, and the patient coaxing of a flame from them would be no simple matter in this drenched and streaming world. Her knowledge of the country guided her almost without conscious thought, and her senses, trained to the keenest perception, functioned automatically. When she halted suddenly, with lifted head, it was as an animal halts, to ratify with his brain an impression faithfully registered by his nostrils or his ears. Cunnembeillee could smell smoke.

She looked about her, her nostrils wide to recover that fleeting fragrance of burning wood and leaves. She found it again, and felt her heartbeats quicken. Now she could see it, too. It was a wraith of smoke, a thin, blue, curling wisp drifting from between the trees not a hundred yards up the hill. She called, her voice cracked and feeble, and began to toil breathlessly up the slope. Now she could see the fire itself—a cheering sight, a joyful sight, set beneath an overhanging rock and blazing brightly with a promise of warmth and security and the blessed comfort of companionship.

She stumbled forward. There could be no one there, for her cry had gone unanswered, but those who had made the fire would return and in the meantime . . .

She stopped dead, frozen in her tracks, her eyes starting from her head, her mouth opening for a scream which was choked in her throat by terror. For the red-headed one was dead—she had seen him die—and yet there he sat, returned in the shape of a child, his red hair, his dark eyes, his white skin—and round his neck, the key!

She turned to run, but her knees gave way beneath her. She huddled on the ground in utter despair, staring fearfully over her shoulder at the apparition, and Johnny, who had been startled awake by her cry, got up stiffly and moved towards her. He could not imagine why she was so frightened. He felt rather annoyed about it. He had been frightened himself, and he had wanted to find the black people so that he could be fed and reassured and cared for; it was no part of his plan that they should be afraid of him. He bent over the cowering woman, and asked, crossly:

"What's the matter?"

She stared up at him fearfully, covering Billalong's body with her own. Johnny felt tears of rage and hunger and disappointment welling in his eyes. He was furious that instead of the friendly, loquacious, cheerful group which he had expected, he should be visited by this stupid, useless woman. He collected his memories, and asked her, angrily:

"Waw murri?"

Her eyes flickered over him uncertainly. This was not the tongue of her own tribe, but she knew it. Where were the men? She looked about vaguely, and shook her head.

It was too much. All Johnny's courage deserted him; all the stubborn self-reliance and initiative which had armed him in his unequal fight against life were overwhelmed by his child's sense of defencelessness in a hostile world. His tears overflowed; he stumbled back to the fire and sat down beside it with his head on his updrawn knees and his arms clasped over it, and wept aloud.

Cunnembeillee, her body still shaken by shiverings which were half from cold and half from fear, stared at him over her shoulder, her mind a dark maze of wonder and confusion. It was true, she was thinking, that one existed as a spirit-child before birth, and that, after death, again in the shape of a child, one ascended by way of the tree-tops to the clouds. But the ways of the red-headed one had never been quite the same as the ways of her own people, and if, instead of ascending to the clouds, he should choose to remain on earth . . .

And he had a fire. . . .

She looked down at Bill, rose slowly and with halting steps edged nearer and nearer to the cheerful blaze. Johnny, lifting a face of incredible woe and appeal, clutched his hands desperately over his stomach, and wailed:

"I'm hungry!"

Hungry! Well she knew that word! Many, many times she had hastened to obey the demand which it made! It had not, indeed, been the red-headed one's habit to weep for food, but then he had not been a birrahlee, as he was now. This demonstration of a thoroughly normal human need reassured her as nothing else could have done, and awakened that impulse of eternal devotion to the practical affairs of life which dwells in every woman's breast. Hungry! Indeed, yes! She was hungry, too!

Her fears allayed by the sound of the white man's tongue, spoken as she had been accustomed to hear it, from the lips of one who was simply An-droo grown young again, she held Billalong out and said: "You take." Johnny, puzzled, found himself cradling a plump brown child in his arms; feeling it shiver, and seeing its teeth chattering with cold, he held it near the fire, and began rubbing it with his own hard, warm fingers. Cunnembeillee nodded her approval and stood erect with an effort, looking round her at the silent bush, grey, dripping, sodden and inhospitable. She saw it as a storehouse full of food, and laid her plans for finding it with the serene confidence and efficiency of a housewife setting forth to market with her basket on her arm.

When they had all fed and rested, she thought, they would find her people, and stay with them for a while as guests of her tribe. And then they would go back, she and Billalong, and the man who was, by the little mystery of death, a child again, to the place which he had made for them far away in the hills. He would open the door with his key, and they would live there in peace, as he had always said. But, in the meantime, there must be food, and only she could find it.

She was so tired that she could hardly stand, but she knew that she could not rest just yet. An-droo, she reflected, had never been good at foraging. He would pass by a good meal a hundred times and never know it was there. Without his cattle, and his fire-breathing weapon, and the strange plants which he caused to come up out of the ground, he would starve. She pushed her hair wearily out of her eyes, and looked down at Johnny's forlorn and tear-blotched face.

She said kindly:

"I go, find food. You wait."

She went, a thin, black figure, shining-wet in the rain. Johnny, nursing his half-brother and chafing the warmth back into his limbs, sat with his mouth agape in the astonishment of hearing his own tongue, and watched her go.

*　　*　　*

Collins, walking with the Governor along the now well-trodden track which led from Sydney to the Lookout on South Head, stooped to break a spray of pink blossoms from a low growing shrub at his feet. Holding it to his nostrils he said:

"I have grown to like this scent."

Phillip nodded.

"There is a wealth of new experience for the nostrils in this country. I find that a scent is something which the memory cannot hold. Only last night I tried to remember the perfume of lilac, and could not. The eye retains a memory, and so does the ear, and the tongue, and the fingers—but the nostrils can tell you only that a scent was pleasing or unpleasing—nothing more."

Collins disagreed.

"I think I can remember some scents. Roses, for instance. . . ." He half shut his eyes in an effort of memory, but the strong strange perfume of the flowers in his hand drifted between him and the elusive ghost of a fragrance which he was trying to recapture, and with a sudden gesture of impatience he flung them down, and burst into what was a change of subject only in the manner of its approach:

"You think it inexpedient, Sir, that I should return to England with you when you go?"

Phillip looked at him quickly.

"I do, Collins. I do indeed."

"I told you, I think, Sir, that my father is very ill? He is too old to survive a severe illness, and . . ."

"I know; I am deeply concerned for you. But believe me, Collins, it would be in the worst possible interest of the colony for you to leave it at present." He was silent, walking on with bent head. How much could he say? How much of his uneasiness might he voice? He turned aside from the path and seated himself stiffly on a fallen log, holding his hand to his side.

"I think we'll go no farther; I'm tired. This is one of the finest views of the harbour, I think. How blue it looks today!"

Collins was silent. He sat down on the ground with his back against the log, and clasped his hands round his updrawn knees. Phillip said abruptly:

"It's impossible. There's no one to take your place."

"Atkins?"

Phillip shook his head decisively.

"No. Later, perhaps; but at this time I am convinced that your presence here is necessary. Indeed, it is only the knowing that you will remain in your present office that relieves my anxiety at quitting the colony myself. Things are not yet as I would have hoped to see them before my departure. I don't need to tell you, Collins, what I have been at great pains to explain to Mr. Dundas—that the continual short rations have been the cause of our slow progress in building and cultivation. But it has had other ill effects—and in the future may have more . . ."

He glanced again at the Judge-Advocate, who picked up a twig and began breaking it into small pieces of exactly equal size. He knew very well what was in the Governor's mind, but caution and discretion—those qualities which had enabled him to live more or less peaceably for nearly five years in a community split by warring factions—kept him silent now. As Phillip's secretary there was little which went on in the colony which he did not know. Most of the official correspondence passed through his hands, and he remembered now the letter in which Major Grose had complained to the Governor of the "miseries" of the men under his command, and asked—almost demanded—official sanction of the measure he proposed to take to remedy them. This was that the Corps should charter the *Britannia* and send her to the Cape to bring back supplies for their own exclusive use. Phillip had been powerless to object, but his reply had been cold. "I cannot acquiesce with you in thinking that the ration served from the public stores is unwholesome; I see it daily at my own table. . . ." he had written. And he concluded with frigid finality: "I am sorry that I cannot with propriety take any official step in this business."

The atmosphere had been stormy since then, and other grievances had not been wanting. The officers clamoured for land, and Phillip was willing enough to give them this. What he was not willing to do was to withdraw convict labour from public works to assign it to the private enterprises of the officers.

"Food," the Governor said suddenly, "is the basis of all things, Captain Collins. Never until I came here and found myself faced with the problem of actual want did I fully realise how all our endeavours fail or succeed by the lack or the possession of food. And I have seen how our black friends, in a land which is not lavish in its sustenance, insure that all shall have enough by denying that any shall have too much. And I have seen how hunger breeds crime . . ."

Again Collins found himself remembering words he had penned to the Governor's dictation: "From the time the corn began to ripen to the time it was housed, the convicts were pressed by hunger, and great quantities were stolen and concealed in the woods; several convicts died from feeding on it in its crude state, when carrying the grain to the public granary. But in speaking of these people it is but just to observe that I can recollect very few crimes during the last three years but what have been committed to procure the necessaries of life."

The Governor's voice was continuing slowly:

". . . and I have thought very often that if there had been some means arrived at in our own land whereby hunger should be made unknown, there might have been fewer of these unhappy people to bring to Botany Bay. . . ."

Collins said uneasily:

"You may be right, Sir. But I must own that they have always appeared to me to be rashly improvident."

"That must be admitted. I confess I have many times been at a loss to know how to deal with them. But I have hoped . . ."

He broke off, and was silent for so long that Collins, waiting for him to continue, looked up and found him staring intently at the western hills. He prompted:

"You were saying, Sir . . ."

"I have hoped that a solution might be found here. I have been convinced that it would be found. We know nothing, as yet, of this country—nothing! Those hills will be passed someday. Who knows but there may be room for not hundreds of settlers—not thousands—but millions!" He stopped again, looking sharply at Collins' rather startled expression. "You find that notion—extravagant?"

"It is more," Collins replied carefully, "than I should have ventured to hope for myself, Sir."

Phillip made a little gesture with his hands.

"It may be that I am over-sanguine. But it is because I have seen a future for this land that I shall leave it, in its present state, with misgivings. I shall hope to return. But in the meantime, Collins, my mind will be quieter if I know that Major Grose is to have—your assistance."

Collins laid his little pile of twigs neatly on the ground.

"In that case, Sir, I shall, of course, remain."

"It is perhaps too soon to speak with such assurance of my own departure." Phillip took off his hat and laid it on his knee. "I wrote to Mr. Nepean a few days ago—a private letter—and informed him that I would wait for another ship in the hope that it would bring me a more explicit permission to return than was contained in Mr. Dundas' letter. But my health grows worse, Collins—almost hourly. If the *Atlantic* should sail without me I don't know when I might have another opportunity. If I find myself forced to leave by the *Atlantic* I shall myself press your claim for leave when I reach England." He lifted his hat and shaded his eyes with it, staring down the hill. "Who is that down there? Can you see them? A man and a woman, I think."

Collins stood up in order to see better, and reported:

"It's Bennilong, Sir, clad in a shirt. And his new wife from Botany Bay, wearing, so far as I can see, some kind of a scarf round her waist, and a handkerchief about her neck. I hear from Immerawanye that she is violently opposed to Bennilong's going with you to England."

"Bennilong," Phillip said dryly, "is not the first man to find out the inconveniences of being held in high regard by the opposite sex." He stood up and put on his hat. "The sun is getting low, Collins; it's time we retraced our steps. I shall have to go rather slowly, I'm afraid."

* * *

How hot it was! The Governor, moving restlessly about the room in which he had spent so many anxious hours, paused by his table to pour himself a glass of water, and drank it thirstily, staring out through the window at sunlight queerly darkened and thickened by the haze of distant smoke. This was good water, he thought; for many months, now, he would not taste such good water again. He sipped it more slowly, oppressed by that sense of loss and melancholy which will assail even the least imaginative of mortals upon performing an everyday action for what will probably be the last time. He felt his mind tangled in a web of chaotic and irresponsible thoughts which yet seemed to conceal, somewhere in their chaos, a firm core of revelation. He thought of the water, and of the smoke blowing in from the country between the coast and the river, where there had lately been so many disastrous fires. Fire—and water. He thought of blackened woods, dark, devastated miles of country which looked as though every leaf, every blade of grass, every living thing, had perished utterly; and he thought of how they would wake again unharmed, even stimulated, after that fierce ordeal by fire. He thought that this was a harsh country, which kept its inner tenderness concealed; a country reticent of its beauty, demanding a wakening of the heart and a new perception in the eyes of the beholder before it spread its treasures for his gaze. Even to himself, who had tried to learn, it had yielded little but a promise. He had felt greatness in it with his senses, and searched for it with his eyes; and though his eyes were not rewarded he still knew that it was there.

How long would it be, he asked himself wonderingly, before people of his race could know it as their own? As aliens they had come to it, and as aliens they would die in it. Would it admit their children? Or their children's children?

They will fight it, he thought uneasily; they will fight it in their impatience because it is not an easy land, a fruitful, kindly, responsive land like the one they have known. His eyes, staring abstractedly at the clear water in the glass, made a crystal of it in which he seemed to watch, like some ancient seer, the smoke and dust of a battle waged by generations against a land which would accept them only when, with difficulty and humility, they had learned that she was not theirs, but they were hers. He saw them, driven by their reckless greed, and by an obscure urge for conquest of so aloof and invulnerable a foe, exhausting her earth, fouling her rivers, despoiling her trees, savagely imposing upon the pattern of her native loveliness traditional forms which meant beauty in other lands. He heard them crying out to her insatiably: "Give! Give!" and was aware of her silent inviolability which would never give until they had ceased to rob.

How did one learn to know a country such as this? Not by building a squalid little England here upon the shores, and clinging to it! Like a streak of light across the cloudy confusion of his mind shot a poignant moment of regret: "If I were a younger man—not ill . . ."

He put the glass on the table and sat down wearily in his chair. "If" was a word he had never cared for much. He liked to take life as it came to him, dealing with it logically, step by step, and wasting no time upon what might have been. He was not robust and young, but ill and more than middle-aged; it must be left to others to seek redemption of that promise which the land had made to him. And suddenly he found himself thinking of the red-haired convict, Andrew Prentice, who had escaped so long ago, and whose strange, heroic death had been witnessed by Mannion and his men on the banks of the Nepean. Where had he lived all these years, and how? What had he learned? Could it be that the land had had more to say to an escaped convict than to the representative of His Majesty the King?

He rested his forehead on his hand and looked down at a paper on his desk—a copy of a return made out by the surveyor-general, setting forth the lands in cultivation at this time—and he read it over idly, already with a curious feeling of detachment. Two hundred and eight acres in wheat, twenty-four in barley, over a thousand in maize. Another hundred and twenty-one laid out in vegetable gardens, and about a hundred and sixty cleared of timber . . .

Five years' work.

He rose abruptly and went across to the window. It was almost time for him to leave. Already the people were assembling near the wharf, a motley crowd of human beings over whose lives he had wielded a power which was almost absolute. Soldiers, seamen, settlers, convicts, natives. His feeling of concern and anxiety for them was so painfully acute that he fled from it, mistrustful, as he had always been, of that sharp, emotional perception which so often disturbed his more practical thoughts; and in a physical reaction to this mental retreat, he left the window hurriedly, snatching up his hat from the table as he passed.

The *Atlantic* would sail in the morning—and by tomorrow evening, he told himself brutally, he would probably be very seasick. This jibe at a failing which had never ceased to annoy and humiliate him was but another crude reminder to himself that he was very mortal clay—another repudiation of that visionary self whose persistent faith and ardour he vaguely resented, and whose light yet found its way through all his sober actions, and lit his cold, official words with vagrant gleams of warmth. He stood in the doorway and looked once more round the room, rather grimly.

"Now," he thought, "it belongs to Major Grose . . ."

* * *

He walked down to the wharf between rows of people. They cheered him, but dutifully rather than spontaneously. They were willing to concede, he thought, that he had striven to govern them justly—even to temper his justice with mercy—but that was not enough to make him loved. It had been necessary for him to be solitary, lending himself neither to quarrels, intrigues, or even to friendships, and he had never felt this solitude more keenly than he felt it now, with the whole settlement turned out to bid him farewell.

Near the wharf the New South Wales Corps was drawn up under the command of Major Grose. But even as he passed, receiving the honours of his rank, he saw that he was far from being the centre of interest, even at this climax of his task.

The centre of interest was, of course, Bennilong. He had been strutting vaingloriously in his European clothes, and wore them with an air which was in sharp contrast to Immerawanye's rather dishevelled appearance, but now he was having trouble with his wife. Gooroobarooboolo was far from being the vixen that Barangaroo had been, but she was not docile enough to stand by and see her husband desert her without a protest. She clung about his neck with an ardour and tenacity which was provoking the crowd to delighted cheers, and Bennilong to embarrassed strugglings. He could very easily have disengaged her arms, and ended her importunities with a few corrective blows about the head, but at this critical moment he dared not do that. Such a thing would anger and offend the Be-anga, who might, even at this late hour, condemn him to remain behind. So he only tugged at her hands, clasped tightly at the back of his neck, and argued with her in fierce undertones:

"Waita koa bag! Mimai yikora!"

She only clung more tightly.

"Keawaran wal bi uwa-nun!"

He repeated angrily:

"Mimai yikora! Kabo bag kanun England-ka!"

At the sound of this hated and ill-omened name she wailed aloud, but Bennilong, seeing that the Be-anga was busy shaking hands with a group of officers, and not likely to observe him at the moment, disengaged himself with a violence which sent Gooroobarooboolo staggering back into the arms of her vociferously sympathetic friends, and sprang into the boat where Immerawanye was already seated. His heart was beating fast with exertion and excitement, and he looked over his shoulder continually at the great nowee which was to bear him across the ocean. The air was clamorous with farewells, and he responded to them untiringly, waving his hat in the air, his teeth and the whites of his eyes agleam in his dark face.

Now the Be-anga was ready at last! Now he was embarking. Now the boat was pushed off from the shore, and the air was white with fluttering handkerchiefs, like the wings of seagulls whirling and swooping above some floating titbit. And he was going, he was going at last as he had always known he would, across the great sea, out of sight, far, far away where no man of his race had been before—he, Bennilong, son of Wunbula who had seen with the eyes of his spirit that on some far distant day his son and the winged boat of the Bereewolgal would come together . . .

* * *

Long after the *Atlantic* had cleared the Heads the Governor remained on deck. There was a sharp southerly breeze blowing; it whipped his coat tails about his legs, and he stood holding his cockaded hat upon his head and looking up at the sky, wondering if the wind were bringing up rain, thinking of the replenishment of the stream at the cove, and of the crops at Parramatta. It was hard to realise all at once that such things were no longer his concern, and he was slightly annoyed to find that he approached the realisation not with relief, but unwillingly, with sorrow.

Watching the shore recede, he thought, "That is the end of my part in it," and immediately reminded himself impatiently that within a year or two he might return. As if ignoring his conscious planning, an inner conviction went on weaving desultory thoughts, half sad, half proud. "Five years of my fifty are all I have spent on it, but my name will be remembered there when it is forgotten in my own land. All my other work forgotten, become small, unimportant; material for some future historian to pad out his monograph upon the founding of the colony of New South Wales. The years at sea, the years in Spain, the years in England; hard work, rigid, dangerous, unforgiving work—but its function was only to lead me here, to this spot, to this moment, looking back at the vanishing infancy of a nation I nursed, but whose maturity I shall not live to see."

The coastline faded, became remote and shadowy, and with its fading the sharp outlines of his mental images faded, too. They became elusive, like the recollection of a dream when one awakens, something living only in the dwindling impact of sensations painfully recalled. Henceforward that land would be only the memory of sounds and scents and impressions which he had stored unconsciously beneath the load of conscious care which he was now discarding. Sometimes in the fresh green of an English spring he would find himself remembering a spring whose young leaves were like rubies; sometimes, listening to the high summer drone of bees in a cottage garden, he would seem to hear faintly, pitched high above their drowsy note, the shrill, triumphant orchestra of the cicadas. Sometimes in the peace and the ordered comfort of his declining years, when his urge to action, like an old hawser, stretched and frayed by long use, was slackening, some tougher strand might still hold tautly, linking him with the violence and the crudity and the suffering of the five years' ordeal which was now just ended.

For it had been an ordeal, and it was over. Firmly as he told himself that he would return, he knew that even if he did it would be to a different function, and a different ideal. For it had been his task simply to insist upon survival, but now survival was assured, and future Governors —himself or others—must face another problem. From now on it would be less the spur of faith that was needed than the curb of wisdom. No, his part was done; and, he told himself with a momentary stirring of weary pride, as well done as had been humanly possible with the poor material provided for him. He straightened himself stiffly, and turned to find Bennilong at his side.

The black man darted a swift, strange look at him. The cheerfulness and assurance with which he had farewelled his friends was gone now, and his eyes, after that one glance at the Be-anga's face, went back to the distant shore, now lying like a shadow along the horizon. There were the high cliffs of Burrawarra, from which, long, long ago, he had watched with Wunbula for the coming of just such a nowee as this one upon which he stood, and his brows wrinkled painfully in an effort to recapture the confidence and serenity of that desire. For a moment he succeeded, borne back by emotion to a time when legends had been truth, and spirits no less real than men, and he saw Wunbula on the cliffs, enormous, his head touching the sky. He saw the lean, tireless legs, the great chest, the upflung head, the strength and the grace and the pride of a man who had never known physical or spiritual humiliation. . . .

Phillip said, kindly:

"What is it, Bennilong? What do you see?"

Bennilong twitched like a startled animal, and looked again, nervously, at the Be-anga. He pointed to the shore, and for a moment, with uplifted arm, stayed motionless, staring, for Wunbula was no longer there. He looked sideways at the Governor, in bewilderment, and muttered uneasily:

"Wunbula . . ."

Phillip, puzzled, shook his head. This was a word he did not know. Bennilong looked at him in sudden earnestness, his dark eyes full of misery. "Bo-ee," he said sadly. "Bo-ee." He made a little upward movement with his hands, and turned away. Phillip, watching him walk along the deck, told himself that this mood was merely a natural reaction of homesickness. Soon, he assured himself, a cheerful and mercurial temper would reassert itself, and Bennilong, that endearing and irresponsible scapegrace, would be himself again. But he looked back for a moment, frowning, at the vanishing shore. Bo-ee. He knew the meaning of that word well enough, and he thought uneasily:

"What is it that is dead?"

EPILOGUE

*I*T WAS spring when Bennilong next saw his native land. From the deck of the *Reliance,* bringing Hunter back to the colony as its new Governor, he watched the harbour unfold as they entered it between the gateways, Burrawarra and Boree, and scanned each bay eagerly as they passed for signs of his countrymen. His senses drank in thirstily the sights and sounds, the scents and colours which, for nearly three years now, had been only a nostalgic memory. There were rocks by the water's edge which he recognised with a sharp delight, and trees whose shape struck with a fresh and exciting impact of familiarity. His imagination sped onward faster than the sails of the ship could take him, so that he saw what lay behind each concealing headland long before they reached it, and linked it with a thousand memories of a life which had been nearly lost to him and was now restored.

Living thus in his senses, he was happy. But when the settlement came into view and he saw the huts of the white people on the shore, and the white people themselves going about their business, or crowding down to the wharf to welcome the new Governor, his mind, beginning to function consciously again, became uncertain, and filmed the bright ecstasy of sensuous recognition with a cloud of doubt.

He was Bennilong, and he had been to England. The whole story of those three long years of exile began to unfold in his brain, clear and complete as many another story of some hero of his race who had performed great deeds. He thought of the long voyage which had brought him to the country of the King—a voyage so long that often he had been afraid, thinking that the ocean was indeed endless, as his people said, and that the white men were spirits after all, having no earthly home. He thought of how the officers had vied with each other to reassure him, to flatter and amuse him and his young companion, Immerawanye, and how the Be-anga, unfailingly kind, had cheered his moments of depression, soothed his moments of alarm, explained with care and patience all those confusing things which had perplexed him in the other ports of call upon the way.

He thought of the place called London to which he had come at last, and of the first days there when amazement had followed on amazement, and fear was never very far behind—for he had known then how great a tribe was the Bereewolgal, and that their magic must be greater and more potent than the magic of his own people. He had lived for a time in an uneasy apprehension, but they had not used their magic against him—at first. They had been kind; they had given him food such as he had never tasted before, and much wine. They had given him fine clothes so that he might be fittingly clad to go and see the King. The King, also, had been friendly, but Bennilong, though impressed by the splendours of his house, had been secretly disappointed in this great man. He was fat; he did not look like a warrior. And, stranger still, his people, though they bowed before him and treated him with every mark of respect in his presence, sometimes laughed at him when he was not there. Often, watching them closely, understanding with his sharp perceptions far more than they imagined him to understand, Bennilong had gathered that they did not consider this King of theirs to be a very wise man at all; on the contrary, it appeared that an evil spirit sometimes inhabited his mind, and robbed him of all reason. Why then, Bennilong had wondered—and once even asked—did they keep him as their leader? Why did they not find a man great in strength and wisdom to be the father of their tribe? But he had been given no sensible reply; to say that this man was a king because his father's father had been a king was simply foolish.

Yes, in London it had been pleasant enough at first. But sometimes it had flashed into his mind that the smiles which everywhere greeted him were . . . Were they true smiles, the smiles of friendship and goodwill? Or was there mockery in them? Were the laughter and applause which always followed his remarks born of admiration and approval, or was there insult in them?

There had been things which happened, too . . .

Even now, thrusting them away into the background of his thoughts, Bennilong felt a hot flush of resentment prickle over his skin. There had been people who drew aside from his touch; there had been raised eyebrows, and wrinkled nostrils. There had been friendly hands upon his arm to guide him, and for these he had been grateful, but there had been others whose touch was not guidance, but hustling, pushing, compulsion . . .

At first he had been made to feel very important, and this was an experience which he had always welcomed and enjoyed. But suddenly, and for no reason which he could understand, everything was changed. He and Immerawanye were taken away from London to another place. Immerawanye had not been present at nearly so many ceremonies as Bennilong, partly because he did not speak the white man's tongue as fluently, and partly because, ever since the voyage, he had not been well. Now, in this other place to which they were taken, he had grown worse. The weather, which had been warm upon their arrival, now became cold, and grey, and damp. There was nothing to do, and they did not like their food.

It would have been a less difficult and confusing time, perhaps, if the Be-anga had been there, but he was ill too, and quite soon after their arrival he had said farewell to them and gone away somewhere, and they had seen him no more. Immerawanye was very miserable, and Bennilong was very restless and angry. Day after day there was no sun, and Immerawanye coughed, and Bennilong said truculently to anyone who would listen:

"Go home. Go home, quick, Bennilong, Immerawanye. England no good, too cold, no sun. Go home quick on boat."

Sometimes they said soothingly, "Soon, soon." Sometimes they said impatiently, "Not yet—no boat yet." Sometimes they only shrugged their shoulders and said nothing at all.

The weather became colder. Immerawanye coughed and coughed. He grew very thin and weak, and lay all day quite still, looking at the ceiling. A white man came, a carrahdy, and performed certain rituals, and shook his head.

Bennilong fumed and fretted, and walked with the feverish impatience of a caged animal where he was allowed to walk. He hated the feel of the soft, wet grass beneath his feet, and he was worried because the leaves of the trees had gone red and yellow, and were now falling off the branches, leaving them bare as bones. He hated the cloudy-soft atmosphere, and brushed his hand continually before his eyes as if he could tear away a veil, and once again see clearly through a bright, hot light. He ached with an accumulation of frustrated desires—for the hunt, for the corroboree, for a woman, for the spiritual life without which he felt himself but half a man.

At first the white people had asked him to sing and dance for them, and he had complied; but now, surlily, he refused. These things belonged to his own land, and here they had no meaning. The ochres and clays with which one decorated one's body were part of that land; streaked and painted with them, smeared with the charcoal of its trees, crowned with the feathers of its birds, one was part of it too. But here the earth was unfriendly to one's songs.

Only at night there was sometimes a gladness which turned to heavier sorrow with the morning. For where Bennilong himself could not go, his Doowee could, and did, travelling more swiftly than the wind, so that it came to its own land and people, and joined them in their hunts and their corroborees. Night after night it fled across the sea to roam with the hunting parties on high, rocky ridges, or to lie across a canoe upon the deep water, and spear the fish as they flashed by underneath. And day after day Bennilong awakened in the dawn, unrefreshed, not to the sight of sky and trees, the sound of children's voices, the smell of burning twigs, the knowledge of a day full of business and enjoyment, but to a square of window framing a grey fog, the sound of Immerawanye's laboured breathing, the knowledge of captivity.

One morning he had seen with a pricking of the hairs upon his scalp that the world without was no longer green, but white. He huddled his clothes on and stared out the window, trembling partly with cold and partly with fear, but searching his memory for a legend of his own people which told of just such a thing as this. How still it was, this white world! How soundless! Silent, and motionless—like death . . . He realised suddenly that there was no sound of Immerawanye's breathing, and turned sharply to look at him . . .

Even now, safely back again in his own land, he shivered with the recollection of that moment. It was not death itself which disturbed him, but the fact that in the face of death he was, for the first time, alone. Death was a tribal matter; the power of the great enemy was reduced by the united spirit of the living tribe. There were many matters which must be performed at such a time, but they were all bound up with the land from which living man had come, and to which his dead body must return. Panic had seized Bennilong in those moments of realisation that here he was powerless to perform the proper rituals of death, and he felt the malignancy of evil powers beat shadowy wings about his head. In the violence of his longing he tried to create what he needed from his inner being—demanded of his eyes that they call up the family and friends of Immerawanye to stand about him, demanded of his fingers that they reach forth and pluck green branches for a burial, demanded of his ears that the clamour of mourning should be heard. To one of his race, delicately poised between a spiritual and a material world, acknowledging no very sharp line of division between what was and what might be, such an effort was as instinctive as the effort of a child to find in its imagination the sanctuary its environment denies. In his own land he had performed such feats many times; there were innumerable scenes and situations which dwelt tranquilly in a memory which did not trouble to ask whether the inner or the outer life had fashioned them. But here, shaken with cold, sharply and nervously aware of the strange white world outside, he had felt himself bound within his shivering body, his creative spirit paralysed and impotent.

* * *

Very slowly the cold season had passed, and the bare, dead-seeming branches of the trees had grown young, green leaves again, and one day Bennilong had heard with delirious joy that he was to go on board a boat, and presently to return to his own country.

Hunter had taken charge of him then, and once on board the *Reliance* his mercurial spirits had leapt from despondency to wild elation. Soon now, soon, soon, his heart had cried, he would see his own people again. He would hunt with By-gone and Colbee and Caruey, he would dance in the cleared circle under the flame-lit trees, he would feel his bark canoe lifting like a leaf upon the swell of the water, and shoot forward by the strength of his tireless arms. He would spear the fish again from the rocks, and cook them over the coals, and eat till he could eat no more. He would stretch himself at ease upon the sand, while the sun made golden the darkness behind his closed eyes. At night, in the warm arms of Gooroobarooboolo, he would know the rapturous agonies of desire, and the slow-rising content of fulfilment. And his people would cry: "Bennilong is home again! Welcome to Bennilong!"

But the ship did not sail. Every morning he asked, "Go? Go today?" He paced the deck incessantly, looking up at the masts as if in hope that even in the space of a moment its white wings might be spread, and the journey begun. The days went by, but he felt them no longer as days, for there was no event by which to mark them. He was burdened and overwhelmed by his first consciousness of Time; life was nothing but Time—endless, meaningless, every dawn a fresh anguish of hope, every dusk a new despair.

Hunter came aboard sometimes, always very busy and preoccupied, but to Bennilong's increasingly sullen enquiries he answered only, "Soon." The warm weather grew cooler, and then cold; Bennilong put on all his clothes, and shivered in the dank sea air. Hope wavered, struggled, died.

He began to cough as Immerawanye had coughed. From the deck he stared interminably at a grey world of fog and leaden water. He gave up pacing, and was still, save for his restless eyes.

Now he began to believe that Immerawanye's fate was to be his, and his misery was again not for death itself, but for the loneliness in which he must meet it—for the strange earth which would receive his body, and the strange stars which would shine above it, for age-old customs lost, and for Baiame half-forgotten, for solitude, that bleakest terror of a people to whom the brotherhood of man in life and death was the firm foundation of all things.

Now the life-urge, once so brave a flame in his robust body and his ardent spirit, dwindled till it was nothing but a spark. There was no longer enough of it to move his legs or lift his arms, and sometimes in his painful paroxysms of coughing he felt that it must be finally extinguished. Now he knew that at last the Bereewolgal were employing an evil magic against him, and his mind became confused and tortured by strange visions of a white man who was pointing the bone at him, and singing not only his death, but the death of all his people. He tried to see the face of this enemy, but it was hidden. He tossed and muttered and held his hand over his eyes, but still the vision was there. Suddenly he was back in his own land among his own people, and there was a great terror in their hearts; they were running hither and thither as if to escape from something, and some were falling dead as they ran, with red sores upon their bodies, and their bodies were so thin that the bones almost pierced the skin. He was standing among them on a beach, shouting to them not to fear, and yet fearing himself. Then he was no longer on the beach, but looking out across the ocean from the cliffs of Burrawarra, and he saw the man with the pointing bone far away upon the horizon. Nearer and nearer he came, his raised arm outstretched to its full length, the bone gleaming in the sun, white and menacing, the air full of his singing magic. Bennilong snatched up his spears and hurled them; never had he flung them so far, so hard, so true. One after another they went through the body of the man as through a pillar of smoke, and fell into the sea. Now all over his own body Bennilong could feel the creeping magic of the bone, and he was filled with a strange and dreadful lethargy, so that his arm would no longer bear the weight of the spears. Closer and closer the man came, now so close and so huge that he blotted out the sky and the sea, and Bennilong, looking into his face at last, cried out in terror, *"The King! The King!"*

*   *   *

After that he had known that the hour was come for him to die. Time still held him imprisoned, but now he seemed often able to watch it as if from a distance; it was as though some part of him had already escaped. To have been so near to death, he thought, looking round the blue, familiar harbour, was something which added wonder to this day of homecoming.

Remember it only for that—to defeat it with this gladness of return. . . .

*　　*　　*

The *Reliance* was dropping her anchor. Governor Hunter paused beside Bennilong for a moment, and glanced down curiously at the black man's face. It was fortunate, he thought, that one of them, at any rate, had lived to come back to his native land. There had been a period towards the end of that interminable delay in Plymouth Sound when he had expected every day to hear that Bennilong was dead. And there had been many times when he had wished heartily that Phillip had never brought his protégé to England. Worried not only by their own delay, but by the delay in the preparation of store-ships for the colony, he had been in no mood to be harassed by bills for Bennilong's expenses, or to be plagued with the writing of letters to the Under-Secretary disclaiming all responsibility for them. Bennilong had been, in fact, a nuisance, and the small diversion which he had caused in London society seemed to Hunter an inadequate return for the months of care and attention he had needed, and for the handsome sum in hard cash which he had cost the Government.

Looking at him now the Governor marvelled, not for the first time, at the recovery he had made. It had dated, there could be no doubt, from the very moment when he had learned that the ship was ready to sail at last. It had been without any particular hope that the news would rally him (for he had seemed to be at death's very door) that Hunter had gone into the semi-darkness where he lay, and bent down to speak to him. No cheerful words, no efforts to distract or encourage him had been of any avail for a long time; he lay very still with his face turned to the wall, his eyes wide open, fixed and glassy.

"Go home, Bennilong." Hunter had said. "Ship ready now."

The dark eyes had moved; Hunter saw their whites gleam as they turned to stare up at him. From that moment he had never looked like dying.

*　　*　　*

David Collins, obeying the invitation of the new Governor to wait upon him in his house, walked up the hill through the starlit spring night, wondering without much optimism how Hunter would cope with the problems about to confront him. In the doorway of Government House he found Bennilong ensconced, very fine in his European clothes, declaiming with affable condescension to a staring group of his countrymen. He broke off and greeted his old friend with pleasure. Collins paused to exchange a word or two.

"You like England, Bennilong?"

The black man shook his head in emphatic denial.

"No, no! Not like England! No good. Cold, no sun, trees wrong, no leaf, dulka wrong . . ." he pointed to the velvety heavens. "There birrong go far away wrong home. Here birrong go all the time one home—there Berai-berai, there Mirrabooka. England Mirrabooka not come. No good."

Collins laughed and patted his shoulder.

"You glad to come back, eh? You tell friends all about the King?"

Bennilong nodded weightily.

"I tell now I come back not let fellow here fight, fight all the time. I tell they put on coat, wash hand before come talk to me here, along Governor. I tell dirty fellow, not like white man." He gave his countrymen a stare of haughty disdain, and Collins, glancing at them with some amusement, wondered for how long they would tolerate without resentment such an air of scornful superiority.

Leaving them, he went inside, and Hunter, hearing his voice, called to him from the room where he was unpacking books and papers from a box upon the table. He waved his visitor to a chair.

"Sit down, Collins. We have hardly yet had time for more than a word. I want to have a talk with you. There are many matters . . ." he glanced up for a moment, frowning, "upon which the opinion of a man who has been continuously in the colony from its foundation will be—of the greatest assistance to me. You are well?"

"My health is good enough, Sir. I have not been able to ask for leave on that score. Nevertheless I had made application even before the late Governor sailed, but it was refused."

Hunter nodded.

"You have been too much needed here."

"The permission was, in fact, granted later," Collins said rather wearily, "but when Major Grose sailed he desired me to stay so that I might help Captain Peterson, who was not as conversant with all the circumstances of the colony as might have been necessary. So I am still here."

"I am glad of it." Hunter lifted the empty box down from the table to the floor, and seated himself opposite his guest. There was a brief silence. Then their eyes met, and Collins said slowly:

"You have been away a long time, Sir."

"More than four years. Four and a half years, indeed. I cannot—I *do* not—expect to find the same conditions . . ."

Collins' smile had little of amusement in it. Hunter, seeing how little, rose abruptly from the chair in which he had seated himself a moment before, and began to pace restlessly about the room. There had been rumours in England. His own Instructions included a paragraph which touched ominously upon "great evils" which were reported to have "arisen from the unrestrained importation of spirituous liquors," and another which significantly directed that convicts assigned to settlers should be maintained by them, and not from the public stores. Yes, he had known that he would be returning to a colony whose problems had grown with its size, but already, within a few days of arrival, he had known it with his nerves as well as with his brain, and there had begun to stir within him a faint and barely acknowledged apprehension. Here in the very room from which Phillip had governed the settlement, he was forced to see himself as inheriting a task begun by that bleak and intrepid little man, and suddenly he began to wonder if he were equal to it. In his long absence he had lost touch with the affairs of the isolated fragment of civilisation for which he was now responsible, but already he was conscious of developments which were disturbing. Almost, even, menacing . . .

He said abruptly to Collins:

"Tell me—how have things progressed?"

The Judge-Advocate allowed a moment or two to elapse before he spoke. He had always been, Hunter reflected, watching him with some impatience, a cautious man, deliberate and judicial in his expressed opinions. He said at last:

"There have been, as you must know, Sir, considerable changes made in the administration. They were not—in my opinion—always in the best interest of the colony."

Hunter nodded, caressing his chin nervously with his fingers.

"Following immediately upon Governor Phillip's departure," Collins went on, "Major Grose directed that the civil authority be superseded by that of the military. I confess, Sir, that this departure from the practice which had always been followed formerly, caused me a good deal of uneasiness at the time. You will remember that there were five magistrates in the colony: the Lieutenant-Governor, and myself, as Judge-Advocate, were, by virtue of our commissions, Justices of the Peace—and Mr. Atkins, Mr. Alt, and the Reverend Mr. Johnson had been sworn in as magistrates by Governor Phillip."

Hunter sat down again and rested his arms on the table, frowning across at Collins.

"So Major Grose and his gentlemen of the New South Wales Corps took command. And then?"

"Then," Collins continued, "there began a state of affairs in the colony of which I cannot feel that our late Governor would have approved. For example, Sir, the sails of the *Atlantic* had hardly vanished over the horizon before the settlers were offering for sale the livestock which had been distributed among them for breeding purposes. They were bought . . ."

"By the officers of the New South Wales Corps!" snapped Hunter.

Collins replied mildly: "At least the animals were not destroyed by them as they probably would have been if they had fallen into other hands. Also, within a week of Governor Phillip's departure, an order was given which made a distinction between the ration given to the convicts and that issued to the civil and military population—which, as you will remember, Sir, had never been done before. This was a matter on which Major Grose had always held very strong views. Even before the Governor left I understand that he had written to the Under-Secretary complaining that the captain of a company should not be expected to subsist upon the same ration as a felon."

"What changes were made?"

"By the first order the convicts, though they still received the same total weight, were to have three pounds less of flour than all other descriptions of people, the balance being made up in rice. Other distinctions were made later."

Hunter nodded gloomily. For a moment he wished that he were still no more than a naval captain, with no greater responsibility than a ship. If he had been able to take this helm of government from his predecessor without a disastrous interval of nearly three years, he might have succeeded in holding the administration to a course already laid down by a more competent navigator of affairs than himself. This depressing moment of self-doubt was followed by a healthier flare of anger against Grose and his Corps of huckstering soldiers—an anger which, if it were not altogether free from the almost inevitable rivalry between the naval commander and the military, had nevertheless a sound basis of reason. He swore to himself that these scourings of the other regiments in the service, these ex-inhabitants of military prisons, these thieving, plotting tradesmen in uniform, should find him more than a match for them.

Collins, watching him, was less confident. Almost from the hour when Major Grose had assumed command, and he had seen with dismay that the civil power which Phillip had so jealously guarded was to be, to all intents and purposes, overthrown, he had nursed only one hope—that Phillip would return. Now that he knew that this was not to be, his confidence failed him, though he was determined to support Hunter to the best of his ability. But he knew the power of the faction which the new Governor would find set against him. Macarthur, for instance, was a redoubtable foe. He said:

"The assigning of large numbers of convicts to soldiers who have taken up farms has had an ill effect on the cultivation of public land. And as they still draw clothing and rations from the public stores . . ."

"That," said Hunter decisively, "has been expressly forbidden by the Government."

Collins smiled again. It had been expressly forbidden before, he reflected, but Grose had made no attempt to discontinue the practice; his laconic reply to the Secretary of State had been merely that the order "would not be put into execution until such time as I am honoured with your further instructions." A conveniently long time, thought Collins grimly. "When the gentlemen were first indulged with grants," the letter had continued blandly, "I gave them ten servants each . . . the public labour has been very little interrupted by their accommodation."

The public labour, Collins thought, moving restlessly in his chair, had been almost brought to a standstill by it, but in the meantime the gentlemen of the New South Wales Corps had flourished exceedingly. He looked again at the Governor. He had aged in these last few years, but he was still a far more robust looking man than Phillip. A far handsomer man, too, with arched, dark brows, an aquiline nose, and a fine, square chin. But at that moment Collins would have given much to have seen on the opposite side of the table a more meagre figure, bending slightly and habitually sideways with the threat or the reality of pain, a face in which sensitiveness was masked, but not entirely hidden, by determination, brows whose faint perpetual frown seemed to bespeak an intense concentration upon inner reserves of strength, a mouth which shut so firmly that it belied the sensual fulness of its lips. It was Phillip, he thought with a sigh, and none other, who was needed here. And suddenly, oppressed by the silence, he said with an effort at cheerfulness:

"I encountered our friend Bennilong at the door as I came in. He is vastly fine in his new clothes. I imagine he'll not again forsake all the comforts he has grown accustomed to for the precarious life of the woods."

Hunter, as if grateful for the change of subject, relaxed, and smiled.

"I should not be so sure. His attachment to the country is remarkable. I assure you that during those months we were delayed in Plymouth Sound I daily expected his death; only our actual departure, I am sure, saved his life. But tell me of the natives here, Collins. How have things gone in that quarter?"

"We have had a good deal of trouble with them, Sir, from time to time. The settlers at Prospect Hill and Toongabbee have been frequently molested. My namesake—you remember him . . ."

"Was he not the husband of one of Bennilong's sisters?"

"Yes —a quieter sort of man than most of them. He was sent on board the *Daedalus* when she sailed to carry provisions to Captain Vancouver . . ."

"Why?"

"Major Grose thought it would afford him an opportunity of learning our language. I cannot say that I found him much more proficient when he returned than when he set out. And his absence was the cause of some disturbance in his domestic affairs, for Warreweer consoled herself with another native—a fine young fellow—and 'Collins' was obliged to fight a duel for her when he came back."

Hunter laughed; the lively interest which he had always felt in the black people still survived, and he began to fire at his guest a series of questions which the Judge-Advocate patiently and explicitly answered.

"They are a difficult race to understand," he concluded. "We have seen them practise the most revolting cruelties, and their treatment of their women must be allowed to be shameful in the extreme. And yet, Sir, consider the account which we had only a week or so since from Captain Broughton of the *Providence*. When they were driven in by bad weather up the coast, and took shelter in Port Stephens, they found there four miserable white runaways who had been most kindly entertained by the natives of that region. They had been fed, and given wives, and treated with every consideration; they assured Captain Broughton that had it not been for the protection of the savages they must have perished. How is one to reconcile such charity with the malevolence they display at other times?"

Hunter shrugged.

"Perhaps there is no very great mystery. We ourselves, I hope, are not incapable of charity—and yet malevolence is not unknown among us either. But tell me of the country itself, Collins. You have had further explorations?"

"There have been further attempts," Collins said guardedly, "to penetrate the mountains. Captain Peterson led one party some two years ago, but he met with no great success. They proceeded up the river from Broken Bay to Richmond Hill, and there transferred to smaller boats which enabled them to enter that arm which flows from the westward."

"I remember it. How far were they able to go?"

"They supposed themselves to be some ten miles farther up than had been reached before. They found the stream narrow and swiftly running, and their way was continually impeded by large rocks and waterfalls and the trunks of fallen trees. Captain Peterson named it the Grose, after the Lieutenant-Governor."

"There was another attempt made?"

"There was—but not until about a year later. It was undertaken by a man whom you must well remember, for he was the quartermaster of the *Sirius*. . ."

"Hacking?"

"Yes. He set out with a couple of companions in August of last year, and was out for several days."

"They found nothing?"

"Nothing but the usual endless ridges of high, rocky land. They saw but one native. I think we may assume that a country which will not even support these miserable people would be useless to us."

"I suppose so." Hunter picked up a pen and began playing with it. "In any case, I understand that we have as much land under cultivation, or suitable for cultivation as we can hope to use at present. There are now a score or so of settlers on the Hawkesbury, I believe."

"It is in that district," Collins said, "that most of the trouble with the natives has occurred. Mr. Mannion was the first to take up land at the river—though he chose a situation rather higher up than where the main body of the farms were placed . . ."

"Ah, yes! So Mannion remained in the wilderness and turned farmer! I must confess I was surprised when first I heard of it!"

"He speaks of returning to Ireland within the next two years, but assured me that he will return, if only for a visit, and to inspect the progress of his farm."

"He is satisfied with his land?"

"I imagine he is well satisfied. The land about the river banks is the best in the colony, and Mr. Mannion has had advantages which are not available to other settlers. He had overseers, livestock and tools of all kinds sent out in the *Sugar-Cane* transport which arrived from Ireland some two years ago, and his farm is by now the most flourishing in the colony. He has a quite commodious house almost completed, and he speaks of moving his household there from Parramatta. But he has had his difficulties, too."

"With the natives?"

"With the natives, and with the other settlers of the neighbourhood, among whom he is not well liked. The Hawkesbury settlement has been a disorderly and troublesome one, Sir, the scene of endless drunkenness, debauchery and violence. It ended in soldiers being posted there continually for the protection of the settlers against the natives—but I feel that the hostility of the natives has not been entirely unprovoked."

Hunter said grimly: "It would not surprise me."

"There was a report about a year ago," Collins went on, "that a native boy had been most barbarously ill-used by the settlers—tied hand and foot, and dragged several times through a fire, and then thrown into the river, where he was shot at and killed. An investigation was ordered, but . . ." Collins threw out his hands and lifted his shoulders with a hopeless movement. Hunter, frowning, asked:

"The charge was not proved?"

"It was admitted that a boy had been shot while in the water. The excuse was made that he was a spy sent among them by his people to discover their strength." Collins paused, and then said with uncharacteristic violence, "I don't believe it!"

There was another long and gloomy silence, broken at last by the Judge-Advocate.

"That reminds me, Sir—there was another strange incident at the river. It must have been—let me see—almost exactly three years ago. You may remember a convict called Prentice who came out with us? A red-headed fellow?"

"I remember Tench speaking of him when I returned from the Cape. He absconded from the settlement, did he not? Taking Tench's best shoes with him, if my memory serves me?"

"That is the man. He was not heard of again, and naturally we assumed that he had either starved or fallen a victim to the natives. But upon this occasion three years ago, Mr. Mannion and his overseer and convicts, at work on the bank of the river, saw him again—and in the most extraordinary circumstances. There was a flood—we had shocking weather about

that time—and a native woman and child were seen struggling in the
water. Our people made an effort to help them, but it was unsuccessful.
Just when it seemed inevitable that they must be swept down the river
to the fall, or else drowned upon the way, this man Prentice burst from
concealment on the other side of the river, and rushed down to their assistance. But he saved them, it appears, at the cost of his own life, for a
floating log struck him and crushed him against a rock. Mr. Mannion
himself told me of the circumstance with some emotion—and indeed it
must have been a distressing sight."

"They were able to be certain of his identity at such a distance?"

"The overseer thought he recognised him, and one of the convicts was
quite certain. He was a conspicuous rogue, if you recollect—powerfully
built, and with a flaming red hair and beard. But there is an odd coinci-
dence connected with the story. He had a child—a son—but you would
hardly remember that . . ."

"No."

"A mischievous, troublesome child, he was, at that time some eight
years old. The mother had been living for some time as—a member of
Mr. Mannion's household. Almost upon the very day when the father
made his mysterious reappearance at the river, the child vanished from
Mr. Mannion's house at Parramatta—and has never been seen since."

"Odd!" Hunter shrugged his shoulders. "It all serves to show, Collins,
that survival *is* possible for an escaped convict. How many of them are
there, I wonder, roaming the woods, whom we have thought dead?"

Collins struck his hand upon the table with an exclamation.

"I had almost forgot to mention, Sir, that there have been persistent
rumours of there being cattle in the neighbourhood of the river. The
natives repeatedly declare that they have seen animals with horns. We
suppose that if there is any truth in this report they must be the progeny
of Mr. Phillip's cattle which were lost during the first year of the settlement."

"Indeed!" Hunter roused himself from his obvious dejection and looked
at his guest with interest and astonishment. "That is something which
must be investigated at some convenient time. Such a herd would be a
considerable asset to the colony; I should think . . ."

He was interrupted by a commotion from outside. So loud and fierce
was the altercation that Hunter and Collins jumped up in alarm, and
hurried out to see what had caused it. They were not in the least surprised
to find that the yelling and quarrelling throng of natives which milled
about the threshold of Government House had Bennilong as its centre.

He was shouting ferociously in his own tongue, his face contorted with fury, but it seemed to Collins that in the tones and expressions of the other natives there was more mockery than rage. They fell back upon the appearance of the new Governor, and Hunter said sharply:

"Why you make noise, Bennilong?"

For one moment as the black man's eyes flashed round to meet his questioner's, Collins could almost have supposed that what he saw in them was anguish rather than anger. He said sullenly:

"All fellow here say Gooroobarooboolo go away along Caruey. Gooroo-barooboolo my woman, live along me. I give fine petticoat, jacket like white woman, bring from England, give Gooroobarooboolo. Now all fellow here talk, talk, tell me Gooroobarooboolo take off jacket, petticoat, tell not want, go away along Caruey . . ." Suddenly his fury erupted again. "I go find Caruey, kill! Caruey bad fellow, dirty fellow, not wear coat, not cut hair." He glanced round the circle of dark faces and stepped forward with a threatening movement of dispersal. "You all dirty fellow! No good dirty black fellow, not come here along Bennilong, along Governor . . ." He broke from halting English into his own rich and expressive tongue, and the faces of his hearers, understanding more clearly, became angry.

They had listened good-naturedly enough to his grandiloquent account of his travels. Indeed, they had listened with enjoyment, for the tongue of the youara-gurrugin was still Bennilong's, and upon his lips any tale gained life and colour. He was Bennilong, who from boyhood had been not unkindly known among them as Kon-kon-taallin, loud-mouth, boaster. A little teasing, a little friendly ridicule had always kept his egotism within bounds, and the joke of Gooroobarooboolo's return to Caruey had seemed an ideal pin with which to prick the balloon of his swollen pride. Anger they had cheerfully anticipated, for Bennilong's tempers had always come almost within the category of tribal entertainments—but there was more than anger here. There was insult and disloyalty. A mutter of resentment ran through the group. They backed away, and as they went one of them called out scornfully: "Bennilong is a white man now! See Bennilong, the white man, with the white men, his friends!"

Collins and Hunter, shrugging their shoulders, went inside. Bennilong stood motionless in the doorway. From behind him the lamp threw his shadow on the ground, and it was, indeed, the shadow of a white man. He lifted his face and looked about him, his nostrils wide to take in the scents of the bush and the harbour, his ears alert for the small sounds of night, his eyes searching and bewildered. He had returned. Here was his homeland all about him—but where was his home?

* * *

Johnny Prentice, clambering out of the creek bed, panted up to the door of the hut, and flung his load thankfully on the ground. Billalong, who had been playing in the creek ran up to greet him, and two dingo pups, excited by the smell of meat, rushed forward and began snapping voraciously about Johnny's prize. He kicked them away angrily, and stood smearing the sweat from his forehead with his arm, recovering his breath.

The weather was very hot, it was a long way from the Nepean, and the huge slab of beef which he had hacked from a speared heifer was a heavy burden for the shoulders of a fourteen-year-old boy. Pushing the door of the hut open he bent again to lift it, hindered rather than helped by Billalong's eager efforts. Inside the hut it was cooler, but Johnny stayed only to fling his meat on the table where, with door and window closed, it would be safe from the dogs, if not from the flies. Then, followed by Bill, he ran down to the creek again, and plunged into the deepest pool. Bathing, to Johnny, was a means of getting cool rather than clean; he had no clothes to take off, for he had soon grown out of those he wore at the time of his escape, and since then he had gone naked. His fair skin had burned to a dark brick-red, his thin body had filled out, and he was growing with the rapidity of adolescence. His bright, dark eyes had acquired the restless alertness of the natives' eyes, and the eyes of the shy kangaroos and wallabies which lived in the hills about him, but his thatch of flaming hair still proclaimed him alien.

It was only lately, during the last two or three years, that he had begun to think about the other life which he had left; now he sometimes sought a kind of contact with it, drawn by a curiosity which held nothing whatever of nostalgia, by going down the Nepean as his father had done, to watch the white settlers upon its opposite bank. He thought very often, too, and with increasing bewilderment, of the transition from that life to this. His memory of that day, six years ago, when he had first encountered Cunnembeillee and Billalong had grown dim, but every now and then, looking at the hut, and at all the things in it, and at the yard before it, and at the cattle, he wondered with a kind of helpless irritation how they had come to be there, and who had made them. He had asked his black friends many times, but always they gave him the bewildering and obviously foolish answer that he had made them himself. Even when he angrily denied it they only smiled, and said that he had forgotten.

It did not really matter very much—and yet sometimes it seemed to matter a good deal. His life was a native's life; he was one of them, speaking their language fluently by now, and accepted by them with a friendliness in which he sometimes seemed to detect the faintest note of . . .

Fear? No, not quite fear. What was it? They asked his advice. When there were disputes they often came to him to have them settled. Sometimes when they made new spears they brought them to him and asked him to breathe on them, and seemed to believe that in some way this made them better spears. Perhaps it did. Johnny was willing to accept the fact, but sometimes he felt that he would like to know *why?* For they did not treat their own boys in this way.

Was it only because he was white? He had no recollection of having seen the natives about the settlements at Sydney and Parramatta behave in a similar manner to other white men. When he wondered about these things he always came back to the riddle of the hut. It must be this, he thought, his possession of the hut, which made him different. There was no doubt that he possessed it. It was his. Its key hung about his neck—a symbol now, for it was never used—and no native ever entered it but by his invitation. Even Cunnembeillee would not move anything in it from the place where he had put it, nor enter it save when he himself was there.

Only Billalong really shared it with him. Wallowing in the shallow creek, with the water trickling pleasantly about his shoulder blades, he glanced at the little boy, now nearly nine, whom, as a plump baby, he had nursed by the fire so long ago. Billalong's skin was almost, but not quite, as dark as that of the natives, his legs were not quite so lean as theirs, and more than ever now his features proclaimed a difference; but to a casual glance he was indistinguishable from the other native children, and Johnny never looked at him other than casually. He was the merriest human being Johnny had ever encountered. His merriment was so spontaneous, so infectious, so constant, that even Johnny's habitual taciturnity sometimes broke down before it, so that he laughed at nothing, merely because Billalong was laughing.

Cunnembeillee did not laugh very much. Johnny had never quite been able to understand her. To begin with, she spoke his tongue a little. That, linked to the existence of the hut, had made him guess that at some previous time she had known a white man, and her necklace of buttons, and the muskets in the hut had convinced him that the white man must have been a lost or deserting soldier. Unable to understand completely, he had abandoned the effort to understand at all, and contented himself with life as he found it. On the whole, he had found it good.

He had slipped into an existence which was almost entirely native, and Cunnembeillee, puzzled, but not ill-pleased, had observed that now, in his second incarnation, the Red-headed One cared little or nothing for those things which had been so important to him before. He no longer toiled all day, digging up the ground and growing things for food, but was well content with what she found, and with the few potatoes and melons which, self-sown, came up year after year among the weeds of their neglected patch. Nor did he ever use his magic weapons now. At first he had merely stared at them, hanging on the wall of the hut; then, as he grew older, he had taken them down and tried to use them, but he never killed anything with them, and his small supply of ammunition was soon exhausted. Thereafter they had hung undisturbed and rusting upon the wall, and Johnny had become quite expert, instead, in the throwing of spears.

In their own little valley the few cattle which Prentice had brought from the Nepean thrived and increased, and Cunnembeillee continued to milk them when they had milk to give, and in lean times Johnny speared one for food and invited their native friends to a feast, though they often brought their own kangaroo meat, preferring it to beef. Those remaining on the Nepean, however, had long ago forgotten that they had ever been domesticated; split into several large herds, they were now so wild that even Milbooroo had resigned himself to doing without the sweet, white drink of which he had once been so fond. Johnny, however, had come to regard them as his own simply because the natives did so, and he was bitterly resentful when the settlers from lower down the river began to make occasional expeditions in search of unlawful beef. He knew that Authority was well aware of their existence, for three years ago he had been informed by Milbooroo that a large party of white men had journeyed from the coast, and had been greatly excited and pleased by the sight of them.

Hunting had become his favourite pursuit, though he subscribed faithfully to the native rule that one must not kill save for food. This was the black man's bargain with the land which nurtured him, and it had been taught to Johnny as to all the other growing boys of the tribes, as a part of those lessons in which they learned to use their spears, and were instructed in the technique of the chase.

Nevertheless, though it was primarily a utilitarian business, Johnny had found that there was an enormous excitement to be had from the communal attack of the kangaroo hunt; it was stirring to be one of a circle closing in upon the doomed animal, closer, closer, while it hopped this way and that, frantic with fear, its sides heaving, its dark eyes wild and brilliant, dashing for the circumference of the circle and then retreating again to the centre, bewildered by the din of its oncoming enemies. Emu hunting was perhaps even more exciting—a solitary affair, requiring patience, cunning, and skill. For Dinewan was a shy creature, and his long legs and his tall neck made it possible to see his pursuer from afar, so that it was necessary to use strategy and guile. Sometimes, keeping against the wind, it was possible to advance within spear-throwing distance by creeping from shrub to rock, from rock to fallen log; sometimes it was better to hide oneself with an uprooted shrub, and move forward imperceptibly, by inches; sometimes an emu skin, with a stick thrust into the long neck, made a disguise in which one might approach openly, mimicking the long, complacent stride of Dinewan himself.

Under the patient and expert tutelage of Milbooroo and the other men, Johnny could now acquit himself well. The hut was his headquarters, but often he left it with Cunnembeillee and Billalong to join one of the other tribes in their nomadic life. They all accepted him, for it was understood that he was not really of any tribe, but a spirit returned in the guise of humanity. They had not been at all surprised to learn that his name was no longer An-droo, but Dyonn-ee, for amongst them the name of one dead was instantly discarded, and never spoken in the tribe again.

Most of the time a few natives lived with them at the hut. Milbooroo was one of these, having a semi-official status as Cunnembeillee's husband. The whole business of the Red-headed One's reincarnation was so unprecedented that it was impossible to fit it into their rigid Law, so they had compromised, recognising that Cunnembeillee must be regarded, at least temporarily, as a widow, and therefore after a due period available for remarriage. Johnny's obvious lack of any interest in the subject had confirmed their belief that this was surely the only sensible arrangement, and now two small half-brothers were added to the oddly assorted ménage at the hut.

In the last year or two Cunnembeillee had observed that Dyonn-ee became more and more like the An-droo he had been before. He began to dig up the ground again, and to plant the small potatoes, by now hardly larger than walnuts, in neat rows; he began to save the seeds from the few melons which had survived, and plant them too. He mended the hut where it was beginning to need repair, and sometimes he went off alone for days down the Nepean, as he had done long ago before he was killed, to watch the growing settlement of the white men on its opposite bank.

It was from one of these excursions that he had just returned, and as he climbed from the stream to a flat rock, and lay there idly throwing pebbles into the water, he was thinking of his mother. For about two years now she had lived in the house which Stephen Mannion had built upon his property, and Johnny had often seen her from his hiding place across the river. He had watched her curiously, but entirely without emotion; in his whole life he had loved no one but Arabanoo and Billalong. He had wondered sometimes where the Mannions were, for he could see no sign of them, though he sometimes noticed two children, a flaxen-haired girl and a red-haired boy, whom he knew must be his sister and brother, Maria and Andy.

But lately the Mannions had reappeared, and for the first time since his escape a queer feeling of restlessness and dissatisfaction had begun to grip him. For Patrick was a gentleman now. He rode a fine horse and was elegantly dressed, and Johnny had heard him calling out orders to the convicts. Miles, too, who looked even younger than Billalong, had a pony of his own. And there had come to Johnny in a sudden vivid and bitter stab of memory the words he had spoken to Patrick so many years ago. "I'm goin' to be gentry, like you!"

Gentry! He looked slowly round the valley, and his eyes rested at last, in a long, hard stare, upon the hut. It was not here, he thought grimly, that he could achieve that old ambition, long dormant but now reawakening. But he would achieve it someday—somehow!

* * *

From down the creek came the sound of shrill and cheerful voices. Billalong leapt from the creek where he had been playing and ran to meet the little group of natives emerging from the gorge and climbing the banks towards the hut. Milbooroo had a young wallaby slung over his shoulder, and Cunnembeillee's basket was well filled with fish from the Wollondilly. Two or three other natives and half a dozen children had come to share the feast, and their talk and laughter mingled with the excited yelping of the dingo pups.

The quiet was shattered. Johnny, from his rock, glanced at them once and then back again, broodingly, at the water. The evening light touched his ruddily sunburned skin to a warmer shade, and lit his tangled mat of red hair till it flamed. The natives looked at him, but made no attempt to intrude upon his solitude, his strange withdrawal. He was Dyonn-ee, a being apart, one of them, and yet a stranger.

* * *

Someone had set fire to Mr. Johnson's little church on the east side of the cove. There was a great deal of frenzied rushing to and fro with buckets of water, but the wooden building was dry and its roof thatched, and it soon became evident that no efforts could save it. Indeed, if close observation had been possible in the confusion, it might have been noticed that the water was not always thrown where it would have most effect, and that some of the convicts were exchanging sly glances of satisfaction. Watching while it flared and collapsed, Hunter found himself wondering grimly whether his recent order enforcing regular attendance at divine service might not have had something to do with its destruction. The children, he noticed, to whom it was not only church but schoolroom, were frankly delirious with joy.

He set his mouth obstinately. If these depraved people imagined that the mere burning of the church would free them from due observance of the Sabbath, they were mistaken. The new storehouse, just completed, should instantly be fitted out as a church, he determined, and next Sunday they should again submit their sacrilegious and rebellious hearts to Mr. Johnson's salutary admonitions.

He was frowning as he stood watching the flames. Three years he had spent now as Governor of the colony, and in his heart he knew himself beaten, but was confused as to the nature of his adversary. He only knew that it was Hydra—a many-headed monster, no sooner smitten in one place than it attacked him from another, so that he spent his time turning desperately from one arduous task to another.

To restore civil authority was not easy in the face of opposition from the military, now firmly established as the colony's first capitalists. To assign convicts in such a way that the public labour was not sacrificed to the demands of the settlers was a knotty problem. To suppress a trade in liquor which was as passionately defended by the exploited as by the exploiters, had been beyond his power. But the middle and immortal head of the Hydra was, he suspected, merely the fact that the mother-country herself did not quite know what kind of maturity she desired for this embarrassing and increasingly obstreperous infant which she had almost accidentally produced. Was it to be a penal settlement for ever, or was it to become a self-supporting colony of free settlers? Lacking direction, it was struggling with this question for itself, and its Governor lived in the dust and heat of a perpetual conflict. And meanwhile, though fresh shiploads of convicts continued to pour in, the arrival of a store-ship was still an uncertain and anxiously awaited event.

The children, capering about in their excitement, suddenly found themselves crowding round the Governor, and shyly backed away. He looked at them with indulgent kindliness. Depraved and infamous as their mothers might be, he thought, these were charming children. Last year over a hundred of them had come, carefully washed and combed and cleanly dressed, to pay their respects to him at Government House. He had thought then, laying his hand on a bright head, bending to hear a laboriously recited text, examining copybooks and samplers, that he had had no pleasanter, no more cheering task to perform during his whole administration. Of some three hundred children then in the colony, he had reflected, there were but few who had not been born in it. Now, turning away rather wearily from the smouldering ruins of the church, he told himself that it was in them, and not in himself, elderly, tired, and discouraged, that the future lay.

* * *

Bennilong, pausing in the dim passage of Government House, pushed the door a little wider, and peered into the room. Chairs, hastily pushed back, were scattered round the table upon which there still stood the glasses from which the Governor and his friends had been drinking when the alarm was given; and in a path of late sunlight falling across the polished wood there were two bottles, one empty, the other almost full, and shining like a star.

Bennilong's tongue ran round his lips, and he glanced over his shoulder. Everyone had gone to watch the fire, to which he also had been hurrying when his eye was caught by that seductive gleam. He stood hesitating, rubbing his hand upon his thigh where there was a dull, throbbing pain from an unhealed wound, thinking of the exciting taste of the golden liquor, and the feel of it running down the throat like fire. But what drew him even more than thoughts of its flavour were thoughts of its power, for it alone, lately, could give buoyancy and enlargement to his spirit, and free him of the misery which lay like a load upon his heart.

He limped quickly into the room and snatched up the bottle. He hid it under his coat, holding it against his body with his arm, and tiptoed out into the passage again. At the entrance door he paused for a moment to peer out into the yard before emerging; there was a sentry on duty, but he was intent upon the fire, so Bennilong stepped forward boldly, knowing that he would not be noticed. Even now, when the last thing he wanted was attention, that knowledge annoyed him, for there had been a time when he never came unwelcomed to Government House, and never left it without friendly farewells.

That had been when the first Be-anga dwelt there. That had been before he went to England, and returned to find himself a stranger in his homeland. From that day, he thought, limping up the hill towards the shelter of the bush, there had been no peace in his heart. Life, once so simple and so enormously enjoyable, had become a long torment of bewildered resentment, a long conflict of opposing loyalties, a long battle between irreconcilable desires.

And when a man is no longer at peace in his heart—aie, how his thoughts fight and strive! Within his mind they turn and twist and writhe like a snake in its agony of death! They will not be stilled, and yet there comes from all their striving no knowledge of a truth to comfort him. Nothing comes from it but passions and moods to shake his body and exhaust his spirit. Gushing up from deep in his heart, like the water of a spring from the ground, comes a love for his own people, and he throws aside his clothes and his white man's ways, and goes to seek them, hungry for the comfort of their companionship, hungry for a peace still remembered, but now insubstantial and elusive as a drift of smoke. And in the camp of his tribe he sees that the eyes of his people are the eyes of strangers; they watch, they judge.

Is a man a birrahlee that he should stand rebuked by their eyes? Now it is fury that rises in his heart, and his words burst from him, and his hand is on his spear, and blood flows. And then, in bitterness, he returns to the great house of the Governor, and the Governor looks at his wounds, and is angered.

"Why do you fight, Bennilong? Always fight, fight. Always trouble. Why do you make trouble all the time?"

Make trouble! Though a man has been to England and seen the King, how shall he find words to tell the Governor that it is not he who makes the trouble, but the trouble which dwells within him, and will not be expelled? Yapallun! Why should a man make a thing which robs his life of joy?

There was a day, long, long ago, when the ship returned from England. Since then the seasons have come and gone, the hot season, the cold season, over and over again, many times. How can a man tell his countrymen who have never left their land that in its scents and its sounds and its shapes and its textures there dwells a rapture so deep that not even the ecstasies of corroboree are deeper? The nostrils have not known the scents until they have known also the smell of fog, the smell of London, the smell of wet grass and unfamiliar flowers, the smells of exile. Then, on a spring day, unheralded, forgotten, the scents of childhood drift back into the nostrils, and in a moment those long years of loneliness are no more than the end of an uneasy sleep, and the joy of homecoming breaks like sunrise in a flood of light.

A man is mind and body, anguish and desire. The mind in torment, the body seeks assuagement—but where is Gooroobarooboolo? She has gone with Caruey. A man says, "Stranger!" with his eyes, but a woman with her whole body can deny a man, and though he fan his ardour and spend his strength she will yield him no joy, and he can win no peace from her. A pink petticoat, a fine jacket, a bonnet from England to cover her dark hair. A day, two days, and she has said with her body that jackets and petticoats and bonnets are no substitute for ecstasy, and she has thrown them on the ground and run to seek Caruey . . .

How strange, how sharp in agony, the wounds of the spirit! Can there be a more deadly insult, a more mortal wound to the pride of a man than that his woman shall find no pleasure in his embrace? Seek out this Caruey! Smarting with the pain of that wound, pour scorn upon his weapons, and mockery upon his manhood—cry out that in England a man fights his enemy barehanded—thus—and thus . . .

Snatch him by the throat, dash your fists into his face as you have seen men do in London. And hear the voice of your people raised against you in anger, fierce and strong. This is no way to fight! Are not the weapons of your forefathers good enough for you, Bennilong? Are not the ancient laws of combat to your liking any more?

Then there comes a hopelessness, a weariness, for man was never meant to strive so with his life. Leave them, leave them! There is no place for you here! Return to the Governor, put on your clothes, sit with him at his table . . .

"Where is your wife, Bennilong?"

There shall be no laughter, no pity for any man, white or black, for Bennilong, forsaken! A laugh, a shrug. She has gone with Caruey—let her go! A better wife, larger, sleeker, more desirable by far, can easily be found when she is wanted!

But at night there comes a restlessness, and the moonlight lies on the ground like water, and the trees are inky black, and their leaves are long and silver and glittering, like little darting fishes. So often, leaving clothes behind, you go back to the listening bush and lie upon the earth looking up at the sky till you sleep, and wake refreshed.

For it is not the earth which denies you, but the men. And the women. The women who once smiled now look mistrustfully away, turn from you, flee from you, mock at you—and the impulse which was then no more than an impulse, becomes a hunger and a dreadful need, and your eyes turn to Booreea, Colbee's woman . . .

To fight with Colbee is to fight with the whole past—its spirit-heroes, its legends, and its Law. They are almost visible there, ranged beside him, and when he flings a spear it becomes a thousand spears, and the strength of his arm is the strength of the whole race of Murri; but you are alone.

Alone, wounded, vanquished. Turn again, then, to the other friends, the white friends, and beg food of them because you cannot hunt until your wounds are healed, and lie alone in the bush, remembering the scornful words of Colbee. "Are these the ways which you have learned in England? Are these the things you have returned to teach us?"

* * *

Pausing among the sheltering trees, Bennilong put his hand up to his mouth, touching his disfigured upper lip, split by the spear of Colbee. He set his bottle carefully on the ground and took off his clothes, tying them into a bundle and slinging them about his neck. His body was scarred by many wounds, and he bent to examine the one on his thigh, still raw, and throbbing painfully. He would not, he decided, return to the white men's camp until it was well—a wound healed more quickly if one left it alone to the sun and the air, and did not cover it with clothes.

He picked up the bottle, uncorked it, and put it to his lips. Even as he drank, that indestructible clarity which governed the thought processes of the primitive mind, that remorseless honesty which came from a habit of self-knowledge, told him that the Bennilong who, years ago, had taken and rolled upon his tongue his first experimental mouthful of this drink, was a better man than the Bennilong now recklessly gulping it down in the panic of his search for mental peace.

Yet how could it be evil? Had not the first Be-anga drunk it, and remained himself, wise, calm, and kindly? No, it was well to drink it. Already its strength flowed through his body, and its potency stirred his mind to new confidence. He was Bennilong. He had lived in the house of the Be-anga, and the Be-anga had treated him with honour, building him a house of his own, clothing him in fine garments, calling upon him for counsel and enlightenment in the ways of the tribes. If he had remained, Bennilong thought, holding the bottle clutched against his chest and walking on blindly through the warm and fragrant bush, perhaps things would not have been so difficult. For in the camp of the white people there was not now the same friendliness and honour which had been shown to him once. They said he was a maker of trouble, a provoker of brawls, and they rebuked him, which was something he would not endure. For all the time, gnawing at the back of his mind, was a contempt for them. They had fed his vanity, and they had showed him marvels. They had been the means whereby he had fulfilled his destiny, and journeyed across the sea to a land which no man of his race had seen before. But he despised them. They were not good hunters; they could not see tracks upon the ground, be they clear as day. There was no valour in their fighting; they never fought as men fight, hand to hand, strength matched with strength, but stood afar off, and killed by magic. They were squeamish, expressing horror and repugnance at certain tribal customs, and yet they held many of their own race in infamous subjection, and inflicted upon them indignities which turned the black men cold with loathing.

They had not one Law, but two, and disobeyed them both. There was the Law of the moon-faced one, and the Law of the King, and they were conflicting laws. The Law of the moon-faced one said that a man must not kill, but the Law of the King directed him to hang his fellow from a tree by the neck until he was dead. The Law of the moon-faced one was a law of gentleness and forgiveness, but the Law of the King was harsh and revengeful. There was no way to learn the hearts of men who professed two such laws, for they could not live by one without denying the other.

And so they denied them both, and having two Laws, lived by none. But without a Law a man is nothing. White man, black man, it matters not—there must be a Law to give direction to his spirit.

Bennilong stopped to gulp a few more mouthfuls, and stood wiping his lips with the back of his hand, looking down from the high crest of the ridge at the harbour spread out below him, golden with the last rays of the setting sun. He thought confusedly:

"Where is my Law? It dwells in the camps of my tribe, about their fires, in their hearts, in the words they speak, in the food they eat, in the tales they tell, in the sacred ceremonies of the men, and in the rhythms of corroboree. It is entwined in their life, which I have lost, and I cannot have the Law without the life. But I cannot find the life again, for it has withdrawn from me; my people do not want to hear me now, and their eyes say, 'Stranger.' They have threatened me, and driven me from their counsels, and in anger I have gone against them with the red-coated warriors of the white men, and threatened them in turn. Now there is no peace such as the first Be-anga desired between his people and mine. For the white men take too much. They take first a little, and then a little more, and yet again a little, and the hunting-grounds of my people are deserted, and their bellies are empty, and their anger rises. Pemulwy of the Bideegal leads them in battle, and five are slain by the gooroobeera of the white man, and between two enemies I stand, and am the friend of neither . . ."

He stumbled on again unsteadily. Now the magic drink was beginning to make itself felt, and reality was blurring. He need no longer strive with his thoughts, nor contemplate that dreadful image of himself facing his countrymen not as one exalted by the white men, but as one destroyed. Now the yellow fluid would restore to him an old contentment, not quite in its ancient shapes, but in dreamlike parodies of them, so that the empty sunshine would be filled with men and battles, and the noise of the surf would seem but the clamour of ancestral rituals, and the wind would bring him voices . . .

His wound was hurting him so much that he stopped, and stood for a moment swaying, looking about him. This was a very familiar place—a childhood place, a tribe place, a spirit place, identified with times and scenes so remote that he hardly knew whether they were born of legend or of memory. There had been one called Wunbula, a maker of songs and images. But there had also been others—great racial heroes whose names filed through his brain, leaving him still unsatisfied, confused. What was this persistent thought of a man, Wunbula, chipping images upon a rock? How clear it was, this thought! Standing still, listening intently, one could hear . . . The sun was hot, hot, and the sand too, so one lay in the shade, and the sound of chipping went on until one grew sleepy. Was this real, or was it legend? Had it happened, or had it been told? Surely it was here, in this very place, close to this very spot, that one called Wunbula had made an image of a boat with wings?

Bennilong stared about him hazily. His mind searched for Wunbula, but when it named him Be-anga, father, it became instantly misted over with the image of another Be-anga, and he rubbed his hand across his eyes, and muttered to himself, stumbling forward again amongst the rocks and stunted shrubs. The habit of a lifetime and the inherited instinct of generations triumphed over his drink-befogged brain, and his bleary eyes still recognised one bush as different from another, still observed the contours of the ground, the formation of rocks, the shapes of the few, wind-tortured trees. His physical identity with the land was still strong in him, but his spiritual life was thrown into utter chaos. He had lost his awareness of eternity, his fellowship with ages past and ages yet to come. He had lost that close and serene communion with mystery by which the inner life of his people was nourished and sustained. Once, he thought, life was whole, like the body of a man. Once the past, the present, and the future were intricately woven together, and with them was entwined the life of man, body and spirit, one life. Once there had been no time but the eternal dream-time, not far away, though it stretched back into the ages, not incomprehensible, though it pushed forward into the future, but one with the everlasting present which dwells in the heart of man. Thus life had been whole, like the body of a man. But now something had assailed it. Change had gashed it like a knife, and the spirit flowed out of it like blood. There had been betrayal—but where was the betrayer? There was an enemy—but what was his name? There was no single man, white or black, to whom he could point in his fury of despair. The very earth had played him false, showing him a land of grey skies and naked trees, and the heavens had deceived him with unfamiliar stars. But worse, he thought, far worse than all, mankind itself had betrayed him. For what was mankind? How clear had been the answer to that question once! With vivid and instinctive symbolism Bennilong saw that answer as a picture of Wunbula, flung up from his memory so that it stood before him, silhouetted against the sea as it had stood upon that summer day so many years ago.

That was mankind. One knew him; he hunted, he fought, he mated, he laughed and danced, he made songs and pictures, and then he slept. No longer. No. What was he now? Bennilong tripped over a root and collapsed on the ground beside a rock, hugging his bottle to his chest and talking to himself. What was he now? He had no shape, no colour. His outline was blurred, his features defaced. His mind was hidden, and his heart divided. His mind was confused and his heart was torn because he knew no longer what he must believe. Yapallun! The unhappiness of man!

He rocked to and fro, and his mumbling became a lament. Such loveliness is in the searching minds of men! Such shapes and colours they have wrought! Such sounds they can make to delight the ear and uplift the heart, such power and magic lie beneath their cunning hands! I have seen many things and many places—I, Bennilong, son of Wunbula who made the songs of his people. Once I, too, made songs, but now no more, for a man cannot sing who is not whole, and words come freely only from the believing heart . . .

And what shall a man believe who believes no longer in mankind? Shall he look into a still pool and see no image there but the image of a cloud and a tree?

He lifted the bottle and held it up, and the rays of the vanishing sun lit it so that it glowed like amber. He tilted it, drained it, and then threw it carelessly behind him on the rock. He heard it splintering to fragments, staggered to his feet, turned, and saw the pieces lying scattered over the image of the winged boat which Wunbula had made long, long ago. He knelt down on the rock, tracing the indented outline with an unsteady finger. He had seen many, many other images of ships since then, and they had looked so real that one held one's breath, suspecting magic; their snow-white sails swelled against a blue sky, and the sea broke upward from their bows in flying spray. This was a very poor image of a ship. Wunbula had indeed been but a poor maker of images after all.

He knelt very still, feeling an exhausting and unendurable sense of loss sweep over him. Here, in this place with the echoes of childhood all about him, he had tried to recapture the eternal dream-time, but it eluded him, and there was nothing in his grasp but a stark and isolated today. Crying out aloud in frustration and in rage, he seized a stone and scratched savagely over the hollowed outlines.

He worked to deface it as long and as fiercely as Wunbula had worked to make it. He worked till the sweat glistened on his body, and his head was swimming. This, he thought, is the evil! This is the thing which has destroyed my peace and the peace of my people, but I, Bennilong, destroy it in its turn! I am great, I am taller than the trees, and stronger than the storm; I am wiser than the fathers of our tribes, wiser than Wunbula, wiser than Tirrawuul, for I have been to England, and I have seen the King. Now I know many things, and I shall teach you what I have learned, and what I have learned is that there is no Baiame, but only God and the King. And I have learned that it is ill to eat with the fingers, and to go unclad, and I shall be your leader, and slay you if you go unclad, and slay you if you do not my bidding, for thus the King does. I have learned many, many things, and I alone can teach you, for you are but naked men of little wisdom, for you have never seen the King . . .

But I have forgotten . . .

From sheer physical exhaustion his orgy of destruction ceased, and his racing brain checked and fumbled in confusion. He looked stupidly at his long shadow lying on the rock, and stretched his hand out to it as if to a companion; but suddenly the sky darkened, and it was gone, leaving him alone. He shook his head, mumbling wearily:

"I have forgotten how to be at peace . . ."

The rock seemed to flow beneath his eyes like water; the ground lurched, and the whole world spun. As he pitched forward, a bit of broken bottle gashed his arm, and blood ran into the defaced groove of Wunbula's drawing. Bennilong lay still, snoring heavily, while the merciful, swift twilight of his land crept up about him to cover his defeat.

The End.

GLOSSARY OF ABORIGINAL WORDS AND PHRASES

Bado ....Water
Be-anga ....Father; also leader or responsible person
Bee-all ....No
Ben-ga-dee ....Ornament
Berai-Berai ....Orion
Bereewolgal ....Name given by the natives to the white men
Lit. "men come from afar"
Biningung bado ....Give me some water
Birrahlee ....Child
Birrong ....Star
Bo-ee ....Dead
Boodjerree ....Good
Bulla murrai dyin ....Two big women
Burul winungailun miai-miai.........Much desirous of young women

Cardalung ....Hot
Coo-ee! ....Come here! Come to me!
Coolamon ....Wooden vessel for drinking, or for carrying food or water
Corroboree ....A dramatic dance, performed with appropriate words

Duggerigai ....White men
Dulka ....The sky
Dyin ....Woman

Ela-beara! ....Exclamation of wonder or astonishment

Gan-to bon bunkulla tetti kulwun? ......Who killed him?
Gan-umba noa unni yinal? ....Whose son is this?
Gatoa bon tura ....It is I who speared him
Gooroobeera ....Musket. Lit. "stick of fire"
Gourgourgahgah ....The Kookaburra
Guioa! ....Good-bye!
Gwee-un ....Fire

Kabo bag kanun England-ka ....Soon I shall be at England
Kai kai karakai! ....Come, make haste!
Kamai ....A spear
Keawaran wal bi uwa-nun! ....You shall not go!
Kia? ....What do you say?
Kuji ....The bee
Kurru ....Clouds
Kuurang ....The tiger snake

Magra ....Fish
Mia-mia ....A bark shelter
Mirrabooka ....The Southern Cross
Morungle ....Thunder
Moo-la-ly ....Ill, indisposed
Murrai ....Big
Murri ....The men
Murruwulung ....Small

Naa-moro ....Compass. Lit. "to see the way"
Na-lau-ra ....Sit down, as a guest
N'ga ....Here!
N'gai-ri! ....Bring it here!
N'gai n'gai pindwagung bado ....I will bring you some water
Ngindigindoer ....Venus. Lit. "you are laughing"
Nowee ....Boat

Parrebuga ....Tomorrow

Teeri-yeetchbeem ....Red-headed one
Thirringnunna ....Hide-and-seek. Lit. "where are we?"
Towri ....Tribal territory

Unijerunbi minku? ....What do you want?

Waita koa bag; mimai yikora! ....I must go; do not detain me!
Waw . . . ? ....Where is . . .
Weeree ....Bad, or wrong
Werowey ....Girl
Whurra, whurra! ....Begone, begone!
Wi! Wi! ....Exclamation of aversion
Wirri ....The sun
Wongerra ....Boy
Wommerah ....Throwing stick for spear; also used for
 other purposes as implement

Woram-woram buna; worambil moium	Go to sleep, sleepy little one
Wutta?	Where to?
Yagoona	Today
Yapallun!	Alas!
Yen-ou?	Shall I go?
Youara-gurrugin	Maker of corroboree songs
Yuroo	Hungry

"Dinga dinga burula,
  Murringa dibura!"

"Burran, burin, bilar bundi,
  Murala berar karni!"

"Plenty of wild dogs,
  The black men are spearing them!"

"Shield of buree, spear and club,
  Throwing stick of berar bring!"